To dear Sarah,
with thanks
+ enthusiasm

A BRAND OF FAITH

D.G.A.Pritchard

ARNICA PRESS

Published by ARNICA PRESS

www.ArnicaPress.com

Copyright © 2021 D.G.A.Pritchard

Cover photo by Sahara Prince

Illustrations by D.G.A.Pritchard

www.dgapritchard.com

Printed in the United States of America.

ISBN: 978-1-955354-03-5

This is a work of fiction. Names, characters, places, and incidents
either are the product of the author's imagination or are used
fictitiously, and any resemblance to actual persons, living or dead,
business establishments, events, or locales is entirely coincidental.

Batter my heart, three-personed God, for you
As yet but knock, breathe, shine and seek to mend;
That I may rise and stand, o'erthrow me, and bend
Your force to break, blow, burn, and make me new.
I, like an usurped town to another due,
Labour and admit to you, but oh, to no end;
Reason, your viceroy in me, me should defend,
But is captived, and proves weak or untrue.
Yet dearly I love you, and would be lovèd fain
But am betrothed unto your enemy;
Divorce me, untie and break that knot again;
Take me to you, imprison me, for I,
Except you enthral me, never shall be free,
Nor ever chaste, except you ravish me.

John Donne

TABLE OF CONTENTS

1. A NEW START

The crocodiles' eyes reflect the flickering flames behind me. I am hauling myself closer to the river inch by inch. I am almost at the bank when hands from above lift me from the path and I am carried carefully – but so painfully - along the small jetty and into a waiting dug-out canoe. The tiny vessel is pushed out towards the middle of the river, cheating the huge reptiles of their supper.

The bottom of the craft is rough-hewn so that splinters grate against my stomach and chest as I lie where they have laid me, in the swill. The tastes and smells of rotten fish, diesel, river-mud and excrement fill my senses as the recurring dream takes hold once again and returns me to that dark journey.

Keeping my mouth above the filth makes my neck ache, the straining muscles sending spasms down my spine. My wretched instincts will not allow the foul water to enter my mouth even though I would welcome the oblivion it might offer.

The kind souls who have dragged me here have thrown sacking over my battered body, hiding my nakedness. Extricating my arms is not an easy task, but I manage to pull them forward and rest my forehead on the back of my hands, as I have done so many times in prayer while kneeling in a church pew or at the altar. When the muscles in my back relax, the pains intensify from the burns, bruises and bones I know to be broken.

From the prone position on my stomach I can see only as far as the feet and mud-spattered legs of the two men who steer the boat. Their bead encircled ankles and the cadence of their words tell me they are from downstream. These are traders who bring fresh fruits and meat to the village in return for carefully harvested soya beans and peanuts. In hushed voices they bewail the fate of their neighbouring village and I glean concern for the vicar they finally came to respect who now lies unceremoniously at their feet.

I am trying to pray, but there is only emptiness where my faith lived comfortably for so long. I try to listen for God's voice but my ears are ringing with the screams of friends I will never see again. Tears are running across my face, making lines through the dirt and adding a sting to the cuts and grazes. Despair, with clammy fingers, creeps across the place where my soul used to dwell.

For some reason, my dream always shifts at this point; the noise of the water slapping the boat's sides and the muffled chatter of the two men is replaced by the gentle songs of non-tropical birds. Thrushes, blackbirds, wrens and blue-tits celebrate the return of Spring to a country garden and I find myself back at my childhood home in the English village of Willenbury. I am in the drawing room, moving towards the French windows, which are open to the thin sunshine. Across the lawn, bending over her beloved roses, I can see my mother. I call to her - the weak cry of a boy whose voice will not break for several years - floats over the lawn.

Mother straightens and turns from the herbaceous border. She is still young, in my dream; a tall, attractive woman with a good figure, pinched at the waist by a green gardening apron. In one hand she holds pruning shears and a pair of gardening gloves, recently removed, while the other is raised to tuck a stray piece of mousy hair behind an ear. Her eyes search the house façade for the source of the summoning voice.

"Robert" she calls. "Is that you? I didn't know you were home already. Where are you?"

My heart contracts, as it always did when my parents focused eager attention upon my elder brother.

"No, it's me, Jack," I try to sound confident and assertive, like Robert. "Can I help you?" I ask. It is a supplication, which goes unheeded.

"Oh, Jack. I thought it was Robert. Is he home yet?" Mother looks at her watch. "No, he can't be, it's too early. He won't be back for another hour at least." She watches my approach across the grass, a carefully plucked eyebrow twitches with annoyance. I inherited my mother's height and was tall for my age, but her grace of movement and her good looks eluded me; my thick spectacles gave me an owlish look and the beakish nose that supported them only added to the effect. I suppose I was not an attractive or welcome sight.

A telephone starts to ring somewhere inside the house. Mother drops her gloves and secateurs and walks briskly towards the open doors. "Now what?" she mutters as she passes her youngest child in the middle of the lawn.

I continue across the lawn and pick up the dropped shears, holding them cautiously, watching the spring contract and expand as my juvenile fingers flex. I have seen mother use them so many times; she wields them with such confidence, snipping at this and that. I decide to emulate her and collect something pretty to give her when she returns.

Advancing into the flowerbed I avoid the prickly rose bushes whose young leaves are pushing reds and greens into the world from dead-looking branches, and step around the bushing hellebores with their pale green bells. I am looking for something special to please mother and consider the delicate blossoms of the flowering cherry, but they are too high to reach. Then I see the irises. The vivid purple buds, promising yellow and white tongues when open, are pushing upwards through spiky green leaves in an exuberance of life. They will make the perfect offering.

I am so engrossed with my work that I don't hear mother's return. I have collected a neat pile of the pretty budding heads and only have two more to snip when I hear her cry:

"What have you done? Stop, stop, Jack. What on earth do you think you're doing? Oh my poor irises," she wails.

I feel the blood rushing to my cheeks and tears rising in my throat. "But they're for you, Mother," I say, pointing to the collection at my feet. "I've cut them for you."

The dream stops here, and I awake with relief to find myself an adult once again, but the emotional mixtures of the two scenes take a while to seep away.

This dream, with its two contrasting segments, still invades my slumber every three or four weeks, even after all this time. It sweeps into my mind, unbidden and unwelcome; slices of life I am not allowed to forget. The childhood scene is easily dealt with, at last, but the start of that river journey opens a minefield of horrors. I have decided that the time has come to confront these specters and exorcise them along with various other demons who plague my waking thoughts as well as those of my sleep. I want to oppose them all and offset them with recollections of joyful excitements and encouraging vitality, and by so doing, to arrive at a conclusion that might justify the great change I have made in my life.

In last week's momentous move from London, I found the boxes of books, photographs, sketches and diaries that I collected from storage when I returned to England. My days spent at both school and seminary college recorded ad nauseam; life as a vicar in Islington detailed obsessively in pages of cramped writing with accompanying drawings. I think of the contrast between the enthusiastic young man who deposited these writings in his friend's well-ordered attic on the eve of his departure for Africa and the dour cynic who collected them some eight or nine years later.

The move also unearthed the tin trunk. I had hidden it away amongst the gardening tools, oil cans, paint tins and so forth that littered the shelves along one side of Stella's garage, next to the highly polished and much loved Aston Martin.

The trunk is charred and warped by the fire, but its contents remain undamaged, a sinister fragment of a former existence. Inside will be my books, notes, drawings, maps and diagrams from those years in Cachonga. Evidence of the evolution of a disparate collection of people into a settled village of farmers and rural entrepreneurs, I suppose. It's a small piece of history, a documentation of the changes to this tiny African community.

During those years in the brown-dry African bush, I used to remind myself of the soft greens of England by writing memories of the surroundings and the adventures of my youth – I suppose those essays are still there, in the trunk, mixed up with everything else.

Next to the trunk, waiting for a home in the cupboards and shelves of my new study, is the battered suitcase given to me in hospital by one of the nuns, to hold my writings from those physically stagnant months. Within are the long screeds written during my months in St. Mary's. Many of the conversations I enjoyed with my fellow patients, and the memories they pulled out of me. All recorded in essays and sketches to pass the long hours of inactivity necessary while our bodies mended.

Next to the suitcase are boxes of papers, slides, lectures and schedules that took me all over Europe and the U.S.A. in my post-Africa life. They are all muddled up with letters from special friends: Thomas, Rufus, Percival and Amrita – even the occasional note from a member of my family.

All these items make pillars of confusion that might topple at any moment. It will take some courage to sift through them but I need to confront the ghosts and, hopefully, to conquer them. So I have decided to organize my notes and flesh them with memories; to dig up atrocities and by exposing them, place them in my past and not allow them to discolor my present. I am hoping that the writings these excavations produce will provide the cathartic exercise necessary for me to make a new start, not just geographically – as I did last week – but mentally and psychologically also.

My hands start to sweat when I look at the tin trunk, now resting under the window, flanked with the other containers of this travail. However, I take courage in my new surroundings. With a study full of light and bird-song and views of a perfect English garden stretching into the surrounding countryside, I am determined to find the strength to fit things together. This is the perfect environment to explore and nurture the unexpected positivity which is returning, albeit tentatively, to my life, in so many unexpected dimensions.

There can be no better place to offset the decline of trusted beliefs with the fluttering phoenix of a different kind of philosophy.

Our rose garden

2. THE TOWERS OF SILENCE

I s it really only a few months ago that I was summoned to meet the Bishop at St. Margaret's, Westminster? It seems much longer that the decision was forced upon me, leading to the move and my present circumstances.

We must have made a strange pair, us two 'priests' confronting each other in the sacristy of the great cathedral: the majestic, opulent robes of the older man, doing their best to conceal the corpulence beneath, contrasting with my own drab clothing and long-shanked leanness. Stella had found a clerical collar at the back of a drawer and insisted I should wear it again, just for this occasion. It was the only sign of my previous calling.

"Stay and take the communion service with me, Jack." Bishop Paul had used his most persuasive voice as he adjusted the elaborate chasuble around his neck so that the ends were perfectly aligned. "You can help me dispense the sacrament and then we can talk some more after the service. There are plenty of spare robes," his arm gestured towards the rail I could see behind a partially open curtain of heavy embroidered silk, "although they are probably all a bit on the wide side for you." His smile creased into his cheeks, lifting the gold-rimmed spectacles whose roundness matched his face. The blue eyes behind them were full of kind concern.

I thought how much the honor that was being offered to me would have meant only a few years ago. To be invited to officiate in such a famous cathedral with such a senior cleric, in the service of the Eucharist.

From much further back in my mind came the picture of the first time I had presided over the altar and participated in the mystery of symbolic transubstantiation. The wonder that had filled my young heart and soul as I went through the sacred motions and prayers before turning to the few bowed heads that made up the congregation, the transformed host held aloft on the paten. In just a few moments the humble wafers had been altered to represent the flesh of Christ and His supreme sacrifice, the evidence of God's love for mankind; and it had been my participation in the ritual that had made the magic possible.

The memory made me emotional and I turned away from the Bishop as if studying the robes on offer. I didn't want the old man to see me mourn my past years of devotion to a God in whom I no longer believed.

"No," the word was unintentionally vehement. "No, thank you Father." I softened my voice with an effort. "It is a kind and wonderful suggestion, but, as I was trying to explain, it is inappropriate for me to participate in the sacrament anymore."

I turned back to face my companion, trying to present a peaceful expression. The Bishop looked older than his seventy-two years as he lowered his large frame into a heavily carved, high-backed armchair. He was visibly disappointed by my refusal.

"But I can come back after the service if you like." I was eager not to offend the prelate. "I would like to know more about your suggestions. Are you sure that someone with my present philosophies would really be welcome in such an august establishment as The Castle?"

Father Paul had chuckled unexpectedly. "Dear Jack," he rose and put a jeweled hand on my shoulder, releasing his squeeze quickly - he must have felt the bones close under his grasp - but he let the hand stay. "You have much to learn about the inhabitants of our special house. Almost all of them have had – how shall I put it – reversals of faith. I think that is the best term – no, I prefer 'expansions of faith,' that's much better.

"In fact, I expect you will find much in common with even the most revered amongst the inhabitants of that institution. God leads us in mysterious ways indeed, ways I don't begin to understand. Many of The Castle's inmates would have had the same reaction as you to the invitation I just made concerning Holy Communion. We nickname the Castle 'the Tower of Silence' as those who live there are welcome to talk between themselves, but their proselytizing days are over, and they are best kept away from a flock. Doesn't that appeal to you?"

"Yes," I answered, managing a smile, "indeed it does. The Tower of Silence, you say – that's a Zoroastrian term, if I remember correctly. It's where they put their dead."

"Ah yes," Father Paul returned my smile with a sigh. "I should have known you would be familiar with the analogy. With earth, fire and water all being sacred to the Zoroastrians, they cannot defile any of them with corpses, so they lay their dead out to the air, on top of a hill, surrounded by a high wall."

The Bishop paused and I noticed his eyes loosing focus, somehow, in spite of his glasses. "I went there once, you know," he added, his voice suddenly hushed. "Such a long time ago, as a young man full of hope and conviction.

"I remember well the flat arid lands around Yazd. It's a place where the dust gets up and throws itself in your face for no apparent reason. Not much to be seen apart from broken mud huts strung across the desert connected by umbilical walls of the same baked mud. It's many years since I have thought of that ancient necropolis in southern Persia. It presented itself to me as a carcass of an organic growth that had died of thirst – or something more sinister. Ever-present in the background were the two hills with broken-toothed crowns of ragged masonry - one for the men and one for the women - within whose circumferences rest the remains of countless dead. Those Towers of Silence, as they are called by the Zoroastrians, as you say, made a deep impression on the young curate I was then."

A shrug of the shoulders brought the Bishop back to the present. "The vultures, sun and wind do the cleanup job," Father Paul smiled again. "Yes, those inside are certainly silent."

"But they are also the ones with the ultimate knowledge," I pointed out. "Does your analogy with The Castle go that far?" I tried to add a note of humor to my voice.

"Well you are ahead of me there, Jack," Father Paul answered with a suggestion of a chuckle. "Come and have supper with me after the service. I would enjoy that. I have another guest I want you to meet. We'll see what we can sort out for your future - after all the options are somewhat limited, I'm afraid."

As I left the cathedral, moving against the small in-coming tide of silent worshippers, I thought how little Father Paul knew of my circumstances. He didn't realize that my options were not as limited as he suggested. I had thanked the bishop for his invitation and agreed to meet around eight, across the Thames, at The Palace.

I was more than ever aware that a decision was imminent, I could postpone it no longer. As I walked along the Thames' Embankment, waiting for the service in the cathedral to end, I thought about my choices.

I could accept Father Paul's offer of a secure future in 'The Castle,' one of the most beautiful houses in the country, surrounded by superb gardens and boasting, as its crowning glory, a magnificently eclectic library. It was indeed an honour to be invited to join the inhabitants of such an establishment, for they are unquestionably among the most interesting and enlightened of men.

Here was the kind of life I had always longed for; the freedom to explore all the different avenues of thought that have been passed down through the ages from so many different cultures and minds. No financial worries; no time pressures or restraints; the kind of Spartan comforts with which I feel at home; an endless supply of wholesome food; solitude when I need it and excellent company when I don't – exclusively male, of course. There were the added attractions of all the books I could ever want, and a wonderful garden to stroll around and in which to ponder. The proposition, for a reclusive philosopher such as myself, was certainly attractive.

On the other hand, there was Stella and the totally unpredictable life she so desperately wanted to share with me, her thought-provoking lover. I tried to imagine how my life would pan out if I chose the sensual option Stella personified. Her brightly coloured rooms are as full of soft furnishings and fabrics as The Castle's would be of wooden refectory tables and pallet beds. The riot of modern art which festoons the interior walls is ignored by the constant flow of chattering visitors, whose conversations are not always inspiring, but who compete stoically with the ringing telephones and the back-ground turbulence of the hi-fi or television.

Then I thought of her garden and the peace I have found there. It is a small space, but large by London standards, and Stella has arranged it to give the impression that it goes on forever. When I had first seen it, I thought of my friend Thomas' lawns that spread around the rectory at Thornton, and of my mother's cherished flower beds at our family home in Willenbury.

Unbidden came the thoughts of the thrill that races up my spine every time Stella appears rushing towards me with the out-stretched arms and big brown eyes I always want to fall into. I thought of the bedroom, with windows open to the garden, curtains flapping slightly, always pulled wide. The bed where I have learned a new dimension of existence and excitement, and the little study she has made for me where her dressing room had been.

The decision was not going to be an easy one.

3. WILLENBURY HALL

I suppose I should start at the beginning and dive into the diaries and sketchbooks from my childhood years. My memories are filled with the church – or should I write The Church? I have no recollection of when I decided to become a priest. The yearning had always been there: to be part of a hallowed collection of people who moved through life with smooth, quiet assurance; people who carry respect, authority, wisdom and a deep inner calm as easily as businessmen carry their briefcases and umbrellas.

At first, tangible religious fervor was unimportant to me. I was a ridiculously frail, bespectacled boy whose elder siblings – strong, tall Robert and vibrant Alice - regarded me with derision. The cool twilight of churches, chapels and cathedrals always felt more like home than the Georgian manor where I grew up. The ecclesiastical smells of distant incense, decaying flowers and damp stones meant peace to my soul, while the smells of home - furniture polish arguing with odours from the kitchen and the scattered dog baskets - made me uneasy. The swishing sound of a cassock over polished flagstones, the snap of sandals on stone steps, the muted mirth of a hidden organ and the rustling of ancient texts were greatly to be preferred to the thrum of heavy music which issued from my brother's room and the incessant garble of television dramas from my sister's part of the house.

Yet our home, in the country village of Willenbury, was mildly grand and very comfortable. The Manor had been in the Bolden family for four generations and my parents, Charles and Elizabeth, had been there since they married in 1958. Robert had been the first to arrive two years later and it was always made clear that the estate would pass to him in its entirety. Alice was born in 1964 and I followed some two years later.

Perhaps it is because Robert has always been keen to flex his proprietary muscles that I failed so completely to identify with Willenbury. I preferred to think that my secular home had become unattractive because the heavy robes and candlelight of the church were calling me to my true abode, and not because I felt out of place at The Manor. Perhaps now, I know better.

Willenbury Hall

The rambling house of my childhood had too many rooms for a modern family who could neither afford nor find the staff that had once occupied its upper floor and the wings that once housed a kitchen, scullery, china-pantry, dairy and laundry.

As a result, the occupants spread themselves at random on either side of the green baize doors. Once we children had left the nursery, we could choose a space of our own amongst the plethora of unoccupied rooms that opened out of long, dim corridors. The only restrictions were the bathrooms, of which there was a sparse number - all with high ceilings, draughty windows, and exposed pipes that gurgled and burped.

The bedroom I chose was the only place in the house where I could feel at peace. Neither my siblings wanted the small north-facing room on the top floor, with its dormer window hemmed in by sharp roof angles. For me, it was perfect. It was a refuge from family chatter and frippery, it was a space which belonged to me.

There were no bathrooms on the top floor, and I had to share one with my sister, Alice, on the floor below. The bath was always festooned with lingerie and the washbasin cluttered with sickly-sweet smelling creams and lotions that made me sneeze. My bedroom was the place where I could invite God to visit and converse, uninterrupted by fears of either of us being ridiculed. Here was my private chapel and I would chatter away to The Almighty without the worry of being overheard.

God, then, was my closest friend and confidant. The Divine Being who could understand the virtues of my soul and appreciate the daily offerings of praise without calling attention to the lack of self-assurance and the physical clumsiness of my youth, thrown into greater relief by being the youngest of three.

In retrospect, I think my mother was fond of her youngest child, even though I didn't have the pizzazz of the elder two – the charm which made her eager to share time with them. Whenever the family did something together Robert would stay close to father and Alice to mother, leaving me trailing behind like an unnoticed after-thought. When they did become aware of my presence, it seemed as if I was never acceptable to any of them. They were always admonishing me for being inattentive and clumsy, or for my general failure to "keep up" physically, emotionally and intellectually. I was familiar with the expression "heir and spare" and reluctantly identified with my role as the latter in every way.

Knowing how passionate mother was about the garden, I used to accompany her onto the lawns and on the woodland paths whenever I could, begging to be of assistance. I think mother was touched by this obvious, and rather pathetic, attempt to win her favor, but whatever jobs she gave me invariably had disastrous outcomes – like the time I was asked to weed a patch of her beloved herbaceous border and carefully removed all the alchemilla leaving the sow thistles standing to attention. There was, of course, the time that haunts my dream when I cut off all the newly budding iris heads – but I have already touched upon that instance. Another time I dug up the strawberries and left the dandelions proudly waving their yellow heads in glorious solitude.

My mother told me quite recently, that she had really tried to like me as a child, but that she couldn't help becoming bored in my company and was always looking for distractions to avoid having to spend time with me alone. " You were my youngest child, I should have doted on you as my friends did on their smallest ones," she told me as I sat at her bedside, a couple of weeks ago. "When Alice went to boarding school, and Robert was already gone, you were the only one left at home. That should have been 'our' time, but we seemed to have so little in common. I couldn't understand your strange ways – all that praying and solemnity. I tried, really I tried. I understand better now," she said with a modicum of remorse, "but at the time you seemed a nuisance, a barrier in the way of a fuller life that I could have lived without you."

Of course this conversation took place now our roles have been reversed. Now she is the one asking me for help and comfort. I understand that mother regrets the sharpness with which she banished me from her garden, but with hindsight, I can see her point.

As I grew up, I was increasingly aware of the distance between myself and my parents. Mother's insistent hugs made us both feel uncomfortable, they seemed forced and strangely unaffectionate. Ironically, any attempt at physical closeness made the divide more apparent. It was not long before bodily contact between us became a mere formality.

My father didn't seem to notice me at all. If, on his way to his study or the library perhaps, we bumped into each other in one of the echoing corridors of the house, he would look at me with mild amazement, then collect himself and ask if I had seen mother, or the dogs, or the housekeeper. It seemed as if no other form of communication was necessary between us, a fact for which I was grateful.

I became used to the idea that my family didn't like me. Robert treated me as if I had no right to be in the house at all. Alice simply ignored me, except on the occasions when I was in the bathroom at inopportune moments when she would hammer on the door and express her distaste in loud tones.

Try as I might to emulate any or all of them, I always fell short of the mark and was left feeling myself to be a mistake. Only with God did I have a relationship of immediacy, love and trust.

4. FATHER EDMUND & ST. BARNABAS

Our family attended Willenbury parish church every Sunday without fail. It was one of those unquestioned disciplines, like placing the fireguard in front of the fire before leaving the room, changing for dinner, and putting the dogs out before going to bed.

St. Barnabas' Church dates back to Norman times and the stones lie heavily in the surrounding earth. Inside the building is a deep quiet with daylight filtering through ancient stained glass depicting even more ancient tales of religious magical events. Fragments of colour decorate the worn font and the screen of carved oak that separates the congregation from the choir and clergy.

The front pew, on the left of the aisle, has been reserved for the family of The Manor since the house was built in the early sixteen hundreds. It would see the Bolden family standing erect in order of height, every Sunday morning at Eleven, like a row of Russian dolls.

Having led the family into church, Father would stand aside as he approached our pew, allowing his brood to file into their familiar positions with silent, bowed heads. He took the seat next to the aisle, for easy access to the lectern when it was his turn to read the lesson.

I can see us all clearly in my mind's eye: father was always the pinnacle of the family line, his grey hair, still flirting with dark brown, wearing an impression like a sunken halo from the recently doffed bowler. Next to him is Mother, whose hat of the day would pay floral tribute to the season's offerings from the garden. Then comes Robert with his thick blondish hair, cut short to disguise the fact that it would not sit smoothly against his scalp. My brother's square features match his square neck and rigid shoulders and his ever-increasing height threatens to upset the symmetry of the family's silhouette.

Alice sits between Robert and myself; her auburn curls are decorated with today's ribbons, as many as her mood dictates. From amongst her locks a fine nose is held high, whether by physical design or social distain is hard to discern, but the ash-grey eyes on either side indicate the latter. Finally, at the end of the pew, next to one of the great ribbed stone columns that support the roof timbers way above, comes my own slender frame with my dark hair combed straight against my scalp and my heavy spectacles balancing on an aquiline nose too big for the thin face.

Being the youngest and smallest of the Bolden family I struggled to peer over the top of my hymnal as the choirboys in their surplices passed by. I was in awe of these boys and fortunately unaware that my dark eyes, magnified by the spectacles and filled with devotion, made me an object of ridicule to the village lads. In spite of their solemn expressions, the real religion of these choristers was to be found outside the village hall, on the football field, or behind the bike shed. I found this out later when I overheard a group of them discussing the latest recruit.

This was after our vicar, Father Edmund, had taken notice of my ardent following of the church services. A contemporary of my father's, with the same air of superiority, he told me that he had recognized the spiritual yearning expressed in my earnest features and remembered feeling the same way when he was my age. His caring attention persuaded him to request that my father allow me to attend Sunday school and to join the choir. Father had looked at the somewhat portly vicar with astonishment.

"Do you think the boy would want to?" he had enquired with an incredulous air that suggested such an offer should be anathema to any proper ten year old. However he gave his consent, and the following Sunday I was duly delivered to the church, ahead of the rest of the family, in a state of curious anticipation.

I remember well the exquisite excitement I felt when first I came to don one of those starched, shining surplices. As I pushed my head through the corrugated choker, a thrill of initiation ran through my slender frame. Suddenly, in the robe of a choirboy, I felt I had stature; even my short-sightedness became relatively inconsequential.

As I grew taller, I was given the honor of carrying the heavy cross from the sacristy to the altar and back again, at the head of the choir. I helped with the communion hosts, watching carefully as Father Edmund bent his large frame at the altar to go through the increasingly familiar motions. The elaborate vestments billowed around the priest endowing his normally unimpressive physique with the harmony of dignity. I wondered how such heavy garments might feel upon my own shoulders and if my slight frame might be similarly transformed in the wearing.

Father Edmund encouraged my spiritual development and became a trusted friend as the years passed. After the Sunday services, I would find him waiting by the font at the far end of the church. We would pass the time of day and then I would ask him about any details of the service, or the content of the day's sermon, which had attracted my particular attention. It was a novel sensation for me to have a proper conversation with an adult who appeared to take my input seriously. In retrospect, I think these discussions made the vicar feel appreciated. Perhaps my genuine enquiries went a little way to make up for the lack of interest shown by other members of his congregation.

"Well, what question have you brought with you today, Jack?" Father Edmund would ask, as we took our customary stances on either side of the font. I would have just emerged from between the vestry's heavy curtains, my country weekend attire having replaced the robes.

"I enjoy the theological challenges you put my way, it keeps me on my toes," the vicar said, one day, after I had been a member of his choir for almost a year. "There's a look of puzzlement you have every now and then during a service, and it is always followed by a question. I saw that expression again today – what have you got for me this time?"

"Well, Father," I began, savoring the coming conversation like a gourmet contemplating a sumptuous meal. "I was wondering about the phrase 'The Holy Catholic Church' in the liturgy. Why do we, as Protestants, confess a belief in a church we left in Henry VIII's time?" I remember this particularly because it is a question I have had put to me several times since becoming a vicar, and I thought fondly of Father Edmund whenever I answered.

"Ah now Jack," Father Edmund's healthy country face produced a large smile. "Now that one I can answer, indeed I am slightly annoyed with myself that you haven't been taught about this already. I take too much for granted, I'm afraid, and assume that points that are obvious to me should be equally apparent to others."

Leaning his elbows on the font edge, Father Edmund continued, his voice taking on the quality he usually kept for his sermons.

"The term catholic, with a small 'c', was first used by St. Ignatius, Bishop of Antioch - the word 'Christian' was also first used in Antioch, as a matter of fact. He was unfortunately fed to the lions around 110 A.D. - so the term must have come into being before that date. It means 'universal' and refers to all followers of the Christian faith. The Roman Catholics are just one branch of a faith that has taken on many vestments – literally, as well a metaphorically," he added with a smile. "In the early days, most of the budding Christians followed the lead imposed upon them from Rome where St. Peter had been martyred and buried. The Emperor Constantine had followed Christ's instructions: "You are Peter and upon this rock I will build my church" and based the foundations of the church on Peter's tomb – here I am speaking literally and figuratively," he added, stressing the second word in case I had not appreciated the difference. He was obviously pleased with his rhetoric.

"To make this new religion more palatable to the masses," Father Edmund was warming to his subject, "the Romans dressed the new church's leaders in clothes derived from earlier religions and used dates for their celebrations that coincided with what had taken place before, in pagan times. Not the Copts, or the Ethiopians, however – but those are other stories for another day. We did the same thing, here in England – the word Easter, for example, comes from Eostre, the name of the Saxon goddess of Spring, and had nothing to do with Christianity until it was adopted by the early church for the Spring celebration of our Lord's rising.

"Our religion today still owes its format to those early Christian days, even though we broke with Rome's particular vein of Christianity so long ago. We are still part of the original, 'universal' church, meaning the broad base of Christianity as decreed by the Apostles, and, of course, by Christ himself. That is the meaning of the word catholic as it is used in the Nicene Creed – the church's first official statement of belief – which we also owe to Constantine."

I remember my puzzlement, but thought my confusion due to ignorance rather than to the strange vocabulary of the discussion. One thing I held on to, that there was another talk to be had on another day. I made a mental note to ask about the Copts and the Ethiopians. In fact, I don't think I ever did, and it was not until I was at St. Augustine's, browsing in that wonderful library, that I found out about their differences.

I think Father Edmund enjoyed our chats as much as I did, I hope so anyway. My ardor for the Church must have appealed to the kindly cleric for he was determined to give me as much help and encouragement as possible. Maybe he knew how much I would need his support to overcome the trials that would accompany my move to boarding school. Pupils with a spiritual bent were easy prey for bullies, especially one with my weedy physique and heavy eyeglasses.

5. BAPTISM DAY AT CACHONGA

These memories of my introduction to choir robes, flowing stoles, starched ruffs and cuffs, and so on, make me think of the excitement, many years later, in my African parish of Cachonga when my riotous congregation first caught sight of garments such as these. The ecclesiastical clothes and trappings had been sent up river, from the capital and tucked away in my hiding place behind the altar, along with so many other things the Bishop assumed I required for my new church.

I don't need my notes or sketches from the tin trunk to remember the chaotic excitement of those weeks. My memory rushes back, through that door of pain, to the enthusiastic commotion of a spectacle that still makes me smile – in spite of everything that followed.

Out in the middle of the African bush I relished being free to teach Christ's message without the trappings of institutionalized religion and was determined that the atmosphere in my small church, St. Thomas's, would be welcoming, homely, friendly and positive. My willingness to incorporate various tribal traditions into my services had won me many converts but I knew my methods to be unconventional and controversial. When I received a message from the Bishop that he was sending his 'Canon Missioner' to visit Cachonga, and to take Holy Communion with us, I panicked. It was time to open the crates and packages he had been sending for so many years and to persuade my congregation to learn a new sense of discipline.

Out of the boxes came stacks of prayer books. A strange gift for a congregation who couldn't read English. There were cartons of communion wafers and bottles of wine with drawings of The Last Supper on the labels, a chalice and paten, large pillar candles, altar cloths with matching chasubles and stoles, a new surplice and a whole set of chorister robes. There was also a large wooden crucifix, with Christ's face distorted in agony, and a beautiful silver dish for the font.

St. Thomas' didn't have a font, nor had there been any christenings or confirmations, hence there had never been the need to celebrate Holy Communion. There wasn't a choir, and I hated the idea of putting a cloth over the splendor of the polished baobab trunk which was our altar, I was also against displaying the crucifix – I didn't want Christ's misery portrayed in my church; I wanted Christ's joy, His love, and – especially – His laughter.

The chief N'anga was called Umboto. I would have called someone of this title a witch doctor before my arrival in Cachonga. It had taken many months and theological compromises to obtain his acceptance of my mission to his village and his blessing upon the construction of a church there. Unlike the other chieftains of the village, Umboto was a wily man of lean build whose sixty or seventy years had taught him how to manipulate the tribe with inflexible subtlety. However, by the time I received the news of an impending visit from the ecclesiastical authorities the old man and I had become firm friends and I did not hesitate to tell him of my concerns.

To my amazement and relief Umboto grasped the gravity of the situation instantly and promised his support in preparing the village to put on a suitable show for the visitor. I explained the significance of the last supper, showing him the picture in the bible, and on the label of the communion wine bottle I had brought to our meeting. I talked of the reasoning behind Christenings, and how and why holy water was used. I described the scene of John the Baptist and Jesus in the River of Jordan, and suddenly Umboto became very excited.

"We, too, have a river," he announced proudly. "We will do the same – you and me together – in the water.

It will be splendid, I will invoke Nyami Nyami, the sacred spirit who lives in river waters, and you shall invoke your Christ. We will make a big celebration, and then everyone will be ready for your communion feast."

I was overwhelmed by this sudden spurt of enthusiasm and soon became equally excited. Together, as the two representatives of God's power on earth, we planned a spectacle that would be talked about, up and down the river, for many years to come.

Baptism Day, as it had been titled by Umboto, dawned fresh and clear. There was no breakfast served that day - although I noticed a tray of something steaming being smuggled into the Chief's hut shortly after sunrise. A procession began to take shape under the strict directions of Umboto as the early morning light became stronger. The villagers were lining up, in order of importance, for the chief to lead when everybody was ready.

I started by distributing the robes to a specially selected group who I felt were the most ardent of my followers. I found I had no chance of persuading the riotous crowd that this was meant to be an occasion of solemnity. The chosen members of the congregation were so pleased with the new vestments and the sudden superiority they acquired along with the robes and starched collars, that a full-scale tribal dance ensued. None of the clothes were as crisp at the end of these gyrations as I would have wished, and some were distinctly muddy. I consoled myself that the important cleric, who was due to inspect us the following week, would assume that the garments had seen many weeks of devoted service.

During the previous few days, the warriors had been busy collecting thin branches and binding them together with strong wire – another item from my shopping list that had been honored by the bishop. They had made a tall mobile corral designed to keep the crocodiles from disrupting our performance in the river. They stood with their impressive bundles at the head of the group.

Umboto was wearing only a loincloth of impala skin and his huge headdress of ostrich feathers.

Sacred Paraphernalia

Complicated necklaces hung around his scraggly neck and there were bright bangles on his upper arms. He was carrying a long carved stick with a decorated dried gourd at the top. Small pebbles on bright strings were attached to the gourd so that it rattled when twirled. I wore my white surplice and the brightest chasuble of the collection recently unpacked, and was carrying the silver bowl. My tin cross was freshly polished and I had even trimmed my beard. As always, both of us were bare-foot.

At a signal from Umboto the chief emerged in the full regalia of leopard skin, feathers and glittering beads that bobbed up and down upon his impressive stomach. With due solemnity he settled on his throne which was ready for him on the royal litter. Six warriors lifted their burden to shoulder height and took their place at the head of the parade. Only the nyoka-boys, whose job was to frighten snakes away from the path with their tapping sticks, were ahead of them. At last the procession began.

When everyone arrived at the riverbank, several warriors placed a specially prepared wooden ramp against the bank, down into the water. Another group proceeded down the ramp slowly, striking the water surface in front of them with the flats of their spears as they went. When they were happy that no crocodiles were lurking in the mud, they unraveled their fence and created a corral of safe water.

I wound my stole around my neck like a scarf, but didn't raise my surplice as, with a solemn nod to Umboto, the two of us walked slowly and steadily into the soft mud of the river until we were waist deep in the water, our toes and feet being gently sucked into the hidden mire. On the bank, on either side of the chief on his throne, four warriors beat on tall drums to add to the drama.

Worried about getting my prayer book wet, I had memorized the passages I wanted to use for the service. I had chosen only the most positive pieces of the prayers and was confident that God would not mind if I did not accuse his flock of innocents of being 'conceived and born in sin' or that they, being 'in the flesh cannot please God, but live in sin.'

Umboto and I had made a careful plan for this performance, and had decided that the Witch Doctor should start the proceedings. After all, this was his village and, I insisted, these were his people, whereas I was only a visitor.

Taking a deep breath, Umboto raised his stick high and rattled the pebbles. He sprayed a gabble of high-pitched sounds across the river surface, towards the throng on the bank. I caught the words Nyami-Nyami, Vadzumi, Mhondoro and Mwari, repeated from time to time, which are the names of the God of the River, the much revered ancestral spirits, and the Gods of the earth respectively, but the rest of the speech was beyond me. It seemed to have a great appeal to the congregation who started to sway and moan and occasionally lift their hands to the sky.

Then it was my turn, and I started with my usual greeting of welcome and supplication to the Almighty God to honor the service. Then, I cleared my throat and pronounced in the most formal tones I could muster:

'Our Saviour Christ sayeth, "None can enter into the kingdom of God, except he be regenerated and born anew of Water and of the Holy Ghost." I beseech you, therefore, to call upon God the Father, through our Lord Jesus Christ, that of his bounteous goodness he will grant you that which by nature you cannot have; that you may be baptized with Water and the Holy Ghost, and received into Christ's holy Church, and be made living members of the same."

I always loved the grandeur of my 1815 version of the Book of Common Prayer, and as most of my new parishioners wouldn't understand the incantations even if they were presented in colloquial English, I indulged myself with the old texts. Upon my signal, everybody said 'Amen.'

"Almighty God, we call upon thee for these persons," I continued, raising my arms and eyes to the heavens, "that they, coming to the holy Baptism, may receive remission of their sins by spiritual regeneration. Receive them, O God, as thou hast promised by thy well-beloved Son, saying: Ask, and ye shall receive; Seek, and ye shall find; Knock, and it shall be opened unto you. So give now unto us that ask; let us that seek find; open the gate unto us that knock; that these persons may enjoy the everlasting benediction of heavenly washing, and may come to the eternal kingdom which thou hast promised by Christ our Lord, Amen."

The crowd shouted 'Amen' and were clearly affected by the scene. Loveness – the girl who had most helped me since my arrival at Cachonga by acting as a translator, now came forward, dressed in one of the choristers' robes. She also walked into the river and took her place between Umboto and myself. In the language of the village, she read out a short explanation of what I had said which we had prepared the day before. Then she translated first the questions, and then the answers, that they all had to make. The responses would be made in English.

Facing the swaying crowd on the riverbank, spreading out behind the Chief, the Elders and the Warriors, I began: "Dost thou renounce the devil and all his works, the vain pomp and glory of the world?" I had decided to omit the part about 'all covetous desires and carnal desires of the flesh' as too difficult for the present congregation to either understand or to follow.

Upon Loveness's instruction, the words rumbled back: "I renounce them all."

"Dost thou believe in God the Father Almighty, Maker of heaven and earth? And in Jesus Christ his only-begotten Son our Lord?

Answer: "All this, I believe."

"Wilt thou be baptized in this faith?

Answer: "That is my desire."

The congregation was getting increasingly agitated. The villagers continued to sway and wave their arms around as they responded. They were all caught up in the atmosphere of the moment, and I caught a glimpse of the Oberammergau style of mass hysteria I had found so disquieting several years earlier – especially as, this time, it was myself who was initiating that disturbing emotion. I remember thinking that there was nothing I could do about it, it was too late to change things now. I had to just let it happen and trust in God that all would be right in His eyes.

Next the Chief was invited to join us in the water, to be the first to be baptised. Chief Mungonie looked extremely uncomfortable with the idea and, after a moment's hesitation, he gestured to his oldest son, Amanzi, to be the first to experience "baptism". Knowing the chief as well as I did, I knew he was afraid, and was amused to note that his anxiety did not preclude him from offering his son and heir to act as guinea-pig.

Amanzi bowed low before his father, and then strode purposefully into the water where I gestured solemnly for him to kneel. With only the slightest delay, Amanzi sank to his knees so that the water came to his shoulders. I then dipped my thumb into the blessed water in the silver bowl and made the sign of the cross upon his forehead.

"I baptise thee, Amanzi, in the name of the Father, and of the Son, and of the Holy Ghost, Amen."

Umboto then dipped his staff into the water and brought it out, shaking it around Amanzi's head so that water droplets scattered from the swinging pebbles.

Meanwhile, I continued my prepared text: "We receive this person into the congregation of Christ's flock; and do sign him with the sign of the Cross, in token that hereafter he shall not be ashamed to confess the faith of Christ and will continue Christ's faithful soldier and servant unto his life's end. Amen"

Amanzi stood up at my instruction, he turned and faced the crowd: "Hallelujah" he screamed at the top of his voice. "I am saved, I have life everlasting," he raised both his arms in the air and concluded: "I am Amanzi."

The whole village went wild with delight, and pushed forward en masse, each wanting to be the next one into the river. The warriors stayed their progress, holding back the throng with a barrier of horizontal spears.

As Amanzi climbed out of the river, the water running off his shining skin, his eyes wide with emotion, his father rose to his feet. With due ceremony the chief turned to his people and spoke to them in their own language.

I looked enquiringly at Loveness who translated quietly, the water lapping at the now prominent dark nipples of the pert breasts that poked stubbornly against her wet choir robe. "He is telling them that he wanted his son to be the first to receive this great blessing, because it was his son who would take over as their leader when he is gone." She suddenly looked straight at me and winked.

It was such an unexpected gesture, and yet so appropriate that I had great difficulty in suppressing a guffaw of mirth.

"He is now inviting the elders to come with him into the river so that they can be baptised together," Loveness continued.

Two large men from the warrior group helped Chief Mungonie out of his throne and down the ramp. His wide skirts floated out on the water as he proceeded towards me, making him look like a giant water-lily.

The Elders, Josiah, Zengali, Moses, Zongarto and Christopher followed behind, each with his own warrior helper.

Umboto and I repeated our performances and the elders bobbed and twirled, shouting Hallellujas and Amens at random moments. The crowd joined in, their cries echoing across the river.

For the next three hours we dabbed and sprinkled the population of Cachonga.

Baptism day ended with another Cachonga feast. This time it was a bull that had been slaughtered the previous day. I had watched with interest as the beast was divided up according to some ancient tribal tradition. All the men of the village had helped to skin the ox, the hide then left in the sun to dry. The meat was prepared for roasting with a dignified performance that reminded me of the gillie and the stag all those years ago in Scotland. The lungs were presented to the grandchildren of the village and the pancreas was divided amongst the herd boys who had looked after the beast. The heart, stomach and entrails were given to the women who placed them carefully into a huge cauldron. Every member of the village would have a taste of the resulting stew after three days cooking. The scrotum of the bull was presented to the chief to be used as a purse for storing his snuff tobacco. The bushy tail was carried with ceremony to Umboto. The horns went to Ngirazi, the leader of the warriors, to be used as blow pipes and trumpets. The meat was then hacked into great slabs ready to be put on spits over half a dozen fires.

When the Baptism Feast was ready, I was invited to eat in the company of the chief, Umboto and the elders; the first time such an honor had been bestowed upon me. While we were eating, the significance of the beef was explained by Josiah.

"Ukama igasva hunozadziswa nokudya" the school master intoned. "This means that friendship of words is not enough; true friendship is proved by the gift of meat, and it is a friendship that goes beyond the grave. Cattle unite the living with the dead. The spirits of our ancestors stay with us in our cattle, and before we kill a beast, application must be made for the mudzimu to move to another animal."

Umboto had been brewing beer for the last week in preparation for this evening's festivities, and now vats of thick, sweet brownish liquid, surrounded by heaps of tin mugs, were set out on tables; a sticky aroma hovered overhead. The singing and dancing that followed went on well into the night.

When all the excitement had finally subsided, and everyone had drifted to their huts, I found myself unable to sleep. As usual, I had pulled my mattress out of the hut and lay gazing at the stars. The ebullience of the day had left me physically exhausted but emotionally I was still buzzing with energy. My thoughts ran over the proceedings and I remember thanking God over and over again for making it all possible and for enriching His flock by so many willing devotees.

I prayed that God did not object to the village's easy transition back to old lore when they returned from the river for the feast. I had said grace before the meal was served, echoed by Umboto, and everybody had chimed

'Amen' in splendid unison. Of the people's love for a God we shared, I had no doubt, so I saw no difficulty in indulging their beliefs in ancestors' spirits in cattle and so on. All spirits were part of God's spirit, I argued to myself, and as such should present no threat to the Christian faith.

The dramatic service had undoubtedly been a huge success, and I had found the villagers' ecstatic response to the baptism itself very rewarding. I had felt God's power and love flowing through me and out to my congregation, and in return the people had sent waves of love and faith, through my outstretched arms, back to Almighty God.

At least, that is how it felt at the time.

6. THE DELIGHTS OF BOARDING SCHOOL

My brother was head boy when I arrived at the famous school that my father had attended - and maybe his father too, I can't remember - but that didn't ease my way into the community in any way whatsoever. During the five years I spent at Rossington, the chapel was my only safe haven. Without the privacy of my own bedroom, communication with The Almighty was at first restricted to hushed whispers in the bathroom, and then stopped altogether when I found I had been overheard, my ardent words horrifically misinterpreted and joked about unmercifully.

Dormitory life was an inferno of humiliations for me, with lewd talk making me feel queasy. God seemed to be totally absent; there was no space for me to consult my best friend and confidant. I felt I had been abandoned in a flesh pit of adolescent fantasies.

However, in the school chapel, I had a raison d'être amongst the familiar, beautiful incantations. Here I could hold my head up above the sniggers and taunts of my classmates, I knew that God would recognize me in his own house, as a true devotee. He would understand my social trials and appreciate my challenges and personal sacrifices.

As at St. Barnabus', I loved the way my surplice flowed as I walked towards the choir stalls. The pride and confidence I felt in the church at home was with me again when I wore the robes at school. The chaplain of Rossington, Father John, who had received a letter from Father Edmund, told me how he watched the alteration in my demeanor as I changed out of the school uniform into the ecclesiastical garments.

"Divine assurance, I call it," the jovial priest proclaimed, as he helped me straighten the billowing cloth before facing the congregation of my school peers. "I never take it for granted" Father John continued, "it's like a new gift every time I don my robes. The Lord be praised for his bounty," he concluded, giving my shoulders an affectionate squeeze. Beyond the curtains that separated the vestry from the main body of the chapel the jeering faces would be waiting.

Chapel happened twice a day during the week and three times on Sundays, but that was not enough for me. I found so many aspects of school life intimidating, I would rather have spent the whole time within the church's stone walls.

When the services finished, I noted how the other members of the choir raced to leave the sacristy. There was an almost panic-driven rush amongst the boys to get out of their robes and away from the sanctity and peace of the church and the presence of Father John. Hence I always found myself alone – apart from the vicar who seemed to welcome my presence - and the tranquility of the place seemed to consolidate the religious experiences of the service in which we had just participated.

Being the weedy brother of a tough head-boy made me an easy target for my peers, especially when the other boys found out that Robert shared their derision for his sibling. The baiting of Bolden Junior became a school pastime.

Dormitory life was the first great horror for me, but there was also the purgatory of the games fields and the changing rooms. Forced to play team sports for which I was totally inept, I found my experiences on the playing fields almost intolerable. The other lads would laugh at my skinny legs and thin shoulders. My blinking eyes, unsheltered by the cumbersome spectacles that had become an unwilling trademark, did little to help the situation. My obvious lack of enthusiasm or talent for games made me an easy target for teasing, as did my obvious distaste for any form of physical contact. My classmates took pleasure in knocking me about - both my body and mind seemed permanently full of bruises as a result.

The worst injury I sustained was on the Rugby field one clear January morning when the grass was still crisp with frost. As usual, I tried to keep myself out of trouble by staying as far from the ball as possible, but this morning it seemed as if all my team members were determined to throw the ball to, or at, me, and to leave it with me, offering no opportunities for a further pass. With the unwelcome ball clasped against my chest, I started to run. The opposition descended upon me en masse and I came down feeling as if I had been shot in the groin as pain spread through my whole body like fire.

The slippery footing was blamed for the low tackle that had resulted in my being headed directly in the crotch. As I was carried off the field with dark blue veins throbbing clearly through the pale skin of my neck and temples, the coarse comments of my classmates drifted towards me:

"Well, he was never going to use the thing any way."

"That'll be the most action that bit ever sees . . ." and so on.

In the sick bay the matron examined my blackening member as I felt my face changing from ashen to puce.

How I wish I'd had Amrita's wisdom then, to help me through the following days. This wonderful lady of Indian descent comes into my story much later, but I can't resist recounting here, her talk to me in the day room of St. Mary's hospital, many years later. We were both trapped in wheelchairs, and I had just given way to an involuntary groan as a shift of weight resulted in sharp pains shooting from my pelvis to my collarbones.

7. AMRITA'S 'LITTLE TOE' THEORY

"How is your little toe today, Jack?" had been Amrita's astonishing question that started the discussion, following my wince of pain. I got used to the value of Amrita's seemingly random questions eventually, but at this time I was still new to the hospital's 'Day Room' and the diminutive, American born, Indian doctor – a couple of years my junior - had not yet impressed me with her gentle wisdom.

"My little toe?" I asked incredulously, unable to keep traces of anger and frustration from my voice. "It's not my toes that are hurting – it's all the stitches around the skin grafts and the wretched 'Hartman's pouch' thing that the surgeon's created. And then, of course, there are the ribs, lungs, the broken femur. . ." a wave of self-pity had engulfed me. I got myself under control after a few embarrassing seconds. "There's nothing wrong with my toe," I concluded with as much dignity as I could muster.

"Well, that's all very well – of course I can't feel mine any more so I have no idea if they're hurting or not." Amrita responded, and I blushed with shame at my insensitivity. "But I was asking about your right little toe in particular. Have you examined it with your mind to make sure that it is in a really healthy state?"

"I don't think I understand what you are saying," I said meekly, feeling very inadequate and upset by my angry outburst towards this delicate lady of courage with her long plait of glossy black hair and deep dark eyes always carrying a soft smile.

"What I'm suggesting, Jack," Amrita continued brightly, as if my outburst had never happened, "is that you move your thoughts and feelings from the pains in your chest, torso and legs, and investigate the state of the little toe on your right foot. Don't look at the toe, or try to touch it with anything other than your mind. Move your mind, in the same way as you can move your eyes, and concentrate on that particular part of your body."

Out of courtesy to my new acquaintance I tried to do as she instructed. I made a physical effort – for that was what was necessary - to drag my thoughts down to a toe that had previously given me no reason for investigation or interest.

"It feels fine, thank you, Amrita," I said after several seconds of careful thought. "I can't find anything wrong with it." I looked at my friend's smiling face in confusion.

"Good," said Amrita. "Now if you're absolutely sure that the little toe is ok, how about the one next to it – that's a much more difficult question. Moving the mind to the fourth toe is quite complicated. See if you can single out that fourth toe and check that it, too, is ok."

I remember so well frowning with the concentration of finding my fourth toe with my mind and examining it as a single entity, and not just as part of my foot.

"I've done it!" I said with a sudden sense of achievement. "I've really separated it out from the others, and it's in fine form, my fourth toe. I don't think I've ever given it such individual attention. What's this all about Amrita?"

"It's just a little exercise I used to do whenever I had pain of any sort." Amrita linked her fingers together and stretched her arms out in front of her. "I shall have to find another gimmick now," she added looking down at her motionless knees.

"You see," she continued, "if you find the strength to direct your mind away from the part of your body which is giving you trouble, the pain is not allowed to dominate any more. Focusing your thought somewhere else is a trick that makes such a movement easier. Toes are useful because they are difficult to single out and it takes a lot more concentration to focus on a toe than it does on say an ankle or a knee. If you work hard at moving your mind down to investigate one toe after another, you will find that the pains of elsewhere go unnoticed for a while, and maybe they will have passed – or reduced in intensity – by the time you allow your mind to roam where it will once again."

I thought carefully about what Amrita had just said. My eyes gazed through the wide windows, down the lawn to the river glinting in the distance, but my thoughts were elsewhere. I returned my mind to my toes – she was right. While I had been concentrating on the state of individual toes, I had forgotten about the tight burning pains of my buttocks and the stabbing in my ribs.

"What a splendid trick, Amrita," I said, returning her smile. "Where does that come from?"

"It's a combination of meditation and yoga techniques I think," Amrita replied. "I discovered it when I was a teenager suffering from terrible period pains. I was experimenting with different ideas, and this one seemed to work, so I stayed with it. Once you've got the hang of it, you can move your mind to anything that takes your fancy – it doesn't have to be part of your body, I just found that was the easiest way to start. Now I can put my mind into the centre of," she paused, looking around the room until her eyes rested on some cut flowers in a vase on the windowsill; "that rose, for instance. I can lose myself among those petals and my body is left without a driver, so to speak, its pains and irritations no longer of consequence."

Just then the doors of the day room squeaked open and Percival – the third member of our 'Day-Room Discussions' – entered, his plastered legs heralding the approach of his wheelchair, their owner visible a second or two afterwards.

"Good morning comrades," as always there was a veneer of humor over the cynicism in Percival's voice. "What is to be the topic of today?"

"Amrita was explaining how the mind can be moved away from the source of pain," I volunteered with enthusiasm.

"Ah, the famous 'Amrita-Little-Toe-Theory,'" said Percival as he was wheeled into position by the nurse Shamiso. "She's a clever girl, isn't she, Jack," he continued, looking at the frail figure with affection. "So much wisdom in so small a person. We can both learn a lot from you, Amrita."

"And I from you, Percival," Amrita had replied, smiling. "And from you too, Jack, I am hoping."

I still wonder if I was ever capable of teaching this wondrous lady anything of value, although we went on to share many adventures.

8. THE MAGNIFICAT

However, in the sickbay of Rossington School, Amrita's wisdom was a long way away in both time and space. The school Matron had none of my friend's gentleness, and her commanding voice brooked no argument. Painkillers were issued along with instructions not to wear underwear or any restrictive clothing until all the swelling had subsided and to report back for a further inspection in five days.

Alone in the dormitory, staring at the vaulted beams above me, I relished the unusual solitude in spite of the throbbing pain. Space to myself was something so rare during term time. Of course, I was dreading the moment when the door would be flung open, noise and commotion accompanying my companions into the echoing room along with their gibes and ill-natured teasing.

Just thinking about that time brings back all the vulnerability I felt as a somewhat weak child who failed to identify with the rest of his peers, even though I wanted to. I cannot help feeling pity towards my former self, knowing that I had meant my comrades no harm, and seeing, now, that their antics on the rugger field must have been carefully planned – and all because I simply didn't 'fit in' whether it was in the classroom, on the sports' fields, in the dining hall or, worst of all, in the dormitory.

From the start of my dormitory life, my contemporaries had been in the habit of comparing each others' reproductive equipment. I would bury my bespectacled nose into one of my many books and do my best not to be distracted. There would be loud and detailed boasts of wet dreams and erections. My reaction was to pray silently that such indignities should be relegated to my coarse roommates while I remained physically, as well as mentally, aloof from such happenings.

As the boys became accustomed to puberty, more and more members of the dormitory achieved sexual fulfillment through shared fantasies. They developed a special game to exercise their newfound prowess: magazine pictures of naked women in positions of extraordinary vulgarity were spread on the floor with the gamesters circled above. They would then encourage each other with sexual comments to see who could get the largest, quickest erection. Masturbation ensued with shouts of excitement and encouragement.

Once, I remember, curiosity got the better of me and I peered cautiously over my book. My gaze of horror and reluctant fascination was caught by the others and a stream of abuse followed my refusal to participate. After that I turned my back on the proceedings, wishing that I could shut my ears to the sounds and my nose to the smell that eventually permeated the room. I was proud that I remained immune to these indecent ideas and undignified physical happenings. I see now what a strange child I must have been, and how easily led to experience sexual feelings in a different way.

As it happened, the injury on the rugger field was the catalyst which introduced me to a new dimension of feeling. Following matron's instructions, I found that there were hidden benefits to the unconfined freedom of not wearing underwear. At first I persuaded myself that it was just relief as the pain receded, but on the following Sunday, as I slipped my treasured surplice over my head and removed my shorts, the feeling of the cool, slippery fabric against my nakedness sent a shiver through me from toe to scalp. I felt a strange prickling at the back of my neck and my afflicted member tightened still further. Throughout the service my thoughts were drawn to the sensation of the smooth, silky material sliding against me as I walked through the church, knelt, sat and stood as the service progressed.

The following Sunday, although I had been given the 'all clear' by the matron, I decided to remove all my underclothes and experience the surplice against my whole body. It was a delicious sensation and I persuaded myself that I was closer to God than ever in this newfound physical appreciation of the holy.

In my defense, I must explain that this idea was given validity by the school Chaplin himself. The church service had finished and, as usual, all the others had bolted and I was the last boy left in the choir room. As I started to disrobe, the door suddenly flew open to admit Father John. The surplice, having been lifted up to my chin, was quickly lowered again over my naked body, as the blood rushed to my face in a profusion of embarrassment.

The Chaplain, a man in his late fifties, with thinning hair and a round somewhat cherubic face, did not seem at all startled by what he had seen. His large, soft hands were squeezing a pile of hymnals against his ample stomach. As he started to place the books on the shelves that lined the walls between the tall diamond-paned windows, he chatted to me in an unconcerned but friendly tone:

"Ah! You have discovered the way to feel the holy against your skin, Jack," he began. "That is a good thing, I do it myself whenever I can." He turned from the bookcase and continued in a conspiratorial tone: "It gives one an intimacy with the Divine, you know, and sometimes that intimacy grows in a very special way, expressing spirituality in a new physical aspect." Father John moved back towards the door. "Just as when the Priest kisses the altar during communion, he is demonstrating a physical love and longing for The Divine Majesty, so that closeness can manifest itself more precisely when you are alone with God." The

Chaplain looked around him before carefully closing the door he had opened so suddenly a few moments earlier. I heard the key being turned and the unmistakable click as the bolt slid into place.

Father John's benign smiling face was turned towards me again. I remember sputtering about my previous injury and the instructions of the school matron, but was stopped by the Chaplain laying his finger gently against my lips.

"Adoration of the Almighty takes many forms," he said, seeming not to notice my still blushing cheeks. "As I pray, I feel God's presence flowing through me" he continued, putting his hands against his chest with outspread fingers. "As long ago as the Middle Ages holy men understood what it meant to have a physical relationship with God. You should read the works of Richard Rolle, when you have time." He was sliding his hands downwards as he spoke, pressing his gown against his chest, against his stomach and coming to rest over his genitals. "He died in 1349, did Rolle, but before he went he wrote of meditations done with the body as well as with the mind. A wonderful mystical and physical experience all rolled into one – that's a pun, dear boy, so you won't forget Rolle's name." His hands had started a rhythmical stroking as he spoke, and now they moved in time to the Magnificat that he began reciting: "My soul doth magnify the Lord; and my spirit hath rejoiced in God my Saviour…"

I watched with a disturbing fascination as the Chaplain's surplice began to rise under his hands until, as he reached the final verse, the cloth was poked out by something underneath so that the hands could grasp it as one might a broomstick covered in a sheet.

"This is a secret sign of true devotion to our faith, Jack." Father John explained conspiratorially, looking down at the development with both admiration and devotion. "You must learn to show your appreciation for God's wonders in this way, and to keep the secret of the Divine Intimacy between you and your God alone. Of course, such a secret is safe with me," the Chaplain went on, "for I am God's representative here in this hallowed place and can help you develop your own physical togetherness with the Almighty.

"Here," he continued in his soft voice, "feel for yourself the power of such communication." Father John took hold of my hands and placed them on the protruding surplice, curling my young fingers and squeezing them so that I could feel the Chaplain's veins pulsing through the cloth beneath my enforced grip. The hardness and warmth surprised me as I allowed my hands to be moved backwards and forwards along the length of the priapic cloth.

The Chaplain had now moved on to the Jubilate Deo, intoning the words mellifluously in time to the movement of the two pairs of hands, quickening the pace of his praises with his head thrown back in excited reverence and then slowing gradually as the final verse approached "world without end, Amen." My hands were released as a great sigh shuddered from the Chaplain's chest and his eyes, filled with a moist look of extraordinary fulfillment, left the ceiling and returned to my own.

"You see, my boy, God's richness is so full. His willingness to fill mankind with his power is sometimes overwhelming. We humble servants must do our utmost to receive his love as best we can, and be ever grateful for the divine proximity he allows to his chosen few."

Turning quickly, the chaplain moved to the door, unlocking and opening it in one swift movement and, looking back at me for just a second, he waved a nonchalant hand.

"Don't forget it's a secret, dear boy. Let me know how you get on with your own Godly communications and if you need any help, you can always count on me."

Then, as suddenly as he had appeared, he was gone, leaving me standing stock still, my arms still outstretched, hands open, as if in supplication, the fingers slightly curled as if sniffing the odor the Chaplain had left in his wake.

9. COMMUNION WITH THE ALMIGHTY

So that is how my puberty and my faith became interwoven. The incident had occurred on the last Sunday of term and I was relieved not to have to face the Chaplain again for several weeks. When I went home, I took Father John's giant secret with me and continued to enjoy genital freedom beneath my ecclesiastical garments at St. Barnabus'. Such behavior had not only been condoned, it had been blessed. However, I did not feel ready to experiment with stroking hands, feeling that God wasn't ready to send His power in my direction just yet, and being unable to dispel the feeling that something wasn't quite right about it all.

Then came the day when, whilst holding the host for Father Edmund during a communion service, my eyes were drawn to a pretty girl kneeling at the altar rail. Her hands were lifted to receive the sacrament. Her elbows, balanced on the polished wood, were squeezing her breasts together inside a low-cut dress. I was fascinated with the way her chest rose and sank with her breathing. On the rise, the round softness of her breasts caught the sunlight as it filtered its way through the stained-glass windows, as they sank, the shadowy cleavage seemed to pull me inside.

As she received the chalice, my view of the girl was interrupted by the vicar's bowed form, and I was filled with impatience for the obstruction to be removed. The girl was getting up as the vicar moved on, she turned those beautiful breasts away from me and proceeded demurely back down the aisle, her skirt undulating against her calves as she walked. As I turned to follow the vicar back up to the altar I caught sight of my reflection in the gleaming silver plate I carried. I hardly recognized the radiance that had come into my face and the gleam that shone behind my glasses. It was then that I became aware of a tightening sensation in my groin and felt the fabric of my surplice against the inflamed tip that had risen without notice.

I tried to push down this uninvited protuberance during a deep genuflection at the altar, but to no avail. I returned to my choir stall and remained on my knees in seeming devotion for as long as I could, dreading the moment when I would have to stand up and take the cross down the aisle, ahead of the rest of the choir, and in full sight of the congregation.

It's amazing, after all these years, that I can remember so acutely my embarrassment when the moment came for me to leave my pew and walk to the altar to fetch the cross. Making the most of the time when I had my back to the body of the church, I arranged the folds of my surplice as best I could to disguise my newly developed manhood. I took the cross from its supports and rested the long handle against myself so that my lower hand concealed the bulge. With stoic determination I turned my back to the altar and began the journey through the church to the sanctuary.

Half way down the aisle my eye was caught by the girl who had caused all the trouble. I felt the cross give a lurch towards her, as if drawn by a magnet, and it took all my strength to maintain its upright position as I completed the walk and was embraced by the heavy curtains that were looped on either side of the sanctuary doorway.

As the other choirboys chattered and laughed in their usual busy way whilst removing their gowns and replacing them with their ordinary clothes, I sat in a corner in wondering silence. Gradually the vestry emptied as one after another the boys went jauntily out to their lives beyond the church. None of them noticed me – my habit of keeping aloof made my silence expected, and not one of them even bothered saying goodbye to the huddled figure at the end of the bench. It was the Priest himself who noticed me, still in my choir robes, alone in the corner.

"Is anything wrong, Jack" Father Edmund asked, coming towards me with a hint of fatigue in a stoop which contrasted with his usually upright posture.

"Can I ask you a question, Father?" I responded, relieved to be with someone I could trust and, of course, he was used to me asking him questions.

"Of course, my boy. What is troubling you?" The priest was all eager concern.

"Is it true" I asked "that God can visit you in a physical sense?" When the Priest raised a questioning eye-brow I quickly continued: "the Chaplin at school explained that some especially religious people could communicate with God in a physical way, could feel his presence in a . . . in something like a sexual way – only not sexual, of course, but spiritual." I could feel my face burning red, and a vein pulsing in my neck so that it might burst. I raised a hand to hide it.

"Tell me what's happened," said the priest quietly, sitting down on a bench opposite me and folding his hands inside his capacious sleeves.

In faltering speech, I told Father Edmund what the Chaplain had told me. "Well, it can't hurt my telling you about the secret, as you must know it too" I started and then went on to talk about what had happened to me that morning in church. The Priest was silent for some time.

Looking back on this scene, after my years of ministering in an Islington parish, I can now see my supplication in perspective. In fact, I think the wisdom shown by Father Edmund that day must have helped me to deal with the problems that came to my door, so many years later, at St. George's.

"Do you consider this to be a spiritual experience, Jack?" the vicar began, obviously aware of the worry in the eyes fixed upon him, beseeching help and reassurance. "Has this ever happened to you before?"

"No, never, and yes, of course I believe it to be spiritual – what else could move a person so completely and in such an involuntary but wonderful way?" I answered rapidly.

The vicar thought for a moment and then seemed to come to a decision. He took a deep breath: "Well, my boy, you must be congratulated. You have today received a special visit. God was with that girl today, and he chose her as a vessel through whom he could speak to you." Father Edmund rose stiffly and looked down at me with as much reassurance as he could muster. "God's magnificence is difficult for us to fathom – it is so immense. He can only show us his powers in diluted forms so that we are not incinerated by the magnitude of his presence. Be content to know that you are following his path; that you appreciate all that is Divine; and marvel at His greatness. In time, other vessels will be provided to assist your communication with The Almighty, but they should always remain within the Church, you understand that, Jack?"

I did not understand. However, I was determined to work it out and make some sense of the explanation. In the meantime, I gave Father Edmund an enthusiastic nod

Tell me," the vicar continued, "the Chaplain at school, what is his name?"

"He's Father John," I answered, struggling to my feet. I was as tall as Father Edmund now, but still willowy and of meager build. "He'll be pleased with my progress in this way, especially after his encouragement. What should I do next, Father?" I queried.

Father Edmund seemed to search for an answer once more. "Do not seek the girl again, Jack," he began. "She was only a vehicle for the Divine, for that moment, just for you. You have been much blessed and you should rejoice in the secret communication that you have experienced." He patted me on the shoulder and turned to leave the vestry. As he reached the door, he looked back over his shoulder, unknowingly mimicking Father John: "Keep this to yourself, Jack, and be joyful" he enjoined, and disappeared into the body of the church.

It's hard to believe that I could have been so innocent, but the truth is that my religious fervor was such that I did not contemplate for one moment any alternative explanation of what had happened. I felt the glow of my religious belief expand within me. I dropped to my knees in the middle of the vestry, clasping my hands to my chest a feeling my heart thudding within. My prayers came unprepared in an outpouring of gratitude and I lost track of time, stopping only when I became aware that my knees were cold and sore against the stone floor. Having changed into normal clothes, I left the church with an euphoric sense of excitement and wonderment.

Upon returning to school a week later, I was eager to share my experience with Father John, but to my surprise, Father John had left the school and been replaced by a stooped, grey-haired man in his early seventies. He had been brought into the school from retirement and seemed none too pleased to be there. Of Father John's whereabouts, no one seemed to have any information. I realize now, with some disquiet, that it must have been my talk with Father Edmund that caused the sudden removal of Father John. Fortunately, at the time, I had no sense of being involved in his disappearance.

The pressure of the forthcoming 'A Level' final examinations filled school life for the rest of my time at Rossington and I absorbed most of my spiritual energy with supplications for assistance. I continued to feel a special closeness with God and treasured this secret intimacy. At last, as my physical frame strengthened, my shoulders squared, and the stubble on my chin grew more insistent on a jaw line that finally had some definition, I looked to the end of my school years with cautious enthusiasm.

10. THE LEATHER TRADE

Having finished school, I was destined to follow my brother Robert into the family business. A fact never doubted by father and never questioned by either mother or myself. I was taught the history of the firm's success and made aware that mine was a privileged inheritance no matter how unpleasant I found it. The rich undulating grassland of our part of England had been beef-fattening country for the previous three centuries - and is still well stocked with bullocks. As meat is easier to transport than live animals, slaughterhouses proliferated in the area with the resulting plethora of hides, offal, hooves and horns. Tanners were busy and the good ones became rich by supplying the leather goods industries that grew up in their wake.

Our ancestors had been tanners with the foresight to learn the trades that made use of their finished product. As well as perfecting the art of producing fine hides, the family had developed its own brand of leather goods. The business had grown and flourishes into the present day.

Visits to the tannery were part of my childhood, but that didn't make them any easier to stomach. I never got used to the smells of the receiving bay, the drone of the flies which would settle upon a fresh skin, still wet with gore, and then land upon my arm to suck the nervous sweat. I hated the brutal noises of the machines that stretched and scraped at the newly cleft hides, the cloying atmosphere of the shed in which the skins matured, the pounding of the hammers and the hiss of the sprays whose chemicals would transform a raw piece of animal into a functional piece of leather with no apparent relationship to a living creature.

Perhaps it was his waiting legacy that made Robert so keen to fuel his inheritance, or perhaps it was just the enjoyment of governing a vibrant business, with a superior product at its climax, that gave him his energetic determination. In any event, whatever spurred him on to share father's enthusiasm for the factory evaded me completely. My brother seemed especially happy when visiting the directors' suites, well removed from the clang and the stink of the tannery and above my station in more ways than one.

I saw father's irritation as he watched my nose wrinkle whenever I was anywhere near the factory and tried hard to stop it. He must have observed also that the relationship between his two sons was anything but close - there was no antagonism, just an absolute lack of empathy. Robert, always an ambitious young man, was keen to join the older generation in business management and production, and the industry embraced his eager entrepreneurial spirit. His squat frame had a strength that made up for his short stature, his abundant hair – then turning from fair to auburn - blue eyes and strong jaw line made him a replica of our energetic father, as my own willowy frame and dark hair mimicked mother's looks. Robert had broad shoulders and a good-sized neck to support the square head that jutted forwards spasmodically whenever he was doing his inspections; whereas I was a tall, gangly youth who needed glasses to bring the world into focus. We had absolutely nothing in common, either physically or emotionally, except for our parents.

My father's brother, Douglas Bolden, ran the leather goods side of the business leaving the tanneries to father, now with Robert at his side. My uncle was a bachelor with no children to follow him into his creation of boots, shoes and other fine-leather goods. It therefore seemed appropriate to all concerned to place me in the retail side of the family firm. So, during school holidays, I was sent to help in the High Street shoe shop of the local market town. Luckily for me, the shop was situated opposite a large church whose dim light and echoing stones were balm to my soul and allowed me to breathe freely whenever I could get away from the sales room. The church boasts an early Henry Moore Pieta within its outwardly municipal structure and I spent many a lunch hour contemplating the massive smooth curves of this splendid piece of sculpture.

After leaving Rossington, I was propelled straight into full-time service in my uncle's business. I now took up a role of authority that hadn't been expected of me during school holidays. I was the heir to the business, my uncle stressed, and must learn to control the finances, and even more difficult, the staff.

I remember well the large airless room behind the shop were lengths of worktables seemed to be escorted by benches, ready to march out of the big double doors had it not been for the stooping craftsmen who bent over them. I enjoyed the workshop with its smells of saddle soap and unctuous oils and sounds restricted to those of studious tapping and the clucking teeth of concentration as the men plied their skills.

Slowly, the finished hides, procured at family rates, were turned into goods for public use and appeal.

Finished Goods

I liked the finished goods and found satisfaction as I checked the shoes' toes and heels, and the seams of briefcases, handbags, vanity cases and shaving bags.

I would run my fingers along the neat rows of stitches, searching out the slightest wrinkle or bump as I placed the goods in their allotted places in the shop window, or packed them into crates for distribution around the country.

My appreciation for the skills of the workshop and for the products they produced did not extend to the shop itself, however. Here I was required to deal with customers who required tactile help in the trying on of shoes. Coming from an undemonstrative family, I was not used to – nor did I seek – any physical contact with my fellow beings. Jostling queues at school had always made me feel uncomfortable and travel by tube, on my annual visit to London to see the dentist, left me feeling dirty and abused. For one who recoiled from the touch of strangers, being expected to initiate contact with customers in such an intimate situation filled me with dread.

Most of the time I managed to engineer things so that I could present the client with a pair of shoes and a shoehorn and absent myself quickly from the scene. Occasionally my uncle would find me amongst the tiers of shoeboxes pretending to look for a particular size or color. I would choose a box attentively and be forced to return to the amphitheater of the shop where, under his watchful gaze, I would find myself on my knees before the ugliness of mankind instead of the beauties of God.

One day an elderly woman insisted that I help her try on a pair of heeled shoes designed for someone of fewer years and with a great deal less flesh. This customer's stomach was such that she couldn't reach her feet, nor could she sit with any attempt at dignity as her large thighs were pushed apart by the bulk above, stretching the too short skirt to extremes. As I wrestled to fit the shoe onto the podgy foot my eyes were caught by the sight of flesh overflowing stocking tops whose reluctant suspenders struggled to keep them in place. There was a hint of old skin and unpleasant moistures in my nostrils causing my stomach to gag into my throat.

That evening I announced to my parents that I wished to leave the family business and go into the church.

The theological college, where I was subsequently enrolled by a tight-lipped father and a mother who wore the expression of just having trodden in something unpleasant, was hidden deep within the Yorkshire moors. The high stone walls, buttressed with brick, that surrounded St. Augustine's were obviously built to keep worldly things out, rather than to keep students in. It welcomed me with gates opened wide, and I felt instantly at home.

St. Augustine's was advertised as a self-sufficient community. Within its enclave was a substantial vegetable garden, fruit orchards, hen houses, milking parlors and cheese sheds to accommodate the ample supplies from the Friesian and Guernsey cows which grazed the fields between the walls of the college and the heather-clad moorland. There was a saw-mill powered by a water wheel, a sewage plant, timber stacks, carpentry sheds, brick kilns, a grain mill, and tool sheds to house the vast array of implements necessary for this un-mechanized organization.

It was here, in those first two years, that I learnt much of what I would later use to guide my errant African flock into re-arranging themselves into a genuine agricultural community.

I think these memories need to leapfrog backwards and forwards to and from Cachonga. It is too painful to deal with those missionary years all at once. Piecemeal, like this, maybe I can get through it and achieve the catharsis I seek.

So now I will look at the state of the village when first I arrived, and the state of myself also – a naive young man who hoped that his enthusiasm and excitement would make up for his lack of experience in the third world. I was exchanging a parish in Islington for one in the middle of the African bush well out of reach of a number 13 bus and a tea-shop called The Priory Café.

11. JOURNEY TO CACHONGA

Arumba is an insignificant country in central Africa. Out of the political limelight, it struggles to obtain recognition even from the world's charitable organizations. As a Christian nation, it finds most of its outside help coming from the church, and I was the latest recruit. After five years of ministering to a parish in North London, I spent four months at a college for missionaries, and now I had my posting and had arrived in Africa.

Four different airplanes, decreasing in size and sophistication, brought me from London to Arumba's capital where I was met by   one of the

Bishop's curates with the unlikely name of Anyway. He was to look after me for the two days I was there, waiting for the bus that would take me to my final destination.

My audience with the Bishop himself was brief but significant. The prelate's flowing white robes made the round shiny face appear densely black, with the whites of his eyes gleaming like slivers of wet marble. He explained quickly that I was replacing a vicar who had allowed his parish to wander back to their pagan past and had finally disappeared into the bush with a member of his congregation. The community had been without spiritual guidance for over a year and my job was to bring it back within the correct parameters of Christian doctrine.

"I want to see Cachonga back in the fold, Jack." the Bishop said, his African accent clipped with tight English over-tones. "If you let me know what you need to re-establish the church there, you have my word that I will get you what you require. It may take a few weeks, but my friend Anyway, here," he pointed to my constant companion, "will make sure that the orders are dispatched. Won't you, Anyway?"

The curate nodded, bowing his head in reverence of his superior. I emulated his motion and expressed suitable gratitude. After a quick and somewhat perfunctory blessing, I was dismissed.

The following day, Anyway accompanied me to the bus terminal. I was immensely grateful for the assistance.

Local bus

The chaos of that place was my first real cultural shock and I would   never have managed to get a place on the bus without my young black friend pushing, arguing and offering tacky notes of the local currency, to secure me a seat. An extra wad of currency extracted a promise from the driver that I would be told where to get off sometime the following day.

The bus set off down the pot-holed road at an unholy rate and I was horribly worried to see my friend shrink into the distance. The vehicle rumbled on for several hours before screeching to the first of many stops. Every time the bus disgorged some passengers, everyone got out to make sure that only the correct amount of items were removed from the over-loaded roof rack. Each stop lasted for over an hour as the baggage, furniture, sacks of feed, chickens, roosters, a goat and many unidentifiable objects were off-loaded and re-loaded amongst a never-ending gabble of instruction and argument from everyone concerned. Sometimes new passengers filled the spaces left by those who had departed, but the bus became emptier as the day turned into night.

Eventually, early in the morning, it was my turn to get out and watch my meager suitcase and tin trunk be handed down from the roof. The latter was heavy, for it contained mostly books, my careful collection of notes from the gardens of St. Augstine's, manuals concerning agriculture in the developing world, and a small collection of tools, nails, staples and string.

I felt dirty and unkempt after so long in the jostling vehicle and my ankles, wrists and neck were covered with insect bites. Much though I had disliked the bus, I remember feeling a wave of panic as I watched it go. I had been abandoned at an unmarked junction of a narrow sand track with the pot-holed semi-tarmac road on which we had been traveling.

The rains were not long finished and the grass was still high, allowing little vision of the endless flat bush country that stretched for miles in all directions. I felt very alone and kept my eyes glued to the sandy track down which the bus driver had promised that my next mode of transport would arrive.

I saw the dust first, then I heard the car's engine, and finally I saw a roofless Landrover approaching, the driver hunched forward over the steering wheel.

"So you're the new padre," I was unsure whether this was a question or a statement made by the short, square white man who had propelled the car towards me with such determination. "I'm Sollis," he continued, thrusting a hand towards the dusty traveller. "It's my job to get you where you're going – or at least as far as the river, after that my friend Boniface has been booked to paddle you upstream."

Sollis looked me up and down without a hint of approval. He was a heavy man, in spite of his small stature, but there was no suggestion of fat about him. I thought he looked like a bull terrier, and his punchy actions, as he swung my suitcase and trunk into the back of the car, added to the similarity.

"Been in Africa long?" Sollis asked me as he gestured that I should climb aboard the vehicle that had been stripped of any suggestion of comfort.

"Nearly a week now," I replied, trying my best to sound tough and confident.

"Thought as much," said Sollis with a sniff. "Well, I have to admire your spunk, coming to a shit-hole like this. At least your new flock is excited about your arrival. Everyone in the village has been cleaning and fussing for the last month at least, so they tell me. I rarely get that far north."

Sollis started the engine and the resulting roar made further communication impossible. I had a full time job hanging on to the door and the dashboard while watching the track ahead. I needed to anticipate the leaps and bounds the Landrover made as it negotiated the obstacle course which was supposed to be a road, otherwise my head would have been battered against the windscreen like a tennis ball on a string.

It makes me smile now, to think of that first journey into the bush. By the time we got to the river, I thought that every tooth in my head must now fall out. Every bone I knew about, and several that I hadn't known until now, felt about to poke through my skin; my stomach muscles ached, as did my arms and legs from the constant bracing. Sollis looked completely relaxed, as if he had just driven to the local shop and back.

"Well, here's where I leave you," he said as he picked my cases out of the back of the car as if they were toys. "A bit dusty, I'm afraid," he added, putting them down and watching a patina of pale brown earth shimmer from their surfaces. "I hope nothing's broken," he added after a moment's reflection.

"Boniface will be here shortly," Sollis continued. "He's the one with the big canoe with a red stripe down the side. He's very proud of that stripe, be careful not to scratch it as you climb aboard.

"Oh, and good luck, padre," Sollis added as he climbed back into the Landrover. "If you need anything at Cachonga, just send a message to me, here at River's Bend. It may take me a while, but there isn't much I can't find if I put my mind to it." With that, he started the engine, did a three-point turn in a space where it didn't seem possible, and disappeared, as he had arrived, in a cloud of dust.

I waited for over two hours for that dug-out canoe with the red stripe. It was to take me on the last lap of this journey from the shady, damp streets of London, with people bustling everywhere, each in his or her own world, to this dry, dusty place without a brick building within a hundred miles and no other human being in sight. Up-stream, I was going, to the village that was to become my home for the foreseeable future.

'River's Bend' consisted of – and probably still does - a small shade hut built some twenty feet from the river bank with a large generator, captured in a cage of steel bars. A small wooden jetty stretches into the mud and out to the river water for just a short span. I had ample opportunity to explore as I waited for Boniface to arrive, but my dislike of snakes stopped me from investigating what might be hidden in the long grass.

Flies buzzed around the damp mud at the river's edge, brightly coloured bee-eaters dived in and out of the littoral shrubs and trees catching equally bright dragonflies as they hovered over the water. What I would later know as a hoopoe bird, with its crest erect, strutted its stuff along the shoreline.

I sat on a rough log, under the thatched roof of the shelter and lent against a supporting timber, my sketchbook in hand. The gentle sounds and stillness were in sharp contrast to the noisy and uncomfortable ride I had just endured. Gradually, I found my doubts dispersing, floating away with the brown river water in front of me; with the resulting relaxation came sleep.

I woke with a start, staring uncomprehendingly at the stranger who was shaking me gently by the shoulder as I gathered my thoughts. Boniface was a tall, thin man with a blue-black complexion, his cheeks marked with two deep scars each side of his nose. He had moored his canoe to the jetty, the proud red stripe mirrored in broken lines on the river's surface. I became very fond of that first canoe.

The journey up river made up for all the discomfort of the previous twenty-four hours. Boniface was an entertaining guide and chatted away as he paddled, pointing out hippos and crocodiles sunbathing on banks or poking eyes and snouts above the water to watch our passage. His knowledge of birds was very impressive, and he took an obvious pride in the beauties of his homeland.

There were cormorants, kingfishers, stilts, rollers, wagtails, herons, Egyptian geese, storks and a couple of magnificent horn-bills, the size of turkeys. A pair of fish eagles called from either side of the river while swifts and swallows chased each other low across the water. We saw many impala too, disturbed from their drinking, looking at the canoe with startled eyes before leaping back into the bush as if on springs.

The air was cooler out in mid stream, and a slight breeze ruffled the river surface in patches here and there. I sat back in the canoe and wondered at everything with delight. I felt closer to God than I had done in years. Suddenly I knew I was in the right place in God's plans for me and felt a deep contentment fill my soul as I sent silent prayers of gratitude and promises into the clear blue sky.

How different were my feelings on my final journey back down-stream some seven or eight years later.

The sun was getting low by the time Boniface turned his canoe towards the steep bank and tied it carefully to a rough jetty of ill-matching logs. He produced a series of long low whistles and then turned to help me out of the canoe. There was no sign of habitation, but a small sandy path led away from the water through the tall grass.

Boniface reached for my luggage. He swung the trunk onto his head with one swift motion, where it stayed as if stuck with glue, the small suitcase was tucked under an arm. "Follow me please, father," he said as he turned away from the river, "and keep a watch for snakes," he added over his shoulder. He walked ahead of me with easy strides, the muscles of his straight back taut, the bright beads around his wrists and ankles contrasting sharply with his black skin.

It was the drums I heard first, a muffled throbbing sound that became clearer as we progressed. Then I could hear the singing – high pitched voices mixed with deep tones ululating through the trees that appeared ahead of us.

"They are ready for you, father," Boniface said. "Your arrival has been anticipated for a long time, there will be a big celebration tonight."

The path came out of the tall grass and I saw my village for the first time. A collection of round mud huts with thatched roofs had been built under a collection of stately masasa and thorn trees. The ground between the huts was padded bare by the passage of many feet. In the centre was a newly lit bonfire, and around it was a crowd of at least fifty villagers, all singing and clapping. To the right of the group were a collection of large drums being thumped with great excitement by tall young men decked out with feather headdresses and animal-skin loincloths.

"This is your welcome, father," Boniface turned and gave me a wide grin of delight. "Everyone has put on their best clothes for you. I sent word earlier that you had really arrived at last, and they slaughtered a goat in your honor – the people have been without holy guidance for a long time, this is a very special day for everybody."

I felt tears prickling my eyes as I looked at the splendid array of shining faces and exotic costumes. Most of the women were bare breasted with elaborate necklaces rising high on their necks, framed by dangling earrings of beads and feathers. Some of the men wore brightly colored robes draped over one shoulder, others, the younger ones, were bare-chested with cloths or skins knotted around their waists. They wore strings of bright beads around their upper arms and carried tall sticks with which they were beating time on the dried earth.

As the new vicar, I was suddenly aware of my shoddy appearance. I had not had a chance to wash or shave since I left the city, and my shirt and trousers showed the strain of two days hot travel through the dust of Africa.

Boniface said something loudly in the local language and then stood to one side, pointing to me with his spare hand. I did my best to stand tall having no idea what was expected of me. Improvising, I gave a low bow, summoning as much dignity as I could, imagining I was in full clerical robes, instead of an open shirt and jeans. This gesture was met with cheers of delight and excited jabbering and a general bustle of movement replaced the singing.

Boniface lowered my trunk from his head and set it down alongside the suitcase. He indicated that I should advance towards my new congregation. "You must pay your respects to the chief before talking to anyone else," he whispered, and pointed towards the crowd.

I saw that the throng had parted to provide a path at the end of which was a large chair of rough-hewn wood. In spite of its crude structure, it was well polished and decorated with a mixture of bones and feathers. Seated on this throne was a large elderly man with grizzled hair under an immense headdress of ostrich feathers. In contrast to the lean figures of most of the other villagers, the chief was extremely fat. His tall frame seemed to have sunk into several rolls of flesh that over-lapped a skirt of decorated lion skin.

I approached with due solemnity, aware of the eyes of the crowd upon my every move. I wished I had asked Boniface for directions as to what to do next, but it was too late now. I stood in front of the chief and repeated my low bow, and then with a sudden thought, I made the sign of the cross, very slowly, in front of the chief's face and intoned a blessing in as deep a voice as I could muster: "In the name of the Father, the Son, and the Holy Ghost, Amen." After a moment's thought I added "Mangwanani" which Anyway had taught me and meant 'good morning' or a 'hello' of some kind.

Fortunately, this was a huge success, and the chief beamed and waved his staff in the air, making the feathers around its handle dance. He shouted something loud and long to which the crowd replied with whoops of delight.

"Chief Mungonie bids you welcome." I was suddenly aware of a young girl at my side. Like the others, her skin had been oiled so that it shone in the low sunlight, her dark nipples were large and soft, a string of beads nestled between her budding breasts. She was looking at me with big dark eyes. "I am Loveness," she said, her English quite precise, "it is my job to translate for you."

"Thank you Loveness," I tried to sound relaxed and confident although both these feelings eluded me completely and I went into the 'bluff-them' mode which had got me out of trouble so frequently in Islington.

I was then introduced to the hierarchy of the village. Next to the chief, the most important man of the village was N'anga Umboto, the witchdoctor. This wizened old man was as thin and bony as the chief was blubbery. He had small, slightly slanted eyes that looked at me with evident suspicion. He was in charge of medicine for the whole village, Loveness explained, and also of the ceremonies that changed young men into warriors.

I remembered the description given by the Bishop and recognised Umboto as a potential rival of serious proportions, in spite of his diminutive physical stature.

Chief Mungonie's eldest son, Amanzi, was next to be presented. He was the deputy chief of the village and therefore head of all the elders except for Umboto. Amanzi returned my bow with dignity. He must be in his early fifties, I thought, and well on the way to attaining his father's prodigious girth.

Next in line came Josiah the teacher, followed by Zengali who Loveness explained was in charge of the cattle and goats – the wealth of the village. And finally there were Moses, Zongarto and Christopher whose distinction seemed to lie purely in their great accumulation of years.

After these formal introductions, came a line of middle-aged men each with a title of his own; then a group of warriors and finally the rest of the villagers pushed forward to shake my hand.

The sun had sunk behind the tall grass when the procession was completed. Loveness then led the way to one of the huts and stood back indicating that I should enter. "This is your house," she said, "It is just for you, all for you." It was several days before I would appreciate the importance of these words for I would later discover that the chief was the only other person to enjoy private accommodation.

"Perhaps you would like to change?" Loveness continued, with appreciated diplomacy. "We have a special feast in your honor this evening which will start when the night approaches."

I bowed low to enter the hut. It was already dark inside and it took my eyes a few moments to adjust. The hut was about ten feet in diameter with a mattress of reeds on the dried mud floor to the left of the door and a bench of patted mud and earth on the right, built out from the wall. My trunk and suitcase had been placed just inside the door – apparently this was home. I turned back to Loveness who had waited outside the door. "Is there somewhere I can wash?" I enquired of my pretty young translator.

Loveness nodded enthusiastically and beckoned. I followed obediently as she skirted the main collection of huts, past what was obviously the village cooking area, where a frenzy of activity surrounded several heaps of glowing coals over which pots were suspended on tripods. The smells were of grease mostly, with a sour overtone that I would later come to know as cassava. The kitchen itself was a small structure of brick and corrugated iron, it did not look particularly hygienic. There was much adjustment needed to my ideas of cleanliness, I decided, if I was to survive here both physically and mentally.

Next to the busy kitchen area was a solitary iron hand pump, the mud around its base was a shiny red.

Our kitchen

There was a large tin bowl underneath the spout, with traces of yellow enamel here and there.

Loveness indicated the pump with pride and walked on to an unroofed structure with reed-woven walls. She pointed to the open door, and I entered, encountered several holes in the ground from which issued the smell of raw sewage, and exited rapidly. She then took me back to my hut telling me that the village would be ready for the celebratory meal at dusk.

The sun's fading rays were streaking reds and oranges across the sky making silhouettes of the tall grass blades. I hurried to open my suitcase and extract the one white robe I had brought with me and a chasuble embroidered with red and gold threads. I hung a large tin cross on a chain around my neck, I had found it at the missionary college, and had been touched by its simplicity. It seemed a suitable symbol for my new life.

The cross glinted softly in the evening light. I brushed my hair, but abandoned the idea of shaving; no time, no water, no mirror – it was the start of a beard I would wear for many years.

The evening was a great success with the village members thrilled by their new vicar's robed appearance. They danced and sang, and served me with a meal of stewed goat, cassava, yams and maize. Only later would I fully appreciate the honor bestowed on me by the provision of such a meal.

I was keen to see the church, but when I asked Loveness to show it to me, that first evening, she shook her head and said "too late, too late."

The next morning, when my request was repeated, I found that Loveness had not been referring to the hour of the day when she had said "too late." It appeared that the large oval hut, that had once been the church, was now occupied by the women of easy virtue of the village, and obviously had been for some considerable time.

There was no trace of embarrassment when Loveness showed me the building and explained that it was now a source of celebration of a different kind. There was still a tall cross of plain timber at one end of the exterior of the building, but all other traces of its former life had disappeared.

I pondered this set-back for a few moments and then announced "we will build a new one, Loveness. We will build a church big enough for everyone."

Loveness clapped her hands in delight and then, following my next request, led me across the village to see the school. This consisted of several rough benches ranged in lines under a large thorn tree. A table with a broken leg was propped against the tree trunk next to a single chair in an equally sorry state. The undisturbed dust of the area was in contrast with the rest of the village compound.

"Well, Loveness," I said, remembering the warnings and promises of the Bishop, "we have some work to do." The challenge of Cachonga had begun.

12. St. Augustine's Seminary

That's enough about Cachonga for now; the mists are forming across my eyes once again. I must step back to the beginning of my path towards becoming a vicar of Christ. Here I have to reach for my diaries, for much of what I learnt within the enclaves of St. Augustine's has seeped from my memory. I rummage in the box for the first of the four books that record my experiences, thoughts, sketches and feelings of those seminary years.

After unpacking the car, my parents and I were shown to my study-bedroom by a young monk dressed in a thick dark brown robe sporting a traditional hood. We had climbed a narrow spiral staircase of worn stone steps to arrive at the top floor of the building where a long, low passage stretched before us. Stooping, we made our way past doors on either side, each with a name plaque of ornate script. The seventh on the left had the name Jack Bolden in the centre, and behind it was my personal space for the next four years.

I remember Mother looking aghast at the whitewashed walls broken only by a tiny window showing faded moorland supporting heavy clouds of varying degrees of grey.

St. Augustine's

The floor-boards were of polished wood without a hint of comfort or warmth apart from a small rectangle of black carpet, no bigger than a hassock, by the narrow plank bed. A pine chest of drawers boasted a pitcher and bowl placed beneath an unframed mirror whose size could reflect only a quarter of the face at a time. There was an empty bookcase against the remaining wall and a plain cross was suspended above the bed's headboard. There were hooks on the back of the narrow door waiting for my towel and the uniform robe I would be collecting that evening.

Mother must have been thinking of the plush curtains, fitted carpets, radiators, a four-poster bed strewn with pillows and dogs, a dressing table covered with potions and lotions and upon ranks of photographs and pictures that made up her own bedroom at Willenbury. A sob rose in her throat. Father caught her distress and uncharacteristically put an arm around her quivering shoulders. I pretended to be unaware of mother's discomfort as I looked around in delight. Here, as in my attic room at home, I could be alone with God and my prayers.

My parents left me in the great courtyard in front of the main entrance of St. Augustine's. The stone façade, with towers on either side of massive wooden doors, glowed bronze in the evening sunshine. Tall windows on the ground floor hinted at grand rooms within and the small windows on the top floor indicated the warren of cells like the one we had just left. In between, lights flickered from first floor apartments whose identity was as yet unknown.

"Well goodbye, darling," mother had recovered her equanimity. "Please don't feel that you have to stick to this strange path you have chosen. You will be welcomed home at any time, should you feel like a change, and we will not delve into your motives, just be pleased to have you back, where you belong." Her voice trailed off as she caught her husband's stern expression and knew he would be thinking of the year's fees paid in advance. She gave me a quick hug and sank into the leather seats of the sleek motorcar that looked so out of place in this Spartan forecourt.

I watched her descent into the car and shrank back as I recognized the leather of the seats and remembered all that had gone into its production. I took the stiff hand father offered and received a short response with an almost imperceptible squeeze.

"Good luck, my boy" father's voice was unnecessarily buoyant, "doesn't look like my sort of place, but if that's what you want, God help us." Then he laughed, "God help us," he repeated, pleased with himself all of a sudden, "of course, that's what you're here for. Well say a few prayers for your family now and then" he finished somewhat lamely and slumped into the car, closing the door with a thump which failed to mask his mutterings.

The car negotiated its way amongst the other vehicles all busy disgorging young men with trunks, suitcases and packages. The gravel crunched under the over-sized tyres as the huge car bore my parents away through the wrought iron gates. Suddenly, I was alone in this new world, and felt a powerful combination of the senses of freedom and belonging at the same time. God had brought his disciple to a new home, and the excitement I felt ran through my body as if injecting me with new strengths. For the first time in my life, I felt independent and alive in every pore with the knowledge that I was doing something that was of my own volition and making.

The tall, grey-haired monk who presided over St. Augustine's was known to all as Father David. He was a man in his early fifties with iron grey eyes that peered from beneath whitening brows the hairs of which curled upwards towards his temples; his eyes glinted sternly but were somehow kind at the same time, which left the beholder somewhat confused.

The name, Father David, was spoken with reverence by all the staff and the students soon adopted this sign of deep respect. The prelate never needed to raise his voice – in fact he didn't use his voice at all for anything other than instruction or prayer. From a man of such standing just a quizzical look was enough to hush a whole room, a nod of assent could make a class smile with delight, and a furrowed brow could, and did, bring the whole college to a state of silent trepidation.

It was Father David who spoke at our first dinner – the grandeur of the room in stark contrast to the simplicity of the food. My notes don't recount his speech, but I remember that he welcomed the newcomers and instructed his returning students to help us as others had helped them when they were new. His dignity and quiet authority filled the room as he spoke and left none of us in any doubt that here was the master of our destiny.

Of my four years' assignment to St. Augustine, the philosophical and theological studies occupied only a small, but vital, part of the first half. Physical labour in the vegetable gardens, fields, lambing pens, carpentry yards, cowsheds, dairy and bakery took up the bulk of the newcomers' time. The ecclesiastical routine of worship three times a day helped bring the community together in knee-numbing fellowship, and the hours in chapel served to put all the physical activities into perspective, which was especially necessary when the weather was blowing horizontal sleet unabated from Siberia to Yorkshire.

It was understood that the secrets of God's requirements from his servants were only to be revealed after such testing times, and we recruits were content with our work outdoors. The somewhat mindless tasks allowed us time to ruminate on the substance of the lectures and assigned readings. The rhythmical labours of sweeping, shoveling, weeding, and even planting, could serve as a type of mantra through which complicated philosophical questions might be digested. As the young tenders of Christ's garden, we were confident that our toil was leading us towards an ultimate achievement - whilst satisfying the more immediate goals of the dining hall and larders.

The classes which interrupted this work were accompanied with long reading lists which kept us all busy in the evenings and gave us something to talk about at meal-times besides the planting of vegetable seeds, the harvesting of the crops, the milking of cows and the making of butter, cheeses, breads and jams.

As the autumn leaves spread their colours over the freshly dug vegetable beds and clogged the slurry drains from the cowsheds, I grew into my new life as readily as I imagine a new starling joins the flock for his first migration. I was migrating also - away from the loud and ugly world of the factory and the tannery, away from the taunts of my class mates at school, away from the home in which I had always felt a visitor. I was extraordinarily happy with my rake, shovel and hoe. I felt that my spirit was at last free to expand amongst generous-hearted contemporaries who cherished their privacy as much as I cherished mine. I had my own space, both physically and mentally, and I enjoyed every minute of it.

The outdoor work continued during the winter months when the coarse robes of the Novitiate, combined with the freezing winds, made me realize the wisdom with which God had allowed men to create underwear; my penchant for genital freedom was tucked away, along with childhood and puberty.

Only at night, in the cold little bedroom that I cherished as my own, did I indulge in a physical communion with the spiritual. I had been to the library and found the works of Richard Rolle that Father John had recommended to me during the strange experience we had shared in the Chapel at Rossington. While these works didn't exactly spell out a physical relationship with God there was enough there to make me feel comfortable with Father John's ideas.

Along the same shelves as Rolle's writings I found a thirteenth century work called "Wooing of Our Lord" where Christ is referred to as "my sweetheart" and "my darling love." A little further along the book case was the first autobiography to be written in the English language by Margery Kempe whose story, written in the first half of the fifteenth century, claimed that Jesus came to her in a vision and told her "I must be intimate with you, and lie in your bed with you . . . and you may boldly, when you are in bed, take me to you as your wedded husband."

It certainly seemed there were authentic precedencies to Father John's actions in the Rossington chapel and I felt privileged that the kindly vicar had entrusted me with a spiritual secret that introduced me to such mystical experiences. There was also the added bonus that such actions kept at bay the "involuntary nocturnal emissions" so disliked by the patron saint of my college, as recorded in his 'Confessions.'

My own confession starts with the purchase of a special silk handkerchief from the college's store, the kind used to cover the communion wafers prior to their becoming part of the holy sacrament. Occasionally, at night, I would settle myself with my knees on the little black mat, my robe about my shoulders hanging loose in spite of the cold, my forehead resting against my left hand, elbow propped upon the bed edge. As I recited my prayers, my right hand would wrap the silk cloth around my manhood and explore Father John's notion of a physical relationship with God.

The day at Willenbury church was always in my mind on these occasions. Once again I could see the girl's breasts, decorated with filtered sunlight. God's gift to be cherished, Father Edmund had reassured me.

As the warmth of my prayers and devotion increased, so the girl's breasts became clouds welcoming me with warmth and love, enveloping me with their soft folds, sucking me upwards and downwards at the same time until the fulfillment of the moment when I could throw myself into the arms of the Almighty with total abandon.

After this, I would stay on my knees for a long time, head sunk onto the blanket, arms spread out on the bed in cruciform, the silk handkerchief dropped heavily to the floor. The stillness of release, the completeness of such a love, these were awesome moments when power and humility mingled and filled every atom of my being.

In retrospect, I cannot condemn my younger self, for I know how genuine were my beliefs, and surely, as far as sexual fantasies go - as I now recognize those performances - mine were of the least offensive kind. Remembering the sensations of the time, and looking into my innermost thoughts, there was nothing smutty about these physical communications with the God of my past. The beauty of the experiences was both mystical and magical. I cannot defend it to outsiders, nor I hope will I ever have to. I remember the great depth of my trust and faith; emotions that only youth could sustain and that inevitably withered, along with the youth itself.

I suppose it was not just the passing of years during my time at St. Augustine's, but the physical work in the garden and on the farm, combined with these intense religious communications, which brought about a change in my physique. My chest broadened; the muscles on my neck and arms strengthened; and my legs, so gangling at school, now produced firm strides. Often I needed to shave more than once a day and the man looking back at me from the tiny mirror showed a face that had grown into the aquiline nose and large glasses. My thick hair was cropped short exposing delicately shaped dark eyebrows over deep brown eyes which held a new confident gaze.

13. EXPANDING IDEAS

As the final two years of serious study replaced the manual labour of the former two, I found the concept of an ultimate goal acquired from my years at St. Augustine becoming less and less distinct.

From high in the library towers I would look down into the gardens and watch the new students dig, plough, weed, and hoe as I had seen shadowy figures watching me.

As I watched, I was turning thoughts over in my mind. I was trying to find a spiritual path, but the more I learnt from my lecturers about man's interpretations of the divine, the less obvious was God's belonging within either an institutional or an academic structure. The 'numinous' core, which I was trying to identify in all the religious philosophies I studied, seemed strangely absent within the refined institutions to which it had given birth.

Diagram of St. Austine's garden

Notwithstanding this confusion; of the presence of God, and of the love of God, I had no doubt. The divine personal proximity I experienced was too strong and too powerful to allow any incredulity. I could sense it running through the many religious philosophies I was studying and weaving with ease through the different denominations of theology. I was excited by the idea that the numinous stayed separate from the variety of names and labels it was given. How it remained un-spoilt by the petty arguments man introduced about seemingly random prohibitions, or modes of dress and deportment. I was recognizing man's intrusions into the divine flow and his eagerness to create divisions to pull away from the central force of creativity and wonder. By dissecting the magical whole, a strand could be given its own identity with its own superstitions and could then be controlled by human forces – the magic of the originating power becoming diluted almost to obscurity. My quest was to recognize the true core of the divine that I felt sure was still at the heart of all the different religions.

As my reading expanded, I began to develop views beyond the theology books in the library. Even then I mixed my compulsory studies with books from the geology, mythology and history sections. After seeking out the works of Rolle and Kempe, the European Middle Ages held a special grip for me, and the accounts of the Crusades found a chink in my own Christian armour. I think it was at this time that I realized that my metaphorical carapace was there to keep Christian beliefs inside my soul rather than to protect me from pagan lances from without, or to help me thrust those beliefs into another's philosophy.

At first I was uneasy with the idea that a man's God was an excuse for physical violence, and rapidly that unease turned to anger that anyone's faith could be so poisoned and so abused. I left the history of the Crusades in disgust.

Geology fascinated me, however, and by mixing some mythical ideas with medieval philosophies, I found excitement in the idea that, over the ages, cracks in the earth's surface have allowed the power of the Spirit - the Numinous, to use just one of many titles - to ignite particular places with mystical powers. These magnetic forces, as the rationalist geologists called them, could easily be interpreted, by the people who lived close to them, as spiritual powers. Who was to say that the cold scientist and the imaginative pagan could not both be right with their ideas? Why not merge the beliefs and pronounce magnetic force fields as expressions of the Divine force that put the world together in the first place?

From the works of Rudolf Otto, I read of the Numinous as the keeper of the collective memory of mankind, the "mysterium tremendum et fascinans" that fills the soul, but surely it was even more than that. Could it not also be identified as the magical and holy power that had produced the original breath of life? In the many tomes I studied I recognized this same power threading through the changing deities, seeping from the earth and seas, rising and setting with the sun and causing the earth to turn within the constellations.

I was enthused with the suggestion that religious buildings had been built on the sites of magnetic force-fields during a time when people still followed their visceral feelings; long, long before education confused things and nomenclature divided the strands of creation and produced factions. Did the special feeling of awe and religious thrill that were encountered upon entering a cathedral come from the architecture that had been specially designed for such an effect, or was God's presence felt through the earth's forces that were there before the edifice was built, and which were then augmented by the structure? Did one feed from the other? The chinks in my Christian armour were expanding as I decided that it is only the names of the Gods worshiped within those sacred sites that changes over time. The power, I deduced, remains there to be used, or misused, with whatever title is the flavor of the epoch.

The power inherent in a place, I concluded, could not be diminished because man tried to enclose that space with an edifice nor could it be captured with specific incantations. On the contrary, surely the buildings and ceremonies were designed to enhance the power, not to control it - and yet all religious ceremonies seemed to have an element of control within them. Perhaps these structures and chants were designed not only to *tap*, but to *trap*, the numinous power as it seeped - or jolted - through the earth's crust and out into the otherwise unfettered atmosphere where it would be available to all. Perhaps, once this energy had been identified, the wish to control it became the driving force - institutionalization of the numinous was the inevitable result. Was I being trained to control the dispensation of divine magic? As far as I interpreted the Holy Scriptures of many different faiths, God was available to all. If that was indeed the case what exactly was the role of a vicar? I supposed the best I could hope for was to be a facilitator – to help those who couldn't help themselves to find the magic that is the God-given birth-rite of all living creatures. Would the incantations I was learning and adhering to the disciplines the Bible taught really help, or were they distractions to provide credence for the administrator? The path of my future was not as clear-cut as I had supposed.

The direction of my studies, roving through many different faiths, had led me to believe that the Numen could be found by any individual who chose to seek boldly and diligently enough, and an opinion was forming in my head that the method of that seeking should be as varied as the people who did the seeking. I did not like the idea that I might be put in a position where I was responsible for dispensing religiosity within strictly defined parameters.

Amazingly enough, at the time, all this made sense without threatening my fundamental Christian beliefs; I was content with the idea that the Numinous was expressed through Christianity. At that time, I loved God deeply, completely, and wanted, with every atom of my being, to dedicate my life to Him. I continued to lean upon Christ as my most true and beloved friend and mentor, and my devotion was constant and undiminished by these discoveries. However, even then, my perspectives were changing and my tolerance of the beliefs of others was becoming not only acceptable but essential as the studies of different faiths provided new ideas without compromising my Christian principles. There was only one God – did it matter by what name He, She or It, was called, or whether He was worshipped in a church, or a mosque, a temple or a shrine, in a forest or on a beach? Slowly I decided that my role within the church would be to help people find a route to their own version of God; to help them identify the numinous in their individual lives and to feel the thrill that such a recognition brought with it.

14. AMRITA AND THE UNDERGROUND LAKE

R eading my notes on these expansions of my religious knowledge and ideas, I have to interrupt my tale once more with the wisdom of Amrita. Suddenly I find myself delving into the dreaded tin trunk with something akin to enthusiasm. I remember an analogy she described to Percival and myself many years after my studies at St. Augustine's and now, reading my diaries from the seminary, I understand why her analogy of the underground lake made such immediate sense to her fellow patient.

Digging around in the trunk I avoid the Cachonga diaries and find my copious notes and sketches from St. Mary's hospital. I flick through the pages until I find what I am looking for.

My fellow patients, Percival and Amrita and I had established a routine - or rather Sister Mary had established a routine for us - whereby we would spend all day together in the day-room, being wheeled in at around ten in the morning and returning to our rooms after supper in the evening. Moving from bed to wheelchair and back again was still a huge and painful undertaking for me – and I suspect for the others - but now that I had a day's discussion to look forward to, the morning effort was worthwhile and positive, and the evening effort beckoned solitude in which to think about and record the day's ideas.

The notes I am looking for specifically, in conjunction with the ideas in my diary from St. Augustine's, are from a day when I found myself in a particularly negative mood. I had been complaining about the stupidity of my former beliefs, deriding the Christian God I had been taught to honor, agreeing with Percival about the incongruous idea of any kind of divine beneficence given the horrors to which all three of us had born witness.

The comfortable silence of deep friendship fell after my outburst. Each of us toying with our own mental and physical wounds and anguish. The emptiness of existence descended on the room in an almost tangible form.

My notes record that it was Percival who spoke next, appealing as he so often did, to the pretty woman –

hardly more than a girl really – trussed into her wheelchair, her eyes studying the hands in her lap. "What do you think about all this, Amrita?" he asked.

"Well," Amrita began softly, "I think it doesn't really matter if there's a God or not. The stories of the Bible, or those in the Bhagavad-Gitā, or the Koran, or even things like the Book of Mormon don't have to be true. What does matter is the quality of what they are offering to the human race."

Amrita raised her eyes to the river view through the windows. "As I see things, there is a collection of energies and wisdoms which have evolved over the ages, the force from which our consciousness springs – and to which it will return.

"My favorite analogy is to view this energetic mass as an underground lake whose waters offer precious wonders to those who can reach them to drink.

"Imagine that every now and then, someone comes along who has the energy, commitment and perseverance to dig himself a well. We will come back to the tools that are suitable for such a task later. Once the well is dug, our special person lowers a cup and pulls up a splash of water: the earth's life force, the essence of existence. He is careful to filter the water he draws forth, eliminating the negative energies and concentrating on the positive ones."

"What does he use as a filter?" Percival was quick to ask.

"That too will have to wait a minute" Amrita answered in her calm voice. "I want to paint the whole picture first.

"So we have our hard-working digger of wells – call him Zoroaster, Jesus Christ, Mohammed, Buddha – what you will. He is sipping his water and telling his friends how good it is. He gives them some to try, and they also think it's wonderful.

"Now the obvious thing should be that they all go away and dig their own wells – but this is not what happens. Someone comes along and wants to know what all the fuss is about. When no-one is looking, he sneaks to the well and lowers his own flask – a flask without a filter.

"Now we come to the sad part of the story. The new drinker sips the magic water and immediately sees the commercial possibilities of such a wonderful liquid. He takes over the well, pushing the original digger away, and begins to dispense the water to those who will accept him as the Controller.

"In time, a pump is introduced into the system - perhaps an orthodox text of some kind? Now lots of water can become available, its direction and profusion carefully monitored. A hierarchy of individuals evolves 'protecting' the well and over-seeing the distribution of the water. The closer you are to the well itself, the more important you are, and the more power you possess.

"In the meantime, other wells have been dug and similar scenarios have emerged. Now we have across our analogical landscape a series of wells each claiming to be the 'One, True, Well' – in spite of the fact they are all tapped into the same underground lake. Fortifications go up to protect each well and to allow only the chosen to partake of its water. Each will have its own filtering system. By the time each cup gets to the faithful masses, it will have passed through many hands. The sacred liquid will have been diluted at each level as the descending hierarchy takes a sip and replenishes the cup with water of man's own design.

"People who have been wooed to one particular well are encouraged to abuse those who attend a different one – and so on and so forth. . . You can see how the scene develops.

"So, why are there not more individuals getting out there with a spade and quietly digging their own little well? One reason, of course, is that this has been prohibited by the big well-keepers. It would allow people to be in charge of their own destiny, they would be out of the communal control. Hence the witch hunts that sweep the world every now and then.

"For me," Amrita continued, "Buddhism encourages individuals with enough spiritual energy to dig their own well. There will be lazy minds following every philosophy, of course, who prefer to have someone else doing the thinking for them, but for the most part, Buddhism suggests the possibilities of personal enlightenment for those who choose to dig."

"And the tools, and the filter?" Percival had not forgotten.

"Well," Amrita replied thoughtfully, "my digging tool is meditation and my filter – well that's the hardest part. The filter is having a correct heart."

There was silence for several minutes. Amrita stopped looking out into the garden and returned her eyes to her lap. Percival and I were used to her pauses and respected them. After a few moments, she resumed her thoughts.

"What I mean," Amrita continued in her soft voice, "is that we should use our mental faculties to expel negative thoughts and concepts and concentrate upon the positive aspects of existence. Of course this isn't easy for any of us," she waved her hand around the room and looked down at her inert legs, "but I believe it is our journey. We must fight the despair within our own souls before we can help others to fight theirs. We must be true to ourselves before we can be true to others."

"Aha," interrupted Percival, "'This above all, - to thine own self be true; and it must follow, as the night the day, thou canst not then be false to any man.' So said Polonius to Laertes. I'm not sure I've got the quote quite right, but you get the meaning."

"What about prayer?" it was my turn to re-join the conversation. Amrita's speech had given me time to compose myself slightly and her ideas had distracted me from painful musings and interested me in a direction that was somehow familiar. "Prayer can be a form of meditation with sentences which are repeated over and over again becoming the same sort of mental aide as a mantra.

"Watch a Roman Catholic with his rosary, a Jew reciting the Torah or a Muslim kneeling and bowing on his prayer mat." I continued, forgetting my former morose state. "They seem to shut themselves into their own private worlds as they go through passages they have learned by rote. Surely that sort of prayer is a kind of meditation – an attempt to cut through the everyday nonsense that clutters the mind and to concentrate upon something 'other.'"

"The trouble with those sorts of prayers, Jack," Amrita was quick to respond, "is that the 'other' in each case is someone else's idea. An idea which comes from a well that is now far away and out of the individual's reach. The 'water' on offer is diluted and corrupted – it has been metamorphosed into an element of control, contaminated by dogma to become a destructive influence instead of a positive one. A force that can be manipulated in the many by a suspect few."

"Yes, I see what you mean," I answered. "It's a good analogy, Amrita, and has given me lots to think about. My problem at the moment is that I can't get excited about your underground lake – I don't think it's there. I just look around at us, at this," I gestured to the world in general, "and think: 'what's the point?'"

My notes end here, for that particular discussion. "The Point" of course is what all these autobiographical revelations are about. Do I come closer to finding it as these pages progress? Thinking about the changes of the last couple of months and the challenges I have faced -

and those that are before me still - amazingly, I feel optimistic.

15. FIRST FRIENDS, FIRST SERMON

In my penultimate year at St. Augustine's, during the months when these ideas were forming, I made my first proper friends who, like Amrita and Percival, became important rocks in my life for the honing of ideas and emotions.

Thomas Allworthy was often to be found in the library long after everyone else had left. – everyone but me, that is. When the monk in charge of closing the splendid vaulted room came to ask remaining students to leave, it was generally just the two of us who needed the instruction.

Thomas' short, sturdy build, together with his lightly snubbed nose and short-cropped fair hair contrasted acutely with my tall and willowy physique, imperious nose and dark hair, worn long enough to cover my collar. We must have made a strange pair as we left the library with books clasped against our chests and eyeglasses glinting – the one thing we had in common.

As these kindly expulsions from the library became a regular event, it was inevitable that we should begin to communicate. A polite enquiry into what the other was researching showed each of us how much we had in common, for we were usually searching for answers to the same questions. This discovery was exciting to both of us and long discussions followed as we shared our finds, doubts and occasionally, our solutions.

It was Thomas who introduced me to Rufus McKinney, who he had known before coming to St. Augustine's. Their parents shared a fishing lodge on Loch Ore, just to the North of Edinburgh, and they had spent their boyhood summers together. This jovial Scot was taller and thinner than Thomas and myself, with blue eyes blinking in a freckled face fringed with russet hair that always seemed out of control. He had large hands that fluttered as if they had minds of their own whenever he got excited about an idea he was expostulating. I had found two kindred spirits and my life was the richer for their company.

As time passed, the three of us learned to trust each other's judgment and soon there was no aspect of philosophy or theology that we didn't feel comfortable about bringing to the discussion table. The intimacy between us came to the notice of our peers and I found myself once again the butt of jokes and the recipient of sideways glances.

"But these are all religious candidates for a life of dignity and devotion" I tried to reassure myself and my friends about our fellow inmates, "how could they host smutty ideas and banal thoughts?" We decided to dismiss the notion, and failing that, to ignore it.

The ringleader of this uncharitable bunch of verbal snipers was called Simon Mountford. He was a strongly built young man of insistent good looks whose habit of brushing his unruly brown hair away from greenish eyes was imitated fervently by the less confident. Personally, I thought that Simon's approach to the Church was similar to my brother Robert's towards his business inheritance. Simon's uncle, having been made a Bishop of an important See, seemed to have imparted a strangely mercurial interest in his nephew's chosen "profession" which was quite different from the aspirations of the other students at St. Augustine's. However Simon's good looks, physical prowess and boisterous geniality made him both popular and admired. He soon had the less independent students of the institution enthralled and eager to share and imitate his ideas.

Simon studiously attended every lecture, but rumors had it that he had works of salacious content hidden within his notebooks, and that he relied upon others to do his papers for him. Strangely these shortcomings only made him more popular and his laughter at the diligence of others appeared to be infectious.

I remember being both surprised and delighted to find that Simon's attitude and remarks had no effect on me at the time. The years of toiling in the garden and on the farm following the break with my family's business and their expectations, had obviously been of benefit. I discovered a new confidence that flourished with my friendship with Thomas and Rufus and their ability to shrug their shoulders when circumstances looked threatening gave me the strength to do the same.

The lengthy discussions held by the three of us sharpened our ideas about how we should proceed with our studies. It was time to choose a thesis topic upon which most of the final year would be based.

For his, Thomas chose the relevance of miracles within Christianity, focusing mainly upon the virgin birth. Rufus was intrigued with how and why Jesus was put upon the cross; and I decided upon my belief in the universality of the Divine Spirit – the Numen, in its many guises - as my chosen subject. These disparate topics might have meant that we would spend fewer hours together, but, as it turned out, we thrived on obtaining objective views from each other, even if our subject matters coincided only rarely.

These weeks of intense study were interesting and mentally challenging but also exciting and rewarding. At no time did we feel the weight or strain of academic pressures usual at this stage of our education. We were just three young men pursuing ideas with energy and enthusiasm and were grateful for the opportunity to explore the dizzying realms of philosophical and theological thought – a world which we found to be full of wonders.

The delivery of our first sermons, however, was a different matter. It was required of students in their third year within the seminary walls, to give a sermon in chapel with the entire congregation of the St. Augustine extended family in attendance. Everybody knew that there were many books of recommended topics, with appropriate texts to illustrate the themes, and guidelines of how the relevant sermon should proceed. However, for their first attempt, the subject matter had to be of the student's own choosing and the content should not be found in any textbook.

Along with all the academic studies heaped upon us novitiates, there were also classes in voice projection and speech presentation. It would be no good, our teacher boomed at us, if we passed into the priesthood without a voice that could be heard in the farthest corner of our churches. Those without good singing voices were at a great disadvantage, and several of the students were assigned extra hours of tuition in this area. I was fortunate in having a decent tone to my voice and a reasonable sense of tune. My biggest problem was finding the necessary audacity - as I thought of it - to allow my voice to ring out and fill a very large space full of people.

Simon was a natural performer - or exhibitionist, we thought, somewhat uncharitably. He was soon heralded as the best in our year for proclamations and sung liturgies. He and I were opposites in that the bigger the crowd he had in front of him, the more he enjoyed himself and the better was his delivery, while I was quite the reverse.

Rufus made the most of his Scottish accent and rolled his R's so that the sound reverberated around the stone walls of the chapel where we were allowed to practice our oratories. Thomas, like me, was neither spectacular nor disastrous. Both of us concentrated hard upon what we were taught and tried our best to put it into practice. Spontaneity and confidence would come in time, we were assured; we just needed enough faith to believe that it would be so.

Now it was time to put what we had learned into practice and take to the pulpit in a solo flight. No-one was allowed to advise on or criticize anyone's chosen idea for their sermon. It had to be delivered untried and untested and judged not only upon its content but also upon its deliverance and originality.

My turn came on a Sunday in the middle of May. The cold weeks of winter had seen me agonizing over my choice of subject and, looking back, I think it was a mark of how much I had matured that I had the confidence, and the daring, to choose my text not from the Bible. A gardening manual was given to every student upon his arrival at the college, and it was from this that I took my quotation.

Thomas and Rufus laughed at my choice, but they were both impressed with my courage in persevering with the idea. I must still have that book, languishing amongst these notes, I suppose.

Of the three of us, I was the first to face the ordeal of the pulpit – and what an ordeal it seemed. Simon had given his sermon the Wednesday before, so I had a hard act to follow. He had spoken with a deep, confident voice, more befitting an actor or a politician than a priest. His gestures had everyone in the Chapel leaning forward in the pews in the eagerness of their listening. Afterwards, everyone remarked how impressive it was that Simon did not appear to have any notes; that the whole thing seemed to explode from him, as if the ideas were coming new to his mind with a special freshness and vibrancy about them.

Thomas said he couldn't remember one word of Simon's speech, but that the delivery had been so good that it really didn't matter what the content had been.

When Rufus and I thought about this statement, we had to agree that neither of us could recall the content either, but we were all of one mind, when we reluctantly admitted that it had been a great success.

And now it was my turn. As recently as the night before, I see from the entries in my diary, I was buoyant about the daring idea of a text taken not from any revered religious doctrine, but from the mundane side of the life that we all lived at St. Augustine's. However, my confidence had diminished throughout the morning and finally, as I mounted the steps to the pulpit during the last verse of the hymn whose end would dictate the beginning of the sermon, it evaporated altogether.

As the strains of the Amen died away, a shuffling ensued as the congregation settled. Much to their surprise, with hands I was trying hard to keep from shaking, I held up the college's gardening manual for everyone to recognize, and placed it on top of the open Bible, spread out upon the polished brass lectern, cantilevered from the edge of the carved pulpit.

Goodness, how it all comes back to me with a tremor down my spine. The topic had seemed so perfect when I had first thought of it in my tiny study-bedroom: to use the unexpected to quicken the interest of a congregation that was tired of hearing the stuttering performances of tyro vicars. However, once there, in the pulpit, I welcomed the idea of an indifferent, somnambulant audience and was loathe to wake it with this unusual choice of text. It was too late now, and taking a deep breath, I straightened my shoulders as I ran my hands over the open book and began:

"My text is from St. Augustine's Gardening Manual, Page thirteen, paragraph six." Clearing my throat in an effort to bring my voice down from the high squeak I thought I heard emanating from my mouth, I lowered my eyes and read: "'When the seed bed is suitably prepared, make an indentation in the soil with the edge of a hoe in a straight line across the designated area; use string and pegs to guide you. The depth of the indentation will depend upon the seed you are planting - refer to the chart on page twenty. Once your trough is ready, take your seeds and insert them at the correct intervals – see chart on page twenty-one. With a rake, gather the tilth from either side of the trough you have created and bury your seeds, pressing the soil down firmly. Water your seedbed until it is evenly moist, but not flooded, and keep watering, if necessary, to maintain a constant moisture level until the first shoots appear. By this time the roots will have developed beneath the surface and will feed the growing shoot from below. If the weather is dry, more watering may be necessary, otherwise let nature take its course. Keep the bed free from weeds. Harvest when ready.'

"What is missing from this text?" I raised my eyes to the rows of faces looking up at me. Father David was in the front pew, as usual, flanked by the round, smiling face of Father Bernard, the Bursar, and the Deputy Head, Father Jeremy, whose long nose made him look disapproving at the best of times.

While practicing my sermon in my room, I had made myself count to ten before continuing after this question had been delivered. I had imagined myself looking slowly and steadily around the congregation, my eyes making a complete circuit of the whole Chapel, including those in the choir over my left shoulder. Now the time was upon me, I only managed to count to three before, with a deep breath, I plunged into my notes and continued: "We are taught how and when to sow a seed, with information handed down from one generation to another, for longer than man can remember. We are shown how to nurture it and encourage its growth. We are instructed how and when to harvest its bounty. Man has learned, through centuries of trial and error, the best way to cultivate every plant that is of use to him. What is missing? What has man not learnt to reproduce and control?

"What is missing is the magic that makes the seed germinate, chit and grow. Of course there are chemical explanations of when and how the change in the seed takes place, however the Why has yet to be noted or explained.

"What is it that makes that seed respond to the care and attention we have been taught to apply? Here is the fundamental mystery of the Divine, the Resurrection and the Life. A seed of oil-seed rape is the size of a pinhead, and yet it can produce a multi branched plant as high as my shoulder and bearing thousands of seeds, in just four months – is that not a miracle? An apple tree loses its leaves in winter and stands as if dead for four months before producing leaves and blossoms that are followed by fruit. Another miracle!

"'Let nature take its course.' The book says – but what exactly does it mean by 'Nature'? Why not use the word 'God' here, why not mention the Divine here in our everyday manual?"

I was warming to my subject now and caught the eye of Thomas whose face bore a wide smile, and I could feel Rufus's eyes sparkling encouragement as I continued: "We are surrounded by miracles of the Divine, and yet we take them for granted whilst our fellow beings are struggling to justify their beliefs. We, who are here to learn how to spread the miraculous nature of God's existence have a book of instructions that omits the absolutely vital role of The Divine, the supreme wonder of God's gift of life.

"Today's intellectuals scoff at tribes who worship the sun, and yet is not the same Divine God, who we love and worship, present in the light strata every morning as dawn appears - and every evening, as dusk falls? Do we not all feel the pull of wonder at watching the moon wax and wane? It is the same Divinity once again that draws us with the magic of creation. God made all that there is, and we are the fortunate inheritors of his munificence. His is the miracle of rebirth with every dawn, and with every green shoot that pierces the soil. His is the wisdom in the relationship he has given us with animals, His is the love shown in every breath He has given us to take . . ."

Well, the sermon continued for a further ten minutes about the everyday evidence of the Almighty and how easy it is to become complacent about the Majesty that surrounds us. My voice had deepened as conviction overcame nervousness and my speech slowed for more dramatic effect as I saw and felt that I had the congregation with me. I even produced a couple of relevant quotes from the Bible that I hoped would tie my ideas into the Christian teachings of St. Augustine's. Finally, I came to a conclusion: "The wonders of God are with us always. Let's not allow life's petty tribulations to blind us to the creative magic that surrounds us. When we walk out from Chapel today, may we appreciate the awesome gifts that are everywhere, which have been provided for our benefit, and for which we should be always grateful.

"In the name of the Father, the Son and the Holy Ghost, Amen."

It was over. The Chapel was as still and as silent as always. The next hymn, "When I Survey the Wondrous Cross," was announced, and the organ began its introduction, as I made my way down the pulpit steps that curved to the aisle. My heart was beating fast, and I could feel the sweat drops on my temples forming into small rivulets which I brushed away with the back of my hand. I reclaimed my place in the choir stalls, standing straight as I willed my fingers to turn the hymn book pages without fumbling. In the years that followed, every time I came across that hymn, all those feelings rushed back at me.

The rest of the service passed in a blur as I recovered my calm. I followed the prayers, answering as appropriate, knelt, stood and sat as required, but my mind was blank, an empty slate from which all had been erased. The numb relief of having the ordeal behind me was balanced by the gradual appearance of nervousness regarding how my great effort had been received.

Once the service was over, my two friends were the first to push their way to my side.

"Well, I hope I can do as well," Thomas said, as he clapped me on the back with the right amount of force to indicate sincerity rather than bravado. "And I hope I can stir them up a bit, as you did. You did a grand job, Jack," he concluded, "very well done, very well done, indeed."

Then it was Rufus's turn. His ginger-topped head was bobbing with enthusiasm, his pale blue eyes watery with emotion. "What a performance, Jack," the Scottish accent made the phrase throb, "that was a real winner. How did it feel, being up there in the turret?"

"Pretty grim," I had to confess. "I can't imagine having to go through that three or four times a week. Do you think we'll ever get used to it?"

"The Church puts out volumes of sermons every month," Thomas reassured me. "This is probably the only time in our lives that we will ever have to speak off the cuff, as you did today. It was brilliant, Jack, honestly, everyone was listening" he enthused, "everyone enthralled - what an achievement!"

The three of us made our way to the dining hall chattering excitedly as we went. The occasional passer-by would clap me on the shoulder with a "well done" or a "good sermon" vocalized with the accompanying positive gesture. I had delivered equally encouraging remarks to so many students before me, that I had no idea as to how genuine these accolades were, but they were there, I mused, why not enjoy them?

The traditional Sunday lunch had never seemed so welcome; I felt as if I hadn't eaten for weeks. The rest of the day was spent rambling across the adjacent moorland, enjoying the spring sunshine. Practicing what I had preached, I reveled in the glories of the Divine God who provided such a vital essence of existence evident in everything around me – or so I thought at the time.

16. TIME OUT

S t. Augustine's, took a maximum of thirty students each year. After the first year, there were twenty-eight left in my class. One student had left in the first week, deciding that this path was not for him, and another had left a week before the end of the scholastic year when his father died unexpectedly and responsibilities fell to him as the family's eldest son.

At the end of my second year, the class was still twenty-eight strong, but then the demanding curriculum began to build and during the third year there were many casualties as exam results began to determine who was a genuinely suitable candidate for the priesthood. By the start of our last year, the class had shrunk to just eighteen and the academic pressures continued out of term time.

During the holidays I would return to Willenbury – where else could I go? Members of the family appeared pleased to see me when I arrived back, but they were all set in their individual routines and, as usual, I felt out of kilter in the house. Fortunately my studies kept me busy and out of everyone's way most of the time.

Robert was doing well in the family business. The conversations at dinner tended to revolve around the day's activities in the factory. My father and brother were growing more and more alike, not only physically, but in the way they spoke and gestured also. They conversed in a kind of business shorthand of which I had no understanding or interest. Mother didn't seem to notice; she paid as little attention to their conversations as she did to mine. She was busy with a myriad of charitable functions and worrying about Alice's latest escapade in London's glittering social world. A world designed to introduce girls from the country to suitable young men during their early adult years.

At the start of my last holiday before St. Augustine's final term, with its demanding exams, I learnt that Alice's 'season' had failed to produce suitable results. One swirling month had led to another and by now Alice had been in London for nearly four years, enjoying a healthy allowance from father and showing no sign of growing up any further. She shared a flat in Chelsea with three friends and made a pretense of attending a modeling college designed for the "modern woman" by which it meant that it taught fundamental IT skills along with the tricks of the cat-walk. Alice was rarely away from town, but every now and then she would appear at Willenbury Hall with a car full of friends all of whom were scantily dressed in ill-fitting clothes of vivid colors.

"Oh, you're all so dowdy in the country," she exclaimed to whoever would listen. Mother would raise her eyebrows as her daughter flounced into the drawing room in a transparent blouse with buttons adrift. "Why don't you come to London and see how the world really buzzes along?"

In a moment of rare intimacy, mother had spoken to me about her concerns for my sister. "I had my time in London, you know," she confided to me one evening after dinner, when Robert and father had retired to the billiard room, and Alice had left the table in a sulk because of the lack of nightlife in Willenbury.

"I did the 'Season' and remember it well." She had refilled her glass of dessert wine and pushed the bottle across the table towards me, the golden liquid undulating as she did so. "Oh, it was a mad whirl of parties and smart occasions when what you wore was going to be responsible for the success of the outing, not what you said or did. The hours I spent going through wardrobes and shopping for just the right pair of shoes and handbag to accompany this or that outfit. Clothes dominated my existence, and all my friends were the same. But I enjoyed it, and, it was at one of the many jostling cocktail parties, where voices echo in tall marbled rooms and nobody can hear anything, that I met Charles, your father. The 'Season' did me well, and we are still hoping for a similar outcome for Alice."

I was flattered by this conversation, allowing me a glimpse into a youth of my mother's I had never bothered to imagine. Suddenly, I felt guilty for not having thought of her as having any past or future other than that of our mother, the mistress of Willenbury Hall.

I got used to some of Alice's more regular friends. Looking through my diary of that summer I remember several of them vividly, and with a mixture of emotions. James and Henry were two sturdy lads who were flexing their muscles "in the City." Their too-loud voices and hearty bursts of laughter at nothing in particular proclaimed their self-satisfaction. They were equally comfortable in their country clothes, elegant eveningwear or the three-piece pinstripe suits they still had on if they came down to Willenbury on a Friday evening.

Jenny, Clarissa and Fiona, Alice's flat mates, were also frequent visitors to the house. All three were Alice clones and they preened and giggled for hours in the bathroom that I was meant to share, and in Alice's bedroom – the door of which was never closed, even when they were in various states of undress, busy trying on different outfits.

I moved my shaving things and toothbrush to the downstairs cloakroom when these guests were in residence. Every morning, while shaving amongst the wellington boots, walking sticks, gun cartridge belts, hunting whips, and waxed jackets, I wondered why English country houses had so many bedrooms and so few bathrooms. Maybe it was something to do with plumbing restraints, and a lack of heating - of course other houses have been modernized, but not Willenbury. However, I had no desire for the house to burst into the twentieth century, let alone into the twenty-first. I was used to the ill-fitting windows, log fires, cold floors and pathetic, clanging plumbing. It was a part of my childhood, and although I never felt exactly close to it, Willenbury with its creaking floorboards and draughty hallways belonged to me – or me to it.

Robert was a great favorite with the girls who he teased constantly with suggestive remarks, making them blush and giggle even more than usual, and James and Henry liked him too. The three young men would go rough shooting together, and come home via the village pub, pigeons and pheasant dangling from their belts.

Alice's younger brother, however, was regarded by her friends as a peculiarity. I kept out of their way as much as possible, but I knew they talked about me by the way conversations ceased abruptly when I entered a room.

Nevertheless, I tried to be friendly to these social gadflies - after all, I told myself, I might have parishioners like these someday, so I had better get used to conversing with them. Perhaps, I thought, if I viewed these unwelcome interchanges as educational, I could deal with them objectively - even gain from them. I realized that the idea of any of this lot attending church was absurd, but I was intent upon charitable thoughts. I reminded myself of the edicts of the professors at St. Augustine when conversations turned to the subject of parishioners and the problems they might bring to their vicar.

I look at my diary with embarrassment when I come to the description of the last afternoon before I returned to St. Augustine's. A series of cryptic comments bring the whole scene flooding back – it all seems so petty, now, but at the time it presented me with a huge personal problem as it concluded in the first sexual experience I had without any religious connotation.

When I walked into the drawing room, that last afternoon at Willenbury, before returning to St. Augustine's, and found Clarissa sunk into an armchair by the bay window, I remembered my determination to view interaction with Alice's friends as educational, and resisted the impulse to withdraw. A tea tray had been placed on the library table behind the sofa. It was waiting for mother to come in from the garden, but she had become distracted, pruning roses in her favorite herbaceous border.

"How about a cup of tea, Clarissa," I asked, approaching the tray with mock confidence. "Mother is with her roses again, and might not be in for ages. It would be a shame to let it go cold." I lifted the embroidered tea-cozy and started to pour from the large silver teapot.

I remember being unexpectedly aware of how shabbily I was dressed. My old corduroy trousers whose beige had faded to grey, and an equally antique blue shirt whose frayed collar and cuffs had lost all sense of color, suddenly seemed completely inappropriate.

"That would be lovely," the girl answered as she flicked absently through the pages of a glossy magazine. Her red skirt was so short it almost disappeared under a long white T shirt with the logo 'I'm blond, so please speak slowly' emblazoned in the same red. The words were sent rolling by the outline of breasts bulging underneath, nipples pressing two pen-points against the tight cotton.

"I'm looking to see if Antonia's party has been written up. It was an absolutely amazing do," Clarissa had a habit of leaning on the first syllable of the many adjectives with which she peppered her speech. "Everybody was there. No wonder they needed Grosvenor House. It must have cost her father a fortune, but then they have lots of dosh, that McRoberts family." She brushed the hair that authenticated the T shirt, from her face in an elaborate movement finishing by tucking a curl neatly behind an ear, checking for the security of the dangly blue ear-ring which might have been dislodged, and fixing me with a keen look. "Do you know them Jack?"

"Not unless they've been to Willenbury." I answered, beginning to feel almost relaxed. "I don't meet any of Alice's London set, unless they come here, like you, Jenny and Fiona." I walked carefully across the deep patterned carpet to her chair, carrying two very full cups of tea. "I put milk in, I hope that's alright. Did you want sugar?" I was increasingly pleased with myself for keeping my shyness so well under control. She would never suspect, I thought triumphantly.

Clarissa reached for her cup as the magazine slid off her knees and lay discarded on the floor, exposing her bare legs. "Thanks very much, Jack," she said, taking her cup while holding my eyes with a steady gaze. "Alice tells me you're a virgin," she went on in the same conversational tone, her eyes dancing with a new twinkle. "Is that true?"

I had difficulty not dropping my cup and saucer, and the concentration required in holding it steady dispensed with the first few dreadful seconds that followed this question. It had been made in the continued tone of polite chatter, as if discussing the weather or the late flowering of the cherry trees this year.

"I don't take sugar, thank you. So how about this virgin thing then, is it true?" My interrogator repeated, as the silence continued.

"I don't believe I have asked you about your private life," I said slowly, staring furiously at my cup of tea whose contents were escaping into the saucer. I was going to continue by pointing out that accordingly she had no right to ask me about mine. But Clarissa interrupted me with her merry voice, chattering away as she stirred her tea with a deliberate slow swirl of the spoon.

"Oh but please do," she began. "There is quite a lot to tell, actually." She placed the cup and saucer on the floor next to the magazine and wriggled back amongst the cushions. "The first time was with the gym teacher at school when I had just turned sixteen. What a handsome man he was, all of us girls used to follow him about with our eyes and giggle when he spoke to us, or even glanced in our direction. His name was Peter and . ."

"Please no!" Against my will I had raised my voice. "I didn't mean that I wanted to know. I don't." I stuttered, bringing the volume down and trying to hide the panic that was screaming to be let loose. "I just meant that you have no right to ask me about mine." Then thinking that I had sounded churlish, I tried a softer tone, "I'm sorry, Clarissa, I don't mean to be rude. I am not used to this kind of conversation, and although I enjoy your company, I really am not interested in your sexual education."

"Oh, but I have so much more to learn," Clarissa insisted. "And I've never had the opportunity to teach a virgin the little that I do know. You're leaving tomorrow, aren't you, so we can't put it off any longer. We might learn from each other. It would be awesome." She used her favorite word, enjoying the first syllable slowly with her tongue.

Now I was seriously bothered. I needed to flee from the room, but wanted to hang on to what was left of my dignity if I possibly could. With great deliberation and determination I sat down in the armchair by the fire place, as far away from Clarissa as the furniture allowed, and placed my teacup carefully on the table next to me.

"Come on, Jack," Clarissa was cooing at me, her eyelids fluttering those long lashes, her sticky red mouth panting slightly. "Let me break your duck. – it would be such fun. You know you want to." She started to rise from her chair.

My panic won the battle; dignity was no longer of any importance. "No," I exclaimed, leaping from my chair. "You're just teasing me, I know you are. Life's just a silly game to you lot. Have any of you a serious thought in your heads? Can any of you talk about anything without sex being part of the conversation?" I swiveled around the armchair and crossed the expanse of carpet to the door in three long strides. The door flew towards me in response to my urgent tug on the handle – I remember it almost knocked me over. "You just want to make me look a fool, well, congratulations, I hope you're satisfied," and I banged the door shut behind me, feeling every bit the clown; an inept apology of a human being.

I could hear the girl's laughter through the thick closed doors. It followed me down the stone-flagged hall, and up the stairwell as I fled to the safety of my room at the top of the house, two steps at a time. I could still hear it when I had closed my bedroom door, leaning heavily against the hanging dressing gown as I turned the key in the lock. I was gasping from the rapid escape and subsequent ascent. "You're a stupid idiot" a voice inside my head kept repeating, "she just wanted to make you look foolish, and you let her," "Yes" I answered the voice, "I let her, I let her."

I did my best to calm myself by taking deep breaths, but my heart was racing and I could feel cold sweat trickling down my spine, leaving a clammy trail like that of a snail.

"What is all the commotion about," I asked myself. "Why am I so upset and in such a physical state. This is all nonsense. I must get a grip." I spoke to myself sternly, trying to look at the situation objectively. I crossed the room to the mirror hanging over the chest of drawers - it showed a tall young man with anguished eyes, wet behind the glasses; not an image I relished or of which I was proud. My nostrils flared with the effort of enforced deep breathing, my cheeks were flushed and sweat sparks prickled my forehead like dew on early morning turf.

It was then that I felt the hot tightening in my groin. "Oh no!" I murmured as I fought to keep images of Clarissa with her T-shirt stretched over ample soft breasts out of my mind. But I was losing the battle. I threw myself onto the bed, turning on my stomach to repress the insistent throb of this unwelcome erection. I began to pray – what else could I do?

"Help me, dear Lord, please help me not to besmirch myself with these unnecessary thoughts of earthly things. I do not need them. I am your true and faithful servant, and will be true to you forever. Help me, Lord Jesus Christ, help me to be pure, as you were when here on earth. Help me . . ." I was fighting to bring my mind to spiritual thoughts, to concentrate on the meaning of the prayers I was intoning, to return the physical and mental attractions to being recognizable reflections of God's love.

The intense anxiety of the last half hour must have exhausted me and, pressing my pelvis firmly against the bedspread, my prayers becoming a mantra of supplication, I drifted to sleep in spite of feeling as if I were lying on a small log.

I dreamt I was walking in the woods that encircle Willenbury Hall. It is early evening and the wood pigeons are calling to each other: "'My toe hurts, Betty' is what they are saying," our nanny had told us children all those years ago, as I waddled after my elder siblings, trying to keep up as they raced across the lawn for tea. Now I can hear the birds' chorus again, "my toe hurts, Betty" they insist.

The cow parsley is in flower, and as tall as my chest as I wade cautiously towards the rhododendron and azalea bushes. I am looking for something, something exciting that makes my pulse rush and my steps quicken. I round a corner in the path, by a big beech tree whose broad low branches make me lower my head. And there she is, that saintly girl, kneeling at an altar rail amongst the flowers and fallen leaves of the wood, her eyes looking down so that her lashes cast shadows on her smooth pale cheeks. The sunlight, dappled by the pale green leaves overhead, makes patterns on those porcelain white breasts. The lacy motif dances as the breeze moves amongst the beech boughs.

I am wearing a vicar's robes. Clasped carefully in both hands is a filled silver chalice, the surface of the dark red wine moving as I walk, reflecting the sun for a fraction of a second as the light shards sparkle around the glittering rim. I stand over the girl, bending slowly and offering the cup to those perfect rose lips as they open in anticipation, the tip of a perfect tongue just visible between the perfect white teeth. "The blood of Christ that was shed for you" I am intoning as I bring the chalice towards her face.

But now suddenly the rosy lips are sticky with bright lipstick; the eyes are no longer looking down, but staring straight up at me. It is Clarissa's face now, her eyes surrounded with make-up, the lashes matted together with mascara. Suddenly I realize that I am naked, and that my member is swelling and rising towards the kneeling girl whose blouse is undone, her breasts spilling through the soft chiffon material. Her hands, with those bright red painted nails, are reaching out to me, not for the chalice but for my priapic organ that is leading me towards her like a man being pulled by a waving metal detector on a mission.

I still have the chalice. I know that I must not spill a drop of this precious liquid. It represents Christ's very blood, and must be drunk with due reverence, every last drop of it. I clasp the chalice with one hand whilst with the other I try to push Clarissa away, my feet scrambling to reverse the direction in which my mortifying member is leading me.

The girl catches my free hand with one of hers, whilst grabbing me intimately with the other, her nails biting the stretched skin like tiny knives of fire. She is falling backwards, pulling me on top of her as I try desperately to keep the chalice upright. A drop of wine spills onto my thumb, and I move my hand to my lips to lick it into my mouth.

Suddenly Clarissa releases me and, reaching up quickly, puts her hand around the back of my neck. With a sharp tug she catches me off balance and I fall on top of her, sinking into the soft flesh of her breasts, feeling her open legs curling around my back I have found a soft, delicate, place to sooth the nail bites. It holds me with extraordinary tenderness.

Both Clarissa's arms are around my neck now, her mouth finding mine and kissing me ardently, her tongue fighting its way between my clenched teeth. Then the sucking begins. Her gentle kiss turns into a fierce tugging, I can feel my tongue being pulled into her mouth, it is going down her throat, I can't get it back. At the same time, the tender place has also turned into a sucking beast and I can feel myself being drawn inwards. As I try to get out, the pull and tug movements make my body jerk, and the precious liquid is jumping around in the chalice. Drops are running down the side of the cup and onto my hand, but this time, I can't lick them off for my tongue is no longer my own.

All at once, there is an explosion in my loins. My tongue is released and recoils into my mouth where it sticks against the roof, as if frightened to show itself again. My head shoots up and my whole body jerks as the chalice slips from my grasp, the red liquid splashing across Clarissa's breasts like a sword wound.

I can hear my own voice wailing as I experience the abject horror of so irreverent a disaster. Clarissa is propping herself up on her elbows, the wine running down to her belly button and below. She begins to laugh. First a light chuckle and then it grows into a cackle so raucous that it wakes me from my torment.

Awake at last, lying on my bed, covered in sweat, I found a sticky warm patch soaking through my trousers onto the bedspread. I lay still for a long time, listening to the creaking of the old house, the birdsong coming in through the open dormer window and the occasional sound of far away voices. Finally, I roused myself, stripped off my clothes, throwing the under-pants and trousers into a corner with disgust, and marched downstairs to my brother's bathroom wearing only a towel.

The cool water of Robert's shower felt good, and I washed over and over until I felt clean again. Dressed in some jeans and a clean shirt, I made up a bundle of dirty clothes and went down to the laundry room, shoving them into the empty washing machine with repulsion. Then I went for a long walk through the park and down to the river where an old tow-path provided a solid footing for letting off steam.

The next day I would be taking the train back to Yorkshire – my trunk was already packed – back to the haven of St. Augustine's. It took a long time to recover from that dream, but I was helped by reading The Confessions of Augustine himself in which, amongst so many other more important insights, he expresses his distaste for his own "involuntary nocturnal emissions." At least I was in good company!

17. FIDDLER'S POND

It was with great relief that I returned for my final term at St. Augustine's, to be wrapped in the security of the stonewalls I had come to love. It was a time of intense study, discussion and solitude in which to ponder the great step we all wished to make into Christ's Ministry. It passed all too quickly, for me, as I found myself increasingly reluctant to face the world outside this sanctuary. I busied myself with the completion of my thesis and research for the oral examination that would follow.

I remember the change in atmosphere throughout our section of the college as the submission date for the theses approached. We all became hushed beneath the pressures of academia and religion, now rolled into one. Even Simon's eyes were less bold and almost pleading as they roamed around the bowed heads in the library waiting for someone to acknowledge his gaze and come to his aid. The students in the three years below us had already gone home, his rumored source of assistance therefore was missing.

Everything changed once these documents had been presented; it seemed even the building sighed with relief. In fact St. Augustine's went into a state of limbo for two weeks while the papers were read and categorized in preparation for the ultimate challenge – the oral examination known as the Defining Discussion. It was upon the results of these two tests that grades of achievement would be given and corresponding individual appointments would be made for those who succeeded in graduating.

During this time, the fourth year students were free to come and go as they pleased. Most went to their homes, but I had no intention of exposing myself to the ridicule of Willenbury at such an important time. I was delighted to find that both Thomas and Rufus were also planning to stay at the college as neither of them wanted worldly worries to interrupt the theological thoughts and ideas which had dominated their minds during the last few months. The three of us decided to spend the time walking in the hills and dales that surrounded St. Augustine. We would camp when appropriate, or return in time for supper as our excursions warranted.

As other students carried their cases down to the forecourt and the family cars mingled with taxis for the train station, Thomas, Rufus and I watched abstractedly from a library window.

"Well there you are," came a voice from behind us, and we turned in total astonishment to see Simon Mountford accosting us, his face beaming. "I've been looking everywhere for you three" he said, with his habitual careless charm. "What are your plans for the next two weeks?"

We looked at each other in bewilderment. "We're staying here – or around here, anyway" said Thomas, recovering his composure. "We thought we might explore the moors, camp out sometimes, get to know the natural surroundings – that sort of thing" he trailed off, not knowing why he should be sharing our plans with someone we had come to suspect was an antagonist.

"Marvelous idea," Simon enthused, "just what I had in mind too. Mind if I come along – I won't be in the way, and I might be able to help carry a few loads that you would find cumbersome? It's exactly what I was hoping to do. When do we start?"

The silence that followed seemed to last forever, but it was probably only a few seconds before Thomas, again, stepped into the vacuum with a throat-clearing cough. "Well we haven't made any definite plans yet, maybe we need some days to study before we start." He was trying to buy time.

"Nonsense" interrupted Simon, "we have studied enough, let's start tomorrow, and if you haven't got a plan yet, let's begin with walking over Igor's Moor. That's a good hike for one day, brings us back here in time for supper, and we'll find out how we get on together. What do you say? How about a start around half past eight, after breakfast? I'll speak to the kitchen staff and see if I can wrangle some picnic lunches. See you tomorrow – well done lads, I think we're going to have a splendid time." And with that he turned on his heel and headed for the Library door, it swished once and he was gone. Thomas, Rufus and I looked at each other in amazement.

"What could I say?" asked Thomas in confusion.

"You did the best you could," I answered, "I was too startled to say anything. What do we do now?"

"Well, it looks as if we have to go along with his ideas for tomorrow," Rufus said quietly. "We have no reason not to. Perhaps it's just as well, then we can agree at the end of the day that it would be better to go our separate ways. After all, we're not exactly the company he usually seeks and he's bound to get bored with us and leave us alone – after tomorrow."

"I suppose so," I conceded reluctantly, "but I don't like it. Why us, for heaven's sake?"

Thomas shrugged "I suppose we're the only ones left. Let's forget about it for now," he said, knowing that it was a futile statement for all of us, "and see what the kitchen has in store for the few who are staying behind."

Breakfast the next morning was a strange affair as it was served in the great dining hall, as usual, but with only the corner of one of the large trestle tables laid for the meal. I had agreed to meet Thomas and Rufus at eight in the morning but they were both there when I arrived at half past seven.

"I can't get used to the idea of not waking at six," said Thomas.

"Nor can I" I replied, and Rufus nodded in agreement

"Perhaps, if we're quick, we can leave promptly at eight before Simon is up, and claim we thought he had gone ahead of us" Rufus suggested.

Thomas and I both grinned.

"A good plan," Thomas rejoined, "let's get a decent breakfast as we probably won't eat again until dinner."

However there was not a great deal on offer that morning. Cereals and fresh bread, with milk and butter from the dairy and jams from the storerooms was the extent of the meal. We filled our pockets with extra rolls to keep us going through the day and snuck out of the dining hall with a feeling of conspiratorial success.

"Ah, there you are." Simon's voice froze the smiles on our faces. "I've been up since five thirty and ready since seven. Look, I've been busy," he continued pointing to the rucksacks at his feet with one hand and waving a map with the other.

We looked at the tall figure leaning nonchalantly against the far post of the great front doors, the crossed legs clad in tweed plus-fours, thick brown knee socks ending in heavy-soled brogues of the same colour.

Muttering apologies we found ourselves rushing towards him, our boots, clumsy from the years on garden duty, making slapping noises against the stone slabs of the Grand Hall.

"Never mind, never mind," Simon's affable voice stopped us short. "It's a beautiful day and we're going to have a fantastic hike. Look," he went on, uncrossing his legs and unfolding the map in one quick move, "here's Igor's Moor with Fiddlers' Pond at its centre."

It was impossible not to be caught up with Simon's enthusiasm as he traced the suggested route with his index finger. I couldn't help admiring the carefully manicured finger nails and found myself pushing my own hands deep into my pockets, squashing the bread rolls.

"If we leave now and take this ridge to the North West we should be there by lunchtime and can picnic by the water," our self-appointed leader continued, his finger moving along the map contours as he spoke. "Then we can come home along the old Roman path that leads back through the village and right to our door, just in time for tea."

So began the first of our three expeditions onto the moors – expeditions that gave a new dimension to my appreciation of the subtle beauties of the English countryside. The damp softness of colour, light and land which later I missed so much during those dry, hot years in central Africa.

When I first arrived in Arumba, my soft English skin had attracted mosquitoes in clouds, but after a few months I barely noticed them. My beard and shaggy hair protected most of my head and face; the muscles, so close beneath my skin, had become tough enough to make what little flesh I had less appetizing to the insects that bred in the puddles around the riverbank.

Cachonga is close to the equator, so the sun sets around six in the evening all year round. Without electricity, there was not much to occupy the darkness except thoughts. The first of my many requests from the Bishop and his trusty Anyway, was for lanterns. They were acquired from down river - along with note-books, pens and measuring equipment. After their arrival I was able to work on agricultural and engineering plans long after the rest of the village had stopped bothering their minds with ideas. I would sit in my hut, papers strewn over the trunk and an upturned crate I used as a table, pencils, rulers and my sketchbook at the ready.

Rondavels

I only slept in my hut when it rained, and that was seldom enough. My pallet of dried grasses spent the day propped against the mud wall. It was pulled down at night and dragged a little way to a carefully

chosen spot that provided the best view of the star-clogged sky between horizontal fingers of a giant acacia tree.

Not often, during those busy years, did I miss the damp soft greens of England, but when I did, I would remember those walks across the Yorkshire moors. The nonchalant, seemingly unintentional, beauty of the hills was very powerful and all the easier to absorb because of the innocence of the young men who wandered them – well three of the young men, anyway.

To help me recreate those splendid walks, I wrote of each one in some detail. Sitting in my rondavel of mud and wattle, with the crickets chattering outside, maybe the sound of a lion roaring in the distance, and the ever-present heat and dust, I sent my mind back to those soggy, magnificent moors.

Simon had raided the college's out-door's department and helped himself to three backpacks which he had subsequently filled to capacity with we knew not what.

"Here are your packs," Simon indicated the three smaller knapsacks. "Let me know if they get too heavy for you and we'll re-arrange things." He swung his own pack easily onto his shoulders. It was almost twice the size of the ones he had given the rest of us but he brushed aside our half-hearted offers to carry it with a laugh.

"Don't be silly lads, I'm much stronger and fitter than you lot, and anyway, I need to earn my place in your company. So let's get going and see how we get along."

Thomas, Rufus and I exchanged puzzled glances as Simon pushed open one of the big oak doors, letting the sunshine stream into the dark hall and splashing the stone floor with a slice of raw daylight. None of us was going to argue about Simon's fitness, his visits to the gym were legendary, and his physique showed the results of regular exercise. Obediently we followed the tall figure out onto the gravel forecourt, through the gates, and turned left into the lane that ran alongside the tall walls of the college.

The morning passed pleasantly enough, Simon kept himself to himself as he led us off the lane and up a track onto the moors. The only time he spoke was to ask after our welfare and to ensure that he was not going too quickly for us, or that our packs were not too heavy. He was solicitude itself and slowly Rufus, Thomas and I all began to relax and feel rather sheepish about our previous resentments and doubts.

The moors opened up before us in the early spring light. The heather bounced under our feet, and the skies seemed full of birdsong as the warmth of the sun stretched fingers into the misty valleys. As predicted, we reached Igor's moor shortly after mid-day. We followed a stony ridge which climbed steadily towards the watershed and, upon arriving at the summit, stopped in wonder at what we saw.

"Igor's Moor is one of the gems of England." Simon said as he swept an upturned palm in front of him. "It is a good three miles from any road and has remained un-spoilt by car parks, litter bins, picnic tables and sign-posted nature trails. As you can see, the hills here form an almost perfect bowl in the centre of which glistens Fiddler's Pond, its color reflecting the sky."

On this particular occasion the sun was shining and the water mirrored the pale blue above. We absorbed the view in silence, enjoying it all the more for the climb we had achieved.

It took a further forty-five minutes to reach the water's edge. Simon led the way around the lip of the pond until he found a spot where the heather withdrew slightly exposing some large, flat rocks.

"Perfect," Simon rubbed his hands together with satisfaction, "now Thomas, let's have your pack first." He helped Thomas extract himself from the encumbrance and began to unload it. The pack contained a large red and white checked tablecloth that had been carefully wrapped around a collection of plates. Knives, forks and spoons were rolled up in matching napkins. A travelling set of salt, pepper, tomato and brown sauces completed the load.

"No wonder it didn't weigh very much," Thomas said as he watched Simon spreading the cloth on the biggest rock and weighting down the edges with stones from the water's brim. He walked over to the other side of the be-decked rock where Simon had put down his own pack and lifted it up. "Good Gracious, Simon, this weighs a ton, you really should have made the weights more even."

"Nonsense," answered Simon, "now come on Jack, let's see what you've got in yours." I obligingly opened my pack and pulled out a large tartan picnic rug.

"Careful!" Simon exclaimed, "there are vital things in there, and they're breakable."

I unfolded the rug with appropriate care to find four cut glass wine goblets tucked within its folds. I placed them carefully upon the cloth and watched the sun sparkles they threw onto the checked surface. I spread the rug over the springy heather with a feeling of disbelief. It was like being on a film set.

Rufus was already reaching into his bag and producing half a dozen food containers, each one had been packed to capacity as could be seen through the semi-translucent plastic.

Simon's pack disgorged yet more containers and when they were all opened, a sumptuous meal was revealed of smoked salmon, quails' eggs, a large roasted chicken, a golden pork pie with castellated crust, some French bread rolls, a fresh green salad with cherry tomatoes and a collection of exotic cheeses.

"I think it's important to pay as much attention to the colour scheme of one's meal as to the flavors." Simon began as he stepped back to admire his display. "To delight as many senses as possible in a single meal should always be one's aim, don't you think? See, we have almost every hue except purple. I did try to find a jar of beetroot or some pickled aubergines, but the village deli didn't have any. I went shopping yesterday, as soon as I knew we were all agreed on today." Simon chatted as he adjusted the dishes on the table-cloth. "So: there are the colours to delight our eyes, I think our noses will find the variety of aromas satisfactory and wonderfully diverse, and as for the sense of touch, the textures of the linen napkins and the woolen rug on the buoyant heather should provide a sufficient variety of tactile feelings; that just leaves the flavors to be judged."

Simon went back to his pack and bent to retrieve yet more surprises.

"But first, we need to celebrate this wonderful morning and thank our dear Lord for the bounty of today."

We all gladly assented to this idea, amazed as we were to hear it from him. We were composing ourselves into a suitable stature for prayer when Simon turned around with a bottle of champagne, sweating with cold, a broad smile on his face. The cork flew out as if from a giant popgun and the pale golden liquid rushed to follow it.

"I'm afraid it's been rather shaken up with our walk," Simon said, laughing as he caught the bubbles in one of the glasses. "Come on lads, don't look so solemn, this is the best way of celebrating with the Almighty that I can think of." He finished filling the glasses, returning to each as the bubbles subsided, and handed us one each.

"Here's a toast to thank the Lord for giving us such a magnificent day and bringing us to such a beautiful place." Simon began in a grave voice that wasn't matched by his sparkling eyes, "and to the company of my new friends with whom I am fortunate enough to share this gift. Thank you Lord" he finished with a flourish, glass held up to the sky so that the sunshine lit up the tiny bubbles. He then drained the liquid in one gulp.

"Ah, the glories of Champagne," he exclaimed, filling his glass again with the same practiced care. "Come on lads, let's see you drink to the toast – or was it not to your liking?"

"Oh, it was fine," I replied softly, "it's just that all this is so unexpected and so grand. We must thank you Simon for all the trouble you have gone to, it's quite astonishing." Whilst talking I found myself fingering the squashed, dried bread we had planned to have for our lunch. The spectacular table in front of me seemed quite foreign, but splendid nevertheless.

We took well over an hour savoring our meal. The champagne lasted only as long as the smoked salmon and quails' eggs, Simon having four glasses to our one. It was followed by a fifteen year old claret "to complement the chicken and the pie," Simon explained, and then diving into his pack once again, he produced a large piece of Stilton, some water biscuits and a small bottle of Port.

Even though Simon drank the lion's share of all three bottles, the rest of us had drunk enough to make us feel sleepy. We were all thirsty from the morning's exertions, and there was nothing else to drink but the alcohol. We dipped our glasses into the water from Fiddler's Pond, but it smelled of the peat from where it had come and minute wiggling organisms could be seen gyrating in the amber fluid – we tossed it back from where it had come.

None of us three usually drank wine, or even beer, except for a sip at Communion or to be sociable on special occasions. This abstinence was for no particular aesthetic or religious purpose - it had just become a habit amongst us - one that had to be abandoned for the moment so as not to appear rude or ungrateful.

The conversation became lively once the alcohol had eased our inhibitions - not that Simon suffered from any - and covered many different topics. I found myself enjoying Simon's company in a way I had never thought possible. Thomas and Rufus were obviously feeling the same way as they laughed at Simon's jokes and entered into lively debates that sometimes flirted with serious issues but mostly rambled from one subject to another without direction.

After dispensing with the Port, the four of us spread ourselves out on the rug, wriggling around to rearrange the heather beneath us, and went fast asleep feeling replete and at one with God and his world.

When the sun dipped behind the rim of Igor's Moor the temperature dropped quickly and the chill air woke Thomas and me almost simultaneously. Rufus was already sitting up, running his fingers through his ginger hair and yawning loudly. Simon was still fast asleep, curled in a fetal position, his blond head bending towards his drawn up knees.

It was nearly five o'clock, and although the days were lengthening now, we would still have to hurry to be back at St. Augustine's before dark. Thomas and I began packing up the picnic things and refilling the packs from which they had come.

"Well, at least Simon's will be a lot lighter now we've emptied everything." I commented. "We'd better wake him up and get moving."

Waking the slumbering Simon was no easy task. He groaned and turned over and told us to "bugger off" a few times before a thorough shaking from Thomas forced him to open his eyes. Once he remembered where he was and what was going on, Simon resumed his position as self-appointed leader of the expedition and we set of at a jaunty pace.

As dusk drew in and the shadows lengthened across the moors, I thought I had never seen a more beautiful landscape. The gentle colours of the heather and gorse had taken on a glow in the approaching twilight, as if the sun had left some of its radiance behind, trapped amongst the spiky foliage. Small birds flew low over the ground and a hawk circled high above. Here was the peace that comes when the evening star shows its solitary spark, a quietness of soul that seems special to this time of day. I began to hum, and then I started to sing one of my favorite hymns, before I got to the second line, Thomas had joined in:

> *The day Thou gavest, Lord, is ended*
> *The darkness falls at Thy behest*
> *To Thee our morning hymns ascended*
> *Thy praise shall sanctify our rest.*

Simon started the second verse with his deep baritone voice, and the rest of the hymn we sang altogether, walking side by side through the heather as the first bats of the evening began their forays into the darkening sky.

The Sun that bids us rest is waking
Our brethren 'neath the western sky,
And hour by hour fresh lips are making
Thy wondrous doings heard on high.

As o'er each continent and island
The dawn leads on another day
The voice of prayer is never silent
Nor dies the strain of praise away.

Forbid it, Lord, thy throne should ever,
Like earth's proud empires, pass away.
Thy kingdom stands and grows forever,
'Til all Thy people own Thy sway.

It was dark by the time we reached St. Augustine's, and the four of us stumbled into the hall in a heap of bonhomie.

"What a day," I exclaimed, shaking Simon's hand fervently. "You must let us know what we owe you for the wonderful picnic. Can we discuss it tomorrow – I'm absolutely beat and ready for bed – I can't even manage supper!"

"Thank you Simon," Thomas was eager to join in, "I agree with Jack about everything – especially the bit about calling it a day. The idea of climbing into bed and going horizontal seems quite exquisite and my feet are desperate to get out of these boots."

"Is it OK if we sort things out with you tomorrow?" Rufus said after adding his thanks.

"There's nothing to sort out, except to decide what we plan to do next." Simon rejoined, throwing his arms around us. "Let's all have a lie in and meet at breakfast around eight – how's that? In the meantime I'm off to the kitchen to see what that lovely little scullery maid has on offer for dinner."

We bade each other good night and went our separate ways, humming as we went.

18. THE SWEET CRY OF HOUNDS

The trip to Fiddler's Pond had been exotic and magical. Against our natural instincts, and to our surprise, the expedition had convinced us that Simon's company was an asset. He knew his way around the moors and had proved to be excellent company. Obviously the lunch he had provided had been expensive and Rufus, Thomas and I were keen to contribute but, at breakfast the following morning, all suggestions of reimbursement were brushed away by Simon with an affluent wave.

"No, no, lads," his voice was louder than necessary and bounced around the large empty dining hall. "I know it was over the top. It was my way of buying into your company. The next time will be nothing like as lavish. I don't mind organizing the food for our forays, I know where to find everything, and I'll let you know the costs each time. How would that be, it shouldn't cost more than a fiver a head, and I'll be responsible for the booze – as I know I am the one who favours that kind of thing. I'll even put some bottles of water into your packs next time, how's that!"

Simon's smile was too engaging to challenge and we agreed to his suggestions that included going on another expedition together, after two days of study and contemplation.

"And to let my feet recover," Thomas added with a smile.

After the unaccustomed exercise of the hike, we were happy to spend the next two days in the library, our physical activity restricted to the occasional stretch, the rubbing of tired eyes and the slow climbing of stairs. Simon was nowhere to be seen, so our studies were uninterrupted and satisfying.

By the third day, however, we were all ready and eager for our next expedition and met Simon on the appointed morning, with excitement, our five pound notes at the ready.

Simon seemed genuinely pleased to see us and gathered our money with embarrassment as we sat down to breakfast together.

"It's Saturday," he said, as he moved the milk and sugar out of the way to enable him to spread the map on the table. "And I happen to know that the Wilburton hounds are meeting over at Muddledock. They're a 'fell' pack, followed on foot by a lot of very fit locals. We can't possibly get there in time for the meet, as it is a good way across these hills, here." He stabbed at the map with his index finger. "But with a bit of luck, they should draw in this direction," the finger traced a curve over a large expanse of moorland inscribed by a myriad of contour lines with not a single roadway or foot path in evidence. "If we leave this trail here, and travel north west, it will be quite a climb, but we may get a glimpse of them before the day is out. What do you say?"

Rufus was the only one of us who had any familiarity with hounds. His family had 'puppy walked' for their local pack for as long as he could remember. He had played with each summer's new pups every year of his childhood, and cried in anguish when it was time for the grown dogs to return to the kennels and fulfill their destiny. His Grandfather had been a keen hunting man, but Rufus had always been put off by the cold and the wet, the early dark of Scottish winters, and the fact that his Mother preferred him to stay at home. His father had sometimes taken him out in the car to watch and there had always been a niggling feeling that he was missing out on something. He met this plan with delight.

"Good idea, Simon," he exclaimed. "Let's give it a go. If we find them, it's a bonus, if we don't, at least we've a purpose to our ramblings. Is that OK with you two?" he finished, turning to Thomas and me, both of us looking somewhat bemused.

"Why not?" I found myself responding. I cared not at all if we found the hounds, but the idea of having a purpose was appealing, and Thomas agreed with a firm nod.

Thus began an astonishing adventure that introduced me to instincts I didn't know I had, instincts made manifest by visceral feelings that were quite new to me. I remember writing about it many years later by the light of my cherished oil lamp, one evening after a particularly grueling Cachonga day digging irrigation channels into the new lands. My parched eyes longed for the damp mists and dragging clouds that crawled over the moors, so far away in both time and space.

There were four small backpacks waiting for us in the hall. "No indulgences today," Simon said in a stern voice that argued his laughing eyes. "Take your pick," he continued, gesturing at the packs, "those three have water bottles, whilst this one has something stronger – which you are all welcome to share." He swung this last up onto his shoulders, slipping his arms through the straps with the familiarity of a soldier.

It was another fine day, and we made good headway through the College pastures and up onto the moors. We walked with easy strides along a well-used footpath that rose steadily away from the village. Soon we could look back at the roofs and chimneys of the hamlet that surrounded St. Augustine's, with the spires and deep pitched gables of the college itself standing like a proud mother hen above the cottages that encircled her.

Simon looked at his compass at regular intervals until suddenly he stopped with us three concertinaing along the path behind him. "This way, lads." he exclaimed, and pitched himself into the heather in a direction at right angles to the path.

The purples, pinks, browns, yellows, greens and reds of the heathers and bracken spread in all directions; uphill and down, ahead of us across the face of the rise, and behind us, towards Rutmoor Beck valley, whose waters could be seen glinting in the sunshine. There were no trees, except way below in the village; only the occasional outcrop of rocks interrupted the sea of soft, springy vegetation.

"*Calluna vulgaris*" pronounced Simon, sweeping his arms wide to encompass the landscape. "Heather to you lot," his voice took on a patronizing air, which he was quick to correct. "Beautiful, isn't it? But bloody difficult to walk through. Just take your time, and we'll stop for lunch whenever you feel like it."

We spread out to tackle the hill as best we could. Sometimes a trickle of water had made inroads into the dense mat, and we could follow it for a while, with squelching noises oozing from beneath our feet, until its course diverged from ours. Occasionally there were animal tracks weaving around the plants, but these also didn't follow Simon's compass heading for very long. Most of the time it was just trial and error as to which plants could be walked upon, and which could not - the latter biting at the intruder's lower legs and ankles.

We were all ready for a break when we reached a ridge that proffered another view of nearly 360 degrees. It was well into the afternoon, and we were all hungry. Finding the least uncomfortable tussock, we sat down and opened our packs, relieved to have water to slake our thirsts. Simon had some water, but he also had a good supply of wine.

"It's rosé, today," he informed us. "Light, sparkling rosé to thrill the pallet and excite the taste buds. How about it chaps, I have two bottles, so there's plenty to go round?"

We each had a glass of the pretty pink liquid, and agreed that it was the perfect accompaniment for the roast chicken sandwiches and slices of cheese and apple Simon had provided.

The conversation was relaxed and easy. We had all forgotten about the purpose of the abandonment of the footpath as we discussed the topics for our up-coming oral exams. Suddenly Simon stopped the conversation with an urgent "Hush." Followed by an even more urgent command: "Listen!"

Across the moors came the distant sound of a horn from the west, followed some seconds later by the sound of dogs.

"Ah the sweet cry of hounds" Simon, leaped to his feet and turned his head in the direction of the noise. "I thought we must have missed them, but they're just over there, and running well from the sound of it. Come on, you three" he called as he threw his picnic stuff into his pack and bounded into the bracken, pulling his pack onto his back as he went. Rufus was hot on his heels.

Thomas and I looked at each other with eyebrows raised. The barking was louder now and, to my surprise, there was something in the sound that sent a prickling feeling round the back of my neck. With an unexpected leap I was puffing up the hill in Simon's wake. Thomas shrugged his shoulders and followed, his face wearing a perplexed, but not angry expression.

"Have you ever seen a finer sight?" said Simon as we arrived at the crest of the next hill with faces flushed from the climb. In front of us the moors dropped smoothly towards a thin strand of water, sparkling in the slanted sunshine. Upon the stream's far bank the land climbed upwards again, clad in the same purple and muted red heather that was under our feet.

Half way up the far hill, running in a thickening line, was a pack of hounds in full cry. The leading hound, nose pressed below the fronds, had a singleness of purpose that was evident even from this distance. The hounds that followed seemed to be both encouraging him forwards and enthusing in the scent themselves. The view from our vantage point was of a single unit made up of various components flowing across the moors. Echoing across the valley came a melody that provoked a primeval excitement.

"Look, there's Charlie," said Simon with his stick pointing to a spot at least a quarter of a mile in front of the hounds – "all foxes are called "Charlie" by the way," he added reverting to his patronizing tone.

My eyes followed the line of the walking stick into the distance. Suddenly I saw a blurred movement amongst the bracken and heather. Adjusting my glasses that had moved down my nose with the exertion of the climb, I focused upon a fox running along the same contour as the hounds with the relaxed lope of a creature confident in his own space. The animal turned suddenly downhill, turned again and disappeared from view.

We stood transfixed watching the hounds as if our eyes were being drawn by magnets. The pack came to the spot where the fox had turned and continued running straight on. Suddenly their cry stopped as the pack spread out in a fan shape. Silently the hounds worked, like a phalanx of soldiers looking for signs of the enemy. Most of them had already doubled back when the hound on the lowest contour started to speak. Like a flock of birds that turns as one, the hounds rallied to the call and the chase was on again.

My heart was beating with excitement. I turned to Thomas and saw my friend's eyes as moist and wide as mine must have appeared. "What is it that moves us so?" I whispered, not knowing why I had lowered my voice.

"I'm not sure," replied Thomas, also in a whisper, "I don't know anything about fox-hunting and I'm sure I should disapprove of what I'm seeing, yet there is something here that speaks viscerally to me. What an extraordinary sensation!"

Some distance behind the hounds, a collection of people could be seen striding through the same heather that was giving us so much trouble. There were about two dozen followers scattered across the hillside all moving in the same direction, all with one purpose. None of them seemed to be having any difficulty with the turbulent going.

Simon and Rufus were steaming ahead of us again, in an effort to keep abreast of the hounds across the valley. They were leaping through the heather with a gusto that seemed to give them balance. Thomas and I stopped our pondering, and tried to follow them as best we could. Soon we also fell into a rhythm, and our feet seemed to learn where it was safe to tread. The cry of the hounds, coming in fits and starts from across the stream, lured us on and we both shared in the exhilaration of our pursuit.

After some twenty minutes of loping across the moor, we came to a road that led sharply down the hill to a village at the base of the valley. The tarmac was very welcome under our feet, especially as hounds also seemed to be making for the village. We were able to slow the pace and walk, four abreast, down the hill to meet them.

"That's Muddledock," Simon said. He was breathing hard after all the running. "They've run right back to where they started. How about that for a bit of exercise, lads? We can get a bus back to College from here; it's much too far to walk now. Let's see what the village has to offer."

Rufus, Thomas and I were all too out of breath to comment, but we nodded and grinned at the mention of a bus back home. Our legs were scratched and our shoulders ached from the pack straps.

19. THE FOX & GOOSE

The sound of the horn could be heard clearly as we entered the village and followed Simon's lead towards the Fox & Goose, a timbered pub that seemed to have sunk into the ground over the centuries.

We crossed the village green with a sense of urgency and entered the pub, which would have been closed at this time of day had it not been for the hunt having met there that morning.

The local pub

There were plenty of others taking advantage of the unusual opening time, and the bar was busy with tweed coated men and women with ruddy complexions under flat caps or head scarves.

Simon ordered in a loud cheery voice: "four pints of your best bitter, please, and a whisky mac as a chaser." I remember his face, flushed under the blond hair, his eyes sparkling with excitement as he took in his surroundings and the people around him.

The landlord having obliged, we were presented with glass tankards of Theakston's Ale that we raised to each other, admiring the way the light struggled to get through the dark liquid. "Cheers, lads, here's to another day in

God's country!" Simon said, and he downed his pint in half a dozen swallows and returned the empty tankard to the bar. Having rummaged in his pocket for the necessary cash, waving away our offers of payment, he picked up the wine glass half full of amber liquid that the barman had left by his elbow.

"So what do you think of the hounds, Thomas?" Simon turned to his nearest companion. Thomas was savoring the bittersweet beer, his upper lip sporting a moustache of white foam. I was enjoying my pint in the same way. My whole body felt rejuvenated, and I thought I had never enjoyed a drink so much or felt better in my life.

"Did they catch the fox, do you think?" Thomas questioned.

"You'll have to ask the huntsman that question," Simon responded. "Probably not, he had a good lead on them and was going well, wasn't he? It's not the kill that we come out to watch, no, it's the hunt itself – the hounds, and how they work. The way the members of the pack relate to each other and respond to each other's cries. Rufus has been telling me of the hound puppies his family used to look after. That's an opportunity to get to know these fellows properly, as individuals, and then later, when you see them as part of the pack, you see how it is made up of individuals, and yet moves as a single entity.

"Almost all of our great generals were hunting men, you know," Simon was warming to the subject. "They would try to have their battalions as disciplined as a pack of hounds, and to move as efficiently, even though they would know many of the troops by name, know their families and their individual histories – they still had to move as one when required."

"There were eighteen and a half couple out today," he continued, "I asked that chap by the door as we came in, he's the kennelman." I raised my eyebrows for an explanation of such bizarre phraseology. "Hounds are always counted in couples, and they always take out an odd number when they hunt" Simon went on, "it's tradition. And there'll be twice that number left behind in the kennels. The kennelman, huntsman and the whippers-in will not only know each hound by name but they will know the names and pedigrees of each of their mothers and fathers as well.

"Did you see, when they over-ran the scent for a moment, checked and then fanned out to search for it, how one hound found the new line, spoke to the others, and the chase resumed?" We nodded above our cherished tankards in response. "Well that hound who found the scent first, his identity will have been noted by both the huntsman and the whipper-in, I expect, and will be written up in the huntsman's report this evening."

Simon paused, looked thoughtful for a moment and then continued more to himself than his audience: "I don't know why I said 'his' identity they might well have been hunting with the dogs today, but could just as easily have been the bitches, may even be a mixed pack – I should have asked" he said to nobody in particular.

Simon re-focused his gaze on his three students, all of us listening attentively. "Hunting is a science and a religion rolled together for these people," he continued waving his hand towards the crowd behind him. "Much more than just their way of life. It's being part of something that stretches back over the centuries, and forward too, if the politicians keep their bloody noses out of things."

"Like being a soldier in a famous regiment – to continue your analogy, Simon?" I queried, surprised at my continuing interest.

"Absolutely Jack, but the members of the hunt staff are more like the officers, and the Masters are the generals. It is the hounds who are the soldiers."

"And the followers?" Thomas asked, using his eyes to indicate the crowded pub full of earnest conversation.

"They are just bystanders, here to watch and judge how well the hunt staff and their hounds perform; to socialize with fellow enthusiasts; catch up on the local gossip; enjoy the freedom of the countryside. All those things, but mostly, they are out to share in the excitement of the chase. Did you not feel a new energy to your legs when the hounds were leading us on? We're here to experience the thrill of being pulled into an unknown adventure, not knowing where we will end up, or how long it will take."

"And to keep out of the bloody way!" laughed a burly man with bushy white eyebrows to match his moustache. He had been waiting at the bar behind Simon, listening to the conversation. "How do you do, chaps?" he said, thrusting an outstretched hand into our midst. "George Fellows, one of the Masters of the hounds of which you were just speaking – well one of the generals, I might say!" And he winked at Simon, stroking each side of his moustache in a caricaturing gesture with one hand whilst he pumped swiftly offered hands with the other. "Followers are always welcome as long as they keep out of the way of hounds and let them get on with the job.

"New to the sport are you?" he addressed the three of us to whom Simon had been directing his excited speech. His greying hair bore the imprint of the cloth cap that was sitting up-turned on the bar. "Well, welcome to one of the finest fell packs of hounds you'll ever have the privilege to follow. William, the huntsman, will be in soon – I'd introduce you, but you won't get a word out of him! He keeps his own counsel and unless you're willing to discuss each hound's ancestry in detail, or the proposals for next year's breeding schedule, you won't get more than a nod and a grunt from him. He's an excellent huntsman, and like all professional hunt staff, he is totally dedicated to his pack – as was his father before him. He used to hunt the Spey hounds." One arm spread out in the direction of the window. "We were lucky to get William, and we do our best to keep him happy."

"What's your pleasure, major?" A barmaid had joined the landlord behind the bar and was leaning on the polished wood behind the speaker, waiting for a break in the conversation. She was a busty beauty in her early forties who watched her client fondly as he talked to us newcomers.

"The usual, please Dorothy, and something for my young friends here?" The bushy eyebrows raised the question for him.

"I'll join you with one of those," Simon responded as he watched the barmaid add the ginger wine to a generous measure of whisky. "Thank you very much, Sir. I'm Simon Mountford. My family is from the South. We hunt with the VWH."

"Ah, the famous Vale of the White Horse," the general responded, as if speaking of something slightly sacred. "Very different country from up here, isn't it? All those bloody blackthorn hedges! You buggers must be crazy crossing that sort of country. My days with horses are over, I'm afraid. Had a bad tip-up twenty odd years ago while out with the Rockwood Harriers – horse caught it's hoof in a piece of wire hidden in the stone wall, came down on top of me. Nasty business.

"What about you lads?" he stopped his reminiscence to attend to the drink order.

Thomas and I both declined, raising our tankards to show that they were both still half full, and thanking him warmly for the offer. Rufus, who looked at his empty tankard with embarrassment, agreed to "just half a pint then. Thank you."

I had noticed the military bearing of our host that was confirmed by the barmaid when she had addressed him. He was amused by Simon's analogy and agreed that it was appropriate, especially as the account of his hunting accident had taken on the somber sound of a casualty under fire. I couldn't help liking the major whose enthusiasm for his sport was proving infectious.

The pub was filling up now, as more and more hunt followers arrived, all red-cheeked and smiling. We raised our glasses to the major and thanked him for his hospitality.

"This is the last day of the season," he said, as we were squashed into a corner of the pub by the incoming tide of hunting folk. "Too bad you left it until now to join us. Be sure you get a meet card for next season – here's the secretary's address," he handed Simon a card, "let her know names and addresses and she'll keep you all informed." He shook our hands energetically once more, and bade us good night. "We always say good night when we've finished hunting," he answered our surprised faces, "no matter what the time of day, just as we always say 'good morning' when we start, even if we join late and it's way past noon. Just tradition, but there you are." The major turned away and was immediately hailed by a group from the other side of the pub.

"What a splendid old boy," Simon exclaimed, and we all agreed.

"Perhaps we should have asked him about the bus times," I was thinking aloud and looking forward to getting out of my boots which were full of spikes of heather, causing my feet and ankles to complain.

"I don't suppose he would have the faintest idea," laughed Simon. "He doesn't strike me as someone who takes the bus anywhere. However, you've got a point, Jack. I'll see if the barmaid can tell us." He started to push his way through the throng, back towards the bar.

It was a good five minutes before Simon rejoined us in our corner, and he brought a tray of beer with him.

"What a scrum," he said, offering the tray around. "The barmaid says there's a bus at half past six, so we've plenty of time for another round. Here you go lads, put the tray down somewhere with the empty glasses and let's move out of this mob." And he led the way, glass held high above the jostling shoulders, out into the late afternoon.

The four of us sat at one of the wooden tables that flanked the pub's entrance, our legs stretched out in front, our bootlaces undone. I took my boots off and worked on picking the annoying blades of heather from my socks with great diligence. I wriggled my toes in delight, sipped the unexpected second pint, and decided that life on the moors was absolutely splendid.

The bus was only ten minutes late. We sat altogether along the back seats like a row of schoolboys. I had managed to squeeze my reluctant feet back into my boots, but had joined the others in leaving them undone. The trailing laces added to the impression of extreme youth as we filled the back of the bus with chatter.

"But isn't it cruel?" Thomas asked the question that had seemed inappropriate when surrounded by the amiable crowd in the pub. "This fox-hunting lark, I thought it was meant to be cruel, yet they seemed such a good lot, those people in the pub."

The question had been directed to Simon, but to my surprise it was Rufus who answered, leaning forward from his seat by the window, his face suddenly animated.

"No!" Rufus exclaimed, in a tone that made us all jump. "Sorry," he said, the vehemence of his voice had startled him as much as the rest of us, "it's just that I have heard this claim so many times before, and it is so terribly wrong."

Rufus took a large tartan handkerchief from his pocket, wiped his forehead and blew his nose vigorously. "Let me tell you why my family raised hound puppies for the local hunt every year," he continued in a softer voice.

"My father found a fox one afternoon where our garden runs into the edge of the wood. It was lying in the bluebells in full daylight and made no attempt to run as he approached. It was looking at him. Father said he had never seen such a dreadful expression as the one that stared at him from those dull eyes. The animal's coat was dull also, and the back legs were laid out in an unnatural position. Father went back to the house to get his gun. He said he knew what the fox was asking him to do.

"After he had shot the fox, father examined the body. It had been caught in a snare, heaven knows how long ago. The wire had bitten into the flesh behind the shoulders and slowly must have paralyzed his back legs. Maggots had already started eating the flesh of his wounded belly." Rufus stopped and blew his nose again. His pale blue eyes were moist with this tale from his childhood.

"The people who own the woods next to us are anti-hunting. Not for reasons of principle, just because they fell out with one of the local Masters of Hounds, and this was their way of getting back at him. They ran a commercial shoot – probably still do – and without the hounds the foxes were giving them lots of trouble with the young pheasants. Their gamekeeper must have set that snare, and probably many others also.

"Father buried the fox, came back to the house and telephoned the kennels. He was not a hunting man himself, polio had weakened his legs when he was a child, but he wanted to do his bit to support the most humane way to control the fox population. The huntsman came to see us a few days later, and being delighted with all the space we had around our house, he agreed to let us have two puppies to look after for them, until they were ready to join the pack.

"Father explained to us children about how the foxhound's jaw is so strong that it can break a fox's neck in a fraction of a second. If a fox is caught out hunting it dies instantly – usually whilst still running. If it gets away, it is completely unscathed. There is no possibility of wounding, and the strongest, cleverest foxes always get away. The maimed, diseased and aged foxes are killed immediately and saved from a lingering death. The Darwinian principle of the survival of the fittest works only with this way of culling. Other methods are indiscriminate and slow. Even shooting can't be guaranteed to provide a swift death. Every man with a gun would have to be a sharp shooter of incredible skill, and with a telescopic sight, if he were to be sure of killing these swift cunning creatures with a single shot. And the fox would have to be stationary. If it is wounded by a misplaced bullet, a painful death from gangrene generally follows."

There was silence in the back of the bus for a few moments.

"But what about the chase," Thomas asked in a quiet voice, he had felt somewhat chastised by Rufus's story. "Surely that's not a bundle of laughs for the poor fox?"

"How do you think the fox gets his dinner?" It was Simon who had taken up the baton. "How do you think the lambs, chickens, ducks and rabbits feel about the chase they get from Mr. Charlie Fox? At least the hounds threaten a death the fox can relate to, and one from which they so often escape, as Rufus has just said. They didn't catch the one we saw today, by the way. I asked someone while I was waiting to talk to the barmaid about the bus times. They lost him in the stream. The clever animal had led them down to the water and must have run along its bed for a good while 'cos they couldn't find the scent after that."

We were silent for a while, each with our own thoughts as we watched the dusk gathering in the valleys and making silhouettes of the hilltops. When the bus dropped us off outside St. Augustine's massive gates, the evening star had appeared again in the clear sky, heralding another fine night.

Back inside, we found a cold supper had been laid out for us in the dining-room. It was very welcome after our interrupted lunch. We chatted over the happenings of the day in a lighter mood from the one that had developed in the bus, and retired early for private night time prayers and the deep satisfying sleep that follows a day of exercise and excitement in the fresh air – well that was true for three of us but I expect in Simon's case, it was more likely to be a visit to the kitchen maid.

20. CHARADES

The next week was split into days of study and days of further ramblings. Simon often joined us in the library now, full of questions and hurried scribbling.

One evening, he brought a couple of bottles of wine to our meager supper table and implored us to help him devour the contents. Wine glasses had been set out on the sideboard which was not a regular occurrence. Why didn't we take notice of this, I have often pondered since. These were now distributed with the usual Mountford flair.

It was not difficult to turn the conversation to the looming Defining Discussions – after all they dominated our lives, thoughts, dreams – indeed our very existence seemed to rely on a satisfactory outcome to these prodigious exams.

"It's most unfair," Simon said, waving away our protests and filling the glasses with ruby-colored wine. "My uncle, you know 'the bishop who must be obeyed,' has insisted that I go first. We have a family Christening being held on Wednesday and he is determined that I officiate in whatever capacity my degree allows.

"And you know how St. Augustine's regards any request from my uncle," he exclaimed, trying to keep the pride out of his voice. "Of course they'll do as the 'Great Bish' requires, so poor old me will have several days' less time to study than some of you and have no feedback from those who have gone before."

Simon had informed us that his discussion concentrated on the necessity of the crucifixion to Christianity. He teased Rufus that his subject would dovetail nicely into Rufus's topic which had now concentrated upon the Trial of Jesus of Nazareth. "Perhaps we should make a joint presentation" he joked one day. Rufus was quick to answer that his research was dealing with specifics about the trial itself and the inevitability of its outcome. He was distancing his studies from the religiosity that resulted from the choice of crucifixion as a sentence for Christ's 'crimes'. Instead he was trying to understand why and how such a situation had become irretrievable.

I was vague with Simon about my subject of the indivisibility of the Numinous. I was still uncomfortable about sharing my personal philosophies with him. So it was with relief that I watched Simon turn his attention to Thomas and discuss the latter's chosen theme of the importance of the virgin birth to Christianity.

I have gone over this conversation – and several of the others that followed – since our time at St. Augstine's, so remember it vividly.

"Come now, Thomas," Simon expostulated, "let me play the Devil's advocate here. Let's pretend I am Father David and I will test you on your ideas." Simon re-filled our glasses and brought out a bundle of notes from which he started to read.

"Is it not true that virgin births were an expected phenomenon of religious leaders way before the birth of Christ?" He started, trying to amuse us by mimicking Father David's solemn voice. "Jesus was not the first to boast a virgin for a mother. Long before Jesus came along, the Egyptians credited the virgin Neith with having brought forth all humanity. Zoroaster also preceded Christ, and it was his virgin birth that led to his being proclaimed the Prophet of the divine Zarathustra. Then there was . . ." he looked up from his notes. "Well Father David is bound to know of others. So why should Christianity have grown when the Parsees, for example, dwindled?"

Thomas had warmed to the game. After finishing a mouthful of turkey sandwich, washed down by the generous supply of claret, he pushed his hair out of his eyes, straightened his spine, and waded into the charade.

"Indeed there have been other virgin births claimed by other religions, all of them relying on the emblem of purity that virginity symbolizes. Even within Christianity itself - John the Baptist, for example is thought to have sprung from a virgin's womb - yet his mother's name has shrunk into obscurity.

"However, these Prophets like Saint John & Zoroaster were heralded as holy messengers only, not as the direct Sons of God.

"With Mary there is the marvel of the Annunciation that is the act of completing the Trinity. By embedding the divine seed in such a perfectly innocent and beautiful place, and with the conception in the virgin womb, the eternal triangle is completed.

"Then there follows the birth itself with the attendant mysteries. Always there is the figure of the Virgin mother at the centre of Christianity, but where is the talk of the mother in the other religions?"

The wine flowed, the conversation also. Simon was at his congenial best. I am ashamed to say that both Rufus and I were drawn into this farce when Simon asked "Come on chaps, what would Father David ask next?" Both of us came up with ideas, and Thomas answered all the questions ably and with great lucidity.

The evening finished with Simon announcing with sombre dignity, that he, as Father David, proclaimed Thomas a thoroughly worthy candidate for the Church and that he would soon see himself standing in the pulpit of Westminster Abbey. We all laughed, congratulated Thomas on his wonderful appointment, and still chuckling we retired for the night.

The other students were scheduled to return the following Monday, so Simon suggested one last excursion for the day before.

Sunday morning saw us all in Chapel for early Mass. The regulars from the village straggled in, the men doffing their hats while the women patted theirs further into their curls with confident pride.

"What a strange habit is this," I remember thinking to myself, "where men remove their head coverings in a mark of respect and the women don theirs for the same reason?" My mind was wandering that morning, looking forward to another day on the moors, and I had to pull my accustomed reverence out of a sleepy corner in my conscience.

With nearly all the students absent, the service was held in the choir stalls. I always preferred sitting on the altar side of the screen. Ever since I had joined the choir in Willenbury, I had felt a sense of achievement in being away from the main congregation – nearer to God, it had seemed then, and it still had a bit of that elevation about it at college.

Thomas was across the aisle from Rufus and me, his head bowed upon his clasped hands, his kneeling body vibrating with fervor. Rufus, my neighbor was in a similar pose, and like Thomas, he seemed absorbed by the strength of his prayers. Simon was sitting behind us, and his deep baritone voice thrummed through the liturgy with a sincerity that was mirrored in his mien, a deep devotion shimmered in his pronouncement of the Creed.

That morning, my mind refused to focus where it should. It wandered around the chapel, circumnavigating the familiar intonations, bobbing up and down as I knelt, sat, and stood as the service required, but empty of the intense feelings that normally occupied my thoughts and feelings during Chapel services.

Hearing Simon's ardent supplications to the Almighty, I could not help dwelling on my previous misinterpretation of a character I had thought to be both frivolous and dissipated. Now I had come to know him better, I had to reshape my views, and I felt guilty about the earlier skepticism. However, we would never be kindred spirits. I didn't know why, exactly, but I was still not entirely comfortable with his company.

Nevertheless, I welcomed Simon to our breakfast table when Chapel had finished and the small congregation had filed past Father David, with hands outstretched and faces full of earnestness. The Head of St Augustine had a softer manner out of term-time, but his beneficent expression did little to hide the solid determination with which the remaining students identified him.

On Sundays when the College was officially closed, breakfasts were particularly meager. The kitchens shut down after dinner on Saturday nights and, with everything laid out for the following day, it remained deserted until early on Monday mornings. That last Sabbath of the break we took advantage of the sparse meal as we discussed how to spend our time for the next day and a half before the others returned and the timetable for the Defining Discussions was published. As usual, it was Simon who came up with a plan.

"There's no point coming back here tonight, gentlemen," he started, "as everything will be closed.

I've checked the weather forecast and suggest we borrow a couple of tents from the stores and trek out well into the moors, camping where we will, and returning by a different route tomorrow. What do you say?"

Thomas, Rufus and I were all in agreement, so we set about the logistics of raiding the outdoor pursuit stores in one of the basements under the main hall. Simon seemed to know his way around the rows of shelves and lockers, and had soon pulled out a large nylon tent with inter-locking plastic rods.

"This'll be big enough for all of us," he chortled, "no need to increase our baggage by taking separate tents. Now we need four sleeping bags, ah here they are." He pointed at some neatly bound bundles, "and a small cooking stove with its own gas supply, perfect." He moved along the shelves collecting a variety of cooking and eating items and four water containers that strapped neatly onto the same back packs we had used on our first outing.

When everything was stowed into our packs, there was still plenty of space.

"We can stop for dinner and breakfast supplies at the corner shop in Thrappington," Simon said, as he handed us some empty food containers. "There's a Pakistani couple there who don't believe in being closed on Sundays, and they have an excellent selection. For lunch, we can buy some sandwiches and things at the petrol station on the A189. We have to cross it if we're heading that way - unless any of you has a different idea?"

All of us shook our heads and our bewildered expressions showed our surprise at Simon's knowledge of the countryside around the College. We had become used to leaving the arrangements for our ramblings to the self-proclaimed leader, and had no reason to either question or complain. Simon had taken charge right from the beginning – the lack of responsibility was a relief for all us, and it was a luxury to just follow along.

The day progressed well enough. The sun made sporadic appearances amongst the low clouds, but we were happy with the cooler air as we climbed away from the main road, our packs flushed with new supplies from the predicted service station.

We stopped for lunch on a flat spot sheltered from the wind by a dramatic cliff of exposed rock. We caught a glimpse of the sky reflected in Fiddlers' pond in the adjoining valley of Igor's Moor. This time the water was the muted grey of a pigeon's breast with the cloud movements mimicking the bird's swelling feathers. To the West the heather-clad hills hummocked behind each other in a seemingly endless progression, the clouds threatening to snag themselves on the uppermost crests.

The talk was once more of the forthcoming Defining Discussions. Simon took his role of the night before and continued for some time to imitate Father David in an interrogation of friendly banter. Then, our lunch being over, Simon suggested we should climb to the summit above the cliff to grasp the greater view.

"You have to experience the full sight from the top, lads. I want to make a few sketches from here, and I've seen the view many times. Watch out for the stream that crosses the path underneath the heather about a hundred yards from the top, it's fed by a spring that comes to light just the other side of the bluff, flows underground again and re-emerges to catch out innocent ramblers. Here," he continued, producing a couple of empty water bottles from amongst the debris of our lunch, "fill these while you're up there, you'll never drink cleaner stuff."

The view had certainly been worth the climb. The cloud shadows softened the already pliable heather that stretched before and below us on all sides. A buzzard, or maybe an eagle, soared over the valley at the same height as we had acquired without the use of wings. Somehow the climb allowed us to share the bird's freedom. We took deep breaths of the moist air and felt exhilarated and humbled at the same time.

We found Simon's stream and, with some difficulty and diligence, filled the water bottles before returning like conquering heroes bringing gifts from the heavens and the mountains to find Simon hurriedly putting away his notepad and pencil.

The afternoon's walk was long but not too demanding and we kept going until dusk got the better of us. In the dwindling light, Simon led the way down a track to the beginning of some woodland. As the land flattened, the heather gave way to grass. We entered a pine forest; the trees seeming to swallow the light, making us stay close together until we emerged into a glade of green. The surrounding firs and larches were tall and straight so that they excluded the sun's fading rays. Darkness was coming on apace. We made camp by the light of a gas lantern whose mantle gave off a soft circular glow attracting surprised insects and seduced moths.

Rufus, Thomas and I pitched the tent while Simon gathered wood and made a fire. There was much laughter amid the shouted instructions from one to another, and eventually the tent was in place with sleeping bags tossed inside and a fire sending shadows leaping into the trees.

A supper of cold meats and French bread was quickly unpacked and devoured. It was washed down with a light beer which Rufus and I shared, a can of bitter for Thomas and some glistening wine for Simon who insisted that an Alsatian Hock was essential to complete this perfect setting.

After the meal, Simon resumed his jovial characterization of Father David interrogating Thomas. The fire faded and the chill air crept along the ground to nibble at our feet and buttocks as we sat around the embers. Simon kept the cold at bay with a bottle of whiskey; the rest of us declined.

"I can't think properly with a freezing bum" Thomas said half an hour into the conversation. "Let's get off the wet ground and go to bed."

"Well it's hardly sleep time yet," said Simon, "but there's no reason not to move into the tent and leave the cold out here. You can't duck out of your questioning that easily – I'm just trying to help consolidate your thoughts for the great day."

Inside the tent we pushed the rolled sleeping bags aside and used them as cushions to lean against as the tent was too low to allow us to sit up straight anywhere but in the middle. Rufus and I were cradling mugs of cocoa, Thomas still had his can of beer and Simon his whisky bottle whose contents were rapidly disappearing via an incongruous pink plastic mug.

Propped up on our rolled sleeping bags with shoulders almost touching and our legs sprawled in opposite directions, Rufus and I looked like a pair of bookends without the books. Thomas sat with crossed legs, his head bowed and shoulders hunched to avoid contact with the tent roof. Simon was lying on his stomach in the tent doorway, his legs stretched outside towards the fire, his head supported on his elbows, face framed by long fingers. The glowing embers of the fire could be seen outside the tent's open flap, behind Simon's shoulders, and gave enough light for us to make out each other's outlines but not the facial expressions.

"So Mr. Allworthy," Simon started mimicking Father David once again, "how exactly does Mary's conception vary from that, say, of Leda whose impregnator was the mighty Zeus himself?"

"Zeus turned himself into a swan to have his way with Leda - I don't think I would put it quite like that if you were really Father David" he added with a chuckle, "whereas The Angel Gabriel was an aspect of the

Almighty, infused with the Holy Spirit, a messenger sent with the Ultimate Gift – hardly to be compared with the randy actions of the promiscuous Zeus. It is the undefiled nature of Mary that appeals. She is pure and thoughtful in her ways, whereas Leda is portrayed as voluptuous and sexy.

"Mary provides a calm and loving way to approach the Awfulness of the Divine. She is a shield against the full magnitude of God. Through the gentleness of Mary, the great power of the Almighty is diluted, or veiled, in such a way that it is accessible to us mortals. She is compassion embodied and has become viewed as an unjudgmental intermediary for man's communication with God."

"But could you not say all the same things about her son, Jesus Christ - is that not one of the main reasons he was sent down to earth, the main function of his ultimate sacrifice?" Simon sounded genuinely interested.

"It is the feminine gentleness of Mary which people find so appealing." Thomas responded. "Mary offers sanctuary, succor and the depth of forgiveness found only in motherhood. So many semi-deities from Greek and Roman mythology were men, and the most powerful avatars of eastern philosophy have male bodies. Look at the seductions put down to Krishna as well as Zeus. Yet no Jesus-type figure emerged from their many couplings with humans. No nubile wench achieved a place, in either the Hindu or Roman pantheons, similar to that held by Mary in Christianity."

"How about Tiresias?" Simon changed his tack, and rather alarmingly seemed to have been doing some research. "If we're talking mythology, don't you think there's an interesting character here? After all Tiresias is claimed by many to be the ultimate authority on the sexual pleasures of the male and the female."

"What on earth has Tiresias got to do with this discussion?" I interposed – for some reason I was uncomfortable with this continuing charade. "From what I know of Tiresias he was a blind soothsayer who lost his sight for watching Athena as she bathed."

"Yes, yes, but he was also turned into a woman as a punishment for something else – I can't remember what," said Simon, tipping the last of the whisky into the pink tumbler. "Towards the end of his life, he was offered the opportunity to revert to being a man if he would like to. He chose to return to manhood even though he proclaimed that women have greater orgasms than men – after all he had been in the unique position to make such a comparison – if you'll excuse the pun," he gave a lewd smirk. "Maybe with age such excitements became less important, or more exhausting. But it's interesting, don't you think?"

"What on earth has any of that to do with the Virgin Mary?" asked Thomas.

"Nothing really," said Simon, "it's just that we were talking about the different aspects of human nature embodied in each sex." His words were beginning to slur together as he edged his body forward on his elbows, sliding further into the tent on his belly. "Always an intriguing subject, don't you think? How women and men feel things differently, or can a man mimic Tiresias and play either side of the sexual divide?"

Simon seemed to be talking to himself rather than to Thomas now, but suddenly his tone changed and he turned his head towards the other side of the tent where Rufus and I were spread out.

"So who's the dominant one of you three?" Simon's question seemed out of sequence - even given the strange turn in the conversation. Thomas, Rufus and I looked at each other in confusion.

"None of us dominates," Thomas volunteered after too long a pause. "We are just three friends who respect each others' ideas. Isn't that right?" He raised both hands in a supplicating gesture. Rufus sat up quickly, causing me to lurch backwards. I recovered and joined him, shuffling, into a sitting position, leaning forward to avoid the tent roof, the confined space forcing the four of us together.

"Absolutely," confirmed Rufus. "We're none of us the dominating sort. What a strange question, Simon, what on earth are you getting at?"

"Oh come on boys," Simon extended his arms to encircle Thomas and Rufus who were now on either side of him in the small circle, whilst staring directly into my dark face opposite him. "Everybody in College knows you're a love triangle. I'm just interested in how you go about your trysts and who comes up with the ideas. Maybe you take it in turns?" he queried the three astonished faces that stared at him.

"Personally I think it's the good old doggy triangle that suits you best. That way there doesn't have to be a leader. It's your very own little Trinity, isn't it? All a bit cramped, of course, and requires considerable balance and a shared rhythm for best effects. Fellatio or buggery, I don't mind, maybe we'll have a bit of both, after all the night is still young. If you let in a fourth member - like the pun - we could have a doggy square which is a lot more stable than the triangle, especially if we all keep the same beat. My God, we could invite two more in and challenge the Turkish cadet." And with that he pulled his legs inside the tent and sat up straight. Still holding Thomas and Rufus tightly around their shoulders he recited:

> *"There once was a Turkish cadet,*
> *And this is the damnedest one yet,*
> *His tool was so long and incredibly strong*
> *That he buggered six Greeks en brochette.*

"What do you say?" he continued, in a jovial voice quite empty of embarrassment. "I've been a good pal these couple of weeks, surely I've earned my place in your circle – or square?" Simon looked from one face to another with his most winning smile spread across his features, a small drop of spittle escaping from the grinning lips.

The silence that followed this merry speech was spiced by the shock registering on our three faces and down our spines. All at once Thomas struggled out of Simon's embrace with a cry of "get off me you disgusting . . . " He sputtered with indignation trying to find the appropriate vocabulary.

Rufus was protesting also: "I can't believe what I think you're suggesting." He also struggled roughly away from Simon's encircling arm. "Why on earth can't people just be friends, good friends? Are you so jealous of our unencumbered friendship that you besmirch it with such lewd suggestions?"

"I knew something was wrong with all this sudden companionship." It was my turn to join the furor, my anger surging through me, but I tried to keep some dignity. "You have it all wrong as far as we're concerned, Simon. Your filthy suggestions have no place here, and you don't either, if that is the way you think of us. You may be drunk, but that's no excuse, you can pack up and leave right now. I'm sure the others will agree that you have outstayed your welcome."

"Oh, so I'm not to be allowed to join in then." Simon put on a sulky expression. "You're going to keep yourselves to yourselves, just the same as always. Well, I have to say I'm disappointed, very disappointed. I've taken quite a fancy to all three of you during these last few days, and I really thought we were getting along famously. It's just as well that things haven't always been like that or I would never have got this far at St. Augustine's."

A hiccup erupted from somewhere deep inside Simon's frame. "Thank God for darling little Edward, he has really saved my bacon over this last year. Such a diligent student, and such a pretty boy with his lovely silky blond hair and those delicious blue eyes of innocence. He was easy to seduce. He thought I was his mentor, and so I proved to be. We went out on the moors one moonless evening, with only the starlight to guide us. He thought we were going to study the constellations – what a laugh!" Simon broke into song again to a tune from Don Giovanni:

> *"Arseholes are cheap today,*
> *Cheaper than yesterday,*
> *Little boys are half a crown*
> *Standing up or lying down.*

"After that the dear boy wrote all my papers for me, and everybody says his – sorry 'my' thesis is a masterpiece. The only trouble is this bloody DD, the Defining Discussion. He can't exactly do that one for me, so I've had to come up with another plan." His voice trailed off, as if someone had gradually turned down the volume of his voice box.

The silence that followed seemed weighty enough to sink the tent into the floor of the glade. It was broken by a deep sigh from Simon who looked from one of us another and said: "Well, you're just a bunch of frustrated faggots, so there's no point in hanging around here for some action – I'll have to see what Mother Nature has on the menu." He had several attempts to stand up before finally exiting the tent backwards on all fours. He then made a show of turning a circle, still on his hands and knees, huffing and puffing as he moved. He stuck his head back inside the tent. "What a waste of a couple of weeks," he declared, "still I quite enjoyed the chase, and who's to say that at least one of you might follow me into the night air and stretch your horizons a bit – not to mention your posteriors?" He looked from one face to another. "Oh well, maybe not. Suit yourselves lads, but it's your loss, I can tell you that, and some lucky sheep's night of pleasure."

With more grunts, Simon maneuvered his body around again and crawled off away from the dying ashes of the campfire. The three of us were silent and quite still for a long time as we listened to Simon's shuffling body-movements and the occasional slur of song.

I was the first one to move and exclaim "Well, now we see him in his true colours. Poor Edward, he must have gone through hell during these last months. Will he ever be able to rebuild his self-esteem? Thank heavens we are all discreet, let's hope Simon hasn't told anyone else about all this."

Thomas and Rufus were quick to agree and our talk based itself around the plight of the first year student who had been caught unawares. We spoke softly and could hear sounds of Simon rummaging amongst the provisions we had left outside and grunting like an obscene wild animal. Soon his grunts turned to groans and then a wail of pleasure slid round the hillside followed by silence.

The three of us inside the tent were equally quiet until Rufus whispered "I've had enough, I'm going to sleep now. Good night you two, and good luck to us all at getting this horrible night out of our memories."

Thomas and I nodded our agreement. We climbed into our sleeping bags fully clothed. It didn't seem appropriate to get undressed. Simon's sleeping bag had been pushed outside the tent entrance and all of us pretended deep sleep when noises proclaimed the return of our tormentor.

The tent flaps opened, and Simon's head thrust itself between the flaps. He slid into the tent on his belly once again, pushing his sleeping bag in front of him and squirming around until he was mostly inside it. Thomas was the nearest, and Simon prodded him with such sharpness that Thomas' eyes shot open.

"Well, there wasn't a single sheep in sight," Simon confided in a stage whisper. "But having looked at you lot and had the conversation about Crufts and all, poor old John Thomas had to do something. In desperation I rummaged in the picnic hamper, and what a success – I found a jar of pickled eggs. Oh don't you worry yourselves, my dears, I tipped out the vinegar and replaced it with the olive oil meant for our salad tomorrow. What a success! But you might think twice about having the eggs with our picnic lunch tomorrow, they now have more protein than you bargained for!

"Oh don't look so po-faced, Thomas, the good Lord wouldn't have given us so much pleasure in using this piece of our anatomy if he hadn't meant for us to give it regular exercise. Jack and Rufus are busy pretending they're asleep – at least you've got the courage to look me in the eye. But you turned down the real Mountford tour de force – what a shame. Never mind, the eggs are a new one for me and my Willie, and one which we won't forget – I've heard of men using jars of chicken livers before now, but I reckon I could patent the eggs-in-oil idea and give those liver boys a run for their money."

Simon wriggled deeper into his sleeping bag, turned away from Thomas and started to snore.

21. THE DEFINITIVE TEST

When Rufus, Thomas and I left the bus outside the seminary entrance, returning from our disastrous night on the moors, we had to dodge between the line of cars bringing students back from their brief sabbatical. It had been a distressing morning, starting as we did by having to climb over Simon's somnolent form in our exodus from the tent.

Simon, fortunately, had been too bleary to bother with any of us as we cleaned up the supper things and loaded our packs without a mention of breakfast. Now that it was light, all we wanted was to be away. All except for Simon, that is, who stayed horizontal, snoring a little too loudly, as we pulled his sleeping bag out of the tent, none too gently, with him still inside it. We collapsed the tent and stowed it ready for travel.

When everything was ready to go we looked at each other in despair.

"You don't know your way home, do you, my little lost sheep?" Simon's voice was disgustingly cheerful and mocking as he lifted his head and surveyed the scene. "Well you'll just have to wait for Uncle Simon to get up and lead you back." He started wriggling out of his sleeping bag, leaving his trousers and underpants within. He stood and stretched in the morning light, throwing his arms up to the trees and arching his back, rocking his hips backwards and forwards in a jerky motion so that his limp manhood bobbed up and down.

"Look what you missed, you miserable spoil sports. Still, we had a nice time in the end, didn't we Willie?" he enquired as his arms dropped and one hand went beneath his scrotum and collected the bundle affectionately in his palm. He retrieved his underpants and jeans from the bottom of the sleeping bag, turned slowly and urinated into the ashes of last night's fire.

"Where's breakfast?" Simon asked, as he zipped up his jeans. "I'm starving."

"We're going straight home," I replied in a flat tone. "Everything is packed up and ready to go. We all want to go back to St. Augustine's as quickly as possible."

"You poor little lambs, who have lost your way" Simon repeated. "Baa, baa, baa" he sang with a sneer.

"Well bugger the lot of you – oh maybe that's not the right expression for this particular situation," he laughed at our stony faces, "I'm hungry and I plan on having a spectacular breakfast – one of the finest in England, actually, at the truckers café just outside Hornington. You are welcome to join me, of course, but if you don't want to" – Simon threw a hand up to stop unspoken words of protest – "you can get a bus from there which will take you back to your safe little world. Come on then, but don't overdo the thank-yous.

"You can carry all the stuff this time," he continued. "I may lose it on my way back from breakfast and where would you be when I tell them back at base that you had everything when we parted?" And with that he strode off without a backward glance, leaving his pack and its contents strewn around the fire.

We scrambled to collect the empty bottles, scattered papers and Simon's deserted sleeping bag and shoved them into the remaining empty pack.

"I'll carry it to start with" I said, "we haven't time to sort things between us, the bastard will leave us behind. Come on." I hoisted one pack onto each shoulder and we scrambled after Simon's rapidly retreating figure.

The rest of the trip had been made in silence until the final descent from the moors to the main road.

"There's my breakfast, down there where all the trucks are parked," Simon said, pointing to a petrol station at the side of the black scar of road that split the moors. There was a huge splat of asphalt beyond the petrol pumps with large lorries neatly parked in parallel lines, and beyond that a low squat building with a large awning above the door upon which was written Annie's Caff large enough for it to be legible even from such a distance. "You are welcome to join me for the best black pudding breakfast you've ever had, or" he added, "you can catch a bus from Hornington, over there." About a mile to the West of Annie's Caff there was a ribbon of cottages and a church discernable between the heather hills.

The three of us turned as one in that direction and began our descent.

"Not even a cheerio?" questioned Simon's mocking voice to our turned backs. "Well at least I've got something from putting up with you lot for all this time – you wait and see. You think you're so bloody virtuous, you make me sick, you sissy bunch of faggots." His voice trailed away as our paths separated and the three of us marched in silence down the hill towards the village.

"What do you think he meant?" I asked Rufus and Thomas as we waited at the bus stop, the four backpacks propped against the shelter wall. "When he said he'd got something, what did he mean?"

Rufus and Thomas both shook their heads.

"Who cares," said Rufus, "let's try and put the whole episode behind us. We have a vital time ahead, we have to focus on what's important and forget what's happened."

"What else can we do?" said Thomas. "I agree, we just have obliterate this nastiness from our minds or it will eat into us. We can't let him do that to us. Let's get back to our studies and concentrate on what really matters."

Back at St. Augustine's, with the throng of nervous arrivals, the atmosphere was full of tension. As we zigzagged between the unloading cars with our camping gear, across the gravel of the courtyard to the service door, we could hear the worried tones of the goodbyes and good luck wishes as the cars drew away.

We put everything back where it belonged on the shelves of the outdoor pursuit room, and threw our rubbish into the bins outside the kitchen door, paying special attention to the disappearance of the pickled eggs into the big green skip. Then we climbed the stairs from the basement to the main hall where there was a throng of students around the notice boards at the far end, beyond the slanting light from the tall windows. The timings of the Defining Discussions had been published.

Only four Discussions were scheduled for each day, two in the morning, and two in the afternoon. As Simon had predicted, his session was on the first morning at eleven.

"Well, I hope his head's cleared a bit by then." Rufus muttered, "Oh hell, there I am in the afternoon, less than twenty-four hours from now."

"Wow, we've got another week, Thomas," I interposed as I found my name for the morning of the last day of the Discussions and Thomas' for the afternoon of the same day, the last one of all. "The luck of the fat priest, eh?" I said poking Thomas in the stomach and grinning. "They always save the best till last. That's bad luck for you, though, Rufus, how about a serious study session in the library after lunch - in about an hour? Thomas and I can put you through your paces, unless you'd rather be left in peace to revise?"

"Thanks guys, that would be great," was Rufus's unenthusiastic response. The reality of the forthcoming ordeal was suddenly upon us - a shard of reality we had managed to avoid during the last few days. All thoughts of Simon were forgotten as we went to our rooms, showered, grabbed a quick lunch in the now full refectory, and reconvened in the library. With hushed voices we worked together on Rufus's topic.

It was with relief that we learned that Simon had left St. Augustine's as soon as his Discussion was over. Rufus had emerged from his ordeal a little pale, but on the whole optimistic about the outcome.

"I seem to have managed most of the questions O.K." he said in answer to our anxious enquiries over a cup of tea in Thomas's small room. "It's pretty daunting to start with, just you and Father David – after all we've never had a one-to-one with the great man in all these four years – but if you enjoy your topic and are confident with your facts, it is amazing how much he knows and sort of helps you along with his suggestions. You definitely feel that he's on your side, so to speak – after the first terrifying ten minutes that is. I certainly wouldn't like to go in there being unsure of my subject."

Rufus stayed on for the following week, helping Thomas and me with our studies and waiting for the postings that would be listed when all the Discussions had been concluded.

When it was my turn, Rufus and Thomas came with me to the Principal's wing, leaving me at the door with a pat on the shoulder and wishes of good luck.

Father David's study seemed larger than I had imagined it, and colder too in spite of the sputtering coal fire in its Victorian grate. In response to my practiced knock - not too timid but not over-confident - the voice had sounded welcoming but tired. "Sit down Jack, by the fire is best, these windows may be quaint but they are horribly draughty and do my bones no good at all. How are you, dear boy?"

"Well, thank you, Father, and how are you?" The response was pathetic, I felt. Should I have said something more meaningful? Was I being judged already? I tried to compose myself as I fumbled with a stupidly small and unstable stool which was the only seat available.

Father David waited for me to re-arrange my long legs. I was trying to be as physically balanced as possible in the hope that my mind would follow suit. I could see my thesis on my examiner's lap, the subject printed in bold in the centre of the page: 'The Universality of The Divine.' He jostled the pages between his neat fingers, straightened them carefully and laid them back onto his knees, beneath a pair of folded hands.

"A charmingly simplistic view," Father David began, tapping the manuscript softly with an extended finger, "and one very popular with the young these days. "Your interview today," he continued in a more serious tone, "is to ascertain whether you are a suitable candidate for spreading God's message through the Christian faith. Recognition of Christ's Holy Father as the one true God is crucial to your being ordained into his church. Do you understand that? Do you believe Jesus Christ to be the true Son of God?"

"Yes, of course," I answered quickly, "but what about other avatars? Zoroasta and Krishna, for example - they have both been recognized by their followers as sons of God, and weren't their teachings all very similar? Well perhaps not Krishna's exactly . ."

Father David interrupted: "My son, my son, I presume this line of chatter is to show me how thoroughly you have studied the heathen faiths, for which I applaud you. All that was in your thesis, and I quite accept the research you did in the writing of, what I believe to be, a most imaginative work. However, let me be quite clear: if you are to administer the Christian faith, then that is where your heart must be – fully and completely dedicated to Christ and his teachings as this Church has interpreted them," - he emphasized the word 'this'.

I was tempted to dive in with ideas of how interpretations of religious texts were being used for secular, rather than spiritual, power - one of my favorite topics when arguing with Thomas and Rufus. I had to remind myself, quickly, that this was my final interview which would judge the last four years of my life at St. Augustine's and that I should restrict interpretations of the Testaments to those to which The College adhered. I adjusted the glasses that always slipped down my nose when I got enthusiastic about a topic, sat very straight and, taking a deep breath, I avowed my deep and eternal devotion to the Christian Trinity and all Its mysteries in a suitably low and reverent tone.

Did I have doubts even then? I try to recreate the feelings experienced during that Defining Discussion, to search for true belief and justify my continuation on the clerical path. Try as I might, I can't separate the need to pass this final exam from heart-felt convictions of devotion to one religious path at the expense of all others. All I do know is that for the subsequent half hour I used only Christian vocabulary from my pantheon of ideas as I filtered my beliefs through the acceptable mesh of the Western Church's theology.

In retrospect, I think the beliefs were all truly there, deep in my soul, only they were normally multi-coloured, and this time I was limited to a monochrome design of divinity. For in my philosophy of religions my thoughts really were full of colours. I could trace the rich maroon of Judaism with gilt edges that swirled as the ideas moved. The Muslim world was swathed with deep purple while the Egyptian Gods were represented for me by obsidian black flecked with glinting gold. Hinduism showed every shade of green shot through with orange, blues and pinks like an ever-moving sari of sumptuous entwining silks. Central America's rich pantheon was represented by bright scarlet in my mind, while Buddhism was displayed with all the shades of blue imaginable, merging at times with subtle mauves into turquoise. Zen Buddhism had its own dark green with flashes of bright gold while the Tao was the steady green of meadow grass in the Spring, rolling in sequence like the ocean waves. Christianity was the pale golden yellow of the rising sun.

Alongside the colours in my mind were the different textures from all the faiths of the world and beyond – each one with its own idiosyncratic weft and weave, but all part of the same immense tapestry of existence.

If I had felt the freedom to expose this multi-faceted gem which I had built - or discovered - in my soul, I would have spoken with more emotion and devotion, but, feeling cautious, I restricted myself to the infusive yellow and the fine linen I felt belonged to Christianity. The sincerity was there none-the-less, and the conviction came through enough to appease my audience.

When I had finished, Father David gave a sigh of relief that he tried to disguise with a cough.

"There you are, my boy, I always knew these liberal ideas of yours were just mental jousting and that there was a stalwart and devout spirit within you that would never swerve from the true path. Are you ready to embrace your calling and join Christ's brethren in Holy orders?"

I bowed my head, partly out of piety and partly because I did not want to look Father David in the eye as I declared my devotion for the path to which I had committed myself. I explained, with perfect truthfulness, that the church had always been my home, and that my years at St. Augustine's had served to confirm and strengthen the beliefs I had always cherished.

"I have found peace here, Father David, within these walls," I continued. "A peace I want to share amongst the people outside who have such little understanding of the wonderful possibilities of divine knowledge. It has been a wonderful experience - to spend time with like-minded souls, away from the distractions of the outside world, sharing our faith and watching it grow."

"Aha, yes," the College Principal responded, "there has always been a monkish slant to your behavior, Jack. How do you think you will manage when you are outside these walls, in your chosen vocation, surrounded by the noises and sights that you have found so upsetting in the past?"

"God will give me strength, Father," I answered, hoping with all my heart that this would prove to be true.

"I cannot say that I am looking forward to my first assignment with unmitigated enthusiasm. I am eager to put what I have learnt here into use, but at the same time I am nervous of my abilities to help people who inhabit a world which I often find dirty, tawdry, insincere and a little frightening."

"You are right to be apprehensive, my son." Father David was wiping his gold-rimmed spectacles on his surplice leaving his eyes unprotected, giving them a bewildered look that seemed quite inappropriate. "You are also right when you say that God will give you the strength to cope," he continued. "He will. You must protect your sensitive soul with a veneer of calm. Never show surprise when your parishioners come to you for help – no matter what you are being told or asked. Anglican priests hear confessions almost as often as our Roman Catholic brethren, sometimes even more, but we are not dressed up in quite the same framework, nor do we have a list of absolutions and remedies handed to us from Rome; but we have to deal with the problems and sins just the same.

"When in doubt, retreat behind your defenses of prayer and remain aloof from mortal struggles. You have conquered your own conflicts well – oh yes, we watch all our students most carefully, and the staff here have been impressed with your self-imposed abstinence from the pleasures that other boys find hard to resist."

I was silent, head still bowed. I could feel the heat rising up my back, to the base of the neck – "please oh please Lord don't let the blood rise to my face," I prayed silently. I made an intense study of a small piece of the threadbare carpet by the toe of my shoe, marveling at the deep reds mingling with faded blues. Father David saved me from further embarrassment by continuing:

"If you think that you will have a non-confrontational existence if you live your life following the principles that we have instilled in you here, think again. You will find the world full of selfish people who have twisted their ideas of good and evil and who will encourage you to do the same. When you refuse, at best they will think you are foolish for not taking advantage of whatever it is they have on offer; at worst they will think you are against them and, because of your profession, will see you as being in judgment against them. This can lead to hatred of you as a defense of their misguided ways.

"Hatred is a dangerous emotion, especially when spiced with jealousy – and there is always a bit of jealousy aimed at those who have the strength to stick to their beliefs. Look inside yourself and you will find the inner strength to deal with these challenges. It will be hard at first, for your inner strength needs developing. Just as with physical muscles, the spiritual ones need exercise to grow and be strong. Your faith, if it is nurtured, will keep that strength growing and you will find God's love supporting you and providing you with the steadfast nature that is required if you are going to remain true to your Christian values and ideas."

Suddenly it was over. Father David was shaking my hand and showing me to the door.

"It won't be long now, Jack, before you start your new life. I shall see you before you go, I expect, but for now let me wish you God's speed in your future. You have been a diligent student and I know you will undertake Christ's work with compassion and strength. Please remember that St. Augustine's will always be here for you in times of need. God bless you."

Father David made the sign of the cross and gently propelled me outside his study door, and then he was gone, the heavy door shutting softly between us.

Over lunch Thomas and Rufus were full of questions, and then it was Thomas' turn to face the ordeal and I found our roles reversed as I joined Rufus to wish our friend luck and watched him go down the long corridor that led to Father David's study.

"He'll be fine," Rufus said confidently. "After all, Thomas is the most studious of all of us."

"And has the best memory," I added, "and the greatest conviction. Well, I mean greater than mine, I think. Sorry, Rufus, I had no right to make that remark."

"But you're quite right," Rufus replied, smiling. "Don't worry about it, you are perfectly right, I agree. Of the three of us, Thomas is the most fervent and the most committed with an unquestioning faith that I sometimes envy and sometimes don't."

"I know what you mean," I answered softly. The two of us were silent for a while as we returned to the refectory where we had agreed to meet Thomas when his Discussion was over.

As expected, it was teatime before Thomas joined us. The kitchen staff had been busy putting out the cups and saucers for some time, and now the steaming metal tea-pots arrived with plates of biscuits and sliced breads and cakes. Rufus and I leapt to our feet as he approached but our smiles of welcome froze when we saw his pale face and heavy frown.

"What happened?" Rufus asked urgently as I pulled the chair out for Thomas as one would for an invalid.

"Now I know what that snake Simon meant when he left us on the hillside." Thomas said in a voice so soft that we had to lean in to hear him. "He stole my topic and persuaded Father David that it was me who had copied him, not the other way around. Remember those sketches he was meant to be making during our trips – now I come to think about it, he always got his paper out after one of our Defining Discussion talks. What he was doing was writing down my answers to his questions. No wonder he kept plying me with queries. He milked me of all my ideas and studies and managed to convince Father David that I had borrowed his notes while he was away one night and memorized them. I didn't know what to say. I was so amazed, all I could say was that it wasn't like that, that it was the other way around, but I had no notes to show him, and of course Simon had shown him his. I was taken by surprise and dismay with no idea of how to combat such treachery. I lost all my thoughts, swamped in a quagmire of mendacity, I couldn't think how to extricate myself.

"The interview ended with Father David saying how disappointed he was that such a good student should rely so heavily on someone else's ideas and research. He told me that, because of my good track record and the merits of my written thesis, he would allow me to pass and to become a priest after the necessary apprenticeship, providing reports upon my behavior were favorable. My appointment, however, would reflect this regrettable shortfall. He had, Father David said, originally chosen a demanding urban parish for me, but now he was going to reconsider and thought a rural setting to be more appropriate and less challenging for someone who obviously shrunk under pressure. What could I do?"

Thomas' head had been sinking as he spoke. He raised it now and looked at his two friends in bewilderment. Nobody spoke. I felt tears prickling my eyes and turned away to blow my nose and try to compose myself. Thomas was such a genuinely good man, an honest, hard-working soul who never criticized or thought ill of anyone. How could Simon do such a thing to him?

"We'll go to Father David and support you," Rufus suddenly came to life and stood up, knocking his chair to the floor in his haste. "Won't we Jack? He can't deny all three of us. You have witnesses Thomas, this is excruciatingly unfair, we can't let that bastard get away with it."

"Of course," I added, vehemently. "We must go straight away and tell him what really happened. He can't believe that snake over you, Thomas, we won't let him."

Suddenly all three of us were rushing out of the room, knocking against furniture in our haste, aware of eyes following us in surprise. We resisted the urge to run, but walked across the great hall at an impressive pace and up the great sweeping staircase that lead to Father David's wing, stopping short at the end of the corridor leading to the study.

"Wait," I said. "We must have a plan; we must make an organized approach, calm and sincere. We have to persuade Father David that this has been a cleverly planned piece of deceit and that Thomas was duped into giving Simon the value of his researches and his ideas."

"We must point out that I never would have chosen to present the same subject as somebody else, if I had known somebody else was doing it," added Thomas. The colour was returning to his cheeks now, flushed by our rapid climb of the stairs. He was endeavoring to sound positive. "Why would I have knowingly copied someone who had already had their Defining Discussion? It doesn't make sense at all."

"Quite right," added Rufus, "but we must have a strategy, as Jack says. We can't all talk at once. How about we start off with you, Thomas, introducing us two as your companions on the hikes with Simon. Say that we have come to support your story – no don't use the word story – your version of events, perhaps. What do you think?"

Several minutes past while we were in earnest discussion forming the plan that we thought would most impress Father David of our veracity. We had just decided on a winning formula when the study door opened at the end of the corridor and Father David's secretary, Father Charles, came out, closing the door carefully behind him and locking it with a huge key.

Father Charles was known to all at St. Augustine's as Bonnie Father Charlie because of his slight stature, bright shining face and fair hair, that would curl if only he would allow it to grow. He was to be seen scuttling about the college corridors at any time of the day, always giving the impression that he was on an urgent mission; head bowed, feet taking rapid short steps beneath his cassock, papers clasped to his chest.

Today, Father Charles had no papers. He turned from the closed door and walked towards us with the usual rapid steps and bowed head. He stopped suddenly when our shoes must have come within his vision. He raised his head in surprise.

"Gentlemen, what are you doing here?" None of us had ever heard Father Charles speak before and his deep voice surprised us, coming from so light a frame.

"We're here to see Father David," I said, a note of intended urgency in my voice. "There has been a horrible mistake that must be put right."

"Has there now?" Father Charles looked from one earnest face to the next. "Well there's not much can be done about it now, unless the good Lord intervenes on your behalf. Father David left, ten minutes ago. He took all his papers with him." The last sentence had a sense of reproach in it. "He won't be back again until after the weekend when the graduates' placements will be published."

"But we must see him." It was Rufus's turn. "It's very, very important. There has been a big mistake. We must see him before he settles on those placements."

"As I said, sirs, you will have to rely on the Lord, because Father David always goes into a reclusive state after the last of the Discussions. Nobody is allowed to interrupt him between now and Monday – and anyway, first you would have to find him, and his reclusive state is just what it says and means – reclusive. Not even I know where he goes for this one weekend each year."

Again there was a touch of hurt in the last sentence and we knew, instinctively that it must be true.

"Is there really no way to reach him before he publishes the placements?" I asked with the most fervent voice I could muster.

"None at all, I'm afraid. I will tell him you were here, if you would like to give me your names, that is the best I can do."

"Well then, trust in the Lord we will, Father Charles," Thomas was trying to sound positive, "but I would be grateful if you would tell Father David of our request this evening." And with that we gave the small monk our names, which he promised he had memorized, as he didn't have either paper or pen with him, and we went our separate ways - Father Charles continuing down the corridor towards a burrow of offices while Thomas led the way, back downstairs.

"As he says, my friends," Thomas said when we were back in the dining hall, "it must be as God wills. It will be interesting to see what the Almighty has in store for me. There may be more to this than meets the immediate eye. Who are we to judge? Let's not spoil our last days at St. Augustine's with bitter feelings. I have an inkling that all will work out as it should and in the meantime let's make the most of our valuable friendships that have been well tested over the last few weeks. We'll stay friends for always, won't we, and what more valuable gift could come from four years on the Yorkshire moors?"

I found myself with my arms around Thomas before I was aware of my motions. Rufus was not far behind me, and we stood in a triangle of limbs for some precious seconds before Thomas burst the band with a laugh:

"Come now fellows, you'll give Simon something to think about if anyone should find us like this. Let's to the pub and celebrate the end of four years and the beginning of new lives for all of us."

The faces of Thomas and Rufus, as they were then, spring into my mind now as I saw them during our last day at St. Augustine's. I envisage the three of us, filing into Chapel for our first ordination – the service that would confirm our graduation from lay-person to deacon, from 'mister' to 'reverend.'

As the three of us knelt next to each other at the altar rail, waiting for the visiting bishop's hands to rest briefly on our shoulders in blessing, I felt a fellowship not only with Almighty God, but with the two men whose company I had so enjoyed and valued through our adventures. I began to appreciate how much I was going to miss them.

After the service, the placement lists were pinned on the notice board in the great hall. We leant forward together, pushed by the crowd of our peers as everyone hurried to find their names with nervous impatience.

"There you are, Jack," Rufus had exclaimed, pointing to my name and alongside it the listing of The Parish of St. George, Islington. "Oh and there's mine – goodness they've sent me to Brixton, do you think they'll understand a Scottish accent there?"

"Where on earth is Thornton?" It was Thomas' turn to join the excited chatter. "I've got 'The Parish of Thornton, Bedfordshire.' Ever heard of it either of you?"

"That's not far from my family home." I was quick to re-assure my worried looking friend. "I think it's East of the M1 by some distance; a really rural area where the planners have defended the green belt with great effect. I'll bet you it's a really pretty place with a Georgian vicarage and roses climbing all over it."

"Spare me the décor, Jack." Thomas interrupted me with uncharacteristic abruptness. "I wonder how I'm going to explain such a mundane position to my parents. They were so convinced I was going to save the world by entering Hell's kitchen and triumphing over Satan. Thornton doesn't sound too hellish to me."

"And so much the better," Rufus put his arm around Thomas' shoulders. "It sounds pretty idyllic if you ask me. And if it's close to Jack's roots, then he can come and visit when he takes a trip home, and you can visit both of us in the smoke and the turbulence of two very different London suburbs."

"I wouldn't call either Islington or Brixton a suburb exactly," Thomas responded. "I think that's the easiest way to upset your new parishioners."

"Well, what would you call them then?" said Rufus. "I'm from across the border, remember, and don't know anything about your great capital sprawl. What do you say, Jack?"

"I'm hardly more qualified than you are, Rufus." I replied. "The only times I've been to London were to see the dentist. Parents usually took us to a show at Christmas time, but it was always in conjunction with those wretched dental experiences, so I never thought fondly of the great metropolis. Maybe we could call them Districts," I suggested after a moment's pause. "I've seen their names on the tube maps – so they can't be suburbs, can they?"

Rows of stuffed envelopes were spread out on a table below the notice board with names displayed in alphabetical order. Inside were the directions and contact numbers of each person's appointment, and instructions on dates and times. A brief introduction to the posting was also included and an explanatory piece as to why Father David had selected this specific assignment for that particular graduate.

There hadn't been any time for intimate talk about the contents of those envelopes. The way St. Augustine's was run dictated that all this vital information was delivered to the departing students only half an hour before we were due to leave. Often the envelopes were not even opened until the newly fledged graduates were far distant from the rolling Yorkshire moors and the tall towers of the college buildings.

The gravel outside the main hall was scrunching under tyres as the three of us exchanged our newfound knowledge as to our futures. We had already swapped home addresses and telephone numbers. Now there was little to do but shake hands, and then abandoning such a formal show of acquaintance, embrace each other with the warmth of true friendship. We separated with vows to keep in touch and tears not far away.

22. THE ISLE OF LEWIS

It was mother who took me to the train for London and my new life in Islington. She was going into town anyway, to collect some dry cleaning, and would be passing the station, she had explained, the night before my departure. We had been having supper, my parents and I, in the family dining room, which seemed smaller than my memories recorded. The conversation had dealt briefly with the career I was undertaking and my having landed an apparently much sought after parish in North London as my apprenticeship placement.

"But you must know something about your position, surely," mother had rejoined to my expressions of ignorance about my first assignment as a man of the cloth. "You say you're going to a church called St. George's to assist a Father Justin in his ministry, but what exactly does that entail?" She sounded slightly exasperated, as if her original questions had been of a token nature that should have been dispensed with briefly - if only I had come up with suitably adroit answers.

"To a large degree, every parish reflects the personality of its vicar," I answered cautiously. "Of course The Church lays down guidelines and there is the framework of the services themselves, but no two parishes are the same. St. Augustine's put great emphasis on how a vicar must adapt his approach to suit his congregation, to encourage new people to attend church whilst making sure he doesn't lose the ones he already has. Father Justin, as I understand it, has been vicar of St. George's for more than thirty years. He will undoubtedly have developed a way of conducting services and visits that fits the people of that neighborhood. So I can't foresee how my daily life will be until I get to know his system. My primary job is to keep an open mind and to learn from Father Justin in such a way that I may be most useful to the parish as a whole."

"It sounds very interesting," my father interposed unconvincingly. "I suppose our parish isn't big enough to justify having a deacon as well as a vicar.

"Oh that reminds me, Elizabeth dear, would you let Father Edmond know that I won't be able to read the lesson the Sunday after next? It's my annual stalking trip to The Isle of Lewis," he explained, turning back to me. "You remember you and Robert came with me when you were thirteen or fourteen, I think."

Indeed, I remembered vividly the weekend of steep hills rising from the sea into sodden grey clouds; the total absence of trees, the sound of water running beneath the sod and squelching underfoot; the peaty smell of Scotland mixed with that of the pony which labored behind the two ghillies. Moorland quite different from that which surrounded St. Augustine's: steeper, wilder, emptier and even wetter.

In fact, this is another damp and incredibly vivid experience that I recreated while I was in arid Cachonga. That day in the Hebrides became a 'rites de passage' for me and re-presented itself in its entirety while I was under the unforgiving African sky. The mosquitoes were zipping past my ears, even the grating of the crickets sounded thirsty, and there was that permanent dust embedded in every crevice of my skin. I needed memories of moisture, and those of the Isle of Lewis were suitably sodden.

During that trip, even at that young age, I learnt something about the dignity of sacrifice that I have used ever since in my performance of Holy Communion. Death, so horribly final, and yet a necessary part of all our destinies, became more understandable and, somehow, more acceptable, after my visit to the Isle of Lewis.

We had started out from the Lodge quickly after breakfast. The clothes Robert and I were wearing had been carefully checked, first by father, and subsequently with an appraising glance from the ghillies who were lined up ready to take the day's clients into the hills. Both us boys were suitably clad in tweeds and brown boots; no flash of inappropriate colour could alert a stag to the invasion of his lands.

Father carried his Holland & Holland .300 Magnum with a casual air that I happened to know was forced. This rifle was one of his most valued possessions and lived at home in a special display case with substantial locks. However that day his demeanor suggested that he never left the house without this extension to his arm.

One of the ghillies stepped forward and doffed a cap of the same tweed as his jacket and plus-fours. "G'morning Mr. Bolden, Sir," he said in his thick Scottish brogue. "M'name's Michael, but the lads, they call me Mick. I'm to be your ghillie for today and this" he continued, waving an arm towards an elderly man whose cloth cap sat uneasily on his white bristly hair, "is Hamish, he's our pony man."

Hamish gave a stiff bow and then turned on his heel and disappeared in the direction of the stables.

"I've found a good stag for you with a powerful set on his head" continued Mick. "It'll be a hike, are you sure your boys are up to it and know how to behave?"

"Oh yes, they'll be fine, or we leave them behind if they prove otherwise, Mick." Mr. Bolden was using the affable voice he kept for employees who had done well in the tannery. "I'll make sure of it," he added giving us an over-the-shoulder glance whose meaning was quite clear.

Hamish reappeared leading a shaggy pony draped in a strange harness, and we set off down the lodge drive at a brisk pace. Father walked ahead with the two Scotsmen and the pony, chatting to his new friend, the confident, soft-spoken Mick. Robert and I walked a respectable two strides behind; neither of us spoke, each being busy with his own thoughts. I don't know what was in Robert's mind, but mine was full of concern that I didn't let father down in any unforeseen way. I had no idea what to expect from the day, but I understood from the general seriousness of all participants that whatever happened, it would be important.

After a little while father dropped back to walk with his sons. He positioned himself between the two of us and began speaking in a hushed tone. "Now listen you two. We've drawn the top ghillie here. Did you see his rifle? It's a Rigby .275. This is no ordinary ghillie, and we mustn't appear unworthy of his being assigned to us."

I did my best to look impressed, although the significance of his statement eluded me. Robert, however, was suitably au fait with the situation to produce the necessary response: "A Rigby .275, but that's the rifle the Queen Mother uses. How could he possibly afford such an item?"

"Exactly, my boy," father raised an arm as if to embrace his elder son, but then dropped it to his side. "No regular ghillie has such a rifle. Our friend Mick here must be something very special to have such a status symbol. He must accompany royalty on a regular basis. We must make sure that we behave in a way appropriate for such an honor, so stay close, but silent. Observe, but say nothing; and make sure that you follow instructions without fail. This is going to be quite a day!"

After several hours of purposeful walking up steep but rounded hills and down again, jumping valley-making streams, and then climbing once more, Hamish and the pony with its strange harness and saddlebags, were left behind, sheltering under the brow of a hill. Father and Mick sank down on all fours and crawled towards the latest ridge before dropping onto their bellies and wriggling through the bracken to the crest of the hill. Robert and I were instructed by urgent hand signals, to follow in a similar fashion at some small distance. The casual atmosphere of a walk in the Scottish Highlands had been replaced with something tense and exciting.

I remember the feel of the spiky heather against my chest and legs and was grateful for the thick tweed. As I pulled my prone body to the edge of the hill alongside my brother I wondered what mystery was ahead of me, making my spine tingle. Cautiously I raised my head and took in the view.

In a slight dip, on the other side of the hill, was a collection of deer grazing busily on the short tufts of coarse grass between the clumps of heather. The clouds seemed almost to rest upon their backs and their coats were glistening with drops of water even though it wasn't raining. At the herd's edge, only about thirty yards away from us prone figures in the heather, was the stag. He too was grazing. His antlers nodded, accentuating the movements of his head as he stripped the grass from its roots with rhythmical bites. The ghillie moved his rifle slowly through the bracken until it was in front of him and father followed suit, his polished Holland & Holland glinting in the grey light. The stag lifted his head, the antlers silhouetted and his jaw suddenly still. I could see the drops of water on the torn grass between his teeth, could sense the brightness of the eyes and the tensing of muscles preparing for speed.

Father's rifle recoiled into his shoulder as the first shot rang out. It was followed immediately by a second from the muzzle of the ghillie's. The deer all scattered down the hillside, the space that had been occupied by the stag was suddenly empty. A still brown shape lay in the grass.

"Why did you shoot?" Father asked the ghillie angrily, adrenalin getting the better of his manners. "I had him perfectly."

"I thought your shot a bit too low and forward, sir" the ghillie answered, his thick Hebridean accent soft but confident. "If you don't get him in the heart and lungs, he'll not die as he should – instantly – unknowing and unafraid. If he runs injured, it could be hours before we can finish him. It's not what he deserves and it's not what we are prepared to tolerate." The ghillie was looking his client directly in the eye. His gaze was steady, somewhat cold, but not disrespectful. "He's still your kill, sir, and the trophy head is not spoiled" he continued, without breaking eye contact, "I was just making sure. We can check the bullets if you like."

Father held the gaze but I could sense his confidence slipping – something I had never seen before. He swallowed almost audibly and after a slight hesitation, he answered "no, that won't be necessary." The words were soft, but came from between his teeth. "You know your job, and as you say, it's my kill." He rose stiffly from the heather and strode towards his quarry.

When we came to look at the dead stag there was a tear in the flesh at the top of the fore-leg from the first shot. The bullet that had dropped the great beast had entered just behind the shoulder, straight into the lungs and heart.

Robert, who had missed the conversation with the ghillie in his haste to reach the carcass, was busy congratulating father on such an excellent shot, and pointing excitedly to the antlers.

My eyes were stinging and I felt bile in my throat as I sat in the heather watching as the second ghillie, Hamish, appeared around the bend of the hill with the pony in tow.

It was what happened next that stayed in my memory most profoundly. Whilst Robert and father were busy toasting the kill with their flasks and discussing where the antlers would be hung upon our return to Willenbury, Mick began his work upon the dead stag. After arranging the body with immaculate care and attention, he took a knife from one of the saddlebags that had been removed from the pony and laid out on the ground near the animal's belly.

The gralloching which followed involved removing the stag's windpipe and then the stomach. This latter was turned inside out so the grass that had so recently been plucked from the turf fell back from where it had come. The emptied stomach was then used as a bag for the other vital organs, which were individually removed and placed within, with a dignity and grace that were awesome to behold. The ghillie acted with deliberate, measured movements, the precision of which reminded me of Father Edmund preparing for, and delivering, Holy Communion. The ceremony – for that it most certainly was – was imbued with the sanctity of sincere reverence, and I found myself amazed by the acceptance of the situation that replaced my earlier feelings of repugnance and distress.

When the gralloching was completed, the carcass was hoisted upon the pony's back, and now the purpose of that strange harness became apparent. The front legs and antlered head hung on one side, the tongue hanging heavily from the open mouth.

The back legs and most of the body were on the other, with the legs tied together under the pony's belly.

The stag saddle

The filled saddlebags were placed on the pony's rump and all that was left on the heather was a large stain of blood and a few bits and pieces of innards unwanted by the kitchen.

"The stags have to be culled, laddie," the ghillie muttered to me quietly as he led the burdened pony past. "It's best it's done properly, and that traditions are honored. This chap had better luck than the bullocks that travel to your slaughter houses on the mainland, but nobody worries about that when they're buying steaks and hamburgers."

Towards the end of my time at St. Augustine's, when working on the steady dignity of pace required for the presentation of prayers, readings and sermons and the solemn gestures required for administering Holy Communion and the Blessings, I had often thought of that ghillie and the confident reverence of his practiced movements.

"Yes, I remember," I replied to father's question, realizing with relief that no further discussion as to my future in Islington was necessary.

The rest of the evening had past pleasantly enough as I listened to my parents discussing the details which made up their day-to-day existence. There was a feeling of familiarity and surprise that so much could stay the same in Willenbury when so much had changed for me.

I don't remember our arrival at the local station the following day, but strangely enough, my mother does.

The last time I visited her, about three weeks ago, she had clutched my wrist with her gnarled fingers, still wearing the splendid turquoise ring father had given her when Robert was born. "Do you remember my driving you to the station, the morning you left home for Islington?" She asked, an unusual urgency in her voice.

I nodded in response, feeling the flicker of a questioning eye-brow.

"I had invented some sort of errand as an excuse to take you into town myself," she continued, still in a hurry. "Why should a mother need to find an excuse for such an important journey for her son? I watched you, in the rear-view mirror, as you took your luggage from the boot of the car – that silly battered suitcase you insisted upon taking and that ungainly tin trunk.

"I remember wanting to get out and give the tall young man my son had grown into, a long, tender, maternal hug – why did I resist the urge? I do so wish I hadn't, Jack. Instead, I remained in the driver's seat and settled for a peck on the cheek through the car's open window.

"The motor was still running, I remember, as I said goodbye - 'Good luck, darling. Let us know how you get on, won't you, and come and see us when you get the chance.' That was all I said, while so much was going on in my heart – a mother's heart. I watched you disappear into the railway station before allowing myself the luxury of tears.

"'I haven't done well for that boy,' I thought. 'He's a good son, really, but so alien somehow. Could I have loved him more; taken more time trying to understand him; spent time just being with him?' Visions of you as a small boy filled my head. Wherever we went, you were always behind me, Jack. I always had to turn around to find you. While the other two were always ahead shouting gaily to each other, you had called only to me. . . 'Mummy, please wait for me, Mummy . . .' That had been your most common phrase. I should have valued the yearning in your little voice, but instead I found it only irritated. I'm so sorry, Jack."

Mother had given my wrist a squeeze as she sighed deeply. I could think of nothing to say.

After a moment, she continued; "I remember feeling a pang in my stomach, not only from guilt - oh yes, that was there, even then - but also from the sadness of missing something irretrievable; that of knowing and loving a child as he grew and changed. One day, you may understand that feeling." She had looked at me questioningly, seeking reassurance as she blew her nose into a fine cotton handkerchief with the initial E embroidered in one corner. She dabbed at her eyes and cheeks, as her other hand moved to take my hand. "Say you forgive me, Jack," she implored.

"There is nothing to forgive," was the obvious response, and the one with which I had dutifully replied. In fact it was also accurate; after all it is hard to miss something you never had. Although I remember vividly wanting to please mother, I had become accustomed to the emotionless relationship that developed between us, and never questioned its validity. These revelations of hers came as a surprise, and I am still trying to put them into perspective. Not long ago there had been her desperate pleas for me to pray for her during her fight against cancer. I fear she gives more credit to what she imagines are my prayers than to the advances of medicine.

However, I am also aware that my mother's long-time-coming faith in her younger son is not something that I wish to jeopardize in a hurry.

Returning to my diary I find myself on the train to London with my old brown suitcase of new clothes suitable for my recently acquired position, and this very same tin trunk carrying my books. I can hardly believe that I am about to start my first pastoral appointment and don't know whether to feel excited, intimidated, or nonchalant. I have a mixture of the first two feelings and am striving for a veneer of the third.

Upon reaching London I took a taxi to Priory Road and the house that was to become my home for, what was then, an indefinite future.

The Church of St. George in Islington is set between two tree-lined streets on a steep hill, surrounded by a graveyard with tilted headstones dating back to the 1600s. The imposing building is approached from Priory Road by a straight flagged path that leads to the Western façade, whose central wooden doors are flanked by statues. The facial expressions of these saints have been obliterated by time and weather, but they exude serenity nonetheless and lighten the grey stone of the rest of the church with their sandy miens.

Over the church's doorway the roof has a high peak and slopes to each side until arrested by substantial pinnacles that anchor this part of the building in the tomb-scattered turf. These elaborate stone spirals would be quite impressive in themselves if it weren't for the central tower of the building whose stature dominates the edifice making the pinnacles appear meager and almost inadequate. To the north of the main building, distanced by several rows of graves, is the vicarage, and towards this humble edifice I turned my steps.

From the front, the house looked like a two story building with the windows of the upper floor filling the spaces under the two roof peaks. I approached the large wooden door, centrally placed between two bay windows, it was of heavy oak with a large, deeply tarnished, brass knocker. Putting down my suitcases, I wondered about the silence of the place. The heavily curtained windows on either side made the vicarage seem asleep, or worse. There were weeds in the pathway and around the door itself a general sense of dilapidation prevailed.

A puff of dust rose around my shoes as I moved onto the step. I tried to raise the knocker, but the heavy circular ring refused to move.

Picking up my bags again, I began to circle the house. Towards the back of the building the ground fell away and revealed a lower floor whose solitary window and door opened onto a small overgrown garden. Continuing around the building, I found a side door of paned glass at the top of two stone steps. There was a curtain inside, drawn across the glass, but here at last were signs of habitation. Two empty milk bottles graced the top step and a pair of Wellingtons the lower one. There was a doorbell with an exposed wire leading up the doorframe and disappearing through the chipped paint into a hole at the top left hand corner.

I pressed the tarnished button and it produced a muffled metallic chime from far away, as if down a tunnel. I waited a couple of minutes before pressing the bell a second time. There were sounds of movement inside and eventually the curtain was pulled back and a thin grey face with a thinner grey beard peered at me through the glass.

23. DREAMS

I have a theory about dreams. My idea is that sleep is necessary for us in order for our brain cells to catch up with the present by storing information about all that has happened in the immediate past. I envisage a giant filing room – the sort that must have existed in legal offices of Dickensian times. Racks upon racks of carefully stowed files not stored in chronological order, but in order of location, or emotional content, or subject, perhaps.

Whenever we go to sleep, and suspend our volitional actions, the department of our brain that is in charge of storage gets on with its job. Sometimes, as files are put together, categorized and sent to their appropriate slots, they brush against other files from other times or even from other lives, perhaps, and the contents of the disturbed files spring alive in the form of dreams, before they are re-captured and put back in their places. If time is circular, and we are in a perpetual samsāra of birth and re-birth, until a final release into Nirvana/Heaven/Obscurity, the possibility arises that some files might relate to an event that has not yet been experienced by the dreamer in their current state - hence the dreams of the future that some people experience.

I mention this theory because I am finding that as I research this or that part of my life in the exercise I am undertaking, items force themselves into my narrative that are quite out of order. Hence at this point of my transformation from a student at St. Augustine's to the position of Deacon in Islington, I find myself wanting to write about a similarly life-changing, and much more painful, transition – that of vicar to invalid. The memory files have been jostled.

I have already written of my recurring dream that starts in the dug-out canoe and then moves to

Willenbury. My memory now has to step into the middle of that dream and recall what happened when that dreadful river-journey ceased, when gentle hands took me by the shoulders and chased the scene of mother and the garden at Willenbury back into the ether.

The hands may have been gentle, but they invoked an involuntary cry as the pain hit me again with renewed ferocity. A burning and tearing sensation seared through my insides.

"There, there, Father," the voice was soft, with a distinctive welsh lilt to it. I thought I must be dreaming again. "We have to get you out of this boat and up to the hospital. It won't be easy, but we have God to help us and to give you strength."

"God!" I remember exclaiming in a derisive tone, turning my head around to express my new-found contempt for the deity I had followed with such complacency all my life. I found myself looking into the soft brown eyes of an elderly nun whose face was flanked by starched white linen. The lines of her pale face were filled with a kindness that had somehow withstood her years of African life. She must have been in her early seventies at least, and of frail build, but her grip on my shoulder was not to be argued with.

I swallowed hard. "Yes, Sister, of course." The words came with difficulty as I withheld the spittle that I wished to fling at the world in general. "But I'm not sure how I can move." I fought the lump in my throat. The subsequent choking rattled down into my stomach and sent a new spasm of pain flying downwards to mutilated buttocks.

"I'm Sister Mary," the singsong voice continued. "I'm here to help you, and there are others on their way with a stretcher. We'll have you out of this boat and up at the hospital in no time. Mr. Umvari himself is on his way," a note of reverence had crept into her voice, "so you'll be well looked after. Just don't move until help has arrived."

What a ridiculous instruction. I had no intention of moving, ever. My position in the slimy fluids of the little boat was, I thought, as comfortable as I would ever be. I could feel the congealed blood, now grown cold and sticky, between my thighs, and knew that, as soon as I made the slightest movement, the blood would flow again. I sank my face back onto my hands and tried not to think about what my rescuers would see when they lifted my covers of sacking.

Sister Mary seemed to sense the depth of my distress. Her soft pale face, with its many wrinkles, wore an expression of understanding that seemed to lessen the pain for just an instant. Although I could not see clearly without my glasses, I could feel kindness emanating from her person, and knew I should surrender to her care.

In spite of her slight stature, the little nun gave instructions that nobody could ignore. The sacking covering my back was lifted by unseen hands and I heard gasps from the hospital staff. Hands moved me so gently – tenderly even - and yet with such pain, onto a stretcher. A clean sheet was quickly placed over me as discussions of horror were hushed and plans made as to how best to transport their burden up from the riverbank and across the lawn to the low-roofed hospital.

Disregarding my protestations, Sister Mary galvanized the boat crew into action and had her patient carried to the hospital where the stretcher with its cargo was placed carefully onto a trolley. I would remain, face down, on that trolley for the next three days.

Three days of being wheeled around, looking at different pieces of scratched linoleum. Into and out of rooms for X-rays, swabbing, sewing cuts, setting bones, bandaging and re-bandaging, and I don't know what else. Fortunately I was on a drip with all sorts of drugs and fluids dribbling into a vein of the back my right hand and as a result, I don't remember much of those long horizontal hours.

I do recall, however, trying to pay attention when the surgeon who had been summoned from the Capital, Mr. Umvari, arrived and began explaining what the operation he was about to perform was all about. The best I could do was to listen with detachment to the kind tones of reassurance with which the large African, in his starched white coat, rendered his speech.

My position on my stomach meant that the surgeon's gesturing hands moved only in the periphery of my vision. They were large and soft, the pale flesh of the palms seeming at odds with the steely black of the knuckles.

After a few minutes Mr. Umvari sat down, tilting his head on one side so as to have a better view of my face.

"Do you understand, Father, what I have been telling you?"

I raised my head a little and turned it towards the surgeon. I remember trying to say something, but not knowing what was expected of me, and having no view of my own to voice, I closed my mouth as quickly as I had opened it and returned my face towards the floor.

"I have been trained in London, you know," Mr. Umvari had misunderstood. "I was at St. Bart's for three years and The Middlesex for another two" he continued softly. "I would have stayed there, maybe have moved to Harley Street and all that has to offer, but my conscience wouldn't let me desert the nation of my birth. I have been back in Africa now for four years. They have flown me up here from the capital especially to look after you. You have nothing to worry about."

I felt a surge of embarrassment and shame that chased my physical pains into the background. "I'm sorry, doctor." I managed to find my voice. "I don't mean to appear ungrateful or distrusting. I just don't really care anymore. You must do whatever you think is right, but please don't bother yourself too much about me. You can care for my body, and for that I should thank you, but my scars are deeper than you can cure. I have a nemesis to deal with and neither the energy nor the will for a fight."

"Be patient, Jack," I think the surgeon did away with the 'Father' title deliberately. "We will get you better. You may not understand just now, but we are all given steps to climb. I am confident that you will reach the top again at some time, but you will have to be patient in your soul - as well as my patient on the table."

The big man gave a soft chuckle as he finished speaking and stood up. He placed a hand on my shoulder with the gentleness of a lover. "I shall be seeing you in a little while," he continued, "but you won't be seeing me until tomorrow. I wish you luck, Jack and a good sleep to see you through. May God be with you."

"And also with you" I replied without thinking. The automatic response made me think of the church in Islington and my first services there when I would follow Father Justin's supplications with my own ardent voice. That was when I had just arrived in London, before I took over the old man's role in the liturgy.

My mind went back to St. George's, via drugs or dream-jostling, I don't know, but all of a sudden I was there. If I raised my bowed head, surely I would see the burnished wood of the choir stalls and, across the aisle of shining tiles, would be the curving wooden steps leading to the pulpit. To my left, the lectern made of a brass eagle, lovingly polished, would be supporting a huge bible on its outstretched wings, and behind me, the organ pipes pushing upwards towards the stone carvings that supported the vaulted roof.

Was it my turn to deliver the sermon, or was Father Justin going to glide past me at any moment with his robes rustling as he climbed to the pulpit which sat like a bird's nest against one of the massive stone pillars of the lovely old building?

The voice of the anesthetist brought me back to the hospital. As usual, my head was resting on folded arms. As I moved my forehead slowly against the back of my hands, avoiding the catheter and the drip, I thought how many hours I had spent on my knees, with my head supported in a similar fashion.

"I'm afraid I'm going to need one of those arms, Jack," said a deep female voice from atop a large pair of bosoms that swung into my limited view and must have functioned as a resonating box. "Just let me help you here," the voice continued as a large black hand lifted my chin from my crossed arms and then set it down gently having removed the left arm and laid it, palm upwards, by my side.

I remember feeling the needle enter the vein on the inside of my elbow. My dreams returned to Islington and the innocence with which I had arrived at St. George's.

24. A NEW LIFE, A NEW MENTOR

My first view of Father Justin, through the misty glass of the vicarage's back door, was of a tired, grey face, frowning in confusion. Now that I know, and love, that man so well, I can appreciate how I must have looked. My close-clipped dark hair must have accentuated my aquiline nose upon which my square glasses rested, matching the shape of my jaw line. I suppose I might have looked quite intimidating – although any intimidation I anticipated would have come from the other direction.

I was dressed with studied casualness in grey slacks, an open shirt and a tweed jacket that – I now realize - made me look as out of place in this urban churchyard as a turnip in a rose-garden. Father Justin's eyes slowly took in the whole picture that eventually included the case and trunk at my feet. A look of comprehension began to replace the confusion in the elderly priest's eyes and there were sounds of bolts being drawn, a key turned, and finally a scraping as the door was opened.

"Father Justin?" I proffered my hand to the bowed figure draped in a faded dressing gown over a pair of jeans and a T-shirt. "I'm Jack Bolden, your new deacon," I said, hoping for some sort of recognition. There was a sense of achievement, and probably pride, in my voice as I used my new title.

"My replacement, you should say," the vicar retorted, staring hard into my face, with little sign of focus. "I wasn't expecting you until this evening." There was a tantalizing pause as he took my hand. "But you're very welcome all the same" he continued, to my great relief. "It's time for me to move on," he muttered in a voice both deep and mellifluous, in spite of his small frame.

I was startled, especially as Father Justin showed no sign of either shaking my hand or releasing it. He just held it in a firm grip.

"No, sir," I insisted, in an involuntary burst. "I am here to learn from you and to help you with the parish. There are no plans for me to take over from you – this is my first placement, I just left St. Augustine's, in Yorkshire, and am a complete novice." Now I was speaking in panic and the words came out staccato-style. "I'm hoping you will teach me with your experience and allow me to benefit from your long-standing appointment. Believe me, Father, I am not here to replace anybody, nor would I be capable of so doing. I am hopeful I can be of use, to help you with your work, remove some of the drudgery, become your student – my words trailed off into an uncomfortable silence.

Minutes seemed to pass, while Father Justin digested my frantic speech – but I suppose it was only seconds.

Eventually he let go of my still unshaken hand and stood back, fixing me with the darting eyes I came to respect so much.

"Well said, young man." My future mentor smiled and stepped forward through the door, any attempt at dignity disappeared as I retreated rapidly, tripping over my cases.

"Steady on now," he cautioned, "and follow me – I'll show you to your quarters. They need a bit of fixing up, I'm afraid, but you're young and shouldn't mind that. St. Augustine's eh, that old buzzard Father David still there?"

"Indeed, he is the Principal," I answered, thinking that I had never thought of Father David as an 'old buzzard.' I was struggling with my bags as Father Justin passed me and descended the steep steps to the garden below. He turned to the small door that I had observed earlier. He stopped amongst the weeds of the garden whose straight lines suggested flagstones underneath, and producing a large key from a pocket of the flapping dressing-gown, unlocked the door with surprising ease. I was following him into the darkness inside but hesitated on the doorstep. There was the sound of a switch and a light went on above the outside door, illuminating me and my bags unnecessarily in the daylight. The next click lit up the inside of the room.

"Come in, come in," Father Justin was beckoning. "It's a bit sparse, but if I know you youngsters, you'll soon fill it with junk. Anyway, compared to St. Augustine's, it must seem positively cluttered."

The room ran the full length of the vicarage and was probably at least half the width. It must have been a cellar once, and only a half-hearted attempt had been made to turn it into a bed-sitting room. There was a single bed at the far end; a chest of drawers was next to it with a mirror above, an empty bookcase filled the space under the window and a tattered sofa leant uncertainly against the opposite wall. A table, with a gas ring at one end and four chairs around the sides, confronted me as I stepped inside. On a shelf above the table perched an electric kettle and an odd collection of plates and mugs.

"The bathroom's upstairs, I'm afraid," said Father Justin, "but you have it to yourself as my rooms are on the first floor – this being the basement, you see, and the main rooms of the house make up the ground floor. There's no wardrobe, but there are some hooks on the back of the door and your church robes will live in the vestry. The stairs are here," he continued, opening a door at the back of the room through which steps could be seen disappearing in a steep climb. "I'll let you settle in, and then please come upstairs and I'll see what I can find the two of us for lunch." Lifting the hem of his dressing-gown, Father Justin ascended the steps and disappeared with a steady slap of rising feet.

I shut the garden door softly and looked around my new home. It's amazing, the clarity of it coming back to me after all these years. I liked the simplicity and was excited about it being all my own space. Ignoring the suitcase full of clothes, I lifted the tin trunk of books onto the sofa. I remember my excitement as I filled the bookcase and stood back to admire my handiwork. I moved a few books here and there, not being satisfied with how they would get on with their neighbours. You can't put William James next to The Egyptian Book of the Dead, I scolded myself, but I was rather pleased to find Rudolph Otto cuddling up to the Tao Te Ching.

I had become distracted, arranging and re-arranging my books, and didn't notice the time slipping past. It was my stomach that brought it to my attention – it had been many hours since breakfast at Willenbury. I was quick to climb the steep stairs to look for the promised lunch.

The staircase led to another door that opened onto the central passage of the ground floor of the vicarage.

To my right I could see to the door whose bell had summoned Father Justin earlier, the daylight struggling to be admitted through the heavy mesh of the curtain that shielded the glass. To my left the passage led to another flight of stairs and the kitchen whose identity was made clear by the sounds of clattering pans and the view of an old gas stove.

Father Justin was not in the kitchen, however. The noises were coming from implements being moved around with some determination by a large lady whose flowery dress and blue apron were doing their best to keep her curves under control.

"Ah, so you must be the new deacon," she said extending a large wet hand and then retrieving it swiftly, wiping it on her apron and extending it again. "I'm Elsie. I look after the old boy in there," she indicated a room opposite the door through which I had emerged, "and now, I suppose, I'll be looking after you as well. Can't say that I object, mind you, we need a bit of youth in this place."

"Jack Bolden," I responded, as hands were shaken busily. "I'm sorry if I've delayed things, I got a bit carried away unpacking my books."

"It's only a cold lunch, so there's no harm done," Elsie said. "Only he'll have had more than his share of the wine whilst waiting for you, but that's a thing you'll have to get used to. On you go, Mr. Bolden – or is it Father Jack? He's in the sitting-room."

I thanked her with a nod, avoiding choosing a form of address. I was trying hard to be self-possessed and to appear confident. Obviously I was a little nervous, but there was also a thread of excitement worming its way through my body. Every pore seemed to be aware of the scale of the transition that was taking place in my life. I felt suddenly grown-up and eager to start my new existence.

Father Justin was seated at a small table in the corner of the large living room that would have been filled with light if the curtained bay windows had been allowed to breathe. The dressing-gown had been replaced by a grey cassock whose folds spilt out of the chair as the priest turned, the wine glass in his hand threatening to lose its contents with the sudden movement.

"Ah, there you are, young Jack. Come and share this simple feast. I heard you meeting Elsie, she's a proper person, dear Elsie, one of the old school, if you know what I mean – but then, at your age, maybe you don't." Father Justin indicated the chair opposite him as he spoke, he was obviously not expecting an answer.

"I'm sorry if I kept you waiting, Father," I began, squeezing myself between the table end and an armchair piled high with books and scattered papers, to arrive at the appointed seat. The table boasted plates of cold sliced ham, thick slabs of bread and some hunks of pale yellow cheese. "I was just unpacking my books and lost track of time."

"No matter, dear boy," said Father Justin in a positively friendly tone. "Bacchus has been keeping me company with this fine claret – a gift from one of our parishioners who doesn't approve of the plonk we use for communion. We still have the regular wine in church, but the claret is much appreciated here, in the vicarage." And so saying he leant across the table, the bottle in his hand, and started pouring the dark liquid into my glass.

"Oh that's plenty, thank you" I cut in as the wine gushed from the bottle. "I don't usually drink at lunch-time; in fact I don't usually drink at all."

"Dear me, dear me," Father Justin looked quite distressed. "I suppose it's all those years at that parched academy in Yorkshire. Well, we'll just have to educate you, my young friend. I have a purpose in life - to emulate our dear Lord's miracle of turning water into wine - only I do it the other way around. It's becoming easier with practice. Still if you're not drinking this fine beverage, what else would you like? I don't think there is anything else other than water, and as you know the London water has been through many miracles each time it re-appears from somebody's tap."

"Water will be fine, thank you. I'll get some myself, don't worry," and so saying I returned to the kitchen and came back armed with a jug and a glass. "Elsie insisted I bring the jug," I explained to Father Justin's raised eyebrows, "I certainly don't plan to drink all that."

"Put a little in your wine, then," my host insisted. "We'll break you in gently. Go on, it won't kill you. It's a shame from the claret's point of view, but it's all in a good cause."

I resumed my seat and topped up the wine glass with water from the jug, as directed. The deep red liquid swirled as it thinned. I raised the glass tentatively and held it towards my companion. "Well here's to your very good health, Father Justin, and to the privilege of working with you."

"Privilege indeed," the vicar laughed out loud. "You tell Elsie that it's a privilege to work for me, she'll have something to say about that, she will." Father Justin laughed again, but then grew solemn. "But I will certainly drink a toast with you, young man, that is to bid you welcome and to thank God for some help with this lousy parish.

"Help yourself to some lunch Jack; it's not much 'but 'tis mine own.'" He pushed the plates across the table. "I'm sorry, I shouldn't have called it a lousy parish, it's not really, it's just that thirty years is a long time to be in the same place and watch people come and go – unfortunately they 'go' rather more than they 'come.' I am serious with my welcome, though. This place needs young blood like yours, and that speech you made upon your arrival was most reassuring. I was dreading being invaded by some ambitious fledgling full of his own ideas.

"Maybe together we can turn things around and bring people back to this lovely church of ours. We'll have a tour after lunch and you can see for yourself what a magnificent house of God we have been given to look after."

"Tell me about the parishioners," I asked, relieved with the last exchange. "I will need a bit of briefing on the regulars – perhaps I should even make some notes." I helped myself to some bread and cheese. The ham was out of reach, so I decided to leave it.

"Well, there aren't that many, but still notes would not go amiss. I'll fill you in this evening, after we have done the rounds at the church. Have some ham, why don't you," Father Justin handed the plate across, "and tell me about St. Augustine's. I was at St Cuthbert's myself, as was our mutual friend Father David, so I'm keen to know what he's done with the place."

My mind went back with affection to the college that had been my home for four years and where my convictions had been honed and my beliefs matured. I was relieved to find myself talking easily to my superior, describing how the years were divided, the general layout of the buildings, gardens and farm, and the moors that stretched away on every side.

"You were sad to leave it," Father Justin surmised. "I remember the feeling – a mixture of nostalgia plus excitement and a bit of fear about what the world had to offer beyond those protecting walls. I can certainly see the benefits of being a monk, although I wouldn't have missed the intimate brush with humanity that this job dictates in the outside world. Did you make good friends there?"

Father Justin was filling his glass with the remnants of the claret. He put the empty bottle down with a thud that brought my attention back to Islington in a hurry.

"Yes, of course, Father Justin, I made some very good friends, as I'm sure you did at St. Cuthbert's. Are you still in touch with any of them?"

"Well, your precious Father David was one of them," the reverent tone of my voice whenever I mentioned the head of St. Augustine's had not been lost on Father Justin. "But I hear nothing from him now, until your appointment came through with its letter of introduction. Two of my closest friends from those days are dead, and the fourth lives in The Castle. Have you heard of The Castle, Jack?"

I confessed that I had not and my attention strayed to my surroundings as my host explained that it was some sort of philosophical retreat for "vicars who have lost the plot," he said with a chuckle, and went on to describe the relevance of such an institution within the Anglican church.

I was taking in the dowdy air of the room and wondering what it would look like if the curtains were opened, and preferably replaced by a more vibrant material than dark brown velvet. Perhaps if there was half the amount of furniture and you could get rid of those dreadful tasseled lamp shades, it could be a workable living area . . . but I should have paid more attention. This was the first time I heard of The Castle. I should have listened carefully.

" . . . So I don't see him anymore, either." Father Justin finished.

"That's a shame," I pulled my attention back to meet the older man's watery eyes. "I hope I can keep in touch with my friends, we spent such a formative time together, and now we are going our separate ways with different challenges for us all. It would be good to compare notes every now and then."

"Absolutely, my dear boy," Father Justin was quick with his response as he pushed his chair back and stood up. "You do your best to remember how important those friendships are, and try to persuade your friends to do the same. Your lives will be the richer for it. Now, how about a tour of the church? I hope you are patient, for I have a lot to introduce you to amongst the stones and carvings of my beloved St. George's."

25. THE CHURCH OF ST. GEORGE'S

It was dusk by the time the two of us returned to the vicarage. The afternoon had started with a walk around the outside of the building, with Father Justin pointing out anomalies in the architecture, his favorite gargoyles and column tops, and the stories behind each one. Inside, the church had welcomed us with light shards from the clerestory windows illuminating dust motes that danced across the aisle in diagonal lines. The tall stained-glass windows at ground level allowed only muted light and kept the rest of the building in shadow. It was a grand edifice whose antiquity and atmosphere made me feel suitably inconsequential.

"You'll come to know this church as a friend, Jack," Father Justin had reassured me. "A good friend and a real home for both the body and the soul. Can you feel the power of the place? These ancient churches weren't built just any-old-where, you know. No, the sites were chosen by those who could feel, really feel, God's energy flowing from the earth's core, back in the Middle Ages, and way before that even. Now in this busy modern world, where tarmac and concrete seal the ground so often, it is hard to believe, and all but a few special people have lost the ability to feel the true force fields. But once you attune yourself to the vibrations, they can manifest themselves in very powerful ways."

We had paused in the centre of the church where the transept crosses the aisle. "Stand with your feet slightly apart for good balance and put your arms out, like this." Instructed Father Justin as he raised his arms, shoulder height, pointing in opposite directions. "Like the crucifix. Now turn the palms up, close your eyes and breathe slowly and deeply. Sometimes I feel the force so strongly I think it's going to pick me up and I'll float off to the roof. Can you feel anything?" He asked after a pause.

I remember being in a state of confusion as I stretched my arms out somewhat reluctantly.

The church of St. George's

Was the lunch-time bottle of claret responsible for this strange speech or was this a normal state for the man Father David had chosen as my mentor? Was he being serious, or was this some sort of trick to find out what his new pupil was made of?

Father Justin was standing as if in a trance, with his eyes closed, his chest rising and falling steadily.

As the moments passed, I remembered my geological investigations at St. Augustine's and my suppositions that magnetic fields could also be viewed as forces of the divine. I closed my eyes and tried to empty my mind, but I couldn't help feeling somewhat ridiculous. I opened them to find the priest looking at me quizzically.

"Feel anything?" Father Justin repeated his question.

"Nothing out of the ordinary, Father," I admitted, "apart from that special feeling of awe I always have when inside one of God's houses, and I certainly feel that strongly here."

"Well done, lad – that's the spirit, yes that's the Spirit, indeed. What you sense is only the beginning of the true excitement that is available. One of my – no our – parishioners put me onto this, her mother is a Druid and she was brought up in that faith and converted to Christianity only recently. Actually," Father David continued after some thought, "converted isn't really the right word – she just advanced slightly to embrace Christianity into her existing beliefs. I'll tell you about her this evening – remind me, her name's Estelle Murchent – although she's about to get married, so she'll have a new name soon."

The tour had continued through the choir stalls to the altar where Father Justin stopped and caressed the heavy cloth with affection.

"Do you know about altars, Jack? I mean really know about them? They are representations of the throne of Almighty God. As we bow before an altar, we are bowing to God who we should imagine seated upon it, gesturing to us with love."

I felt embarrassed that my studies at St. Augustine's had omitted such an important piece of ideology. Father Justin didn't seem to notice however, he was busy straightening the wrinkles from the altar's elaborate mantle with its decorations of heavy brocade; pleased to have a new audience for his enthusiasm.

"Every altar has been lovingly made and is meant to contain relics from a Saint or two," the vicar continued. "Tiny pieces of ancient holy beings are introduced into the stone before it is blessed by the Bishop and consecrated to God. Most people think of them as just a piece of furniture that gets dressed up in different colors at different times of the year, but they're a lot more than that.

"In the Middle Ages they used to put relics into all sorts of constructions, you know, not just altars." Father Justin continued. "Bridges for instance, often had holy relics incorporated into their structures so as to be sure they wouldn't collapse. There's a very old bridge I know on the upper Thames that still has a hole in the masonry where the relics of some saint or other were stowed. There's a bridge between Caversham and Reading which is said to have a relic from King Henry VI who was canonized before the Reformation changed things around. They've probably replaced it with some horrible modern thing by now. In fact the sixth King Henry must have been divided up pretty well - there's meant to be another relic of his somewhere in the bridge that gives Bridgnorth its name." Father Justin turned from the altar, his right hand lingering upon the cloth as if reluctant to leave.

We moved on to the sacristy, behind the choir stalls, on the south side of the church. I was shown my part of the great wardrobe where my newly acquired garments would live. Across the aisle, behind the organ and the north choral pews, was a small chapel dedicated to St. John of the Cross, with some large stone tombs along the far wall.

"There's so much to look at, and so much to tell," Father Justin said proprietorially, "but you have plenty of time ahead of you to digest it all carefully and acquaint yourself with St. George's idiosyncrasies. Have we not a wealth of beauty here to look after, Jack? Are we not greatly blessed to be able to call this grand edifice 'home'?"

I was quick to agree. Father Justin's fondness for every corner of the building was as infectious as it was moving. My neck ached from studying the many wonders of the roof and I was glad when Father Justin led me back to the massive doors, letting the soft light of dusk creep over the stone slabs as he opened them.

Having locked the doors behind us, with a key the size of a serving spoon, Father Justin led the way back to the vicarage.

"I know," he said sadly as he watched my eyes follow the great key as it disappeared back into the folds of his cassock. "God's house should always be open, but we have had precious things stolen from within, and since then, it has always been locked at night. It's a sad sign of the times, Jack, but one that cannot be ignored.

"Dinner will be at eight." Father Justin turned to me as we approached the house. "Now you have time to yourself for a while. Don't forget your notebook when you come upstairs, I'm going to make a list of parishioners to talk to you about over our meal."

"Thank you for a wonderful afternoon," I said as Father Justin stepped over the milk bottles and entered the vicarage, indicating that I should take the outside steps down to the basement. "I'll see you at eight, then, my notebook at the ready." This last was said to a closing door with the inner curtain hiding the priest's retreat.

26. ST. THOMAS'S OF CACHONGA

I returned to my room, filled with emotion. It had been an unexpected honor for me to have Father Justin share the intimate love he felt for his church, so soon after my arrival. Indeed, I felt privileged by the friendliness and trust I felt sure such an action indicated.

Now that I am reviewing these notes in my new, charmingly airy, study, I can feel time slipping backwards through the fingers that hold the papers. With the memory of Father Justin's devotion to St. George's so fresh in my mind I cannot help thinking about my own love – obsession, perhaps – for the structure of worship I created in Africa. I called my church after my dear friend back home at Thornton with my few personal possessions carefully stored in his attic.

St. Thomas's church had neither the antiquity nor grandeur of the edifice in Islington, but it was built with love and claimed the same kind of grip upon my soul as St. George's did upon Father Justin's. And of course, there was my altar – it may not have housed any relics of saints, but it was beloved by the whole congregation, and by myself most particularly. The conception and subsequent creation of this building and contents had not been without difficulty.

Upon arriving at Cachonga, the re-establishment of the church, both physically and in spirit was obviously my first priority. It was expected of me, and was my most fervent desire. I realized that I would be judged on the success or failure of this mission not only by the people of the village, but also by the church leaders in the capital, most especially by the Bishop who would be responsible for sending me everything I needed.

So, my first task, as the community's new vicar, was to seek permission from the chief and the elders to build a new church, to appeal for laborers and for the felling of trees. This was obviously not going to be straightforward. I soon found out that the elders specialized in prevarication. While my request was being contemplated, however, the chief agreed to let me use the school area for church services.

I moved the wooden cross from the end of the brothel and tied it with a rope of sisal to the thorn tree in front of the benches. I mended the table so that it could stand on its own, and covered it with a bright cloth I purchased from one of the village women. Upon this I set my bible every evening and gave a short service, in English, adding local words as I learnt them. I concluded the proceedings with a prayer asking God to bless the people of Cachonga and listed the names of the chief, the 'doctor' and the individual elders for special attention.

Loveness had helped me write the names of the village hierarchy on a piece of paper that I kept at the back of my bible for easy reference. I used phonetic spelling where necessary, and never ceased to wonder at the strange mixture of African and European names which came so easily to these people. The elders enjoyed hearing their names woven into so solemn a prayer, and even Umboto, the 'doctor,' took to attending the services, standing slightly to one side of the gathering, leaning forward in acknowledgement when his name was spoken. On Sundays I wore my white surplice and gave a full service of Morning Prayer, complete with a short sermon.

Whilst waiting for decisions to be made about the building of a proper church, I occupied myself by learning about the village farming techniques and the daily routines of different members of the community. I could see many areas where things could be dramatically improved, but kept my council. I was determined to earn the people's trust and confidence before I started all the projects I knew could improve life for everyone in the village.

Knowing that requests would take a long time to bear fruit from the capital, I sent a letter to Sollis via Boniface who came to the village every fortnight or so. I asked him to procure certain seeds and tools along with bags of cement and to send the bill to the head of the Christian Church of Arumba.

I made several drawings of the church I wanted to build, which I proposed calling St. Thomas's, and these I showed to Chief Mungonie on a daily basis. I would change some detail or other every morning, to provide a reason for asking the chief's opinion and advice, and also because new ideas presented themselves to me during the hours of darkness in my hut. N'anga Umboto was always present at these meetings, but he sat in the background and stubbornly refused my requests for his opinion.

In this way I managed to keep the project of the new church at the forefront of the endless deliberations the tribe's elders indulged in every day, but I knew I would never get anywhere without Umboto's approval.

The day after my arrival I set about learning the local language. Loveness was a patient teacher. She had been raised by my predecessor since she was a toddler, after being orphaned, she told me, and had been taken away with him and his 'wife' when they left the village some four years ago. She had attended a school in 'a distant place' and had only returned to Cachonga last month to prepare for her long anticipated marriage to one of the elders, Josiah. She wanted to be married in a proper church, so was keen to help me in any way she could. In answer to my question, she thought she was thirteen or fourteen years old.

I tried to remember which of the elders was Josiah, but they had all blurred together somewhat. What I did know was that not one of them could be younger than sixty-five, in fact most of them seemed wizened well beyond that age. In addition, all of them had several wives already.

I decided, with reluctance, that this was a problem for another day. It would be a contentious issue and one about which I could do nothing just yet. As long as there wasn't a proper church, Loveness had insisted, there would be no marriage, so I had some time. I decided to dismiss the distressing situation from my immediate list and file it in the 'too difficult' department.

Loveness told me that most of the elders spoke a little English, and understood quite a lot, but that they were reluctant to admit this, the chief especially was perfectly capable of having a conversation. However, knowing how delighted everyone was with my eagerness to learn their language, I struggled on.

I had been quick to understand that Umboto was not a medical doctor in any sense whatsoever. In the local language, I learnt, his title 'n'anga' meant he was recognized by all as a traditional healer, a priest of a non-specific religion, a magician and probably much more. Loveness went on to explain that Umboto commanded even more respect from the villagers than the chief. I subsequently discovered that his medicines consisted of various sorts of alcoholic beverages mixed invariably with hallucinogenic herbs.

It was Umboto who was in charge of who the girls of the village should marry and the size of the dowry appropriate for each match. It was Umboto, again, who decided when goats and cattle should be mated, sold or slaughtered, which crops should be grown and when they should be harvested. It was not surprising that such a man should be deeply suspicious of my role in 'his' village. He viewed my repeated requests for his assistance with the design of the new church with obvious skepticism.

At night, I spent many hours staring into the star-filled sky, trying to find a way to win Umboto's friendship and support, and slowly I came up with what I hoped would be a winning plan.

During my time at St. George's, I had been given lessons in dowsing for power lines by Estelle, the lady with the Druidic mother, of whom Father Justin had spoken on that first day. I had brought with me, to Africa, the dowsing rods she had given me and after much clandestine searching I felt that I had identified two lines of power crossing on a small hill, about half way between the village and the river. In spite of its being some distance from the village, I considered it to be a perfect spot for a church. It was surrounded by thorn trees and had a special mystical feeling about it.

My plan was to involve Umboto using the 'if you can't beat them, join them' philosophy, by branding my dowsing as just another kind of magic. "Why not?" I thought - and indeed I had no better explanation.

With Loveness's help, I asked the medicine man for his assistance in searching for a suitable location for the church using my 'supernatural rods.' Umboto looked at me with one wizened eyebrow raised. I explained that I needed his help in communicating with the Earth Spirit.

"What has our Mhondoro to do with your Christian God?" Umboto asked suddenly, in heavily accented English.

I stared at the old man in amazement. "You speak English," I exclaimed and immediately regretted expressing my surprise. I quickly continued in the most matter-of-fact tone I could muster.

"Well you see, doctor," I chose my words with care, keeping a reverential cadence, "my understanding of the Christian God is that He manifests himself in many ways. We are most familiar with Him being 'made flesh' and dwelling amongst us as Jesus Christ, but he needs to communicate with many people, on many different levels.

"'God created heaven and earth,' we are told." I continued, pausing frequently for Loveness to translate. "He loves this earth and cares for it by putting part of his Spirit here, in the soil, to look after it and render it fertile. This part of God's spirit is given many names. In South America it is known as the Goddess Pachamamma and here in Cachonga you know it as" – I paused - "Mhondoro?"

Umboto nodded.

"I recognize your Earth Spirit, Mhondoro," I continued, trying to sound natural, "as you recognize the Almighty God who made all things – including Mhondoro, or of whom Mhondoro is a part.

"I'm sure you agree that great care must be taken not to upset any aspect of God's spiritual powers, and hence I have asked for your guidance in this important decision. I believe your ability to communicate with this aspect of our mutual God is greater than mine. I am only a visitor here in Cachonga, but you, N'anga, have this soil as part of your soul."

I had spoken slowly, but I was not confident that Umboto understood everything. I was not entirely sure I understood myself, it was, after all, quite a complicated concept I was trying to explain, but, as I spoke, I understood that it was one in which I believed completely and with passion. I was amazed and surprisingly elated. I had never put it into words before.

Loveness, seated between us, did her best to translate, but I was now convinced that Umboto and I were strangely moving along the same wavelength, and that translations were becoming increasingly unnecessary. The witchdoctor was too curious to turn down the invitation and agreed to accompany me the following day.

Umboto, Loveness and I left the village early the next morning and I tried to explain the working of the rods as we walked. We stopped at my chosen hill and Umboto watched me as I walked forwards slowly, the rods extended in front of me. He must have noted my concentration and subsequent delight with the sudden swivel of the rods as I came to a particular spot. I repeated the action from a different direction before handing the rods to Umboto with careful instruction to hold them lightly and let them move as they would.

"Listen to what the earth is telling you, Doctor," I said softly, remembering Estelle's gentle instructions. "Be open to the forces that come from within the earth and which travel upwards, through the rods, through you, and beyond. Feel the message of God which Mhondoro can make available to you."

As Umboto moved slowly forward with the rods in his hands, I prayed energetically for God to reveal Himself. I was startled from these supplications by a shout from Umboto and looked up to see the witchdoctor shaking with excitement. The rods had lurched in his hands, springing inwards with such rapidity that they almost connected with his thin frame.

"It is here," Umboto was recovering his dignity. "It is here that the spirits wish us to build our church. The spirits of our ancestors, the Vadzimu, tell us so. We must build here, and without delay."

So it was that I obtained all the necessary approval for the location and construction of the church of Cachonga in spite of Chief Mungonie's disapproval of the chosen location being so far out of the village – he was not a man to take exercise.

Not long after the momentous day with the rods, I set off into the bush with a group of young men, called 'the warriors', led by Umboto himself, to choose the trees to make the frame of the church. There was much singing and enthusiasm as we went, so that most of the children decided to join the party.

The warriors carried spears as well as axes and formed a circle around the children and me as we moved away from the village. The African bush is full of dangers, the young men assured me with due gravity, and it was the job of the warriors to protect the weak from snakes, lions, leopards, elephant, buffalo, and so on. Umboto skipped ahead with an agility that amazed me, his magic evidently strong enough to keep him safe from marauding predators.

Three days after the tree felling had begun, a 'Ground Breaking' ceremony was held at the proposed building site to ask the spirit-of-the-land's forgiveness for disturbing the soil where the church was to be built.

The previous evening, in my little service, I had used as my text: Exodus chapter nine, verse twenty-nine, in which Moses claims "the Earth is the Lord's" to remind my flock of Christianity's claims to the soil. For my Psalm I chose number thirty-three giving weight to verse five: ". . the earth is full of the goodness of the Lord." I spoke with fervor of my anticipation of the following day when the first piece of earth was to be moved to make way for God's new home in Cachonga. I hoped my enthusiasm, tinged with religiosity, would be infectious, and from the reaction of the congregation, I decided that things were going well.

Understandably, there were no guidelines from St. Augustine's or the missionary college for the ritual we were about to perform. It seemed diplomatic to ask Umboto to lead the ceremony – he probably would have done anyway, but by suggesting it myself I hoped to bolster the fledgling feeling of mutual respect I was nursing so carefully. Together we planned the ceremony in some detail. It was to be the first of many joint ventures into the spiritual world of Cachonga.

The two of us, each dressed in the robes of our calling, made a strange pair as we led the procession from the village to the chosen site on the appointed day. Everyone had put on their best clothes, and I found the singing and chanting that followed us up the hill genuinely uplifting. I was carrying the heavy wooden cross, keeping it erect so that any resemblance to the journey to Calvary might go unnoticed. The witch doctor carried his feathered staff with equal dignity.

Umboto took centre stage when we arrived at our destination. There was a small delay in the proceedings while chief Mungonie, whose throne had been held aloft on a specially built litter, carried by six strong warriors, was settled into position under the biggest of the stately thorn trees which would one day encircle the church.

The ceremony began with Umboto calling upon Mhondoro with supplications for understanding and offerings of various kinds, waving feathered wands and rattling gourds full of beads. He lit a neat pile of charcoal and a small trail of smoke rose into the clear sky. Umboto weaved around the fire in a trance-like state with a mixture of excitement and gravity.

I had spent many hours trolling through the bible to find suitable texts for such an event. I hoped to include enough Christian over-tones to keep up with Umboto and to work my own beliefs into a powerful harmony with those of the spirit medium, without compromising his belief and faith in any way – or my own, come to that.

"Hurt not the earth" I quoted from Revelations chapter seven, in a stern voice to echo Umboto's opening prayer. And through the rest of the performance I interjected biblical quotations whenever the witchdoctor paused for breath: "The earth is the Lord's, and the fullness thereof" I claimed loudly quoting Psalm twenty-four, echoed in Corinthians I, chapter ten; and later, from I Samuel, chapter two: "the pillars of the earth are the Lord's and he hath set the world upon them."

Umboto danced upon the hill that was soon to become a building site. The villagers swayed and chanted along with the witchdoctor, and added "Yeh, Amen" in loud tones whenever I finished speaking. The chief waved his approval with his rod of authority, rolls of fat quivering with each movement. The ground reverberated with the stamping of feet and the air was filled with joyous noise.

The ceremony finished with Umboto hurling himself to the ground with tears streaming down his face as he thanked Mhondoro for the permission that had apparently been forthcoming amidst the excitement. I gave a closing quote from the twentieth Psalm: "Before the mountains were brought forth, or ever thou had'st formed the earth and the world, even from everlasting to everlasting, thou art God" I intoned, and then gave the blessing, with all the elder's names - by this time, I knew them by heart.

The double act had been a success. The chief and the villagers descended from the hill in high spirits and a celebration meal, almost as generous as that which had been served upon my arrival, was enjoyed by all. The foundation of St. Thomas's Church of Cachonga had begun.

It took nearly three years to build St. Thomas's. However I remember remaining remarkably buoyant through the many frustrations because I was convinced of God's blessing upon the project. This gave me the patience necessary to cope with the many delays. There was also a multitude of other projects to keep me busy, now that Umboto and I could work together.

It was hard to envisage the building until the last bundles of thatching grass were placed over the burgeoning church's carefully trussed skeleton. Beneath the sharply pitched roof was a mud and timber edifice of impressive proportions, with large glassless windows, rounded at the tops. I had sent for whitewash from the

The Baobab tree

capital, and Sollis had been as good as his word in procuring it plus a multitude of other items. He sent large tubs of paint up the river with Boniface. The interior of the building began to shine.

During one of my frequent ramblings into the bush, looking for suitable areas to be turned into fields, I found the remains of an ancient baobab tree. It was some distance from the village and, with the help of all the warriors, several oxen – and Umboto, of course – we brought the ravaged trunk into the church where it was lovingly carved and polished into the most wonderful altar I ever saw. I remembered Father Justin's description of what makes a true altar, and considered our baobab to be one of the finest offerings God could ever be expected to use as a throne.

That is how St. Thomas's, Cachonga began to take shape, but now I must return to St. George's and the start of my life as Father Justin's deacon.

27. MY NEW FAMILY

The promotion from student to deacon had not really registered in my mind. I realized that the Parishioners of St. George's would expect a professional member of the clergy and I certainly did not recognize myself as such. 'Father David would not have assigned me here, if he didn't think I was capable,' I kept telling myself. Obviously I prayed to God for reassurance but waves of self-doubt assailed me as I nervously explored my new surroundings.

The slope upon which the St. George's vicarage was built meant that the drawing room, which stretched the length of the building, was seated directly onto the ground with the old front door - never used - leading directly into it, the heavily curtained bay windows bulging on either side. Beyond the drawing-room, and parallel with it, came the central corridor with the kitchen at one end and the glass-paned side-door at the other. On the far side of this dark passage were two more rooms that sat above my basement flat, with the staircase rising between them. One of these, the nearest to the outside door, was Father Justin's study, the other was a dining room with the kitchen next to it at the end of the corridor and the stairs that led up to the first floor.

Father Justin emerged from his study when he heard me climbing the basement staircase, the night of my arrival, and was waiting for me when I emerged through the door at the top.

"We're eating in state tonight," the old priest said as he gestured towards the dining room. "Elsie's done us proud, in your honor, young man. It's done her good to have someone new to cook for - there's more than a touch of the maternal in our Elsie.

"You're probably not far in age from her own son who's away in the army. Father David's report says you're twenty-two, is that right?" I nodded, feeling a twist of nervousness with the knowledge that there had been such a document. "She has a daughter too, quite a bit older than you," the priest continued as we entered the dining room and Father Justin motioned to my place at the near side of the polished mahogany table. "She's married and lives up North somewhere and has yet to make Elsie a grand-mother, a cause of much irritation to our dear house-keeper."

Dinner had been left on a hotplate atop a splendid Victorian sideboard at the end of the room. Father Justin's carver chair was at the head of the table facing the door. My place had been set looking towards the room's only window which must have a view to the church when not concealed by more of the same heavy curtains that cut the drawing-room off from the outside world. On the wall behind me was one of two large faded hunting prints showing hounds meeting in front of a grand mansion. Its twin was hung over the sideboard and showed the hunt in full cry across an English landscape of hedge-crossed fields and tall elms. As I helped myself to slices of roast chicken and a plethora of vegetables, my mind flicked back to the day in Yorkshire when I had followed the chase for a while. How different were those wild moors from the almost manicured fields portrayed in these pictures.

With our plates filled and on the table, Father Justin stood at his place and bowed his head. "Let's take it in turn to say grace, shall we?" he said, his eyes looking up from beneath his lowered brows. "I'll start, to give you time to think of something interesting to say for tomorrow.

"Dear Lord," Father Justin's voice had dropped an octave, and reverberated around the small room, "Thank you for bringing my new friend Jack to share Your parish of St. George's with me and to share my meat and drink also. May he enjoy the spiritual sustenance You have shown me in Your church and the physical sustenance we are fortunate to have upon our plates. Amen.

"Short, sweet and to the point, that's what I like," the priest concluded as he sat down, spread his napkin on his lap, and attacked his chicken with enthusiasm.

I had brought a notebook and pen with me, as instructed, but it lay undisturbed on the table as we ate our dinner and sampled more of Father Justin's much admired claret. Elsie had placed a jug of water alongside the wine bottle on a silver salver in the centre of the table and I was touched to find that she had put a glass for water as well as one for wine at my place. No such extra vessel was required for my host, I noticed.

The conversation over the roast chicken consisted of Father Justin asking me what I thought about various sculptures and other works of art we had seen together in St. George's that afternoon. Fortunately I had only begun to formulate an answer before the priest provided an answer himself, enthusiastically pointing out how perfect such a statue was for that particular corner of the church, how well suited was this carving to that column top, and so on.

I was aware that the priest was making the most of his captive audience, and it occurred to me that life must have been lonely for the old man who seemed to have shut himself away from the world in this shrouded house.

When we had finished a pudding of tinned peaches and cream, Father Justin put his empty bowl on the sideboard and returned to the table with a cup of coffee, poured from an awaiting flask. He had also collected a small liqueur glass and a bottle of port produced from a cupboard of the sideboard, disguised to look like two drawers. I put my own bowl next to his and, declining the offered coffee and port, returned to my seat, aware that the conversation was about to change.

The last of the claret was evenly distributed between the two wine glasses. Father Justin leaned back in his chair, one hand resting on the carved arm, the other slowly twirling the stem of the wine glass, his eyes watching the liquid as it remained stationary within the turning goblet.

"And now to our parishioners," the priest began, his eyes still focused on the wine. "We haven't many regulars, but those that we have will form a sort of extended family for you, so you had better know something about them before they descend upon you – and descend upon you they will, I'm sure."

I opened the notebook, pressing my fingers along the spine to make it stay flat, and picked up my pen in expectation, waiting for the new silence to end. The ticking of a distant clock could be heard, and the faint sound of traffic to remind me that we were living in a city.

"Let's start with the benefactor who brings this lovely wine," Father Justin seemed to wake from a distance. "George Stanhope, and his wife Virginia, are both regulars of our Church – indeed one gets the feeling that Mr. Stanhope claims the place as his own, and not just because of its name. He reads the lessons every Sunday and passes judgment on the suitability of my sermons. It is mostly because of the Stanhopes that I have been able to keep to the old prayer book and bible. I use these two worthies to defend my decision - to remain with the ancient texts - to the Bishop on the rare occasions he shows any interest in St. George's. He's always trying to make me 'move with the times' and bring my parish into the modern world.

"George Stanhope is a successful businessman who is deep in the world of finance. He's told me many times exactly what he does, but it is so alien to me that it is of no interest whatsoever, and I'm afraid my mind drifts when he is explaining the machinations of various funds and so on, so I can't help you much there. It's enough for you to know that he is very successful – he's bound to drop lots of hints to that effect, so just look impressed. It's what I do, and has worked so far! His wife hardly says a thing, but when she does it is always to offer to bake cakes for a fête or a Christmas fair or something awful like that, and the indications are that we should hold such functions and that I am remiss not to do so. I believe her to be a good woman at heart but one without an opportunity to develop a mind of her own.

"The husband, meanwhile, is always very fervent in asking the Almighty for forgiveness, as our prayers dictate. He spends just a bit longer on his knees than anyone else muttering and nodding his head against the pew top. I somehow feel that he is using the Church to get a clean slate for the coming week, putting last week's activities safely into the 'forgiven box', and feeling justified to start the same mistakes all over again. Perhaps that is why he is so successful in the City. Maybe I'm being unjust, you'll make your own mind up, I expect. But there you are, that's Mr. and Mrs. Jolly-Respectable-Stanhope."

Father Justin finished his claret in a single swallow and filled his port glass in one appropriately fluid movement. I was aware that my host's verbosity was increasing in proportion to the decreasing level of the wines. I made a few notes on the Stanhopes and topped up my wine glass with water from the thoughtfully provided jug.

"Who shall we have next?" Father Justin raised his eyes to meet mine for a brief moment before returning them to his slowly turning glass. "Mrs. Simmons, I think.

"Helen is a single mother with two children. Sam, who's thirteen or fourteen, and Sandra who must be around ten. The lack of adult company in her life makes her lonely. She is very protective about her children, over-protective if you ask me.

"Like Virginia Stanhope, Helen's ideas are well-founded but she has far more about her than poor Virginia. Sometimes she brings me a casserole for my supper, a sort of donation towards her salvation! No, I shouldn't say that, she's a good soul and is doing a good job bringing those children up on her own. They all three come to church every Sunday and the kids don't fidget, which is a great bonus.

"Lorna and Edward Jackson have two children under ten. Edward has just done a bunk with the au pair girl, so I don't think you'll be seeing much of him, but poor Lorna is going to need our help. It happened about three weeks ago, and Lorna comes to church with puffy eyes. She's a good-looking woman but, like most mothers, hasn't got the waistline to compare with the Swedish nanny with whom Edward has absconded. Lorna was working at the local library before this happened, and enjoying the independence, but she's had to give that up now that she has the children to look after full-time again. It's a double disaster to lose both your husband and the nanny together.

Father Justin refilled his port glass. "I mentioned Estelle Murchant to you this afternoon, the lady whose mother is a Druid. She's a really splendid person, highly intelligent – she's just finished a PhD in something impressive to do with bio-chemistry – and is very pleasing to the eye. Estelle is about your age, may be a little older, and is getting married in a couple of months – at St. George's, of course. I have met the fiancé once when they came to organize the reading of the banns. Can't say I liked him, but then I'm not getting married to him. He's a tall chap who's just a bit too sure of himself to make you feel comfortable and has the unlikely nick-name of 'Chicago.' Anyway, Estelle seems very happy with him, and that's all that matters.

"Then there's a young man called Philip – I don't know his last name. He must be in his late teens but pretends to be older, not very convincingly, I must add. Philip is an enthusiastic alcoholic. He is always hanging around waiting to pester me with questions about how he should deal with the demon drink and various other substances that his peers offer him.

"I would have a lot more patience with Philip if I felt that he ever listened to anything I said. And if he came to church properly, I suppose. He just turns up ten or fifteen minutes before the end of the service and thinks I haven't noticed, then he pounces on me as the congregation leaves. I think he is after a quick fix to his problems – you know the sort of thing confessionals offer - an admonition followed by instructions to say a few Hail Mary's or the like, and then you're off the hook for a while. Maybe you'll be more successful with him than I have been.

"There's a girl called Tracy who is usually in Philip's wake, although she does attend the whole service, probably just to 'bump into' Philip afterwards. She can't be more than fourteen and she often pops into church on her way home from school. I'm never really sure what she wants, but she seems to enjoy the peace of St. George's and I like her for that.

"Dahlia is another kettle of fish altogether. This piece of dynamite is in her early thirties and is bringing up three children on her earnings as a lady of the night. She brings them all to church on Sundays accompanied by her mother who also lives off Dahlia's ill-gotten gains. The kids are immaculately turned out by their grandmother while poor Dahlia has often come straight from 'work' with smudged make-up and tousled hair shoved under an improbable hat.

"I have a lot of time for Dahlia, or Dilly as her friends call her, and find it hard to look upon her as a sinner. She is one of the most generous hearted people you will ever meet. And I say that not just because she drops off the occasional bottle of whisky every now and then!"

I looked up from my busy note-taking to find Father Justin smiling at me across the table. My eyes had been fixed on the moving pen, trying not to smile as both the vicar's vocabulary and complexion became increasingly florid as the port was consumed.

"We also get cakes delivered here quite regularly from a woman called Charlotte Littleton." Father Justin continued, leaning back in his chair and addressing the ceiling. "Another single mother this one, with a daughter called Sally of about thirteen who still has the imaginary friend of her younger years. Charlotte has got her knickers in a twist about this – I think I'll pass her on to you to deal with as soon as possible, I'm fed up with telling her the same things over and over again."

My head shot up from the notebook. "What do you tell her?" I asked, the worry in my voice undisguised. The reality of dealing with these people on a one to one basis descended on me with some force.

"Oh it doesn't really matter what you tell her, Jack. She's another one who never really listens. She's just after someone to talk to and something to talk about and Sally's imaginary friend fits the bill and will probably stay there until something else comes along."

I didn't feel very comforted by this, but there was no time to worry about it as Father Justin, having re-filled his port glass, was continuing his descriptive list.

"Elsie, you've already met, there doesn't seem to be a Mr. Elsie, but I've never enquired. She talks about her children sometimes and never mentions a husband. It's so valuable to have a housekeeper who doesn't natter all the time, I hesitate to break the spell by asking questions. After all, in our profession, it is for people to come to us with their problems, not for us to dig trouble out of them for our own amusement.

"And then there's Rosie," Father Justin paused and gave a sigh. "I've saved Rosie until last because she really is a very special member of this family.

"Rosie is a black girl of ten or eleven, at the most, and she spends more time here at St. George's than she does either at home or at school, and has done since she was about four. She likes to help me with whatever I am doing in the church, which is not always convenient, but I give her a duster and set her to polishing things and that seems to work. Often she just sits on the front pew, her legs swinging, looking around her; she just likes to be there, and I can understand that and admire it in one so young.

"The trouble with Rosie is, she talks. A stream of verbiage spurts forth every time she catches sight of me.

But I'm fond of the little thing and flattered that she should form an attachment to an old humbug like me. I've learned to filter out the prattle, it has become like the sound of the traffic outside, a background buzz that is quite re-assuring somehow. I think she will be thrilled to have another member of her family and I know she will win your heart as she has won mine."

"What about her parents?" I looked up from my notes. "Don't they worry about her?"

"Rosie's part of a big group. They all come from Jamaica, and have lots of relatives all living in the same house. Everyone seems to know that she comes to St. George's and are happy to have her out of the way and in a safe place. Nobody's ever come to find her, but Rosie tells me they know where she is – because obviously I've asked her – and they don't mind as long as she's home in time to do her chores. Mostly these involve looking after her younger siblings. I think it's to get away from them that she comes here.

"Anyway, that's enough for you to be going on with. There are other people who drift in and out, but I've given you most of the regulars. It's a relief to have someone to share them with."

"Yes, thank you very much, Father." I closed my notebook carefully. "It is very kind of you to introduce these people to me like this and it will help me enormously, I know. I just have to remember who is who now, when I meet them. I think I'll do a little crib sheet to keep with me until I've got to know them all properly."

"Good idea, Jack," Father Justin replied. "Put something down on a single sheet of paper you can keep folded in your pocket. Then you can produce it surreptitiously with your handkerchief, and have a quick squint whenever you need to.

"I look forward to hearing how you view our extended family when you come to know them all.

Tomorrow is Wednesday and we have an early morning communion at seven-thirty. We never get more than one or two. Why not be a member of the congregation tomorrow, and we'll work on our double act in time for Sunday?"

"Thank you, Father, that sounds like an excellent idea," I answered with relief. "It's been a long day, with a lot for me to digest, so if you'll excuse me I shall retire and work on my crib sheet. It is a relief that I won't have to be "on duty" tomorrow, and very considerate of you. May I bid you a goodnight?" I collected my notebook and pen as I stood up, "and thank you for an amazing day, and most especially for making me feel so welcome."

"Father David was right about your sensitive nature, Jack, and he was right to send you here. I feel we will get along well, you and me, and I don't feel as threatened as I have done ever since the Bishop told me that he was requesting a deacon to help me with the parish. I wish you a very good night. Let me know if you are missing anything vital."

I remember making my way downstairs to my spacious apartment, feeling suddenly very tired. I made myself scribble a brief crib sheet of my notes to put into my pocket for the morrow, should they be needed. The notebook itself, I put amongst the books on the top shelf under the window. I would not look at it again until I was packing my bags some seven years later when I would find it in amazement and realize how innocent I had been upon my arrival in Islington and how much I had learned and changed since the evening of its writing. I also wondered if I could have done things differently and avoided the upsetting occurrences that led me to leave this wonderful parish and seek work as far away as possible.

28. SWEET SUGAR

Father Justin's splendid description of our regular parishioners was an invaluable help to me in those first few weeks and beyond. As I came to know each of them in turn, I was increasingly impressed with his subtle understanding of their characters. His insights allowed me to face the challenges of being the new deacon of St. George's with more confidence than I had imagined possible, and slowly my earlier fears melted away.

One by one these people became part of my life. During my time in hospital, in Africa, with my fellow immobile friends, Percival and Amrita, we passed the time by sharing stories of our past. When I was asked why I left my first parish, to which I was so devoted, I found I had to tell them about each of the people who had contributed a part to my leaving – apart from Estelle, who had no part in my exodus - but I was eager to tell them about her, the ley-lines, the dowsing and her intriguing magic.

When I was first questioned as to what brought me to Africa, I answered as vaguely as I could. Neither Amrita nor Percival would let me off the hook. The best I could do was promise to tell them the story of my years at St. Georges piece-meal. That bought me time, but I knew I had to produce something new for them each day, so every evening thereafter, I turned my attention to the people of Islington who had been so much of my life for seven years. Each of them contributed something to my life and some of them became very relevant to how my philosophy has changed. All were part of my decision to move away.

As my mentor had anticipated, the first of the parishioners to make my acquaintance was the Jamaican girl, Rosie. Late in the afternoon of that first Wednesday

I was at the lectern, polishing the head of the brass eagle whose outstretched wings supported the Bible's angled resting place when the heavy Western door of the church creaked open. Sunshine leapt onto the stone flags and silhouetted a slim figure against the bright churchyard outside. The little girl came bouncing towards me.

"Hello, Father," came a call, as the door swung closed behind her with a muffled thud followed by a sharp click as the brass latch snapped home. Without the light her figure was obscured but her voice was loud and clear. "I'm Sugar," she announced proudly.

One thing that comes back to me with sharp clarity was that I was suddenly aware of a change in the church's atmosphere. The building seemed to have lost its habitual ability to mute the tones of conversation. The girl's voice bounced off the stone walls and pillars as the tight black curls bounced on her head, as if on springs. She skipped between the lines of pews towards me, one hand held out to tap the carved pillars at the end of each one. "Father Justin told me you were coming. This is my home too – well, I really live at 16 Holly Lane, but God is my true Father, so I reckon this is my real home."

I descended from the lectern, proffering a hand from my cassock's sleeve as the bundle of energy stopped in front of me. The girl took it gravely and shook it with slow deliberation. "My name is Jack," I said, "and I'm pleased to meet you. What can I do for you?"

"Oh, I just come to chat, and help sweep and dust if needed. Father Justin said that you would like to hear all my stories, because he has heard them lots already. He said you would be looking forward to my visits."

"And so I am, Father Justin was telling me about you just last night, during our first evening together."

"Oh" she responded with an unexpected air of delight, "what did he say?"

"Only that you would be coming in, and that I would enjoy your company," I answered lamely, suddenly unsure of myself with this youngster – what had I ever had to do with children? St. Augustine's had given us no guide as to how to talk to twelve year olds. However, my answer seemed to have done the trick, because it produced a big smile of white teeth in the girl's round, ebony face. She hopped onto a nearby pew, her legs swinging, her feet a good six inches above the floor, as she continued to chatter in the steady stream of one who is not yet old enough to know that perhaps everybody isn't interested in what you have to say. I was amused at how accurately Father Justin had described just such an encounter.

"However, he called you Rosie, not Sugar," I continued in some confusion.

"I've never been called Rosie by anyone other than Father Justin," she continued without drawing breath. "No, I'm Sugar. Sugar Sweet to Pa, Sugar Candy to Ma, Sugar-Sugar to my sisters, and Brown Sugar at school. It's just Father Justin who won't call me Sugar. You can call me what you like."

"Do you mind that school nick-name?" I asked, as I returned to polishing the eagle's head before moving on to the wings of the great brass bird.

"No, I like it," replied the girl. "It's because I'm black, you see," she explained with importance, as if shedding light on a mystery and letting this newcomer into a special secret. "And I'm proud of my skin which, Pa tells me, is soft and smooth and gorgeous and . . ." The girl's voice trailed off and her eyes misted over and looked distant again as she stopped speaking.

"You can call me Rosie, too, if you like," she resumed.

"Rosie it is then," I said trying to sound relaxed and friendly, which was not at all how I felt with this alien conversation. I needn't have worried however, because the girl continued her prattle with only the briefest pause to acknowledge my comment.

"My second name is Parker. Pa got the name from a smart pen that was in a briefcase he brought back to the house one day, long ago, when we still lived in the warm, where the sun shone all day.

"Pa said someone had given him the shiny briefcase with all sorts of things in it including a really smart wallet – which I only saw that once. There were a lot of important looking papers too - which helped the pot come to boil faster, on the fire out back, where Ma did all the cooking. Pa threw away that briefcase, and the pen that had a case all of its own, into the slop bin, of all places, but I got them out when he wasn't looking. I cleaned up the leather as best I could. I got it shining again, although the slops had changed its color in patches. It still looked really smart.

"I tied string round the handle and put baby Louisa's blanket in the bottom and pulled her around in it all day. It made a perfect sledge, that briefcase, with the shiny brass hinges holding the lid up at whatever angle I chose, to keep the sun off the baby's face."

Rosie stopped, and I saw her eyes were out of focus as she gazed, not at the lectern in front of her, but back to the Jamaican sunshine and the briefcase sledge she had been so proud of pulling around.

"The pen never recovered from the slops. It didn't ever write, but it looked so smart in its dark blue case with the shiny material inside. There was a dent in that material which fitted the pen perfectly, and a little white stretchy band to keep it in place. I used to keep it under my bed with the card that Grandma had given me the last Christmas before the Good Lord took her. One day Pa found me admiring it, but he wasn't cross, he just laughed and said "that's a good name, Parker" - it was written in gold on the lid of the case, and on the pen itself. "That's a very good name, I think we'll keep it" and so we did, because when we came to leave the sunshine I was given my very own passport with Rosie Parker as my name."

Having finished polishing, I picked up the Brasso tin and my dusters and descended the steps with care. Unsure how to proceed with my new visitor I sat down next to her on the edge of the front pew.

I had no need to worry, for Rosie was off again, chattering away about who had said what to whom at school that day, how she had too much home-work to do and how her teachers just didn't understand how much time she had to spend looking after the rest of the family.

As the child prattled on, I found my mind wandering around the church. I was thrilled, really thrilled, to know that this was my church. Not only my place of worship, but a spiritual home and my first place of work – for following God's Will. And here was this little girl, my first genuine parishioner, accepting me as Our Lord's representative on earth. I was suddenly over-whelmed with humility and grandeur at the same time. There was such a rush of emotion into my soul that I had to pray.

"Excuse me," I interrupted the stream of chatter. "Would you mind saying a few prayers with me? I feel God's presence so strongly, and I would like to share this special moment with you, if you don't mind?" I was already getting down onto my knees.

"That's OK Father Jack," the girl sounded as if she were giving me permission, "I have a special relationship with The Almighty and am used to the strength of God's presence, maybe that's why you can feel it, I bring it with me wherever I go."

The phrase "special relationship with The Almighty" sounded strange in so young a mouth, and was said as if quoted from someone else, or from a book, maybe. I was young, new to my job - should I have listened more carefully?

"No, I'm happy to share your prayers, Father. Please carry on," she said with strange authority.

I had reason to recall this conversation some time later, but at the time, it just seemed an unusually confident admission of faith, and one I was happy to embrace. I remember the fervor with which I started to pray with this small girl perched beside me. I gave deep, deep thanks to The Almighty for bringing me to St. George's and was busy asking for God's help in justifying my existence as a servant of The Lord. I became totally absorbed with these supplications and it was some time before I remembered that I was not alone. My companion said 'Amen' several times during my dissertations, probably, in the hope that I had finished.

With a last big Amen said jointly, the two of us rose. I was trying to decide what to say when the girl turned to me and laid a hand on my arm – it was an inappropriately protective gesture.

"God has heard your prayers, Father Jack, and I'm here to tell you that you are in the right place and that The Lord is pleased with you being here."

"Well, thank you," I responded, "it's good of you to have shared prayers with me, and I apologize for them being so self-centered, I'm afraid I got a bit carried away. Is there something, or somebody, you would like me to say a prayer for?"

"No, thank you Father," the girl replied. "I say my own prayers, but thank you anyway. I have to go now, but I'll be back. Look after yourself while I'm away, and we'll chat again tomorrow."

I was amazed to hear such a speech from the child – surely it should have been me directing those words to her? Anyway I returned her cheery wave and found I was indeed looking forward to her visit the next day.

Rosie was good to her word and visited the church every weekday, as Father Justin had said she would. I never minded her interruptions and enjoyed having her follow me around the church as I attended my duties, telling me about her family and the daily happenings at school. Unusually, the girl spoke in a voice that was not hushed by the sanctity of the building and had the ordinary ring of normal conversation.

I would look with amusement at how Father Justin scuttled out of the sacristy door when he saw Rosie arrive. Although the priest was genuinely fond of the girl, he was happy to pass on her distracting presence to his protégé and retire to the tranquility of the vicarage. I got into the habit of finding specific things for her to do in one corner of the church or another. She attacked the tasks I gave her with delight and I thought her visits brought the charming brightness of innocence into the building – I remember that with anguish now.

29. LONELY LORNA

Lorna Jackson, whose husband had recently decamped, as my crib sheet informed me, was the second person from Father Justin's introductory list that I encountered after Rosie's initial visit. A tall lady in her early thirties, I guessed, came into the church on the Thursday afternoon, two days after my arrival at St. George's, and found me in the sacristy.

"Oh, I'm sorry," the distraught young woman said when she saw a stranger turning to meet her, "I was looking for Father Justin." Her pale face made her brown eyes seem unnaturally large, her cheeks were pinched by the way her painted lips kept compressing and twitching with nervousness.

"I'm Jack, the new deacon;" I was quick to reassure her. "Can I be of any assistance? I'm afraid Father Justin isn't here just now."

"Oh, how do you do, Jack, I mean Father Jack," she stuttered. "I'm Lorna Jackson and I was very much hoping for a word with the vicar." Her sentences had a staccato urgency to them. "You see, I need his help. I need to talk to him. I thought he would be here. He must be here." Lorna collapsed onto the narrow wooden bench that ran along the sacristy wall, beneath the row of hooks and robes. Her head dropped, the abundance of shiny brown hair tumbling around her face. She burst into tears.

It was at this point that I took advantage of the situation and nervously consulted my piece of paper. 'Abandoned wife with two children' I had written alongside her name. Instantly I remembered Father Justin's description of the wasp-waisted au pair and the errant husband.

"It's just that I have no-one else to turn to," Lorna was blowing her nose into a handkerchief that looked none too dry.

"I'd like to help, if you'll let me." I approached the dejected figure cautiously. "I have come to share Father Justin's parish and to join him in ministering to the parishioners. He has told me of your plight – not as a matter of gossip, you understand, but as a matter of business between the two of us. Well, between the four of us really – Almighty God, Father Justin, yourself, and now me" I continued in as soft and professional a voice as I could muster. "Just as doctors will talk together of a patient's physical problems, so Father Justin has spoken to me of the parishioners' difficulties of their souls. I assure you I am only here to help and any conversations we may have will remain within these sacristy walls, and with God, of course."

"So you know what Edward has done to me?" She asked with a quick upward glance. I nodded in reply and was about to speak when she continued: "I don't understand it, I just don't understand it. Now he's become even worse. He's moved back into the house as if nothing had happened, except that he sleeps in the guest room and shows far more interest in the children than he ever did before. And he's absolutely horrid to me. All the time, he's horrid, horrid, horrid – as if it's me who's behaved badly, not him."

There was silence in the sacristy, with only Lorna's sobs filling the emptiness, as I struggled to find the correct response. I was floundering, but then suddenly words just seemed to come without forethought, the sentences following each other all on their own.

"As I understand it, guilt manifests itself in different ways, Lorna." I found myself saying. "There are so many things it is not for us to understand. Life isn't fair, but that doesn't mean there isn't a Grand Scheme somewhere – we can only see a short space ahead and behind. There must be a reason for this new move. Maybe your husband has moved back to build a bridge between you both, after all you have been married for quite some time, Father Justin told me, and have two children. ."

"That's just it." Lorna interrupted, her voice shaking with emotion. "He's after the children. The only reason he's come back into the house is because he is trying for sole custody of our children. His argument, so my lawyer tells me, is that I want to keep my job at the library whereas Helga – she was their nanny before . . . Helga is happy to look after them all the time – after all that is what she was employed to do.

"Edward has come back to the house in order to drive me out. If he succeeds in making me leave, his argument for taking the children from me is strengthened. I have done nothing to deserve this,

Father, I have been a good wife, and wanting an interest outside the home doesn't make me a bad mother."

"Of course it doesn't." I put my hand softly onto Lorna's shoulder. "You shouldn't blame yourself for another's folly."

"But I don't understand why he has to be so incredibly unkind to me. Isn't it bad enough that he lusts after another woman, that ten years of marriage have been forgotten – even denied. He's now saying that he never loved me, that all this time it has been a charade – and that's not true, I know it's not true.

"You wouldn't believe how this man - who has been my friend, lover and confidant, the father of my children, - could turn into something so destructive and beastly. He criticizes me in front of the children all the time. Everything I do is wrong or somehow dishonest and dirty. He is constantly trying to bring me down in their eyes. It's evil, what he is doing, really evil, and it's upsetting the children enormously. To lose my husband and my marriage is bad enough, but he's intent on stealing the children and my home as well. It's the destruction of my whole life."

There was silence again for a few moments as I explored various avenues of thought and Lorna exchanged one sodden handkerchief for a clean one from her handbag.

"Are you familiar with the Hindu concept of Karma?" I had chosen my theme. "It suggests that what we build up here on earth, in one life, dictates who and where we will be in the next."

"But I'm a Christian, not a Hindu," protested Lorna quickly. "Is Karma part of the Lord's teaching?"

"No, not exactly, but perhaps it's just a question of vocabulary." I was trying to convince myself of this argument as much as Lorna. "The important thing is not for us to set ourselves up in judgment on anybody, leave that to The Almighty. We must look after our own path and be proud of our perseverance at resisting the urge to retaliate. We must not allow someone else's sins to breed sinful thoughts and deeds in ourselves."

"Well, I may be able to keep the deeds under control, but sinful thoughts regarding the bastard are filling my mind. I'm still cooking his meals for heaven's sake, and doing his laundry."

"Pity the man, that's the best route to take," I decided upon a new tack. "And, if it makes you feel any better, it's also the most belittling. You can stand tall within yourself, you can look yourself in the mirror when you're cleaning your teeth every night, and not wince at what you see. Give a wink at your reflection, because you must know that Edward won't be able to do the same.

"It is probably the fact that you are behaving so reasonably that makes him so angry. Every time he looks at you 'turning the other cheek,' so to speak, there must be a twist of guilt in his soul. If you look at it that way, it is your fault that he feels so bad, and he'll take that out on you as and when he can."

"Do you really think that's what makes him so horrible?" Lorna took on a pensive air, her eyes studying her clasped hands and the twisted handkerchief. "If I had behaved badly, had affairs and was drunk and disorderly, as he has been to me, then he would feel justified in hating me, wouldn't he?" She raised her eyes, a light of comprehension spreading across her face; "and he could do so and not feel bad about it."

"Exactly," I nodded. "But as it is, he knows that there's no way he can account for his actions before God or anyone else. He has an uphill struggle ahead of him, whichever path he takes, and a lot of baggage on his shoulders to weigh him down. It may seem very hard on you at the moment, Lorna, indeed it is. But there is a light at the end of the tunnel – it's not for us to know the length of that tunnel, just to have faith in the existence of the light.

"So remember, every time you feel that hurt and anger welling up inside you," I continued, thinking of Thomas and his philosophy for dealing with Simon's treachery, "turn those feelings into pity. You don't have to forgive him," I lifted Lorna's hands from her lap - along with the clasped handkerchief - and she stood up from the bench, our faces only inches apart. "Just feel sorry for him and the dreadful journey he is building for himself. Live in the present; cope with each minute in turn. You are strong, Lorna. You will get through; and remember, no one can alter the fact that you are the mother of those children. You carried them in your womb and endured the pains of childbirth and the joys that follow. Your closeness to the children cannot be challenged."

Lorna's eyes were still brimming with tears, but they were no longer tears of anguish.

"Thank you, Father," she whispered, her eyes darting from one of mine to the other, not knowing upon which to settle. "I think you have just saved my sanity. May I come and see you again?"

"The doors of God's house are always open," I said in the same soft voice and then changing my tone and unlocking our eyes, I turned towards the sacristy door, "but sadly here they have only to be metaphorically open, I'm afraid. Since the gold cross was stolen from the altar two years ago, Father Justin insists that the doors are secured when nobody is here. However, you can always find either of us in the vicarage if we are not in the church."

I watched Lorna Jackson walk down the aisle towards the great Western doors. She had straightened her spine and was carrying her head high, her shoulders back. The big door moved inwards easily at her pull, the grey light of a drizzly day making a silhouette of her body as she turned and raised a hand to me. I was still standing at the sacristy door, and waved back with a deep sigh of relief. My effort in pastoral work seemed to have passed quite well.

As I returned to my duties in the church, I felt a sense of elation growing inside me until I had no option but to collapse onto my knees in the nearest pew and offer thanks to Almighty God. Gratitude poured through my clasped hands, rising towards the altar and Father Justin's image of the Almighty seated upon his throne I offered deep-felt thanks for the help I felt to have received in dealing with this initial dialogue, followed by renewed thanks for bringing me to St. George's, plus thanks for the support I was getting from Father Justin, and above all, thanks for guiding me towards the path of being one of His vicars here on earth. I was doing God's will, I could feel it in my very bones, and unworthy as I was, I knew that I had become a vessel through which divine love could reach out and help others. It was an exquisite experience – and one I still cherish in spite of the change in my philosophy.

30. INTRODUCTIONS - MY FIRST SUNDAY

Most of the other regular parishioners met their new deacon following my first Sunday Matins at St. George's. When the service was over and the crosier had been returned to the sacristy, I took up my position next to Father Justin, outside the church door, where the path leads down to Priory Road. I was doing my best to appear calm and confident while my fingers fiddled nervously with the crib sheet in my pocket.

Helen Simmons and her children were the first to emerge from the twilight of the building into the weak sunshine. They said their hellos to Father Justin with impatient looks in my direction.

"You must be Sam, and this has to be Sandra," I said, having taken a quick look at my notes. "How do you do, I'm Father Jack." I was startled by what I had just said. The statement sounded amazing to me - I was almost expecting them to say "no you're not, you're just that clumsy creep Jack Bolden who couldn't do anything right . . .". The two children and their mother accepted my introduction without a blink however, and took my hand, in turn, with serious expressions.

"Welcome to St. George's," said Helen. "I hope you'll be very happy here, I know Father Justin will be pleased to have some help. He is always so busy. Please let me know if there's anything I can do to help. You know, mince pies at Christmas time, cakes – that sort of thing. I would love to be more involved with the parish. Perhaps, now you're here, we can get something social started amongst the regulars of the church – we might manage to involve new people as well."

"That sounds wonderful, Mrs. Simmons," I responded, trying to sound enthusiastic, and marveling once again at the accuracy of Father Justin's descriptions of the members of his flock.

"Oh, please call me Helen," the lady's eyes were sparkling with delight. "Now Sam and Sandra, you must get to know Father Jack, he is here to help and guide all of us – isn't that true, Father?"

"Well, I'll certainly do my best," I responded. "You know where to find me if you want anything."

The trio moved on down the church path as other members of the congregation pushed forward.

"Good morning, Elsie," I said to the only person in the body of the church to whom I didn't need an introduction. "It's good to see you 'off duty.'" I gave her Sunday best attire what I hoped was an appreciative glance.

"And good to see you 'on duty,' Father." Elsie replied, blushing slightly as I admired her hat. It turned out she had bought it the day before, especially for the occasion of my first service. It was a lucky comment.

Next in line were Mr. and Mrs. Stanhope, easily identifiable because, as anticipated, George Stanhope had read the lesson. They each shook my hand with respect; Mrs. Stanhope glancing only briefly at my face while her husband gave me a penetrating stare.

"I hope you're not one of these progressive types, Jack," said Mr. Stanhope, who obviously felt that the omission of the word 'Father' showed his long-standing superiority. "We can't be doing with any of that dreadful modern vocabulary in this church, you know. Kings James's version of the bible has stood the test of time, and there's no reason to change it now. I hope you agree?"

"I like the magic of the old texts," I answered truthfully. "They have a mellifluous quality that appeals to the spirit. Even if the words are sometimes obscure in today's world, the meaning and the mystery come through, don't they?"

"Yes, just so," the financier had responded with a smile. "Good to know you're on our side. Father Justin has protected this parish well; it would be a shame to see all his hard work swept away. Good." He said firmly, and followed his wife down the path with the air of one who has concluded a satisfactory interview.

Dahlia, her mother, and three children, were easily spotted from Father Justin's descriptions. The two girls came out of church on either side of their grandmother who clasped a hand from each firmly in hers. All three were appropriately groomed and dressed for the Sunday service. Behind them came the controversial Dilly with a small boy holding onto her with one hand while the other was attached to his mouth by the thumb. Dilly was tripping along on high heels, her strides limited by the tight skirt she wore that came down not very far, so that her steps and those of the toddler matched perfectly. Her ample bust was well displayed in a shiny blouse whose buttons struggled to keep control. The large, round face was beaming through the make-up and her red-streaked hair fighting for freedom from a bright yellow hat that swayed as she walked.

Father Justin did the introductions as I came under the two ladies' inquisitive scrutiny. They both wished me well as we shook hands. The two girls shyly obliged their grandmother's insistence and gave their hands politely without raising their eyes from their shoes. The little boy just shook his head and shuffled his feet when Dilly tried to offer the hand she was holding.

"Please don't worry," I was quick to intercede as the child's face puckered towards a scream. "Another time will do just as well. It's good to meet you Mrs. . ." I faltered upon realizing that I had not heard a surname.

"Oh call me Dilly, please Father, everyone does," the woman rescued me with a big smile that revealed a smudge of lipstick on a front tooth. "We have been looking forward to your arrival. I know Father Justin will be glad of the help, isn't that right Father?" Dilly turned her attention back to the older priest, but he was busy talking to a tall young woman with a striking face framed in a halo of light blond hair.

"Never mind," said Dilly, "I've had my go with the priestly hand-shake already, now it's Estelle's turn. I hope you'll be happy here at St. George's, Father – you know you're awfully young for me to call you Father – do you mind if I just call you Jack?"

"Not at all," I answered with relief. I was finding this ordeal even more testing than I had imagined, and it was good to have someone talk to me as if I was just another human being, instead of somebody from another realm.

"Hello, I'm Estelle." I was watching Dilly moving away along the path, pulling her son behind her. I brought my eyes back in a hurry and produced my hand for the next young woman to shake. "Father Justin tells me that you're interested in learning about ley lines."

I panicked for a moment while I tried to visualize my crib sheet. Of course, this was the lady whose parents were Druids and who had got Father Justin all excited about power lines in the earth's crust and so on. There had been no warning about the large brown eyes that seemed to hold my entire being in their gaze.

"Yes indeed, Estelle." With an effort, I brought myself back from the depths of those eyes. "How good to meet you, I'm Jack Bolden, and I'd love to learn more about the power places. I studied geology quite a lot when I was at College and have some ideas of my own about force-fields, faults in the earth's crust, and so on. Father Justin says you find them right here in this church."

"This church, and just about every other church," Estelle's eyes continued to act like magnets so that I could not drop my gaze. "I would be delighted to introduce you to them," she continued. "Maybe some time next week, if you are not too busy. I could come by on Tuesday afternoon if that would be alright."

"Splendid," I responded quickly. Indeed I did feel as if some major geological plate had shifted beneath my feet, so that I had to shuffle to keep my balance. "I'll look forward to that."

"'Till Tuesday, then," said Estelle, letting go of my hand and eyes at the same time. She turned and followed Dilly and her family down the path towards the street lined with parked cars.

"This is Charlotte Littleton, Jack," Father Justin's voice brought my attention to the next person in line, "and her daughter Sally."

I stretched my hand towards a woman of my own height, in her early to mid thirties, I estimated. She was well dressed in a tailored suit of pale mauve that accentuated the vivid blue of her eyes. She was looking at me with much interest, tucking wisps of light brown hair behind her ear.

"How do you do, Mrs. Littleton?" I said rather predictably, "it's good to meet you. And you too, Sally," I disentangled my hand from the mother and offered it to the tall girl who stood somewhat apart, looking at me suspiciously from the corners of her grey eyes. She had long straight hair the color of light straw around a face boasting the subcutaneous plumpness of youth.

"Shake the vicar's hand, Sally," said the mother crossly, "Oh and please call me Charlotte, Father," she continued. "Don't mind Sally, she's a little shy, that's all."

As if to contradict her mother, Sally turned suddenly and took the offered hand with confidence.

"How do you do, Father Jack?" she began, "allow me to introduce you to my best friend and confidant, Peter." Sally indicated the empty space at her side.

"Oh, for heaven's sake, don't start all that again, Sally. Please excuse her, Father, she's far too old for this sort of thing." Charlotte pushed herself between her daughter and me as she spoke; filling the space that had been indicated. "She'll be a teenager next month – don't pay any attention to her, we just try to ignore it" said Charlotte, her quick reaction demonstrating the error of this statement.

I remembered the imaginary friend problem Father Justin had warned me about, and made a sudden and unexpected decision. "Hello, Peter," I said, stepping around Charlotte carefully "I'm delighted to meet you and look forward to getting to know you better." I was addressing the empty space that had been recreated between the daughter and her mother. "Please ask Sally to bring you to see me whenever she has the time, I would be delighted to talk to both of you."

"It's no use indulging the child like that," Charlotte interposed, not noticing the look of surprised gratitude that her daughter directed towards me. "I'm taking her to a psychiatrist next week; I've had more than enough of this ridiculous pantomime."

"It's good to meet you, too, Charlotte," I managed to maintain a steady voice as full of friendship as I could muster. "Father Justin tells me that you might be willing to help organize a church bazaar or something, if we felt there was enough interest here at St. George's."

With the help of my crib sheet, I had struck just the right note, and Charlotte was suddenly a-buzz with ideas for this or that social function. She prattled on for some minutes before realizing that she was holding up the exodus from the church of other members of the congregation. "We'll talk again, when we're not so rushed, Father. I shall look forward to it."

"And so will I," was my not very convincing response as I tried hard to smile a good-bye.

After Charlotte had swept past, I lent towards Sally and said in a low voice: "don't forget what I said, you'll both be very welcome to come and see me - any time."

Sally gave me a conspiratorial nod and a smile of trust that went straight to my heart. I would have said more but a young man with a spotty complexion and blood-shot eyes was pressing towards me with hand outstretched.

"Hello, Father. I'm Philip, one of Father Justin's regulars. I've been looking forward to meeting you," the young man concluded brushing a greasy lock of dark hair from his eyes with the other hand.

I didn't remember seeing Philip in church during the service in spite of using every moment between prayers and during the hymns to observe the members of the congregation, trying to ascribe names to their personages. Then I remembered what Father Justin had said about Philip always turning up just before the service finishes.

"Ah yes, Philip, how do you do?" I tried to sound genuinely interested. "Indeed, Father Justin has mentioned you as being here almost every week. It's good to meet you, my name is Jack."

"Yes, I know, Father," the youth kept hold of my hand with a sense of urgency and seemed to be trying to rub the sweat from his palm into my own. "I'm so pleased you've come." Philip lowered his voice, with a cursory look over his shoulder to the older priest who was busy talking to a young girl with a distracted expression on her face. "I need someone closer to me in age to help me with my difficulties. I don't think" and here there was a jerk of his head in Father Justin's direction "older people understand the problems of this generation. And I need help, father. Please may I come and see you sometime, if you're too busy just now?"

"Of course, Philip, that's what I'm here for." I said with a sinking feeling in my stomach. "It's difficult immediately after a service, obviously we have our priestly duties to perform, but any other time. I can always be found, either in the church or at the vicarage. I hope I can be of some help."

"Oh I know you will be, Father. Thank God you've come. I feel better already just knowing you're here. I'll come and find you in the week. Thank you again."

Philip moved off down the path, back to the street, 'and back to the pub' I thought remembering Father Justin's description of the lad, and the memory provided me with the identity of the girl who was now approaching.

"You must be Tracy," I offered my hand to the somewhat over-weight teenager who shuffled up to me with the clumsy self-consciousness of puberty.

"How did you know?" asked the girl with a sniff that I would learn accompanied most of her sentences. "We 'aven' met before, 'ave we?" Tracy's North London accent ate various consonants as she spoke, notably the h's and the t's.

"No, no," I assured her, "it's just that Father Justin has told me about your being one of his favorite regulars at Sunday services." I was lying again, but knew that the Good Lord would approve of such petty falsehoods when they were aimed at another's wellbeing.

Tracy was delighted with this answer and brightened visibly. She stood up straighter and adjusted a ridiculous fluffy pink thing on her head that I supposed was a hat. It squabbled with the maroon color she had chosen for her hair that week, but she seemed pleased with it and patted it fondly.

"Oh, how nice," she trilled. "I'm looking forward to your first sermon – I think I've 'eard all of 'is several times over. See you next week, then." And she was off in rapid pursuit of the shambling Philip.

"Well, that's the lot for today, Jack," Father Justin looked relieved. "You were quite the celebrity, and certainly took the heat off me. I think I'm going to enjoy having you around. What did you think of them all?"

"I think the descriptions you gave me the other night were absolutely spot on." I replied gratefully. "My crib sheet came into good use, and I can't thank you enough for such an accurate briefing. Lorna Jackson didn't show, did she?" I asked, thinking of the meeting with the distressed lady earlier in the week. "I hope she's alright."

"Well, she knows where to find us if she needs anything," Father Justin turned to go back into the church. "Come along, let's finish off in here and go and enjoy one of Elsie's splendid Sunday lunches. She doesn't come in on a Sunday, of course, but she always leaves something exciting in the 'fridge.

"Do you want to have a go at Evensong? Lorna might well pitch up for that, and a few other stragglers usually come in on a Sunday night."

"If you don't mind, I'd rather wait until next week," I answered quickly. "There's so much to take in at the moment, and I haven't prepared a sermon. Can it wait?"

"Of course, Jack, I quite understand, and don't blame you at all." Father Justin also seemed relieved.

The two of us collected the prayer books from the pews and piled them carefully on a shelf by the font. We closed and locked the great western doors from the inside, picked up the collection bag from where it had been placed next to the crozier, and left the church through the sacristy door to the path which led straight to the vicarage and our waiting repast.

31. FORCES OF ENERGY - ESTELLE

The following Tuesday afternoon, I was sitting at the big oak table in the sacristy, busy composing my first sermon which Father Justin had requested for Evensong the following day. I heard the click of the brass catch on the great west door followed by the clipping footsteps of a woman's heeled shoes.

There was a light knock at the sacristy door, it opened, and a blond head appeared into the light of the room.

"Can I come in?" Estelle Murchant asked somewhat unnecessarily, as she closed the door carefully behind her. "We did say Tuesday afternoon, didn't we?"

"Oh yes, I'm sorry, I'm afraid I completely forgot." I stammered, cross with myself for not handling the situation more professionally. How could I so easily admit to forgetting the arrangement made briefly, but so enticingly?

"I can come back another time, if you like," Estelle started, a look of disappointment glinted across the brown eyes I had found so absorbing on Sunday.

"No, no, please don't." I suddenly panicked at the thought she might leave. "I'm sorry about being so absent minded. There's a lot to take in with a new parish and everything," I was stammering like a teenager, but somehow I managed to reassure her that my interest in her visit was genuine.

"Actually I'm really looking forward to learning about the mysteries Father Justin said you have shown him," I said eagerly. "As I told you on Sunday, I was seduced by geology while at college and like to believe that there is good reason for so many cultures to have worshipped the Earth as a divinity. Earth goddesses have many names – always female, as far as my studies have taken me. The Cherokee call her Mon-a-lah, the Babylonians have Ishtar, the Egyptians, Isis.

"I think Pachamama is my favourite name for her." I couldn't stop the babbling. "It is used by the indigenous people of Bolivia and beyond. Sacrifices have to be made before every disturbance of her surface - whether for a simple path or a major highway, a furrow for planting potatoes or a pit dug for the foundations of an emporium. Where shall we start?" I ended somewhat lamely.

"Well, it seems you have a lot to teach me, too, Jack." Estelle was smiling with delight, the fleeting look of disappointment replaced with a sparkle of anticipation. "But why not mention of the Virgin Mary? Surely She is the Christian equivalent of the Great Earth Mother. She comes to us, with her great beneficence, in her role of the ultimate mother. In Mary's son we have the natural cycle of death and resurrection mirrored in the seasons and in the plants that wither, die and spring up again with new life.

"I shall look forward to hearing more about your Pachamama, I was expecting you to know about Aphrodite and Demeter, even Cybele and Astarte perhaps, but your studies have led you much further afield."

How grateful I felt for my varied interests at St. Augustine's - I stood a little taller. "Indeed, Estelle," I answered, my confidence returning. "I do know of those names, and of the Romans' Goddess Maia who the Greeks call Gaia, Hera or Rhea. They are all symbols of fertility and resurrection." It seemed we had started a kind of tennis game, lobbying names at each other, trying to prove our knowledge and interest in myths far and wide. "But I confess, I had never included our Blessed Virgin amongst them," I continued with genuine surprise. "That's such an obvious idea I am ashamed to have failed to recognize it, although such a view would hardly be encouraged at a theological college."

Estelle laughed softly. "No, I don't suppose it would," she said. "My mother has always referred to Silbury Hill as 'the womb of the earth mother' – you'll have to meet her sometime," Estelle continued. "She lives at Avebury, next to Silbury Hill. Have you ever been there? Well, we'll have to put that on our agenda," Estelle answered my shaking head. "The hill resembles a belly swollen in pregnancy, and its origins are still a matter of considerable debate.

"But to return to the present introductory lesson in ley lines," she continued after a brief pause, "have your studies ever brought you across Feng Shui?"

Again, I shook my head, trying to concentrate on Estelle's words rather than watching the fluidity of her movements as she walked around the sacristy, her hands fluttering. She was telling me of the ancient Chinese idea of the Ch'i. "This was their word for the lines of energy that pulsate from the earth's core, through the crust, and out into the atmosphere.

"Like the complicated web of nerves that allow a human being to feel on many different levels, so the Ch'i allow the feelings and powers of the living earth to emanate to a level where they can be detected, channeled and used by mankind."

"That's what scientists call magnetism, isn't it?" I was searching through my memories of time spent in St. Augustine's library.

"Yes," Estelle answered, "as you know, different cultures have different names for the same magic. Wouivres is another name for these phenomena, and there's Pneuma and Prana –"

"Oh, I recognize 'Prana'" I interrupted with enthusiasm. "That's Hindu isn't it, meaning 'breath'?" I was back in the game.

"Yes – well that and more. Prana is the vital power of life for the universe and everything within it. Man cannot live without breathing, nor can the universe exist without Prana - the energies and forces that are indicative and essential to life in all its forms.

"Anyway, let's see what we can find, right here in St. George's." She walked over to me, and with all the naturalness in the world, she took my hand and led me through the door, into the main body of the church. "We'll start in the centre where I think there's a ganglion of energies that are strong enough for even a beginner to pick up."

The next couple of hours were the most fascinating I had ever experienced. Estelle had started by taking off her shoes. "My stockings are much thinner than your socks," she said after I had also removed my shoes. She tried unsuccessfully to hide a smile as I rearranged the right sock in an effort to hide the hole by my big toe. "I think you would be better barefoot. You need to let the forces run up through these ancient stones and into the very fibers of your being. I am already receptive, so the stockings aren't going to interfere in any way, but a newcomer like you needs all the help he can get."

We then proceeded to walk slowly over, or stand still on, almost every stone slab of the central aisle and those in the small chapel of St. John of the Cross. I tried hard to banish my thoughts and to concentrate on the visceral feelings that Estelle assured me were available from the stones, through my feet, into my inner being. I remember vividly being unsure whether the excitement I was experiencing was due to the proximity of the ley lines, or of my alluring teacher. But I didn't care either way. I just abandoned myself to the experience and felt enlivened and depleted at the same time.

Having identified the various kinds of ley line forces, Estelle went on to explain that, in addition to the meeting of many lesser lines of energy in the aisle of the church, there were two exceptionally powerful ones that crossed under the altar. This intersection, she insisted, was the reason for the altar's placement, and the altar in turn, defined the choice of site for the whole church. One was a male line, and one a female.

"I'll explain about that later," she assured me. "This is a complicated and powerful initiation and you can't be expected to learn everything at once. You have to start slowly by just learning how to feel. Once we have that sorted, we can analyze the feelings as they come to you, but we've a way to go before then."

After exploring the entire church I found I could indeed feel certain energies stronger in some places than others. I found it enormously exciting and immensely tiring. I was also hungry, and summoned up the courage to ask Estelle if she would like to join me for tea at the Priory Café across the road from the church.

"What a lovely idea," Estelle answered enthusiastically. "I'm starving. I skipped lunch today so as not to be late, so a cup of tea and one of their splendid currant scones would be very welcome."

Sitting in a corner of the café with a tin tea-pot between us on an orange waxed cloth, Estelle reviewed the lesson of the afternoon - her pupil eager to learn.

"I know there's a lot to take in," Estelle said, stirring her tea thoughtfully. "I hope you didn't mind – I get a bit carried away on the rare occasion I am asked to proselytize. Of course, that's your job," she said smiling, "you're meant to do it all the time; but I'm just a lay person – like the pun?" and she laughed. I thought it was the most beautiful sound I had ever heard.

"Father Justin was right when he told me you wanted to learn, wasn't he?" Estelle's voice was suddenly full of uncertainty.

"Oh absolutely," I answered eagerly, although I couldn't remember my friend being so insistent about the subject. "I've learnt a lot today, maybe too much. I shall have to digest all that I can remember and let it settle. I'm sure I will have lots of questions for you, but just now everything's a bit of a jumble in my head.

"You said that there are lots of churches, like this one, situated upon these lines. How did that happen?"

"Not just churches, but all kinds of places of worship from many denominations, even the Masonic lodges – or perhaps especially those." Estelle paused and her mind seemed to travel some distance before she continued. "Mark stones – boulders of significant weight and size – were placed along ley lines by our ancestors in a time without date, and many of these became the original 'foundation stone' of churches and cathedrals. "Lots of the Roman church altars were built on, or even made of, these significant stones. They are markers of magic places. Why should it matter by what name that magic is called? The stones pre-date the buildings and the

Christian epoch but have been assimilated into the new doctrine."

"I remember thinking along those lines - whoops, there we go again - in college," I said enthusiastically. "It occurred to me then that a building like that of San Sophia in Istanbul, for example, remains just as holy whether it is inhabited by Christians or Muslims."

"Yes, Hagia Sophia has indeed remained impervious to the doctrines practiced within." Estelle hit the ball back. "It was built by Constantine as the pinnacle of Christian worship, then converted into a mosque in the 1600s, I think. I can see I will have to do some revision before our meetings in future," she added with a laugh.

"Anyway", Estelle continued, "to return to these special stones. Did you know, for example, that St. Peter's name was actually Simon? He only became known as Peter after this proclamation from our Lord recited in Matthew XVI, 18: "thou art Peter, and upon this rock I will build my church." Peter was not even a name until then – it comes from the Greek word 'petros' which means a rock or a stone. Could Jesus have been identifying His favorite disciple with one of the Mark stones which were ancient, even then?"

I nodded, remembering my talks with Father Edmund. Estelle had certainly won that game, and now it was her service, it seemed, she was not the only one who would need to revise.

"Most of the churches in Britain were built on sites of pagan worship, sites that were determined by the forces we are trying to recognize today, forces incapable of being harnessed by nomenclature. Why else would Patrick, the Bishop of the Hebrides all those years ago, insist that churches should be erected on the same sites as the menhirs which populate those remote islands? It was the normal practice of the time.

"Do you know Bede's 'Ecclesiastical History'?" Estelle didn't wait for an answer. "In it he quotes a letter to Abbot Mellitus from Pope Gregory written in 601 AD with instructions that pagan temples should be converted to Christian churches rather than being razed to the ground. This was not just a clever way to encourage the pagans to combine their ancient ideas with the modern vogue, but a recognition of the power places extant on those sites and a desire to use that power within the vestments of the new faith.

"London is full of ley patterns and alignments marked by churches. I'll be happy to walk some of them with you, if your interest persists, once your recognition facilities are stronger."

"I'd enjoy exploring the lines of London churches - that sounds fascinating," I answered enthusiastically. "I'm sorry not to be more intuitively receptive. If I practice, will I get better?" I asked, more to keep the conversation going than for instruction.

Estelle assured me that I would and promised to continue the lesson the following week. "We'll see how you are at dowsing," she said, smiling. "That's a good way to learn about channeling the powers."

I was beginning to relax and enjoy Estelle's company when she suddenly leant across the table and spoke to me in an entirely different tone.

"Father, may I ask you about something completely different?" Her voice was now low, almost conspiratorial, and I was aware that it was the first time she had used my title. "I've been wanting to ask someone about an experience I had about six months ago, and finally, I think I've found the right person."

I hoped I was nodding in an encouraging way in spite of my guts tightening with worry about my qualifications for such questioning.

Suddenly, our roles were reversed. Now Estelle was the supplicant, and I found myself, uncomfortably, as the one from whom advice was being sought.

"The story is this," Estelle began. "I was visiting some friends of mine in Derbyshire, they have three small children – George is seven, Belinda is five, and Rupert had just turned four. Rupert is my godson. I was there for his birthday.

"I volunteered to take the children for a walk in the dales while their parents had some peace and quiet. We set off after lunch full of high spirits and left the village by a narrow footpath between two houses. There was a big dog, chained to a stake in the garden to our right. It was an Alsation-cross-something, by the look of him, and he was very unhappy about our progress alongside his fence. He was barking and snarling and pulling at his chain.

I encouraged the children to hurry past, and the older two ran ahead up the steep path towards the hilltop. It was a narrow path, with bracken on both sides and the occasional rock, so I had to watch my footing. I was hastening to catch up when I heard a scream from behind me."

Estelle paused, her face suddenly pale. She dabbed her upper lip carefully with a napkin.

"I turned to see Rupert frozen on the path behind me. He must have been a good two hundred yards away." Estelle was speaking quickly now, her voice barely more than a whisper. I had to lean forward to catch the phrases. She was staring hard at the crumbs on her otherwise empty plate.

"I will never forgive myself for having left him so far behind, but then the others were at least five hundred yards in front, and I'm not a mother, I don't have the built-in understanding of risks that apparently comes along with the birthing of a child.

"The dog had broken its chain, jumped the small fence. and was charging up the hill towards little Rupert. I saw the scene in horrible detail, the full horror of the situation descended like a shroud, I couldn't move."

I swallowed audibly in a silence that seemed to stretch forever. Then just as I felt I should say something, Estelle continued. "There was suddenly an awful noise. It was as if a banshee had been let loose, mid-afternoon, outside an ordinary Derbyshire village. It was the most dreadful sound I have ever heard and I had no idea where it was coming from. It made the hairs on the back of my neck stand erect, it made cold sweat run down my spine, sides and legs. It made the dog's movements slide into slow-motion.

"You probably won't believe this, Jack," Estelle began again after another agonizing pause. "But that sound emanated from me. I do not remember moving a limb; in fact I was frozen with terror when I saw the scene. But the next thing of which I was conscious was that I was there, between the dog and the child, and the sound was retracting down my throat.

"The dog froze in front of me. It was close enough for me to touch - I could feel its hot breath against my legs. The animal was bushy-haired with fear, its tail jammed between its back legs. When I regained some sort of focus, I found I was staring at his eyes, and then, suddenly, he dropped his massive head. He turned around with a dreadful whimper and slunk back down the path."

I had stopped breathing, feeling suspended somehow, in another dimension. How could I possibly offer advice? I gazed at Estelle, until she raised her eyes to mine.

"What I want to know, father," she said slowly, "is whether there is a visceral side to spirituality. My movements on this extraordinary occasion were completely involuntary, and also beyond my physical capabilities.

"When the dog left the scene, I became like a deflated balloon. I was a wreck both physically and emotionally. Rupert, bless his heart, gave a great yelp of joy and ran off after his siblings, leaving his Godmother in a heap on the hillside. I struggled to get up and grope my way to follow him.

"Forces had moved through me, Jack, greater than anything I could have imagined, way beyond cognitive instruction. So what happened? Can I think that I was an instrument of God's for just a couple of seconds? Should I be humbled or filled with hubris? Should I be frightened or enlightened?"

There was a long silence. It was now my turn to study crumbs on plates. I had no idea how to respond. Then, as my face reddened, I thought of the sexual outpourings I was in the habit of executing in the fervent belief that I was expressing utter devotion to God. Certainly I believed in the power of God to manipulate the physical aspects of His creations, but how could I communicate anything like that to Estelle?

Eventually I took a deep breath and addressed Estelle's question as best I could.

"Of course you are an instrument of God, Estelle," I started. "We should all consider ourselves so to be, and I think there are elements of both humility and pride in recognizing this. God made us in his image and likeness, after all. It would be ungrateful, and show a lack of appreciation, not to grasp the positive aspects of such a marvel."

There was a long pause before I found the strength to continue. "I have to admit to envying you such an experience. There are not many people who can lay claim to being physically moved by Almighty forces."

"My mother says differently," Estelle said. "She is the only other person to whom I have related that story. She claims that the forces that moved me were the powers of raw instinct – powers of the earth which education dilutes. She is a Druid, after all."

"But who says that instincts and the earth's forces are not the powers of God?" I asked with genuine confusion.

Estelle looked thoughtful, "I don't know," she answered slowly. "I'll have to ask her about that. Of course, that makes complete sense.

"Oh, Jack, why did I not realize how simple the wonders of the world can be if you can attribute them to the same source, no matter the name. Thank you."

I gave a sigh of relief. My question had been spontaneous, and seemed to have been a better reply than any I might have come up with after hours of careful thought.

I was genuinely thrilled to have found a kindred spirit with whom I could explore some of the ideas I had nurtured at St. Augustine's; and what a deep and intriguing parishioner Estelle turned out to be. There was excitement in conversing about strange and wonderful powers with someone who didn't dismiss them as spurious; someone who knew more about these forces than my own studies had allowed; who had experienced them herself; someone from whom I could learn.

We said our goodbyes outside the café, with me telling Estelle how much I was looking forward to our next meeting, when she had promised to introduce me to dowsing. I watched her turn away from St. George's and walk purposely down the puddled pavement, her bright hair moving softly in the wind of her steps. At the corner she turned and looked back. I hadn't moved, it was as if her departure was severing something precious. She must have seen me watching her for she raised a hand with a friendly wave and I reciprocated before turning in the opposite direction and heading home. I had a lot of mental, spiritual and physical feelings to digest plus an unusual spring in my step.

32. THE CHALLENGES OF CHARLOTTE, SALLY AND PETER

During the couple of weeks that followed my first Sunday, one by one the parishioners took up my offers to be available to them with any difficulties they might have.

I had already been visited by Rosie and Lorna; Estelle had made her memorable visit on the following Tuesday, and on the Wednesday, straight after the early service, I had a visit from Charlotte Littleton.

After our encounter in the porch on Sunday, I had added to my crib sheet, 'neurotic mother and even more neurotic daughter, Sally, and the pretend friend Peter' alongside her name. My heart sank as she opened the sacristy door following a short, rapid knock. She closed the door behind her in a conspiratorial manner that filled me with foreboding.

"Oh, Father Jack, I'm so pleased to have found you on your own," Charlotte started, speaking rapidly. "Father Justin is a dear man, of course, but he is reluctant to speak to Sally about this problem we have with her and her stupid imaginary friend. I do so need your help and support to get her out of this childish phase. It is making me – I mean her – the laughing stock of all our friends and associates. You will help us, won't you?"

I looked at the carefully dressed and coiffed woman in front of me. There was nothing casual about how Charlotte Littleton presented herself. Her eyebrows had been plucked into perfectly matching curves that gave her a slightly surprised expression, her lips were painted with precision and her face wore a patina of makeup to suggest a perfect complexion. She must have had Sally very early in life, I thought, as she didn't look older than thirty, and her figure, well displayed by a tight fitting blue skirt and matching blouse, was that of someone even younger.

"Of course I will try to help if I can," I said as I pulled a chair out from against the wall and indicated for her to sit down. I turned my own chair around from the desk so that we sat facing each other across the flagged floor. "Can I get you a cup of tea or coffee?" I volunteered; hoping the time spent fussing with the kettle would give me space to form a plan of some kind.

"No, thank you, Jack – is it alright for me to call you Jack? I don't mean to be disrespectful, but . ."

"Of course, that's fine," I stepped into the hesitation. "Now, how exactly do you see me being able to help?"

"Well, Sally is more likely to listen to you than she is to me. Heaven knows, I have tried so hard to get rid of this fixation – and that is what it is, Jack, a fixation that has become an obsession. It's quite ridiculous for a girl of her age, you know she's twelve now, to have such a . ."

"Yes, yes, I know," I did not want to hear the whole saga again. "If you want me to help, you will have to allow me to speak frankly." I paused; did I have the courage to speak my mind, even if it might cause distress?

"Well, of course, I expect you to speak frankly." Charlotte's plaintive expression was replaced by one of irritation. "I wouldn't expect or want anything else. What exactly do you mean?"

"Well," I started slowly, unsure I wanted to look at Charlotte as I spoke, but knowing that it was necessary if my words were to have any weight with her. "I can't help feeling that it is not so much for Sally's sake that you wish this imaginary friend to go away, as for your own."

Charlotte gave a gasp, and I was quick to continue. "Please understand me, I am not criticizing, just wondering if Sally would be so insistent upon keeping her friend so prominently before you if it didn't provoke such a strong reaction. After all, there are many vices a lot worse than having an imaginary friend. What possible harm can it do her? There is a chance that she is unwittingly using it to get your attention, and if that is the case, you have to admit that it is working."

"Well!" Charlotte's voice exploded out of her. "I never thought I'd find myself under attack in my own church. Here I am coming to you for help, and you turn things around and attack me like this. It's outrageous. Where is Father Justin, I want to speak to him at once."

"I expect he is in the vicarage." I made sure my voice kept the same quiet, even tone. "I thought you wanted me to speak frankly. Would you prefer to have an advisor who simply says what you want to hear instead of what he really thinks? What good would I be as a helper, if I only said what was acceptable to the questioner? What value would I have in God's church if I did not try to be truthful? Believe me, Charlotte, I mean no offence, I am simply trying to be objective and offer the best view I can to help both you and your daughter, Sally.

"This friend of hers, Peter isn't it?" Charlotte nodded her head, her lips pressed together too tightly to allow for speech. "He can only interfere with your relationship with your daughter if you allow him to. You know he doesn't exist, and so does Sally. I am just suggesting that the credibility this invention gets comes more from your reaction to his supposed presence than from Sally's theatrics."

The silence in the sacristy seemed to settle on the hanging robes and the shiny stained glass window panes. It crept across the floor like an autumn mist and brought with it a similar chill. Charlotte was staring hard at the stone slab in front of her feet that were pressed together under tightly clasped knees.

"I realize that you cannot do a 180 degree turnaround and agree with the pretense all of a sudden," I continued as softly as I could. "But what if you stop reacting to Peter's infiltration into your family life? Just don't rise to the bait, so to speak, and see what happens. Also" - I decided that I might as well go the distance as I'd braved it out this far - "perhaps you should look at your lives together. Yours and Sally's I mean. Try to find out why your daughter is trying to get your attention in this way, why she wants a third presence in your family circle. You should not blame or criticize either your daughter or yourself, just try to step back from the situation that has captured you in such a negative way, and discover what really lies behind it."

There was still no reaction from the seated figure whose hands were clasped around her knees and who had started to rock slowly backwards and forwards.

"Have the two of you been on holiday lately?" My question seemed pathetically mundane, but it was all I could think of, and something had to be done to hold the silence at bay.

Charlotte shook her bowed head.

"Well, that might be a starting point." I tried to make my tone light and conversational. "Peter would come too, of course. But you could handle that if you put your mind to it.

"I tell you what," I paused, waiting for some sort of reaction from the taut frame opposite. "I will have a chat with Sally, and perhaps, if you could spare just a weekend for the two of you, where she has you all to herself, I could persuade Peter to leave you both alone. What do you say?"

I moved to the shelf with the kettle and cups and busied myself preparing some coffee in order to stop the panic I could feel building inside me. Charlotte had to be the one to combat the silence this time.

The kettle started to hiss as the water began to heat. I clinked a teaspoon against a mug spooning in some instant coffee. Bizarrely the sounds helped to ground me and gave me confidence.

The kettle came to a boil, and still no sound issued from the bent figure who continued to stare at the floor, her rocking body coiled as if to combat pain.

"Are you sure you won't change your mind about a cup of coffee, or tea?" I was trying to sound casual.

Charlotte suddenly sat upright. Then she stood slowly, and advanced across the room until she was looking directly in my face. Her eyes narrowed slightly, the immaculate eyebrows drawn together.

"Alright, I can see where you're coming from, and I'm prepared to give it a go – but only if you will really talk to Sally. I can't do this all on my own. Where on earth am I meant to take her? I haven't got the time. I play tennis every Saturday morning with the girls, and we have lunch afterwards. Sundays, after church, there's always a gang around for lunch. During the week, I have to work. When can I fit her in?"

"Perhaps, if you really are serious about dealing with this problem, you should make it a priority and let the tennis and lunches go for a weekend." I ventured in as soft a voice as I could muster – didn't she see how excluded her daughter had become from her life? I would have backed away, but the shelves were against my back and I could feel the remaining mugs vibrate with my movements.

"You tell me when you can find the time for Sally, and I promise to have a talk with her before you go away." My voice was stronger now.

"But I always have time for my daughter," Charlotte leaned even closer so that I could see the tiny cracks in the make-up on her cheeks. "What are you suggesting – that I am a lousy mother?"

"I'm suggesting nothing of the sort." I tried to imitate Father David in his tone of authority, remembering one of my college lessons on dealing with difficult parishioners: when you are expected to defend your words or actions, take the initiative and attack instead. "Why would you come out with a question like that?"

Charlotte's face began to crumple. The corners of her carefully painted mouth turned down, the bottom lip began to quiver, her eyes –still fixed on my own – filled with tears which began to course their way across the powdered cheeks.

That was it. My heart melted, and I placed one hand upon Charlotte's shoulder and with the other, allowed my fingers to carefully stroke the tears away from one side of her face.

"A real friend is someone who you can trust to help you through times of trouble," I began gently, thinking of Thomas and Rufus. "Someone who will stand at your side and tell you the truth, even if it is unpleasant, but because they are your friends, you can appreciate the value of their words. True friends are hard to find. Maybe it is because Sally hasn't got any that she has made one up. Maybe it is better to have a 'Peter' to confide in than to have your trust misplaced and to face the hurts that results from being let down. Peter can never let Sally down. I will never let you down," I finished, not knowing quite why or how I had come to say that.

"So, what you're saying," Charlotte started quietly, between suppressed sobs, "is that Sally has created Peter because she doesn't trust anyone else?"

"Perhaps," I answered, "or maybe because she's lonely. After all, you can never be lonely with an imaginary friend. Perhaps it's a combination of many things. Certainly you can have nothing to lose by trying to get closer to her, as long as she will let you, of course.

You will need to be patient, but mothers always know how to be patient with their children, and how best to love them." I was unsure about this, especially when I thought of my own mother, but I carried on. "Maybe you need to show that love a bit more. Just because you know your love for your daughter is genuine, doesn't mean that Sally does. Perhaps you should find a way to convince her of its presence and strength. Making time especially for her would be a good starting point."

"Oh dear," Charlotte wiped the tears off her other cheek, and moved back to her chair and the handbag she had left against it. "I'm sorry I was cross, Jack." She continued as she rummaged inside the bag and produced a white-laced handkerchief reminding me of the mother I had just been thinking about. "I expect my anger was really directed at myself, and not at you.

"You're right, of course. I suppose I do spend a lot of time with my friends, but that's because Sally is so distant with me, and there's always that wretched pretense between us. I will try hard to do as you suggest, but only if you keep your promise and talk to Sally on my behalf."

"I'll talk to Sally," I replied. "But only when you tell me that you have your trip organized. Perhaps if you let me know when you plan to go away, I'll invite her round the day before. How would that be?"

"That sounds a bit like blackmail," Charlotte responded, but she was smiling as she said it. "I'll see what I can do and let you know. I suppose you think I'm weak not to be able to sort this problem out on my own, but being a single parent isn't easy, and I know I don't do it very well. I will try to be stronger and sort out the priorities in our lives."

"That's something you don't need to do on your own, Charlotte." I suddenly felt as if she had missed the central core of my argument. "You are not alone – you have Sally, and the priorities you need to define are for both of you, not just you. As you have said many times, Sally is old enough now not to act like a child, she is also old enough not to be treated like a child. Perhaps she might even be included in the choice of venue for your excursion?"

"Ok, ok." Charlotte almost laughed. "You've made your point, Jack. Actually, now that I've got used to the idea, I'm quite excited about it. Sally's always loved horses, maybe we can find somewhere for the weekend with lots of horses."

"That's the spirit, Charlotte," I said, marveling at the depth of that simple phrase, and relieved to have her agreement. "Involve her in everything. But don't be put off if Peter puts his 'five eggs' into the discussion. Be prepared to listen to the ideas she feels 'he' should suggest rather than herself. It's a defensive mechanism, this Peter thing, and is bound to take a while to become unnecessary. If you are to earn her trust, you have to take Peter along as far as possible. I will do my best, once the holiday is planned, but bite your tongue and realize that where Peter wants to go is really Sally's choice. Your agreement will be all the more powerful if she thinks you are accepting Peter's suggestion."

"Well, I'll give it a go, Jack." Charlotte picked up her handbag and returned the handkerchief. "Thank you so much for your help."

"Thank me only if the plan is successful," I answered, taking her arm as she turned towards the sacristy door. "I'll be waiting for your signal as to when I should invite Sally to help me with leaf sweeping, or something. May God give you patience and the powers of understanding, dearest Charlotte, and may your spirit be lifted so that you too might benefit from this special weekend."

We had reached the door, and I held it open as Charlotte brushed past me a little more closely than necessary, and went down the two steps into the church.

"I'll see myself out, Jack. I will enjoy having the church to myself for a few moments. I am all excited now, about this plan, and feel more positive than I have for ages. Keep your fingers crossed for me. I'll let you know how I get on."

"I'll keep them crossed for Sally as well," I answered stubbornly. "The two of you have some interesting times ahead, and I wish you both God's blessings. I will await your dates, and now I must return to the sermon I was trying to write. Good luck, Charlotte, and thank you for seeing yourself out. Take your time. St. George's has much to offer."

I closed the door softly and returned to my desk. I turned my chair round to where it belonged, but didn't sit down. Instead, I knelt on the stone slabs next to it, balancing my head and hands upon the desk top. I needed reassurance – I had been speaking without planned thoughts, out of my depth regarding the subject matter, nervous about my irritation and with my unpremeditated suggestions.

"Dear God, help me to follow the path You have chosen for me. Help me to hear Your voice and recognize Your guidance. Help me to be worthy of Thy calling, Help me, please help me to do what is right, in Thy name."

I found it impossible to work on my sermon any more. Fortunately it was mostly finished, nothing spectacular, just an honest reaction to the text Father Justin had given me from the ninety-first Psalm, which was a favorite of mine anyway. I would put the final touches to it later. Right now, it was time to follow my mentor to the vicarage and divest myself of the responsibilities of my profession for a while.

I had promised Charlotte that I would never let her down – but in the end, of course, I did.

33. SAM

I n between the mother and daughter, came Helen Simmons's young son, Sam, who could hardly bring me challenging questions, I thought. I was wrong, and for the first time – but sadly not the last - I became really agitated and worried about advising so young a parishioner on such a personal matter.

I delivered my first sermon at evensong on the Wednesday after my arrival in Islington. I think it was well received by the six members of the congregation, and I was happy not to have had a larger audience.

With relief, I retired to the sacristy following the service to be congratulated by Father Justin before he scuttled home via the small side door. I tidied up the vestry and was removing my surplice when I heard the heavy clunk of the Western door and the sound of footsteps echoing towards the sacristy.

My pastoral duties were not yet finished, it seemed. I hurried to pull a dark blue sweater over my shirt, straightened my hair and reluctantly moved through the sacristy door to the main body of the church to meet my next challenge. There was a small figure advancing, which, as it came closer, I recognized to be that of Sam Simmons.

"Hello Sam," I said - the relief of finding so uncomplicated a parishioner giving my voice an extra shade of welcome. "What can I do for you today?"

Sam shuffled his feet and peered steadily at the floor immediately in front of him. "Can I ask you something personal, please father?" he said in a small voice.

"Of course," I responded, although my heart lacked the assurance of my voice. "Come into the sacristy, we won't be disturbed in there" and, with leaden feet, I led the way back from where I had just emerged.

With foreboding and a sense of déja-vu I repositioned the two chairs and tidied the papers on my desk. I moved my coffee cup to one side while indicating one of the chairs to Sam. "Would you like a cup of tea or coffee?" I asked, aware that I didn't have any drinks here that might appeal to the fourteen year old.

Sam shook his head as he climbed onto the chair. "No thank you father." His eyes remained focused upon his shoes.

There followed a silence that I thought would last forever until, suddenly I felt unnecessarily impatient. I cleared my throat, "Now," I was trying to sound gentle and interested but my feelings were running in contrary directions, "what was it that you wanted to talk to me about?"

"Is it true that when you talk to a priest, he cannot talk to anybody else?" Sam asked, with a quick upwards dart of the eyes.

"Of course," I reassured the boy while my heart sank wondering 'what on earth have we got coming now, and how long is it likely to take?' The strain of my first sermon had left me tired and, having been too pre-occupied to eat much lunch, I was looking forward to my supper.

"Well, I'm in trouble with my mum," the boy started, and the vision of Helen Simmons shot into my mind along with a picture of the crib-sheet which had 'over-protective mother' written beside her name.

"What sort of trouble, Sam?" I asked cautiously, trying hard to sound beneficent.

"She found my magazines," Sam explained with a sudden burst of courage, as if everything should now be crystal clear.

As the silence continued, I was forced to ask: "which magazines, Sam?"

"My secret mags – my friend James finds them for me, the one's with pictures of sexy women. The ones that show ladies as you don't usually see them." The speech had come out reluctantly, and then all at once he rushed: "the ones I masturbate over" and stopped suddenly as if the words had ejaculated themselves uninvited into this hallowed space, mimicking his supposed crimes.

Immediately, my mind went back to those noxious nights at Rossington and the anatomical pictures that had littered the dormitory floor. I felt a shudder of revulsion, and then again a wave of relief that Sam's was not such a drama as might have been supposed from his initial reluctance to talk.

"So, your mother found the magazines, and she's cross with you, is that it?" I was trying hard not to sound patronizing, without success, I fear.

"She's furious," sputtered Sam. "She says it is the work of the devil, and that I'll go to the hell, I will, if I keep doing it. But it's hard, Father Jack, very hard, not to let the feelings that surge up inside me explode. These pictures help me to get them out. Am I committing dreadful sins? Has the devil really got hold of me? What should I do? And please promise me you won't tell anyone."

I promised rather absent-mindedly, I'm afraid, being unsure what to say in response to Sam's enquiries. I was trying to hear the Lord's voice telling me how to proceed, but no celestial ideas presented themselves. Once again I would just have to muddle along, and hope for the best.

"It's certainly not the devil's work, Sam. Be assured of that, and you haven't assigned your soul to hell, not at all. I believe this is all part of puberty and is the normal behavior of boys, sorry, young men, of your age."

"Did you do it?" Sam was eager for reassurance.

"No," I answered carefully, "but then, Sam, I had a different calling from most people. I dedicated myself to God very early in life, so magazines of this sort didn't appeal to me."

"Are you a faggot, then?" Sam slapped his hand over his mouth as if that part of his anatomy had functioned unbidden and needed reprimanding.

"Certainly not," I was suddenly really angry. I took a deep breath and reminded myself that this was quite a reasonable question under the circumstances and I had no right to be so agitated and - it suddenly occurred to me – had no proof to the contrary. This last revelation took me aback, and I lost the train of thought I had been pursuing with which to sort out Sam's problems. I pulled myself back to the present situation with some effort, promising myself that I would deal with my own uncertainties anon.

"I thought we were here to discuss your problems, Sam," I returned to the fray. "I am comfortable with myself and with my love of Almighty God. My feelings are not a cause for anxiety, so let's return to yours.

"As I see it," I had found a path that seemed appropriate, "your mother is accusing you of dealing with the devil, when in fact you are just dealing with puberty, the way most boys do.

"In my opinion, and I stress that this is just my opinion, I believe that an act that does one person good and does not do anyone else any harm, cannot be deemed to be evil. I suppose it depends quite a lot on what you are thinking about as you masturbate" I found the word distasteful and was irritated by this prudery. "That's what probably dictates whether it is a positive experience for you or a negative one."

"Oh, it's always very positive," Sam was quick to re-assure me. "But it has nothing to do with religion. I mean nothing at all. It's just, I don't know, it's just - necessary."

"Well, Sam, it all seems very natural to me, and I stress again, that as long as it doesn't do anyone else harm and that your intentions are not base, there can be no evil in it."

"Can I tell my mother that you said it is OK?"

This took me aback somewhat. I decided to be courageous and replied: "If your mother has worries on the subject, certainly you can tell her to come and talk to me about them." I was not feeling anything like as confident as I hoped I sounded, and was gambling that Mrs Simmons would be far too embarrassed to confront me on the subject.

"Thank you, Father. You have been a great help. When you first came here and told me and my little sister that we could come and talk to you whenever we felt like it; I didn't realize how greatly I would appreciate the offer. I don't believe that I'm a bad person, but these feelings arrive uninvited and it's a lot easier to go with them than to try and shut them in. Anyway, anything that feels so good, can't be all bad, can it?" Sam fixed me with a questioning eye in which there was more than a trace of laughter – or was it excitement?

I disentangled our eyes with some discomfort. "Look, Sam, just be as discreet as possible. It isn't right that you should antagonize your mother like this. I may not agree with her reaction to what you are doing, but you must respect her sensibilities. It can't be easy for her to bring you and your sister up on her own, and especially you being a boy, she will not be able to empathize so readily with your problems." I wasn't sure that Sam would be familiar with the word empathize, but he hadn't the chance to edit my words. "You have to realize that you are the man of the family, and as such should act in a responsible way and be a help and support to your mother, not a worry."

"Yes, I understand what you're saying, Father." Sam was ready to obey, now that he had been given a guidance that he found acceptable and understandable. He also seemed to grow taller as I spoke of him being a man. "I will make sure mother doesn't find any more mags, and I am very grateful for this talk and to know that if she does give me a hard time again, I can tell her to talk to you. Thank you very much.

"I feel a lot better now than when I came." Sam got to his feet and moved to the door as if to make his escape. "I was so worried that you didn't really mean what you had said about us coming to see you, and now I know you're for real, the world has suddenly got a whole lot easier." He went out of the door, and then turned back briefly.

"I'll see you later, and thanks again," said Sam and allowed the sacristy door to thump closed behind him.

I had no choice but to return to my knees by the desk after Sam had gone. Not so much to ask for help regarding my words of advice, this time, as to beseech The Almighty to restrain Sam's mother from coming to see me.

At the time, I was genuinely worried about the caliber of the advice I had given the boy, but more upsetting still was the possibility of having to discuss masturbation with the neat and dignified Helen Simmons. Indeed, I was so distressed about the idea that I forgot all about my promise of secrecy to Sam and asked Father Justin for help that evening during supper.

As usual we were sitting opposite each other across the dining table. Elsie had left a shepherd's pie simmering on the hot plate with a dish of carrots alongside, and there was an apple crumble with a jug of custard to follow.

Father Justin asked after my 'day at the office,' as was his wont when we sat down to dine. It had been my turn to say grace, a challenge less grave than during our first couple of days together. These pre-prandial prayers had become a favorite of Father Justin's and it was now a habit between the two of us to find something different and evocative to say each evening, the piety of the speech dropping to third place behind the importance of wit and originality.

That evening's hasty composition had been delivered as follows: "May the shepherds who came to your birth, Oh mighty Lord, and who, in their wisdom taught us to eat their pies, share with us their reverence and humility as they have their provender. And may the stable that gave Our Lady shelter for the mystery of your birth be blessed along with this facsimile in edible form that you have provided for our repast. Amen."

"Bravo Jack," said father Justin laughing. "That was quick thinking, unless Elsie told you beforehand what was on the menu." I shook my head and tried to look offended by the suggestion.

"So how has your day been," he continued, "any parishioners with interesting problems for you to solve?"

I told him briefly about Charlotte Littleton's visit and glowed under the praise he gave me over the suggestions I had made and the courage he said I had shown by confronting the lady with some home truths.

"Then Sam Simmons came to see me, Father," I continued when most of the shepherds' pie had disappeared from our plates. "His mother had told him that masturbation was the work of the devil and he wanted to know if I thought the same."

Father Justin gave a great guffaw that made him choke. His eyes were watering as he took repeated sips of his wine. "Well, well, well," he sputtered through his mirth, "and what did you tell the young lad?"

I summarized the discussion and waited for my companion's opinion.

"Good work, Jack. Yes, I think you did well there too. I must say it's not what one expects on a peaceful Wednesday evening. Yes, I think you acquitted yourself and your church well."

"But what if Sam's mother takes up my offer and comes to me to condone her son's smutty behavior?" I asked nervously. "What am I going to say then?"

"Just reiterate what you told Sam," Father Justin replied, his eyes twinkling with merriment. "But don't worry, Jack, Helen will be far too embarrassed to talk to you about such a thing. I'll bet you six bottles of wine to a glass of water that she never does - how about it?"

I ignored the offered wager, not being as amused by the conversation as Father Justin and my doubts regarding my ability or worthiness to be giving advice suddenly erupted.

"I keep praying to the Lord for guidance, Father," I said, all in a rush. "I have no idea how to address these problems, most of which are quite alien to me. How do I know if I am saying the right things?"

"Don't you worry about young Sam Simmons, or his mother Helen for that matter." Father Justin realized that it was not appropriate to dwell on the jocularity of the situation. "You must have confidence in your calling and in God's ability to use you as an instrument of instruction.

"If Helen should ever raise the subject, and as I have said, I think it extremely unlikely, you should express the view that frustrations not expunged in this way will probably erupt in another; and this other way could be a lot worse than the one he is using at present. It could even become a permanent part of her son's personality – aggression, for example. You can always suggest plenty of physical activity – sports and so on. It is only a phase, after all."

Once again, I remembered the dormitory at Rossington, and then the dreadful night on the moors with Simon. I had doubts about the validity of this last sentence. I kept my counsel however, and was relieved that the conversation seemed to have finished.

After supper we repaired to the drawing room where it was our custom to sit in the two big armchairs and read until we felt like retiring. Father Justin had not gone straight to his chair, however, but busied himself at the bookcase, the index finger of his right hand following along the book titles. Having found what he wanted, he extracted a large book with a faded pink binding. He brought it over to where I was sitting in one of the shrouded bay windows.

"Going back to Sam's little problem, Jack," he said, "don't let the physical side of life upset you. I think you handled the situation very well – excuse the pun," he added with first a smile and then a chuckle.

"Your friends the Hindus have a healthy idea about communing with the Divine through physical pleasures. Have a look at this sometime," he continued, handing me the book he had chosen from the selves. "The Kama Sutra is a religious document, as far as they are concerned, and shows their ways of getting close to God by loosing hold of their humanity through the glories of sex. Actually, you don't need a partner to feel that sort of closeness with the Almighty, but it's bound to help.

"I've never tried it myself, but it's something I can't help regretting just a little, although I am fortunate in being able to feel that sort of super-natural intimacy without needing sex or drugs. Still if the end result is the same, the different ways of approaching the Divine shouldn't be looked upon critically. What do you think?" The old man had returned to his chair into which he now sank, placing his hands on his knees and peering across the room in expectation.

I felt the blood rising to my cheeks during this speech. I had given up my physical relationship with God some time ago, but still felt rather uncomfortable about the idea. The actions had been justified at the time, and indeed I still remembered the depth of religious fervor that my nocturnal sessions had inspired within my soul, but I had out-grown the need for such actions now, and could find myself close to God through mental activity alone.

I placed the large book carefully on the floor next to my feet. "Thank you father, I shall put it on my list of religious works to be studied. I am working on Geoffrey Farthing's explanation of Theosophy at the moment," I held up the book that had been on my knees. I knew that I sounded pompous and more than a little ridiculous, but was hiding behind the only prop available.

"Well, let me know how you get on with it, Jack," Father Justin's eyes had started to twinkle again, "I shall be interested in what you make of it." He picked up the periodical that waited for him on the arm of the chair.

We passed the rest of the evening in silence until I extricated myself from the ample armchair and picked up the proffered book. I tucked it under my arm along with my book on Theosophy. "Well, I'm off to bed" I said, "this Theosophy is very fascinating, I will let you have a look at this book, when I've finished with it. I would be interested to hear your views." Blushing, I realized I had paraphrased Father Justin's last comment. "Good night, then" I finished, rather lamely, and left the room as my mentor offered me similar wishes and waved a perfunctory hand without lifting his eyes from his reading.

34. AFTERNOON TEA

It was at least a fortnight after my conversation with Charlotte Littleton before she sent me a note saying that it was Sally's birthday the following week – she was turning thirteen. A riding weekend in Wales had been booked as her present. The writer reminded me of my part of the bargain and signed herself, 'affectionately, Charlotte.'

Not knowing how to persuade Sally to spend a few minutes with me alone, I took the problem to Father Justin and together we made a plan.

The next day was Sunday and, as usual, Charlotte and her daughter attended the morning service. After the final hymn and the blessing, the priest and his deacon stood side by side at the great western door shaking hands with our parishioners as we always did.

There was a steady drizzle outside that morning, making the tombstones glisten, tiny drops of moisture shone like miniature fairy lights along the cobwebs that threaded their way through the grass. The two of us stayed within the porch as the congregation emerged. Hands were shaken, pleasantries exchanged and a quick goodbye as each group or individual left the porch.

The column of people exited into the damp, umbrellas snapping open and being raised above the departing heads as they glided along the path and dropped out of view down the steps to Priory Road. I felt as if members of my flock were parachuting into enemy territory from the safety of the church and that Father Justin and I were their commanding officers sending them forth with the best armor we could provide.

Charlotte had thoughtfully lost her handbag and remained scuffling in her pew. Sally was busy telling her that she hadn't brought it that day, so obviously she was not going to find it. Charlotte finally agreed with her daughter, that she must have left it behind after all and they joined the back of the queue.

"A little bird tells me you're becoming a teenager next week, Sally." Father Justin had his hand on Sally's shoulder and was bending towards her in an avuncular pose. "Well, there's a tradition at St. George's that I have a little chat with all my parishioners who reach this great stage in their growing up, so now it will be your turn."

Sally's expression turned from the smile that had greeted the statement about her birthday to a look of defiance. She tried to extricate herself from the priests restraining hand.

"Oh, it isn't as bad as all that." Father Justin said with a chuckle not letting go of his grasp. "But, oh dear," he continued with a sudden look of dismay. "I'm so busy this week," he gave a dramatic pause before continuing. "I know, perhaps our new deacon can have the chat with you instead. How would that be, Sally?"

A look of relief spread across the girl's face as she looked at me. I had just finished saying goodbye to her mother. I raised my eyebrows in mock surprise and shrugged my shoulders at Sally with a questioning look, which I hoped was also friendly. Father Justin released her shoulder and patted the girl on the back. "Find a time to suit the two of you," he said as she moved away, "and if you can't arrange anything, then I'll make sure to find some time myself the following week." He turned into the church and disappeared.

"Well, I don't know what that was all about," I lied, somewhat unconvincingly. "Any way I was hoping you would come to visit. When do you think you could spare a few minutes?"

"I'll have to ask Peter." Sally was looking at me cautiously.

"Of course. Is he here now?" I asked.

"Yes, he comes everywhere with me, don't you Peter?" Sally indicated the space to her right.

"Well, can we ask him right now, then?" I said quickly. "How about after school tomorrow?"

There was a pause while Sally consulted the space next to her, not with words, but with gestures of the hands and head.

"No, Peter has football practice on Mondays, and I have netball. But Thursday would be alright for both of us."

"Thursday it is then," I answered as brightly as I could. "How about a cup of tea in the Priory Café at around four-thirty? Father Justin didn't say we had to meet in the church, and I have a soft spot for their currant scones." This made me think of Estelle with a warm feeling of excitement.

Sally shrugged her shoulders in reluctant agreement and with a "come on Peter" directed at nowhere in particular, she was off down the wet path in pursuit of her mother.

I gave a lot of thought about my date with Sally on the coming Thursday. I went to the library and found a few books on child psychology and read everything I could about imaginary friends. In all the quoted cases, there seemed nothing decidedly negative about the idea. A combination of time and puberty seemed to dispense with the problem eventually, and there were no recommendations other than to let the syndrome run its course as quietly and calmly as possible.

One book in particular spent as much time discussing the effects on the parents of this phenomenon as on the exhibitor. "A mother, especially, can become unconsciously jealous of her child's choosing an imaginary person in whom to confide instead of herself" - the author claimed – a Professor of Child Psychology at Edinburgh University –and gave over two or three pages to descriptions of the parents' reactions to the syndrome rather than to the child's.

I found this particularly interesting, and wondered how I could use this information to help both Charlotte and Sally without infuriating the former and losing the trust of the latter. As always, it was to God I turned for help with the dilemma - what an irony that now appears to me - and yet again found myself floundering on my own.

On the Thursday afternoon, I arrived at the café early and organized a table set for three in the corner by the window. It had been raining earlier, but now the sun was making its presence felt through the slow-moving clouds, turning dull puddles into sky-mirrors and causing the wet pavements to shine.

From my frequent visits to the tearoom, I had got to know the various waitresses of the Priory Café. Today, Vera was on duty. A bustling lady in her early sixties, she busied herself making her customers feel cared for. Short and rather plump, she wore her apron with pride and this attire, combined with the round glasses which perched on the end of her nose, reminded me of Mrs. Tiggy-Winkle. In my thoughts I referred to her, affectionately as Mrs. T.W. but not to her face. Addressing her by her proper name, I explained the relevance of the third place, which was to be laid but would remain unoccupied. She listened with nods of motherly understanding.

"Poor little dear," she said, "she must be missing something at home in order to fabricate a friend like that. Don't you worry, Father, I'll play along alright. What's the imaginary friend called?"

"Peter," I answered, "but I don't think you should know anything about him, or Sally will know we've been talking about her."

"Right you are, then, Father. Leave it to me, I'll be the soul of discretion, you see if I'm not." Vera gave me a pronounced wink, which was not at all comforting or reassuring. She went to fetch the place settings.

Charlotte and Sally were still some distance from the café when I spotted them making their way along the pavement. They were walking with rapid strides up the hill towards the church, on the far side of the street. Charlotte looked at her watch and grabbed Sally's hand, the better to pull her along. I looked at mine, it was already five minutes past our allotted time.

When the two hurrying figures reached the arched gate of the path leading up to the church, they turned towards the café, threaded their way between the parked cars, looked carefully up and down the hill, and made their way across the road. Stepping over the puddle by the curb, they crossed the pavement and entered the café.

I rose from the table and started towards the door. Charlotte had seen me and was pushing Sally in front of her, through the tables.

"Oh, I'm not staying Father," Charlotte said, eyeing the table laid for three. "This is to be just the two of you – that's what Father Justin insisted on" she said falteringly. "I've got some shopping to do. I'll be back shortly after five, will that be alright?"

"Yes, of course, Charlotte," I shook her hand and then patted her on the shoulder. She looked like someone who could use a big hug, but a pat was all I could offer. Her distress was in sharp contrast to the calm indifference shown by her daughter. I thought of the books I had been reading and couldn't help feeling sorry for her. "That will give us plenty of time for our tea, scones and cake – I've ordered a proper tea for us, I hope that's OK with you, Sally?"

Sally gave me a shy smile, extricated herself from her mother's grip and squeezed past to take a seat at the table.

"Don't worry, Charlotte, everything is going to be fine," I suddenly found myself feeling unusually confident as I led her towards the door. "Give us three quarters of an hour - that should be plenty of time. Would you like me to order some tea for you when you come back?"

"No thank you, Father. Oh, I do hope you can do something about this wretched 'Peter' – it's been driving me to distraction. I did as you suggested and invited him along for this riding weekend, and now she wants me to rent a pony for him as well as for her – I don't know what to do, I really don't. The whole thing is quite ridiculous and I am finding it very hard to go along with it, as you said I should."

"You're off tomorrow, aren't you?" I said, as we reached the door.

"Tomorrow after school, yes. We should be at the riding centre in time for supper. I don't know why I let you talk me into this crazy idea. It's all going to be so embarrassing."

"No, it won't, Charlotte." I spoke firmly but – I hoped – kindly. "Just wait and see what happens this weekend. I am optimistic that it could be a new beginning for both of you." I was tempted to say 'all three of you' but thought the humor might be unappreciated. I closed the door softly behind the reluctant mother and turned back towards Sally who had made herself comfortable in the chair with its back to the tea-room.

I sat down opposite my guest, the empty place between the two of us. "Of course, the place wasn't for your mother anyway," I began, indicating the vacant chair, "it's for Peter. Thank you both for coming, I've ordered the tea, it should be here any minute. How was school today?"

Sally fidgeted with the chair next to her. She pulled it out, pushed it back in, took the napkin from the plate and spread it carefully on the seat. "There, that should be fine," she said regarding the scene with her head on one side. "School was O.K. I suppose – the usual taunts from the bullies. I came top of the class in geography, you see, and they don't like that. Geography is Peter's favorite subject and he helps me with my homework, that's why I always do so well. The others are angry, but it's not my fault they haven't a Peter to help them."

"I ask Jesus for help, when I'm stuck with a problem," I suddenly found a new approach to the subject - maybe God was helping me after all. "It's a great comfort knowing that you have a really good ally who you can trust in all ways, isn't it? I always count myself lucky for the faith I have in Jesus, it means I'm never alone and no one can upset me because I have his love and friendship to support me. Is it a bit like that with Peter?" Oh, how these words would come to haunt me.

"Yes," Sally answered with enthusiasm, "only Jesus is for everyone, and Peter is just for me – he's my own, very special friend."

"I find that people get embarrassed if I start talking to Jesus out loud." I had found a theme. "Even though I'm taking holy orders and work in the church, it still makes them uneasy. You're right when you say Jesus is for everyone, but not everybody realizes that, not everybody knows they have such a special friend. You, for instance, Sally, you have two special friends, Peter and Jesus. That's good - Jesus had a best friend called Peter during his time here on earth.

"However, you choose to talk to Peter more than to Jesus. But Jesus can wait. He has infinite patience, and even though he is there for all of us, he treats us with individual attention, love and care. Divine beings can do that. I hope you'll discover that for yourself one day.

"But in the meantime," I had been drifting from my chosen message, "we have to be discreet about our special personal friendships, if they make other people feel ill at ease. Do you understand what I mean?"

"No," said Sally stubbornly, "what's the point in having a friend if you have to keep it a secret?"

Just then Vera arrived with a tray laden with sandwiches, slices of cake and scones. A teapot, milk jug, sugar bowl and little dishes of butter, jam and clotted cream completed the load and were all solemnly placed upon the table.

"Now, how does the young man like his tea?" Vera held the teapot and hovered it over the cup in the middle of the table. Sally looked at her sharply, and then at me – I could feel the blush rising to my face.

"We'll help ourselves, thank you Vera," I said quickly, picking up a plate of sandwiches and passing them to Sally.

Vera put the teapot down with a thump of disappointment. "As you please, father," she said, with an air of an actress interrupted at the start of a performance. She turned and bustled back towards the kitchen.

"You pour the tea, Sally, please," I said, leaving the choice of two or three cups being filled to her. "I have a little milk and two sugars. Oh good, there are plenty of egg sandwiches, they're my favorite." I helped myself to a couple of tiny, carefully cut sandwiches. "Now where were we, are yes, discretion – do you know what the word means, Sally?" Vera obviously did not, I thought to myself.

"Doesn't it mean keeping things secret?" Sally answered, as she maneuvered the teapot with great concentration. I noticed that Peter didn't get any, and thought that a good sign.

"Not exactly," I answered. "It means being careful not to upset other people. It means avoiding saying or doing things that you know will cause hurt, anguish or embarrassment. I avoid bringing Jesus into conversations, for example, because I know it makes other people uncomfortable. So, although I talk to Him all the time, I keep the conversations within my soul, not out loud. That way nobody else knows, and I have Him all to myself.

"Did it ever occur to you, Sally, that your mother might be jealous of Peter?"

Sally stared at me in amazement, her sandwich arrested in mid air, her mouth opened slightly to receive it. "What do you mean?" she said, returning the sandwich to her plate uneaten. She leaned forward, took another sandwich and put it firmly on the empty plate between them. She was making a point.

"You're about to be thirteen, Sally. You're no longer a little girl, and I am not talking to you as a little girl. I need this conversation to be just between you and me – and Peter of course – it is not meant for anyone else, do you understand that, and are you happy with the idea?"

"Of course," Sally sat up straight in her chair. "You're right, I'm not a child any more, and I'm perfectly happy with an adult conversation. As you say, I'm thirteen now - my birthday was yesterday, actually - and I take a size twelve dress."

This last piece of information meant nothing to me at all, but I realized, by the way she said it, that it was a declaration of her grown up status - beyond question. "Yes," I continued, leaning across the table towards her, "but are you happy about this conversation remaining between just us?" I gestured around the table.

"Go ahead, Father," Sally looked me straight in the eye. "I'm grown up enough to know how to keep a secret – how to be discreet, too, I think."

"Splendid, Sally, I knew you would be, but thought I should make it absolutely clear." I coughed nervously, pushing a piece of cake around my plate with an absurdly small fork. "The truth is, Sally, I think – and I must stress this is just my personal opinion, and I haven't spoken to anyone else about it – I think that your mother is jealous of Peter."

Sally was about to interrupt, but I raised a hand and continued. "Mothers find it hard when their children stop coming to them for comfort, advice, friendship and love. It has to happen to everyone as their children grow up. They have to learn to let go. But they never stop loving their children, no matter how old they are. That sort of love is always there.

"With your mother being a single parent, and you an only child, the bond between the two of you must be especially strong, and what I'm suggesting is that, quite unknowingly, maybe your mother resents your having found someone else to do all the things that she would like to do for you herself. Do you see what I mean?"

Sally was staring at her plate where the sandwich remained. She didn't speak.

"Growing up is a difficult and complicated business," I continued, not sure where I was going now that I'd delivered the main thrust of our 'adult' conversation. "Not just for the young person concerned, but for his or her family also. Adjustments have to be made as a child becomes a girl, the girl becomes a young lady, the young lady becomes a woman, and so on. Your mother has to adjust to your not needing her all the time, she has to come to terms with the fact that you will confide in other people, that you are no longer dependent upon her for everything.

"What I am asking you, Sally, when I mentioned discretion, was that you consider your mother's feelings when you discuss things with Peter. She probably doesn't realize that she is jealous of Peter, but you know he makes her angry, and I'm sure it's all because she loves you, as only a mother can. She may not tell you very often, but then perhaps, you don't give her the opportunities you used to – you have made a new life with Peter, a life from which she is excluded. Her anger may come from the unhappiness she feels inside at loosing you. Do you understand what I'm trying to say?"

I stopped in a panic. Tears were running down Sally's face, her head bent low, her hands in her lap twirling the napkin through her fingers.

"Here," I said pulling a handkerchief out of a trouser pocket and passing it across the table. "Wipe your eyes, and blow your nose. I'm sorry, I didn't mean to make you cry. This is a very difficult conversation to have, and any grown up with sensitivity would be crying by now – as a matter of fact I'm tearful myself." This last was not strictly true, as I felt my mother had not been distressed in any way by my growing up.

Sally used the handkerchief as directed and raised her head. She gave her hair a shake and squared her shoulders as she passed the handkerchief back.

"Thank you," she said, more to the handkerchief than to its owner. "What you've said actually makes quite a lot of sense to me. Mum has always been reluctant to let me go to do anything on my own, and you're right, she has always been very angry about Peter. But he's my friend, and I'm not going to give him up."

This last sentence was said with defiance, as she picked the sandwich from the plate between them and ate it steadily.

"But you don't have to give him up." I was quick to reassure her. "All I'm suggesting is that you are discreet about him, as I am about my relationship with Jesus Christ. I know He is always with me, but I don't lay a place for him at the table or talk to him loudly in front of other people.

"Peter can still be your friend, but why not make him your secret friend. He can still accompany you everywhere, but perhaps he can sit on your knee, or behind you when you ride, that sort of thing. That way you can keep him close to you without upsetting your mother. You know, Sally, I really feel that your mother misses having you all to herself – she'll have to get used to it, of course, but may be you could be a bit more gentle with her. Try to talk to her, as you chat with Peter now, and keep your conversations with Peter until you are on your own.

"Can Peter read your thoughts, Sally? I mean can he tell what's going on in your head, even if you don't speak out loud?"

"Of course he can," Sally answered. "That's how he talks to me, but I like to talk to him out loud."

"Do you think you could try, just for this weekend, to talk to him only in your head, so that your mother won't get upset?"

"That's being discreet, isn't it?" Sally answered.

"Being discreet, and being very grown up," I was quick to point out. "Discretion is not something you expect to find in a child. Do you think you and Peter could accommodate such an idea, that you both could be more diplomatic about your relationship and keep it as a special secret between just the two of you?"

"I'll have to talk to Peter about it, of course," Sally answered, putting a piece of cake onto the middle plate. "But I don't like the idea of making Mum unhappy, even though she is very tough with me a lot of the time."

"Maybe she won't be so tough on you if she feels that Peter isn't occupying all your attention. Peter, I know is a real friend to you, and as such he can't want to see you causing your mother distress. I'm sure he won't mind pretending, with you, that she's as important to you as he is. Why not ask him right now? You can practice talking to him in your head, the way he always talks to you."

Sally gave me a quizzical look. She munched thoughtfully on a scone, and then suddenly turned to the empty chair, her head tilted on one side, wisps of fair hair falling across her face. She brushed the strands aside as her head nodded a little, shook a little, then nodded again. Finally she returned her gaze to me.

"Peter is happy to give your idea a go – just for the weekend, and then we'll decide what to do next. You are right about him not wanting to upset Mum. Peter wouldn't deliberately upset anyone."

"I didn't think he would," I said piling cream and jam onto a scone with a sigh of relief. "Thank you Sally for listening to me. I do hope it all works out for all three of you. I know your mother has put a lot of effort into arranging this weekend; it's just another way of her saying how much she loves you. Hugs say a lot also, and don't feel you're ever too old for a hug – your mother certainly isn't, so how could you be?

"Anyway, tell me about the riding centre you're going to - have you been there before?"

By the time Charlotte returned from her self-imposed exile, I had heard all about the riding centre they were about to visit. Sally went on to tell me about how much she loved being with the ponies and all the different things she hoped to do with them in the future. She was chatting away happily when her mother came to collect her.

I got to my feet as Charlotte approached the table. "Well we've had a splendid tea, Charlotte," I said, "as you can see from the empty plates. Sally has just been telling me about the place you're going to tomorrow. It all sounds very exciting, although I don't know one end of a horse from the other, myself. I'm looking forward to hearing all about it when you come back."

Sally rose also and lent towards the empty chair with an outstretched arm. Then she caught my eye, and let the arm drop. To my amazement, she winked at me. I could feel a big smile creasing into my usually solemn face, and beamed at the girl as she straightened, turned and greeted her mother. "Hello, Mum. Did you have a good time shopping and, - where are all your bags?" she enquired as she put her arms around her mother's neck and gave her a kiss on the cheek.

Charlotte was so amazed she couldn't answer straight away. Then she looked at her daughter with delight, and then at me. There were tears in her eyes. "Oh I couldn't find anything I liked," she responded finally to the shopping question, "so in the end I didn't buy anything. We should be getting home soon, Sally, there's lots to do before we leave tomorrow. Thank Father Jack for the tea, and we'll be getting along."

I moved around the table to accompany them to the door. Catching Vera's eye I made a scribbling gesture; she nodded and pulled her order pad from the pocket of her apron.

"Have a great birthday weekend, Sally," I put an arm around the girl's shoulders and gave her a gentle squeeze. "Are you going to be riding also, Charlotte," I was eager to keep the conversation light.

"I haven't made my mind up yet," Charlotte answered. "It depends on the horses and what they have planned for us. I don't want to be holding Sally back, she's very talented, you know, given how seldom she has done this sort of thing."

"Well, I look forward to hearing how you've both got on. How about tea again next week? I won't be seeing you this Sunday, but give the vicarage a ring if you feel like a reunion." I smiled as I waved them both goodbye and turned back into the café in search of Vera and the bill.

Scones at The Priory Tea Room

I had prayed long and hard for guidance as to how to talk to Sally about the imaginary Peter. I knew there was a risk, speaking to her about her mother, but could see no other way to lift the girl's obsession and make her look outside herself. On the whole, I thought, it had gone well, as long as Sally could be trusted to keep the conversation to herself. Charlotte's faith in me would be totally shattered if she learnt about the nature of our talk.

That evening, back on my knees in the basement flat, I again sought confirmation from the Almighty that I had done the right thing. I had been following Father David's premise that God would lead me through the emotional quagmires of the parishioners, even if I wasn't aware of being so guided. I waited a long time, kneeling on the wooden floor, head bowed against the side of the bed, to hear - or rather to feel – some blessing which would ease my mind and give me confidence that I was, indeed, doing God's Will. I was never sure that any came through, but then berated myself for not recognizing the blessings that must surely be there. God would not desert one of his own. Jesus must be with me through all, otherwise . . . No, there could be no otherwise.

I wrote about this episode while in St. Mary's 'Day Room'. My two incapacitated friends were eager for new topics of conversation and had demanded a description of my parishioners and their problems. In retrospect, I suppose these dives into a past I had long ceased to think about were beneficial for all of us. It amused Percival and Amrita and it allowed me to exorcise doubts and difficult experiences while distracting all of us from our physical pains and limitations.

I remember clearly the afternoon in which I described the episode. The stark African sunshine which hit the bay windows was such a contrast to the dim light of The Priory Café which I tried to recreate for Percival and Amrita. The scene seemed so very far away emotionally as well as in time and place; the cozy, rather self-satisfied, young vicar I was speaking of seemed to have no relationship to the dour man who was now telling the tale.

I began with my research into the imaginary friend invention where I found many positive elements quoted about the syndrome - all having to do with filling emotional and social gaps in a child's life, rather than attention-seeking ploys. By its very definition, an imaginary friend could be easily manipulated to support – or even deliver - any argument about which the real child is shy or uncomfortable to confront themselves. With an imaginary friend as a constant companion, loneliness is impossible, and isolation by one's peers therefore cannot exist even as a threat. Another advantage is that the most intimate of confidences can be 'shared' without fear of disclosure and ridicule. In an argument, a child is never alone in their defense or attack, and therefore can never really lose.

What I remember most vividly about relating this story at St. Mary's, was being struck with sudden anguish. The research I was talking about, I suddenly realized, was the story of my own childhood, adolescence and beyond.

"What's wrong, Jack?" Percival told me that my face had suddenly contorted.

"Well," I said slowly, "as predicted, Sally did grow out of needing her imaginary friend. I've just realized that I too have finally outgrown mine. It just took me a lot longer than Sally.

"I actually used the analogy of the love and confidence I had in Jesus Christ to Sally, to explain that I knew how she felt. At the time I thought this just a clever guise. I am shattered, all of a sudden, to realize this wasn't an analogy at all, it was a truth.

"All those years of believing there was someone to whom I could confide my inner-most thoughts, to whom I could turn for succor and counsel, who listened to me, guided me and looked after me. My imaginary friend of all those years, called: Jesus or God. And the great irony of it all is that I prayed to my imaginary friend for guidance in how to deal with Sally's. It's almost laughable."

There was silence in the day room for some time as dusk fell upon the garden, night crept up the lawn from the river and the crickets began their descant to the bull-frogs' bass.

35. THE PROBLEM WITH PHILIP

During my first few weeks in office in Islington, my nervousness abated as I participated in the regular services of the church. Sometimes I would be the server, helping the vicar with the communion hosts, and sometimes Father Justin would ask me to lead the service while he sat back, watched and listened.

As time passed, I spent more and more time in front of the congregation, intoning the prayers, giving the sermons and administering the sacraments and blessings. I learnt to give more meaning to certain phrases by lowering the timbre of my voice, to talk and move slowly where emphasis was necessary, and to speed things up at points where the congregation was bound to get restless.

Every morning, before breakfast, I said my own private prayers, kneeling at the side of the small bed. I would thank God for making me one of His servants and ask for help in fulfilling my duties. Then I would rise, don my cassock with a small thrill and sense of achievement, and climb the stairs to meet the new day – the skirt of the robe held in one hand, my prayer book in the other. It was as if, when I put on the collar and robe of my calling, I became a different being, one with assurance and inner peace; and one quite removed from the self-conscious, nervous youth of school and college days. Father Justin always welcomed my appearance at the breakfast table with enthusiasm and we would plan the division of the day's work over toast and marmalade.

The relationship between Father Justin and myself was growing in mutual appreciation and our friendship communicated itself to our parishioners with very positive results. Father Justin remarked upon how much lighter the atmosphere had become during the church services, and how more people lingered to chat when the worship was over. We had even managed to attract and keep a few new followers.

"At this rate we'll be doing Christmas fairs and summer fêtes," Father Justin had exclaimed after a particularly busy Sunday service. "And for the first time in my life, I think I'm quite looking forward to them."

"We'll have a band of happy helpers, if you do decide to go ahead," I answered, "and I think it would do well to bring the community together in a social atmosphere rather than just a spiritual one."

"Go ahead and organize whatever you want, my boy." Father Justin answered, "but I shall leave you to keep those worthy ladies off my back with their cream teas and endless cakes." And then, after a pause, "but I'll look after George Stanhope and his wine, plus Dilly and her Scotch can be my department also – maybe we could have a bottle stall!"

"You see - you're involved already." I laughed with delight. "It's no use pretending it's going to be all my doing."

As the weeks merged into months, I continued to grow into my new family – as Father Justin had described the parishioners – with cautious progress. Rosie was always one of my favorites, but I became attached to others as well. With Philip, however, I always had difficulty. There was something about the pale, emaciated lad that was very hard to like. I did my best to keep uncharitable thoughts at bay, but it was an uphill struggle that required many a supplication to the Almighty for assistance. There was something unhealthy about him, something that needed a good dose of fresh air and sunshine.

Although the lad was in his early twenties, it was impossible to think of him as being any more mature than the thirteen year old Sally, or even Rosie, who was only twelve.

It was usually early evening when Philip descended upon St. George's. He would sidle into the church, as if the door would not open far enough for him to enter properly.

At Philip's request, we would sit at the back of the church, near the wonderfully carved stone font that dates back to the twelfth century. During our discussions I spent most of the time examining the intricacies of the leaves and flowers that some ancient artisan had painstakingly chiseled around the font's lip and sides.

The first time Phillip told me that he was no longer good enough for this world and that he would soon be standing face to face with his maker, I was seriously distressed. I placed my hands on the boy's shoulders, turning him so that we faced each other, peering deeply into the narrow, bloodshot eyes. Surely there must be something in there, I prayed, that could be pulled out of the mire to set this troubled spirit onto a healthy and fulfilling path.

"It's no good, father." Philip had wailed, "I can't cope without the drink, and when I drink I get bad, really bad. I don't want to be bad. I want to be good, but I have to drink. The world will be better off without me. I just have to find the right time and place. Then it'll be all over, and nobody will care, or even notice."

I did all I could to dissuade the young man from this chosen route; to explain God's love and powers of forgiveness; to point out all the positive things Phillip had in his life compared to so many others.

"You have your health, Philip, with a full set of working limbs and senses. You are young and strong" - 'well physically strong, anyway,' I thought to myself - "and have your whole life ahead of you. A life you can make into something joyous, or one you can allow to slip into despondency. It's your call, Philip – why even contemplate such a negative move when you have so much that is positive? Don't you see that what you are contemplating is an insult to The Almighty who gave you so many attributes?

"I genuinely feel," I was warming to the subject, "that it is up to each one of us to celebrate the great gifts of God by enjoying them to the full, as a way of praising the Lord and showing appreciation for his generosity. What you suggest is to flout His great kindness and fling his greatest gift – life - back at Him. You must sort this out, Phillip. Can drink really be all that is to blame for this morose disposition, or is it the devil himself who has crawled into your guts and dined on your courage and love of life?

"Take stock of your thoughts and ideas. Root out and destroy these loathsome ruses that are the devil's own." I was beginning to get carried away, becoming uncharacteristically charismatic – but I couldn't help it, I was in a panic. "Find your courage again, Philip, and use it to conquer this evil. If you feel that drink is exacerbating the problem then turn yourself away from its temptations. Find comfort, instead, in the wonders of God's world around us. There is so much to see and do for good if you take the trouble to look properly."

Together we prayed for guidance, strength and help, and when he left, Philip assured me that he felt a little better and stronger. He would try to reform himself along the lines suggested and would be looking for further encouragement and assistance from me very soon. A prospect I did not relish.

That evening, over supper, I asked Father Justin for his advice on what I could do when Phillip returned.

"Oh, he's been threatening suicide again, has he?" the elderly vicar said between mouthfuls of pork pie and salad. "Don't get too perturbed about it, dear Jack, I told you he was a problem. The wretched lad just wants attention and gets it by misbehaving when drunk or bothering us with his threats. He is a sad case and certainly not an easy one. He pays absolutely no heed to whatever you say. The moment he's out of the door, he's straight down to the pub. Let me ask you – did he come to talk to you at shortly after five and stay for about an hour?"

I reflected upon the timing of Phillip's visit. "Yes, I think you're right. In fact the clock was chiming six as he left."

"There you go, Jack. Phillip works at the service station down the road. He finishes work at five, and has nothing to do until the pubs open at six. That's when he puts on his emotional displays for us to deal with. Who else will put up with his morose mental wanderings, and who else will pay him the close attention he craves?

"Try not to worry too much about the lad. I know it is difficult, and you'll soon run out of things to say to him. Let's hope that the adage of 'those who talk about it never do it' is correct, as far as his suicide threats are concerned. Certainly he's been on the same theme ever since he first walked into St. George's, several years ago. I remember well being as concerned as you are now, after my first meeting with him.

"Let's put him out of our minds during dinner at any rate, or we'll both get indigestion. Have some of this lovely claret – George has found a new favorite - it's only a second growth but drinks like a first. Gruard Le Rose is the name of the chateau, it's a real winner, so smooth and so subtle on the tongue."

The wine accordingly diluted my concerns about Phillip and the evening's talk moved to more positive topics.

In time, I allowed myself to get quite cross with Philip, but nothing seemed to change, and the lad still came into the church two or three evenings a week, and was always there on Sundays, closely followed by the girl Tracy.

36. DELIGHTFUL, DELICIOUS DILLY

Dilly was at the other end of the spectrum from Phillip when it came to my affections for the parishioners of St. George's. This wonderful bundle of energy with her vivacious smile and bright attire always brought laughter into the church.

Dilly's first visit found me at my desk in the sacristy, one late afternoon. I heard the click of the western doors swinging shut followed by the tripping sound of a pair of high-heeled shoes coming ever closer.

"Coo-ee" was the unexpected salutation that heralded the visitor's approach. It was followed by a rhythmic knock on the door and Dilly came into the vestry before I had time to answer.

"Hello Dahlia," I rose to greet her, pleased to see such a bright vision disturb the permanent dusk of this part of the church. Only the lamp on my table fought the dimness of the high-ceilinged circular room whose single window depicted the scene of St. George and the dragon with such intricacy that the outside light found it hard to make any impression within.

Dahlia was dressed in a bright red mini-skirt atop patent leather, high-heeled boots of the same color. Her blouse was of a startling purple under a jacket of light blue. The make-up above her large eyes reflected the shades of her attire and her hair fanned out from her face in waves of auburn curls.

"Oh please call me Dilly, – especially if I can call you Jack." She spoke in a bright voice with laughter bubbling beneath the surface. "You did say I could didn't you? It's ridiculous," she continued as I nodded assent, "to call someone 'father' who must be six to eight years younger than yourself. Any chance of a cup of tea," she added looking pointedly at the top shelf of the bookcase where the necessary paraphernalia for making and serving both tea and coffee was kept.

"Of course," I turned quickly, pleased to have something to do. The kettle had just been refilled from the tap outside the South door.

"How do you like your tea, Dilly?" the name sounded ridiculous to me, but it made my visitor smile with obvious delight.

"Milk and no sugar, please," she answered. "I hope you don't mind my coming for a chat. But I've been a bit down in the dumps recently - which is out of character for me, and very bad for my job. So I thought I'd come and get rid of some of my worries on you, as I haven't anyone else who I can really talk to whose objectivity and discretion I can trust."

"That's my job, Dilly," I responded, trying to keep a note of pride out of my voice, "and also my pleasure, I'm sure. Aren't we lucky, those of us who choose a profession that we enjoy?" The blood came rushing to my face, as I realized what I had said. I tried to hide my embarrassment in a fit of coughing, and then, pulling myself together with what shred of dignity I had left, continued: "you certainly brighten up the place and I'm delighted that you feel happy to talk to me. As I intimated - what else am I here for?"

Dilly took her mug of tea and busied herself trying to sip the too-hot liquid to disguise the giggles that I could see rising to her lips. "Yes, and I'm grateful," Dilly put down her mug and looked at me with unnerving candor. "I like you already, Jack. You are completely different to dear old Father Justin in whom I have confided for the last five or six years. There is always something wistful about Father Justin when we have our chats, as if he might have, or could have, or wished he had. . . .

"Perhaps it would be helpful if you knew a bit about my background?" Dilly asked, suddenly losing her confidence and seeming unsure of where to begin. "I wasn't always in my current line of work," she continued when I had nodded agreement to her suggestion. "I imagine Father Justin has told you the nature of my profession – the oldest in the world, and all that." I nodded again, not daring to speak, or more accurately, not knowing what I would say if expected to contribute to the conversation.

"I had a turbulent adolescence – I suppose everybody does – but I had been blessed - or cursed - with these things" Dilly indicated her impressive bosoms, "and got more than my share of attention from members of the opposite sex. However, I had my principles and refused to lose my virginity until I was married. As a result of these high morals, I was married at seventeen to a Lothario of twenty-six who was intent upon stealing my jewel. I thought he was wonderful. He was good-looking, suave, sophisticated - or so I thought - and most important of all, every girl I knew threw herself at him. He chose me. We were married with my mother's blessing – which I had to have as I was under eighteen, and my father died when I was fifteen – and we went off to live happily ever after in Bayswater.

"Well, that was all fine until two months later I found I was pregnant. Of course Tony pretended to be pleased as punch – mostly I think he really was pleased, but pleased with his potency, not with the reality of the situation. I used to watch him brag to his friends in the pub as my belly started to swell. I was quite proud at first – no that's not fair, I was very proud – but then I started to get tired before he did and wanted to go home to sleep. The closer we got to the birth, the less I saw of him and by the time little Fiona was born – that's Fifi who you met – the wretched sod had buggered off with a girl with a waist like the one I had had just nine months earlier. Sorry about the language, Jack, but believe me it's appropriate."

I shrugged my shoulders and smiled. Dilly was leaning on an empty part of the shelf that ran along the edge of one wall. She was framed by hymn-books on one side and prayer-books on the other. Now she moved to the chair opposite mine, and we sat facing each other. She put down her empty mug. "Would you like some more?" I asked, jumping up again.

"No thank you, Jack, that was fine thank you." She waved me to be seated, definitely in charge of this interview. "To be honest I'd much rather have a glass of whisky."

"I'm sorry, Dilly," I raised my hands in a gesture of helplessness. "There's nothing like that here."

Dilly gave a broad smile. "Have a look in the second drawer down on the left." She was pointing at the big oak chest over by the casement where the robes hung.

I raised an eyebrow of enquiry, Dilly nodded encouragingly. Obediently I stood up once again, feeling a little like a Jack-in-the-box - a thought that made me smile as I approached the heavy piece of furniture. It was divided into two rows of deep drawers. I had never had cause to open any of them.

Just as Dilly had predicted, there was a bottle of Scotch and a couple of glasses where she had indicated. I turned back towards her with the bottle and one of the glasses held aloft.

"Well, you know your way around here better than I do. Do you think Father Justin will mind?"

"Don't be silly, Jack, it's my whisky. We're lucky there's still some in the bottle, although it doesn't look as if he's left us much. I usually bring one over every couple of weeks, but I haven't been here for almost a month. You must be a good influence on Father J. I'm glad you've come, Jack – for my sake if not for yours. But you've only brought one glass," she concluded with a note of disapproval.

"Thanks, but no thanks," I responded quickly, as I re-took my chair. "I'm happy with my tea. Would you like some water?" I added, pouring what was left of the whisky into the glass.

"No thanks, ducks. This'll do just fine, thank you," said my colorful visitor, shifting in the chair like a mother hen fluffing her feathers over a brood of chicks. "Now, how far had I got?"

Fortunately for me, Dilly didn't wait for an answer. I had lost the thread somewhat with the surprise of finding the whisky.

"Ah yes, the abandoned wife with a screaming baby. Well it wasn't Fifi's fault that she cried – all babies cry, I know that now, but at the time I was terrified. I had no knowledge of babies whatsoever, I was eighteen, a single parent and an unwilling slave to the little creature who was more precious to me than I could ever have imagined.

"Mum came to the rescue. You met her last Sunday, she's still my salvation, but then I have become hers also, in a way.

"As I said, my father died when I was fifteen and mother coped by getting a job at the dry-cleaners. We lived in a council flat and money was very precious, but Mum always made sure I had what I needed for school, and I think she was relieved when Tony came and took me off her hands. Now she had me back again, and Fifi to take care of as well. Tony had emigrated somewhere, and we never saw him again or got a penny from him. I moved back with Mum, I looked after Fifi during the day while mother was at work, and then I went out to work behind the bar in a local night club until three in the morning.

"I guess I must have got my figure back by then, 'cos I was getting a lot of attention from the guys on the other side of the bar, especially after midnight. One night one of them, who had been asking me out over and over again, offered me a hundred pounds if I would accept his invitation. I was horrified, and told him so. So he offered me five hundred. Suddenly everything seemed very different.

"Here I was, a lonely eighteen year old scraping pennies together to buy my daughter little things that mothers like to buy, sharing a bedroom with my baby and taking it in turns to do the weekly shop. I was tired of being grown up, I wanted my youth back, and most of all, I wanted that five hundred pounds.

"So that's how it started. Soon Mum gave up working at the dry cleaners so that she could look after Fifi full time and I could get the sleep I needed to keep looking good. I could buy fine clothes, and that meant I looked more expensive and was more expensive. I started to bring in decent money.

"Then I met Charles. Here was someone different who wanted me all to himself. He bought me a flat in Chelsea and all our financial worries became history. Of course I couldn't have Mum and Fifi with me, as he might appear at any time. But I had enough money to rent a bigger flat for them, here in Islington. I visited them lots and took them on excursions most weekends and whenever else Charles was home with his wife.

"Charles is the father of Christopher – Chrissy we call him – and Rupert. He moved us into a bigger flat as the children appeared and when we needed child care – so that our time alone was not disturbed - along came

Mother who he paid without any interest in where I had found such an accommodating and caring nanny.

"Life was pretty good until one day a strange woman turned up at my door. She just barged in, saw a photograph of Charles holding Chrissy as a baby on the sideboard, and went berserk. She smashed whatever she could, I had to ring the porter to come and help get her out of the flat.

"So, Charles's wife was a serious Roman Catholic and divorce was out of the question. Charles had to abandon his second family. All of a sudden I lost the flat, and we all moved here to Islington. He is meant to support the children, and to be fair, there are monthly payments into my bank account, but they come from the wife's account, not his. The payments certainly help, but they're not enough now that the children are growing. So I went back to work.

"Now, the reason for this visit," Dilly picked up the bottle, saw that it was empty and put it down again, "is to share my worries about my capabilities of being able to earn as much money as we need.

"Mum long ago adjusted her belief pattern to justify what we were both doing to pay the bills, so she's very supportive and does a wonderful job with the children. The trouble is that most women have time to make themselves look good, and to keep looking their best. Other women have time to pamper themselves, while I only have time to pamper the male ego – and that's a full-time job I can tell you.

"That's what makes you so different, Jack, you don't seem to be a slave to your ego, in fact there's no sign of an ego at all – but I digress." I shifted uneasily in my chair, about to protest, but mercifully, Dilly continued.

"Anyway, you see what I mean. I haven't time to cover myself in face cream, have massages and manicures. Mum helps me as best she can, and I have a fantastic wardrobe, mostly thanks to Charles, but I am getting older and my face is beginning to show wear and tear. What I need is an elixir of youth – I know C of E doesn't offer that as a regular service – but just having someone to talk to seems to take years off my life. What else can I do?"

The silence that followed this question brought me up with a start. I had no idea what sort of help I could offer. Her story had been very touching, and I understood why Father Justin had said that he couldn't think of her as a sinner.

Dilly was the first to break the silence. "You're on your way to being a curate, aren't you, Jack? Isn't that the next step after deacon?" I nodded. "I looked up the word 'curate' in the dictionary," she went on. "Do you know what the definition is?"

"No, I'm ashamed to say, I don't" I admitted, feeling particularly pathetic.

"It means 'one to whom the cure of the soul is committed'" Dilly said, looking at me intently. "Can you do that for me, Jack? Can you cure my soul?"

"Your soul doesn't need curing, Dilly," I let my thoughts run freely, hoping Father Justin's previous advice was sound. "You are a generous-hearted woman who is part of a loving family. What we have to find is a way for you to make money that doesn't drain you physically and which you can enjoy. Have you thought of looking for another type of employment?"

"Yes, of course," Dilly was quick with her response, "and Mum looks with me, but we cannot find anything, for which I am qualified, that pays so well. After all, Jack, my qualifications are pretty limited. I left school at sixteen and have been having children and keeping men happy ever since."

"You'll have to let me think about it for a bit, Dilly," I had no idea where to go from here. "You've given me a lot to ponder and I'll need to pray to Almighty God to see if a solution presents itself. That's what I always do when I need a friend to talk to and some advice - I pray. Sometimes answers present themselves in strange ways, and it takes me a while to realize that I have indeed been given a response, although I didn't recognize it as such straight away. Then it is necessary to reappraise the situations and the solutions that have appeared. However, I have faith, Dilly, and so must you have, or you wouldn't be here now, or bring the family to church every Sunday. We must look to our faith and be patient. Something will present itself to help you out. We'll look together, have faith together, pray together. And then we'll be patient and wait."

"Well, I hope you're right, Jack, I really do. The trouble with my faith is that it works for my mother and my children, and I'm happy to pray for them. But given how I earn the money to support them, I don't feel confident in praying for myself."

"Come on then," I stood up and kneeled down, right where I was by the desk. I gestured to Dilly to do the same, aware that it was now my turn to conduct the conversation. I placed my elbows alongside my books and papers, clasping my hands together I looked at my guest expectantly.

Dilly put down her empty glass in a hurry and scrambled out of her chair. She struggled to kneel in her tight skirt, but finally joined me with her head bowed against the desk's surface.

"Almighty Father," I began. "Please look on your subjects here in your wonderful church of St. George's and help us to find the paths which you would have us follow. Guide us, merciful Father, so that we can avoid sinful ways and walk in thy light with the confidence that you will be at our side at all times, leading us in the direction of your choice.

"If we have sinned against Thy righteousness, we pray that you bring your forgiveness and your understanding into our lives to cheer us as we strive to stay on the course that you have chosen for us; and that we can praise Thee with joy for the love and happiness you bring to us in this strange and demanding world.

"Through our Lord Jesus Christ, Amen."

"Amen" echoed Dilly, in a hushed whisper.

I stayed on my knees for a few moments after I had finished speaking, head bowed upon entwined fingers. When I got to my feet, I was surprised to see Dilly's face still bent upon her hands, a trail of tears glinting on the cheek closest to me. Then, with an effort, she stood up, wobbling on her high heels as she smoothed her skirt over her thighs. She turned away from me and picked up the handbag she had left by the chair. Having found a handkerchief, she blew her nose loudly, wiped her cheeks and turned towards me.

Suddenly I found myself engulfed in Dilly. Her arms encircled my neck, a wet cheek pressed against my face, a large bodily presence squeezed itself against me.

"Thank you, Jack. Oh thank you for that. That was beautiful, and I feel better already. I promise I will spend more time looking through the 'situations vacant' section of the Evening Standard, and let you know what I find. But in the meantime, if you can find time for me in your prayers, I will feel so much stronger knowing that you are on my case and working upon the cure of my soul.

"Thank you, again," she detached herself slowly, "and please let me come and talk to you again. I'll tell you how I've got on with creating a new life. For the first time, I think I'm ready for a proper change and that one might really happen."

That was the first of many meetings during which this exotic creature and the dull conventional deacon became firm friends. If our relationship hadn't ended as it did, we would be friends still.

37. LINE DANCING WITH A DIFFERENCE

My parishioners continued to visit - I note that I am writing about them now with a sense of sole ownership that's not at all justified. Their problems were many and varied but I did my best to deal with them although not always with success. There was one, however, who didn't bring me problems, at least not for some considerable time, and whose company I always found both interesting and enjoyable.

After my initial meeting with Estelle and our bare-footed wanderings around the church, I had been looking forward to the promised return visit. Certainly I was not disappointed, on the contrary, my psychological boundaries were about to be significantly stretched. The next time she came to see me she brought a diagram of the church drawn in impressive detail on a piece of graph paper.

"I have had this plan ready for ages," she explained somewhat tentatively, "but never really fancied doing the explorations on my own. Now that you seem to share my interest, I'm eager to get started, making use of your assistance, if that's alright with you."

I nodded enthusiastically. The plan, she explained, was to do a careful search of each square, and if we found power lines present, we would map their course on the graph paper, using different colors to identify the various forces. This would take some considerable time of course, but, she assured me, it was a wonderful way for me to learn and if we persevered, we would end up with an overall view of all that the church had to offer.

That was how our regular Tuesday appointments began. Gradually my receptivity improved and I became more adept at interpreting the feelings that seeped up through the cracks in the ancient stone floor. Not only did I learn to feel the church's different auras, I began to recognize them individually as well.

Our meetings always finished with a discussion of our latest finds at the Priory Café with pots of tea and scones daubed with jam and cream.

As the weeks passed, our chart took on a third dimension - crisscrossed by colored lines - a distinct pattern was emerging. When the design we were creating became quite balanced, Estelle announced that it was time for us to explore outside the church. "We will need some dowsing rods," she said, with some excitement, "to find the extensions of the lines we have charted inside. I will bring a pair next week. Your feet have learned to read the energies of the stones, let's see if your hands can become as receptive and interpret the magic which seeps through raw earth."

The following week, I was introduced to another experience of the inexplicable and intriguing; I became acquainted with both male and female ley lines.

Estelle's dowsing rods were two innocent-looking pieces of wire bent at right angles about a third of the way along their length.

She held them at the bend with the shorter pieces cradled in loosely cupped fingers, her thumbs resting on top so that the longer stretches of wire pointed towards the ground, about twelve inches apart.

I watched as Estelle began her slow and deliberate walk, a motion I was familiar with from our investigations inside the church. The rods lay still in her hands until, to my amazement, they suddenly sprang towards each other, overlapping in front of her in an urgent motion. It happened as Estelle approached the North Eastern corner of the church.

"Here, you hold them, Jack," Estelle had retraced her steps and the rods were once again inactive. She handed the two pieces of wire to me; showing me how to hold them, shoulder width apart. The rods remained inert in my fingers as I moved slowly forwards.

"They look like bits of bent coat-hangers," I exclaimed, trying to keep the skepticism out of my voice.

Estelle laughed, "that's just what they are – or what they used to be. Metal coat-hangers make excellent dowsing rods.

"Now, try to hang up your mind, Jack. I can't teach you to dowse, I can only show you how it works for me. You have to find the ability within yourself to let the earth's forces connect with you – as you have done inside the church. Just try to be receptive and intuitive and concentrate on the ley line idea. You know how to do that by now.

"The strength of your concentration is all important," she continued. "If we were dowsing for water, you would be thinking hard about rivers, lakes and so on; if we were dowsing for gold or oil, then our thoughts would be more mercurial. So put everything out of your mind except for the power lines you know to be here, somewhere. It's just a question of finding them."

I felt Estelle watching me as I proceeded cautiously towards the church. Out of the corner of my eye I could see her; head tilted slightly to the right, her steps keeping pace with mine. "Don't hold them so tightly, Jack" she reached out gently and adjusted the positioning of my hands. I remember being unsure whether it was the rods or my body that vibrated at her touch.

"Now just walk slowly, don't look for anything specific, this is not something to be seen with the eyes," she instructed gently, her voice taking on the sing-song lilt of the Welsh which she usually tried to conceal. "Let all your thoughts leak away, other than those seeking messages from deep within the earth. Open yourself, and let the rods act as a conductor, an amplifier, if you like, of channels of communication you have always had, but which have been stifled by the education and enculturation of our modern world."

I continued to place one foot carefully in front of the other between the big stone tombs, trying to follow instructions. I was attempting to empty my mind of everything, but Estelle's proximity made that difficult. I decided to concentrate on the oneness of the universe that seemed so obvious when I was with her, and the serenity that her company produced in my world. My eyes, fixed on the path ahead, began to lose focus.

Suddenly the rods jerked in my hands with extraordinary energy. It was as if there were invisible strings on the tips that pulled them forcibly towards each other. It was so sudden and so strong a sensation that I exclaimed out loud.

"Good gracious, Estelle," I looked in amazement at those brown eyes that always made my heart flip. "That made me jump. It's quite amazing, isn't it? I had no idea such a force could be so sudden and so strong."

"This is the male line," Estelle said, smiling with delight. She pointed to a space in the Church wall, between two buttresses. "It enters the church at the corner there, runs straight under the altar – or more accurately the altar has been placed directly above it – and continues in a south-westerly direction to St Mark's church in Myddleton Square, Clerkenwell, and then on to Lincoln's Inn and The Aldwych before reaching Westminster Abbey. It continues across the river, but I haven't researched any further.

"This power line is not as intense as the famous Michael Line. Do you know about The Michael Line, Jack?" Estelle added - she must have noticed my look of bewilderment. "It's a particularly strong line that may encircle the whole globe for all we know. The first place I know of its appearance is Skellig Michael — an extraordinary piece of black rock that rises from the sea like an obsidian pyramid, eight miles off the south-west corner of Ireland – but I've heard it said that it has been found in Iceland. It can be followed in a straight line through Cornwall and St. Michael's Mount, across the Channel to Mont St. Michel and it continues diagonally across France to Sarca di Michele in the Italian Alps. This monastery was started in the tenth century. It is perched on a mountain top which forms an important link between France and Italy and has been dedicated to St. Michael for longer than memory can tell."

Estelle leaned against a big rectangular tomb that rose three feet out of the churchyard grass. She ran her finger across the lichen covered stone to illustrate her story. "The line goes to San Michele di Monte Gargano on Italy's heel," she continued. Here the Archangel himself appeared to a bishop somewhere around the fifth century. The result of the visitation was the construction of a sanctuary in a place where the Earth Goddess already had a subterranean shrine. The power source was already there. The bishop just changed its name, and the Michael theme was continued.

"Still in an absolutely straight line, the ley carries on through Delphi, Athens and Delos and ends – or rather begins depending upon where you start – at Mount Carmel in Israel. I will show you on a map sometime - it's quite extraordinary and very exciting."

"Now I am with you," I interjected with enthusiasm. "Mount Carmel is mentioned in the Bible - the first Kings, I think – as the site of a battle between the priests of Jaweh and Baal. Elijah was responsible, I seem to remember, and the priests of Baal were scattered."

I was staring down at the rods in my hands. It felt as if a force from the ground had pushed them around, turning them to their present position alongside each other. They were vibrating slightly – or was it my hands that were doing the trembling? I couldn't tell.

"What are they telling me?" I asked, feeling rather foolish.

Michael's ley line

"They are telling you where the ley line is and the direction in which it is running. Look," Estelle moved in front of me, standing only a little distance away from the rods. "The ley runs this way," she moved her hands backwards and forwards in line with the turned rods. "You were crossing the line at right angles, and the rods are showing you where it is. This is a very strong line, that's why I chose it for your first try, Jack. Once you get the feel of this one, you will be able to pick up more subtle lines also.

"Now come and meet, the female ley," continued my teacher as she led the way to the East of the church, "and, with luck, you'll see what I mean."

Here the stained glass windows formed a semi-circle behind the altar within, the images rising in splendor to a peaked roof of intricate carvings. I had studied this face of the church many times, often with Father Justin at my side. The old priest had waxed eloquent over this carving or that, suggesting whose faces they might represent.

"All the stonemasons, from the middle ages onwards, used local people as the subjects for their carvings," Father Justin had enthused. "It was their habit to make the ugly gargoyles resemble people they didn't like. Those worthies for whom they had respect were represented as saints, and somewhere, there is always the sculptor himself, a self-portrait for us to discover, like the three dimensional torso which stands out from the pulpit in Chartres. That's a perfect example."

This time, however, I was not arching my neck towards the sky but studying the ground instead as the rods began to dance once again. This was not the same urgent pull of before, but insistent nevertheless. The rods pointed towards each other and swayed slightly backwards and forwards.

"There she is," laughed Estelle with delight. "Let me introduce you, Jack. This is the female line whose confluence with the male line is exactly where the altar stands. These two lines together give off powerful currents that would have been easily recognized by our forebears and would have dictated the positioning of this church. The female has a more gentle force than the male, hasn't she? But as with all women, her gentleness is a show of strength rather than of weakness."

We continued walking slowly around the church as I pondered on her ideas. Estelle showed me where the two lines exited the building – the female ley came straight down the aisle and out below the great Western doors. It amused both of us to find the male line heading directly for the Priory Café.

When the lesson was over, Estelle led me back inside the church, through the tall portals, into the dimness. I was acutely aware of a new caution with which I was walking. Now that we had identified the leys so acutely, it seemed wrong to stamp or plod over their routes. I placed my feet with soft precision and was careful not to scuff my shoes against the stones. Looking again at the chart we had been working on I began to understand why Estelle had used a deep maroon color in some squares and a pale blue in others. The two colors formed an appropriate purple where they crossed under the altar.

Inside the building, our searches continued and Estelle held forth with a lesson in power recognition and appreciation. I was excited to find that I was beginning to understand viscerally now - ideas were being absorbed by an intelligence within my body, rather than being analyzed by my mind. It was an extraordinary experience – and one that I have been able to replicate many times since.

We paused in the transept, standing quietly, feeling the incipient power course through and around us. "Once you have been shown the door, and pushed through it, or passed willingly into the portal, it is much easier to find a second time," Estelle promised. "The more frequently you use that door, the more obvious it becomes." Estelle had resumed her instructor's role.

"Almost all religious buildings were started with the siting of the altar – or its equivalent. Once this place of power had been identified, the layout of the church was set out around it, incorporating power lines. Ancient churches were built with love, devotion – passion even - and all these positive human energies augmented the powers of the lines. Through years of worship, this collected energy is further enhanced by the prayers and devotions of the occupants who unwittingly act as conduits between the spiritual energies and those of the earth's currents; forces that travel in both directions.

"Over time the strength of the conduits varies, but the foundation energies remain ever-present. Certain individuals can carry these energies from one place to another and spread them amongst humanity. Some of these saints have enough energy within themselves to be self-sufficient; others need to find appropriate places to recharge their powers. This is an ongoing situation, there are still saints among us – we just need the time and receptivity to recognize them, and to listen."

I was intrigued. "It must be this collection of energies over centuries that gives the great medieval cathedrals their aura of wonder and sanctity, then." The idea of eons of prayer offerings seeping into the stones of buildings and shining out again into a cathedral's atmosphere, appealed to me. The concept was intimately pleasing.

"Yes, of course, Jack, you are quite right. Those buildings are permeated by the influence of centuries of worship - as well as by the natural powers of magnetism that seep through and into their massive floors and walls. But it's not only in the great cathedrals. You can feel it here, in St. George's also."

I found myself nodding enthusiastically. Estelle seemed to have finished speaking; she was standing in the little chapel of St. John of the Cross now, studying part of the elaborate ceiling. I'd left my jacket on the back of the first pew, and reached for it, feeling ready to cross the road for tea and eager to continue the conversation and pursue these exciting ideas. However, Estelle turned quickly and held me back.

"Just a minute." The hand on my arm tightened. "Could we stay here a bit longer? I want us to exchange roles for a while and for you to instruct me, as your calling suggests. Would that be alright?"

"Of course," I was bluffing – my confidence vanished as the familiar feeling of panic and inadequacy leapt to my stomach. "Shall we sit here in the chapel, or would you rather go somewhere else?"

"Here's perfect," Estelle nodded, and sat down promptly on the first pew before the small altar which supported a gleaming brass cross with fluted tips. It had been Rosie's polishing job of a few days before, and she had performed the task with her usual diligence.

Estelle looked down at the big emerald ring, flanked with diamonds, which she always wore on her left hand. Of course I had known that she was getting married, but Father Justin had not mentioned any such celebration in the church's diary and I had avoided asking her about it.

"Dear Jack," my teacher-turned-parishioner began as I felt my throat contract. "I want to ask you a great favor – well you and Father Justin also, I suppose. I want to ask you for a blessing on my forthcoming marriage. I have not been married before and had my heart's set upon a ceremony here at St. George's, but Chicago won't have it. That's my fiancé's name, I know it sounds silly, and everybody thinks it's his nickname, but in fact that is what he was christened. His mother was reading a book about the mafia when he arrived into this world, and liked the name of the city. So there it is.

"Anyway, Chicago has been married twice before – you know we can all make mistakes, and he's obviously had a difficult time, but now he is sure that this is the real thing. The trouble is that we can't be married in church."

"You can always have a church blessing," I said hoping that I was showing an enthusiasm I was far from feeling. With a jerk similar to that experienced with the dowsing rods, I realized how strongly I felt against this suggestion. With an effort I pushed the feelings aside and tried to adopt the tone and expression of the professional Curate.

"A formal one, I mean," I continued, "with a congregation, flowers, choir, anything you want. A service that is so like the real one that few notice the difference." I was talking too fast trying to disguise my panic. I took a deep breath and tried to slow down.

"It would be necessary to have had a registry service beforehand, of course, just to satisfy the civil servants, but as far as our Lord is concerned, the real one will be here, with us, where it should be." Who was I trying to reassure – Estelle, or myself?

"I know, I know," Estelle was wringing her hands, the extravagant engagement ring hampering her movements. "Chicago won't have it. He's an agnostic, you see, and insists on a registry wedding, as small as possible, and then a huge party somewhere fashionable enough to attract the press. That's why I am asking you for a blessing – not on Chicago and me together, but just on the concept of our union, for me to cherish."

I remember being struck by the feeling she was not telling either me or herself the whole problem. I decided that silence might be the best way to encourage her to keep talking. The church was still and quiet except for the spattering of rain drops which had begun to fall on the roof high above and on the stained glass windows beside us.

I studied my shoes with great attention, noticing the scuff marks on the toes from praying on my knees and the frayed end to one of the laces. My mind was drifting so that when Estelle next spoke it made me jump.

"I don't know" - there was that phrase again - "there's just something not quite right. In theory everything is perfect. I have a man who is proud of me and of my accomplishments. He has an understanding of how much I have achieved and encourages and congratulates me in turn. He is wonderfully good looking and can charm anyone in the world, even my mother." A smile lightened up Estelle's features and transformed the already lovely face into someone immensely engaging and attractive. "But . . ."

This time the silence stayed. I took her hand gently – the one without the ring - and, not daring to look at those deep brown eyes, stared at her strong fingers instead as they lay unresponsive in my palm. "We'll make a plan of some sort," I promised her. "I'll talk to Father Justin and between us we'll come up with something to show God's blessing on this marriage. By next Tuesday we will have worked something out and then it will just be a matter of your choosing a date."

"The civil service is tomorrow," Estelle's voice was just a whisper. "But I feel better knowing that we have something planned." Her hand suddenly tightened in mine. "I'll let you know when would be a good date, and yes, please, work on something with Father Justin so that we're all ready to go." She looked at her watch and her voice returned to normal.

"Goodness, look at the time, I'm afraid I'll have to miss tea today." Estelle jumped to her feet, grabbing her handbag and dowsing rods. "Here, Jack," she said impulsively, thrusting the rods into my hands. "I want you to keep these, I have plenty more, and you did so well with them today." She leaned towards me and kissed me lightly on the cheek. "Thank you for everything, Jack. I'm sorry about the tea, but we'll make up for it next time." She turned and almost ran out of the church, the heavy door clanging shut behind her.

I never saw her in St. George's again.

38. OBERAMMERGAU A PILGRIMAGE OR A PRODUCTION?

It was 1990, the year of the next ordination for St. Augustine's graduates of 1988 and Father David had planned a surprise for his alumni. There is a famous Passion Play performed in the Bavarian village of Oberammergau at the beginning of every decade. Father David had arranged tickets for a selection of his past students to join a coach trip to experience this event.

Father Justin had received a letter from his old college friend some six weeks before he decided to tell me about it. He was waiting to make sure he could endorse the project, he explained, and apparently my steady industry within the parish had assured him that he could.

The first I knew about it was one evening in early January when Father Justin passed me a journal open at an article about the famous play. We had finished supper and were seated in chairs drawn close to the fire, the winter cold kept at bay only slightly by the thick closed curtains of the sitting room.

"What do you think about this, Jack?" he enquired. "I went to the Passion Play once, when I was about your age. I found it an extraordinary experience."

I took the article with interest, and read it carefully. "It sounds really amazing, Father," I said, looking up from the journal. "But it's hardly possible for me to go, Easter will be busy here. Indeed, I'm not sure I would like to make such a trip on my own."

"Well, hardly on your own, Jack," Father Justin said, with a twinkle in his eye. "God would be with you, as always."

I was not overly impressed with this consolation. "No," I repeated, "I couldn't be away from St. George's at Easter."

"Well, it may be an opportunity you can't afford to miss, Jack – after all it only happens once a decade, and it seems that your friend and mine, Father David, has ideas for you - and your friends" he added with a smile "to celebrate the year of your next ordination in style." He passed Father David's letter across to me. I was totally amazed by what he had said; I took the letter and absorbed the contents slowly.

"Is there a list of the graduates he intends to send on this trip?" was my first question, after the reality of the situation had dawned on me.

Father Justin smiled. "Yes, and don't you worry, Thomas and Rufus are both on the list."

"Can I see it?" I asked, trying to hide an anxious note from my voice.

"Certainly," answered the priest with surprise. He handed me a second piece of paper. "Of course I cannot guarantee that the people whose names are there will all be able to go. Their superiors have to sanction the idea, as I have for you, but I did check that your two friends had also been given the nod of approval by their mentors."

I read the names with trepidation giving a sigh of relief when I found that Simon Mountford's was not among them. The idea of spending a whole week anywhere near that unpleasant man would have put me off the trip and I was sure that both my friends would feel the same.

I passed the paper back to Father Justin with a smile. "Well, what an unexpected idea," I said. "It sounds quite astonishing, and a great treat to be able to attend with the approval of the Anglican Church itself."

"Not only approved but also sponsored by the Church," Father Justin replied. "It is your good fortune to be seeking ordination in a year in which the play is performed. Don't you worry about St. George's, I've managed Easter on my own before, and I will manage again. Especially as this should be the last time I will be called upon so to do."

I glanced at my friend and mentor with great affection. Suddenly I was looking forward to the adventure I was to share with Thomas and Rufus although I had little idea of what was in store.

That's how it was that in the spring I found myself aboard a coach alongside my chums for our great spiritual adventure to Oberammergau in Southern Germany and to the monastery in Ettal where we would be staying. We had much to catch up on, and chatted excitedly for almost the entire voyage which passed pleasantly enough apart from a rough channel crossing.

It's a long drive to Oberammergau, not to be undertaken in a single day. The coach stopped at a monastery near Ludwigshafen for us to spend the night in a municipal looking building of grey concrete annexed to the main chapel. We shared the monks' evening service and meager supper before retiring to sleep in dormitory-style bedrooms with our fellow travelers, all clergy of one rank or another.

The following day, after matins, we set off again full of excitement. Soon the arable landscape gave way to undulating vineyards and then, as the slopes grew steeper, to the sharper meadows of the Alpine foothills. The air had grown significantly cooler.

As the coach began its climb into the mountains, the countryside slid backwards in time as the seasons receded from the green of spring to the brown and black-and-white of winter. The grass, decorated with yellow cowslips and pale mauve crocus in the lower meadows, lost its color along with the flowers, and turned sandy and then brown until it was lost altogether under a snow pack in retreat. There was no hint of warmth in the distant snowy peaks that could be glimpsed every now and then as the coach left the autobahn and took to the mountain roads.

Paintings adorned the white sides of village buildings, as we climbed the murals changed from rural scenes to more religious themes. The oompah-oompah of the music playing from the coach radio also changed and became interposed with hymns, psalms and prayers as we moved from one local radio station to the next. None of the passengers felt it appropriate to ask the coach-driver to turn the radio off, although, as few of us spoke German, the relevance of the religious-sounding verbiage was lost.

The house paintings were now almost entirely of saints. St. Francis, with his entourage of children and animals, seemed especially welcome to the occupants of our coach. However depictions of martyrs quickly overtook the friendly patron saint of travelers, with St. Sebastian an obvious favorite. He was displayed in all his gory glory in a painting that covered the whole side of a large two storied building in the centre of one town - an edifice which housed a bank, a hair-dresser and a shop selling children's clothes. The grizzly embedded arrows that were depicted protruding from all over St. Sebastian's body, each with its own bloody rivulet, and the agonized expression on the saint's face, made this huge painting strike me as inappropriate, and somewhat obscene amongst the day-to-day commerce of the place.

Once the coach stopped at a set of traffic lights alongside a huge freestanding crucifix, which dominated the little town. A brightly colored flyer advertising a pop concert caught my eye; it was pinned into the wood, just below the bloodied feet of the enormous Christ.

"This must be what happens," I thought, "when people live with all this pain as part of their day to day décor. They must become immune to the deep messages displayed, otherwise they couldn't go about their daily business without crumpling in penitence every few minutes." I wanted to ask my friends for their views, but Thomas and Rufus were busy with a discussion of their own and seemed oblivious of the gore pictorially represented around them.

By the time we reached Garmisch-Partenkirchen, I had become more accustomed to the ghoulish paintings in the otherwise picturesque Alpine villages. There were larger-than-life renditions of the crucifixion jockeying for attention with Pietas in full Technicolor. The agony on the faces of both Jesus and his mother, Mary, at their most personally private and painful moments, seemed to compete for the sympathies of an audience who were busy going about their day to day activities, apparently unmoved by the painful scenes that rose above them.

At last, the coach rounded yet another hair-pin bend and we saw the cream colored abbey of Ettal with its magical domed church sitting like a bubble in the mountain's lap. We were approaching our destination.

After being shown to small rooms with beds carved into the stone wall of the mountain, we were summoned

to the abbey's Grand Hall, which doubled as a refectory.
The monk who had shown us to our sleeping quarters
had told us that we were to receive a welcome address
from the abbot himself, and that we should hurry to
attend. Dropping our bags, we obediently followed the
busy little man through a maze of corridors to a massive
timber-roofed Hall.

Refectory tables had been pushed to the sides of this
cavernous room. Soft lighting came from rows of iron
candelabras hanging on long chains from the steeply
pitched roof. Candles had been replaced with light
bulbs, but the effect was still gothic and impressive.

Visitors straggled in from various corners of the hall
– there were three other coaches parked alongside ours
outside - and were ushered to a cleared space between
the long polished tables at one end of the room. At the
other end of the Grand Hall the floor was raised, making
the tables in that part of the room seem like props on a
stage.

The sound of a small bell ringing caused the
gathering to stop their chatter and look up expectantly.
A heavy arched door swung slowly open and a
progression of choirboys entered with appropriate
solemnity, the leader shaking a small brass bell.

Behind the boys in their starched white ruffs and
blue over-garments came a great body of monks in plain
brown cassocks with white rope belts tied to one side,
the ends dangling to the floor. They ranged themselves
in lines behind the boys, facing us. Their ranks parted
briefly to allow a tall man with stooped shoulders and a
hooked nose to pass to the front.

The boys also made way for this old man whose
presence walked before him. He was dressed in the
same somber garb as the other monks with an identical
plain brown cross hanging around his neck. It swayed
slightly as he walked. The gnarled fingers of his large
hands were clasped loosely in front of him. When he

came to a halt in front of the line of boys, one of the tassels of his belt continued to brush the polished wooden floor in a steady swing. He was facing his audience, his deep-set eyes roving around the gathering.

"Good evening brethren," the voice broke a silence that the old man's appearance had somehow forced upon the company. "I am Brother Ignatius, and have the honor to be abbot of this wonderful house of our gracious Lord and Heavenly Father." He spoke in English, the German accent soft on the speaker's tongue, his words strangely powerful for so frail a man.

"Most of you will know bits of the story of our little mountain town here in Bavaria." The abbot spoke slowly and clearly, addressing the gathering with a well-practiced mixture of formality and familiarity. "But perhaps there are some who don't know it all. So I am going to tell you a little of our history, even if you have heard it before, for it is a history which has brought you all on this pilgrimage."

Father Ignatius looked around the room once again. And then, very much in the manner of a kindly grandfather reading a well-known bedtime story to a favorite grandchild, he began his tale.

"In the early 1630s Bavaria was swept by the Black Death - a horror similar to the bubonic plague that went through much of Europe. Some of the villages and towns in the area were completely wiped out; others had maybe just one or two people left alive.

"Ober Ammergau, as it was then known, had enforced a strict quarantine restriction around its mountain location and was completely untouched by the disaster that ravaged the rest of the country. Then one night, a lonely father called Caspar Schuchler, who had found himself outside the quarantine barrier when the Black Death began, crept secretly back into the village to visit his wife and his children. In the pockets of his person he unwittingly brought the catastrophic plague.

The citizens of the mountain sanctuary fell ill and began to die."

The monk paused and looked around his audience with a serious expression. "Soon there were not enough people left living in the village to bury those who had died." Another pause added weight to the drama. "The stricken community grouped together in their church to pray for the forgiveness of the sins that had brought this disaster to their homes and families. Sins which they could not identify but which they acknowledged must have been committed for such retribution to be necessary.

"They prayed and prayed, collectively and individually. Their priest chastised them, and himself," said Brother Ignatius nodding his head slowly, "over and over again for the wickedness which had brought this plague upon them."

Then the monk's tone changed. His voice became lighter and his words lost their ponderous intonations. "In one of the many offerings made to the Almighty, the small collection of survivors promised their Lord that, if they were spared, the village would perform a Passion play every ten years as a token of their repentance and for the glory of God. They would all share in Jesus' sufferings with a re-enactment of his last days of mortality and the first that followed his resurrection.

"As the story is told," the abbot looked brightly over our heads, "from the moment the promise of the Passion play was made, the deaths in the village stopped. Those who had already become afflicted recovered; and there were no new cases of the fatal illness. God had listened to the people of Oberammergau." The monk's voice was raised in excitement. "He had heeded their prayers and accepted their offer of penitence.

"And so, every tenth year, the villagers of Oberammergau perform their play depicting the return of Jesus to Jerusalem, His trial and dreadful crucifixion,

His wondrous resurrection and, eventually, His ascension into heaven. There are also a famous collection of 'tablaux vivants' representing scenes from both the old and the new testaments." Brother Ignatius was warming to his subject with obvious enjoyment. "One of these represents the scene of Moses lifting up the serpent in the wilderness, binging God's mercy down upon his people in an act of salvation similar to the sudden cleansing of the plague-ridden village in 1634."

The Abbot went on to explain that all the performers of the Passion play had to be inhabitants of the village, and as many of them as possible should take part in its production. That was part of the sacred agreement. "Now there are over two thousand villagers who are involved, including hundreds of children and the play has expanded to last for over seven hours," he proclaimed, "but with a three hour interval in the middle, so don't get too worried about its present length, I assure you it will all pass too quickly.

"As the number of spectators increased" the abbot continued, so the little village has built bigger and better stages and began to spread the performances over five months instead of five days to allow as many of the faithful as possible to share in the experience.

"Over six and a half million people come to watch our special spectacle now," the old man said with obvious pride. "The first package tours began as long ago as 1870, and now," he spread his hands out to indicate his audience, "you see for yourselves how the pious continue to flock here to be part of the celebration of the original great miracle.

"Our village has dedicated itself to the Glory of God and to the Passion of his son, our Lord and Savior, Jesus Christ. We monks, here in Ettal, are greatly blessed to live in such a holy place. We marvel at God's mercy, which was showered upon this area so long ago, and can still be felt so immediately today.

"Gentlemen," he paused, the gravity in his voice hanging heavily on the word, "gentlemen, you have come from all over the world to participate in this glorious spectacle. Prepare yourself to be moved by God's mysteries, to feel His presence here, with us in these mighty mountains, and to indulge your spirits with the many wonders you will experience. Welcome, gentlemen, welcome."

The monks, standing in ranks behind the speaker, had been so still and silent they had seemed like a vast sculpture. Now, they suddenly came to life and repeated the last three words as one voice. The greeting rumbled across the room and reverberated over our heads, the voices of the choirboys seeming to float in the air after the deep tones had gone.

Someone amongst the guests said "Amen," and then everybody was saying Amens and showering blessings towards the monks and each other. It was a deeply moving moment, when a feeling of strong religious unity bound us all together in humility and devotion.

By the time everyone had returned from evensong in the domed chapel that formed the heart of the abbey, both architecturally and emotionally, the refectory tables had taken up their habitual places and had been laid for supper.

"This reminds me of St. Augustine's," I said to Thomas as we shuffled along the benches with plates of sauerkraut, onions and mashed potatoes retrieved from a large buffet table at the end of the hall.

"Yes, it's somewhat grander, of course," Thomas replied, "but every bit as cold. There didn't seem to be many blankets on those tiny beds, did there?"

Rufus joined us and agreed that there did not. We decided that it was part of the monastic experience and should be enjoyed for what it was.

"And for how much we'll appreciated our comforts when we get home," added Thomas.

In fact, we all slept remarkably well in the garret-styled beds and woke full of anticipation for the day ahead which started with the monks organizing us into small groups according to how we were sitting at breakfast.

Two mini-busses were to take the groups in relays into town where the visitors were free to explore and absorb the atmosphere, walk in the mountains or through the narrow streets of the village. They should find somewhere to have an early lunch and would be collected at twelve-thirty and taken to the amphitheater where the performance would begin at one in the afternoon.

Oberammergau looks like a typical Tyrolean village from a distance, with steep roofs and tall wide chimneys rising like medieval bulwarks in a castle town. Towering over this idyllic scene, however, is a hotel, as vast as it is ugly. Built close against the mountains, it dominates the village. I remember feeling that a malevolent presence brooded there, emanating from so much concrete. It did not sit comfortably amongst the surrounding rock and the delicate shapes of the rest of the town buildings.

Averting our eyes from the barrack-style building, we concentrated on the approaching village with anticipation. As we drew closer we could see that almost every building had huge multi-colored murals decorating them from the ground up to the chalet-style eaves.

The bus dropped us at the entrance to the village and returned for the next group. The three of us joined the small crowd that was walking purposefully up the mountain road. As we entered the village I thought the savage subjects of the paintings detracted from the beauty of the artwork that had looked so attractive from afar. I found myself studying the pavement in front of me feeling intimidated by the blood and gore of the scenes depicted on the walls around us.

Most of the shop fronts mirrored the murals. They were full of carvings and paintings of the crucifixion, occasionally interrupted by Pietas showing similar expressions of extreme distress.

There were carefully carved crucifixes in sizes that ranged from those that could fit in the palm of your hand to huge structures rising to over ten feet. They were made of simple polished metals, wood, and even of plastic. Some of them were painted with vivid bloodstreams shining deep red from Christ's feet, hands, the hideous gash in his side, and in trickles down his face from the various crowns of thorns which competed with each other for verisimilitude and horror.

The three of us fell silent as we walked along. We entered one shop that catered for tourists and churches alike. Towards the back, where the roof was highest, there were larger-than-life sized statues of various saints, including the obvious favorite, St. Sebastian, this time in three dimensions with arrow shafts at nasty angles protruding from all over his body. One statue of a manacled Christ was so tall that his crown of thorns had been carefully fitted into the apex of the room. Christ's raised eyes seemed to be studying the rafters with distress - as if the building was responsible for his pain and the roof might collapse at any moment.

In another shop there was a bank of Madonnas in escalating sizes along one entire wall. Some of them held the baby Jesus with loving care, some stood erect with hands outstretched, some cradled Christ's body, fresh from the cross. The carvings were stacked so neatly and in such profusion I was tempted to pick one up to see if the whole wall would then disintegrate in a tumble of wistful faces. I resisted this childish urge, trying to make myself into the responsible person I was meant to be: a deacon of the church, approaching ordination.

The most amazing thing about that shop, however, was the ceiling, from which hung literally thousands of crucifixes. They were of many different sizes and colors, each with its own impaled Christ. They dropped towards the curious shopper like stalactites in a cave.

Back on the street, pausing to cross a side road, I was bemused to see a shop window full of life-sized statues of martyrs staring, with tortured faces, across the street. Answering their gaze from the shop window on the other side of a pedestrian walkway, were more statues, but this time they were models in a dress shop. The plastic fashion models had painted lips curling in smiles as artificial as the rest of their faces. Their arms and legs were set in sensual poses to better show the desirability of the slinky dresses with which they were draped. Opposite, the carved wooden faces of St. Stephen with his stones, St. Sebastian full of arrows and Matthew the Evangelist with a halberd embedded in his chest all had eyes staring balefully across at the fashion models which seemed to wave back at them cheerily.

"Come on Jack," Thomas was tugging at my arm. "Look what this one's got." Rufus was already at the next shop. His bent form was studying a set of carvings depicting the nativity. The carefully carved figures that surrounded the crib were all familiar, but the novelty that had attracted Thomas and Rufus was that the biblical characters were all portrayed as Bavarians. The shepherds wore lederhosen and had brought mountain goats to the crib; Joseph sported a trilby style felt hat, complete with feather, a high-collared jacket with embroidered trim and matching plus-fours; the three kings were paying homage in flowing cloaks decorated with edelweiss; and Mary, was leaning towards the crib elegantly attired in a pinafore dress over a puff-sleeved blouse.

"How strange is that?" queried Thomas, showing his find with some delight to add to my bewilderment.

"Well, why not," said Rufus as he straightened away from the window. "I know it looks really ridiculous, but if you think about it, what better way to help children identify with the Christmas story than to dress the characters in familiar clothes. Now that I've got over the initial surprise, I think it's rather a good idea."

Thomas and I both frowned at our friend, then we all started laughing. Suddenly the over-load of visual images dispersed in a guffaw of merriment, we laughed and laughed. Passers-by looked with astonishment at the three of us deacons jiggling about on the street corner, giggling like schoolgirls.

Finally the laughter subsided and we made our way across the street to a 'bierhaus' for some much needed refreshment.

"I don't believe it," I started as the door closed behind us, gesturing to the huge crucifix that dominated the opposing wall and the paintings of Christ's journey to Calvary displayed on wooden panels behind the bar, just above the rows of inverted bottles of whisky, schnapps, and so on.

The air inside the pub was steamy and dark after the bright chill of the outside, and heavy with the smells of sweat, cheap cigarettes, and beer. The customers – of which there were many – all seemed more interested in looking down into their tankards than upwards at the décor.

"Don't start me off again," said Rufus, who was wiping his eyes after the merriment of a few moments before. "I'm exhausted with all this laughing, and more than ready for a drink in spite of . . ." he trailed off, his eyes roaming around the busy pub and back to his friends. "Mine's a pint, please," he added with a broad grin as he saw me pulling a wallet from my jacket pocket.

The three of us enjoyed a pleasant half hour quaffing beer and exchanging thoughts about the strange things we had seen. There was much laughter and comradery which accompanied us as we made our way towards the auditorium.

The play started promptly at the appointed hour. We were sitting together in a row of tiered seats, with many more behind, and an even larger crowd of heads in front. A great arched roof covered the audience, but the Athenian-styled stage was open to the sky, the mountains rising behind providing an impressive backdrop. The sky was thick with cloud and a cold wind did its best to disburse the warmth that came from the over-head heaters.

The atmosphere in the auditorium was unlike anything I had felt, or even imagined, before. There was awe, excitement, worship, anticipation and a strange blanket of sanctity spreading itself across the crowd who waited in respectful silence.

As the play started and the scene of Jesus' arrival in Jerusalem began to unfold, I was caught up with the dignity and wonder of the enactment. I marveled at the discipline of the children, some who seemed less than six years old; at the obvious devotion of all the players; and at the delicate portrayal of Jesus himself. The cast had been carefully chosen and the costumes were immaculate, down to the smallest detail. The throng of actors bustled gently around a very placid donkey, parting and closing again like a school of fish.

The production was indeed impressive and I found myself following the acts one after the other with delight. The tableaux vivants, which interspersed each act – presumably to allow the massive cast time to change – were also quite spectacular. The people who created these static scenes went to their positions quickly and silently in the dusk. When the lights returned, the audience was presented with a completed three-dimensional picture of a significant biblical scene. Abraham and the Ark of the Covenant; Moses parting the waves, with the entire tribe of Israel behind him; Isaac and his willingness to sacrifice his son – with an arch-angel staying the knife surrounded by lesser angels of one sort or another, and so on. It was all beautifully done, and again, the discipline of the cast was extremely impressive.

It was hard to realize that so much time had elapsed when the interval was called. Night hovered behind the mountains as we made our way to tables set out behind the amphitheater, laden with cold meats and salads, fruits and cakes.

I found I was bubbling with excitement as to how much I was enjoying the performance, but, to my surprise, I found my friends subdued and thoughtful. I was suddenly aware that the atmosphere around us was somber rather than enthusiastic. People were speaking in lowered voices, movements were slow and deliberate. We took our places at one of the long trestle tables and I looked from one of my friends to the other in confusion.

"What and amazing play," I began, in an effort to re-establish a hint of normality. "Can you believe all those little kids behaving so perfectly, and for such a long time? It's tremendously impressive, don't you think?"

"Tremendous is the right word," Thomas eventually replied, gazing down at his plate as if it had arrived before him by divine intervention. "What a privilege it must be for all of them to partake in something so sacred. No wonder their discipline is so finely honed. It's a wonder . . . " His voice trailed off into silence.

Rufus was quick to agree, and I found myself left out of the conversation as my two friends talked in near whispers of the experience they were sharing.

"But they do it almost every day for five months," I tried to get some reality into the conversation. "That's what I mean as impressive discipline. They all look as if today is the only performance that matters. It is really amazing – and they are all amateur actors, to boot, just people from the village."

Thomas and Rufus turned their heads slowly towards me. "They are not acting, Jack," Thomas pronounced carefully, "they are taking part in something sacred, full of the mysteries of our faith, full of the real powers of Our Lord and Our God." He looked at Rufus for confirmation.

"I agree, absolutely," Rufus was nodding his head carefully, as if any sudden motion might break the spell. "This is akin to participating in Our Lord's final days, we are on the same journey to Calvary; we will be crucified along with Him - we will all save mankind, together."

I was stupefied. What had happened to my friends? "But it's a play. A good and impressive production as I have said, but it's still just a play."

My two friends shook their heads slowly. Rufus reached out an arm and laid it across my shoulders.

"Let go, Jack," he said softly. "Let these wonders enter your soul – become a part of it, feel it in your bones. Look at everyone," he continued with an expansive wave of the other arm. "This is not entertainment, Jack. It is a religious experience of great magnitude. You have to join the throng; you can't miss out on something this awesome."

I looked around at the people who were sharing our table, and those on the tables that spread out into the distance. Everyone was eating with bowed heads. Conversations were muffled; nowhere could you hear a chuckle or a laugh.

I seemed to be the only one who was aware of the distance that had suddenly sprung up between us. I was bewildered and confused. Why was I so different from everyone else? Why was I here?

As these questions descended upon me I felt a reeling sensation, as if I were losing my balance. Bowing my head I got on with the meal, preferring to ape the subdued and sanctimonious actions of my friends and neighbors than to get up and shout: "what's with you all? This is a play for Christ's sake" and then as I thought of those words and saw them in perspective I had difficulty in controlling a sacrilegious giggle. I was isolated in my confusion and suppressed merriment.

As the audience returned to their seats and the play continued, I found it hard to enjoy the artistry as much as I had done in the first half. I was trying hard to open myself to whatever divine energy was motivating everyone else.

By the time Christ arrived at Calvary and was hoisted aloft, I gave up my attempts to emulate my peers. Looking sideways at Thomas I could see tears streaming down his up-turned face, his hands were clasped together with inter-laced fingers, his knuckles shining white with the tension.

Beyond Thomas, Rufus was equally transfixed. He was rocking slowly backwards and forwards in his seat, his hands cradling his head. He was crying uncontrollably, murmuring "no, no, no, no . . ." over and over again.

Looking around me, I saw the members of the congregation - for that is what it had become, rather than an audience - were all equally moved. Men were swaying, sobbing, clutching their hair, wringing their hands – never could I have imagined a scene of such mass distress.

"I'm alone here," I thought. "I don't feel this experience the way everybody else does. What is it that grabs these people and pulls them into the realm of hysteria, and why am I not with them? I observe, but everyone else participates. Do I want to be otherwise? Do I have a choice?"

I tried to put these questions away and looked for the genuine appreciation I had experienced earlier. However, the more I watched, the more I just saw actors rendering scenes with polish and technical excellence. I continued to enjoy the spectacle, but it never ceased to be anything other than what it was – a carefully choreographed play, a performance with style. Each scene and tableau was portrayed with expertise, imagination and skill. No expense had been spared in the scenery, costumes, make-up, lighting, sound production and so on. It was a first-rate theatrical presentation. But, surely, that was it, in its entirety.

How could all these people be engulfed inside the performance, becoming a part of it – and more astounding still – believing they were a part of the original scenes these actors were portraying?

Eventually, much to my embarrassed relief, the great passion play came to an end. Jesus had risen from the dead, amongst ululations from the audience. The resurrected Lord had performed many wondrous things and finally ascended into the heavens with the help of ropes and pulleys, I assumed, and the audience rose with him. People leapt from their seats, throwing their hands in the air with ecstasy. I followed suit, so as not to be the only one left seated, but I didn't know how I was expected to act and my feelings told me I was behaving like an idiot.

Fortunately my two friends had eyes only for the stage. Again, tears glistened upon their cheeks, but this time in joy and humility rather than with the pain and suffering of the crucifixion, and with the unbridled joy of the resurrection.

The kafuffle took a while to subside. The actors faded away, the lights went up, blotting out the stars that had been visible behind the mountain backdrop, and still the audience swayed and moaned with delight and excitement.

I was turning to go, but the people between me and the aisle showed no sign of moving. Thomas and Rufus were similarly rooted in their places, hands clasped together or raised above their heads, weeping without restraint or embarrassment.

Eventually the ushers persuaded the throng to move and herded us carefully towards the massive gift shop that filled a space between the auditorium and the car-park.

The many cash tills were fully manned, but still there were queues at each one as people waited to buy tapes and videos of the performance. There were models of all the main characters, posters of the tableaux vivants, your very own plastic crown of thorns to display - or wear perhaps? My mind was reeling.

Clerical clothes of all sorts hung in rows. There were communion sets that varied from cheap and tacky articles to elaborate and hugely expensive vessels depending upon the metal used and the gems displayed. Each set had its own carrying case with specially molded foam to cradle the chalice or ciborium, monstrance - deluxe versions only - and pyx. You could buy thuribles, mitres, crosiers – and, of course, any amount of crucifixes and pietas.

I watched in bemusement as Thomas and Rufus fussed over which tapes to buy - the full set of six covered the whole production; which videos, posters etc. Keeping my hands deep in my pockets I moved slowly for the exit. It was like watching sharks at a feeding frenzy, all these "holy people" tussling for the best buys. I felt sick and turned away, out into the fresh air of the car-park to wait for our turn in the bus.

My account of this experience is somewhat expansive because I received so many questions from Percival and Amrita when I was relating the story that the details multiplied as I recalled the different scenes so vividly. It was a milestone of some sort in my ecclesiastical career, I suppose, but not as a powerful religious happening but as a realization as to how different I was – and still am - from my peers, as far as theological philosophy is concerned.

It was the first time I personally experienced the type of mass-hysteria I had read about in my studies at college. I didn't like it then, and I still find it frightening. Perhaps I should refer to it as mass-hypnosis? I don't know, but I have seen it since, in a variety of places, and even when it has a strong Christian flavor, I am still uncomfortable about this willing suspension of man's reasoning faculties.

Following my description of the event to my fellow patients, and voicing my doubts and misapprehensions, I found kindred spirits who brought me out of isolation on this subject. We discussed the situation as objectively as possible, trying to recognize the positive elements of this kind of collective brain-washing, while realizing how malevolent a tool it could be in the wrong hands. Adolf Hitler was mentioned more than once, as were the leaders of the men who had caused our injuries.

39. ORDINATION

"I know what you mean, Jack," Father Justin's words were soft as he replaced his wine glass carefully upon its coaster. "I have often wondered at how people manage to suspend their sense of reality so quickly. How is it that rational thinking can be so easily put aside?"

I was grateful to be home. The journey back had passed without mishap, but I felt dishonest throughout as I tried to emulate my friends' Oberammergau experiences. It was with relief that I talked to Father Justin over our supper of a cottage pie that Elsie had made especially for my return.

I hadn't intended to tell my mentor of the upsetting nature of the trip. I was worried my reaction would seem ungrateful and inappropriate for a deacon approaching ordination. However, the old man was not easily fooled, and he knew me well enough to see through the smoke screen of enthusiasm I was putting up as I described the brief holiday in the mountains.

Under Father Justin's quiet questioning, I found pretense evaporating and my true feelings spilled out as from a lanced boil. I was much relieved to see Father Justin nodding his head sympathetically as I spoke of my horror at the macabre nature of the murals and shops in Garmisch, Parternkirchen and in Obberamergau itself. The gross commercialization of my faith had made me feel sick.

"And the play itself?" Father Justin asked softly as the descriptions of the villages and shops faded away.

Taking a deep breath I told the vicar of my genuine appreciation of the artistry of the production and of the grand and exciting atmosphere the players managed to produce. Pausing to eat my supper - and to buy time – I watched Father Justin fill our glasses with the Stanhope's claret of the month, wondering how to proceed. Finally, with a deep sigh, I reported my failure to empathize with the production in the same way as everyone else.

"There was a kind of group hysteria all around me, Father," I said. "Eyes were glazed, not only with tears, but with some strange sort of force that transported people into another dimension – so that in some way they were no longer responsible for their actions. Even my dear friends, who I know so well, were moved to the point of feeling Jesus' pain – or rather the pain portrayed by the man playing the part of Jesus. It was all very confusing for me.

"I know it was a wonderful experience, and please don't mistake me, Father, I appreciated the trip enormously and found it fascinating, but as a personal religious experience for my soul, I'm afraid I missed the boat."

To my great relief and surprise, Father Justin applauded both my honesty and my ability to detach myself from the crowd – although I had done so somewhat unwillingly.

"Just because everyone around you acts in a particular way doesn't mean you have to join them, Jack, and doesn't mean that you are wrong. I'm impressed by your having maintained a rational view of the whole thing, and I believe you to be the stronger for having done so."

"But, Father," I interjected. "I am having doubts now about my ordination. If I can't feel God's divinity as so many others can, how can . . . how can I continue trying to teach His word?

"You know how I am always pleading with God for help with the advice I am asked to give to our parishioners. I have spoken to you of my feelings of inadequacy and the continuing absence of any help from The Almighty. Maybe the church, which has been my home for so long, is not the right place for me – but if it isn't, God help me, I don't know for what else I am suited."

I had been speaking into my plate. Taking a gulp of wine, I slowly raised my eyes to the Priest who returned the gaze with affection and sympathy.

"Ah, Jack," he began softly, "how well I remember those very feelings myself. Rather like a man about to step into matrimony having a last minute panic, I also almost turned away from my ordination. My feelings of unworthiness came from many directions, and my doubts niggled away at me like parasites.

"My mentor, Father Matthew, who also guided Father David, by the way, listened to me well before trying to set me straight. I may not remember his exact words, but the spirit of his speech is with me still." Father Justin reached for the decanter of port on the sideboard behind him.

"Father Matthew explained to me that my doubts and worries were signs of my humanity and as such to be examined and noted but not to be feared," he continued, filling his port glass carefully. "Doubts should act as an anchor that can steady a speeding boat that may be heading unknowingly for a reef. Not to stop it, just to slow it down a bit, so that the mind at the helm has time to see the hazards ahead and to steer the right course.

"You never conquer your doubts, Jack, or if you do, new ones arrive to fill the gaps the old ones have left. However, you can learn to live alongside them; to keep them contained so they do not blight your true knowledge but keep it in perspective. You need to learn to heed their warnings from time to time and to analyze where they come from. Use your doubts to your advantage by allowing them to keep over-zealous fantasies at bay and to hone your religious thought to its essence.

"How can anyone who claims not to have any doubts about the intangible nature of our beliefs - all of which are beyond scientific proof - possibly be qualified to help their parishioners?" Father Justin looked at me steadily, but it was clear this was a rhetorical question, and I said nothing.

"Someone who claims to have only the clear sky of unquestioned belief cannot help those who bring clouds of negativity with them when they come to ask for help. Those in trouble never come to us when the first cloud approaches, no they wait until there's a full thunder storm raging in their emotions, and then they want help from someone with genuine understanding of their fears and worries. Not some pontificating idiot who takes the "holier than thou" stance with the surety of his convictions and is incapable of empathy.

"Descartes made the famous declaration: 'cogito, ergo sum.' The full quote is sometimes rendered as "dubito, ergo cogito, ergo sum. That missing first word is the essence of our friend René's philosophy. It is 'dubito' that puts existence into perspective for him; the only thing that was beyond question for Descartes was that he was capable of doubt."

Father Justin sipped his port thoughtfully. "As the Bible teaches us: God manifests Himself in different ways to different people," he continued. "It is not for us to demand a particular type of relationship with The Almighty. You are a good man; an honest man who genuinely cares for people. There's not a selfish or false bone in your body. You have the most giving heart I have ever met, and you offer yourself to assist others without restraint. That generosity of spirit is an aspect of God's grace within you, and one which is more profound than any kind of group hysteria which can be brought about by introducing collective hypnosis to less objective minds.

"Your ability to lay down your weaknesses before people is one of your great strengths. No wonder our family at St. George's has taken to you so readily. You identify with their problems without criticism or judgment, you tell them all the reasons why you don't think you are worthy of giving advice, and then you give the best advice they could possibly get from anywhere. You can't let a talent like that go to waste.

"Besides," Father Justin paused to refill his glass. "The more realists there are within the Church, the more chance we have of instilling morality within the population without being called all sorts of old-fashioned names.

"It's one thing when a crowd suspends their belief in order to embrace a particular occasion, such as your passion play, but it's quite another when people do so on a regular basis – every time they read the Bible, in fact. There are many seemingly sensible and educated people who want to believe that everything written there is real, and not an elaborate metaphor, or just some random quasi-historical story. They suspend their rational minds and persuade themselves that these writings from two thousand years ago are sacred facts. How can that be?

"No, Jack. The church needs young people like you now more than ever. It needs honest men with their own sense of what is right and the courage to speak out and say so when necessary. Men – and women," he added after a moment's pause, "with motives which are genuinely unselfish and good.

"You have a calling, Jack. You can't turn a deaf ear to such a summons. Our church will crumble if people like you don't stick with it and set it on a modern track."

I had never heard Father Justin speak for so long and was deeply moved by the speech. I remember feeling humble, proud, and grateful all at the same time, and tried to find a way to communicate these sentiments. My efforts were brushed away.

"Oh, stuff and nonsense," said the elderly priest. "We all need a bit of a push now and then. Why don't we go together to Wipples tomorrow and sort out your robes for the ordination, I never pass up an opportunity to visit that extraordinary emporium."

Wipples, the London tailors where most of the Anglican priesthood acquire their garments, was indeed a splendid place, more of a shrine than a shop. Arriving at the highly polished double doors of dark mahogany, with gleaming brass handles, gave me the same sense of awe as I felt when entering a cathedral. Inside, the glassy wooden floors, with an ever-present smell of wax reminiscent of incense, matched the very large counter that dominated the room with the importance of an altar; an old fashioned, gleaming cash register taking the central place of honor. The reverence with which the staff handled their wares and the hushed tones in which mundane questions were asked and answered in liturgical tones combined to strengthen the feeling that there was a sacred element within the walls.

Father Justin greeted the staff by their Christian names with easy familiarity. He soon had two men of about my age running around opening drawers, taking down hangers and spreading garments across the counter top with loving caresses.

I found the whole scene as amusing as it was fascinating. I only managed to suppress a strong desire to laugh because of a sense that any show of mirth would be considered sacrilegious and disrespectful. I let Father Justin make all the decisions and allowed myself to be twirled in front of the largest tryptic of mirrors I had ever encountered, wearing one set of robes after another. I was surprised at the images that confronted me.

Mirrors were not something that played a big part in my life. The only one I had at St. George's was a shaving mirror, reminiscent of that in my room at St. Augustine's – it allowed for only a small percentage of my visage to be seen at a time. The vicarage walls were covered in dour prints; there wasn't even a mirror in the sacristy. At the barber's, I always busied myself with magazines, giving my reflection the briefest of glances to nod embarrassed approval to the man with the brush and scissors. So I was quite unfamiliar with the full-length three-dimensional images that looked at me from the huge, ornate mirrors at Wipples.

When had the gangly youth changed into this mature man? I remember regarding myself with both surprise and interest. My nose, which had always seemed too big for my face was now in proportion with a strong jaw and wide forehead. Gazing back at me were eyes full of quiet confidence, the dark-framed glasses no longer seemed inappropriately large and my abundant black hair surrounded a strong, lean face, slightly bronzed from the hours I spent gardening. A tall physique with squared shoulders and upright stance showed the robes to great advantage.

The reflections of both kinds were interrupted as more and more garments kept appearing; there were surplices, chasubles, cassocks, stoles and all sorts of exotic habits. It wasn't until Father Justin suggested I try on a bishop's mitre that I realized the old priest was enjoying himself at the expense of his protégé.

And expensive it certainly was. Father Justin was aware that my father, in an uncharacteristic gesture of support, had volunteered to buy the necessary trousseau required by a newly ordained man of the cloth. With a grand flourish, and to my astonishment, Father Justin wrote my father's name and the Willenbury address, to which the invoice should be sent, without a moment's hesitation.

The acolytes bowed with respect, gathered up the paperwork, and handed me my new wardrobe packed in immaculately wrapped brown-paper parcels, neatly tied with fine white string. Father Justin led the way out through the double doors and the hushed interior of refinement was replaced by the noisy traffic of central London approaching rush hour.

Father Justin set off down the street at a good pace, with me striding behind, juggling my parcels. Only a block away from Wipples, Father Justin took a sudden left turn into a mews and disappeared into a pub with the unlikely name of The Fox & Vivian. I followed, ducking my head through the low door, into an equally polished interior of a completely different kind from the one we had just left.

This time it was the lovingly rubbed bar and draft beer pump handles that stood in for an altar and central cross, and the smell of hops and spilt ale that replaced that of incense. A large barman with a round red face was holding court, already pulling a pint at Father Justin's request.

"Bishop's Finger" Father Justin said as he handed me the dark brew with its froth threatening to overflow the dimpled glass. "Most appropriate after our afternoon's activity, don't you think?" He picked up the second pint that had appeared on the bar top and raised it carefully: "Here's to you Jack," he said with a sudden serious mien; "to many rewarding hours in your new robes, and to a long and fruitful life in the church."

The old vicar took several gulps from his glass, his tongue carefully removing a foam moustache as he replaced the glass tankard on the bar top with a sigh of satisfaction.

I nodded my thanks and returned the salute, drinking the amber liquid with equal enjoyment.

"We might as well hide out here until the rush hour is over," Father Justin continued as he fumbled in his pocket to pay for the beers. "There's never a trip to Wipples which isn't followed by a visit to The Fox & V. It's a tradition."

We found a table in a corner and spent a pleasant hour chatting about our life at St. George's before catching a series of packed underground trains back to Islington and were home in time for Elsie's supper. Afterwards, I unpacked my parcels with feelings of delight and excitement that I had not expected, and hung the robes carefully in the little wardrobe. Suddenly, the misgivings about my ordination had evaporated and I was looking forward to 'Petertide' just a few weeks hence, at the end of June, when the ordination would take place.

My father, mother and Alice drove into London for my big day - Robert apparently had a social appointment in the country that demanded his attention. I was not so much disappointed by the absence of my brother, as I was astonished by the presence of my parents and sister. This unexpected show of family support made me feel slightly uncomfortable, but I was determined to banish negative thoughts and encounter the day with positivity. I greeted my family outside the cathedral where the ceremony was to be performed with warmth and affection, and amazement when I realized that, for the first time in my life, they were proud of me. I was also touched to see that many of our St. George's parishioners had made the effort to dress up and travel to the City to support me.

Elsie had travelled with Father Justin and myself; upon arriving, I was greeted by Lorna, Charlotte and Sally, Estelle, and Dilly wearing a huge floral display on her head that made us all laugh.

The ceremony itself was long and complicated with several different components. First there were graduating students becoming deacons, as I had done, then the deacons who were being promoted to the priesthood, and finally there were two priests who were becoming canons.

Father Justin was at the bishop's side when it was my turn to kneel at the altar rail. He joined in 'the priesting' by putting a hand on one of his protégé's shoulders while the bishop touched the other one. The choir was singing something beautiful – I don't remember what - accompanied by an organ of huge stature, the drones of the bass reverberating through the cathedral. The bishop was chanting something grave in a deep voice.

Like some sort of automaton I went through the carefully rehearsed motions as if watching my body from outside, somewhere in the distance, with only a mild interest in the proceedings. I came away more conscious of the rustle of my new clothes than aware of any sense of spirituality, but I definitely felt enlivened and excited in a way I had not anticipated. The appearance of my two families, dressed as for a special occasion, meant more to me than I could have imagined.

On regaining my pew, I sank to my knees in an effort to absorb what had just happened. In two short minutes, I had become qualified to celebrate Holy Communion on my own, to give blessings, perform weddings and to absolve sins – and yet I felt just the same as before. I prayed to be worthy of this new authority, beseeched God for help with the awesome responsibilities and expressed my never-ending gratitude for a multitude of wonders.

40. CHATTER OF DIFFERENT KINDS

Following my ordination, life at St. George's went on without any outward sign of change. Only Father Justin and I noticed that I was taking over more and more of the services now that I was able to deliver them in their entirety. My outward duties as curate were really no different to those I had as a deacon, but the greater depth of responsibility I had undertaken was always with me.

Rosie's visits were still a regular feature of life at St. George's, however. In between counseling the adult parishioners, it was a relief to let the chattering of this young girl fill the church with a banter to which no response was required. All I had to do was welcome her, assign her a task with a duster or mop, and ask her a question. Then she was off, filling half an hour, or more, with inconsequential stories – or so I thought.

"Tell me about your family." I remember saying one sunny afternoon in late spring. We were in the churchyard, I was trimming the grass around the grave stones whose weight had tilted them at arguing angles over the years.

Rosie was perched on a lichen-covered sarcophagus, dangling her legs as she did when on the pews, watching me wrestle with some convolvulus that was insistently curling around a headstone. Two cherubic heads, with wings fanning out behind them and clouds billowing beneath, were wearing wreaths of the green foliage.

"Well, there's baby Jo," Rosie started, "he's just six months old, and everybody's thrilled because he's a boy. I don't know why, he's just another baby with nappies that need changing and food that needs mashing up. More washing and work for me, and he cries all the time." She gave a big sigh before continuing.

"Then there's Clara-Belle, she's three and learning to do most things for herself at last – but she needs watching all the time or she's bound to come to grief, so Ma says.

"Emma-Lee is five now, and I take her to school most mornings along with Louisa who was just a baby when we came to London. She's seven now. Pearl is ten, and she helps me quite a lot with the house, cooking, washing and all. But I'm the oldest, and I'm in charge and responsible if anything happens to any of them."

This last was said in a matter of fact tone, without strains of either hardship or hubris. It was just the way it was. I paused in my battle with the bindweed, aware that the prattle had stopped and that it was time to prompt the next phase.

"What about your mother?" I posed, more to keep Rosie occupied than out of interest.

"Ma works nights at the club." Rosie replied, and cheerfully took up her narrative. "She has to leave every evening at five to be there for six. It takes her an hour to get ready, and we all have to stay out of the way, except when she calls for her tea. When she's ready to go, she looks wonderful – so tall and covered in bright colors, with bright lipstick and blues and purples above her eyes. Her hair is bushed out, with ribbons hidden amongst the curls. She has high shoes that I couldn't begin to walk in – oh, she's really something special, is Ma. You should see her, Father Jack, when she's ready for work, she's pure magic. I want to look like that when I grow up and have cupboards full of bright clothes and high-heeled shoes, as she does."

I had won the battle with the Morning Glory – 'what a name to give such an invasive plant,' I thought, as I moved to use a rusty trowel to dig out a family of dandelions at the base of the headstone.

"She doesn't get home until nearly daylight, my Ma." Rosie went on. "It's hard working nights. I often hear her and Pa shouting and bumping around their bedroom, which is above my room. Then she has to sleep all day, so that she's ready to go back to work again in the evening. Sunday she stays at home, but poor Ma is always too tired to do much on a Sunday, that's why she doesn't come to church. She says I spend so much time here I can pray for her, so she doesn't have to.

"I love to bring her meals on a tray on Sundays and to sit by her in her bedroom and sort out the jars and pots of make-up. They're always in such a mess, all over the dressing-table, and when I've got them all neat and tidy, she lets me try some of them."

So it was that I learnt a little of Rosie's life when she was not following me about in and around the Church. She was a breath of fresh air after Philip's morose alcoholic ramblings, the demands of Lorna, Sally and Charlotte, and the gap Estelle's absence had created in my life. The wonderful thing about Rosie was that she never expected anything back. The occasional nod, or a prompting phrase would keep her going until it was time for her to wave a cheery goodbye as she closed the lytch gate and skipped off up the hill to the family duties of which I was learning so much.

It was understandable that, during the school holidays, Rosie's visits became less regular, but then they became a rarity. Once or twice she visited the church, with her siblings in tow, swathed in a heavy overcoat in spite of the warm weather. She was busy with her family duties, she explained, but would not forget to visit me whenever she could. I remember smiling to myself at the way in which this little girl, with responsibilities way beyond her years, worried that I might miss our chats, even though they were so one-sided.

As time passed and my commitments to the grown up parishioners who beleaguered me increased, I failed to notice how Rosie's visits ceased altogether.

Tracy didn't really qualify as a grown up parishioner, I had thought, until one day I found her kneeling in the empty church, right at the back, close to the font where my chats with Phillip took place. She sat up at the sound of my approach, the light struggling through the stained glass windows glinting on wet cheeks.

With a deep sense of foreboding, I sat down beside her. "Is there something you would like to talk about, Tracy?" I was trying to keep my voice soft and non-demanding, to keep the irritation I was feeling well hidden.

"Oh please, Father Jack," the girl began with a whisper. "I need your help, well, God's help really."

"God is listening to you Tracy, never doubt that. He hears your prayers and has brought me here, to this corner of the church, for a purpose." How I wished I could have felt sure about that. Duty called, and I tried to sound encouraging as I asked: "How can I help?"

Upon reflection, I had no idea why I had suddenly chosen to investigate this particular spot in the large church. My feet had brought me there unbidden and it had been with surprise that I had found the kneeling girl amongst the neat rows of hymnals and prayer books. There had been no sound of any door opening or of footsteps that usually echoed across the stone slabs and gave me warning to be 'on duty.'

"I'm pregnant, father." Tracy's declaration threw me into a panic but the girl didn't seem to notice. It was as though a damn of resistance had been breached as words spilt out of her in a rush.

"Social Services say I'm too young to be a mother. They say that my whole future will be ruined – you know what they say about puppies not being only for Christmas, well it seems the same is true for babies. They say if I act now, it's a simple operation and my body will be back to normal in no time at all. The whole thing can be paid for by the National Health and I can resume my life at school without missing more than a couple of days. No-one will ever know."

The girl took a gulp of air and went on again. "Whereas if I keep it – and doesn't the church say I should – my future is locked into early adult-hood, no more school, no prospects for a financially secure future – and so on.

"What should I do, father Jack? What does God want me to do?"

Not for the first time since I began my ministry, there was a moment of crisis in my soul and panic in my heart. What should I say to this girl of fourteen - fifteen at the most? Of course the Social Services argument had a lot of sense in it; far more than any alternative argument I could think of. But there was a life in this discussion. A foetus with a beating heart; a human being; part of God's creative genius; a living soul. How could I advise its termination?

"What do your parents say?" I was buying time.

"Mother calls me a little slut and keeps going on asking who the father is. I won't tell her, because I don't want to tell him – it's my problem and my decision. Why complicate things even more?"

There was no indication as to whether this lack of communication with the father was to protect someone, or if the girl actually didn't know the identity of the man whose act had resulted in this quandary.

"What about your father?" I asked softly.

"He's not fussed," Tracy replied. "He knows it will be an extra mouth to feed, but we'll get more money from the Social Services, and we might be able to use the new baby to get us a house instead of our flat. He says he hopes it's a boy."

A small hole in the stone slab at my feet had caught my attention. There must have been a tiny pebble in the rock, in another age, to have left such a clearly defined indentation, I thought. The geological puzzle seemed immensely attractive and I longed to explore it and not to confront Tracy's predicament.

"What do you want to do, Tracy?" I was aware that I was still stalling. "What do your heart and mind tell you to do?

"That's easy," the girl's short laugh was grating. "My brain tells me to get shot of the thing pronto and get on with my life. My heart says I can't. My heart says that it's my lot in life to be a mother to whatever this turns out to be. Sometimes my brain seems to be winning, and then the heart steps in and shuts the brain out. I don't know what to do, father Jack. That's why I'm here, in this church, talking to you."

The weight of responsibility I had felt at my ordination crashed onto my shoulders like a mantle of lead. How could I pass judgment on something as vital as this – oh yes that was the right word – vital, indeed it was.

Where was the St. Augustine manual telling how to cope with a matter of life and death like this? Philip's threatened suicides were bad enough, but now I was being presented with another scenario of greater magnitude, in that Philip's threats were just that – threats - and I was doing my best to parry them. There was no doubt in my mind as to how to advise Philip. Here, however, was a terrifying choice being put at my door where my own life would remain relatively unaffected by what I chose to say, and another life – or may be two – would be changed forever.

Of course I knew what the Scriptures taught and the route I was duty bound to recommend to the girl, but at the same time I saw that the argument from the Social Services made a great deal of sense as far as Tracy's life was concerned. I prayed silently for help and ended up with a middle road solution, which I recognized as being more of a cowardly way out of the dilemma for me than a conclusive answer for Tracy.

"Why don't you go back to the social services and talk this situation through with them once again, Tracy? I can't recommend a road for you to take. It's something that I'm afraid you must work out for yourself, but please bear this always in mind: God is gracious in his forgiveness, he knows you to be a genuinely good person and he loves you as only Almighty God can.

"Let Him guide you during your discussions with the Social Service people – remember they are God's servants also. Know that he will support you, whichever decision you make, and give you the necessary strength to go down whichever road you choose. Keep God in your heart, Tracy, and keep your dialogue open with Him through prayer. He will not abandon you."

We sat in silence for some time, apart from Tracy's sniffling. "Would you like me to call Father Justin to talk to you?" I asked, feeling that I had let her down, and eager to dilute the responsibility. "I'm afraid I'm very new to this job, and maybe someone with more experience would know better how to advise you."

"No, thank you." Tracy's answer surprised me with its urgency. "I'm frightened of Father Justin. He would never understand. You're different, Father Jack, I knew you wouldn't be angry with me. I hoped you'd tell me what to do."

"Oh dear, Tracy, I'm afraid I've let you down rather, haven't I?" I said in a low voice, feeling totally wretched.

"No, not really, Father. I think you've told me it would be all right to follow the advice of the Social Services – that's what it sort of sounded like, anyway. I have to tell you that I am as relieved as I am surprised. And you have given me great comfort in telling me that God will understand and forgive me. I believe I now have the strength to go ahead and put all this business behind me and get on with my life. I have learnt a big lesson, Father. This mistake will not happen again."

"No, well, I'm sure . . " My voice trailed away as I realized I wasn't sure of anything any more. "Look, Tracy, you know this conversation is safe with me. It won't go outside these walls. Take your time, reflect carefully, talk to your parents – as they already know of the situation – and to the Social Services again. Then you can make up your mind and trust in God to show you the right path."

"Time is just what I haven't got, Father." Tracy was quick to answer. "If it's going to be done, it has to be in the next three days. I know I've left it late to come and talk to you, but I was frightened you would tell Father Justin, and I just couldn't bear that. You won't will you?"

"No," I said with great reluctance, I had been relying on the older priest's review of the situation and his instruction on how it could have been better handled in case – God forbid – such an occasion should be repeated.

"Promise me, Father Jack, please promise me you won't tell Father Justin." The girl must have picked up my hesitation.

"I promise, Tracy," I said with a deep sigh. "I promise, your secret is safe with me." And I knew it would be.

Tracy stood up suddenly and threw her arms around me. "Thank you, father, thank you so, so much. You are my savior, and I will never forget your kindness and your honesty in talking to me like this."

"No, child," I regretted the epithet as soon as it was uttered, "I am not your Savior. It is our Lord Jesus Christ who is your Savior, who understands your travails. Have faith in His love and follow his guidance."

"Bless me, father. Please give me blessing before I leave this wonderful church where I have found such sanctuary." Tracy plumped down on her knees on the stone slabs by the font, and bent her head.

The next thing I knew, I was standing before her and giving the blessing used at the end of every service. I made the sign of the cross and prayed silently to God for forgiveness of my own sins, rather than those of the girl in front of me.

After Tracy had left, I spent a long time on my knees in the little chapel of St. John of the Cross, asking forgiveness for my wrong-doing to the unborn, unwanted foetus that Tracy was carrying to its destruction. Slumped against the back of the pew in front of me, I felt exhausted by worry and the deep fear that I had not acted according to God's will. I prayed and yearned for understanding and enlightenment regarding this difficult situation. Surely the girl needed time to grow up and form a life of her own before being asked to donate it to the encumbrances of children. I prayed for Tracy, herself, that she should be forgiven for her ignorance and innocence, and that she might love God all the more for His support. Perhaps she might trust in the Lord to find her a suitable partner to stand by her when she matured enough to be ready for parenthood.

"Oh Lord, please give me the strength I need to carry on the ministry you have given me." As always, back then, I was fervent with my prayers. "Help me to hear your voice when I am asked for advice. Please help your humble servant who is so acutely aware of his short-comings and ignorance of the ways of your strange but wonderful world. Let me hear your voice, please, please let me hear your voice." This last was beginning to become a mantra for me.

41. OLD TRADITIONS, NEW IDEAS

This incident with Tracy, which worries me still, has reminded me of another young girl, torn between duty and desire. I am back in Africa, again.

I loved my life at Cachonga. The lack of luxuries worried me not at all – in fact I barely noticed it. It's only since my return and my travels throughout Europe and America, instructing future missionaries, that I realized, from the questions that were raised over and over again, how very basic was life in the bush.

One of my regular friends by my hut each morning

In this remote village, I was enlivened in a way that I had never before experienced, with goals I could visualize clearly, and saw no reason why they could not be achieved as long as there was enough hard work, energy, perseverance, and, of course, patience.

I was being a soldier of God in a far more tangible way than I had been during my more conventional pastoral life in Islington. The satisfaction that came from the success of the smallest achievement filled me with happiness and I met every new day with excitement.

There was only one area in this new life that made me uncomfortable - unhappy even - the custom of wedding young girls to old men. Loveness had become like a daughter to me – she reminded me of Rosie, of course.

My relationship with the young girl who, as translator, was a constant support during all my endeavors, made me understand what parental love must feel like - an extra dimension of giving and protective tenderness. I knew that all children grow up and leave home, and that I would move away some day, but, like any parent, I cherished the here-and-now love experience and hung on to every detail of her changing, growing life. Her intended marriage to Josiah, who had many children older than this new bride, filled me with horror; I found it difficult to deal with the man in a civil manner. So I made it a duty to get to know him and his six existing wives who ranged in age –I surmised – between twenty and fifty. Loveness would be wife number seven by the time she was barely fifteen.

Josiah was in charge of education in the village, and it was obvious that nothing had been done since my predecessor left. He was a relatively well-educated man, aged somewhere between sixty-five and seventy-five, and perfectly capable of teaching the young of the village, but he needed motivating, and I decided to make this motivation part of my mission. Obviously the children of the village needed to be educated, but I was using this valuable cause as a means to get to know the man who was to claim the honor of my young, and much valued, helper. He was a tall, thin man with a dignified air and his gentle acquiescence to my involvement indicated a twinge of guilt, perhaps, in the way in which he had let things slip at Cachonga. There was now a whole generation of young children without any knowledge of either reading or writing.

When I offered my help by suggesting the provision of a blackboard and chalk, Josiah sighed in resignation and agreed that these things were needed, but that they would never be forthcoming.

It took a while, almost two months in fact, but eventually a blackboard arrived via the Bishop's office, courtesy of an aid agency somewhere far away, along with chalk, slates, exercise books and pencils. Josiah began to look at me with a mixture of admiration and irritation. His life was no longer one of complete idleness.

Winning the trust of the people of Cachonga had not been easy. I spent a lot of time, energy and, above all patience, to achieve it, and I was always aware of how fragile my position was with the hierarchy of the village. I desperately wanted to maintain the present relationship with the Chief and the elders, but my dislike of the status quo regarding marriages was becoming harder and harder to ignore. With the church nearing completion, Loveness's wedding day was getting ever nearer. I decided to approach the magician Umboto once again, and ask for his help.

With the start of the new church and the re-establishment of the village school, Umboto's reservations about me seemed to have diminished. While he was still suspicious of the changes happening around him, The witch-doctor relished the way that everything appeared to be done through him and had convinced himself - along with everybody else - that it was his mind that generated all the new ideas, that their implementation was all done through his authority.

Nervous of letting anything slip past him, Umboto got into the habit of visiting my hut every evening, before the sun went down, to talk and to study the drawings I was making and the manuals from which the ideas had come. Loveness was frequently called in to help whenever I had difficulty explaining a particular concept to this man of magic. When I acquired a paraffin lantern – a gift sent from Sollis – the evening talks grew longer.

During these discussions, Umboto was constantly on the look out to discover the secret agenda he suspected me of nurturing; to be ready to expose whatever scheme I had in mind for my own aggrandizement; and to thwart such a plan, whatever it might be. However, as the weeks passed, and one after another of my suggestions became ideas of his own, I began to glimpse moments of respect from the great man. It appeared that I was genuine in my wanting to help Cachonga develop. Bit by bit, he learned the various plans I had in mind and made them his own. It was Umboto who then presented the various projects to the elders, taking pride in being able to explain, in detail, all aspects of the latest venture.

Now, with Loveness's wedding on the horizon, I had to test Umboto's trust and use it as best I could.

It was evening, and as usual the revered N'anga had stopped at my hut to discuss agriculture and learn about a new scheme I had mentioned earlier that day. It was a lure with which to put my ideas on matrimony to the test.

I lit the paraffin lamp with due ceremony and the two of us sat opposite each other, as was our custom – Umboto on the earthen bench, me on my grass mattress – with the lamp, supported by the tin trunk, in the middle, a stack of books at the ready.

"N'anga Umboto," I addressed my new friend with his full title. "May I talk to you about something that has been troubling me?"

Umboto straightened and nodded with due solemnity.

"May I talk to you as a friend, dear Umboto?" I was choosing words and tones carefully, trying to hide the nervousness.

Umboto looked worried for a fraction of a second, and then nodded his consent.

I started talking about the excitement of seeing Cachonga beginning to modernize; how there was potential in this village to become a symbol of developing Africa, and if this was accomplished how money would become available for all sorts of further improvements. How other villages should, and probably would, need Umboto's help to grow in the same direction, how Umboto would put Cachonga on the map as an example of how the smallest African village can improve the lives of its people better than the big cities. How progress can and does have a place in Central Africa.

Umboto got a bit lost in the middle of this speech and called for Loveness who, as usual, was waiting just outside the hut entrance. She took her place, sitting cross-legged on the floor, between us, and translated in her calm, soft voice. Umboto was growing taller by the minute as my speech became intelligible to him.

So far the plan was proceeding well.

"My question to you, dear Umboto, is" I continued after a suitably dramatic pause, "are you happy with this presentation of yourself to the world as a 'modern man,' the leader who pulls his village from medieval times onto the threshold of the twenty-first century."

Umboto spoke gravely, and Loveness translated: "I understand that it is my calling to do this thing of which you speak, vicar, and I am ready," he declared with due solemnity.

"That is good, N'anga," I replied, "I had expected nothing less. However there are certain tribal habits that might need to change, if you are to acquire recognition as a modern man, and if Cachonga is to receive the funding I believe it deserves."

Loveness translated by rote. The witch doctor shrugged his shoulders and indicated for me to continue.

"Well, there is the initiation rite required when the young men are around eleven or twelve, I think, to turn them from boys to warriors." I was using a foil. "In other parts of the world," I paused again, this time only to allow Loveness to translate; "circumcision is performed when a baby boy is only a few days old - and the killing of a great beast is not considered to be essential to maturity." Again a pause for Loveness's interpretation, her tone was taking on a new edge of interest. "The warriors here are a wasted resource" I continued. "The village needs competent and strong workers, not young men who sit around sharpening their spears. You could transform the farming here overnight if the warriors were prepared to view working in the fields as honorable. Only you can make that change."

Umboto listened carefully as Loveness translated. He nodded slowly. "I shall think about what you have said," he pronounced.

I did not wait for the translation. "Oh, yes, and there's another thing," I added quickly. "People in what is known as 'the civilized world' do not approve of arranged marriages, that is to say, of marriages where both the bride and the groom are not entirely happy with the idea." I stopped and nodded to Loveness to translate. She was looking at me with wide eyes that had suddenly become watery. She turned to Umboto and translated the message.

"Also, it is not considered appropriate for a man to have more than one wife, however, I can see that we have to allow present culture to adapt slowly, and a man who already has many wives should be able to live out his life as he had anticipated." Again a nod to Loveness, who hesitated before translating.

"What you can do, to show the world how things are changing here, deep in middle Africa, is to assure the world that this is a tradition of the past, and one which has been outgrown by the present modern day people."

Loveness translated with a new speed, looking directly at Umboto as the words sped from her lips.

There was a long pause before Umboto repeated: "I shall think about what you have said." Again, I didn't wait for a translation. It was a phrase with which I had become very familiar.

"And now, my dear friend," I continued in the most natural tone I could muster, "I want to tell you about some ideas expressed in this book" I tapped my much thumbed copy of 'Organic Farming in the Developing World.' "About how we can multiply the yields from agriculture in this village so that Cachonga will be the envy of the whole country."

Loveness's tone, as she translated, had lost its enthusiasm.

I went on to explain to Umboto how the small area of cleared bush behind the village, which was the extent of Cachonga's farmland, was not sufficient to feed an expanding village and grow enough crops with which to trade. I was sure that Umboto would agree that maize, rape and cassava were not the only crops that could be grown. That there were lots of possibilities that neighboring villages had not thought of that Umboto could get going with success.

We talked for another hour as I showed Umboto pictures and diagrams in the cherished book. "We won't have access to pesticides and manufactured fertilizers, nor the money to purchase them; so we might be able to obtain Organic certification," I explained, and then added with suitable emphasis: "it will give our products a higher value when sold in the cities."

Umboto looked from my face to the book and back again, his eyes wide with either disbelief or excitement, I couldn't tell which. "I shall think about what you have said," he repeated solemnly, before leaving the hut and going out into the darkness.

As my role at Cachonga was officially only that of the village vicar, I was not included in the daily deliberations of the chief and elders – a relief really as I had no desire to sit having talks during daylight hours when there was so much to be done. However, I was impatient to learn of Umboto's progress and busied myself in the vicinity of the chief's council hut the following morning.

The chief and the elders had discussed Umboto's latest idea of bringing Cachonga into modern times. It turned out not to be the up-hill struggle that I had anticipated. All the elders already had half a dozen wives, at least, and found the up-keep of all those huts, and, presumably, many other demands from their spouses, to be physically and financially draining. They had all agreed with alacrity not to acquire any more wives and to restrict men of the next generation to one wife each. It was noted that this change would also improve business at the brothel, which paid dues to the chief, so it seemed a satisfactory arrangement all round.

The proposed marriage of Loveness to Josiah was never mentioned again. Instead, Loveness became the old man's assistant at the school and began to teach the children English. Looking back on this, I'm still proud of this achievement - regardless of what Loveness later became.

42. FLYING WITH THE ANGELS

During the early days of my priesthood, it was a great boon to have Rufus comparatively close. Our parishes were very different, but our problems were the same as we grew into our responsibilities. We would meet every four or five weeks at The Australian, a pub somewhere between Knightsbridge and Chelsea, half way between our two parishes, and exchange stories of our experiences and the resulting worries or delights – usually the former.

One such interchange sticks indelibly in my mind, not the least because the first time I recounted it to Percival and Amrita, they were so amused and delighted by the tale that I was asked to repeat it several times during the following weeks and months. Any time we found ourselves confronted with a quagmire of despondency, one of them would say "come on Jack, tell us again about Winston's magic." Hence my notes of the story Rufus told me were refined several times as I remembered details previously omitted and embellished those already told. It also held within it the mystery of de-corporealisation, an experience that all three of us had experienced during different life-threatening moments. Thankfully, with this tale, there was none of the angst that accompanied our own near-death experiences

It had only been about three weeks since my last meeting with Rufus when he telephoned with a note of urgency in his voice, saying it was time for another of our get-togethers. I was only too happy to comply.

As usual we met promptly at half past six in the evening. and, furnished with a pint glass of frothing ale, sat ourselves in a booth towards the back of the pub.

Rufus listened with an edge of impatience to my inconsequential news. I noticed the Scotsman fidgeting on the bench reminiscent of a high-backed pew; his fingers tapped the sides of the glass tankard, already partially drained, so that I curtailed my description of Elsie's habit of hiding things. "It's her way of telling me to be tidy, I realize that, but it's quite infuriating when you are in the middle of writing a sermon, and all of a sudden you can't find your notes or the passages you're researching, and so on." My companion was obviously not enthralled.

"Somehow I feel this mundane domestic trivia is not holding your attention, Rufus," I said with a smile. "What's on your mind?"

"I've been let into the secret of St. Luke's success." Rufus lent forward across the beer-smudged table and gave a deep sigh. He shot a quick glance in my direction and then returned his eyes to the froth-lined glass in his hands and the amber liquid waltzing in the lower half. "The only thing is, that it really is a secret, and I shouldn't be telling you – but if I don't share this with someone sane, I'll go mad." Rufus lifted his eyes once more, and this time did not lower them. "I've always been grateful for our friendship, Jack, growing as it has from our shared experiences over the years, but never more so than now, when I really need someone to talk to, someone I can trust implicitly."

"What on earth have you found out, Rufus?" I lowered my voice instinctively and shifted to lean forwards in conspiratorial fashion, the better to catch the tale.

"It seems that when Father Henry first came to St. Luke's," Rufus began – Father Henry was his mentor, as Father Justin was mine; "the congregation was almost non-existent - just a few old biddies and one black family who always sat at the back. The old biddies had swooped upon the new vicar - well you know how it is – but he had to work hard to get the black family to trust him. He kept inviting them to the church hall for refreshments after the services, or to the vicarage itself, and eventually, one day they accepted."

Rufus had drained his glass and lifted it as he stood up. "I think I'll have another, how about you Jack?" he said, and receiving a nod, he crossed the wooden floor to the bar.

I watched my friend in a detached manner - a tall Scotsman leaning against the bar, turning his head in search of the barman. His red hair was not as bright as it had been when we first met, but was still orange enough and unruly enough to attract attention. His freckled face had lost the flush of youth and wore a lean, mature mien. He was a good-looking man, I suddenly thought, and the self-confidence that had grown with his faith and the success in his job, made him a striking figure altogether.

Rufus returned to our booth and set the slopping beer glasses down with steady hands. For the next hour we stayed with heads bowed towards each other as the story of St. Luke's unfolded.

When the black family had accepted the vicar's invitation, Rufus explained, there had been nothing prepared in the church hall, so Father Henry took the group to the vicarage. The leader of the family was a tall man called Raymond, with him was his wife, Rachel, and three or four children, plus his young and rather beautiful sister, Pearl. They found some tea and biscuits for the women and kids while Father Henry and Raymond each had a glass of port. The conversation started off somewhat stilted, but after the children had found a game of Ludo and the women had started to chat to each other, things got a bit easier.

Father Henry said that he wanted to pick Raymond's brains about how he could get to meet more of his parishioners – not to insist upon their coming to church, but just so that he could feel part of the community. He said that he felt ostracized at the moment, with people in the area shunning his presence. Even when he went shopping his friendly 'good-mornings' were met with silence, shrugs and suspicion.

By the end of the conversation, Raymond had promised to think about how he might help. Rachel suddenly joined the conversation to which she had obviously been listening. She suggested they hold a gathering - a picnic in the park, or something like that – where Father Henry could get to know everyone on a casual basis.

"But get rid of that" Pearl joined in, pointing to the vicar's dog collar. "Any sign of authority is viewed as suspect around here, and it would be easier to get people to talk to you if you dressed like everybody else."

Rachel was as good as her word and, after the service on the following Sunday, she told Father Henry that there was to be a communal picnic in Brockwell Park next Saturday evening, from six onwards, and that he was expected.

Rufus talked in a low voice, without hesitation. As he recounted Father Henry's tale, I felt included in the story, as if it was all happening just outside my window and I could watch it unfold.

It was mid-summer and the sky would stay light until after ten. There was a carnival atmosphere to the park when Henry joined the group at around seven on the Saturday evening. He had dispensed with his clerical collar and decided to get rid of the title also and to be just plain Henry for the duration of the evening. As instructed he was wearing jeans and an open-neck shirt and had deliberately omitted to shave that morning. He had thought of acquiring a T-shirt, but decided that if he'd managed to get to his mid-fifties without one, he could continue to do so. He hoped he looked suitably casual in spite of this and was relieved to find that he was not the only person in a conventional shirt, nor was his the only white face in the group.

More than a dozen families had gathered in the centre of the park in between some playing fields and a pond. Someone had organized a game of cricket with a mixture of children and adults. Henry stopped to watch; he had always been fond of cricket and had played for both his school and the theological college he'd attended.

As the tall bowler came thundering towards the wicket, Henry recognized Raymond. Having unleashed the ball at some speed towards a boy of about fifteen, who managed to deflect it satisfactorily, Raymond caught sight of Henry and gave him a friendly wave.

"Ah splendid," he said, and, abandoning the game, he strolled over to Henry and enveloped him with a large hot arm around the shoulders. "Hey, everybody, this is my mate Henry. Fancy a bit of cricket?" he said turning to his captive, "we're short one on the batting side."

"O.K." answered Henry, relieved to have a raison d'être and pleased that he had resisted wearing his normal shoes in favor of a pair of trainers.

Raymond returned to his end of the pitch and bowled a spinning ball, knocking the bails off the stumps to a flurry of cheers. The boy shrugged and turned to Henry.

"It's all yours, Pop," said the youngster as he handed Henry the bat and bent to undo the pads which were hanging loosely around his legs.

Henry didn't have time to think, except to acknowledge privately that the title Pop had not been to his liking. He found himself surprisingly pleased to be back at the crease, tapping the bat on the park turf and watching Raymond as he walked slowly away from him.

Raymond turned and bowled an easy ball. Henry widened his shoulders and gave it all he'd got. There was that splendid crack of leather on willow that thrills any batsman, and Henry watched in amazement as the ball lofted into the sky, fielders running and calling to each other under its trajectory. It came down beyond any of them and bounced into the long grass.

"That's a six," shouted a huge chap in electric blue shorts and a yellow T-shirt that proclaimed 'I'm the Greatest' in bold red letters across the chest. This was Winston, captain of the batting team, who held his arms aloft in triumph and then bounded up to Henry and slapped him on the back.

"Keep it up, Pop, you can bat for us any time," he shouted enthusiastically.

Raymond started bowling fast and furiously and Henry batted with increasing success until, out of a mixture of courtesy and fatigue, he offered his bat to the next chap in line, a white lad of about eighteen who looked none too pleased with the gesture.

"No need, no need," said Raymond. "The barbecue's on the go and I'm ready for a beer. Anyway, you're bound to have scored enough runs to clinch the game. You can really belt that ball, Henry, I'll make sure you're on my side next time."

"Not a chance," said Winston. "He's ours, and we're going to keep him."

"It's been years since I played," Henry answered shyly to the congratulatory pats that were raining down on him from his teammates. "Thanks for letting me join in. It's good to know there's life in the old dog yet." The newcomer was immediately engulfed in the community as a celebrity, all initial embarrassments dispensed with.

The picnic was a grand affair with families bringing out tins and trays of food from cooler bags that seemed to materialize from nowhere. A gas-fired barbecue was loaded with sausages and hamburgers and a table had been erected alongside with relishes and sauces of all shapes and sizes, plus banks of bread rolls. Brightly colored rugs were spread on the ground; paper plates and cans of drink were everywhere.

Amongst all the provisions, Winston had produced a large cake-tin full of chocolate chip cookies that he was handing around over the heads of the children. Henry had a weakness for biscuits and followed the tin around with his eyes in anticipation. Instead of the cookies, however, he was handed a large hot-dog and a can of beer which he consumed eagerly while nodding to people to whom Raymond was introducing him. His success with the cricket had worked like a magic passport and everyone was welcoming him with enthusiasm.

The evening wore on as the sun made its slow descent and the shadows lengthened. The ducks and swans left the centre of the pond and squabbled for places around the perimeter. Well-fed young children snuggled into laps while the older one's started a game of soccer. It was well after nine o'clock, but twilight was still only a suggestion.

Henry was chatting to a group of men who had taken up residence on two matching blue and red rugs. They were discussing legendary cricketers from their childhood when the cookie tin made another appearance. This time Henry was determined not to be missed out, although he had to reach across his neighbour, who had helped himself and was passing the tin the other way, to ensure success. Perhaps it was the beers - he had been trying to keep up with the others and had lost count of how many he had drunk - that gave him the boldness to make that reach, and to grab a handful of cookies, in case he didn't get the chance again.

There was a slight lull in the conversation, and Henry looked up from his hoard with embarrassment, like a schoolboy caught having more than his share of cake.

"Well, I still think Botham is the best of the bunch by far." Henry decided to bluff it out by returning to his side of the conversation. "Remember that test match in South Africa – he showed the rest of the players up, on both sides." As if to complete his argument and show the gang he was not ashamed of his cookie seizure, he popped the first biscuit into his mouth whole.

The group seemed to think his actions tremendously funny, although Raymond didn't share in the giggles. "Yes, Botham certainly had his moments," he answered Henry, watching him carefully. "I think he's my favorite player too."

Henry watched the different shades of darkening blue cross the sky in the East, as the evening star shone just above the trees. He munched on his cookies slowly – they must have been in the tin for too long, he thought, as they were a bit musty – and thought how grateful he was to Raymond and Rachel for allowing him into their group. He hoped to establish some good relationships with the crowd before revealing the nature of his profession.

As the conversation drifted and the sky darkened, Henry thought he had never before seen such delicate colors washing across the evening sky. He could sense the world turning as the sun slid away and the evening star rose, chased by its fellows. The fabric of the rug was extraordinarily soft under his supporting hand and the can of beer he was holding with the other was sweating beautiful drops of water, disfiguring the beer's name like a mirror in a fair ground. He watched as each drop made its way down the side of the can, leaving a trail like a miniature snail in its wake. A drop fell onto his jeans, just above the knee. The water spread out into the fabric, following the lines of stitches with precision. Every detail of every movement and color and light were dramatically apparent.

Then the music started. Someone had set up some huge speakers attached to a shiny black box with red knobs on the top. The sound seemed to come from everywhere at once; it pounced on Henry and picked him up from the rug. It ran through his body like an electric current, the heavy beats of the base and drums taking over from his heart to pulsate the blood out to his hands and feet, up to his head and into his hair – he could feel each follicle making every strand sway in time to the beat; feel the energy extending to his finger- and toe-nails. He had never been so aware of being alive.

Henry found himself supported by Winston on one side of him and Raymond on the other. The three of them were swaying in time to the music, the large, black faces of his dancing partners drifting in and out of Henry's peripheral vision.

The vicar had never suspected that he was such a fine dancer. His body drifted with the music, making wonderfully graceful movements, which felt delicious. He was dancing with lots of different people, all of whom were laughing and smiling, and he laughed and smiled back. What a really friendly bunch he had found, he thought he would stay all night, letting the music float him along.

Raymond and Winston had other ideas, however, and at some point, the two of them informed the sandwiched Henry that it was time to go home.

"We're coming with you, Pop," said Winston in his deep, vibrating voice. "Don't worry, you won't get lost." Henry found himself propelled along by his new friends who had linked their arms across his back.

The moon had risen by this time and it was bright enough to cast crisp shadows of the trio on the grass in front of them. "We'll never catch them," Henry commented to nobody in particular. "Look how they outpace us, clever things these shadows, always just out of reach, but attached to us at the same time."

They reached the edge of the park and the streetlights threw shadows of their own, jockeying for position with those made by the moonlight. "Look, they've multiplied and are dancing with us." Henry was delighted as the men's shadows revolved around the walkers when they passed under one light and went on towards the next.

Suddenly, it seemed, they were at St. Luke's great oak doors that led straight onto the street from the Western side of the church. The vicarage was just a little further along, at the end of a path through the cemetery.

Henry stopped by the doors with such determination that his two supporters had to stop also. "Gentlemen, we are at The House of God," he said solemnly. "My House of God, to be precise, and I insist upon you joining me inside. Be my guests, let me show you St. Luke's and its many wonders." So saying, Henry produced a large key on a chain hung around his neck. It was quite a business trying to extricate it amongst three pairs of arms and any number of hands all trying to unbutton his shirt and negotiate the chain over Henry's head.

Eventually they succeeded and Henry held the key aloft with pride. It was a truly magnificent key and it slid with ease into the truly magnificent lock. The three men listened with awe as Henry turned the key and the barrels of the ancient lock could be heard slipping into new positions. Now it was the turn of the great iron ring that hung above the keyhole; Henry seized it with both hands and with one swift movement, born of months of practice, he turned it anticlockwise. There was a satisfactory sound of the latch being lifted and the great door slowly began to move away from them, into the porch.

There was deep blackness inside, but Henry was quite undeterred. "Wait here boys," he said confidently and walked up the two steps and into the darkness.

"What do we do now?" Raymond asked Winston, who shrugged his shoulders. They both stood still, gazing at the black mouth of the church into which their charge had disappeared. A few moments later, lights came on both in the porch and in the inner church whose door had also been opened. Henry was standing in the aperture, beckoning them to come forward.

"I forgot to mention that he's a vicar," Raymond whispered to Winston.

"Oh Sweet Jesus" Winston replied as they advanced.

"Yes, indeed, my dear friend Winston," Henry had heard his protestation. "This is His home – metaphorically speaking of course. Jesus is at home in every church and in every heart that will let him in. And this is my home also, and yours as well - if you will allow it."

"Bloody hell, he's a God-botherer right and proper is this one." Winston hissed to Raymond, hoping that Henry didn't hear this time. But he needn't have worried, because the vicar was off on a tour of delight as he ushered his new friends into the church having shut and locked the great door behind them.

"How the hell do we get out of here?" Raymond asked the bewildered Winston as he watched the great key being returned to its original hiding place.

"He's bound to want to go home soon, isn't he?" asked Winston.

"I don't know," Raymond responded dismally, "he had a whole slew of cookies all at once, and he's not used to them. Anything might happen, we have got to see him through. Let's just stay here, by the door and wait for him to calm down."

So saying, the two slumped into the back pews on either side of the aisle. Winston picked up a hassock and used it as a pillow as he lay full length along the polished wood. Raymond stretched his long legs out in front of him and propped himself against a brass rod clipped to the pew's end.

It was morning when they awoke. The early sun was shining through the stained glass windows behind the altar, filling the choir stalls with a myriad of colors. The church lights were still on, the door still closed behind the two waking men, and there was no sign of the vicar.

"Where's he gone?" Raymond was shaking Winston by his massive shoulders. "Winston, come on, we've got to find him and get him home before anyone discovers what's happened. Wake up, Winston, for God's sake, I need your help."

Winston obliged by stretching his massive bulk and letting rip with farts that echoed around the church.

"Don't do that in here," Raymond's voice sounded suddenly upset. "It doesn't matter what your thoughts are about religion, show some respect for other people's."

Winston looked at his friend in surprise. "Hey, man, you're serious aren't you," he said with a chuckle. "Well, I'm sorry, I don't mean no disrespect. I always have a good fart in a morning; it sort of gets me going. Where's that crazy bugger of a vicar gone to?"

"You look that side, and I'll search over here," said Raymond indicating the two sides of the church.

"Oh no you don't," Winston answered quickly. "You're not leaving me alone in this place. It gives me the creeps. I'm staying with you. We can search the place together."

Now it was Raymond's turn to chuckle. "You're serious aren't you?" he mimicked. "So there might just be something here after all, eh? Well, stick close to me and I won't let anything hurt you" he laughed, and he was off to the left of the aisle still chuckling as Winston moved his great bulk with amazing speed to keep up with him.

They found Henry curled up in fetal position behind the altar. He was fast asleep, his face fixed with a peaceful smile.

"We'll have to wake him up," Raymond said, tilting his head as he looked down at his vicar fondly, as he would a sleeping child. "Do you think he'll still be high?"

"No telling," answered Winston. "But, you're right, we've got to get him home" and with that he knelt down and softly nudged Henry's upper shoulder.

"Wake up, Pop," said Winston, his deep voice suddenly finding the echoes of the great church. "Time to go home."

After several more shakes of increasing vigor, Henry opened his eyes. He looked at Winston and Raymond in confusion for a moment, then sat up and looked around him.

"Oh my word," he said as he got to his feet. "Raymond, Winston, where did you go? I have had the most wonderful night of my life. And I mean just that – a night filled with wonder. There were angels, and arch-angels, flooding down from above the altar and filling the central aisle." His arms made an arc moving from the rose window towards the Western door. "Their singing filled the church with the most beautiful sounds I have ever heard. I was on my knees at my pew, over there, and they lifted me up and carried me high up into the roof – see those carvings." Henry pointed to the stone heads that disguised the main truss supports of the church roof, "I have spoken with each and every one of them. That one there, third from the right – I think it's St. Stephen – there's a crack in the stonework at the back of his neck, we must get the stonemason, for we can't have his head falling off in the middle of a service.

"And I had never noticed that tiny window," Henry continued, as he emerged from behind the altar and almost ran down the aisle. "Over there, above the font, it's hidden by the regimental colors. The rush of angels made the flags move, as if they had returned to the battle field, and all their colors shone like new, and suddenly I could see the window – from up there you look straight across the roof-tops. It's a splendid sight.

"Gentlemen, I have had an amazing experience. I don't claim to understand it yet, but I know you are somehow responsible, and I thank you from the bottom of my heart."

"It's time to go home now," Raymond spoke softly but firmly. "Your house-keeper will be worried if she comes to work and finds the house empty. If we leave now, we will have you home before she arrives to make your breakfast."

Rufus stopped speaking, looking at his empty tankard thoughtfully.

"My round," I said, extricating myself from the story and returning to the present with reluctance. I rose quickly and went to the bar and ordered another couple of pints. The stout publican whose shirt sleeves were rolled to the elbows showing tattoos of anchors on each forearm, collected a couple of dimpled glass tankards and took them to the beer pumps. While I watched the amber liquid foam into the glasses, I thought of Father Justin and my introduction to St. George's.

"Sometimes I feel the force so strongly I think it's going to pick me up and I'll float off to the roof." Father Justin had said when talking of the forces Estelle had shown him in the church – and me too, subsequently, of course. Perhaps Father Henry had imagined the same sort of thing - with the magic cookies providing verisimilitude.

Hurrying back to the booth with the drinks, I was eager to hear what happened next. Rufus accepted his beer with a nod and had several large swallows before resuming his narrative.

Father Henry, Winston and Raymond left the church and made their way up the path to the vicarage. Henry produced an insignificant door key from his trouser pocket and let them in through the back door. "I'm starving," he said, "let me invite you both to breakfast, we've got all sorts of goodies in the 'fridge. What do you say?"

So it was that Mary-Jane, the house-keeper, found her employer dressed in her apron, cooking bacon and sausages when she came to work at seven-thirty that morning, while two large black men sat at the tiny kitchen table looking embarrassed and shy.

"I'll finish off now, Father," she said, looking at the mess of pots and plates that littered her usually immaculate kitchen. "You go off to the dining room and lay the table. I'll bring breakfast through when it's ready. What were you going to do with these eggs?" she enquired looking at a collection of yolks, whites and bits of shell in a bowl.

"Scramble them, of course," answered Henry, "but I'm delighted to let you do it, Mary-Jane. Your eggs are legendary and I confess to being a bit out of my depth in here."

"I should think so too," said the tall woman. "And I'll have my pinny back if you don't mind."

Henry stopped in the doorway to take the apron over his head and handed it to her with a look of apology.

"This way, gentlemen," he beckoned to Winston and Raymond who were already on their feet. "We will leave Mary-Jane to her empire. The dining room is through here."

They all agreed that the breakfast consumed in the vicarage that morning was one of the finest meals they had ever eaten. Mary-Jane had excelled herself, acknowledged by many compliments, and the empty plates were testimony to the fact that the huge meal had been a success.

It was half past nine by the time Raymond and Winston made their goodbyes. "You have to come back and see me again" Henry insisted. "There's much I want to talk to you about, but first I need to ponder upon what has happened and try to put it in perspective – if such a thing is possible with miracles. This experience has changed my life. I feel elated in a way I can't properly express. Promise me you'll come back?

"How about us having a drink together after Evensong on Wednesday? "Don't worry, Winston," Henry added with a laugh as he saw Winston's worried face. "You don't have to come to the service, just meet me when it's finished, around seven – what do you say?"

"Sure thing, Pop." Winston answered too quickly.

"No, I'm serious," said Henry in a solemn voice. "Promise me you'll come, both of you. I'm not going to proselytize, just have a chat. No pressures – but please promise me you'll come."

The two men duly promised and they shook hands.

Raymond turned as he was leaving. "I'll be seeing you later this morning, 'though, Father," he said. "Don't forget it's Sunday, and Pearl and Rachel will be busy getting the kids all polished up ready for the service."

"Whoops," said Henry, looking at his watch. "I'd better get a move on. I can hardly stand in the pulpit looking like this. See you later, Raymond, and you on Wednesday, Winston." He waved them down the path, closed the door softly and went upstairs to shave and change his clothes.

There were the usual three elderly ladies at the following Wednesday's Evensong and a young couple who sat towards the back, their shoulders always touching, holding hands and whispering together. Henry went through the service, his new sense of rapture carrying it forwards as if he had a congregation of hundreds.

Raymond and Winston were waiting for him outside, on the pavement, as Henry bade his little flock goodbye.

"Come on in, while I change," he said to his two new friends. "It's all right, Winston, nothing's going to hurt you," he laughed at Winston's sudden look of uncertainty.

The two men followed Henry into the church and up the aisle towards the sacristy. They stopped at the transept and looked with surprise at a scaffolding tower that had been erected behind the Southern choir stalls, next to the organ.

"What's going on, Father?" asked Raymond, indicating the scaffolding.

"I've got the stone-masons in, as I said I would," Henry answered over his shoulder as he entered the sacristy. "It's just as well I did too," he continued, his voice muffled as he pulled his surplice over his head. "They say that head could have fallen at any moment. It could have caught the organist, or a member of the choir – if only we had one. That's what I want to talk to you two about – I want to fill St. Luke's as it should be filled, not only with a congregation, but with a choir, organist, church wardens, the whole lot, and I think, together we can do it. What do you say? Will you help me?"

Father Henry came down the sacristy steps, straightening his hair with his hands. He had removed his dog collar and was wearing an ordinary blue shirt tucked into his black trousers.

Raymond and Winston were still standing in the nave, looking at the scaffolding with bewilderment.

"So there really was a crack at the back of St. Stephen's head," Raymond was speaking slowly. "A crack that couldn't be seen from the ground? How did you know it was there, Father?"

"I told you already," Henry was quick to reply. "Surely you haven't forgotten – no you can't have, because you remembered that it was St. Stephen. Mind you I had a bit of a problem convincing the stonemasons to have a look. They were reluctant to put that scaffolding up just on my assurance that the job needed doing. They insisted that there was no sign of any fault visible from below. I had to promise them I would pay, even if there wasn't a crack, so they indulged me – and there it was, a really dangerous crack, at that. They're very respectful to me now!"

Raymond and Winston were looking at each other with an air of disbelief. Winston's huge jaw hung slightly open, Raymond was rubbing his temples slowly with both hands. They made their way carefully through the choir stalls to the bottom of the scaffolding and looked up, eyes squinting.

"Are we going to have that drink?" Henry's voice came echoing up the church from the big open door. "Don't you worry about St. Stephen, he's secure from decapitation now. The masons have just a bit of tidying up to do, but the danger is over. They're going to check all the other heads, while they're here, just in case I missed something while I was flying around. Are you coming?"

Rufus paused, and slowly raised his eyes from his glass. I realized that I had not touched my beer; I was just staring at Rufus in amazement.

"What on earth was in those cookies?" I asked when I finally managed to speak.

"I'm just coming to that," said Rufus. "It's quite a story, isn't it?"

43. THE DAY ROOM

While I am here in my recollections I am reminded how my telling of this tale, many years later, was interrupted by my fellow inmates of The Day Room - the two people who would have such an impact on my life. My introduction to them, and to that place - which became both a prison and a sanctuary - is very clear in my mind.

The first time I was put in a wheel-chair is still a painful and clear memory – even after all this time. I was sitting in an inflated rubber ring, propped up with a series of pillows. A pair of crude wooden half-crutches had been wedged under my armpits and down to the seat of the chair. They had been specially made for me, I had been told, but they were bruising me badly. I tried to shift my weight away from them but the pains from below shot upwards like knives. I decided to take the lessor of two evils and give the crutches the respect they deserved. My left leg, encased in plaster from the ankle to the hip, stuck out in front of me on an extension from the chair. Sweat was bubbling across my forehead until it trickled down my cheeks. I was exhausted, humiliated, and altogether negative about the move from my bed.

"Well," Sister Mary looked at me with a sense of satisfaction I did not share, "you see, you don't have to spend the rest of your life in bed. Bravo Shamiso and Rosemary," she said turning to the two nurses who stood, panting slightly, on either side of their patient. "You've done a brilliant job - in spite of a somewhat uncooperative patient." The smile that accompanied these words took the sting out of their suggestion, but I knew I had not made the move from bed to wheelchair an easy one. The pain was one thing to deal with, but the anticipatory fear of it was even more debilitating.

"It will get easier, Jack," Sister Mary continued turning her smile towards me as the two nurses moved the drips from their bed-side hangers to those already fixed to the wheelchair like antennae. "The first time is always the worst, and that's behind us now. You'll see, every day will bring improvements – you just have to look for them and not to concentrate on the ugliness of the pain and discomfort."

Sister Mary moved round behind the chair and I heard a click as she released the brake. "Come along, I have some people who are looking forward to meeting you, and it's time you had a change of scenery." She started pushing the wheelchair towards the door held open by the small nurse, Shamiso.

"Oh, no, please, Sister Mary, I'm not ready to see people yet." I remember so clearly trying to keep the note of panic out of my voice. "I need more time. It's only been a few days since the operation. I'm not ready, not ready at all."

"Rubbish," snorted Sister Mary. "I've never heard such a fuss. Believe me, Jack, you are more than ready to put all this in perspective and to stop feeling as if you're the only one in the world who has encountered tragedy." The words were spoken sharply but edged with kindness.

I felt a rush of self-pity and my throat constricted; tears pushed behind my eyes as I wondered how anybody could be so callous and not understand the depth of the damage done to me – both emotionally and physically. I swallowed hard, eyelids tightening. Why were these nurses, who I had come to trust so completely, suddenly being disruptive? They seemed to have turned against me, their care and understanding disappearing behind a barrage of bossy insensitivity. I just wanted to be left alone with my misery and pain.

Despite my protestations I was wheeled along a wide corridor lit by skylights through which the purple blossoms of Jackeranda trees could be seen against the blue African sky. There were rooms on either side and I caught glimpses of other beds festooned with tubes; prone or seated figures were gazing blankly into the distance in front of them.

At the end of the corridor, a pair of double doors led into a semi-circular room with a large bay window. overlooking a well-tended garden with lawns sloping down to the river.

Shamiso and Rosemary had gone ahead and were holding the doors open as Sister Mary and I approached. "This is our Day Room," my driver announced with a note of pride in her voice as she pushed the unwieldy charabanc through the doors. "And here we have my very good friend Percival," she turned the chair towards a good-looking white man in his mid-thirties, also in a wheelchair, with both legs plastered in the same way as the one of mine. His right arm was bandaged from below the elbow and was too short by the length of a hand.

Sister Mary swung the chair around before I had a chance to say anything. "And my other very good friend, Amrita," she pronounced as another wheelchair came into view holding a small Indian woman, in her mid-twenties by the look of her pretty face, wrapped in blankets with no outward signs of injury.

"Amrita and Percival," Sister Mary said with a note of anticipation in her voice, "I want you to meet my very good friend, Jack." Having positioned me so I was looking out towards the garden, between the other two whose chairs were facing each other, she applied the break. She had created a semi circle of wheelchairs in a curve converse to that of the windows.

"Welcome, Jack," it was Percival who was first to speak. "We've heard about you and have been looking forward to your being well enough to join us here. Amrita and I have just about run out of conversation after the six weeks we have shared. We are in need of new territory."

"Nonsense, Percival," Amrita's voice was soft, with an American twang that caught me by surprise. "You and I will never tire of our conversations, but all the same, it is good to have you here, Jack, and I, too, bid you welcome."

"Well thank you both," I found it less demanding to speak to these two strangers than I had anticipated. The words came easily and, in spite of my fears, I was suddenly excited about having fellow beings to talk with

— as if a new slice of life had returned from beyond the grave. "Have you both been here that long?"

"I have been here for six weeks and four days," said Percival in a monotone, "and Amrita for over two months, I think."

"Two months, more or less," Amrita answered. "I'm not as specific as Percival. And you, Jack, arrived just over a week ago, is that right?"

My panic returned in a rush as I looked over the garden, down to the glinting river. "Did you see me arrive?" I asked.

"No," Amrita answered. "You came here at dawn, so we have been told. Neither Percival nor I frequent the day room at such an early hour."

I didn't know why the idea of people watching my arrival should upset me so much. The indignity of it all, maybe – but why should that matter? I gave a sigh of relief.

"So, what happened to you, Percival?" I needed to know what horrors bound the three of us together without the option of leaving.

Percival's story was told quickly and quietly, without emotion. He had been working as a paramedic in a small town out in the bush. One day he had been called to a house where a woman was in a dreadful state after being beaten up by her husband. They got her into an ambulance and brought her to the hospital. As he, and two nurses, were moving her from the stretcher to a trolley the husband arrived with an axe in his hands.

The man went berserk, smashing whatever was between him and his screaming wife. Before he could be stopped by the hospital's security services the man had killed the two nurses who were trying to protect their patient, amputated Percival's right hand, broken his legs both below and above the knees with the flat side of the axe and then beheaded his wife.

"I have been trying to put myself into the firing line of life for over five years now," Percival added calmly, "and still the ultimate relief is withheld from me. What I have left just gets worse" he finished, a calm smile on his face that made the horrors he had just recounted even more macabre.

I could find nothing to say. I looked at Amrita who was staring out into the garden. After a few seconds, without prompting, she began her tale – again in a monotone voice of flat normality.

"I was born and raised in USA," she began, "in a rambling suburb to the North of Washington D.C. There is a large Indian community there and I benefited from the great combination of the gentle philosophy of Buddhism and the wonderful go-for-it attitude of America.

"I always wanted to get to know the country of my ancestors and to contribute in some way. To use the advantages I had - by growing up in The States - to make lives easier for those not so fortunate. I set my heart on becoming a doctor.

"After graduating from Georgetown Medical School, I followed my dreams and went to India to ply my new trade in places where it was much needed.

"I was two years in India – pretty much all over the country – when I heard of Asian communities in Africa suffering from persecution. I came here to help.

"It was while I was involved in moving some injured people from a town to the North West of here that a gang of rebels found us. Most of the men were killed – you know what they do, these people?" she turned her eyes from the garden and looked at me properly for the first time. I nodded, unable to speak as my own horrors rushed back at me.

"When they found me," Amrita continued in her soft voice, "they indulged in a gang rape – I will spare you the details. There were very many of them. Big men, small men, some were just boys, others with plenty of experience and their own way of doing things. All were strong and merciless. I passed out before they had finished, and I suspect they left me for dead. They had broken my back and I am now paralyzed from the waist down."

Amrita's eyes had returned to the garden. The last sentence was delivered in a flat voice without a trace of emotion of any kind.

The barrage of emotions rushing through me as these tales were told made me nauseas. I knew that hearing their stories, said in such matter-of-fact tones, should put my own tragedy into perspective. Sister Mary had insisted upon my meeting these two fellow patients for a reason. I had become obsessed with my own misfortunes and had allowed a cloud of self-pity to grow until it engulfed me. Now it was time to disperse that cloud – to get rid of it altogether, as these two amazing people must have done with theirs, but I was not sure that I had either the strength or the courage necessary to succeed.

Percival gave a theatrical cough and I realized that silence had lasted for several minutes. Looking up I found both my companions looking at me expectantly. Percival raised his remaining hand in a gesture of query and invitation.

But my story can wait, I'm not ready for that yet.

Several weeks after my introduction to the Day Room, I was re-telling Rufus's tale of Father Henry's 'flight with the angels'. Percival had intervened and taken over as the story teller.

"But I've been there," he said with some excitement, causing me to stop my account mid-stream. "I have also 'flown,' but there were no accompanying angels for me. Mine wasn't anything like such a positive experience –

although, to be fair, it wasn't negative either. A sort of non-committal suggestion of a journey that might take another path.

"It was in the hospital, when everything went so terribly wrong. I remember a man with an axe, much screaming and blood and bodies scrambling, falling, fading. I felt a lifting sensation, and suddenly I could see the gory scene with a bird's eye view. I was un-detached, free of both emotional and physical pain, just floating in a great quiet.

"From my vantage point, somewhere close to the ceiling, I could see a body lying on the floor with arteries pumping such bright blood all over the place, spraying the white uniforms of those who came to help. For some reason I was impressed with the brightness.

"The distance between myself and the scene below was increasing but I could still see security guards, doctors and nurses rushing around. There was a collection of concerned people gravitating towards what I now realize was my own body – a body to which I was no longer attached in any way; not physically or emotionally. As I rose higher, I watched with mild interest as tourniquets were applied and people scurried to find needles and bags of fluid. I remember watching them looking for suitable veins into which they could insert their life-saving drugs.

"The vision finished there – but I do remember it most vividly. Your father Henry must have left his body in a similar fashion. From what I've learnt since, he was lucky to come back to it."

So much of Percival's account was familiar to me that I joined in with a mixture of surprise and fascination. "I too have been there, now you come to mention it, Percival, only a few weeks ago." I found myself explaining to my friends and to myself at the same time. "I also remember the feeling of floating upwards. It was as the morphine took over, before my operation. I hadn't identified that strange sensation with father Henry's account - now you tell me your experience, it all makes perfect sense.

"There was no point in fighting the drug, I had no wish to anyway. There was a spiraling sensation, and then I found myself observing the scene from above, just as you have described, Percival. I remember being mildly concerned that I would get tangled up with the light bulbs dangling from the ceiling. But that was momentary, as I continued to rise.

"With the same detached interest you mentioned, I watched a prone body, framed between a doctor and a nurse; a sheet was draped over the patient's back; his head cradled in some sort of frame that kept him looking at the floor; there were suspended bags of liquid on each side, filling various tubes that disappeared under the white hospital gown. Other tubes disappeared under the bed into sinister looking containers. It made an interesting scene. The freedom from pain and physical limitations made me giddy, and I felt as if I were spinning in space, catching snapshots of the universe around me.

"There was a dragging sensation of great weight as I recognized the body below me as my own and felt myself returning to the crippled mess on the stretcher. The pains came back only fleetingly before I lost consciousness again."

Amrita was not to be left out. "Well, I'm afraid my experience of decorporealisation was darkly different," she said in her usual hushed tones. There had been quite a pause, the kind of silence only possible between friends who are deeply comfortable with each other's company.

"Your experiences seem so light, as if releasing you into something bright. Mine was a downwards suction. It must have happened at the point of my ordeal when I lost consciousness and my mind was full of hatred and anger and my body filled with pains.

"Like you, I saw the scene from afar and felt no relationship with what I was watching, but I did feel emotion. A barrage of negativity filled my soul – for that is where I believe myself to have been – in my soul. I was immersed in blackness, sinking into a turbid morass of swirling evil. I was being offered the opportunity to 'get my own back' – that is the only way I can describe it. I remember fighting for peace. I just wanted to let everything go, to be away from the horror and not to wish for any kind of retribution. I just wanted to be free, to let it all go away, and not to remember.

"The next thing I knew I was in a hospital bed – a position we are all familiar with. Laced with tubes, surrounded with caring people, but oh so very much on my own, in an unfamiliar body of which I was in control of only half."

Looking at this conversation now, in such benign circumstances, I feel rather guilty about my present serenity. Then comes to mind the recently visited story of Estelle's involuntary translocation which saved the little boy from a vicious dog. Was that another experience of mysteries beyond our present understanding? That time, however, her body had moved with her. It's all so fascinating. I must look into these phenomena more closely, and explore the instances of alternative personas, such as those presented by 'imaginary friends' and by people who use theatrical guises by cross-dressing or puppeteering, for example, to communicate ideas too sensitive to be presented by their normal selves. And then, of course, there are those who use a deity . . . Where does the 'mysterium tremendum' start and the machinations of the human imagination end – do they merge into one another, or are they a product of each other?

44. WINSTON'S MAGIC

It's time to return to The Australian pub in Milner Street and Rufus's tale regarding the success of his church St. Luke's. He had asked me what I thought of his story.

"Astonishing," I replied, eagerly. "Please go on."

Rufus took another gulp of beer, wiped his mouth on the back of his sleeve and continued his tale.

Raymond and Winston had joined Henry outside the church door in silence. They watched him lock the big oak doors and return the giant key and chain over his head and back inside his shirt. Then, following the vicar's lead, they crossed the street, into the sun's slanting rays, and walked to the next junction where 'The Queen's Head' was already spilling its clients onto the street. Groups had gathered around tables set out with bright umbrellas advertising a make of champagne in red and white swirls.

"Do you mind if we sit inside?" asked Henry, I want to find a corner where we can hear each other speak, and it's going to be loud and crowded out here in the evening sunshine. What will you have, gentlemen?"

Henry bought a round of drinks, a pint of best bitter for each of his friends and a lager and lime for himself. He brought them to the corner table they had chosen where his friends had taken bench seats at right angles to each other. Henry sat on a stool, with his back to the centre of the pub, completing the triangle.

"You're uncharacteristically quiet this evening, both of you," Henry started, pushing the drinks across the table. "I hope I haven't got you worried by asking for this meeting? No?" he added, as the two heads shook in unison, "splendid. Well let me tell you what I've got in mind – I'm very excited about all this, and I hope you will humor me and hear me out."

Winston and Raymond shifted uneasily on their seats. Winston licked his lips nervously, the pink of his tongue contrasting with the blue-black of his complexion. Raymond stared fixedly at his beer and then, with an effort, he raised his eyes and nodded to Henry. "Go ahead, Father," he said with a new reverence in his voice, "let's hear what you'd like us to do."

"Well," Henry moved his stool a little closer to the table, and gave a furtive look over his shoulder, "first I'd like to ask you a couple of questions – just between us, you understand."

The two members of his audience nodded slowly.

"I realize that I must have taken some sort of drug on Saturday which allowed me to have the mystical experience in St. Luke's. Do you mind if I ask you what it was?"

Winston and Raymond looked at each other uneasily.

"Go on, Winston," Raymond said, "the Father's told us this is all in confidence, isn't that right, vicar?"

"Of course," Henry answered. "Why all this sudden formality? On Saturday I was Henry at best, and more frequently heralded as Pop?"

Winston ignored this last question and, upon being nudged by Raymond, he started to speak. His voice was so soft that Henry had to lean into the conversation and watch his mouth carefully to be sure he understood what was being said.

"It was those cookies, Father – I mean Henry. They were hash-chip cookies as well as chocolate-chip cookies. We tried to keep them away from you, but you grabbed a whole handful and there was nothing we could do about it. Some of us like a cookie every now and then, to lighten things up, take the edge off worries, that sort of thing. We had one before the food, and then one afterwards, but you – you took a whole lot, all at once, and we didn't know what to do about it."

"We're really sorry, Father – Pop – Henry . . ." Raymond joined the conversation nervously. "We just didn't know what to do, so Winston and I, well we just kept you company, that's all, to see that you were alright."

"Oh, please don't be sorry, you have done me a huge favor. Are you familiar with Huxley's book, 'The Doors of Perception'? No, maybe not," he continued as they shook their heads. "I have had a momentous mystical experience, and it happened because my doors of perception were blasted open. I could see, hear, feel – probably even smell, although I don't remember any smells – in another dimension, and now I know that dimension is there, I don't need your cookies to experience it again.

"When I was walking around St. Luke's that evening, I became filled with The Spirit in a most amazing way. I have tried to analyze the feeling since and the nearest I can come is to say that it was an intensification of all my religious beliefs. Beliefs were transformed into certainties in a way I had not experienced before. God the Father, God the Son, and little insignificant me, created in their image and likeness, capable of immense love and fulfillment. It was wonderful, quite wonderful."

Henry stopped speaking, his eyes misted over as he recalled the magical experience of flying with the angels and being at one with the spiritual forces that had seemed to flood the church that night.

"What you have enabled me to discover," the vicar continued in a soft voice, "is that religious understanding can be aided, at a visceral level, by a little bit of help from cookies such as yours. I heard God speaking to me through instinct rather than through thought. All the education stuffed down my throat from an early age had blocked those instincts – your cookies blew away the blockage. Do you understand what I mean?"

Winston was studying his empty beer glass with great deliberation. Raymond, who had also finished his drink, looked at his companion for help and, finding none he replied: "yea, sure, Father, how about another drink, I think it's my round."

Henry looked at his untouched lager. "I'm fine, Raymond, but you two look as if you need some replenishment. I'll wait until you come back, because I need your views on what I have to suggest."

Raymond shuffled out of his seat, reached for the two empty glasses, and made his way to the bar.

"I've got to go to the Gents, father, I mean Henry." Winston stood up so suddenly he knocked the table, spilling the lager and lime. "Oh, I'm so sorry. Should I get you another? I won't be a minute."

"No problem, Winston," assured Henry, "it's only a splash, and I was too busy talking to drink it anyway." He produced a startlingly white handkerchief and mopped the table and the glass carefully. "Don't worry, I won't continue until you're back."

Winston didn't look very reassured by this statement. He disappeared through a dark opening to the side of the table that advertised 'toilets' in elaborate gold script. It was some time before he came back, and when he did so, Raymond was at his side. Both men cradled new pints of beer as if they were life-savers.

"Now gentlemen," Henry was eager to continue once his companions had regained their seats. "What I am going to suggest to you both is slightly unorthodox, but I believe it will be worth the bother.

"On behalf of St. Luke's parish, I would like to put in an order for some of your cookies, Winston."

"Listen, Henry," Winston was suddenly on safe ground. "If you want to buy some of my stuff, no problem. Just tell me how much you want and I'll work out a price for you. But you shouldn't take too much at once, you know, all that flying around ain't good for you."

"Thank you, Winston, but it is not for me that I want to buy the cookies. I have been shown 'The Doors of Perception' and now that I know they are there, I no longer need a cookie, or anything else, to show me how to find them. I can open them at will. My communication with The Almighty continues to grow and to inspire me.

"Tell me," Father Henry's voice took on a practical edge, "how long does it take, after you have eaten one of your concoctions, for the world to shift a little?"

"Twenty minutes, half an hour may be." Winston looked at Raymond for confirmation. His friend nodded his head.

"OK then," said Henry. "What I suggest is this. St. Luke's starts a new 'get to know your neighbors' drive with coffee or tea and cookies before matins every Sunday. We have two sorts of cookies, yours for the grown-ups and straight chocolate chips for the children, and we'll need someone to control which cookies go where and restrict the powerful ones appropriately. Nobody must know about this but us, of course, so you see why I need your cooperation.

"After the 'tea and biscuits' everyone goes into the church and I start the service. Believe me, my services have been really exciting since my experience last Saturday – what did you think about my sermon on Sunday, Raymond?"

Raymond grunted with enthusiasm, hoping that he wouldn't be asked to recall anything of last Sunday's service through which he had slept soundly after the shenanigans of the previous night.

"By the time we are half way through Matins, religious fervor should be increased within the congregation, courtesy of the cookies. It is then up to me to make sure that the rest of the service is something wonderful. If I get this right, and with God's help I will, we should have people returning to our church in droves. St. Luke's can be full again, and with the collections we make we can afford an organist – and more cookies. What do you think, gentlemen, will you help me?"

"And that's how it all started," Rufus gave a huge sigh as he finished his story. "Father Henry's plan worked a treat, and Winston and Raymond encouraged their friends to come and find out what was going on at the church. Soon the church hall was full to bursting before every Sunday matins.

"To be fair to Pop Henry, as they all call him, he has delivered his side of the bargain. He produces the most exciting services and the atmosphere in the church is really awesome. We have a professional organist now - the collections every Sunday are massive and pay for far more than just the cookies - and kids are queuing up to be in the choir – our choirmaster used to play in a pop group. It is all quite splendid – but . . ."

"But it's illegal," I finished the sentence in a whisper. Rufus nodded in silence.

"In his support," Rufus started again, "Henry, with Winston's help, has devised a system of about four levels of cookies. Newcomers get the strongest ones and then the amount of hash per cookie declines depending upon how many services someone has attended. At the lowest end, the cookies are merely placebos where just the idea is enough to send the people into a spin once the service begins. It is this working out which cookies to give to which people that has necessitated Henry telling me his secret. I kept trying to be helpful and give the wrong tin to the wrong people." Rufus paused and stared thoughtfully into his glass. "Anyway, Jack, what do you think I should do?"

A smile started unbidden across my face, which then, uncontrollably, turned into a grin. I could feel mirth seeping up inside me as I started to chuckle, and before I knew it I was laughing out loud. Rufus looked up in surprise at what must have been an uncharacteristically merry face. All of a sudden, he was laughing too.

The two of us sat opposite each other and laughed richly and deeply. We laughed until tears were streaming down our faces; I had to take off my glasses and reach for a handkerchief. Rufus was slapping his hand upon the table, rocking backwards and forwards so that the booth shook. It was several minutes before the merriment subsided.

"My round," I proclaimed, standing up on rather shaky legs. "This definitely calls for another pint. Same again, Rufus?"

Rufus nodded and watched me adjusting my glasses, the unstoppable broad grin pushing my cheeks upwards so that they refused to sit straight. A lock of hair had come adrift with the laughter, I could feel it curling onto my forehead above my right eye, but had to leave it as my hands held the empty tankards.

"I've never seen you enjoy yourself so much, Jack." His rueful tone was countered by a pair of sparkling eyes.

Retuning from the bar, I put the foaming tankards carefully onto the table. "What a splendid story, Rufus," I said. "How long do you think this has been going on?"

"For about four years now. Father Henry never takes any of the stuff – he's only had it the once, but that experience was enough. Even Winston and Raymond don't take it any more – the fact Henry knew about that cracked carving without being able to see it from below has scared them off the stuff. They look on Henry as some sort of magician – a Christian magician, of course, and they never miss a service now.

"In fact more and more people are enjoying the placebo cookies and getting just as high as they did when there was hash in them."

"What would happen if you stopped using the stuff altogether?" I asked the obvious question.

"Well, of course that's the plan," Rufus answered. "None of the congregation are meant to know it was in there in the first place, but Raymond and Winston must have suggested it to enough people to get them to go along, at the beginning, so now the reputation is there."

"And very successful it is too, by the sound of it" I said, not without a hint of jealousy. I took a long pull at my pint, wiping the foam from beneath my nose with a handkerchief. "If the special ingredient is indeed being phased out, what harm can there be in continuing the tradition of tea and cookies before each service.

"You've told me before about the interactive services you have at St. Luke's, with all sorts of local celebrities making appearances – I was always jealous of your happy enthusiastic congregations, indeed I still am, although I can't see Father Justin agreeing to such a plan as your Pop Henry's.

"Legal or illegal, Rufus, your vicar has filled his church in a very positive way – you have no choice but to continue as you have been for the last couple of years and 'go with the flow.' Have you ever tried it yourself?"

"No, I haven't," Rufus's voice took on an offended tone. "My relationship with The Almighty is deep enough as it is. I don't need any help from that stuff."

"I would be curious, all the same," I answered thoughtfully, aware that our friendship suddenly didn't seem as intimate as I would have liked. "Seriously, though, if all is going as well as you say, I can see no reason to rock the boat. If you are worried about being discovered, leave the stuff out of the cookies for a couple of weeks and see if there's a difference to the services.   If you can do without it and still maintain the high spirits, then you've nothing to be concerned about.

"Thank you, Rufus, for sharing this with me, you have brightened my day and given me lots to think about.

"Don't look so serious," I continued – to the amusement of my friend who said he had never seen me anything but serious until now.   "You've got a big success on your hands." I insisted.   "The important thing is to keep it alive and growing – you've got to be inspired along with Father Henry.   Let go of your worries and enjoy it."

"That's really something - coming from as intense a person as you Jack.   And I must say I've enjoyed seeing you laugh" Rufus answered with a smile.   "It's true, that before I was let into the secret I enjoyed Henry's services enormously, and he's let me join in quite a lot with the gaiety.   Worshipping should be a positive experience, and if you could see the faces of our congregation both during and after the services, you would approve, I know you would.   It's just, now that I know what has been behind it all, I'm not sure of my moral ground and whether or not I should continue to be a part of it."

"Have you talked to Father Henry about your concerns, Rufus?   Perhaps you should," I continued as my friend shook his head silently.   "He must have grappled with the moral question himself before he embarked on this unconventional course of action.   Why not ask him about it?"

"Yes, I suppose you're right," Rufus replied thoughtfully.   "I don't want to appear negative, that's all. I admire Henry greatly, and I must admit that he has turned that community around – from what I am told – in a wonderfully positive way.   There is no more violence in his parish, the families look after their youth and push their energies in positive directions.   The churchyard is taken care of with well-tended graves, even though the occupants have no relatives living in the parish by now, and there are flowerbeds and borders all over the place.

"There is a gang of splendid ladies, both black and white, who clean and decorate the inside of the church every week – you should hear their chatter and laughter as they dust and polish and weave garlands around the pulpit. Father Henry is both popular and revered. The story of his flight with the angels has seeped into Brixton's cultural history and he's quite the celebrity."

"What do you make of that part of the story?" I asked, "did Henry tell you about it himself?"

"Yes, of course he did," Rufus answered, "it was the pivotal part of the whole idea. He talked about it with as much excitement as if it had happened yesterday, with sparkling eyes and waving arms. It was infectious, his fervor, I was swept up with the idea and have never thought to question it. Strange things happen when you're dealing with religion – you must have found that yourself, Jack?"

I felt it appropriate to nod at this point, but once again I was confronted with the sensation that I was missing something of magnitude in the pursuit of my profession.

"I have no doubt that Father Henry is genuine about what happened, and I don't try to explain it – as you just suggested, I go with the flow," Rufus continued.

"But I've been feeling more and more uncomfortable about the cookie business. It has helped me enormously to be able to talk to you about it, Jack, and I feel a weight off my shoulders, especially given your positive response. I will talk to Henry about it, and see if we can't stay with the placebo route alone. I would hate to be visiting my superior in jail – and think what the press would do if they found out - he would be de-frocked for sure, and me along with him, I suppose."

"Yes, of course, Rufus, you're right to be worried." I felt my face resume its habitual serious expression. "You must talk it through with him and find a solution with which you are both happy – a solution that's within the law.

"I haven't read Huxley's 'Doors of Perception' – I've heard of it, of course as the inspiration for the successful pop group who called themselves 'The Doors' – but I have read another book of his called 'Island' and there's something similar there about drug-induced religious experiences. I must dig it out and read it again. I must say, I am rather envious of Henry's mystical journey, aren't you, Rufus? Nothing like that has ever happened to me, not even during ordination."

"My religious feelings are real enough without needing hash to show me the way" Rufus replied with a touch of pomposity. "I think I have found the way, hence my taking orders and following this way of life. I have an intense relationship with my God and I'm not sure I could manage any more excitement. Maybe when I've been around for as long as Father Henry – after all he's a good twenty-five years further along the path than we are – maybe I'll feel strong enough to experiment, but not yet. I've got all I can handle at the moment."

I could not help but reflect upon my own spiritual relationship with the Almighty, and of how Father Justin had suggested that sex was another way through the walls of enculturation – hence the Karma Sutra. I could feel myself blushing and raised my glass to hide the sudden perplexity.

"Well, it's been an eventful evening, for sure." I was looking at my watch. "Thank you for sharing all that with me, Rufus. I shall wait with interest to hear the next episode. I'm afraid I've nothing as exciting as that to report from Islington, although I have been dowsing for power lines – that's the earth's natural forces I'm talking about, not electricity cables" I added quickly, noticing the quizzical expression on Rufus's face. "That's not something you do every day!"

We agreed that the ley line story would have to wait for another time. The sky was dark now, the streetlights casting their yellow glow along Milner Street. Outside the pub we shook hands, and then suddenly gave each other a generous embrace. "Good luck, Rufus," I said, holding my friend away from me by the shoulders. "Let me know what happens – oh, and one more thing. Before you ask Henry about the situation, have a word with God also, see what feedback you get from that direction. It's what we would advise our parishioners, and often forget to do ourselves."

"You're quite right, Jack," Rufus said with a soft chuckle. "Good for you, I shall be talking with both my superiors, and I'll let you know what they have to say. Thanks for being such a good sounding block, I really do feel a lot better about everything."

It was time for me to head North and Rufus to go South, back to our flats in the basements of two very different vicarages.

45. A Very Different Hospital Visit

It was autumn and, apart from the dour yews, the trees in the churchyard were turning their leaves into an argument of yellows, reds and browns. I hadn't seen Rufus for several weeks but he had telephoned me to say that all was proceeding according to plan. He had spoken in a Mafioso style of code that made me smile.

I was busy in my little garden, raking fallen leaves into colorful heaps. I was working with a steady rhythm, remembering the months spent in the gardens of St. Augustine's, when I heard the gravel path scrunch - it was a warning of an intruder.

I looked up to see a woman approaching with quick, deliberate strides. Her tall frame, swathed in a full-length military style blue coat, was held erect, and the confidence of her steps told of a decisive nature and a youngish body. Her black face was mostly hidden by a large brimmed, blue felt hat that matched the coat and kept her curly hair in order.

"Father Jack?" the tone resonated with a question to which she was already sure of the answer. "My name is Rosanna Todd and I am a doctor. I have come to talk to you about a patient of mine by the name of Sugar Parker – do you know the girl?"

I was suddenly on the back foot. I was in my own space, master of my own little patch, but that didn't stop my confidence being swept away with my visitor's abruptness of manner, the surprise of the question, and most of all, by the striking blue eyes that looked at me inquiringly from beneath the hat's brim and seemed so out of kilter with the black face.

Something about Dr. Todd's stance made me feel as if I were in the dock; my rake was now at my side as if standing to attention, and my position at the bottom of my sunken garden added to my involuntary air of servility. Her enquiry had seemed more like a summons than a question and the intensity of those eyes, framed by the tightly curling black hair, made me stammer an answer.

"Yes, I know Sugar, although we call her Rosie here at St. George's, but I haven't seen her for quite a while. I hope she isn't ill," I added lamely, "seeing that you are a doctor . . " my words trailed away.

I remember the urgency with which I tried to recover some sort of equanimity. I had been far away with my thoughts of St. Augustine's vegetable garden and now I felt that a beautiful Grand Inquisitor had arrived to find me unprepared and clumsy.

"She's not exactly ill," my visitor replied, in a crisp, professional tone, "she's just given birth to a still-born child. We can't find out anything from her apart from it all being 'God's Will'. We have no idea who the father of the child might be. She had a bad time in the delivery room, and is very weak both physically and mentally. She has told me that this is her church, and that you are her vicar. I have come to ask for your help."

Having agreed to visit Rosie with Dr. Todd in attendance, I made my way to the hospital around noon the following day. I had reacted to the news from Dr. Todd first with total amazement, then disbelief, and finally with deep sadness. Had I failed my talkative little friend? Had I not been there for her when she really needed help? Had I missed something in her merry stories that might have prepared me for this?

I took the tube to South Kensington and walked along the Fulham Road until I reached the hospital. The doors of the main entrance were in full use as a tide of humanity pushed its way into and out of the building. Inside, the hospital was full of foreign noises - rubber soles squelched against linoleum, swing doors sucked themselves together, distant telephones seemed to be ringing each other, trolleys with groaning loads went past me with antennae of plastic bags. I didn't know then how accustomed to those things I was to become so many years later.

The doctor had given me the name of the ward and, following the many arrows directing me this way and that I found Rosanna, as I had been instructed to call her, waiting for me at the entrance. She looked taller in her Doctor's starched white coat and without her hat to control her swirling hair. The blue of her eyes seemed greyer than when she had spoken to me in the church garden and heavy with responsibility and concern.

"I've asked Sister to put Sugar in the sitting room and to make sure no-one else is there" she told me, catching my arm gently and giving it a slight pull in the direction she was pointing.

We made our way through another pair of double doors and were confronted by a large room with mismatched armchairs arranged in a semi circle around a television that stuck out from the wall on a metal arm - like some electronic praying mantis. It was switched on, of course, showing a collection of people arranged in a mirror image of the armchairs around us. A group of earnest celebrities were taking part in a talk show of some kind; they were staring into the hospital sitting room, as the armchairs stared back into the square condensed space.

Rosie was huddled in the furthest chair underneath a faded mustard-colored blanket.

"I can't change the channel. I don't want to listen to this stupid stuff. Why won't they let me go back to bed, and I don't like being here on my own" she started wailing as soon as she saw us. Her eyes were enlarged from crying and her cheeks shone with recent tears like a soldier's polished boots. She seemed far too small and pathetic to be making so much noise.

"Well you're not alone any more, Sugar." Rosanna interrupted her. "Father Jack is here to see you, and so am I. We're going to have that chat you promised me."

The patient looked at me with a mixture of bewilderment and suspicion.

"Hello Rosie," I said, sitting on the arm of the chair next to her and taking one of her hands gently. "I hear you've had a horrible time and I've come to see if I can make things better in any way. I've come to remind you that God loves you and cares for you, even if it doesn't seem much like it at the moment. I've come to pray with you and see if, together, we can find a way to understand what has happened."

Rosie's dark eyes were fixed on mine, her lower lip was quivering and suddenly she was clinging to my arm, climbing out of her chair, the blanket slipping to the floor as her thin legs pushed her tiny frame into my lap. Her chest heaved with sobs inside the green hospital smock as she buried her head into my shoulder, pushing my jacket aside with her nose, wetting the thin shirt with her tears.

"It's God's will, it's God's will, just as Pa always said, but why does it have to hurt so much, and why does Ma call me a slut, and why is everyone so rough when all I've done is what God wants?"

I looked at Rosanna with one hand raised in a help-seeking gesture whilst the other stroked Rosie's shaking back, my fingers getting tangled in the tapes which kept the bed gown loosely closed over her tiny frame.

Rosanna knelt down beside us and carefully pulled the child upright on my knees. Gently, she took the two small hands with the bitten finger nails from around my neck and held them in a firm grip with her left hand whilst her right hand reached for the girl's chin and turned the blotchy face towards her.

"Sugar, God has sent Father Jack to help you," she said, ignoring my raised eyebrows. "You have always told me that this has all been God's will and that nobody should question you about the secret you share with Him. You said you couldn't talk to me without God's permission, and Father Jack is here to give you that permission, aren't you, Father?"

I opened my mouth to speak, but not knowing what to say, shut it again, staring at Rosanna over Rosie's dark curls.

"Now that he's here," Rosanna continued, using the most formal doctor's tone she could muster, "I want you to tell me how you managed to get pregnant. Father Jack and I both love you and care for you very much, Sugar, and we are here to help you get better and to be strong again, and for that to happen we must make sure that you don't get pregnant again. We have to know that you understand how and why these things happen, then we can stop them from happening again – you don't want this to happen again, do you, Sugar?"

Rosie was staring fixedly into her lap. She shook her head but said nothing.

"Tell us what happened, Sugar, please" Rosanna used a softer voice as she tried again to tilt the child's head to look up at her.

"It's God's will, it's God's will, it's God's will" Rosie repeated as if she were chanting some sort of mantra.

"How do you know?" Rosanna decided upon a different tack.

"Pa told me," Sugar whispered.

"What about your Mother, Sugar?" It was my turn to be persuasive. "What does your mother say?"

"Mother still says I'm a slut – but I promised Pa I wouldn't tell anything, so she must think what she will. That's what Pa says."

There was a pause in the room apart from the squabbling on the television. Rosanna got up and walked to the machine. She turned it off and came back to the tousled child on my lap. We must have formed an incongruous heap in the sagging armchair into which we had subsided. The doctor had a different expression on her face - a mixture of up-set and anger.

"Tell me Sugar," she said in a matter-of-fact tone, "when do you and your father share your secret chats."

"Mostly around dawn, before Pa goes back to his room. You see, I am the oldest," a note of pride crept into the little voice, "I have my own room in the back of the house, where the pantry used to be.

"But I mustn't tell you these things," Rosie looked up in a sudden panic. "Pa will be so angry, I don't want him to be angry, not ever again. I promised him, I promised I wouldn't tell."

"No, of course you shouldn't tell" Rosanna replied in what she hoped was a reassuring manner. "You're not supposed to tell any ordinary person, but Father Jack and I are different, you know that. You can tell us anything and everything and we won't tell anyone else, but it will help us to help you. Indeed, having Father Jack here proves that it is God's will that you talk to us, remember, that's what we agreed last time we talked?"

I felt something sharp against my shoulder and realized it was Rosanna's finger prodding me urgently. I felt a mixture of betrayal and anxiety as I obediently confirmed Rosanna's pleas.

"Come on Rosie, there's nothing to be afraid of here, God has sent us to help you, and you must trust us not to let you – or Him - down. Tell us about these chats you have with your father," I said with reluctance. I did not like the way things were going, a very uneasy feeling was growing inside me.

We waited, the girl's shuddering and gasping tugging at our hearts. Suddenly she gave a deep breath and nodded. Rosie began to whisper, her head was bowed again, hidden in her hands with fingers pressed against her eyelids.

"God loves me in a special way, you see," pride returned to the child's voice and she spoke with a rush of sudden confidence. "He comes to me two or three times a week, after I've put the others to bed and Pa has come back from the pub. Pa tells me that I am God's very special girl and we share this very special secret. I cannot see God, but I can feel him, and he feels me."

I remember staring hard at a brown spot on the green linoleum floor, I didn't want to hear this. Anger was rising with icy fingers from my stomach through my chest, into my throat. I swallowed hard to keep the emotion at bay and tried to breathe normally so the child on my knee would not notice my distress.

"Pa brings God to me when I'm in bed," Rosie continued. "I turn on my side, and Pa holds me tight, from behind. He holds my chest to keep me still, both hands where I can see them so that I know it must be the Lord's hand that is hot and hard against my bottom.

"The Lord is good to me, but He needs to know that I am good inside and out, so most nights he feels right inside me to make sure there is no badness there. Pa has to hold me tight to stop me moving – the first time it hurt a lot, but Pa explained that was because there was badness inside, and the Lord would have to get it out. As the nights past, it stopped hurting, but Pa still held me tight, so that my nipples hurt sometimes with his squeezing. Whilst the Lord is doing his exploring Pa moves around a lot and grunts most terrible, but that is because The Lord has to check him out too – although how that happens Pa won't explain. It's private, you see."

Through the blur of anger and horror in my mind I remembered Rosie, the first time I met her in St. George's, when she had called the church her home. She had said then that she had a special relationship with the Almighty, and I had noticed the strangeness of the sentence. Only now did the full significance of the statement hit me. Should I have realized earlier, was I somehow to blame for allowing this horror to continue? These thoughts would haunt me over and over again.

"Sometimes I haven't been very bad and the Lord blesses me quickly" Rosie was talking easily now. "He leaves me to sleep, with Pa snoring in my ear and me feeling the blessing oozing out of me and making my thighs sticky. Other times, I must have been very bad, because it takes a long time for the blessing to come and seems to cause Pa a lot of trouble too because his huffs and groans go on for ages. Pa leaves me every morning, before Ma gets back from her Club. It's just before he goes that we have our chats – or rather he chats to me, I don't have much to say as I know so little. I don't even know what sins I have committed for which I need such cleansing, and that shows just how bad I am."

As Rosie's revelations began to spill out, Rosanna turned her back to us. Her doctor's coat was taut across her shoulders as she wrapped her arms around herself. Her shoulders started to shake as the tale continued, her head dropping onto her chest.

I found that I was rocking Rosie gently, making the chair springs creak. My mind had gone numb and, with my hands around the child's waist and shoulders I couldn't wipe the tears that were running down my face. There was a deep cold anger in my chest that threatened to burst out and scream and yell all on its own.

Rosie had finished speaking, and her sobs had changed to sniffles. I was stroking her softly again, saying over and over again: "it's alright, Rosie. It's alright."

But it wasn't alright, a voice in my head was shouting. How could this evil have all been perpetrated under the guise of God's will. How, and why, could God have allowed this to happen, and to go on happening?

I tried to pray, but no words came. I looked around the room helplessly, as if somewhere in that tawdry area there should be an answer. Rosanna had turned back towards me and our eyes met.

"What do we do?" I mouthed the words to the doctor over Rosie's bowed head.

Rosanna was shaking her head at me when there was a noise outside in the hospital corridor and a large man pushed his way past the ward sister and into the room. Sweat beads stood out on the puffy round face that was so black it was almost like polished dark blue. The man's eyes were wide, the whites contrasting vividly with the dark pupils. In one hand he carried an incongruous bunch of flowers, with the other he was pushing the nurse aside.

"I'm sorry, doctor, I told him not to disturb you, but he insisted." The nurse had followed the man into the sitting room.

"She's my daughter, I can see her if I want to," the man said addressing the ward sister, the heavy Jamaican accent giving a sing-song lilt to the belligerent tone. "I have my rights, as a father, and you are out of order to get in my way." He turned and looked at me as I continued to cradle Rosie in my lap and at Rosanna who was standing tall, her starched doctor's coat giving her the authority she needed.

There was a moment of hesitation as Rosie's father narrowed his eyes and looked from the doctor to me in my dog-collar and back to the doctor.

"You are all out of order. It's none of your bloody business. Leave us alone the lot of you, I want to know how my daughter is, and I don't need any of you lot around to get in the way."

There was a heavy silence in the room until Rosie gave a great sob and pulled her head up from my shoulder. "Hello, Pa," she said softly.

Rosanna was the first to speak: "Of course" she said, "actually I was just leaving, but Father Jack will stay a bit longer, won't you Father? I will see you later, at the nurses' station. Come on Sister," she said to the nurse, "we have paperwork to attend to."

I understood my instructions, although they were unnecessary as there was no way I was going to leave Rosie alone with her father. Later I would look back at this moment and be amazed at how unfazed I was about facing this man who I knew to be a monster. The strength that came to me seemed out of character, as did the surge of aggression I could not deny. My arms were still wrapped around the trembling girl, holding her securely but tenderly. The irony of this paternal protectiveness struck me briefly as I focused on how to handle the conversation.

"So they call you 'father' do they?" The big man seemed to have sensed my feelings. " I suppose you're the one little Sugar's been spending so much time with in that spooky old church she likes so much. Well you're not her father, so that title has no sway with me. I'm her father, and nobody can take my child away from me. Not you with your silly religious get-up, nor your doctor friend there, nor these damned nurses. Now get the hell away from my girl and leave us alone."

Rosie was disentangling herself from my arms. She climbed off my knee, straightened her hospital gown and ran to her father, throwing her arms around his legs. "Oh Pa, I'm so glad you've come. I wanted you to meet Father Jack, so don't be angry that he's here. He's only trying to help me."

"Well, I'm all the help you need," Rosie's father said with a softness that surprised me. He was stroking his daughter's hair, and bent to kiss the top of her curly head.

I felt a surge of disgust. "But of course, she doesn't know," I reminded myself, "and he doesn't know that I know, although by his abusive tone I think he suspects. Dear God, help me," my thoughts ran wildly, "please, please tell me what to do."

I stared at Rosie and her father, murmuring endearments to each other, then suddenly made a decision.

"Rosie's been telling me about her special relationship with The Almighty," I began. I was relieved to find my voice was steady as I fixed my eyes on Rosie's father as he lifted his head and stared. The man's eyes narrowed before they dropped to his daughter. He pushed her away from him, holding her roughly by the shoulders.

"I told you to tell nobody," he hissed. "You stupid child, what have you done?"

I was quick to step forward until I was standing right behind Rosie, my face only a couple of feet from her father's.

"As one of God's representatives here on earth, Mr. . ." there was a pause while I realized that I didn't know the surname – and then Rosie's story of the stolen briefcase and the pen came back to me. "Mr. Parker, I feel that I have every right to know of how God manifests Himself to my parishioners. Rosie has a lot to learn, it seems, and we all have a lot of praying to do."

The silence in the room was heavy; the malevolent look that was aimed at me seemed to go right through me and out the other side. I stood my ground and met the gaze steadily.

"I don't think it advisable for Rosie to convalesce at home," I continued. "She has told me of her duties in the household, and she needs a complete rest. A change of scene would do her good. She can come and stay in the vicarage, maybe."

"So you want a piece of the action too, do you." Rosie's father spat back. "Well you're not bloody having it."

My hands flew from my sides in an involuntary movement of speed and strength that took me by surprise. I was only just able to stop them whirling into the leering face as, with a physical effort, I forced my fingers to clasp themselves together in a totally inappropriate attitude of prayer.

"Well maybe Dr. Todd will have a better idea, Mr. Parker," I managed to speak through a tensed jaw, "or the Social Services, I understand they are usually the people to deal with this kind of situation."

"I don't want to go with no Social Services people," Rosie spun round and looked up at me in genuine distress. "They take you away from your family, those people do, they destroy the bonds that keep us altogether," the child was reciting something she had either been taught or had overheard, "they don't want us blacks to have a proper place in society. I'm not going anywhere but home, where I belong."

"See," said Mr. Parker with a note of triumph in his voice. "What are you going to do about Rosie's wishes, she's meant to be the most important person in this conversation, she's the one we should be listening to. Now you tell the vicar, Rosie, where you want to be and who you want to be with. You wouldn't like to be anywhere without your Pa, now would you?"

Rosie turned back to her father and re-coiled her arms around his legs. "Nobody's ever taking me away from you, Pa. Nobody!"

I didn't know how to respond. I could no longer hold the man's stare and moved my eyes, circling the room, as if somewhere in the corners of the ceiling there might be an answer.

"Another thing you gotta think about, you interfering zealot," Mr. Parker's words came out with spit in them; "is that I'm the bread-winner of this family. Rosie's got younger sisters, and a brother coming up. Who's going to pay for everything if I'm not? Oh yes, her Ma works the clubs, but she keeps her money, it's all I can do to get her to buy the kids some clothes every now and then. No, I'm the one who pays the bills."

My reply was involuntary: "it's those younger one's I'm worried about, look what's happened to Rosie" I was stuttering, the anger suddenly re-kindled and only on the edge of control.

"There's nothing wrong with our family, is there Sugar?" the man pushed his daughter gently away from his legs with one hand and tilted her chin with the other one. "You wouldn't want to be anywhere else than with the family, would you?"

Rosie's eyes filled with tears. "No, no, Pa. Don't let them take me away. What would the others do without me – it's been hard enough for them this week having to cope with Auntie Bessie, I know, Emma-Lee's been telling me. You've got to let me go home," she said turning her back on her father and looking up at me, "you've got to."

I suddenly felt defeated. "Rosie, I just want what's best for you, that's all" I said rather lamely, "and you need time to get well."

"What's best for me is what's best for my family," she told me proudly; and again there was that sense of recitation. "Why don't you speak to Ma about it all, she would be real upset if she thought I wasn't coming home."

"Should we talk to your wife on the subject?" I couldn't help the cheap jibe. "What do you think she would feel about all this, if she knew what's really been going on?"

"Oh, no," Rosie was quick to intercede, "Ma's not to know the secret. God would be really angry and do something horrid to Ma. We can't tell Ma."

"Why do you think that?" I was quick to raise the question before Rosie's father had a chance to speak, although Mr. Parker didn't look in a hurry to re-join the conversation.

"You tell him, Pa. Tell Father Jack why we can't tell Ma."

The silence had returned, but this time it was Rosie's father who could not hold my gaze. The sound of the second hand of the big clock over the doorway counted the moments of anguish. I waited.

"This has nothing to do with you," Mr. Parker suddenly exploded. His eyes had become blood-shot and seemed to swirl in his head. The veins at his temples were throbbing visibly. "Why don't you just fuck off back to where you belong in your stupid church and leave us to get on with our lives. You know nothing about us, and we don't want to know anything about you. Just take your sanctimonious shit and stick it up your arse where it belongs.

"Come on Sugar, let's get your things, we're getting out of here."

"I'm afraid it's not quite as simple as that." A new voice entered the conversation as Dr. Todd entered the room and I realized, with relief, that she had been there all the time. "Your daughter has to be released by a doctor, and that isn't going to happen until we think she is fit and ready to go. By bringing her to this hospital, Mr. Parker, you have relinquished your control over Rosie. She is only thirteen, and we have the power and the authority to keep her away from you until we think it is safe for her to go home."

"This is a conspiracy, isn't it?" Mr. Parker swirled from the doctor. "I'll see you both in hell before you take my Sugar away from me. Don't you worry, darling," his voice softened as he turned to his daughter, "Pa won't let anyone take you away. We're a family, and that's the way we're going to stay. I have to leave now, but don't worry, I'll be back." He straightened his back and looked at Rosanna, who had now moved beside me. His eyes widened to include us both in his glare. "Oh yes, I'll be back, and when I come, I'll have my lawyer with me. You two had better watch out." He turned on his heel, pushed the swinging door so hard that it hit the wall with a bang, and was gone.

Rosanna and I looked at each other as Rosie started to wail. At the sound, both of us dropped to our knees to comfort her and words of encouragement and love poured down on the sobbing girl in a rush.

Eventually, Rosie stopped crying, looked up at first one, and then the other of us and said: "I missed lunch, and I'm awfully hungry, do you think we could find something to eat?"

I gave a huge sigh of relief, while Rosanna laughed out loud. "Of course, sweetie. Come on, we'll go to the kitchen and see what they can do for you. What would you like best of all?"

"They do some really good omelets here," Rosie responded as, upon invitation, she climbed onto Rosanna's back. "Am I going to have another of those wonderful piggy-back rides?"

"For sure, Rosie, all the way to the kitchen. What do you fancy in that omelet then, should we ask them for chicken, ham, maybe some cheese, what's your choice?"

Rosanna hitched the child up on her back and was half way out of the door before she remembered me.

"You've done a marvelous job, Jack," she said. "Can you wait a little bit longer while we get Rosie some lunch? I'll be back as soon as I can, we need to talk."

I nodded at the disappearing back, watching Rosie's little body lurch along in time with Rosanna's strides. The tapes of her hospital gown were stretched across her naked back, small brown buttocks protruding above the doctor's locked elbows. I felt another shock of revulsion and anger before slumping into one of the armchairs, gorge was rising in my throat and I had to make a physical effort not to be sick.

It was nearly half and hour before Rosanna returned, and by that time the adrenalin had subsided and I felt exhausted and empty.

"Here, I've brought you a cup of tea, Jack. I thought you might use one after your sterling battle with that dreadful man. How on earth are we blacks meant to get on in the world with people like that around?"

"It's got nothing to do with his color, Rosanna, you know that." I said, taking the tea with a grateful nod. "I'm afraid there are some extremely unpleasant people walking around in white skins also. Mankind hasn't come very far for all the technology in the world, has it? There are still a lot of beasts in our midst.

"What can we do about Rosie?" I continued. "I've been thinking, we only have her story. If her father denies any wrong-doing, how can we prove anything. What happened to the baby? I never thought I would thank god for an infant's death, but this time it must be seen as a blessing. Should we ask for a DNA test to be done?"

"I don't know, Jack. I wish I did." Rosanna had moved one of the big chairs so that she sat facing me. "I've been trained to heal people's bodies. I'm totally out of my depth with this. Perhaps you were right to suggest the Social Services, they must have come across stuff like this before, unpleasant though it is to contemplate. I've never had much time for them in the past, but I don't know where else we should go."

"Except to the police?" I shuddered at the thought of filling in forms with this dreadful accusation. "But once again, we haven't really any proof – and as you say, neither of us are used to dealing with this sort of thing."

There was a pause while I stared into my tea and Rosanna studied her shoes. "And another thing," I continued, clearing my throat, "we promised Rosie we wouldn't tell anyone, and now we have to break that promise. She'll never trust anyone again, and it's very unlikely that she'll talk to anyone else as she has talked to us, especially with the rubbish her father has been threatening her with. Rosie obviously has a terror of the Social Services. If she denies what she has told us – there's nothing to go on at all."

"But we have to do something," Rosanna cut in. "We can't just let things carry on. How about talking to Rosie's mother about it? Maybe a simple act like having all the children sleep in the same room would be enough to solve the problem."

"No, that beast will find a way. If we don't do anything, it's as if we've condoned his ghastly behavior – Rosanna, I wish I knew what we should do. I feel drained, useless, helpless and very frustrated."

"You've a right to feel drained, Jack," Rosanna said, getting up and placing a hand on my shoulder in an unexpected gesture. "I was so impressed with how you handled that conversation. I panicked, I'm afraid, and knew I wasn't going to be any good if I had to stay in the same room as him. You're the one who faced him." She gave my shoulder a squeeze and I felt a welcome rush of warmth. She sat down again.

"Thank you, Rosanna. I was just following my instincts – although not as far as I would have liked to." I began to realize how much the doctor's praise had meant to me, I sat up straight and drank my tea. "And thanks for the tea, also. You were right, I did need it."

"I suppose there is always the dead baby, as you pointed out, Jack," Rosanna said with a shudder. "But I imagine we would need a court order to get a DNA test done, and without Rosie's testimony there won't be a case to go on. This is a nightmare."

"What about telling Rosie the truth?" I suggested without enthusiasm. "She's thirteen, it's amazing she hasn't worked it out for herself already, given how the kids at school must have chatted."

"I think that might be the answer," said Rosanna, "but I think her mother should tell her, not us. If that bastard of a father of hers wants to keep this 'within the family' perhaps that's the best way – the only way – to deal with it. At least he won't get off scot-free if his wife knows what's been going on. But who's going to tell her?"

"We're going to have to involve the Social Services, Rosanna," I said after a few moments thought. "As you suggested, they're probably used to this sort of thing, God help them. Even if we haven't any proof, at least there are two of us as witnesses to Rosie's story; that must count for something. Let's give it to them to sort out."

There was a sudden beeping noise and Rosanna removed a device from her breast pocket and pressed a button. The sound stopped and she stood up quickly. "I've got to go Jack. I think you're right. I'll contact the necessary people - they work here in the hospital all the time. They'll probably give you a call, if they need to. Can I have your number – I'm sorry, I really have to go. If you could spare a few moments to say goodbye to Rosie . . . She's in the Swan ward – second on the left, down this corridor, and the first bed on the right."

I nodded, searching through my wallet for something to write on. Rosanna produced a pen from alongside the beeper in her pocket and I scribbled my number on the back of a dry-cleaning ticket.

"I'll go and see her right now and talk of normal things," I said. "Give me a ring when you can, and good luck."

The two of us shook hands, a sudden formality reasserting itself into our relationship. I held the door open for her and the doctor walked swiftly off to the left, while I turned to the right and headed for the Swan ward and my diminutive parishioner.

46. VOICE OF EXPERIENCE

The scene in the hospital left me badly shaken. I blamed myself strongly for not having noticed Rosie's condition or questioned her absence. I scolded myself that I had been too busy being pleased with my treatment of the other parishioners, and had abandoned the most vulnerable of them all.

Father Justin noticed the change in my demeanor at dinner that evening, and it didn't take much persuasion to coax the story out. We were in the dining-room, as usual, having finished our meal and stacked the plates on the sideboard ready for Elsie in the morning.

We had been talking about the forthcoming charity sale that Lorna had persuaded us to hold in the church the following weekend. I must have been monosyllabic in my contribution to the conversation, and Father Justin wasn't used to being the main protagonist in such a discussion.

The senior vicar reached for the port, filled his glass, and replaced the cut-glass decanter carefully onto its silver-edged coaster. He had long ago given up offering me any port but was encouraged to see that I had started doing justice to the wine Mr. Stanhope kept bringing to the vicarage.

I was staring into my recently emptied glass, turning the stem slowly between my fingers, and looked up, startled, as Father Justin moved the tilted bottle of claret into my vision. I did not object as the glass was refilled.

"All right, my boy," Father Justin returned to his seat, the claret bottle set down gently next to the port. He had never addressed me like that before, and the affection in his voice caught me by surprise. "What's happened?" he continued. "Something has affected you strongly, and I think you should talk to your vicar about it – that's still my job, you know, I haven't handed everything over to you yet. Now tell me what it is that has distressed you so."

"It's that obvious, is it?" I smiled - I had thought I was putting on a bold front and was touched by the uncharacteristic kindness with which the older man spoke. It was not that Father Justin wasn't usually kind, it was just that we had always kept our conversations briskly professional and had never allowed emotions to creep into discussions except in a most light-hearted way.

I told Rosie's sad tale, cautiously at first, and then all in a rush. My voice rose in anger as I described the intervention of Rosie's father and the role the wretched man had played in his daughter's dreadful experience.

"I blame myself greatly, Father," I stated flatly when I had finished the account. "I should have been more observant, more attentive, more interested in the poor little girl, but you know what she's like, always chatting away. I only listened with half an ear, and never noticed all the clues she kept giving me. She was always talking about her special relationship with the Almighty – I never realized the import of what she was saying."

"And what would you have done about it if you had understood and found out the situation sooner?" Father Justin interrupted the self-recriminations. "No-one sensible could have imagined what was going on with Rosie from her carefree attitude and happy disposition. I know her as well as you do, Jack, and although I haven't seen her for a while, I'm sure I wouldn't have caught the awful implications of her chatter either."

"But that's the point, Father" I replied rapidly. "I hadn't seen her for over two months. Why did I not think it odd when her visits stopped? Why didn't I go in search of her and make sure that she was alright?"

"I say again, Jack," the vicar suddenly looked older as he lent towards his protégé, his eyes watery behind his glasses, as he pronounced each word slowly. "What would you have done about it had you known earlier?"

I looked at my mentor, my gaze moving from one of the old man's eyes to the other as if desperately searching for an answer to the question he had posed. There was none forthcoming, just a slow blink of empathy.

Suddenly I realized that Father Justin had been faced with problems of such magnitude before, perhaps many times. I was acutely aware of my youth and inexperience and had a glimpse as to why my superior now shut himself away from his parishioners.

The silence lasted for quite a while. I could hear the ticking of the grand-father clock in the hall, and the tapping of twigs against the windowpanes as the breeze buffeted the darkness outside. Father Justin lent back in his chair, but his eyes remained fixed on mine, his face impassive and patient.

It was the patience that got to me in the end, and I stood up abruptly, pushing my chair back with a grating noise. I strode towards the door, and then turned and came back, grasping the chair back with hands clenched so that the knuckles showed white with the strain.

"I don't know, Father. I just don't know, but I feel I should have been able to do something," agitation was giving an edge to my voice.

"But now you do know about it, and you still don't know what to do." Father Justin paused and took a thoughtful sip of his port before continuing. "The situation is at least somewhat simplified now. The baby was born dead, so there's one element of the problem that doesn't have to concern anyone. The father is aware of the doctor's and your knowledge of his role. Something has to happen now, and the problem will be dealt with, whether you like it or not.

"If you had known earlier, you have to ask yourself what you would have done about the pregnancy. Would you have told the authorities? Would you have tackled the father? What could you have advised regarding the baby itself? There are all sorts of ramifications to all these questions. Fortunately you were spared all that and we have to face the fact that it was probably better for you not to have known about this horror earlier."

Silence returned to the dining room as I stared gloomily at the shiny table, so lovingly polished by Elsie every day. I could see my reflection in the swirls of the wood grain, my glasses glinting as I tilted my head.

Finally I looked up and took a deep breath.

"Be that as it may, father, I have still let Rosie down."

"It's the world that's let Rosie down, Jack, and her father in particular. You're just a small part of it; but a positive part, because you are there for her now. You have stepped into the scene and given her something to hold on to. It's what happens next that you should be looking towards, not chastising yourself about the past. The future is where you are most needed. Now we have to make a plan to see how best to do God's will in helping with what lies ahead - both for you and for Rosie.

"How was she when you left her?" he concluded.

I thought of Rosie, sitting up amongst a bank of pillows in a ward of children each with their own problem. The curtains had been three-quarters drawn on both sides of her bed so that she had privacy without being alone and she could still see the television perched on a high shelf across the room. She was fiddling with the ear-phones that had become tangled with her thick, tight curls. She was so absorbed in the program that she hadn't noticed my approach and looked up in surprise when I pulled a chair up close to her bed and sat down.

"Oh, she seemed fine," I answered, finding it hard to look at Father Justin again without the risk of tears springing to my eyes. "She was far more interested in something on the telly than in talking to me. I must confess, it was a relief.

"I made sure she was comfortable, and I left. I said I'd come back and see her tomorrow – with this collar, I don't need to be restricted to visiting hours, so I can go when there's no chance of meeting any of her family. I don't know how to speak to them."

"Well, go and see Rosie tomorrow, then," said father Justin, "and talk of nothing in particular. Let her feel that all is returning to normal. She has to get her health back. She is just a child, and children heal a great deal faster than adults, both physically and emotionally. After all, as far as she's concerned, she hasn't done anything wrong. You will be astonished at how she will put all this behind her and get on with life.

"I'm afraid this will probably affect you and Dr. Todd more than it will Rosie during the years to come," he added thoughtfully.

"After your visit, why not take a couple of days off," Father Justin continued. "You've hardly left the parish for more than a few hours since you came, and it's certainly time you did. Why not visit your friend from College, the one who has a country parish somewhere. It would do you good to get away, and I can hold the fort for a bit – just as long as you're back for the weekend and Lorna's wretched charity sale."

I looked at my superior in amazement. It had never occurred to either of us that we could leave St. George's, even for a short time. The most travelling I had done since my arrival – apart from the trip to Oberammergau - was to visit Rufus in Chelsea and Thomas in Harpenden – the two central places between us. Both Rufus and I had travelled to Thornton for Thomas' wedding, but we had managed the trip in a day with little opportunity to talk to the bride and groom in any depth.

The only other time I had seen my friends together was on a Monday near my last birthday, when both Thomas and Rufus had come to St. George's as it was a convenient middle point between their parishes. We had a wonderful few hours together reminiscing about St. Augustine's, comparing notes on parishioners, and wondering about the innocence with which we had been allowed out into the world; an innocence that was eroding rapidly in all of us.

Suddenly I was eager to get away, and a visit to Thornton seemed an excellent idea. I remembered the village and the vicarage only slightly, it had been over three years since the wedding, but I knew it was pleasant and rural and quite unlike Islington. I found myself looking at father Justin with affection.

"That's a wonderful idea, father, and I am most grateful to you for suggesting it. Yes, I would love to see Thomas and get to know his family and his church. They had a second child very recently, but I couldn't get to the Christening – it being on a Sunday.

"I could visit Rosie tomorrow morning and then take the train straight afterwards – I'll go and telephone Thomas now and see if it's convenient. If you'll excuse me, that is."

"Of course, Jack," father Justin smiled as he watched enthusiasm return to my face. "You can work on your sermon while you're there," he said to my retreating back, "you'll be in the pulpit on Sunday and I shall expect something inspiring from your visit to the countryside."

47. Back to Thornton

Thomas had been delighted with my proposed visit and insisted upon driving into Newport Pagnell to meet me at the train station.

"The buses are few and far between, Jack," he had insisted, "and I had plenty of time after early communion. Perhaps we could do even-song together, it being a Wednesday?"

"Sounds like a busman's holiday," I laughed in reply, but agreed anyway.

The Thornton Vicarage

"We had to bite the bullet and swap the lovely old Rover for this thing," Thomas said as he guided me through the station car-park and pointed at the elderly Volvo estate ahead of us. "A family car for a family man."

"Well you look very well on it, Thomas," I told him with a smile.

"Oh, you mean this," Thomas patted his stomach. "Yes, Sandra's a marvelous cook, but we take lots of exercise and I'm trying to keep it under control."

"No, I didn't mean that, Thomas," I was quick to defend myself. "Not at all, you're in splendid shape. I meant your general demeanor seems wonderfully buoyant."

"Well, it's true, we are greatly blessed. Your namesake and godson, was two last month and the new baby is a delight. We christened her Alicia Sarah – Sandra's mother's called Sarah, and apparently I had a great Aunt called Alicia, but we only found that out after we had chosen the name. A lucky coincidence, my father was delighted!"

We had reached the car and Thomas moved the baby's chair as he spoke, placing it reverentially in the back along with my small suitcase. He ushered me into the passenger seat.

"It's so good to have you here, Jack," he said, closing the car door with care. "Sandra was so excited when I told her you were coming," he continued as he climbed behind the wheel. "She's busy nursing little Alicia, of course, so you'll have to take pot luck with meals. Little Jack and I are in charge of the kitchen at the moment, but we have a lot of fun and the supermarkets make everything so easy these days."

It was a forty minute drive from the station to Thornton through curling roads with immaculately tended fields on either side. The fresh air felt good in my lungs and I felt myself relaxing as I left the troubles of St. George's behind me. I listened to Thomas' delightful, uncomplicated chatter about children, dogs and general household chores – all so unfamiliar to me. I had no domestic obligations in Islington at all; Elsie did all the shopping, the cooking and the cleaning. On her days off, she left cold meals wrapped in cling film, all ready to be placed on the table, and when she came back she tackled the small pile of washing up which her charges had left ready for her. Dirty laundry went into a basket and was returned neatly ironed and folded, sheets were changed every Monday. Perhaps I should give Elsie more attention, I thought, be more grateful for all she does to allow Father Justin and me such freedom from trivia.

Thornton is a pretty village with the church and vicarage at its centre. The former reminded me of St. Barnabus in Willenbury, only this one had a wooden spire built atop its grey stone tower. As we drove past the church, Thomas looked at it with affection.

"She's beautiful, isn't she?" he said. "The stone part dates back to Norman times and the slightly magical wooden spire was added a couple of centuries later. I always think it looks a bit like a wizard's hat," he chuckled.

I recognized the proprietary excitement in Thomas' voice as he spoke of the church; I felt the same about St. George's. It was good to be able to share so much, so easily, and without having to talk about it.

Turning right off the road, Thomas drove the car up a short gravel drive behind the church and stopped in front of a Victorian vicarage of grey stone with a sharp pitched roof and dormer windows. As I had predicted, all those years ago at St. Augustine's, there were climbing roses arguing around the front door with honey-suckle riding piggy-back on the briars, reaching up to encircle the first floor windows. The heavy oak door swung open before the car had stopped and Sandra, a baby in her left arm and a toddler holding onto her right hand emerged onto the front steps.

Sandra was not pretty, but the wholesome nature of her friendly face, her open gaze and a smile that made the freckles on her nose dance, made her a natural beauty. Jack, the toddler, left her side as soon as Thomas got out of the car, and ran eagerly towards his father shouting "Daddy, Daddy" at the top of his voice. Sandra used the newly released hand to return a strand of auburn hair behind an ear and shake her pony tale loose from the green apron that encircled her neck and covered her yellow blouse and blue jeans.

"Welcome, welcome," Sandra walked carefully down the front steps as she spoke, leaning forward to watch her feet over the bundle she held so lovingly. "It's good to have you here, Jack. Thomas has been over the moon ever since your telephone call last night. What do you think of your god-son?" She gestured towards my namesake who had climbed into Thomas' arms and was busy getting sticky fingers all over his father's glasses. "Hasn't he grown?"

"Hello, Sandra," I came around the front of the car and cautiously bent over the bundle to give my hostess a kiss on each cheek. "He's quite the young man, now, isn't he? Well, Jack, how about shaking hands with your godfather?"

I have no experience with little children and felt awkward and patronizing as I spoke. However the child seemed to respond and, having been put down by Thomas who was eager to polish his glasses on a flamboyant red and gold handkerchief, walked solemnly towards me with his right hand outstretched.

"Well that's very formal, I must say," said Thomas laughing as his son and best friend shook hands with grave expressions on both our faces.

"This is a serious relationship," I replied, "and one which I hope will develop into a serious friendship." I lowered my eyes to meet those of the little boy who was looking up at me. "I take my role as your godfather to be an important one, Jack, and look forward to our journey together into God's wondrous world."

"Well come on in," said Sandra. "It's nearly Alicia's feeding time, and Jack has been waiting for you two to take him to the village shop to buy supper. Isn't that right, Jack?"

The boy nodded his fair head, and as he did so the sun caught his hair and showed streaks of his mother's auburn mixed in with the blond.

"Is he going to be a red head, like his mother?" I asked.

"He might well be," answered Sandra. "His eyes are already turning from blue to grey. Still, he's a good looking chap whatever color he ends up with on his head." She tousled the boy's curls as he dashed past her into the house.

"Come on Daddy, supper-shopping, supper-shopping" he called as he disappeared down a long narrow passage that ran the length of the building.

My small leather suitcase in hand, I followed Sandra upstairs as she chatted away about new decorations that were needed in the house, and especially in the guest room.

"It all looks very comfortable and grand to me," I said truthfully, as I looked around the airy high-ceilinged room into which I had been shown. The two tall sash windows looked out across well-tended lawns and flowerbeds to a stand of high trees. It was a delightful vista, and I felt instantly comfortable with the room, with the house, and with my friends.

My stay at Thornton did me the world of good. I accompanied Thomas on his daily chores, both pastoral and domestic, and relished the lack of responsibility as I listened to the parishioners' problems and questions.

The church-goers of the village were mostly middle-aged and comfortably well-off. There were a couple of elderly widows and an old couple in their eighties with the charm and manners of a past age. There didn't seem to be anyone under about thirty-five.

"The younger generation only appear at Christmas and Easter, or for marriages, christenings and so on," Thomas replied to my query. "They commute to The City mostly and are not here during the week. I don't seem to be able to get them interested in attending regular Sunday services, but they are always ready to help with fund-raising activities, the garden fête, that sort of thing. I worry that if we put pressure on them to come to church more often we will lose their support altogether. But I am sad not to have the children as part of our services.

"Sandra had a Sunday school going for a while, with lots of exciting games amongst the prayers, but it had to stop when Alicia made her presence felt, and there was no-one else willing to take it on. Perhaps she will re-start it when she's stopped nursing the baby."

"We have very few children also," I admitted. "And the one's we do have all seem to want some special attention that they don't get from either their parents or a church service." I told Thomas a little of the demands of Charlotte's children Sally and Sam, but it wasn't until Friday evening that I felt ready to talk about Rosie.

Jack had gone to bed after I had read him his favorite *Thomas the Tank Engine* story and Sandra had gone upstairs straight after supper in preparation for another night interrupted by nursing Alicia. So Thomas and I were on our own in the 'drawing-room each ensconced in a large armchair in front of the fire, cradling a full glass of Rioja, the remainder of which was in a bottle on a low table between us.

We had been discussing the various demands made by our parishes and by individual members of the congregations and sharing doubts as to our qualifications in answering some of the personal questions we were asked.

"Our tutors at St. Augustine's never really helped us with the intimacies we should expect from our relationships with our parishioners, did they?" Thomas said as much to the smoldering fire as to me. "I never gave this side of the ministry much thought, and yet, of course it is the most important part of our job, really. We were so busy fussing about sermons, intonations, the singing bits – remember the singing lessons, Jack, weren't they a laugh – the depths of our personal faith and so on. We quite overlooked the most important aspect of our job, namely helping people on an individual basis, not just through the church services. Being there for them when no-body else is, or perhaps, when nobody else will do. Do you know what I mean?"

"Absolutely, Thomas," I answered enthusiastically, "and nobody told us how to react to the human situations that are so foreign to us. At least you have Sandra with whom you can discuss female issues in confidence – I just have Father Justin, who's a dry old stick and always tells me to follow my instincts. He has suggested most strongly that God is guiding those instincts, but I get huge waves of doubt, like the time I advised the girl Tracy to listen to the social services about her unwanted pregnancy – I as good as condoned her getting an abortion."

Thomas turned his eyes from the fire and looked at me in amazement. "What did you say, Jack?" he enquired.

I proceeded to tell Tracy's story and my reaction to it. I finished the tale with a description of the anguish I had felt whilst praying to The Almighty Father after the girl had left the church, and my inability to discuss the matter with Father Justin. "After all," I added somewhat lamely, "I had given Tracy my word that I wouldn't tell him, or anyone else come to that, but it was quite a while ago now – Tracy goes to college next September – and you don't know the characters involved, so I'm sure God will forgive me for sharing this burden with you."

Thomas nodded but said nothing. He turned his eyes back to the glowing logs and was sipping his wine thoughtfully.

"I had a pregnant woman asking me for advice once also," he started. "But it was a totally different situation, and I gave totally different advice. This was a married woman – happily married, I might add – with two children already, a boy and a girl. She and her husband had been using some sort of contraceptive device, but in spite of that, she got pregnant.

"One of her children was already in school full-time and the second, the daughter, was due to leave kindergarten and follow her brother very shortly. My parishioner was looking forward to regaining her freedom and was hoping to go back to working part-time - she was a florist before the children arrived. She told me how much her marriage depended upon her being independent once more and not having to nag her husband for help with the children, and so on."

Thomas put down his wine glass gently and got up to prod the coals with a shiny brass poker before adding another log to the fire. He replenished our glasses before sitting down again and continuing his story.

"She was asking me to sanction an abortion, but I couldn't. This lady was in excellent health, the family had plenty of money, I just couldn't condone such an act on what seemed to be a purely selfish whim – and I told her so.

"She was very angry with me, even though I tried to soften my remarks with emphasis on God's generosity and abundance and love and all that stuff – you know. She accused me of being an insensitive chauvinist who thought all women should be kept for breeding purposes only except when they were looking after their men folk. It was quite a scene!

"Like you, I prayed long and hard when the meeting was over – she left saying she would not be coming back to this church as long as this vicar was in residence. But at the end of the day, she didn't have the abortion and she has been decent enough to seek me out and thank me for my advice. She said she couldn't imagine life without Rupert, he was an absolute joy to the whole family, and please would I be his godfather and christen him in our church. She also added that they had employed a nanny and she was now conducting a small floral business from her home."

We were silent for a while. My mind was in turmoil – was my friend berating me for the advice I had given Tracy, even though Thomas knew how much it troubled me. I was about to plead my cause once more when Thomas resumed his speech.

"Of course that is an entirely different scenario from the one you have described to me with the girl Tracy. I hope I would have had the courage that you had to advise her as you did. I'm sure you did the correct thing – even though it's not something to advertise within the family of the church.

"As I understand it, Tracy was still in school. She had plans to complete her education and go on to better things. Plans that a baby would have destroyed – not just for a few months, but forever. She also had no money with which to buy the myriad of things a baby needs and greedy parents who were prepared for her to sacrifice her future so that they could have a larger council flat. She didn't know who the father was – and I take it that there was no suggestion of immaculate conception?" Thomas smiled at me, I held my hands up in a gesture of both surprise and incredulity. "No, I rather thought not," Thomas said with a grin which lightened the atmosphere in a flash.

"So you see, I agree with you, and am impressed with the strength and compassion which is evident in the way in which you dealt with the situation. Here, by the fire, in cozy Bedfordshire, after a lovely supper and sipping a very fine Rioja - always my favorite - it's easy for me to say. But if I had been confronted, as you were, without warning and without a textbook to guide me – I wonder what I would have done. I am sincere, Jack, in saying that I hope I would have done the same thing."

My eyes were moist with emotion. "Thank you Thomas, you are a good friend," I said, after buying time sipping the wine and adjusting my glasses, "and it's such a relief to be able to share these worries with you like this. I still find it hard to know what is really God's will and whether or not I am following his commandments. There is a great deal of uncertainty in my life at the moment and, I have to confess, I am struggling with it."

"So Tracy's predicament has not been the worst problem for you?" Apparently Thomas knew me well enough to understand that this had only been the prologue to my concerns. "What was it that caused you to come to Thornton with so little notice? Not that both Sandra and I aren't thrilled that you did, but it is uncharacteristic of you nonetheless, and I suspect there was a catalyst behind the visit."

"You're quite right, Thomas," it was now my turn to stare into the rejuvenated fire. "It was Father Justin's idea for me to have a few days away. I fear I let one of my young parishioners down very badly and have let God down at the same time. This is another instance when you have to ask how tuned in you are to The Almighty's instructions. Why did I not hear the cry for help from little Rosie? Where was I when she needed my assistance and support which should have been evident from her absence at St. George's rather than her persistent presence?"

So I told Thomas the whole story from when Rosie had first entered the church to find the new deacon, to when I left her on Wednesday morning in the children's ward of the hospital.

During the tale, Alicia's muted cries could be heard from upstairs, followed by the sound of creaking bed-springs from the room overhead, the opening and closing of two doors and subsequent silence. The clock at the end of the passage struck eleven o'clock, and the fire gave up its flames and sank into ashes once again.

Thomas listened attentively to the story, sometimes nodding, sometimes shaking his head, always encouraging. When I finished he was still for a while and then got up to put another log on the fire, turning to me when he had finished.

"Well, that's quite a story. How lucky I am to be here in Thornton. When I got this parish, you remember, I was very upset. Now, with Sandra, little Jack and Alicia, with an old-fashioned English community, surrounded by farmland that makes you notice the weather and the seasons with piquancy, I am grateful to Father David – yes, even to that disgusting rogue Simon, for the living I have here.

"Your people in Islington – and the congregation with which Rufus has to deal – they are totally beyond my ken, and I would be grateful if they stayed that way, but I don't suppose they will. City people are spilling into the countryside more and more these days, and with them come their different moral standpoints and habits. I worry for the children I am bringing into this world. Can I assure them of the decency of life with which we were brought up? Can I know that our morality will stand fast against what is amounting to an alien invasion?"

I could not help smiling at this unexpected reaction to my tale of woe and horror. Thomas shook himself and said: "that's a dreadful story, Jack, I admit. However I fail to see where you, personally, have gone wrong.

"Let's take the tale piece by piece." Thomas turned his wine glass slowly between his fingers. "First, there was Rosie's entrance into your life, she obviously enjoyed your company and you continued to provide the church as a home for her, just as Father Justin had done before you.

"You say you didn't hear her cry for help – but are you sure there was one? After all, in her eyes, what had Rosie done wrong? I admit her lack of perception into what was really happening during those nocturnal visits from the 'Almighty' is difficult to credit. But then she was such a child when they first started – only eight, you said - heavens, she's still only a child and this has been going on for over four years. She trusts and loves her father – and from the sound of it, she still does. She trusts and loves her God also. What a horrible mess! What will happen to her psyche when she is old enough to understand the dreadful nature of her childhood experiences?"

"I don't know," I admitted. "Perhaps that is where I have to deliver some answers for her – although heaven knows what they will be."

We sat in silence for a while, staring into the fire, each with our own thoughts.

"What does Father Justin say about all this?" Thomas enquired after pouring the remainder of the Rioja into the two glasses.

"He says I have to be there for Rosie in the future, and not to dwell on the past. I think he's as upset as I am, but I get the impression that he has dealt with things as ghastly as this before. Not just the same, of course, but of equal unpleasantness. I think that is why he has withdrawn from the parish as much as he has, and why he is so glad to have me on hand to take it over. I'm just not at all sure I want to take it over if this is the sort of thing I have to deal with.

"I don't feel qualified – it's the same story over and over again. I am desperate not to make mistakes that might cause harm to someone. I pray all the time for guidance, but still feel that I am left to sort things out on my own. I don't feel I have done well with this Rosie mess."

"It sounds to me as if Father Justin is a wise old bird," Thomas answered softly. "And I agree with his view of looking forward and planning to be there for Rosie as time passes. I just don't know exactly what that will entail. I understand your concern, and wish I had a smart answer. Let me sleep on it and pray about it, and see if I can come up with something before you leave tomorrow."

"Thank you Thomas," I smiled across at my friend and suddenly felt immensely tired, and there was something troubling me over and above Rosie's story that I couldn't quite identify. It had something to do with Thomas' comments on her innocence and credulity.

"I'll take the afternoon train, if that's alright with you, Thomas," I said, standing to stretch my back and neck. "I have a sermon to work on in the morning – maybe we can work on one together? What have you in mind for this coming Sunday?"

I lay awake that night, my mind uneasy. Thomas had put his finger on a point in Rosie's story that had troubled me from the beginning, but that I had never allowed myself to confront. I would have to deal with it now. It was Rosie's unquestioning acceptance of the filthy sacrilegious explanations made by her father for his nighttime visits.

Thomas had been right to point out Rosie's extreme youth when first this dreadful practice had begun – she can't have been more than seven, eight at the most. She had often said how her father encouraged her love of God and her visits to St. George's must have been an offshoot of that encouragement.

I remembered also my studies at St. Augustine's of writers such as Margery Kempe who relished a physical relationship with Jesus. "I must be intimate with you, and lie in your bed with you . . . and you may boldly, when you are in bed, take me to you as your wedded husband" she claimed the Lord had said to her in a dream. That was over five hundred years ago, and my mind dwelt tentatively upon what exactly Margery Kempe had experienced.

It was Father John who had instructed me to study the works of Kempe and others. Father John of my early years at Rossington who had encouraged the worship of the Almighty in a physical way. Father John who had suddenly disappeared.

For the first time I wondered about the school chaplain's disappearance and my talk with Father Edmund at Willenbury. I could feel my face rushing red in the darkness as I turned uneasily on the pillow. I began to sweat – was it with shame, embarrassment, guilt, or all three combined?

I had been thirteen or fourteen when the incident in the school vestry had taken place, and it wasn't until now that I looked back on it and my own credulity and innocence. How could I wonder at Rosie's?

The question of my sexuality was one I avoided. I well remembered my anger with Sam when the boy had suggested I was gay. What did my nocturnal exercises mean when – encouraged by Father John - I used a spiritual vision for inspiration rather than a human one, and felt the pleasurable release to be an expression of a spiritual desire instead of a carnal one?

I got out of bed. The cool air felt pleasant on my body, still moist with disquiet. I walked to the window and looked out across the moonlit lawn to the darkness of the trees beyond. An owl hooted somewhere in the distance, but otherwise all was quiet in the windless clear night. Slowly I lowered myself until my knees met the wooden floor, and bent my head onto my hands that rested on the windowsill. I began to pray.

As usual, my prayers started with expressions of love and devotion to God. I made an effort to still the small voice of confusion that niggled at the back of my mind with these protestations of affection. I then went on to thank God for the great beneficence shown to this unworthy servant. My homespun liturgy continued as I listed the personal gifts God had given me and for which I owed eternal gratitude: my health, my family and friends, my work in God's church, my wondrous relationship with the Lord Jesus Christ - there it was again - and my humble position in God's infinite plan.

Then came the most earnest part of my daily prayers: my supplication for guidance in carrying out the work of Almighty God. Now I was including myself in those who needed help and direction. "Please, please, dear Lord, show me a way to find fulfillment in the carrying out of your will; and to understand my physical body as I strive to increase my spirituality. Give me the grace to be able to hear your commandments, to accept your guidance and find confidence in my actions."

My prayers continued for well over an hour and I only noticed the pain in my knees when I came to stand up. The floorboards were cold, hard and uneven and had left deep indentations in my skin. I rubbed them gingerly, and then stretched my arms up in the air, throwing my head back to relieve the neck and shoulders. I felt cleansed and whole and new. As I climbed back into bed, I felt a rush of reassurance about nothing in particular and fell asleep almost immediately.

The following morning the family breakfast was busy and noisy and it wasn't until Thomas was driving me to the station that we had time to talk.

"I have prayed long and hard, Jack," my friend began as the car was eased out of the vicarage drive, "to find answers to the many questions you are being asked to solve. How I wish I had been given a guide-book of ideas and answers, but that has not happened – yet." He added the last word with a smile. "But I do feel, very strongly, that God is using you well and that you are following his mission with wisdom and imagination.

"I am so impressed, Jack, with your resilience and creativity. St. Augstine's did nothing to prepare us for any of the problems you have encountered, and yet you're coping with strength, compassion and love. You should be proud of yourself, Jack, proud of how you have dealt with all these difficult questions and keep your head up high.

"Thornton will be always here for you, Jack. I'm glad you came, grateful and flattered that you shared these traumatic encounters with me. I shall continue to pray for guidance and for us both."

By the time we got to the station I was feeling a completely different person from the one that had arrived just a couple of days earlier.

My new energy and positivism came back with me to St. George's. Father Justin welcomed me warmly and congratulated me on the sermon Thomas and I had concocted on the morning of my departure from Thornton amongst little Jack's chatter and endless cups of tea. The two of us had found the idea of delivering the same discourse, at the same time, in two such different parishes, intriguing and exciting and had worked together enthusiastically.

The text we had selected was of Jesus as "The Light" and our homily exhorted the idea of an electric bulb left burning through the day and going unnoticed in the sunlight. So was God's love and guidance always present, but only looked for by human beings in their darkest hours when it could be seen in its true brightness to show the way. We would exhort our congregations on the value of daily acknowledgement of the eternal presence of God's love and watchfulness, rather than waiting for the darkness before recognizing the Light of God's love – and so on and so forth.

My exuberance evaporated, however, when I went to visit Rosie on the Sunday afternoon. Her bed in the hospital was empty and the ward sister explained that her family had insisted upon taking her away and had found a doctor to sign the release papers.

"The child was eager to be back home," the friendly nurse had said with the sing-song accent of her native India. Her head bobbed from side to side as she continued: "Rosie has made a remarkable recovery, and there was no physical reason for her to be kept here any longer. Dr. Todd is off this weekend, so it was young Dr. Roberts who signed the papers."

"Was Dr. Roberts familiar with the case?" I asked nervously.

"He consulted the notes on Rosie's records, examined the child carefully, and had to agree with the family that she would probably recover better in the loving care they promised to give her at home.

"Rosie's whole family came, on Saturday morning, you've never seen such a gathering, and they all wanted her back. Her little siblings especially, it was a really sweet scene. I'm sorry you weren't here to see it for yourself, Father, I'm sure you would have approved." The nurse smiled broadly as she recounted the story.

With reluctance, I went to see the hospital registrar and explained that I was Rosie's vicar and wished to visit her at home as she wasn't strong enough to come to church yet, "and it's Sunday, . ." I finished rather lamely.

I already knew the street where Rosie and her family lived, but I did not know the number. Having gained that information I forced myself to follow it up and visit the wretched place. I had decided to trust in the Lord to guide me in what I would say when I got there, for as I set out to retrace my steps to Islington, my mind was blank.

However, as it happened there was no reply when I knocked at the door of number 15, Elizabeth Road. There were plenty of children playing in the street, their shouting voices mixing North London accents with those of the West Indies and Africa. I turned to watch them as I waited in vain for the door to be opened.

"No use waiting there," a woman's voice from behind me made me jump. I turned to see a large woman, probably Jamaican, I thought judging from her brightly colored dress. "They've all gone. Packed up and left, lock, stock and stinking barrel, yesterday afternoon."

I felt my heart sink. "Where have they gone?" I asked feeling relieved and worried at the same time in equal portion.

"They wouldn't say. Fancy that, being neighbors for more than five years, and suddenly off without a word. One of the kids told me that the father had been offered a really good job somewhere else, and that was it. But I can't see it. He was a lazy good-for-nothing, and nobody was going to entice him away with a decent job. Anyway, who cares, it'll be a whole lot quieter here in the evenings without them." The woman crossed her arms about her ample bosom and looked satisfied with her explanation.

"They probably owe on the rent, or something like that, to up and away so suddenly with no telling where they were off to," she concluded.

I turned and looked through one of the grimy front windows. The room had been cleared. There were a few pieces of crumpled paper on a dusty floor and a lonely sock still showing the shape of the small foot that had occupied it. Otherwise the room was bare.

"It doesn't look as if they're coming back." I said more to myself than to the neighbor.

"Not a chance," said the woman with obvious pleasure. "They took everything that wasn't nailed down, even the light bulbs. Was there something you wanted?" She enquired, sticking her head forward in a way that made me appreciate the validity of the word 'nosey'.

"I just came to see Rosie," I said somewhat reluctantly, "she hasn't been well."

"Knocked up, you mean," said the woman with continuing satisfaction. "No, we'll be better off without that lot, if you ask me. I'm surprised to see a religious gent like you enquiring after them – hope for a redemption did ya?"

"Thank you for your assistance," I answered as pompously as I could. "If they do ever come back, please tell Rosie that her vicar came looking for her, she'll know where to find me." I managed a false smile, and felt the woman's eyes on my back as I returned the way I had come.

"Well, there's an end to it," Father Justin had said when I returned to the vicarage and told him what I had discovered.

"There's nothing more you can do unless the social services choose to ask you to elaborate on the statement you've already given to them. I don't suppose they will let the matter drop – the family are bound to surface somewhere and want benefit money, then the authorities will find them - if they can be bothered.

"It's out of our hands, now Jack. You must put the whole episode aside unless and until the Good Lord decides to bring Rosie back into our lives. And I think that to be unlikely. You did your best, Jack, God knows that, and He knows how much you care. Now we have to leave everything to his divine judgment."

After a moment's pause he added: "Elsie's made us one of her splendid orange sponge cakes. Come and have some tea and tell me how Lorna's charity sale went this morning."

48. CONCERNS

As I had been explaining to Thomas, Father Justin was handing over more and more of the daily running of the parish to his young curate. The elderly priest had offered me a handsome desk in the sitting room, but I preferred to work at my own table in the basement. A telephone extension had been connected so that I could run the business side of the church without disturbing the senior priest who was becoming more and more reclusive.

I was proud of the charming garden I had created around the flagstones outside the basement flat. In summer I would work with the door wide open and from my desk I could see across the well-tended flowerbeds and up the bank to the crooked gravestones under the tall sycamore trees. In the winter I would close the curtains as soon as the light began to fade and move the electric fire closer to my feet to battle the draught that came from under the door. When it was really cold, I would take my papers and books upstairs in the evenings and sit by the fire, next to Father Justin. The two of us could sit together in silence for long periods with the comfort of friendship making idle chatter as unnecessary as it was undesirable.

However, all was not as well as it seemed. I was now twenty-seven years old and, without realizing it exactly, I was becoming increasingly dissatisfied with life at St. George's. The first rush of excitement and enthusiasm had passed and the congregation had barely altered since my arrival. Oh, there were one or two additions, and the Christmas fairs and summer fetes were attracting new faces, but they never stayed long enough to be part of the community.

The sermon Thomas and I had composed together had been the first I had done from scratch for quite some time. I used to delight in composing my bi-weekly treatises but now they came more frequently from the Church of England's ample supply of ready-made lectures than from my own ideas.

Meetings with the parishioners were still an important part of my ministry, but I no longer felt a sense of achievement from them – things seemed to stay much the same and my advice, whether right or wrong, was rarely heeded. I spent my time fighting off invitations to dinner, picnics in the summer, even to see a movie - that was Dilly. I didn't want to socialize with any of the parishioners and preferred a monkish life in the rectory with Father Justin, Elsie and the books providing all the company I desired.

Rosie's fate remained a sharp barb in my conscience and I battled to banish her memory as Father Justin repeatedly told me I should.

As the months passed, Father Justin must have noticed my increasing dissatisfaction and restlessness and, quite unexpectedly, decided it was time for me to take a holiday. I became aware of this one evening when he dropped a collection of travel brochures onto the dining table as we sat down for one of Elsie's legendary cottage pies. "You haven't been away since the trip to Oberammergau, before your ordination," he remonstrated. "It's time for you to have a change of scene. Not just a fleeting visit to Thornton but a real break to somewhere exotic.

"We're not very busy here in June. So I thought if you could see us through Corpus Christi, and maybe the week after, you could get away without causing too much chaos. After all there isn't anything particularly special in the church calendar until Assumption Day in August."

"What about the church fête?" I asked, looking at the heap of magazines with distrust. "I have to be here for that."

"And so you do, most definitely," Father Justin agreed. "But that isn't until the end of July. You could take two weeks off at the beginning of June and still be here to quell the squabbles of the stall-holders!"

"You're serious, aren't you?" I looked across the table at the man who had become more of a father to me than my biological one had ever been. "Are you sending me away?"

"Yes, and no," was the answer, after a pause. Father Justin dropped his eyes towards his steaming plate of minced beef and mashed potato and picked up his fork. "I am asking you to go in the short term so that I have more of a chance of keeping you in the long term.

"Things are not right for you just now, Jack. I can tell. I have been there myself, and if someone had given me a shove and sent me away at just the right moment, I might not have made some of the moves I did - moves I have lived to regret.

"So I feel it my duty to push you into a holiday, and this time it should be a holiday just for you. Forget taking your friends, that's not an option. Go somewhere that interests you. Be unashamedly selfish and choose something that you want to do for no other reason than that you want to do it. It's a challenge!" he added, with a chuckle. "I wonder if you've ever thought of doing something just because you wanted to do it."

I thought for a moment. "Well, I went to St. Augustine's," I eventually responded. "That was quite a thing for my family to come to terms with. As a matter of fact, I don't think they ever have. How many times have any of them visited me here at St. George's?"

"Well," Father Justin forked a chunk of pie into his mouth, and drew his breath in sharply to diffuse the heat, "apart from your ordination, I met your mother once, right here at the vicarage."

"She was delivering some mail." I answered, trying to suppress a belligerent tone from creeping into my voice. "A journal from St. Augustine's which must have been at home for a good while, otherwise they would have sent it here, and a letter from Father Edmund, our village vicar, wishing me luck in my first appointment – also at least six months old. She didn't even ask to be shown around the church, just wanted to see my room so she could picture her youngest if she chose so to do."

"Both your parents came to your ordination, and wasn't your sister there too?"

"Yes, but that was more of a social occasion than a spiritual one as far as they were concerned. I suppose my father wanted to see that his money had been well spent and that I was off his books, so to speak."

"Now then, Jack," Father Justin spoke softly, but with reproach, "that is neither a charitable nor necessarily an accurate view. They were there, and they were there for you. You should be happy with that."

There was a pause and Father Justin took advantage of it by tucking into his cottage pie once more. I remember staring angrily at nothing in particular, then I reproached myself, sighed, and answered. "You are absolutely right, Father. I apologize for allowing such perverse thoughts into my head. I did appreciate their coming to my ordination more than I may have told them. I should do something about that, I think."

"Perhaps," said Father Justin when he had finished another mouthful and washed it down with some of Mr. Stanhope's claret. "But that is not what we are meant to be discussing.

"I have gone to great trouble to acquire these glossy magazines for you, all of which, the travel agent who produced them assures me, are just what you want. I can't vouch for that, of course, but you will do me the courtesy of perusing them at your leisure, and I expect to have your views by the day after tomorrow at the latest."

I looked across the table with disbelief. "You really are serious, aren't you Father?"

"You're bloody right I am," Father Justin exclaimed with a vocabulary and vehemence that startled me into realizing just how determined my mentor was about the idea. "Now get on with it, and don't speak to me again until you have chosen your destination."

We continued our supper in silence. I spread out the brochures in front of me and looked from one title to the other as I ate. 'Budget tours of the Mediterranean,' proclaimed one with a picture of a coastal town tumbling down to a bright blue sea dotted with yachts. Another had pictures of low white houses, also along a coastline, with brightly decorated camels strolling along the shore. "Morocco, a Land of Mysteries" it declared proudly. One, titled "The Wonders of Ancient Egypt, from Aswan to Giza" had a startling picture of massive columns stretching to a vivid blue sky, with ant-sized people at their feet, gazing upwards.

"That's Luxor," said Father Justin, gesturing towards the magazine with his fork. "I went there once when I was about your age. An extraordinary thing happened as I was walking through that temple. I found myself muttering some sort of chant, and my feet turned suddenly right down a passage, leaving my tour group. Then, without choice, I turned left into another passage that led straight to the grand altar.

"I'd been there before, Jack. I'm sure of it. My body
– or more likely my spirit – remembered some sort of
ritual I used to perform on a regular basis. It was very,
very strange, and I wasn't at all comfortable with the
feeling. The hairs on the back of my neck rose as I
approached the central room, and I felt shivers all over.
There was a great fear waiting for me in that room. I
broke the spell by taking myself well away, into the
sunshine, and abandoned the rest of the tour. I was
soon distracted by dozens of hawkers selling fruits,
beautifully embroidered linen, shawls and so on. An
interesting experience, but one I was not keen to repeat."

"What about this one?" I asked, pointing to a
brochure decorated by huge structures with steep steps
on all sides, leading upwards to nowhere. There were
wide swept streets between massive platforms of sandy
colored stone, all under a cloudless sky without a touch
of green anywhere. "Mayan Mexico" it proclaimed.

"Well, that's wrong, for a start," said Father Justin
pointing to the title. "The tourist office is obviously
after alliterative affect rather than an accurate one, for it
wasn't the Mayan's who built Teo Ti Huacan. That's a
fascinating part of the world, Jack. And you could go
South from there to Tikal in Guatemala where another
ancient city, of similar size to this one," he tapped the
brochure with his finger, "is still being liberated from the
jungle."

"Well, you've certainly given me plenty to think
about, Father," I said. "I need to get used to the idea of
going anywhere at all first, and then, perhaps I can
decide upon where to go. It's very exciting, and I am
most grateful to you for your endeavors on my behalf,
and, even more, for your caring.

"It will make a bit of a hole in my savings, I'm afraid,
so I'll have to think about that also."

"And what are you saving for?" Father Justin asked
with a smile. "You never go anywhere or do anything

that costs money. I don't think you've bought as much as a new pair of socks since you've been here. You must have plenty of money saved up, and what better way to spend it than to expand your mind with a completely new experience?"

I laughed and withdrew a foot from my shoe and showed Father Justin a large hole on the heel of my sock. "You're right there, Father. I just never get around to shopping, and I usually have some socks from Father Christmas, but this year I got handkerchiefs instead. Mother obviously thought I needed a dramatic change in my life!"

I replaced the shoe and stood up, collected the brochures together with deliberate care and looked at Father Justin with deep affection. "Well, if you'll excuse me, Father, I think I'll take these downstairs and look through them thoroughly."

"You better take this with you also," said Father Justin, handing me the wine bottle. "I shall be moving on to the port after this," he nodded towards his wine glass, "and the claret won't keep until tomorrow."

"Thank you Father," I said smiling. "I'm not sure the wine will help me make a decision, but it will certainly provide encouragement." I tucked the brochures under an arm and, with the wine bottle in one hand and my glass in the other, made to leave the dining room. Somthing held me back and I turned as I reached the door. "Thank you again, Father," I said softly, looking across the room at the priest who seemed to have shrunk into his chair. A new intensity of fondness for the old man filled me. "I'm still a bit shell-shocked by all of this," I confessed, "but feel the kindness behind your actions and I am touched and humbled by it."

"Oh, stuff and nonsense," said Father Justin, but he was blushing as he said it. "Off you go now and get on with it. I look forward to hearing your decision in the morning. Good night, Jack."

49. EXPANDING HORIZONS

As a result of that night's deliberations, I signed up for a package holiday to Central America. I would start in Mexico and travel South, through Guatemala, and fly back from Costa Rica, all in just two weeks. The transport, accommodation and excursions were all organized and paid for in advance. I would be one of a group of twenty – a coach load – 'complete with English speaking tour guide' - the brochure boasted.

The holiday was much more interesting than I had anticipated. On many occasions during the tour I had time to reflect upon the reasons behind Father Justin's unexpected suggestion. Had I really become dissatisfied with my life in Islington, and if so, was this holiday going to turn things around for me?

I remember being slightly nervous about leaving St. George's and the vicarage that offered such a retreat from the world and had become so much of a home to me. However, I felt a creeping excitement as the day of my departure drew nearer. This sense of anticipation was encouraged by the parishioners who were tripping over each other to give me advice, inappropriately garish holiday clothes, travel guides, and even some sun-tan lotion – this last a tentative offering from Philip. Dilly gave me a Spanish phrase book.

There was also an uninvited tussle about who should take me to the airport; in the end it was Dilly who won due to some logistical fact with which she managed to trump both Lorna's and Charlotte's efforts. Philip's offer of accompanying us was turned down promptly due to lack of space in the car. Charlotte was appeased by being awarded the job of collecting me upon my return, with Sally eager to be included. Lorna had to make do with looking after my garden. All this went on behind my back - I would learn about it later - and the plans were presented to me as a fait accompli.

Mexico was a whirl of noise and brown dust. My group consisted of a couple of spinster sisters in their sixties from Derbyshire; two middle-aged couples from Sussex who went everywhere together; an American family from Texas with two teenage girls and a disgruntled, overweight boy of about ten; a soft-spoken Canadian man of my age, called Frank, and his girlfriend Sue; and a group of six Chinese girls in their late teens who chattered constantly like a flock of incomprehensible starlings.

When it was not possible to be alone, I spent most of my time with the Canadian couple whose company I began to enjoy. Occasionally one of the Chinese girls would come up to me and ask a question in careful English while her friends giggled and nudged each other in the background.

The group's first excursion was a visit to Teotihuacan. I was in awe of the wide wind-swept streets of the deserted citadel and the steep-sided pyramids that had caught my attention on the travel brochure. I strolled around the vast spaces trying to envisage the hustle and bustle of the place in its heyday and wondering what beliefs had led to the sacrifices that had been carried out with so much pomp and cruelty. With whom or with what was this ancient civilization trying to communicate from their tall towers and astrologically placed pyramids? What calamity had swept all the people into total oblivion while their buildings remained relatively unblemished? The place was full of intriguing mysteries that made me feel slightly uncomfortable.

While waiting for the group to gather at the end of the visit, I watched a local girl sitting on the car-park wall. A pair of huge dark eyes, set in an amber face of perfect proportions, were concentrated on a large Sisal plant. As I watched, her fingers bent a spine from the top of one of the spikey leaves with careful deliberation until it snapped almost all the way across. She pulled the sharp thorn down the back of the leaf with care, unpeeling a thin string of fiber all the way to the bottom. This was then cut in one swift movement with a tiny knife that glinted in the sun. The girl held aloft the thorn with its attachment for a moment's inspection. Satisfied with what she saw, she went quickly to work using her newly acquired needle and thread on a cloth she was weaving; a cloth as delicate as lace.

My attempts to share this observation with others in the party were unsuccessful. There was the usual bustle of urgency to get back into the coach; a shuffling for room to stow newly acquired Mexican hats, pan pipes, plastic models of the pyramids, and so on, accompanied by loud discussions of the different wonders of this dramatic place. The girl's skill and ingenuity were unnoticed by anyone else and I tucked the vision into my memory like a gem to be taken out and admired at a later date.

The other excursion that made a great impression on me during my time in Mexico was the visit to the country's modern cathedral; an incongruous edifice built on a hill outside the capital city, over-looking the great urban sprawl.

Local legend has it that an angel descended from the clouds, a few hundred years ago, bearing a message from God and from his son, Jesus Christ. A lowly shepherd was the sole witness to this wonder, and to him the angel gave a sacred portrait of the Son of God, painted by the angels, or, perhaps by the Heavenly Father himself.

A cathedral was built on the site of this miracle to house the holy painting, but, as the years passed, the building's foundations slipped so dramatically that it had to be abandoned. The whole conventional Spanish-style edifice, with two towers flanking the main doors, now lists to starboard as dramatically as the tower in Pisa.

Once it had sunk beyond recall, the cathedral's entrails had been surgically removed and given places of honor in a new building erected alongside, at right angles to the old.

This modern edifice, a statement of the modern Roman Catholic faith, is shaped more like a mosque than a church, its low rounded body in dramatic contrast to the traditional upward-reaching building at its side.

The nation's holiest possession, the mysterious painting of Christ, is hung above the altar. From the main aisle there seems nothing out of the ordinary about its position, but when approached from the side, a clever gap is revealed between the altar and the backdrop upon which the painting is hung. Closer inspection shows a sunken walkway hidden below and behind the altar with a moving surface. Pilgrims, of which there are thousands, can be advanced, whilst praying, either standing or kneeling, without being seen by the congregation, without interfering with any service that might be in progress, and without being able to over-stay their allotted time: for there is a never-ending queue of supplicants outside.

I watched in amazement as the faithful were duly carried along with eyes raised towards the painting, a look of wonder filling their faces. The suspension of rational belief and the subsequent ecstasy apparent in the wide eyes reminded me uncomfortably of Oberammergau. During the three or four minute electrically controlled journey - for which the pilgrims may have waited several hours - the worshipers were transported into a realm of ecstasy way beyond my comprehension.

Another similarity with the Bavarian experience presented itself when we left the cathedral and were ushered into a line of shops selling all sorts of religious paraphernalia. Outside the official stores were many stalls and hawkers trying hard to get attention. I looked at their wares with the same sense of nausea I had experienced in Austria.

Father Justin had insisted that I leave my clerical collar behind for my holiday and travel without any sign of my profession. "Just be yourself for a while, Jack," he had instructed, "find out what you are really like when you are not presented to the world as a vicar. It is too easy to hide behind the trappings of our calling. This journey of yours must take place on the inside as well as the outside; for the next two weeks, you must be simply Jack Bolden, tourist!"

Now, going through the shops, with vendors swinging pendants ranging from a small simple cross to an elaborately jeweled crucifix the size of a large pizza, I was grateful for the advice. I watched in amusement as a Catholic priest from somewhere in Europe, his dark robe collecting grey dust as he walked, was besieged by a crowd of hawkers who pushed their wares towards him in a clamor of excitement. Embossed briefcases were opened, showing everything you need to perform a mass-on-the-move, chasubles of ornate embroidery were waved like flags, one man had a collection of Bishops' crooks and another had several miters stacked on top of each other, their glass 'jewels' glinting in the sunshine.

"What a circus," I thought, fingering my open collar and waving a hand in dismissal to the one vendor who assailed me with rosaries. The man shrugged his shoulders and went off to join the throng pursuing the visiting priest.

My inner disturbance was further enhanced by the Chinese girls' appearance, for they climbed aboard the coach bedecked in sombreros bought from the same man who sold miters. My concerns were taking a sharper focus as I surveyed the trappings that obfuscated the really important heart of religion.

From Mexico the bus took us on a long and bumpy journey into Guatemala and the small town of Flores where we were staying in a whitewashed stucco hotel with cramped rooms and unreliable plumbing. From here we were to visit Tikal, a site on the same scale as Teotihuacan, except that only a small portion of Tikal has been uncovered from the jungle, the majority of this great ruin still being submerged beneath soil and foliage. There was plenty of scope for the imagination here.

The group was instructed not to wander about without company, as bandits hid in the lush flora and tourists had been both robbed and abducted. This information reduced everybody's enthusiasm somewhat but the day was a success and passed without dramas.

I attached myself to Frank and Sue, the Canadians, and the three us explored the various paths with excitement. A long climb up rickety ladders took us to the top of one of the tallest towers of the site and gave a view over the seemingly solid jungle canopy below, from which two other strange edifices reached for the clear blue sky.

I found myself strangely moved by the experience. Having seen Teotihuacan, I could visualize what Tikal must have been like, and found the hidden grandeur even more intriguing than that which had all been scraped clean and exposed in Mexico, as if secrets were waiting for the right person to find them. I had a sudden urge to find a trowel and start liberating the buildings from the grip of rampant foliage

The drive to Guatemala City was hot and dusty. The jungle pressed in on both sides of the road, so there was little to see apart from the occasional village where peasant life seemed not to have changed for centuries.

The air was clammy with humidity and irritability spread amongst the travelers like a disease. I was relieved when I could shut the door of a tiny hotel bedroom and be alone with just one or two cockroaches for company.

The holiday finished with two days in San José, the Capital of Costa Rica, with tours of various municipal buildings and a visit to a near-by coffee plantation on the itinerary. By this time I had had enough of being part of a group. I needed space and time to myself, so made excuses to avoid all planned activities. In glorious solitude I strolled through a myriad of narrow streets, free to wander wherever my footsteps led.

Which is how I arrived at the Cathedral Square.

It was a religious holiday that day and many people from the farming areas had come into the City to join the processions. Decorated statues of various saints were carried from one church to another around the metropolis with a crowd of followers chanting and dancing behind each one.

In the centre of the city, I was intrigued to see 'brujos' setting up their stalls in the forecourt of the huge cathedral that dominated the main square. These rural magicians were plying their trade in town as part of what was obviously an ancient festival from before the Christian era, now absorbed into the dominant Catholic faith.

A large, shifting crowd had gathered outside the cathedral filling the space between the brujos and the western façade of the building. A temporary balcony of scaffolding poles and planks had been erected stretching the entire width of the cathedral, effectively sealing off the doors. Four priests were walking to and fro along the planking issuing holy water to the crowd below them in a most unusual way. Each priest had a plastic bucket in one hand, and what looked like a small kitchen hand-mop in the other. They were using these mops to sprinkle the holy water – incongruously contained in the bright little buckets - upon the mass of people who moved like surf on a beach towards and away from them.

I ducked under the scaffolding and entered the dark cavern of the cathedral's interior through the one door that had been left ajar. Closing it carefully behind me, I leant with relief against the cold, hard, wood as the noise and confusion outside wilted away.

I needed to find God and the inner peace which quiet, private, prayer always brought. The fanaticism of the scene I had just left, and the cheapening of holy values through mass distribution had upset me. There was no attempt to connect any individual with the divine, no mystery, no magic. Could those people really believe that water dispensed this way could cleanse their souls?

What was even more worrying was that the answer was clearly written on all those faces – whenever a splash of water hit someone, they cried out with a delight bordering upon ecstasy. The hands of the faithful were either stretched out or busy making rapidly repeated signs of the cross over their chests. Once splashed, they continued the gestures as they joined the wave of people moving away, allowing those pressing from behind to move forward.

Inside the unlit cathedral all I could make out of the interior of the great building were various clusters of pin-prick lights. Slowly, as my eyes adjusted to the dark, statues of various saints emerged from the gloom, with rows of candles twinkling at their feet. The church was very tall, with rows of stone pillars disappearing upwards into darkness. The high stained-glass windows did little to illumine the interior, their dark colors all portraying dark subjects. The air was chilled and heavy with silence.

I gulped at the quiet and sat down at the edge of one of the long wooden pews, taking long deep breaths of the cool stillness, each one seeming to heal my disquiet.

I pondered the scene I had just left. Why did it worry me – this blind faith of a crowd, verging upon mass hysteria? First Bavaria, then Mexico City, and now again, here in St. Jose - the sense that believers were being manipulated; were surrendering their capacity for rational thought; voluntarily giving up their individuality and allowing judgment to be dished out on their behalf. Each member of the crowd seemed to have given up his or her responsibility of thought with an eagerness that I found almost unbearable. Here was a frenzy of mass indoctrination whereby members of the congregation willingly opted out of any genuine communication with The Almighty, any real understanding either of themselves or of a personal relationship with God.

A few years later I would recall this scene and view it in a different light. It was during Baptism Day in Cachonga when I found myself doing much the same thing as the priests here in St. José, only this time I was enjoying it as much as everyone else. Had I been too harsh with my views of the people of Costa Rica? What happened in Cachonga had been a tremendously positive experience for all concerned and, when I recalled the trance-like expressions on the people's faces outside the St. José cathedral, I realized that they, too, were positive in their simplicity, and that I had been wrong to be so critical. But at the time, I was uncomfortable and distressed.

My musings were interrupted by a junior priest in a long flowing white robe and a strange floppy hat of red felt sewn into a complicated quadrangle. He came hurrying down the aisle carrying a bucket of water in each hand; his incongruous sneakers squeaked on the slabs as he walked. He stopped when he saw me and spoke rapidly in Spanish.

"No habla Español," I managed, and then added somewhat lamely "English, tourist" and raised my hands in a gesture of apology.

The young man raised his eyebrows in surprise. "Closed," he said loudly and emphatically, swinging one of the buckets so that the precious water splashed onto the floor. "Church closed. Out," he added sternly as he looked hard at the intruder and then at the small puddle by his feet.

I thought for a moment, and then turned slowly and made my way to the door, the young priest hard on my heels muttering in Spanish. I was contemplating trying to explain to the young man that I was also a man of the church – but I decided against it. "Our followings are cut from different cloths," I thought to myself as I opened the door, blinking in the sudden harsh light. I ducked under the scaffolding planks and was swallowed back into the crowd.

I turned to watch the young priest climb onto the make-shift balcony with a bustle of importance. Buckets were exchanged without a hint of ceremony, and the older priests continued to dip their little mops into the water and sprinkle the crowd while the young man returned into the cathedral. The blessings continued in an unbroken stream of sonorous Latin while the crowd wept with emotion as they reached for the sacred droplets.

Only a few feet from this scene, people were crowding around the five or six brujos who had installed themselves against the railings of the forecourt. Each was sitting cross-legged with a pile of smoldering coals in front of him. People were thrusting feathers, bangles, necklaces and talismans of various kinds into the magic men's hands. These offerings were received solemnly with large, gnarled fingers, and placed on dented tin dishes, hanging from chains, to be held over the coals. While the laden dishes swung in the smoke, the men gabbled rapidly and unintelligibly in high, excited voices, the steady drone of the priests' Latin incantations audible in the background.

"Where is God in all this?" I wondered to myself. I strolled among the good-natured crowd, amazed at the two occult philosophies rubbing shoulders so easily. I had wanted to go inside the church to pray and enjoy a solitary moment with God. The brusque dismissal from the cathedral had shaken me. It was as if it were God, Himself, who had shooed me away in such an unceremonious manner.

I left the central square with the jostling crowds and found a small garden with benches among some weary-looking shrubs. I sat down to gather my thoughts. When I managed to focus my eyes I found myself staring at sweet-wrappers and empty cigarette packets around my dusty shoes.

The next day I would be returning to England and the welcome damp and low clouds with which I felt at home. I made an effort to view my holiday in perspective, juggling all the many images and experiences and wondering what I had learnt.

In the end, I decided that the most useful aspect of the tour had been to expand my horizons and put bits of my life in perspective. Islington had been reduced to just another part of the great London metropolis instead of the focal point of my existence. The problems faced by those parishioners were paltry when viewed alongside the states of poverty and deprivation experienced by so many people in the countries through which I had been travelling. Did I really belong there? Was God's plan for me to spend the rest of my life massaging middle class egos and organizing church events that were more social than spiritual?

And of God? What had I learnt about God? Visions of the vacant upturned faces below the holy painting near Mexico City came back to me, followed by the hungry eyes of the street vendors selling religious baubles as if they were sweets. The eager visages of the crowd just now, the trance-like expressions of the brujos as they wove their spells; the unquestioned credulity of people en masse, eager to absorb hope, desperate for reassurance in the harsh world in which they live, and apparently easily manipulated by people clothed in authority. People who were really just the same as them, with no more spiritual power than anyone else. It was all a show, I decided sadly, just another act in the circus we make of our lives. The numinous was nowhere to be found in all this nonsense.

Perhaps this was the beginning of the mental journey which has brought me to where I am today. It was definitely responsible for the next momentous move in my life although, obviously, I didn't know that at the time. My mind was still a jumble of impressions and questions as we started our journey back to the familiar.

Looking out of the 'plane window while flying out of St. José small villages interrupted the jungle only rarely as the 'plane swerved to fly North. Glimpses of the two major oceans of our globe were caught between tipping wings with only the thin and vulnerable bridge of Central America separating them. We would be changing 'planes in Mexico and from there back to London.

Charlotte and Sally met me at Heathrow with bright smiles. I was too tired to either resist or return their embarrassed hugs and followed the two of them meekly to the car park – Sally having taken charge of the luggage trolley. The mother and daughter chattered brightly on the way home, asking me lots of questions and, fortunately, not waiting for answers.

50. PROBLEMATIC PROPOSITIONS

In the months following my return from Central America, my doubts regarding my efficacy in Islington grew instead of diminished. Indeed the holiday had the reverse effect of that envisaged by Father Justin when he suggested it.

This went unnoticed by the senior priest who was becoming increasingly reclusive. It seemed he had missed me more than had been anticipated and now, assuming that any wanderlust in his Curate had been dealt with, he took less and less interest in the running of the church that had been his raison d'être for the last forty years. He was happy to leave all the services to me and didn't even ask to look over proposed sermons any more.

Later Father Justin would tell me that he could not help worrying that the new found enthusiasms of the parishioners seemed to centre on me personally instead of around the church and the faith for which it had been built. The summer fête had been a great success, as were the coffee mornings that I had initiated, the special festival services I introduced, the Christmas fair and so on. 'You seemed to be doing an excellent job, Jack, but I could sense a gathering storm."

Unaware of my mentor's concerns, I found myself more and more left to my own devices while feeling less and less sure that the path I was treading was the correct one. St. George's parishioners remained about the same. I had lost my two favorites when Estelle and Rosie disappeared, both leaving an impression of unfinished business and a sense of failure. Those who were left behind did not seem to be progressing in any spiritual way, although the sense of community that had developed within the parish was a definite improvement.

Things took a turn for the worse at the beginning of 1995. First there was a visit from Lorna, one late afternoon as I was preparing for Evensong.

After a light tap on the sacristy door, Lorna entered in a fluttering state of nervousness. Recognizing the symptoms of distress, I prepared myself for the latest episode in her travails. I had already been through the traumas of Lorna's divorce and had thought things should be more positive now for her and for her children after she had won the custody battle. In our last discussion, some three or four months earlier, she had agreed that she was ready to make a new start.

"What's gone wrong now?" I mused to myself as I began making her welcome by pulling a chair out from under the desk and switching on the electric kettle.

The speech upon which Lorna then embarked had obviously been rehearsed many times. It was delivered carefully, sometimes with eyes downcast, at other times with her looking straight at me with large grey eyes filled with supplication and – what I was eventually to realize – love.

Yes, Lorna started, she had agreed with me that a new start was needed; that she should put all the hurt of her marriage behind her, enjoy her children and look towards the future with positivity. Together, we had agreed on such a course and she was doing just that. However, along the way, she had discovered that the only way forward for her and her children was to confess that she had been in love with me since our first conversation together. The love had crept up on her, taking her by surprise, but now it was the sole motivating force in her life. Her children needed someone they could trust unequivocally, who they could love without fear of rejection – and so did she. I was the only one who could fill that role and she wanted to know if I might possibly reciprocate her feelings, and if not now, then if I would be prepared to 'give it a go.'

I was as much surprised by this revelation as I was uncertain how to respond. I liked Lorna well enough, but the idea of living with her and her children filled me with horror. Where would be my space, my tranquility and my ability to shut the door on the outside world? Surely this was not what God had in store for me? I had not yet fulfilled the promise to serve that I had made at my ordination: I suddenly realized this with powerful clarity – I had God's work to do in places other than Islington with its comfortable middle class problems and ideals. How could I explain this to Lorna without shattering her world? I was not the man she loved, I was an apparition, I had become what the parishioners wanted me to be. I needed to break free.

Some of this came out in my garbled response in which panic threatened to break out at any second and send me flying from the sacristy, from the church, from Islington – but to where? To my amazement I found myself telling Lorna that, since my holiday, I had wanted to change my position and to preach to the less fortunate on this earth, that I was considering becoming a missionary and helping communities grow in more ways than just the spiritual. That I was not ready to settle in this parish, or anywhere else, until I had accomplished more of God's work.

Lorna had listened quietly, her eyes filling with tears that ran down her cheeks and splashed into her lap. Her gaze cut into me. I spluttered apologies, assuring her that there were far more suitable men for her and for her children; that she must have faith and someone would turn up when it was right, that God had a plan for her. She only had to believe. . . but I knew I was lying. I felt I was letting her down, although I realized such a feeling was unjustifiable. What else could I do? It was Lorna's expectations I was disappointing, not my own.

Lorna finished the meeting by getting up without a word, walking across to me and kissing me lightly on the cheek. She had then turned and walked out of the sacristy, letting the door close behind her on its own. I listened to her footsteps echoing away, and to the main church door closing with its familiar swish-clunk noise. Only then did I resume breathing.

I had barely recovered from this upsetting interview when Charlotte repeated the scene just six weeks later, with only a slight change in the script.

After my experience with Lorna, I recognized dangerous signals as soon as Charlotte accosted me in my garden one Saturday afternoon. I had been busy splitting the Alchemilla plants when she had arrived with a flask of chilled homemade lemonade and two glasses.

I felt the freezing sensation in my emotions that Lorna's revelation had triggered as I listened to Charlotte explain how I was the only person in the world who her daughter, Sally, respected. How I had rid them of that silly imaginary friend where psychiatrists had failed, how she knew that she had fallen hopelessly in love with me, how I was the only one who could fill the missing gaps in both her life and that of her daughter. How she needed me as her husband as badly as Sally needed me as a father.

This time I was not surprised to hear myself play the missionary card. It was a speech totally unplanned, and yet it appeared as if by rote.

Charlotte was as tearful as Lorna had been, but her sadness was tinged with anger as she accused me of being happy to let Sally float through the dangerous years of adolescence without a father-figure to guide her.

I found my resolve strengthening rather than diminishing under such an onslaught. While being as gentle as possible I spoke firmly, and with a new sense of purpose. I was fighting for my freedom – a freedom to pursue God's will - and was sure that Charlotte's suggestion was not on the Almighty's agenda for me.

This new resolve became further cemented in my psyche when I received a visit from Sally herself the following week, in the sacristy as I was preparing for Evensong.

At first I assumed that Sally had come to press her mother's cause, but it soon became apparent that hers was a totally different mission.

Sally was now fifteen, soon to be sixteen. Though young, she was wise, so she claimed, and knew what would be best for her as she entered her adult life. She had a present to offer to the right candidate – her virginity, which, she assured me, was still intact. In fact she had been keeping it just for me.

Sally went on to explain how I alone could have managed to separate her from her friend Peter. It was then she had fallen in love with me and knew that I would and could be better than any other friend, that I could indeed be both a friend and a lover. She had to wait nearly three years to be able to tell me of her plans. Next week, she would turn sixteen and her gift would be ready.

Things seemed to be getting completely out of control, especially when Sally offered to join me with my planned missionary work about which she had heard from her mother. "No, no, no," I wanted to shout at her – but I didn't. After several deep breaths I did my best to explain that I wasn't ready to enter into any sort of romantic or sexual relationship with anyone. I had much to do along the path that God had chosen for me before I could contemplate such things. I was flattered by her offering of course - although that is certainly not how I felt - but that it was inappropriate and that she needed to pray for guidance as to how she should proceed. I would pray also. I was floundering, and I knew it, and was keenly aware that she knew it too.

The interview ended with a pathetic attempt on my part to persuade Sally that, just because I didn't return her affections - or couldn't at this stage in my life – that others wouldn't, and that she should be very careful to whom she should offer her 'gift'. I showed her out of the church and found myself locking and bolting the great front doors after she had gone – a ridiculous gesture given that Evensong was due to be celebrated in less than an hour.

My vanity was not engaged by these declarations as I was well aware that none of the supplicants knew anything about the real me at all – and I wasn't too sure I did either. They were in love with my position and my ability to listen – a professional necessity rather than a virtue. None of our conversations had ever dwelt on any subject other than themselves. They were in love with the idea of Jack Bolden, but not necessarily with Jack Bolden himself. Still, it made life difficult and strained; the relaxed, friendly atmosphere I had worked so hard to produce in church was under serious threat. And it was about to get worse.

After a recovery period of about three months, Helen Simmons was the next to assail me with her affections. As with Lorna and Charlotte, she used the vulnerability of her children to throw guilt at her vicar.

"Sam used to be such a problem, but ever since his talk with you, father, he has been an exemplary son" Helen enthused. "Sam has more respect for you, Jack – if I may call you that – than for anyone else on earth, and Sandra also seems to think that you have all the answers. It is hardly surprising that I have fallen so deeply in love with you."

"I haven't got the answers," I had wanted to shout, but managed to keep my voice subdued. "I don't even know the questions. Please, dear Helen, you must not be hurt when I tell you that I am not planning to stay here in Islington for much longer. My time here is nearly over, and I have a lot to do before I am ready to settle down.

"Please believe me when I tell you that I am truly sorry not to be able to take up your wonderful suggestion. There will be someone more appropriate coming along, when the time is right. You must trust in the Lord that this will be so. I am not the one. I'm so sorry, so very sorry," I ended lamely.

It was not over yet, only three weeks later Tracy presented me with a proposition. I had not seen her since she had enrolled at university. Shortly before Christmas, she reappeared in church to tell me that she is now ready to live with the love of her life. I had promised her this would happen to her sometime, when she was older, and that she would be able to have a child at the right time, with the right person. Now, she explained, she was ready and had no doubt that I was that right person. She even indicated that this had been my suggestion, when I had endorsed her going to the social services with her unwanted pregnancy. She had kept herself for me.

I could find no solace in prayer for all this unwanted attention. I was causing hurt and disappointment to so many people – people I was here to help. How had everything gone so horribly wrong? Why had my world been turned upside down, my good will been so misunderstood? How could I redeem the situation? Where was God with the answers?

While I was in the middle of these supplications to God, Dilly presented me with another problem early the following year.

I had relied on this splendid parishioner to provide some light relief amongst the dramas of the less liberated spirits of the congregation. How I would have loved to share the recent declarations of love with her, and asked for her advice in an area of the heart with which I had no experience, and which was her forte. Of course that was not an option, but it was with no sense of foreboding at all that I reached into the drawer where the whisky bottle lived when she stayed on after evensong, asking for a chat.

Dilly and I had established a routine of 'catching up' with Dilly's progress in her job in the library. It was the only time that I ever drank whisky, but it was part of the tradition, and I enjoyed the personal touch it gave to our talks. Dilly was different from the others, she was stronger, more interesting, and – I had to admit - far more attractive. Not that any of that should make a difference to my pastoral care.

On this particular evening, Dilly was looking even more enticing than usual. Her low-cut blouse showed off the soft amplitude of her breasts, her waist was as pinched as her hips were broad. Her calf-length skirt moved with more attraction than any short garment could have achieved.

I thought she looked terrific, and told her so – suggesting that her new look was due to the healthiness of her new life.

Dilly laughed. "Well, Jack," she responded, "do you really think it is thanks to the library that I look so well? It is true that I am enjoying my new life, and so are the kids and my mother. I owe you a lot for your guidance – more than you appreciate."

Dilly's voice dropped an octave with the last sentence and panic surged into my chest. "Oh no, not again, not Dilly, please not Dilly," I prayed.

Dilly rose as she spoke, she put her glass down carefully upon the top shelf of the bookcase. She was close to me now, very close. She raised her hands, and her fingers started caressing my neck. Her breasts were pressed against me and my eyes were drawn down between them as if by a magnetic force.

I felt a stirring in my loins and could feel the blood pulsing through my groin. I was in trouble.

Carefully I took Dilly's hands from the base of my head where the fingers of her right hand had started to invade my hair. I pushed her away, gently yet firmly, because I knew I could not stop the bulge growing in my trowsers, and that Dilly would feel it, pressing against her, if I didn't act swiftly.

Grateful for the ample folds of my surplice, I turned away from Dilly and pressed my torso against the bookshelf. It was not a pleasant feeling as I tried to extinguish the exciting sensations. I had to abandon Dilly to fend for herself while I dealt with my own problem. Hearing a choking sob, I turned to see her crumpled into the chair from which she had risen just a few moments before.

Between her tears, Dilly confessed that she had never felt so safe and so free as when in my company; that she knew she had fallen in love with me, and that she would like to be the one to introduce me to the glories that the sexual world has to offer: glories to which an older woman would be the best guide, especially this woman, who knows and loves him without question. "You have given me back my self-respect, Jack, you have given me a decent purpose in life, and you are that purpose."

Dilly went on to explain that she had talked to her mother and her children about her feelings for me, and they all agreed that it would be wonderful if I would consider changing our relationship to cement her new, virtuous life.

I was distraught by what I selfishly could only feel to be a betrayal. Not Dilly as well? Was there some sort of conspiracy? "Please God, Almighty, not Dilly as well" I prayed again. But I knew it was hopeless and I was on my own to deal with this latest disaster. I looked at the mascara-smudged Dilly and my heart melted with compassion as my manhood twitched to be released.

Suddenly I was the one who was sobbing. Loud, inarticulate noises were issuing from somewhere in my chest and throat. I dropped to my knees and hugged Dilly to me, whispering over and over again, "I'm sorry, I'm so sorry."

We stayed that way for quite some time, swaying backwards and forwards as our sobs subsided. Finally Dilly disentangled herself from my embrace and stood up. She straightened her skirt, brushed her cheeks with the back of her hand, and looked down at me.

"I'll be going now, Jack. Please try to forget this conversation," she paused, "but, if you ever change your mind, please let me be the first to know." I was still on my knees when I heard the sacristy door close.

Perhaps the most distressing scene amongst all these protestations of love and anticipated obligations came from Phillip. This was a visit as unexpected as had been Lorna's and the first signs of confusion and panic.

"I know you've been having trouble with your sexuality, dear Jack," Phillip was being uncharacteristically loquacious, as he propped himself against the top shelf of the sacristy book shelf, "but believe me, it will all be so much better when you admit your hidden desires and enjoy the sexual freedom that is everyone's right.

"I felt just the same as you before I met Don, and he explained to me what homosexuality is all about. I am a much more complete person now, and I know in my soul, that there is only one person with whom I want to spend my life, and that is you – my friend and confidant over all these years, the only person who has not condemned me for anything, who has always been there offering support – and, I believe - love."

I had to reassess my upset at the physical excitement that had threatened to interrupt my conversation with Dilly a few weeks earlier – suddenly it became a reassuring asset. I had been accused of homosexuality a number of times through school and university days, and it was good to be able to look Philip in the eye and tell him without hesitation that he had misread the situation. While I had been happy to reassure Philip in the past, and to try to redirect his ways, I had done so only as part of God's work within the parish of St. George's and not from any other motive whatsoever.

This time, when I told Philip I was leaving the parish, I really meant it. I was ready to go, and, it appeared from my panic-driven statements, that I was going for a missionary appointment. All that remained was to tell Father Justin – a prospect that did not appeal to me at all.

"That's the price of your success, Jack," Father Justin said when I explained the reasons behind my decision to leave. "You gave those people faith not in God, but in yourself. You are a tangible force, God is intangible. You have provided your parishioners with everything they need, only in human form rather than in divine shape."

"But I didn't mean to" –I was beside myself with disbelief, anger, frustration – a barrage of emotions I was ill-equipped to deal with or even to recognize. "That's not what I'm about – surely you know that Father? Surely you can't think that I have deliberately disillusioned people in this way?"

"No, Jack, of course not," Father Justin's voice was kinder now, and softer too. "I'm not suggesting for one minute that you have done this deliberately, but innocence is seductive, and innocence and purity in a good looking young man like you is a force without limits – you cannot blame yourself, but nor can you claim no fault. It is one of those strange incongruities that beset the painful act of growing up – an act that doesn't finish until the grave.

"I'm afraid you will have to adapt your philosophies and your actions to take into account what you have learnt here. I don't expect you to stay – that's a personal tragedy for me, but one I quite understand. As a parent has to grasp the pain of letting a child go, I honor you with the same freedom.

"'Go forth and multiply', the good book tells us, and while I don't give you exactly the same instructions, I do give you leave to have a life of your own wherever that takes you. In fact rather than just give you leave to go, Jack, I give you instruction so to do.

"I have been reviewing my life, also," the old man continued in a quieter voice. "I have been seeing how my actions have been restricted, all my adult life, by living within the confines of other peoples' requirements. Maybe that is the lot of a priest - I always thought so - but now I'm not at all sure that such a life-limiting sacrifice is actually what is necessary in this job. In spite of my efforts, I can't say that I have succeeded in making any one person particularly happy.

"So you go with my blessing, Jack. Your time here in Islington is over, I accept that. You will leave bruised and broken hearts behind, but that can't be helped.

"I understand your disenchantment with the Christianity of the Western world," Father Justin continued, in a more conversational tone. "I agree with a lot of what you say. It is too late for me to move my thoughts radically at this stage of my life. I am comfortable with my own company and my own version of the Christian faith. However, you are young and intellectually strong enough to keep a genuine faith without the woolly trappings that threaten to douse the fire of true belief. You should use your gifts to enlighten others, and your choice of missionary work seems as appropriate as it is bold."

The older man paused, and then added: "I only ask, Jack, that if you care to, you will let me know where you are and what happens in your life – a visit every now and then would be even better."

51. ESCAPE TO ARUMBA

It was Father Justin who recommended the missionary college that I attended for six months after leaving St. George's. It was a splendid Victorian building surrounded by various outhouses, reminiscent of St. Augustine's, except for its situation alongside a busy main road, surrounded by industrial estates.

Whilst there, I attended lectures on all sorts of aspects of living in the developing world, and how best God, and a community, might be served in both secular and non-secular ways. I was quick to dismiss the instructions on how to maintain Western cultural standards while living in the bush – changing for dinner every night and not allowing staff to call you anything other than 'Sir' or 'Reverend' - and in so doing, discovered that I had firm ideas about what I wanted to do. I concentrated on learning manual skills, especially carpentry, and took several courses in how to improve farm production in tropical lands where there would be no recourse to modern equipment, fertilizer or chemicals.

When I moved from St. George's, I took all my books to Thornton where Thomas agreed to store them in the vicarage's attic, my drawings, sketches, diaries and notebooks too . My glossy wardrobe from Wipples I left at Willenbury, taking only one set of clerical robes with me. At the college I purchased the burlap cassock and the tin cross that would become my trademarks, along with some strong boots and a collection of manuals on all sorts of things - sewage management, building wells, basic welding and electrical skills, and so on.

The college authorities observed my preferences and were happy to agree to my request to be sent somewhere remote and primitive. "We have far too many vacancies in such areas," the principal had commented. "I just hope you will not regret your choice."

Having received my posting, I sped to the library to find out everything I could about the small, central African country of Arumba. There was little information about the country itself, but plenty about the warring political factions of its neighbors who were constantly threatening invasion. I was not concerned with politics but hungry to learn of the tribal traditions in the rural areas; I wanted to be sure not to upset my new congregation by being unaware of local customs. Of the nation's political problems I gave not a thought.

My agricultural studies proved to be a good investment, and, far from being upset by the lack of facilities at my final destination of Cachonga, I leapt at the challenges the village presented.

I have already made reference to parts of my journey away from Islington and the middle-class aspirations which had entrapped me. I wasn't just leaving England, I was leaving Europe and the modern world, everything with which I was familiar and from which I wanted to escape. The long journey of airplanes, cars, more aiplanes, buses, Landrover and canoe made the transition between cultures and expectations more obvious and all the more exciting.

When I first arrived in this insignificant Arumbian hamlet, up-stream from nowhere in particular and on the way to nowhere at all, it was a tiny ramshackle place. A single path led from the small swaying jetty up a hill and down into the plains. The bush stretched for as far as the eye could see around the small cluster of rondavels, a couple of corals and a few insignificant arable plots was all that constituted the village of Cachonga.

CachongaVillage diagram

While I was establishing myself as a bona fide but non-threatening vicar of the Christian faith and working hard at cultivating friendships with the powerful people of the village, I spent fruitful hours studying the agricultural issues the land presented.

The existing small arable area required a lot of irrigating in order to produce anything other than veld grass. At best it produced only just enough to feed the people of the village of whom only the Chief and his son Amanzi were fat. Every day, water had to be collected from the kitchen area via a hand-pump that produced only small spurts with every hefty heave of the handle. The precious liquid was then transported in a steady procession each morning by the women of the village carrying pathetically small containers.

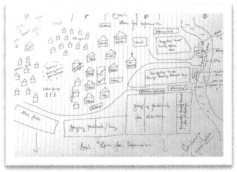

CachongaVillage five years later

I would watch the silhouettes of these straight backed women, made taller by the buckets on their heads, their bare breasts swinging as they walked to and from the pump. There had to be a better solution to the problem – if only the growing plots were closer to the river.

When the women weren't watering the fields, they were off to the river to do the washing. Children with long sticks and the important title of 'nyoka-boys' ran in front of the chattering bunch. Their job was to hit the grass roots on either side of the path as they went and to call out with fearsome shouts. There were many snakes hiding, I was told, and they needed to be frightened away. Nobody was ever allowed to walk to the river without the nyoka-boys leading the way.

The other danger facing the washing crew and by anyone wanting to bathe - I was alone in this practice - was that of crocodiles. Although the steep bank gave Cachonga a certain amount of protection from these giant reptiles, the women did their washing on the single rough jetty and needed to bend down to the river surface to rinse the clothes. I learnt that two women and five children had been lost to crocodiles in the four years since my predecessor left. Part of my responsibility seemed to be to keep these slimy predators at bay. Apparently it was expected of me, and given my desire to wash every day, it was also desirable.

The help of Umboto, the village witch doctor, was once again necessary to deal with this crocodile threat. Umboto was in charge of the 'warriors' who seemed to be too important to help in the domestic life of the village. With a considerable effort, I managed to persuade these capable young men that it was an act of courage - as I truly believed - to go in front of the women to the river, and to hit the water surface with their flat spear-heads to ascertain whether or not

crocodiles were present.   Only after the warriors gave
the all-clear would the women then proceed with their
washing - and me to my bath. The warriors would also
be responsible for protecting the women and children
from possible attacks by hippo, lion, leopard or elephant.

Eventually I was given two warriors by Umboto; the
young men came with long sullen faces – quite out of
character for these proud and energetic people.
However, on their fourth day of what they thought of as
belittling work, while slapping the water as instructed, a
submerged crocodile had leapt into view, grabbed a spear
and pulled its owner into the river. The warrior had let
go of his spear and leapt from the water with great speed
and little dignity.

Fortunately I was present and heard the commotion.
I was quick to congratulate the young man on his
courage and bravery in tackling the fearsome creature on
his own - it was indeed a monster. The warrior looked at
me, first with suspicion and then with delight. His erect
posture was restored, and after that, the washing party
was escorted with at least six warriors, all of whom
stressed the danger to which they were exposing
themselves for the good of the village.

After I had been at Cachonga for well over a year
and had finally managed to secure a site for the new
church and start its construction, I took another
controversial step. I wanted to create agricultural fields
closer to the river. Once again I enlisted Umboto's help
because the acquiescence of Mhondoro, their Earth
God, was needed in allowing the villagers to dig the land
between the river and the hill where the new church was
slowly taking shape.

"'One generation passeth away, and another
generation cometh: but the earth abideth for ever'" I
quoted from Ecclesiastes, in a deep, serious voice as
Umboto looked at me quizzically. "We are only the

caretakers, and I think we can please the Earth Spirit aspect of our God, the one you call Mhondoro, by turning this piece of barren ground into somewhere productive."

It was an obvious place for growing crops, I explained to the witch doctor. From various manuals I adapted diagrams of how water could be directed from the river into channels to the suggested growing area with the use of a bicycle with wheels suspended – a peddle pump in fact.

By sitting on this ingenious device and peddling hard, someone - a suitable warrior, perhaps - could cause water to be carried up the bank from the river. I was busy experimenting with scoops made from gourds fixed to a conveyor belt. As the peddling power was transferred to the belt by the use of a pulley, the scoops would dip into the river and be carried upwards. The top of the belt's journey would be over a hopper situated on a specially built bamboo platform. As the belt turned, the water would be tipped out into the hopper before the scoops started their downward journey back to the river for replenishing. A pipe would descend from the hopper to carry water to channels leading to the new fields.

That was the idea, but I had yet to perfect the scoop plan as all my efforts to date had spilt more water than they had collected. It was a work in progress, I explained to Umboto.

In this instance the village Brujo was quick to understand the concept and to claim it as his own. With his approval, applications were made to Sollis, and to the Bishop, for such a machine and advice sought as to which sort of pumping mechanism would be best. We also asked for seeds for all sorts of different crops, and ideas as to what would sell in the villages and towns down-stream.

I made long studies of the books that had become my second and third bibles: "Rocks for Crops" and

"Organic Farming in the Developing World." I was excited about using the natural sources of phosphate, potassium and lime that could either be mined in the vicinity or produced by the villagers themselves through the growing of plants suitable for composting.

Some of the crops these books suggested, such as sunnhemp, were to be grown purely to fix atmospheric nitrogen in the ground and to be used as composted fertilizer for the valuable crops of wheat, barley, maize, sun-flowers and soya beans the following year. Pigeon peas, I learnt, were invaluable as an inter-crop with other plants. Although their peas were not everybody's favorite delicacy, they did produce a protein-rich food supply while fixing nitrogen in the soil at the same time.

With a ready supply of water, I explained to Umboto, the village could grow crops such as tomatoes, chillies, green peppers, and all sorts of herbs that would sell in the towns and cities. The money could then be used to buy things like a generator and fuel – Cachonga could have electricity! Maybe even a tractor?

The concept of producing more than the village could use was not easy for any of the elders to grasp, nor was the idea of planning more than three months ahead. To grow a crop which was of no value in the year of its planting and harvest was incomprehensible. Surprisingly, however, Umboto was enthusiastic about the plans and told the chief and the elders that here was an opportunity to improve life for everybody in Cachonga. As always, he took full credit for the suggestions but I had no difficulty with that, and was grateful that things were going in the right direction. Work on the new arable area started almost immediately so that the ground would be ready for planting as soon as the irrigation machine arrived.

Zengali, the elder in charge of the cattle, didn't escape my plans. With Umboto at my side, I showed the elders my book on livestock rearing and explained how cattle, goats and sheep could benefit from being corralled and their rations monitored. I had requested some clover and grass seed, along with those for the crops and told them how clover, like sunnhemp and pigeon peas, could fix nitrogen in the ground and thus help the grass to grow and provide more nutrition for the animals.

By creating large paddocks and grazing them in rotation, the manure could be easily collected, and the beasts would fatten if they didn't have to walk so far for their fodder. They would still have to come into the 'bomas' or 'kraals' at night, for the tall, solid walls of these enclosures, built with vertical logs, tied to each other with ropes of hide and sisal, kept the stock safe from the big cats, wild dogs and hyenas. The day paddocks would also need guarding, but it should be easier for the warriors to control. The village had lost two calves already since my arrival, each time because the herd had become spread out across the bush. Whenever lions were sighted or heard in the vicinity, Umboto now ordered his men to spend the night by the bomas with fires and drums to persuade the beasts to go elsewhere for their suppers.

Boma

Sollis had sent several manuals explaining the virtues of different kinds of peddle pumps and I spent many hours pondering over the selection. Eventually I abandoned anything with scoops or cups as all my previous experiments with these had been unsuccessful and decided on a 'rope-and-washer' design. It was simpler than the alternatives and less-expensive, so I was hopeful that my request would be granted, and indeed it was.

Once the decision had been made concerning the essential ingredient for our irrigations system, I was impatient to get started. It seemed to take ages for the device to arrive, but eventually Boniface arrived with a collection of strange boxes along with the requested seeds and some unexpected new tools to help till the soil and weed the crops. Finally work could begin in earnest.

The old arable area was sown with grass and clover and the warriors were dispatched into the bush to find long branches to make fencing, while the women concentrated on sowing the new crops. My job was to assemble the essential machine that would enable water to be peddled from the river. It took me a while to work everything out and several false starts, but eventually the machine was ready for its inauguration ceremony. It was an ingenious device consisting of a tube through which a rope with washers was threaded. Knots were tied above and below each rubber washer to stop them from slipping and to keep them about a meter apart. The diameter of the washers matched the diameter of the tube. The rope went in a continuous loop up through the tube, around the back wheel of the bicycle whose tyre had been replaced with a suitable metal groove, then back down to the water. There was a stand to support the bottom of the tube above the riverbed and a guide to ensure the rope returned directly into the tube as it rotated. Water was trapped between the washers and tipped out at the top of the tube into a collection tank on the top of the bank. This 'tank' was made from half an oil drum implanted into the ground enough to stop it wobbling, with a hose attached at ground level to take the water into the first part of our distribution channel.

At least that was the idea. As I fiddled about with knots, rope, tube, stands and so on, I was not convinced that our investment would work. There was only one way to find out and I persevered with my labours.

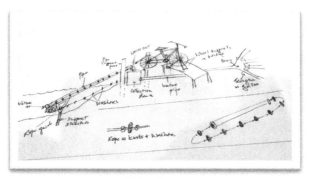

Water Pump

I was eager that the warriors should look on the tedious task of peddling for water as an honour, so Umboto and I planned a suitable 'show' to invest the rather mundane machine with awe and grandeur. We decorated the handle-bars with flowers, made a circle of palm fronds around the base, and summoned the village.

The drummer warriors led the procession from the village beating a steady rhythm. Next came Chief Mungonie, carried high on his throne by six strong men. The elders followed in some sort of shuffling order, and then the rest of the villagers flocked behind with children running in all directions. Umboto, resplendent in the full reglia of his office, and I were waiting by the suspended bicycle with its train of rope and washers. I was still in my burlap cassock, somewhat smudged with grease, but I had polished the big tin cross that always hung around my neck and it shone in the sunshine with a welcoming gleam.

I had taught my choir of school children to sing the Hymn 'All Things Bright and Beautiful' especially for this occasion and the words rang out, spiced with an

African lilt, into our new world. My English classes for the last month had concentrated on the words in the hymn so that when they came to perform at this great moment each child actually knew what he or she was singing about. My heart swelled with love and pride as we sent this message of appreciation and devotion into the wide Cachonga sky.

Next it was the turn of Umboto and the drumming and dancing warriors to make their noise and gyrations to the delight of the crowd spilling around the site and now swaying and stamping along with the performance.

Finally the head warrior, Ngirazi, marched solemnly towards me and mounted the machine with great dignity, sitting tall in the saddle, his hands on the handlebars, one foot on a peddle, the other balancing on the ground. I placed a garland of flowers around his head and turned to the Chief.

Mungonie raised his staff high in the air so that the ostrich feathers bounced. He brought it down with a thump so that the men carrying the litter upon which his throne rested flinched. At that moment, Ngirazi lifted his foot from the floor and started pedaling. A hush fell on the crowd as the rope began to move and the washers dipped into the water one by one and began their return journey up the tube to the top of the bank. When the first water splashed into the sump a huge cheer went up and everyone began to clap and dance. It was a splendid atmosphere and already the other warriors were forming a line, waiting for their turn for the honour of pedaling. The sound of the water splashing as each washer turned to start its downward journey was the most beautiful sound I had ever heard!

A goat had been slaughtered the night before and the smell of roasting meat wafted towards the crowd from the village, but nobody wanted to leave. Each warrior tried to outdo the one before and in less than an hour the sump was full and the first water sent trickling along the carefully prepared gullies to the furrows of the new fields. Farming in Cachonga had entered a new phase.

As the months passed and the farming enterprise flourished the warriors were kept busy in many different areas. The church was taking shape slowly but surely, there was the irrigation to keep going, the livestock to guard and now the precious seedlings and mature crops needed protecting from the bush pigs and baboons who liked to help themselves to the fruits of the villagers' labors. Hedges of thorn branches had been built between the fields and the bush, but this deterrent was not always adequate for these determined creatures. Chilli plants were grown alongside the hedge, as these were the marauders' least favorite crop – you could always tell when a baboon had stolen some chillies, as whoops of anger and cries of dismay echoed through the bush, causing much mirth amongst the field workers.

With Loveness's help I had bartered with a neighboring village to swap a few goats for some sheep, and several beef cattle were exchanged for milk cows. The village now had milk from nanny-goats, ewes and cows. A new hut was built by the corrals as a dairy, and the production of butter became so prolific that pats were sent for sale downstream every day.

Crop wastage, such as maize stalks and weeds from the herb fields, was spread across the dried mud floor of the bomas. Whatever the livestock didn't eat was trampled into the dung and urine every night and quickly transformed into rich compost to dig into the freshly tilled ground or spread on the growing crops.

After only two and a half years, sacks of dried tomatoes, marjoram, thyme, chillies and coriander were accompanying the butter down-stream where Sollis had taken to acting as both distributor and banker for the village. He was also responsible for making sure all the charitable goods that came from the capital made it as far as Cachonga with as little pilfering as possible. I think Sollis's respect for me grew in proportion to his increasing business, income and general sense of well-being.

All this activity along the river made Boniface quite a wealthy man also. One day he arrived at the newly extended Cachonga pier in a wide fibre-glass boat, complete with an outboard motor. He showed me his new pride and joy with a proud grin. I put on a show of delight, my eyes filling with tears when I saw that Boniface had christened the boat "Father Jack". In flowing letters of royal blue the name had been painted on both sides of the bow and across the stern. Flattered though I was, I could not help missing the splendid, silent canoe, with its proud red stripe, which had first brought me to Cachonga.

Another result of this steady trade was that Cachonga began to attract itinerant workers. Strangers used to be a novelty in the village, but now there was a steady stream of people looking for work, and there was plenty of work to be done.

As they prospered the villagers abandoned their meager huts to the new-comers and built larger ones around the church. The original hub of the village became 'the poor end of town' and my new splendid church, now central, was the pivotal point of all activities - it even doubled as a schoolroom during weekday mornings.

Josiah and Loveness's classes had grown too big for the paltry area they had used before, so I encouraged them to move to St. Thomas's - I even gave classes to the adults myself. We propped the black-board against the altar and used the space and benches to hold classes at each end of the building. The congregation of St. Thomas' grew along with everything else, so with the services and the lessons, my beloved church was always busy.

The chief was getting richer, the elders began to put on weight, the children looked healthy and were ambitious with their learning. The warriors dug ditches and tilled the soil, the women planted seeds and weeded the crops. When harvest time came, everyone in the village helped to bring in the bounty. I was in the middle of everything - always encouraging, always positive, always with another idea up my sleeve. These were happy and fulfilling years for me, so different from my years in Islington, and I thanked God fervently for every new day.

52. ENVOYS BEARING GIFTS

The Bishop's envoy, the Canon Missioner, was a tall, thin man in his mid forties. Father Merciful, as he introduced himself, arrived in full clerical dress, seated on a pile of crates and oil drums in the back of Boniface's boat. He was accompanied by a young man of about nineteen dressed in neat dark clothes.

Here were the visitors who would report back to the Bishop about my success or failure in bringing back Cachonga to the Christian fold. Coming towards me were the reasons for our mass-baptism ceremony, and the envoys who would accredit or discredit any future requests for provisions. I watched their approach with trepidation.

I had hoped the visitor would be a white man, not because I missed white company – I did not - but because I was uncomfortable with Umboto's part in the scheduled ceremony being understood by a fellow countryman from the city. There was a danger that the Christian flavor of the service would appear diluted – or even corrupted.

Father Merciful looked exhausted from his journey. I remembered my own trip, and was impressed that this priest had managed to arrive looking so smart. I bade him welcome and was introduced to Jamu, the young assistant, who had picked up two small suitcases. I led them with pride along the path towards the church, my plain cassock swishing around bare ankles, the tin cross tapping against my chest.

"Our service is scheduled for four o'clock, Father," I stopped where a track led off to the entrance of the church. "So we have nearly two hours. Would you like to wash and have some refreshment while we wait? If you're not too tired, I'd love to show you round."

"I've been sitting for far too long, Father Jack." Merciful's voice was a rich bass, "and I have been looking forward to seeing what you have achieved with all those packages we have been sending you."

"Splendid," I answered quickly. "We'll leave the church until later then and I'll explain how we built it. Let me show you where you are spending the night and we can get rid of those suitcases."

Umboto met us at the edge of the village. He made a low bow and, in his own language, welcomed the visitors on behalf of the chief.

Father Merciful turned to me in confusion. "I'm from Mozambique, and Jamu is from Kenya. I'm afraid neither of us speaks the local language, I assumed everything here was done in English."

I held back a desire to throw my hands up to heaven and thank the Lord for this happy information, and it gave me great pleasure to translate Umboto's message. "Of course the school is busy teaching as many people as possible to speak English," I said when Umboto's speech was finished, "and thanks to all the books, black-board, chalk and slates you have sent up, we are coming along well. But I still prefer to rely on a girl called Loveness to translate important things for me when we are in church or at any other important occasion, just to make sure everyone understands what's going on."

"Very sensible," Father Merciful was quick to respond. "It seems like a wonderful way to get everyone involved: after all some of our Christian messages are quite complicated.

"You seem to have a great rapport with the witch-doctor," he continued, "that is an amazing achievement, and one that I think is truly unique. Was it hard to convert him?"

I hesitated, "well, it took a bit of time," I said thoughtfully, and then added, "of course spiritual understanding can be accepted in different ways, and I have tried not to diminish his high position in the village hierarchy by setting myself up as his superior. We work as equals, or if anything, I am his subordinate. After all, he is a great deal older than I am and this is his village and these are his people."

Father Merciful looked confused and was about to pursue the topic when I continued in a hurry to suggest that the visitors should stay in my hut, as I was happy sleeping under the stars. I took off at a steady pace in the direction of my tiny home with the two visitors jogging to keep up.

I still lived in my original tiny dwelling, although the elders had all moved away into larger homes nearer the church. My neighbors were now the new workers who had come to Cachonga for jobs. Wives and children had quickly followed, and my end of the village was always full of chatter and activity. I led the way through a group of children playing some sort of circular game amongst shouts of 'hello Father Jack,' and indicated my house to the guests.

Father Merciful bent his head and entered the hut followed by Jamu with the bags. I watched from the doorway as the strangers looked around them at the bare floor, mud walls and thatched roof. The earthen bench had a neat row of books along its length, mostly to do with agriculture, and a couple of DIY manuals. There was a cross, made of two small branches bound together with hide, on the wall opposite the mattress. My tin trunk served as a table to support the precious paraffin lamp.

"I'll get another mattress brought round," I said. "I'm afraid we weren't expecting you, Jamu, but you're very welcome just the same." I turned to Father Merciful: "will you both be alright in here, or should I try to find another hut?"

"This will be perfect," the priest answered unconvincingly.

"Not quite what you're used to, I'm afraid," I tried to look at my house through the eyes of an urban priest and wondered how these two would cope with the washing facilities. "We have little use for luxuries here," I added rather lamely.

"So I see, Father. But Jamu and I will be fine here; after all it's only for one night."

I started the tour of Cachonga with the corrals and the dairy. I showed the visitors the former arable land where we had now sown the grass and clover seeds which the Bishop had sent. I explained that enough pasture was now being grown to allow the village to make hay in addition to providing grazing. As a result, the size of the herds had been increased.

We watched a couple of cows and a nanny goat being milked, and two women showed them the butter churns and pats that had also come from the capital. Large wedges of butter were ranged along a stone shelf.

"We have to transport the milk and butter at night," I explained, "so it can get to Sollis's cold boxes before the sun's up. We have a steady routine now and all the local villages have fresh dairy produce almost every day. We are hoping to have eggs to sell soon," I added, pointing at a row of rough chicken coops behind the dairy. "There's some of the wire you sent two weeks ago, Father, it keeps the hyenas away from our hens at night."

We continued the tour past the kitchen area of large open fires under tripods with black pots hanging heavily. We passed the old hand pump, and I explained how the irrigation device I had requested, for bringing water to the crops from the river, had meant that this pump only had to supply the villagers and the livestock now. I apologized briefly for the primitive lavatories as we passed them and explained that most of the villagers preferred to go off into the bush. "It's usually possible to find somewhere with a nice view, if you walk a decent distance. Makes the whole process a lot more pleasant, although it's not safe to go out of the village at night, I'm afraid. I've never actually seen a lion, but I've heard them often enough."

Father Merciful had a quick look inside the latrines. "Perhaps we should approach one of our charities to fund a septic tank for Cachonga?" he enquired.

"Oh, that would be wonderful," I responded with enthusiasm. "We would have to pump it out ourselves, I'm afraid, so we might have to wait until the village has electricity, and we would need a suitable pump, of course. Then we could compost the effluent . . ."

"Well, I'll see what I can do," the Canon Missioner interrupted quickly. It was obviously some considerable time since his family had become urbanized.

I was thrilled to have someone to whom I could show off all the achievements of the village, especially as I believed it to be the Bishop's appeals to charities that had made so much of these improvements possible. I was especially proud of the herb and vegetable fields, and the crops of wheat, rye, maize, cassava, beans, millet, soya, and barley. This last was being grown to improve the quality of the village beer that up to now had been made entirely with maize.

"The amount of protein the villagers have in their diet has improved dramatically since you sent us the first batch of seeds to get this lot going," I said gesturing towards the well-tended fields. "We do two crops in twelve months – you see the soya being planted here, that follows straight behind the harvesting of the wheat and rye. You should see the improvement in the people's skins and general stature. This is the healthiest village for miles around," I added, hoping that the more successful picture I could paint, the more vital supplies would be forthcoming from the capital.

The tour complete, apart from the church, I rushed back to change from my cassock to my surplice. I had forgotten to look up the church calendar to see whether I should be wearing the green or the purple stole. I chose the green one, straightened my hair with my hands, gave a loving rub to my tin cross and re-joined the visitors.

I had an attack of stage fright as I led my guests towards the church. Umboto and I had been forced to hold a second dress rehearsal for this service, only yesterday, after the first had been an absolute disaster. Everyone in the village was determined to be included and the excitement, as the hoard of ecclesiastical trappings emerged from behind the altar, had been impossible to contain. There had been a fight for the choir robes resulting in several having to be mended and all of them needing a wash. I had been upset at the time, but when the second rehearsal took place with Umboto in charge of the discipline, I realized that the robes now had a well-used look, which, under the circumstances, was an improvement on the clean starched robes that had been unpacked.

Another setback had been the disappearance of the communion wine. A pile of empty bottles was later discovered somewhere in the bush, and a group of warriors were strangely ill the following day. Fortunately I had taken one bottle to my hut in order to show the drawing on the label to Umboto during my explanation of the communion service – that would have to suffice. The empty bottles were carefully washed and I collected them into a box to give to the visitors to take back to the Capital. They could draw their own conclusions as to where the communion wine had gone.

All had preceded reasonably well with the second rehearsal, but I was still nervous as I led the visiting vicar towards my beloved church. I had already asked Father Merciful if he would do me the honor of conducting the service, with me in attendance - there was no-one else I could trust to handle the holy sacraments apart from myself and the visiting padre - and besides, I had become uncomfortable with certain groveling elements of the service. I did not want to be the one who accused the congregation of "not being worthy . . " Fortunately, Father Merciful had accepted and seemed flattered by the request. However he had not prepared a sermon, so relied upon me as the priest of the parish of Cachonga to deliver one of my own.

There was a small crowd around the door of the church. It parted as the three of us approached. I was busy explaining how the building had taken shape, the various problems we had encountered during its construction, and how God had showed us how to proceed. I paused when we reached the entrance, from inside came a babble of excited voices.

"We decided to make this service a bit of a harvest festival, as well as Holy Communion," I told Father Merciful. "Everyone has been working hard reaping the rye and the wheat so the soya could be planted in good time. The harvest was good enough to fill our stores and still have enough to send twenty sacks to the trading post at River's Bend. It seemed right to celebrate and thank the Almighty for his beneficence while you are with us, for God has manifested his generosity to Cachonga via yourself, the Bishop and the various charities with which you are connected.

"Welcome to St. Thomas', Father and Jamu" I concluded and stood back to let the older man enter first. It was then that I noticed that Jamu was absent. This seemed strange, but there was too much else happening to allow me to dwell on the occurrence for long.

I couldn't imagine how Father Merciful judged the creation of the Cachonga Church. I doubted if the Canon Missioner, in spite of his title, had any other bush churches with which to compare St. Thomas' – as indeed I hadn't when I designed it. I was also aware that the Bishop's envoy was used to the grand cathedral in the capital, built by Europeans in colonial days. However, this was no ordinary rural parish church. "No it is a much greater concept than just an ecclesiastical building," I told myself, "it is the true heart of a community, of men and their souls; it is God's house in the middle of nowhere, where everyone is welcome and should feel at home."

As Father Merciful stepped into the church, the clogged congregation grew quiet. More than a hundred heads turned to look at the visiting padre, and I watched carefully as the guest absorbed the scene that confronted him.

The giant crucifix had been hung on the wall behind the altar that was now draped in a cloth of embroidered gold and green. Two pillar candles – which amazingly enough had been lit – stood on either side of my centrally placed bible and Book of Common Prayer. I had arranged stooks of wheat, rye and maize to frame the altar, and there were more at the edge of alternating benches and at the entrance. Corncobs were set in neat stacks on the altar and the blackboard easel which doubled as a lectern; along with the stooks, they lined the aisle between the benches.

A piece of acacia trunk had been stood on end, just inside the doorway, on the right. It was about chest height and the silver font bowl had been set on its top. This was also filled with golden cobs of maize.

Warriors had been on duty all night and all day to stop the baboons from helping themselves to this bounty and from relieving themselves within the open-windowed edifice - a favorite trait of this particular member of the simian family.

The 'choir,' resplendent in their robes, stood on either side of the altar. The paten and chalice reflected the candlelight waiting expectantly beside the bible.

The lowering sun sent shafts into the building through the oval openings, and I thought the packed church, with its decorations of fecundity, looked absolutely magical – in spite of the suffering face of Jesus on the cross.

On the whole, I decided, the service had gone well. Umboto had agreed to wear a white surplice, but had rejected the blue cassock that should have been underneath. He had decided against the ruff also, preferring a necklace of tusks around his neck instead of the starched double collar. Of course, the ostrich feather headdress and the shell-adorned staff were not to be discarded, and I knew well enough not to mention how they might appear inappropriate to the visitors.

Umboto stood to one side of the altar, in his fantastical outfit, facing the congregation and chattering to them at intervals as he 'translated' the proceedings.

For the Epistle, I had chosen a piece from Deuteronomy, chapter twenty-eight, and read with as much gusto as I could: "Blessed shalt thou be in the field. Blessed shall be the fruit of thy body, and the fruit of thy ground, and the fruit of thy cattle, the increase of thy kine, and the flocks of thy sheep. Blessed shall be thy basket and thy store. Blessed shalt thou be when thou commest in, and blessed shalt thou be when thou goest out."

For the Gospel, I read the story of Jesus with the loaves and fishes and pushed from my thoughts Rufus's comment from St. Augustine's days when he had said "all I can say is, He must have been a very delicate carver!"

I had dismissed the possibility of the Chief and elders coming quietly to the altar and going down onto their knees to receive communion. I had already explained to father Merciful that there was only one bottle of communion wine left, and so had decided that only the most important people of the village would actually receive the holy sacraments, and that, as there was no altar rail – yet - it was my practice to take the wafers and wine to the congregation, as they sat along the front benches. The Canon Missioner had nodded understanding, although his eyes did not nod with the same message.

The administering of the Holy Communion had gone better than I could have imagined possible. I had accompanied Father Merciful, with the sacraments, to the front benches of the church, and together we gave 'the body and blood of Jesus Christ' to each of the occupants. Umboto followed behind with his own mumblings and waves of his staff, and everybody seemed genuinely moved by the experience.

There followed a general blessing of the whole congregation with symbolic gestures of holy offerings to the crowd. There were ululations from the women and deep groans of emotion from the men. An infectious atmosphere of spirituality filled the building and the people within. I felt that it was an extraordinary experience, and hoped that father Merciful and Jamu, if he had turned up, would feel it also.

The text I chose for the sermon of this inaugural harvest festival and Holy Communion service, was taken from Psalm ninety-six, verses eleven and twelve: "Let the heavens rejoice, and let the earth be glad; let the sea roar, and the fullness thereof. Let the field be joyful, and all that is therein; then shall all the trees of the wood rejoice." I remembered my first sermon, while at St. Augustine's, and repeated it here, with only minor modifications. I kept it as short as I felt was allowable, and let Loveness and Umboto take it in turns to translate the ideas. I finished with another quotation from Psalms number sixty-five, verse nine, to connect this first Holy Communion service with the baptism day of only two weeks before:

"Thou visitest the earth, and waterest it, thou greatly enrichest it with the river of God, which is full of water: thou prepares them corn, when thou has so provided for it."

The service ended with the choir - a group of a dozen children ranging from ten to fourteen led by Loveness - singing the same hymn we had practiced for the previous event. Their rendition of 'All things bright and beautiful.' was the extent of the participation of 'The St. Thomas' choir,' apart from the sonorous 'Amens' and 'Hallellujas' that punctuated all that had gone before. Each child held a hymn book out in front with appropriate solemnity, even though Loveness was the only one who could read well enough to understand the meaning. Our rehearsals and practice paid off, and the hymn made a suitable finale.

Once the blessing had been given, I walked down the aisle with Father Merciful on one side and Umboto on the other. We stood next to each other at the doorway, shaking hands and exchanging enthusiastic impressions of the service with the members of the congregation. The crowd lingered outside the church, not sure about what they should do. The chief and the elders came out last, the warriors waiting with the royal litter; standing tall and flushed with importance.

As Chief Mungonie climbed aboard his litter, I heard the distant noise of a motor, and wondered what Boniface and his boat were doing here at this hour.

A procession formed behind the litter with Umboto and us two priests being next in line, followed by the elders and then the rest of the villagers. Dusk lingered around us, obscuring the bush beyond the fields, as we made our way to the village centre and the celebratory feast that was waiting for us. The cooking fires sparkled in the gathering gloom, but the torches had not yet been lit, which made me twitch a little with annoyance. The darkness swallowed any hope of a ceremonial arrival.

Suddenly the procession stopped. I was surprised to see Jamu and Boniface standing in the middle of the path ahead of the chief. They were blocking the way, causing the procession to come to a confused halt. Before anyone could make enquiries, father Merciful spoke:

"Are you ready, Jamu?" he asked.

"All ready, Father," Jamu replied.

Father Merciful left his place behind the chief and squeezed past the warriors with their heavy burden to stand with Jamu and Boniface. "With your permission, Chief Mungonie," he said, bowing low, "we would like to present Cachonga with the latest donation from the Western charities to the Christian church of this country which the Bishop, in his generosity, has designated for your village."

Jamu and Boniface had disappeared behind a hut as the Canon started speaking. The sound of a motor was suddenly apparent in the background.

"Let there be light," announced Father Merciful with theatrical magnitude, and a string of a dozen or so light bulbs came to life hanging from an electric cable that stretched across the village centre from an acacia on one side to a eucalyptus on the other.

There were gasps of amazement from the crowd. Some people fell to their knees, ululations filled the air. I grasped Umboto's hand, for no apparent reason, and found myself shaking it hard. "We've done it," I said to my friend, "we've arrived. Now we have power, there will be no stopping Cachonga. Poverty will be a thing of the past. We are on our way!"

At some point during the celebrations that followed this great event, Father Merciful explained that he had brought the generator and all the necessary equipment, plus a supply of fuel, upon instruction from the Bishop. However, his orders were to return with everything still in its crates if he found Cachonga unworthy of yet another large contribution to its welfare.

"We have sent so much up-river to this village," Father Merciful went on. "While we had great faith in what you were trying to achieve, various voices in the background kept suggesting that it was impossible for one man to make so many changes in just a few years. Hence, I was sent up to see for myself, and I am relieved and delighted to be able to report back to my superior that not only is Cachonga worthy of the generator and lighting but also, I shall be putting in a request for a whole lot of other things – starting with a septic tank and some lavatories!"

I asked father Merciful if we could say grace together to commence the meal that steamed from the pots before them.

Father Merciful had welcomed Jesus, God's light to the world, to their feast. I had added a coda of one of my favorite biblical quotation from Habakkuk chapter two, verse fourteen: "For the earth shall be filled with the knowledge of the glory of the Lord, as the waters cover the sea."

Amens and Hallelujas filled the air. People clapped and sang, and after eating there was dancing to the drums for which Cachonga was becoming famous. I sat on a log with a gourd of Umboto's beer in my hands and sent prayers of gratitude to the Almighty for the happiness I was feeling through every part of my mind and body.

53. The Tide Turns

Father Merciful and Jamu left the next morning. I found it hard to say goodbye to these messengers from God, with all the beneficence they had at their disposal. I had already thanked Boniface for his industry in helping to install the generator and for the vote of confidence the boatman had given to father Merciful during the journey to Cachonga about which I had heard later from Jamu.

Father Merciful and I had spent over an hour together before he left, during which I had been able to articulate my feelings for Cachonga for the first time. I had told Father Merciful briefly about my previous parish in Islington, and how unsatisfactory I had been, in my own mind rather than that of my parishioners, as a 'minister of faith.' And now, here, in this village, how I felt I had been given the Zen equivalent of an 'un-carved block.' At last I felt worthy of the responsibilities I had undertaken at my ordination. I was achieving something, here in Cachonga, or rather I was helping God to work his wonders in a place that was previously unreceptive. The people here now look to me for help, on both spiritual and material planes, and I am but a conduit for the Almighty. They see joy in the church services "the natural uninhibited joy that city people seem to have lost," I expanded, father Merciful nodded slowly.

I paused, "I mean 'city people' in the Western world, Father, I know nothing of how churches work in your parish." Had I gone too far? This heart-felt explosion of feelings was so uncharacteristic, but then I hadn't had a kindred spirit with whom I could talk since I left St. Augustine's, apart from father Justin, and that was several years ago now. I tried to explain this to Father Merciful by way of an apology.

"Father Jack," the Canon Missioner responded with a voice full of feeling. "It has been a privilege to have met you and to have shared in the wonderful service you orchestrated yesterday. I admit I was skeptical about your success in the many areas you have sought to change. But now that I have been here and met the amazing cast of characters you have managed to work with so well, I am filled with admiration for what you have achieved. I am looking forward to returning to the Bishop with so much positive information, and I have no doubt that you will receive whatever you feel Cachonga needs to keep the community growing in such a wonderfully Christian direction. You are an inspiration to us all."

While pleased with this accolade, I couldn't help feeling a twinge of guilt about some of the short cuts I had taken as far as assimilating the people of Cachonga into Christ's church were concerned. I knew very well that I would have achieved very little without the support and commitment of Umboto, and presumed that as "God moves in mysterious ways" this would all be understood - somehow.

As Father Merciful and Jammu were boarding the 'Father Jack' for the start of their journey back to the capital, the priest turned to me and said: "I have heard rumors of gangs of thugs from neighboring countries invading our lands. Be vigilant, Jack, I know you are far from any political activity, here in the bush at Cachonga, but still, keep an ear to the ground - and it wouldn't hurt to make some emergency plans, without alarming anyone, of course."

I thanked the visitors for their concern and assured them that, thank heavens, political problems had no part to play in the small world of this village.

"Well, just in case," Father Merciful said as the boat moved away from the pier, "please make a plan."

I watched the boat move out into the river, turn its bow south and head off downstream. The visit was over, and now I could get back to building and expanding all the ideas which were going so well, but which needed constant supervision and encouragement, it was time to get back to work.

I wouldn't have had it any other way. I was thriving with the positive energy which buzzed through the village. Nobody had to be encouraged to work, everyone was eager to play their part – especially as the original villagers did less and less of the manual labour, leaving the grubbiest jobs to the new-comers. Their new responsibilities were in the dairy, the drying sheds, the packaging huts, the ever-growing school and so on.

The women no longer had back-breaking work weeding the fields or carrying water – some of them even had servants of their own to do their laundry, clean their huts and cook their meals. Cachonga was developing a class structure with the chief, Omboto and elders being the aristocrats and the original village workers becoming a middle class while the in-coming folk created a working class grateful for the work, homes and the security of decently paid jobs.

The enthusiasm from everyone involved was palpable and the lines of men being turned away from the village every day kept those who were employed concentrating on doing well and gave them a pride and an identity.

Cachonga was being recognized down stream and the compliments and money that came back up the river gave the villagers a strong sense of community and self-esteem.

I can see all that in retrospect. At the time, I was too busy following up new ideas and expanding every aspect of the community. My parish was growing and evolving and I had a wonderfully satisfying life. I thanked God almost continually for my good fortune.

During the next few months I put my mind to maximizing the use of the generator. The old hand pump was dug up and an electric pump arrived to bring water from the well. It had been purchased from Sollis with the money earned from the sales of our crops. For the first time we had bought something that came from our own industry and not as a charitable donation. Along with the pump came an irrigation expert to set it up and teach the warriors and myself, of course, how it should be used.

Tendai Ngapasare specialized in rural development, but had never heard of Cachonga until the order for the pump came through. He looked somewhat out of place in his pressed trousers and smart shirt, with the name of the irrigation company emblazoned across a breast pocket. However, he must have come from hereabouts, because he could speak the local language.

Tendai wandered around the village and its compounds with a sense of wonder. "How did all this happen, this far up-river?" he asked with a sweeping gesture. "I grew up just thirty miles downstream and never knew anything like this existed."

"Progress, I suppose," I answered somewhat wistfully. I had been thinking a lot lately about what God and I had set in motion in this back-water village. I had been worrying ever since Boniface replaced his beautiful silent canoe with the fiber-glass boat and an out-board motor. Did the boatman still see impala and elephant as he cruised upstream, I wondered, or did the animals hear the engine in good time and vanish before the boat's arrival. I shrugged my shoulders with discomfort and returned to the manual Tendai had brought about the workings of the electric pump.

Of course it was wonderful to have electricity in Cachonga, but with it had come an end to the jungle noises of the bush that had been the constant background to village life. The whooping of the cranes and the chuckles of the hoopoe birds were now drowned out by the coughing and spluttering of the generator's engine that gave an impression of perpetual anger and argument. At night, when it was finally turned off, I could hear the crickets and cicadas once again, and, when the rains came, the frogs and toads with their multitude of wooing songs, but you had to walk a good distance from the village now if you wanted to hear the birds by day.

I berated myself for these doubts. I had read enough anthropology to be familiar with the 'noble savage' concept and refused to allow myself, or this village, to be pushed into a box or category. I listened carefully to what Tendai had to say and took copious notes on how to get the best from the twin wonders of generator and pump.

"Are you not worried, all the way out here, with what is going on in this country today?" Tendai asked as we walked back to the river and the salesman's ride home. "The village seems remarkably undisturbed and undefended."

"Should we be disturbed and defended?" I asked in surprise. "We have many strong warriors who guard our crops and animals from lions and elephants – not to mention the thieving baboons. We have fires, thorn hedges, drums, spears, and brave men. What else had you in mind?" I asked, pride giving my voice a bit of an edge. I did not like a stranger questioning the ability of Cachonga's splendid warrior group.

Tendai hesitated; he stopped walking and turned to face me - this strange white vicar with his straggly beard, bare feet, homespun cassock and crude tin cross.

"Lions, elephants and baboons don't carry AK47s," he said in a flat tone. "It is not God's four-legged creatures of whom you need to be afraid. How I wish life could be as simple as that. No, Father, you need to be aware that 'man's inhumanity to man' stalks our borders and can infiltrate at any moment. You should know what is going on with the world."

"They shall not hurt nor destroy in all my holy mountain" I quoted from Isaiah, chapter eleven, verse nine. The phrase had come to me unbidden. I had faith in its surety.

"Thank you Tendai," I said in a softer tone. "Thank you for your help with the pump, and for your caring for our village. I will continue to pray that the world will leave Cachonga alone to grow and to flourish. We are one of God's communities; that should be all the defense we need."

"I pray that is so," answered Tendai. We had reached the pier and Boniface was eager to be away. We shook hands, and with a wave to the boatman and the salesman, I turned my back on the river and returned home.

The electric pump in the central well changed the lives of so many women in Cachonga. Suddenly, with the fitting of a hose and a series of troughs all coming from the capital, there was no need to spend two or three hours a day carrying water to the village and the threshing and winnowing of grain was now being done by the new-comers. The women grew idle. In spite of my begging them to spend more time in the dairy, school, packing sheds and so on, they found it difficult to alter a regime that went back to their forefathers. They began to put on weight.

Umboto and I could not spend too much time worrying about this change in routine. The village had suddenly become inundated with refugees from up country where dreadful things had been happening. We were told of entire communities being wiped out by brutal gangs who had no respect for any kind of law. Neither the country's nor God's values were respected in any way by these marauders, and of the atrocities they committed – I chose to disbelieve such revolting tales.

Every night I preached at evensong, and the church was getting more and more crowded. One night I had taken as text for the sermon the first two verses of Deuteronomy Chapter thirty-two: 'Hear oh earth, the words of my mouth. My doctrine shall drop as the rain, my speech shall distil as the dew, as the small rain upon the tender hay, and as the showers upon the grass.'" I extolled the congregation with assurances that their gentle and beneficent God could not allow the horrors that were being reported. "We must have faith," I called out in a loud voice, with what I thought to be the power of God running through every fiber of my being. "We must have faith, and our God will not let us down."

The following day, Zengali came to me, worried about his livestock. He told me he had heard of paramilitary gangs rampaging through the country to conscript 'soldiers' for their armies. "They are killing everyone over thirty," he stammered, "and taking the young away to corrupt one way or another. This roving 'army' needs food, and they steal everything they can find. If they hear of our stock, they may well come to get it."

I had never seen Zengali this motivated and, for the first time, I felt an element of doubt creeping into my psyche.

At evensong that day I prayed for God's protection against all evils. I gave a sermon on the strength God gives to his people in times of trouble. 'Have faith and you can be stronger than any army' I promised.

Last of all, and in quite the wrong place for a conventional evensong, Loveness and I sang the ninety-first Psalm which we had practiced earlier that afternoon:

"He that dwelleth in the secret place of the Most High, shall abide under the shadow of the Almighty.

"I will say of the Lord, He is my refuge, and my fortress: my God; in him will I trust.

"Surely he shall deliver thee from the snare of the fowler, and from the noisome pestilence.

"He shall cover thee with his feathers, and under his wings shalt thou trust: his truth shall be they shield and buckler.

"Thou shalt not be afraid for the terror by night, nor for the arrow that flieth at noonday.

"A thousand shall fall at thy side, and ten thousand at thy right hand; but it shall not come nigh thee.

"Only with thine eyes shalt thou behold and see the reward of the wicked.

"Because thou hast made the Lord, which is my refuge, even the Most High, thy habitation,

"There shall no evil befall thee, neither shall any plague come nigh thy dwelling.

"For he shall give his angels charge over thee, to keep thee in all thy ways.

"They shall bear thee up in their hands, lest though dash thy foot against a stone. . . ."

The congregation had left the church filled with calm and optimism. I went to my hut praying that I might feel the same, and with just cause. My peace of mind was further troubled by a visit from Umboto when the witch doctor calmly announced his intention to visit his family somewhere far away. He would be gone for quite some time, he was leaving immediately, and the Chief and his entourage were going with him.

"But that will leave us short of warriors," I was very upset with the idea. "Chief Mungonie can't walk any distance without his litter, and it takes at least six strong men to carry him."

Umboto shrugged his shoulders, "it can't be helped," he answered in a matter-of-fact tone. "There is an important family wedding in the village of Mungonie's birth. He has to be there. I'm sure you'll manage without us, you have your God, after all." The witch doctor turned quickly and left the hut. I never saw him again.

So it is time. I have now to record the facts. This is the reason I started this collation of memories. I have dodged around the story for too long and can put it off no longer. I need to exorcise the horrors that have followed me all these years.

It was just two days later that shouts were heard from outside the village. The noise from the generator meant that the distress calls didn't reach the ears of the villagers until those that were crying out came into sight.

"We are surrounded," came the frenzied cries. "They are everywhere. Help us, what should we do?"

I had been weeding a patch of coriander seedlings and straightened to find myself confronted by a crowd of frightened faces, it was Loveness who had spoken.

"We must go to the church," I said, without any forethought or reason. "'Under the shadow of Thy wings shall be my refuge, until this tyranny be over-past'" I quoted from the fifty-seventh Psalm. "Everyone to the church."

Nobody moved until I dropped my trowel, and turned towards St. Thomas'. I marched with determination, the skirts of the heavy cassock swinging around my feet, the tin cross, as always, bouncing softly against my chest. The villagers rushed behind me, hushed by the gravity of the moment.

When we reached the church, I stood to one side and ushered everyone through the rough hewn doors. There were more people coming in a frantic rabble, I waited.

A collection of crop workers and warriors were stumbling along the path towards the church. There was an eerie silence to their approach that I found most disturbing. As the group grew closer I made out a gang of about fifty men at the back and around the sides of the moving huddle. They were dressed in faded fatigues and sported machine guns as if they were children's flags on a day out at the seaside. They were herding the villagers in a fashion that made my blood run cold. I began to pray.

Amanzi was amongst the first to reach the church door. He pushed past me without a pause. Warriors who usually stood so tall, rushed past with heads bowed and shoulders shaking.

When the last villager had pushed inside the already crowded church, I stepped forward and stood in the doorway of my beloved St. Thomas' holding my cross up, into the face of evil.

In the glinting eyes of the men who advanced I saw the same frenzy I had witnessed in Oberammergau and San José, only this time the frenzy was filled with a malevolent passion.

"This is God's house," I was shouting. "You cannot bring your violence into God's house." I was trying to block the way of at least fifty men. I was alone, standing for everything I believed in. I could not fail.

"Well it seems that your God is not at home" laughed the man at the head of the invaders, a heavy draught of foul fumes issuing from his mouth as he spoke. "You best get out of the way padre, Mungutu himself is coming" the heavy man spoke the local language with a strong accent as he pushed me with such force that I crumpled against the door jamb. I recovered quickly and sprang back, but the invaders had already surged into the church and were pulling people out of the building.

A strong arm pinned me against the door as my congregation was pulled out in a steady stream. Each individual was thrown to a throng of invaders. They were stripped naked and put into groups according to their ages and sex.

The sky was full of smoke and heat before I saw the flames. The village was on fire. The crops were burning, and then, finally, they set the church alight using a whole can of petrol from the generator store.

I was the only one left, pinned against the door by a mighty, foul smelling arm, as the baobab altar started to smolder. Tears ran unheeded. I kept trying to pray, but words choked in my throat and thoughts fused in my brain. Another man came and joined my captor. "We are Mungutu's Champions," he spat at me. "You are now part of the great Mungutu army."

"Or you can die," hissed the original assailant.

Mungutu's thugs lined the naked men up in front of the burning church. The men's hands had been tied behind their backs, their ankles lashed together with heavy rope. The women had been herded off towards the river apart from Loveness and two other young girls who had been led in the other direction.

I was as yet unfettered, but my arms were pinned by the two huge men who squashed me as they shouted and gesticulated instructions with their non-restraining arms. A strong odor of unwashed, sweating flesh was in my nostrils. It was a raw animal type of smell that I would not have recognized as human had not the two sources of the aroma been at my sides.

My mind hurt. It is a hard sensation to try to express: the pain was excruciating as I watched the abuse of people I had come to think of as family, and with the sight and smell of my smoldering church. I hadn't known a mind could feel such pain. Where had they taken Loveness? I could hear raucous mirth amidst shouts of encouragement coming from the group who had taken her away. Then there was the scream. The voice that so recently had been singing hymns with the sweetness of a Spring dawn now rent the air with a single, sharp wail.

My body made an involuntary lurch to free itself.

"Want a bit of the action, do you" one of my captors said laughingly as he yanked my arm behind me increasing a knife-like pain which ran from the tip of my shoulder diagonally towards the lower spine. "A nice little piece, your friend, but you'll have to wait your turn – if there's anything left by the time the boys have finished with her." He paused, and then with a wink to his comrade, he leaned towards his captive. "Let me tell you what they'll be up to."

While the man on the left held my jaw in his massive hand to keep my head straight, the speaker to the right put his mouth to my ear. I could feel his spit running down my neck as the man spoke in a wet stage-whisper, his voice showing the enjoyment he was feeling as he spoke:

"Our comrades over there, they've got a routine, you see. Jonah, he likes young pussy, the younger the better. While Alfonse, he likes the back passage, a real anus he is, in every way." He drew back to allow a deep belly laugh to work its way through his large abdomen and out into the chaos of shouts and screams that surrounded us. "And then there's Bernard, he goes for the mouth – but not until he's put banana leaves over the bitch's teeth – he learnt that trick the hard way and now he never embarks on one of these jollies without a ready wad of fresh, green leaves." Another guffaw joined the riot of sounds.

"Zeik & Sonny, they just like to watch, but they help the lads by holding the meat still so that they can all three have it away at the same time. It's teamwork, that's what it is. We teach them these skills at an early age, in the training camps, and it works a treat. This bunch, they've got it down to a fine art and can make their pleasure last a goodly while now – unless the bitch splits of course."

I could feel the sweat of fear and horror running down my back, soaking the lines of pain caused by the position of my arms. Tears must have been running as a salty taste was on my tongue mixed with the bile that was rising in my throat. The pressure in my head threatened to explode.

"Don't worry, it'll be your turn soon," the man used his free hand to take hold of my right buttock, he pinched a handful of flesh beneath the coarse robe. "You're to be the dish of honor, today."

Both the men began to snigger, and then stood up straight as their commander approached, once more squeezing me upright between them so that all three of us appeared to be joined at the shoulders, standing to attention.

"They're ready for you, Commander," my raconteur addressed his Chief, a note of reverence evident in the coarse voice. He indicated the line of pathetic prisoners who were gibbering with fear as the thugs poked at them with bayonets to make them stand straight.

Mungutu came over. "What have we here?" he asked.

"This one's for you, sir," replied the man who had as yet restricted his comments to grunts and sniggers at the other's words. "We found him in there," he indicated the remains of St. Thomas'. "I think it could be fresh meat," he said, eyeing his boss as a spaniel might look to his master for praise when it returns with a pheasant in his jaws.

Mungutu stepped up close. I stared into the wide, blood-shot black eyes in horror. The men wrenched me straighter still as Mungutu reached up with both hands and, with a gentleness that was more chilling than any rough treatment could be, he carefully opened my cassock. Starting at the top, he worked his way down to just below my waist, savoring each button. Then he pulled the robe carefully away from my chest revealing the tin cross hanging on its rough chain in the centre.

"Oh nicely decorated, lads" he said in a soft voice that was completely out of place with his huge frame and cruel mouth. "That's a nice touch." He picked up the cross and turned it carefully between his large stubby fingers that looked sticky. "But I don't think we'll keep this trinket" and so saying he gave the cross a savage tug. The crude chain dug deeply into the back of my neck before it split. Mungutu threw the cross onto the ground where it fell amongst the red ashes of the church, glinting softly among the glowing coals.

"Yes, I'll enjoy this one, but we have some business to attend to first." He was turning towards the line of prisoners when a thought struck him and he turned back. "Get those off," he said pointing to my baggy pants, the draw string of which was now exposed through the open robe, "and get him ready. I won't be long." He gave me a long peering look as he ran his tongue over his already wet lips. It looked enormous, that tongue, much too big even for that huge face – amid all the horror, I found myself wondering how all that flabby flesh could fit inside the quivering mouth.

Mungutu's men had arranged the line of prisoners roughly according to age. Of those who had not managed to escape there were six elders, and a dozen or so young men aged between twelve and eighteen.

The commander spent a few moments with the men guarding the prisoners, pointing at the elders and laughing with his troops whose eyes followed his every movement with devotion. He then stood back and indicated to his henchmen to proceed with his instructions.

Any attempts to pray evaporated as I watched in horror as first Amanzi, then Josiah, Zengali, Moses, Zongarto and Christopher had their manhoods sliced away and the severed pieces pushed into their mouths. As their bodies slumped into the dust, blood gushing from the open wounds between their legs, their moans turned to splutters. Pathetic choking and gurgling sounds joined the chaos of burning timbers and the screaming of women and children.

The young men were sobbing and pleading with their captors. They each in turn went down to their knees, eyes wide with terror, babbling devotion to their new masters, if they were to be given that option.

Mungutu stood above them, a look of satisfaction on his round, shiny face. He spoke to them in their own language; turning his back on the dying men he had just watched being mutilated while their lifeblood oozed its way through the sand to form a grotesque puddle close to where I, their vicar, was being held.

I could not hear what was being said, but from the gestures of Mungutu and the frenzied nodding of the heads of the youngsters, I knew these gentle people were being recruited for a life of violence and horror. They were children no longer, and would be turned into the sort of men who were holding me so tightly.

Flies buzzed around the spreading pool of blood. The heat from the smoldering church caused it to bubble slightly at the edge. I could feel the stench of death in my nostrils and felt the bile pushing into my throat once more, my guts rumbling with revolt.

Mungutu's men, upon a sign from their leader, cut the ropes that held the young men's hands behind them, and with a gentleness that was excruciating to watch, they pulled the young men to their feet, patted them on the shoulders and led them away from the scene of gore.

Mungutu turned slowly, a big grin on his face. Once again, that massive tongue slid slowly over his lips. A dribble of saliva found its way into the creases around the plump chin and fell onto his chest as he approached his prey.

"Right lads, I'm ready for this pretty morsel now. Let's have that robe off and see what the gift looks like out of its wrapping."

The men pulled my robe over my head and pulled my pants away from my ankles where they had fallen. They dropped my cassock on top of them, next to the glowing ashes of what had once been my church.

As the captors held my arms away from my sides, pulling in opposite directions, two other men appeared, doing up their flies as they approached. They grinned and laughed along with their comrades as they looked at my pale white body stretched upright in front of them.

Mungutu looked at his victim and very slowly raised a grimy hand towards me. He began stroking me, murmuring something soft and unintelligible at the same time. He caressed my face, slowly moving his stubby fingers around the eyes, down the nose, tracing the contour of my lips. He took my chin in his hand and wrenched my head up to look him in the eye. He smiled. It seemed the embodiment of evil that smile. My mouth was dry, I had no breath, I was dizzy with fear and disgust as my tormentor's hands slid carefully down my neck and onto my chest where the blunt fingers found my nipples and twisted them with sudden savagery. I made no sound, my jaw clenched rigid with the effort not to scream, but I couldn't stop the tears as Mungutu's hands went lower.

"Well, what a nice little collection we have here," Mungutu crooned as he cupped my scrotum in one hand and stroked the accompanying member with the other. "A little lifeless just at the moment, but we'll work on that another day. No point in rushing things, we have plenty of time ahead of us, my lovely, plenty of time, and I can teach you many excitements you will never have dreamed of.

"Look what I have to offer you," the big man said, undoing his flies and letting out the bulging manhood which had been pressing hard against his zip. "This," he said, looking down with pride and affection at his erection which pointed straight up, as if in a salute, "is known by my troops as "Mungutu's Monster." He gave a guffaw of delight. "And today, it is your good fortune to experience the power and the glory it can deliver.

"Ok lads," Mungutu gestured to the four men. "Let's have him."

I was turned round roughly by the men so that my back was towards Mungutu and his throbbing pride. One of them doubled over in front of me in a much-practiced move, his hands on his knees for support. The other two pushed my upper body down onto their comrade's bent back passing my arms forward to the fourth man who took my hands and pulled steadily. The original two captors each had a hand on one of my shoulders while the fingers of their other hands slid down to my buttocks and pulled them apart.

I felt the bile rising again, and knew this time I would not be able to stop it. My guts churned with spasms of fear and horror. I could feel the hot tip of Mungutu's monster pressing against my rear as his torturers pulled at me, chuckling with glee.

"Here we go lads," Mungutu's voice was rich with anticipation, as he nuzzled against me with increasing pressure.

All at once I felt the vomit spurt from my mouth and at the same time liquid feces squirted out, covering the priapic member and shooting into Mungutu's open trousers.

There was a shout from the man underneath as yellow puke curled round his neck, oozing towards his bent face, and a scream from Mungutu who sprang back as if stung.

With a string of oaths Mungutu looked at his besmirched pride. His fury needed an immediate outlet, his eyes were sweeping around in anger until they must have noticed the tin cross glowing amongst the ashes.

For a big man, Mungutu could move very quickly. He picked up my abandoned cassock and wound it around his hand so that he could pick up the cross without burning himself. It sizzled against the rough cloth, and then he pressed it with all his anger against the part of me he had just tried to enter.

I had no idea what had happened. I was struggling to keep my balance as the man I had been leaning on ducked from under me as vomit slid around his neck. As the searing pain of the red-hot cross pierced through me, the man in front let go of my hands, and I fell full length into the dust, the smell of burning flesh all around.

Not satisfied with what he had done, Mungutu rearranged the protective cassock and carefully picked the cross from between my seared buttocks. Skin came away with it as Mungutu admired his handy work. Then with a new wave of savagery, he carefully turned the trophy and pushed the long end of the cross as deep into me as it would go.

Now there was blood gushing everywhere, there was pain radiating through me to an extent that I didn't notice the kicks as my torturers let loose around me with their grimy boots. Blackness finally descended, and I felt no more.

When consciousness returned, the sun was low in the sky – a yellow blur amongst the smoke and ash of what had been Cachonga.   Feeling returned slowly to my limbs and with it so many pains that I wanted to be sick again, but there was nothing left for me to spit but blood.

The burning sensation that filled my torso was such that a desire to put myself into water overcame all other feelings. The River! If I could just get myself to the river, perhaps the burning would be quenched – and if the crocodiles got me, it would be a welcome release.

I had fallen onto my arms, and my body had protected them from the vicious kicks that had pummeled everywhere else. I managed to get them out in front of me and started to pull myself along through the blood-soaked sand. It was very slow going, one of my legs was broken, just above the knee from what I could make out, maybe below the knee as well, but the pains were everywhere so it was hard to tell. Stabs of pains from my chest let me know that various ribs were in pieces, but nothing mattered as long as I could get to the cool water.

I did not look towards the mangled bodies of the elders.   I kept my eyes on the inch of sand under my nose. The path to the river was just around the corner and I concentrated all my efforts on this pathetic progress.

After just a few yards, I had to rest, breath coming in awkward gasps, each one sending new pains darting in all directions. As I lay there panting, I caught sight of something green. I raised my pounding head to look. Without glasses it was hard to identify this incongruous piece of color, and I crawled forward until it came into focus.

The green turned out to be a couple of banana palm leaves with teeth marks punched into the fleshy fibers.

But there are no banana palms in Cachonga, my brain was puzzling – and then in a rush I remembered the gruesome description of what the men were planning for Loveness. Once again the mental hurt overwhelmed me. How could I ever forget the promises I had made to that girl: that God would take care of her, and everything would be alright – just as it had been for the elders? Just as it had been for me?

But now was not a time for thinking. I resumed my crawl. It must have taken over an hour to drag myself inch by inch along the path that usually took just a couple of minutes to traverse. I had done this trip so often, but this time there were no children running ahead of me, their snake-sticks at the ready. What had happened to all those bright smiles, the laughter that used to guide me along the path to the river? All was silence now, except for the incessant buzzing of the flies that swarmed around me, and the flapping of a large-winged bird hovering menacingly overhead.

It was the crocodiles' eyes that I saw first. Even without my glasses I could make out small globes of yellow catching the last rays of the sun. They seemed to be floating upon the water, just the eyes on their own. I could count six pairs reflecting the flickering embers behind me. With luck, I thought they might all be adults. I was relieved – at least with so many, death should be quick. I continued edging my way towards the bank.

Suddenly the sound of shouting and the smack of paddles hitting the water surface disturbed the dusk of evening. I was pulling myself onto the lip of the bank, where the sand met the rocks that boarded the river.

"No, no, don't send them away . ." I tried to call out but the words wouldn't come and the extra gasping made my head reel. Someone was sending the crocodiles away, someone was interfering in my hard fought exit route from pain.

I didn't see the big canoe as it nudged against the pier, but I heard the gasps of the men who ran towards me and the confused gibbering of their speech laced with the sing-song accents of the tribes who lived downstream. I heard the crackle of a two-way radio and one of the men spoke loudly in English:

"Yes, we've found the vicar. He's still alive, but in very bad shape. He has been badly burned and looks as if he has several broken bones.

"Yes, yes, we will do what we can, but please send for help, he needs serious medical attention. We will bring him in, we should be with you around dawn.

"No, there's no sign of anyone else alive, and the village has been totally destroyed. I'll leave a burial team to wait for the police." The radio crackled once more and was silent. The men reverted to their native tongue.

Strong arms reached down and tried to lift me, but my involuntary cries stopped them, and the discussion started afresh. I didn't care. "Why don't they just leave me here to die," I thought. I didn't want to live with this pain – and it wasn't just the physical torture from which I wished to rid myself. Death was not just attractive, it was necessary – my body needed to follow the mental and spiritual deaths I had already undergone.

Someone arrived with two long poles, and in spite of my groans they managed to get them underneath me and with much care, they carried their burden and placed me carefully in the bottom of a shallow boat. One of the men laid some cloths over me with care and gentleness, then they pushed off into the dark river and started paddling back the way they had come.

54. SPECIALIST SURGEON MR. UMVARI

I remember little of the days that followed. The trolley I had been placed on when removed from the boat had became my permanent bed and was wheeled from one room to the next as various attempts were made to clean my bloodied legs and attend to the many cuts and bruises of my torso.

X-rays were taken of my chest and pelvis, complete with the embedded cross. My broken leg was set between splints, a drip was set up to administer morphine and various liquids to keep me hydrated. Nurses were careful to explain to me what was happening and why but my mind drifted in confusion between ministries at St. George's and Cachomba.

Mr. Umvari, a specialist surgeon from the country's largest hospital in the capital, arrived the day after I was admitted.

"I told the staff here not to touch any aspect of this brutalism," the doctor told his patient, his crisp English accent belying his large African frame and round black face. "And I was right to do so. They were eager to try to help you, but from their description of the injury I felt sure that the cross would have to be removed surgically to avoid any further damage, and, now that I am here and can see you and the x-rays for myself, I am satisfied I gave the correct instructions.

"I have arranged for an anesthetist to be here first thing tomorrow. I will come and see you before you go into theatre to explain what has to be done. Until then, I'm leaving you in safe hands."

Mr. Umvari was back again the next morning, his dark western suit replaced by a surgical gown that reminded me of the surplice I had worn in Islington.

As promised, the doctor had come to explain what the operation he was going to perform was all about. I was listening with detachment to the kind tones of reassurance with which Mr. Umvari rendered his speech. My obligatory position on my stomach meant that the man's gesturing hands moved only in the periphery of my vision. They were large and soft, the pale flesh of the palms at odds with the steely black of the knuckles.

"The cross needs removing with great care," Mr. Umvari began, "in order to minimize the damage to healthy tissues and remove those that have been burned and can no longer function.

"There are important muscles called 'levato ani' which support the rectum. These will have been damaged, or even destroyed, but, if given the right treatment, they should repair themselves.

"The entire musculature of the anal canal will need time to heal and rebuild; the perforations in the sigmoid and descending parts of the colon will need sutures; any damaged parts will have to be removed and the healthy pieces re-connected. This procedure is more straightforward than it sounds – it is what we do when removing pieces of colon that have been affected by cancer. There is plenty of spare colon in the body and it can continue to work properly even if several inches have been taken away.

"I know you won't understand all this, Jack, but I need you to try. It will help if you are mentally prepared for what is going to happen to you."

Mr. Umvari paused, waiting for some sort of response, but when none was forthcoming he continued speaking in his soft, clipped voice.

"I won't know the extent of the damage until the cross is removed, but I do know that the only chance we have for all this to heal properly is for me to fit you with a colostomy bag.

"If all goes well, this will only be a temporary state of affairs," the surgeon went on quickly. "By creating a diversionary colostomy we exteriorize the bowel and stop the fecal stream from being able to contaminate both the injured internal tissues and the external burns between your buttocks. It will allow me to seal off the rectum making something which is known as a Hartmann's pouch."

Mr. Umvari walked towards the window and looked at the swaying branches of the jacaranda trees. He turned back and approached my trolley once again to resume his speech.

"My plan is to do what is called a double-barrel colostomy in the ascending colon, as this is the easiest kind to reverse. It will take a bit of getting used to, but if you're lucky, we'll have everything back to normal in three or four months time, maybe less. You will need at least that time for the exterior burns to heal anyway and your broken thigh and leg, of course, and your ribs.

"You have a lot of healing to do, Jack, but heal you will, and there's no reason why you shouldn't lead a perfectly normal life again. In that respect you are a great deal more fortunate than most of the other patients in this hospital."

But Mr. Umvari did not know about the great black hole in my soul where my faith, my God, my life's structure had been for all my life, until now. When it was time for the operation, and the anesthetic took hold, I could feel myself falling into that hole, falling slowly at first and then faster and faster until all around me was impenetrable blackness.

When I came round, I found myself facing forwards for the first time in what seemed to be forever. I tried to bring my eyes into focus and then remembered that I had lost my glasses. I was propped up in the bed so I could see around me. I looked down at my hands, brown and calloused from work on the farm; they were lying limply at my sides. A catheter taped onto the back of my left hand was being fed by a tube rising to a bag suspended on a metal frame beside the bed. Then I looked carefully at my right hand; there was something in it, something small and white with fingers of its own; fingers that were curled around mine.

Sister Mary felt the movement and turned quickly from the book she had been reading. Grasping her patient's hand a little tighter, she rose from her chair and moved so that she was within my vision.

"Welcome back, Jack," she spoke with an expression of joy in her voice. "I knew you wouldn't let us down.

"The operation has been a success," Sister Mary lifted my hand and clasped it with both of hers. "Mr. Umvari has had to fit a colostomy bag, as he told you he would, but he says that it is only temporary, to allow things to heal as they should.

"Don't panic," she added quickly as I felt my eyes widen and my face go paler as I began to remember all that had happened. It's a fairly routine procedure," the Sister continued, "and although it takes a bit of getting used to, it is by far the safest way to stop infections.

"You have had the very best treatment, it has been a privilege to work with Mr. Umvari, and I am totally confident that all will be well. It will just take time," Sister Mary paused, "quite a long time, I'm afraid."

I mumbled something. My tongue was heavy, my throat dry, my thoughts scrambling for some sort of understanding of what Sister Mary was saying.

"Now, very important, Jack," she continued, looking steadily into my eyes. "Can you hear me?" I nodded slowly. "And can you understand what I am saying?"

I nodded again. I felt that I could understand the words, but not necessarily their meaning. However, I managed to give Sister Mary's hand a squeeze.

"Splendid," she responded with a smile. "Now we don't want you moving around and upsetting the skin grafts and stitches, and we don't want you hurting either. So the anesthetist has fixed you up with an epidural – it's an anesthetic administered into your spinal cord by a needle, and this drip here feeds into that needle." She pointed to a bag and tube on the other side of the bed from the one leading into my hand. "The result is that you cannot feel anything below your waist at the moment. You are not paralyzed, do you understand me Jack?

"It's very important that you understand and are not frightened by this wonderfully merciful drug. It is used a lot during childbirth, and for operations like the one you have just undergone.

"You have to keep as still as you can because you have broken ribs that need to mend, and one had punctured a lung just a little, but no permanent damage has been done, and all should heal well, eventually. However, I'm afraid you are going to be very sore for quite a long time.

"Now, if you feel strong enough, Jack, Mr. Umvari is waiting to see you." Sister Mary lowered my hand back onto the bed with a gentle motion, our fingers still entwined. "He has to go back to the capital as soon as possible, but I know he wants to talk to you before he goes. Shall I go and find him?"

I was bewildered by what I had heard. My head ached when I moved my eyes, I felt waves of unhappiness and nausea washing around me threatening to either drown or suffocate me. I watched, as if from a great distance, as sister Mary carefully removed her fingers from my hand.

"Can I go and fetch him?" she repeated, her bird-like head tilted slightly to one side as she looked steadily into her patient's eyes.

"Yes," I was surprised to hear myself speak. With effort, I returned the Sister's gaze. "Will you come back?" I asked, an involuntary tremor of anxiety in my voice.

"Of course, Jack," Sister Mary leant towards me and kissed me lightly on the forehead. "We are family now, you and I. We will be together for quite some time, and I am looking forward to getting to know you properly. I won't be long, just try not to worry." She left the room quickly, shutting the door quietly behind her.

Alone in the silence, I struggled against the clouds of anguish that came crowding in on all sides. I could hear Loveness pleading with me for help, heard my own voice giving her calm promises of reassurance. I heard her desperate screams, and that long painful wail that had torn my heart to shreds and shattered the faith I had relied upon for so long. Would I ever stop hearing that sound? I closed my eyes; behind the eyelids, as if on a movie screen, came the scenes of the elders as they dropped one by one in their pools of blood, gurgling and choking on their hideous gags. I opened my eyes again in a rush of panic. There was a strange sound in the room, a banshee howl that seemed to rush around the ceiling, making the curtains flutter and the pendant light sway. It was an unearthly sound that struck me with a new fear until I traced its source and, closing my mouth, stopped it.

Maybe I lapsed into unconsciousness, or perhaps I slept a bit, for the next thing I knew Mr. Umvari was standing at the bedside looking down at his patient with professional pride.

"Well, I'm very pleased with you, Jack," the surgeon began. "It will take a while for you to adjust to this situation, and I know the incision looks very raw, but, believe me, you will get used to it. I have briefed Sister

Mary and she is very competent. She will make sure nothing goes wrong in these crucial early days when infection must be kept at bay and the movement of the colostomy tube minimized.

"I'm afraid it will be several days before you will be allowed to leave your bed, but at least you're sitting up now and no longer looking at the floor. We can't keep the epidural going forever, but you are sitting in a rubber ring that should help the pain and I've left plenty of pills to keep you as comfortable as possible. You're lucky to have those, they are in short supply in this part of the world, but I am under orders from your headquarters to make sure you get the best treatment available.

"If all goes well, I'll be seeing you again in a few months, maybe sooner, to put everything back as it was. It just depends upon how quickly the skin grafts take and everything else heals up."

The surgeon walked slowly around the bed, his eyes never leaving mine. "How are you feeling?" he questioned.

I couldn't trust myself to speak. I was afraid if I opened my mouth another great howl of anguish and despair would rush into the outside world.

"Don't try to speak," Mr. Umvari broke the silence with the unnecessary instruction. "Try and have faith, Jack. As I said to you before, you will get better and there are others in far worse circumstances than yours, and without the drugs that you have.

"It is time to start rebuilding. I know you have many to mourn," he hesitated, he must have seen my eyes mist, "but there is still much good for you to do in this world.

"I have been hearing a lot about you, Jack, since I've been here," Mr. Umvari continued, trying to ignore my fraught stare. "It seems you made a real success of binding a disparate set of people into a genuine community. You are much admired in the vicinity, a hero in fact. You should be proud of what you have achieved."

I looked at the surgeon in disbelief. I could feel the tears running unheeded into my beard. I raised a hand in a gesture of futility.

"Well, anyway, I'll keep in touch with the hospital and Sister Mary will let me know how you are getting on." The surgeon looked at his watch. "If there are any problems, I'll find time to come back and sort them out, but I'm pretty sure everything will be perfect on the physical side." He leaned down and took my limp hand from the bed.

Suddenly I was afraid to let this man go. I caught hold of the surgeon's fingers and felt the strength return to my muscles as I squeezed a response to Mr. Umvari's handshake.

"There, that's better," the surgeon said, smiling. "Look after yourself and you'll mend quickly. You're young and strong and very fit. You'll be fine."

Mr. Umvari disentangled his hand. He stood up and gave me a long straight look. "I will be back before you know it, but right now I have people in worse states than yours waiting for me in the capital." He turned and walked out into the hospital corridor without looking back.

55. PUTTING THINGS INTO PERSPECTIVE

I have already filed an account of my introduction to The Day Room and my first encounter with fellow patients Percival and Amrita. At my request they had told me their dreadful stories, and now it was my turn to tell them mine.

I remember well my reluctance to do so, but their expectant faces gave me no choice. I took a deep breath and began my tale. I described briefly my beloved Cachonga and the change that had happened there during the eight years since my arrival. How Mungutu's gang had destroyed it all, committing atrocities along the way – "you know the sort of things they do," I said glancing at Amrita briefly, aware that I was mimicking her words.

"And then Mungutu did this to me," I spread my fingers, lifting my hands to indicate the present predicament.

"What exactly is 'this'?" asked Percival, after a pause had lasted long enough to indicate that I had no intention of continuing.

I looked at him and thought angrily 'how could this man be so insensitive as to press for details?' Then I looked at Percival's bandaged arm where his hand should have been. My eyes moved involuntarily down to his plaster-cast legs sticking straight out in front of him on the wheelchair's extension. I remembered Mr. Umvari's words about how I should be able to lead a normal life again one day, 'unlike many others in this hospital' and I acknowledged, deep within myself, that this man had a right to ask such questions.

I delivered an involuntary sigh and answered Percival. "He took the cross that he had torn from my neck and thrown into the smoldering embers of my church, and branded me with it across my buttocks. Then he shoved it up my rectum" I stated in a voice as empty of emotion as I could muster.

Amrita was staring out of the window, her eye-brows drawn slightly together as she watched a weaver bird stripping fibers from a yucca tree. She said nothing, but her eyes were moist.

Suddenly Percival produced the most unexpected sound. He laughed. A deep, rumbling belly laugh.

"Well, my friend," he gasped, "now I understand why everybody whispers about your injuries: so much more distasteful than a severed hand or a broken back."

I winced with the horrid truth of this statement and felt again a wave of guilt for the insignificant nature of my complaints compared with the suffering of my companions.

"At least you fared better than King Edward II," Percival was still grinning. "Remember? Popular belief is that, because of his homosexuality, the poor bastard was put to death in 1327 by having a red hot poker thrust up his arse. No St. Mary's hospital for him."

I looked at Percival in astonishment. Then suddenly I was laughing too. My broken ribs protested and I had to hug my sides gingerly to reduce the pain. There was a huge rush of relief - as if the vocalizing of my trauma had allowed me to let it go in some strange way. By spitting out the story, I had externalized the anguish, or at least some of it. It had been a cathartic experience and I felt a shift in my perception of existence. I realized with sudden clarity that I had allowed my own devastation of mind and body to become the predominating experience of all that was going on around me – but it wasn't. My personal vision was changing. And now, with these writings, I hope, it will change again.

This was the first of many exchanges of stories that passed between us over the next few months. One phrase of Percival's first story kept niggling at me. In his explanation of what had happened to him, Percival had said that he had put himself "in the firing-line of life." It took a couple of days before I found the courage to ask Percival what he had meant by such a strange statement.

"Yes, it was a silly thing to say, really," Percival answered. "We all have our histories, but I confess to be interested in yours, Jack. So, if you tell me what brought you to Africa, I will reciprocate. Is that a fair trade?"

I nodded assent without enthusiasm. I was staring out into the garden, down towards the blur that was the river. I was becoming used to the indistinct world in which I was living without my glasses, the lack of clear lines in my vision seemed appropriate to this new life.

"Ready when you are," Percival interrupted my meandering thoughts.

"I'm not sure where to begin," I said with a sigh.

"How about at the beginning," Amrita urged gently. "You know we have plenty of time, after all none of us are going anywhere in a hurry."

I was not used to talking about myself and needed repeated promptings to unravel the psychological journey that had brought me to Cachonga.

By lunchtime, arrested by many questions from both Percival and Amrita, my tale had only got as far as St. George's and my introduction to Father Justin. I had never talked so much in my life, but the enquiries that came from my two new friends made me think carefully about what I had done in my life – perhaps for the first time.

After lunch I began telling my audience about the parishioners I had inherited with the appointment to Islington. I omitted Rosie altogether, I just couldn't bear re-living all that, but I enjoyed talking about Estelle and how we had dowsed for power lines both inside and outside the church.

I told of the splendid Dilly and the fawning Philip. We laughed together as I related Sam's worries about masturbation and of Mr. Stanhope's attempts to buy salvation with bottles of claret.

It was while talking of Sally and her imaginary friend, Peter, that I suddenly stopped. I had been recounting my advice to Sally's mother, Charlotte, about how belief in this fictitious person wasn't doing Sally any harm, that the imagined presence provided company, comfort and support to the child. I had assured Charlotte that her daughter would inevitably grow out of this pretense sooner or later. Why not go along with the idea for the moment and let it run its course.

I have already recorded how the similarity between Sally's friend Peter and my former friend called God suddenly asserted itself, making me feel sick and pathetic. But I am stronger than that now and, in time, am confident that I will be able to view all of this as part of an interesting, and well-intentioned, learning curve.

It was not until the next day that I was able to remind Percival of our trading agreement.

"Well, you didn't actually get to the end of your tale, Jack, but we can come back to that. You gave a good innings, so I suppose it is my turn."

Over the next couple of hours, Percival told his story. He had grown up in Sussex, been educated at Charterhouse and Cambridge and trained to be a teacher of literature. He married at twenty-six and he and Sylvia were expecting their first child when they stopped at an off-license in Hampstead to buy some wine on their way to a dinner party.

Three youths entered the shop while the couple were choosing a suitable bottle; one of them had a gun. They ordered the man behind the till to give them all his cash. The shopkeeper must have had an alarm button by the register, for even while he was fumbling to pull the notes out of the machine, a siren could be heard approaching from a few streets away.

The boys panicked, grabbed the money and fired the gun indiscriminately around the shop as they ran. The shop-keeper had ducked behind the counter and Percival fell to his knees pulling Sylvia with him, but a stray bullet found her swollen belly. In spite of the efforts of the paramedics who were called to the scene, Sylvia died as the ambulance was approaching the hospital.

Percival confessed that he had become obsessed with the idea that it should have been him who had taken the bullet and not Sylvia and their unborn child. He abandoned his teaching career and, impressed with the paramedics who had tried so hard to save his wife, he trained to become one. With such qualifications he sought the world's trouble spots, putting himself in the firing line while trying to help others. He had spent time in Palestine, Bosnia, the Congo and Rwanda before coming here, to Arumba.

"Like you, Jack, I've enjoyed Amrita's underground lake analogy, but for me also there is no lake. No spirit water could hydrate this dried-up soul of mine. For me there is only the dust of decay, the grit and sand of a death that continues to elude me.

"I think I finally threw away the last vestige of hope in the existence of any positive force when myself and two fellow paramedics were called to a school following an incident of 'ethnic cleansing' in which one group had massacred another - as happens so frequently on this dark continent of sorrow.

"What we found in that school will haunt me forever. A pile of young bodies heaped without dignity in the school gym. Grotesquely twisted limbs, staring eyes in fly-blown faces, hands cupped in pleading gestures. And worst of all – the reason for our having been called – the bizarre hope of a life still breathing as a little girl's abdomen could be seen moving at the bottom of the heap of corpses.

"As the three of us grappled with the bloated bodies, scrabbling to unearth this tender hope of life, the smell of rot, decay and putrid death seemed to fill our minds as well as our throats with bile so that our brains seemed to gag. When we reached the pathetic body, the moving belly burst open – it was the seething of maggots within that had caused the movement. The life here was not of human form."

We sat in silence for a while. A grey heron landed on the lawn with outstretched wings, folding them neatly as his feet met the grass. The large bird swiveled its head slowly before striding purposefully towards the river. A cormorant who had been drying its wings on the pier, took to the sky.

"No wonder I'm an atheist," Percival continued after a while. "If there was a God who loves us, why does he allow so much suffering in the world? There is an argument that says if our lives were hunky-dory-ticketti-boo, we would not need to look for a God. Few people turn to religion with fervor when everything is going smoothly for them. The God of the Bible, and his Son, are always making the point that they are championing the cause of the poor and the oppressed. Is that because the affluent and powerful aren't that interested in promises of better things to come?

"Maybe you're one of the exceptions, Jack," Percival added watching as my eyebrows arched.

"Maybe I was," I corrected him slowly. "In fact I most definitely was. I realize now that I had an almost entirely trouble-free childhood, although it didn't seem that way at the time. And yet, the church was always more of a home for me than the house in which I lived with my parents and siblings. I can't explain it, and now I can't begin to understand such unquestioning faith. What fools we can be."

"Innocent fools, Jack. You should not chastise yourself about your earlier beliefs." Percival responded.

"I believe your heart has always been a kind and giving one, Jack," Amrita added, "and I think it still is. I agree with Percival, you should not be so hard on yourself."

Suddenly I began to cry. The tears were totally unexpected; they just appeared without warning, running down my cheeks, into my beard. Sobs, deep and painful, erupted from my diaphragm, making my damaged rib-cage throb with pain, surging up through my throat. The emotional pain was even worse than the physical. Anger consumed me completely, and then it was pain, then anger again before the pain took over once more.

Percival and Amrita remained silent, looking steadfastly though the window at the view of the garden sloping down to the river that glinted sullenly in the morning light.

When the explosion finally abated, I was left with an immense sadness, the deep, unfathomable sadness of loss that produces nothing but emptiness. My hands were making involuntary grabbing motions as if they were trying to catch a falling object. My whole body ached with loss, the emptiness clutched at my lungs so that I gasped for breath. My vision was gone, just blank whiteness stared back at me. There was nothing.

As the minutes ticked by and I became aware of my physical self once again, with all the pain it contained, objects began to manifest in my vision, and I could hear a soft voice chattering, with the nonchalance of a church coffee morning.

"In my philosophy," Amrita was saying, "there is no room to struggle with the impossible concept of an omnipotent and omniscient deity being entirely benevolent. There is a force of existence, call it what you will, which has caused us to be here, in the 'now'. We must appreciate this 'here and now' for what it has to offer.

"Look at the three of us; all damaged; all fighting fear, pain, and immense losses of one kind or another. What have we to look forward to without the passion and energies of our earlier years? The easy path is to sink into despondency, always looking for what might have been, but we cannot allow ourselves to be so tempted.

"I think that if there is a devil, his most powerful weapon is despair, for it is from despair that all sorts of negative possibilities present themselves with alacrity and credibility. We must not allow despair any space in our lives. Right now, we each have our challenge. Despair is easier to keep out than to remove once its tentacles have coiled around our psyches. We must not let it in. The physical challenges that face all of us are nothing compared to this mental battle that each of us must wage every minute of every day.

"The world cannot give us back that which it has taken away, but it can give us new experiences, within the parameters that now threaten to restrict us. We must fight those restrictions, banish them with determination and courage, win against the odds. We have spirit, we have soul; we are part of the amazing energy field that spins us all around in this extraordinary universe of activity. We must find ways to expand our horizons mentally even if we are limited in what we can do physically.

"Our only hope is to accept the wonders of 'now' and to filter the positive elements from the darkness, so that we can live in the light and follow the light. The Tao of Now, if you like."

There was a pause and then Percival spoke: "the 'mynah birds in Huxley's book 'Island' were always chanting 'here and now, boys, here and now.' Living in the moment, for the moment, was one of his central themes."

"Percival has been teaching me about the wonders of literature," Amrita's voice was brisk and positive. "Not just English literature, but the great writings from Russia, Germany, France and my own country, America. He is working on a reading list for me. I concentrated so much on medicine during my school and university years that I missed out on the magic of fiction. He has given me a new path of interest and excitement for which I am very grateful."

"You had better give me that list too, please, Percival." I interjected, grateful to Amrita for pulling our thoughts away from Percival's tragic description of despair, and my own unexpected outburst of mourning. "I don't think I have opened a novel since exams at school when I was sixteen."

"I'm sure we have a lot of tales we can share between us," Percival said in a flat voice that told of his struggle to leave his memories. "There are no books in this hospital and no games either, so we will have to make our own" he continued with a deep sigh. "If neither of you is familiar with the great world of literature, then I will be able to poach ideas from all over the place, I will have an advantage. Having been a teacher of the subject, I've indulged in most of the great writings at one time or another."

56. TALL TALES TO TELL AND BE TOLD

So it was that our stories took on a less personal nature and I was relieved not to be required to describe the circumstances that caused me to leave Islington. I apologized for having read very little fiction and therefore having few stories to contribute.

"Nonsense," was Percival's reply. "A man of your profession must be well acquainted with the Bible at least, and there's plenty of fiction in there for you to relate to us. All that begetting and so on, plus plenty of fire and brimstone. How about the story of Noah for example? There's one full of imagination and drama. Or the Garden of Eden? What about the cruel command for Isaac's sacrifice? Or God's fast-forwarding the Earth's creation into seven days – that's a good yarn, Jack. Take your pick.

"Amrita, here," Percival continued, his voice beginning to thaw as he warmed to his theme, "she tells stories from the Bhagavad Gitā and the Rig Veda and presents wonderful poetry from The Upanishads. She will tell you stories of Hanuman, the mischievous monkey god, and of the Lord Ganesha with his elephant head sitting harmoniously upon a man's body. Sensual stories of the Lord Krishna and frightening tales of Kali the Goddess of Death."

So that is how the tradition arose between the three of us. We would tell each other tales every day and then discuss the implications of the stories. As he had intimated, Percival had a great advantage over Amrita and myself and his enthusiasm for the adventures he related and the information he gave of the authors caught us in a web of enthrallment.

Through Percival's eyes Amrita and I were introduced to Tolstoy, Dostoevsky, Stendhal, Victor Hugo, Hawthorne, Melville, Samuel Clemens, Faulkner, as well as so many of the great British and Irish writers and poets.

I did my best to keep up with my friends, and our days passed without much attention to our injuries. While our minds assimilated each others' views, our bodies were left to heal, but it was a slow process, and my nights were still full of screaming and the smell of burning flesh. The fate of the Cachonga parishioners haunted my drowsing and sleeping hours. Every morning it was a new challenge to adhere to the instructions of Sister Mary: to concentrate upon the improvements each day might bring rather than to be taken over by the emotional and physical agonies of the past.

Looking back on these seemingly endless days at St. Mary's, there are many stories that stay with me. Amrita's tale of the man seeking enlightenment is one of them. An old Buddhist analogy of how before the pilgrim set forth on his journey he looked around him at the trees and mountains, all clearly defined, sitting solidly upon the ground. Once he had set off on his quest and was pursuing his Nirvana, everything lost its defining lines and became muddled and confused – mimicking my life without glasses. At the end of the tale, when our hero reached a state of enlightenment, everything returned to how it had been before – trees were trees and mountains were mountains once again, as they had always been. The journey had brought him back where he had started; his newly enlightened soul realized he had not needed to travel, the great change had happened within.

I remembered also the day when Percival teased me into telling the tale of the crucifixion and the resurrection.

I did my best to remember all the crucial details of the story, telling of my visit to Oberammergau at the same time. When I had finished, Percival asked me for my views on the resurrection, such a vital - he chose the word carefully- part of the great Christian myth.

"Well, up to now, I suppose I just took it on faith," I said. "However, after what has happened to persuade me that. . ." I paused, and then continued with a different tone, one of flat bitterness: "like you, Percival, I now feel that if there is such a thing as an omniscient and all-powerful God who allows human beings to behave in unholy ways at the expense of innocent people - then I don't want to be offering Him obeisance." My voice had taken on a note of delinquency. "On the contrary, I turn my back on such a deity." There was a pause, before I spoke again in a quieter voice: "So I'm no longer sure what I think about the resurrection, or anything else, come to that."

"Well, I've got some ideas on the resurrection," said Percival, causing me to look at him with eyebrows raised. I was relieved to be off the soap-box and intrigued that such a confessed atheist should have views on this most religious of subjects.

"First let me say that I believe Jesus Christ to have been a good man." Percival spoke as if he was reading a prepared script. "A very good man, but I have grave difficulties with what institutionalized religions have done with his philosophy.

"Remember Dostoevsky's Grand Inquisitor chapter in The Brothers Karamazov? Oh no, I forgot – but don't worry, it will be on your lists, both of you, and quite near the top. You should spend special attention to Ivan Karamazov's story of Christ coming back to Earth in the middle of the Spanish Inquisition when religion was used so efficiently as an instrument of fear; as a raw and cruel weapon of control. Man's ability to subjugate his own kind - clothing greed for power in a mantle of myth - was never more forcibly demonstrated. Oh, and when you read it, be aware that it is Ivan who is telling the story and not Alyosha. That's important too.

"Anyway, I digress. Now, there's a theory that appeals to me as to how Jesus beat the death rap at Calvary, and it goes like this.   Remember Mary Magdalen offering Christ a sponge while he was on the cross?"

"Yes," I said, "it had water and vinegar in it and was lifted to his face on a spear, a gesture of compassion and love in the middle of anguish."

"Yes – something like that," agreed Percival. "Well, what if that sponge had more in it than water and vinegar? Could not the vinegar have been used to disguise something stronger – after all why else would you offer vinegar to a man already suffering enough?" Percival grimaced, and stuck out his tongue.

"What if the sponge was infused with some kind of opiate that Christ could suck out and which could put him into a deep coma, mimicking death? You know, the sort of drug that Shakespeare's Juliet took with such ill-fated results.

"Do you remember how Christ died well before either of the two thieves who were being crucified with him? How the Roman soldiers had to break the thieves' legs so that they could no longer support themselves and they died through suffocation as their ribcages sank into their lungs? Christ's legs were not broken as he was deemed to be dead already.

"Now, what happens next? Christ's body is taken down with great care and gentleness. It is removed to the sepulcher and anointed with oils – perhaps oils with some healing properties? Then he was wrapped in burial cloths – cloths that would work well as bandages for that gash in his side. He is then laid to rest, and rest is just what he would have needed to regain his strength when the drug wore off.

"Have you heard this theory before, either of you?" Percival asked his audience, we had both been listening attentively. "No," he answered for us, as we shook our heads, "well it's been around for a long time, but, for obvious reasons, it doesn't feature much in religious literature. The idea makes quite a lot of sense to me – but then you see, I don't really mind whether the resurrection is true or not. What does matter is that the concepts Christ brought into the world were genuine and good with or without the conquering of death bit."

"What about the Ascension?" I queried. "How is that explained in your version of events?"

"I'm not sure about that bit, Jack," admitted Percival. "Perhaps Christ had just had enough of all the controversy and decided to disappear from dangerous proselytizing and go back to his carpentry in disguise. Perhaps he really was carried away on a fluffy cloud – but I have to say that's a bit hard to swallow and I prefer to envisage him returning to a life of fitted kitchens! I saw a graffiti splashed across a wall in Kilburn once saying: 'cancel Easter, they've found the body.' I thought it rather amusing at the time."

The arrival of Shamiso with our supper caused the discussion to wither away. I tucked the ideas into my memory somewhere, for a later review, and turned my attention to the bowl of chicken curry that had been set before me - and now, here they are, again!

57. Unexpected Visitor and Gifts

"You're having a visitor today, father," Sister Mary announced one morning as she came to take away my breakfast tray. "So we need to make you more presentable. I've called in the local barber and you're having a hair-cut, and he'll trim that beard while he's at it."

"Who is coming to visit me?" I was perplexed. I couldn't imagine anyone who would be interested in visiting me.

"There's an envoy from the Bishop coming, a Father Merciful, you know him already, I believe" Sister Mary answered lightly, as she put the tray on a chest of drawers by the door and returned to the bedside. "So we will have you looking neat and tidy if you please, I'm not having him telling the Bishop that you are not being looked after properly."

I had learnt that there was no use trying to dissuade Sister Mary from anything to which she had set her mind. I submitted to the difficult and painful experience of having my hair washed and cut, using Amrita's trick of thinking of other things to remove my mind from the parts of the body which still caused me to wince, sweat and, occasionally, to cry out.

Percival and Amrita had become part of my life at St. Mary's, as had all the members of staff with their wonderful patience and gentleness, but was I really ready, I asked myself, to meet someone from outside? Someone who knew all that had been lost?

I knew I had no choice, so resigned myself to the meeting; but I was not looking forward to it. Father Merciful was due to arrive shortly after lunch and, with my resigned agreement, was to join the three of us in the day room. An extra chair was added to our semi-circle, the only one without wheels.

Amrita and Percival wanted to know all about the Canon Missioner and greatly enjoyed my description of the sudden baptism and service of Holy Communion that the envoy's visit had initiated. The story made me wonder what had happened to Umboto and Chief Mungonie and I could not stop a pang of bitterness at their desertion. However, at least those two rascals were still alive and free – unlike all those they had abandoned.

We were just finishing our lunch when we saw a boat moor at the hospital pier at the bottom of the garden. The three of us watched as the boatman sprang from his craft and gave a hand to a tall figure dressed in a dark suit, in spite of the hot sun. He wore a large panama with a black ribbon, the white of the hat and of his dog-collar framing the lean black face. He turned and spoke briefly to the boatman before climbing the steps to the neat lawn and the equally neat figure of Sister Mary who was waiting for him with an outstretched hand. The two chatted together as they walked towards the hospital and disappeared from view around the corner towards the main entrance. The boatman and his helper were busy dragging a large box up the lawn behind them.

Father Merciful was as ill at ease with our reunion as I was. He was obviously distressed at the sight that met him when he entered the day room and was introduced to Percival and Amrita.

He looked at me sadly. I realized that the vibrant vicar he had last seen bustling around his jungle parish, full of strength and vigor, coppered by his life outdoors, was now a thin, pale wraith of a man with haggard lines in his face and a haunted look in the once sparkling eyes.

I felt sorry for my visitor as I watched father Merciful trying to deal with the situation. I could see waves of pity flooding through the Bishop's envoy for the three injured souls with whom he was confronted.

Percival and I still had plastered legs sticking out in front of us. My good leg had dressings above the knee where skin had been taken for the grafts. Percival's arm was no longer bandaged, but the stump had an angry look from where the skin had been sewn together.

The three of us had become used to each other's physical hurts. Percival had adjusted to his stump eventually and only became aware of it now, when he saw the expression of father Merciful's face. He slid it under the light sheet that covered his lap.

"I'm afraid none of us can stand to make you welcome, Father Merciful," I said, trying to sound relaxed. "So it's best you join us by sitting down." I indicated the empty chair between Amrita and me. "It is good of you to come," I added. "Are we far from the capital? I'm afraid I have no idea where we are, apart from being 'down-stream.'"

"It's a two day journey," Father Merciful was grateful to find a topic of conversation not laced with painful thoughts. "I had business with villages along the way, so it was all very harmonious. I have brought you something, Father Jack." He handed me a small package.

I opened the parcel without a twinge of curiosity, my fingers working automatically. Inside was a pair of glasses in a smart leather case. I looked at them - a mild interest was stirring. Very slowly I raised them from my lap and put them on, gasping as the world sprang into focus. For the first time in over six weeks, I could see clearly. I turned to the visitor in astonishment. "How?" was all I could manage.

"Your parents had them made up from your last prescription. They arrived last week, hence my visit today. The Bishop arranged it all."

The thought of my parents made me hiccup with emotion and suddenly I wanted to cry like a little boy. I controlled myself, with an effort, as I gazed around me seeing sharp edges where I was used to smudges.

The day room needed painting, there were moss patches on the walls and peeling paint in one corner. The windows hadn't been cleaned for a long time, but the garden beyond was a real treat in its new-found clarity. The sun sparkled on the river that had previously been only a blur, every blade of grass seemed individually wonderful, the petals on the roses were so delicate, the fallen jacaranda blossoms made mauve patterns in the shade. It was a beautiful sight – I found I was smiling.

"Please thank the Bishop for me," I said quietly. "You have no idea what a difference it will make for me to see properly again. I am really very grateful."

Father Merciful beamed with delight for a moment, and then the serious expression returned. "We all feel so awful, Jack, so very, very sorry . . ." His voice trailed away, and he coughed nervously.

"Yes, well," I paused. I had no idea what to say, but I didn't want to hear Father Merciful speak either. "I'm not strong enough to talk about it" I continued, in a panic, "so, if you don't mind, we'll speak of other things. How is life in the Capital?"

Father Merciful took a large pale blue handkerchief from a trouser pocket and blew his nose. "Much the same as ever, Jack," his voice sounded relieved and grateful. "I have brought you all something else, if you'll excuse me for a second." He rose and left the room quickly. Percival, Amrita and I looked at each other, but said nothing.

The large box that had been pulled up the lawn by the boatmen was now dragged into the day room by Father Merciful, with Sister Mary pushing from behind. They pulled and pushed until it was in the centre of the room.

"I'm afraid we couldn't get everything on Sister Mary's list, but we've had a good try, and found a few other bits and pieces as well." Father Merciful opened the top of the box to reveal several stacks of carefully packed books. The three of us gasped with amazement and delight.

"I found the list you gave Amrita," Sister Mary said to Percival. "So I sent a copy to the Bishop and look what's happened," she indicated the large box.

"We raided the University library, and put an advertisement in the paper," Father Merciful said. "Most of these have been donated by the white community, and one of my Asian friends gave these," he said, picking up the top three books and handing them gently to Amrita who took them with shaking hands. Her eyes filled with tears as she looked at elaborate editions of the Bhagavad Gita, the Rig Veda and the Upanishads.

"Now I have a list for you, Percival," Amrita spoke in a quiet voice full of emotion. "Father Merciful, you are certainly living up to your name, you have no idea what a difference these books will make to the long dark evenings when we are in our rooms. We will no longer be alone."

"But you have never been alone," Father Merciful answered equally softly. "God has always been with you." He turned to me as he bent to the box once more. "This is from the Bishop himself, Father. He chose it especially for you, and has inscribed it. It's a great honor," he added as he handed me a large leather-bound bible with gold edged pages.

I took the bible obediently and nodded. I did not dare to speak for I risked shouting with anger instead of appreciation. I did not open it to see the inscription.

Father Merciful put a hand on my shoulder and I was relieved by my visitor's lack of understanding of the true situation. I put the bible down gently beside my chair.

"And for Percival," Father Merciful broke the silence which had suddenly become heavy. "Some wonderful old lady has sent you her entire collection of Dickens. She says she has nobody to leave the books to who would really appreciate them and sends them to you with her love." He produced a superb set of green leather-bound volumes and piled them onto a table next to Percival that Sister Mary had moved into position.

"Oh, and this is for you also," Father Merciful held up an enormous book. "The complete works of Shakespeare," he announced with excitement.

"Give that one to Jack," Percival said quickly. "My table is getting crowded."

I was grateful for Percival's understanding. It helped to have a book in my lap that wasn't the Bible. I opened it cautiously and began to turn the pages. I was pushing away the anger and bitterness that had rushed upon me, and I was winning slowly.

"We've been putting this collection together for some time," Father Merciful was chatting away unaware of the drama going on inside me, "but felt it would be unkind to send the books until Jack's glasses had arrived. As it happens, the wait was worthwhile, as quite a few of these volumes only came to us in the last few days.

"I'm afraid we failed on the Dostoevsky and Stendhal, but we did find a copy of Moby Dick, and there are all sorts of other books in here that we thought you might enjoy. I will leave you to go through them all after I've gone."

Father Merciful straightened and looked around at his audience. I was busy peering at an illustration from 'A Midsummer's Night Dream' of Bottom with the donkey head and trying to align it with Amrita's description of the Hindu God, Ganesha, with the head of an elephant.

Percival was stroking the Dickens' collection with his remaining hand. Amrita was turning the pages of The Upanishads with mesmerizing gentleness. Both of them had tears running down their cheeks. The silence in the day room was complete.

Father Merciful absorbed the emotions of the three of us and knew that his journey had not been in vain. He would be able to report back to the Bishop and to all the people who had donated these books that they had been well received and provided solace to stricken souls.

"I will leave you now," the benefactor said softly. "And I will pray for you all three every day, and so will the congregations of this country. God will see you whole again," Father Merciful hesitated as he glimpsed Percival's stump and the stillness of Amrita's legs. I could see he regretted his last sentence. "We must have faith," he continued with urgency, "we must, we must. We have no choice, there is no acceptable alternative." The Canon stopped in confusion.

"Thank you, father," I filled the space left in the air by father Merciful's sudden silence. "And please thank the Bishop and everybody else who has contributed to these amazing gifts. Please try to explain how much the books mean to us, and how much these glasses mean to me. I am very grateful. If you could get word to my parents also, that would be kind. I'm afraid I'm not ready to communicate with the outside world directly, you will have to be my envoy."

"And mine, also," Amrita whispered, "I'm afraid the surprise has caught me off-guard. I am really grateful."

"As am I," added Percival, in an uncharacteristically small voice. "If I ever get to walk again, I would like to come to visit the wonderful lady who has sent this collection. Could you arrange that for me, father?"

"Of course," father Merciful was moving towards the door. "I can think of nothing she would like more. I will make sure that you meet her.

"I will try to return in about six weeks, so if you think of anything else I might be able to bring to you, please tell Sister Mary and she will make sure I know about it. No promises, of course, but you must be confident that I will do everything I can."

The courtesies of goodbyes were exchanged, and Father Merciful left the day room. We watched his descent to the river, accompanied by Sister Mary who waved him away as the boatmen helped the visitor aboard and then pushed their craft out into the main body of the river. The motor started and the boat puttered off down-stream.

The Gifts of Books and Spectacles

58. THE JOYS AND SADNESS OF PROGRESS

S ister Mary put herself in charge of the books. She dispensed them like a school matron with sweets, making sure no-one had a bigger share than the others, or had too much at any one time. She only allowed her patients to have their apportionment in the bedrooms, so the routine of the day-room remained the same. As none of us were in charge of our own movements, there was no chance of smuggling volumes here or there.

Occasionally Sister Mary would bring a book into the day-room at the urgent request of one of her charges who wished to quote something particular to the others. She would then stand over the orator until the passage had been found and read out before gathering up the volume with due reverence and spiriting it away.

Every morning now, we had new ideas to share and explore. An enthusiasm had crept into our conversations, similar to that which had accompanied my introduction into the enclave. Our discussions covered every imaginable topic and ranged through the centuries and across the globe.

Even Percival sounded less cynical, and when it was time for his legs to come out of plaster and he had to spend an hour every morning and afternoon with either a physiotherapist or a trainer of some kind, he resented his time away from the day-room and wanted to know what he had missed.

For me, the gift of the prescription glasses had brought an extraordinary change to a life of blurred pain and confusion. Clarity had returned to my vision; were my thoughts clearing also? Did seeing things in perspective physically help me see more clearly in my mind? There was so much pain for the loss of a people I had grown to love, and who had loved me; for my life over the past eight years with everything I had built, for my on-going physical sufferings and, most of all, for the loss of my faith.

Up until a few months ago, I had enjoyed the certainty that there was something grand and wonderful to lean on throughout my life. Something I thought was as unquestionable as it was invincible. The discovery that such a support had failed when it was most needed had created a vacuum in my soul. The ghastly emptiness this revelation had created was slowly being covered by a hard scab grown from a matrix of horrors and hurts. This unbidden plug had promised to seal the traitor called faith into a psychic sepulcher forever.

Very slowly, however, during the months I spent with my fellow sufferers in the day-room, things had begun to shift again. The scar of the black hole where my soul used to be no longer seemed an impenetrable carapace. It had begun to change into a fallow plot where new ideas might be grown. Amrita was sowing the seeds and Percival was adding the fertilizer to this freshly-tilled ground. Something new was growing, quite alien to my former beliefs, but present in some form or other.

One day Amrita and I found an extra chair had been put out in the day-room where Percival's wheel-chair was always parked. As we waited for our friend to finish with his torturers – as he called the physiotherapists who put him through his ordeals – we discussed which visitor might be coming to occupy the chair – perhaps Father Merciful was coming back.

"I do hope he's found 'The Brothers Karamazov'" Amrita said. "Percival is always going on about how everybody should be made to read this book at least once every decade. Not because there is anything different in the book each time, of course, but because the reader will have changed and will find new lessons from the same text. Percival has not read it for fifteen years; he is overdue for his 'fix' and wants to know, now that he has altered, what new wonders Dostoevsky has in store for him."

I was about to reply when the nurse Nolisa came into the day-room. She stood to one side, holding the door open as Percival entered slowly. Sister Mary was supporting his right arm, and under the left was a crutch upon which he was leaning heavily. The look of concentration on Percival's face was almost comical, but the delight he must have seen on the faces of his two friends inspired him. Percival stopped for a minute, panting slightly. He looked at Amrita, then at me, and then at Amrita again, and, for just a moment, his face broke into a smile before the concentration returned. Very slowly, Percival and Sister Mary approached the chair and shuffled around until the patient was in the right place to sit down.

Nolisa left her post at the door and came to Percival's right side. Carefully she removed the crutch and replaced it with her shoulder, her arm encircling Percival's back. The two nurses lowered themselves slowly until their cargo was seated, then they stood back to admire their handiwork.

Amrita and I started clapping simultaneously. Both of us were awash with excitement and admiration. We all knew there was a long climb ahead of Percival, but he had started the journey, and the sense of achievement was shared, empathetically, by his friends.

Amrita and Percival were equally encouraging to me when the time came for my operation to attempt a reversal of the colostomy. Only then would I know if the healing process had been successful enough to allow me to lead a normal life once again.

Mr. Umvari had returned nearly four months after the original operation explaining that the reports from the hospital had told him that I was not ready to undergo further surgery until now.

The reversal operation had been a success and slowly my body began to readjust and the angry hole in my side to close. The process was as unpleasant as it was painful, but as Mr. Umvari had foretold, I was lucky enough to be able to look forward to a life without physical handicaps.

During the months that followed Percival learnt to hold a crutch under his right armpit, clamped in place with his stump pushed into a specially designed cup. In time, his left crutch was replaced with a walking stick, and then finally his muscles grew strong enough to carry him with just one elegant cane – yet another present brought by father Merciful.

Meanwhile I had also come out of plaster and begun the long road of physiotherapy and exercises towards walking again. I had a huge advantage over Percival because only one of my legs had been broken and, of course, I had the use of both hands. My friend, however, had a six week start so that the two of us were soon undergoing similar treatments and exercise programs together.

Sister Mary relaxed her rules on when and where the books could be read and allowed Amrita whatever she wanted as she sat on her own gazing down to the river.

One morning, as Percival and I returned to the day-room from our treatments and exercises, we found Amrita in a heap on the floor in front of her chair. She was sobbing softly.

Percival and I looked at each other in horror as we hobbled towards the bundle of arms and legs. Percival lifted Amrita's head with his hand, I remember thinking I had never seen a more gentle gesture.

"See if you can lift her, Jack," Percival said with soft urgency. "Take her under the arms. I cannot bend that low. Careful now," he added unnecessarily.

My own physical problems were forgotten completely as I maneuvered myself between the fallen figure and the empty wheelchair. I managed to bend until my arms were around Amrita's waist. How delicate and fragile she was. As I lifted her slowly, the small body began to unwind, Amrita's hands reached up to Percival who was still cradling her face in his one hand, tears were running down his face now too, but he made no sound until we had succeeded in getting her back into the chair. Then he buried his face in her hair and began to sob.

I didn't know what to do next. I was awash with emotions – there was a deep sadness at Amrita's plight, and at the same time a sudden joy in the appreciation of the relationship that obviously existed between my two friends. Had either of them been aware of it before this moment? I didn't know and didn't care – a deep and touching affection had now been declared to each other, without a word.

"I'll go and fetch Sister Mary," I said softly, and, as neither of my friends seemed to hear me, or see me even, I shuffled from the room.

As I made my way down the long corridor towards the nurses' station I tried to settle my thoughts into some sort of order. The charge of emotion that had so suddenly been displayed had left me feeling slightly giddy and unbalanced, as if the Earth had shifted slightly on its axis. I straightened my spine as I shuffled along, and raised my head feeling my facial muscles moving in an unaccustomed way – I realized I was smiling.

Sister Mary leapt from her desk as I moved slowly through the door to her office.

"What's wrong?" she asked in a startled voice as she rushed towards me. "What's happened?"

"Amrita has fallen from her chair," I said softly. "Percival and I managed to lift her back again, but her legs don't look as they should," I added, suddenly remembering the strange angle of one of Amrita's feet.

"Why didn't you ring the bell?" Sister Mary's voice had a tinge of worried annoyance. "We would have come straight away. Nolisa," she called, "come quickly, I need you in the day room. Shamiso, fetch the stretcher bearers, hurry both of you."

I reached for Sister Mary's arm as she tried to brush past me and touched her gently. "Don't hurry too much, Sister," I said. "Something wonderful has happened in the middle of the tragedy of our lives."

Sister Mary looked at me in astonishment. "I don't know what you're talking about, Jack. Amrita may have broken something; she may have internal injuries, she cannot feel, so she cannot tell us. We have to investigate quickly, I must go at once." She turned quickly and hurried away down the corridor.

By the time I reached the dayroom once again, two men had arrived with a trolley. As they pushed it past me, the wheels made a slight squeaking noise, and I looked at it with a sudden surge of loathing. The memory of my first three days at St. Mary's came rushing back at me with that awful squeak. I had been wheeled from room to room on that same wretched vehicle, my vision blurred and restricted to the movement of the floor beneath my prone body. I swallowed hard and returned my thoughts to the present.

The nurses were busy with Amrita's feet and legs. Percival was at her side, one of her hands sitting comfortably in his.

"I'm so sorry, Sister," Amrita's voice was soft and musical. "I have been very stupid. I suddenly couldn't resist a desire to stand, and for some reason, I thought I could."

"We must take you to X-ray, Amrita," Sister Mary's voice had only a veneer of the matter-of-fact tone she used every day. "I'm sure everything is alright, but we have to make sure.

"I don't think we'll be needing that trolley after all, lads. Now our patient is back in her wheel chair it seems silly to move her again. Please go and warn X-ray that we will need them to be ready in five minutes."

"I'm coming too." Percival made the announcement quietly but with a voice of authority.

Sister Mary looked up in surprise and caught Percival's calm gaze. Her eyes dropped to the two hands, and then she looked across the room to where I stood in the doorway. I nodded slightly, but it was enough. She returned her attention to Amrita's legs, but I caught the glimpse of a smile as she dropped her eyes.

Things changed from the day of Amrita's fall. The future had always seemed forbidden territory to the patients of St. Mary's whose attention had to be kept in the present in an attempt to lose the past. Now there was a glimpse of purpose and the reality of decisions to be made, plans to build. The three of us cautiously began to look ahead.

The physiotherapist had been trying to show Percival pamphlets about prosthetic hands ever since he started his treatment, but her patient had always pushed them away with irritation. Now he was showing a reluctant interest in what the pages had on offer and I was encouraged one day to find him studying one of the pictures with deep concentration.

"If I am to look after Amrita properly," Percival said looking up, with a note of defiance in his voice, "then I need all the help I can get." He picked up the leaflet with his good hand and waved it towards me. "These things look awful, but if they mean I can lift her safely, then I must learn to use them."

Amrita was coy in her happiness. She struggled to accept Percival's love, as a child might find it difficult to believe that Father Christmas had heard all her pleas and answered with effusive generosity, bringing gifts way beyond the requests.

At first, fearing disappointment, it was easier not to believe in a situation that had presented itself unannounced, so Amrita had denounced it. However, Percival, who had been taken by surprise by his sudden show of tenderness, was like an uncorked bottle of suppressed emotion. He insisted that she accept his love, that it was real and everlasting, that he never wished to be separated from her, nor would he allow anyone else the privilege of looking after her.

Finally, and after much persuasion, Amrita gave up protesting that it was unfair for Percival to spend his life attached to a cripple. She accepted his love and confessed that she had been in love with him from the time they first met, but had resigned herself to the fact that she could never ask anyone to love her in return. She also confessed that her parents had been trying to have her moved back to Maryland where the nearby naval hospital in Bethesda might find ways to help her, but that she had refused to leave St. Mary's until Percival left. She did not want to sacrifice a moment of being with him. Now, it seemed, they would leave together.

Suddenly I was excluded and realized I would have to face my future alone. Life without my two friends seemed impossible; it was something I had never considered, in fact I hadn't thought of a future of any kind. There had been a 'never-never land' quality to our months in the day room. A healing time when each day merged into the next under the ever-present African sun with the river at the bottom of the garden always moving with no sign of either coming from, or going to, anywhere. To look ahead to a world outside this hospital was a frightening concept, but one – I now knew - that had to be faced.

It was Father Merciful who provided me with a strategy for a life beyond St. Mary's. On several of his previous visits he had asked me about future plans, and made various suggestions, only to be met with a blank stare of incomprehension so complete that the priest had found himself averting his gaze and quickly changing the subject. Now, at last he found me more receptive and ready to listen to the plans the Bishop had for me.

As Amrita and Percival began to arrange for their journey to the USA, I sought permission to accompany them at least as far as the capital, and asked Father Merciful if there was somewhere we could all stay together until the necessary arrangements were made to allow Percival to go to America.

When the day came for us to leave St. Mary's the whole community turned out to say farewell. Both Percival and I had been taking walking lessons around the garden during the previous three weeks and were getting stronger and more confident every day, encouraged by Amrita who would follow in her wheelchair pushed by Nolisa or Shamisso.

Percival walked with the aid of a frame that he managed to control with his one hand. Eventually, I could manage with just one walking stick. It felt good to have the sun on our faces and to feel the breeze, thick with moisture, as it moved from the river's surface to jostle the jacaranda leaves into a sultry sway.

As we walked down the garden for the last time I found my new confidence evaporating and a sudden panic gripped my stomach. I stopped and turned to Percival and saw my fears reflected in my friend's eyes. We both turned to look back at St. Mary's and the windows of the day room, now seen from the other side. We were leaving a sanctuary and, like small boys leaving the nursery to be packed off to boarding school, there was a physical, as well as an emotional, yearning to stay with the safe and the familiar.

"What are you two looking at?" Amrita's voice was cheery and buoyant. "Another adventure is beginning, and I, for one, am looking forward to it. Let's get on with it, shall we?"

Percival lifted his head and I saw him straighten his back and set his shoulders square. The amputee pushed his walking frame to one side as Amrita's chair came towards him with Nolisa in charge. As they drew alongside Percival reached out and gently stopped the little nurse with his hand.

"Let me, please, Nolisa," Percival said as he maneuvered himself behind Amrita. "I think we could modify the controls of this machine so it can be driven by just one hand, let's see. We'll need a single bar between the two handles and the brakes moved to the centre, I'm sure we can find someone to do it for us. But until then, I'll just have to manage like this." And so saying he proceeded to push Amrita along cautiously, with Nolisa fussing alongside.

With what I hoped was equal conviction I too turned my back on St. Mary's and walked slowly forward towards the river. I was pulling courage from the soles of my feet, upwards, slowly, until it reached my chest and my breathing returned.

When we reached the jetty the throng of well-wishers made way for us and I looked in amazement at the familiar boat that bumped gently against the wooden pier.

The 'Father Jack' had been freshly painted and gleamed in the sunshine. There were ribbons attached to any fitting large enough to hold them, and streamers running down into the water. Boniface was standing at the bow, a look of sober excitement on his scarred face. Suddenly he rushed forward and threw his arms around me and began to sob. He murmured "oh, Father, oh Father," over and over again.

I gently disentangled myself from the tall man's grip. Unaware of my own tears, I tried to calm the boatman and found myself muttering words of reassurance that came from instinct and not at all from my mind.

"Oh, I'm sorry, Father," Boniface wiped his cheeks with the back of his large hands, the strange pink of his palms catching the sun. "It's so good to see you, you have no idea. We have all missed you so much – those of us who are left, that is," he added softly. "I wouldn't let anyone else take you down river, not for anything in the world. It is my honor and I have waited for this moment for many months, always asking, always hoping that it would be soon. And now it has arrived, this wonderful day when Boniface can once again have his most important passenger in his boat."

It was hard to say goodbye to the team who had worked so hard to get us three injured souls back in action. None of us could speak to Sister Mary. Long embraces had to suffice and it was the delicate nun, herself, who pushed each one of us away in turn, with gentle insistence.

"Get along with you now," she said, ushering us onto the boat and supervising the positioning of the ramps for Amrita's wheel chair. "You mustn't keep the bishop waiting. If you've a mind to write, it would be grand to hear how you're getting along. All of us here at St. Mary's would like to know we're not forgotten."

"You will never be forgotten," I managed to say, and Percival nodded his agreement, emotion gripping his vocal chords into unaccustomed silence. "We can never thank you enough, Sister," I was struggling to keep my voice steady as the memory of the last time the nun and I had been on the jetty thrust itself back into my mind.

Suddenly - partly from habit and partly to appease the lady who had been my strength for so long –I found myself adding "may God bless you." My hand made an involuntary movement to make the sign of the cross, but I stopped it in mid air where it seemed to hang suspended for a second or two before sinking slowly back to my side.

"Amen" resonated from everyone standing around the jetty. The sound echoed across the river and then fell into silence.

"And may He be with you, also, Father. With you all," Sister Mary sang in a high, loud voice, and she took the painter from the bollard herself and threw the rope into the boat. "God's speed to both the Father Jacks" she called as the craft moved out towards the middle of the river.

We three former occupants of the day room clung on to the view of St. Mary's as it slid away as the river bent. The hospital disappeared first, then the lawn shortened until finally there was just the jetty left, crowded with people, all waving. Suddenly, as if somebody has turned a switch, it was all gone and we were out on the feisty waters of the river we had watched for so long whose waters were at last going somewhere and taking our new lives with it.

59. THE CHAOS OF THE CAPITAL

The journey down-river took just over four hours. As soon as the boat was in the middle of the fast-flowing water Boniface put the motor on tickover and let her glide with the current. He had a smart helm wheel now in the middle of the boat, and he kept one hand idly twitching the polished wooden spokes to keep us mid-stream. I stood beside him watching the banks slide by.

"Sometimes I miss my canoe," Boniface confessed quietly. "I'm very proud of my new boat, of course, Father Jack, but I miss the wild animals, the birds, and the feeling of togetherness I used to have with Nyami-Nyami. I don't think our river God likes diesel engines as much as the paddles that used to caress him and help us ride his powers. These engines push against his will and churn waters that were best left undisturbed. On homeward journeys I use the engine as little as possible."

"Most eloquently put," I answered, putting a hand on my old friend's shoulder in a gesture of understanding. I breathed in the sound of the water lapping at the boat's prow, my eyes scouting the skies and tree-tops for fish-eagles. I felt a momentary resurgence of love for the African bush as a herd of impala raised their heads from drinking to watch the boat and its occupants slip past.

Percival was with Amrita at the stern of the boat where the wheel chair had been roped into a secure position. They too were watching the banks drift past, Amrita holding Percival's hand and nodding enthusiastically as he gestured now and then with his stump, at things that caught his interest.

I couldn't hear their conversation, but sensed the warmth of their togetherness from the way their bodies moved and the ease with which they handled each others' disabilities. I turned my eyes back down-river just in time to catch some pied king-fishers playing 'catch' across the river's sheen.

"I don't want to dwell on the past, Boniface," I said suddenly in an unanticipated burst of conversation. "But I don't know when I will see you again after today, and I know I will regret it if I don't ask you about what happened to Mungonie and Umboto, and to any of the young warriors who were taken. Do you know?"

It was a while before Boniface answered. I let the time pass uninterrupted, staring steadily ahead.

Eventually, with a deep sigh, the boatman started speaking in a voice so low I had to bend to catch the words.

"The warriors who were taken, and the women too, have all joined the rebel forces. We neither see them nor hear from them, and to be honest, now we don't want to. Their reputation is enough that villagers just flee, leaving everything, if they hear that Mungutu is anywhere near."

Boniface paused, concentrating upon the river ahead. It was several minutes before he continued. "Of Mungonie and Umboto we know nothing at all. Everyone in the neighboring villages was so upset when they heard what had happened at Cachonga and how the Chief and his witch-doctor had abandoned the village just before the invasion, without taking anyone with them, or warning anyone . . ." Boniface stopped again, breathing deeply. "There's nobody would take them in or make them welcome now," he continued eventually. "We don't know what happened to them. Some say they crossed the border to the South, some say they went to relatives in the North. Nobody knows, nobody wants to know."

We were silent for a while, each busy with our own thoughts and memories. I was trying to prepare myself for the answer to the next question.

"And Loveness?" I asked in a voice barely above a whisper.

"You don't want to know, Father." Boniface answered in a hard voice, his face set forward, staring at nothing in particular.

"Is she still alive?" I had to know.

"Oh yes, she's alive alright Father; but don't you go looking for her."

There was another pause, this time so long that I gave Boniface a nudge of impatience with my elbow.

"She is Mungutu's favorite, so they say," said Boniface, reluctantly. "It is Loveness who plans the raids, who supervises the executions and chooses the children to be conscripted into their foul practices.

"I'm sorry, Father, I had not meant to tell you. But if I don't, you might try to find her. She has rejected everything you ever taught her and is known now as the destroyer of all things Christian. It is said that she is never happier than when she is torching a church."

I stopped looking for fish-eagles. My head slumped, my eyes focusing on the new leather shoes Father Merciful had brought on his last visit. I wondered what my uncle would make of the careful stitching which went across the toes and diagonally down to the heels. My mind was wandering, it was choking upon what I had just heard, my body felt floating-light and dreadfully heavy at the same time. Pain came rushing back in a torrent of mental torture that made me lose my balance. I steadied myself on Boniface's shoulder, took a deep breath and decided to make a stand against this ultimate foe - despair.

With considerable effort, I raised my head and forced my eyes to look ahead once again, although it was hard to bring things into focus. I concentrated on my breathing, willing the air into my lungs and out again in a steady stream. I counted the breaths steadily in my head, and when I got to twenty I stopped, turned to Boniface and said:

"Thank you, Boniface. I know that can't have been easy for you. You were right, I would have looked for her if you hadn't told me, so better to know now than to waste time and energy in a fruitless endeavor ending in even more hurt . . ." My voice trailed off into silence.

The boat took us to a town about fifty miles north of the capital. The river had become crowded with ferries, trading boats and water taxis. Boniface pulled The

Father Jack into a busy maze of piers and jetties where the sudden mass of pushing humanity made the three of us gasp in dismay. After so many months of our own space and quiet, the weight of pushing bodies and outstretched hands, the noise of clamoring voices supplicating, selling, demanding, arguing and pleading made us shrink into ourselves and remain huddled together in a collective panic.

Somebody from the crowd suddenly jumped on board having pushed his way to the front with a great deal of determination. With a sigh of relief, I recognized Jamu, Father Merciful's acolyte from the day of the first Holy Communion at Cachonga. He was stronger now, a fully-grown man, with square shoulders and a confident demeanor.

"Oh, Father Jack, how relieved I am to have found you," Jamu stretched out his hand eagerly. "I have been searching every boat that's come in for the last two hours, and that's not easy amongst this rabble, I can assure you.

"Hello, I'm Jamu," the young man turned to my companions, eager to make a good impression, his extended hand suspended in confusion as Percival unthinkingly held out his stump.

Amrita grasped the offered hand quickly, "I'm Amrita," she said smiling, "and this is Percival. We have been Jack's companions for many months."

"Yes, of course, you're expected. The bishop himself is looking forward to meeting you. Tonight you must rest, but tomorrow he hopes you will be his guests of honor at a dinner in the palace itself. We have all been eagerly awaiting your arrival."

Jamu turned again. "It is so wonderful to see you again, Father. The tales of what you achieved at Cachonga have swept the country; you have become quite the hero. The bishop is eager to hear of all your achievements first hand, and has set up a schedule for you that is far too busy for someone who is still convalescing. I have told him, over and over again, but he will not listen to me. You will have to tell him yourself."

Indeed, the days that followed were a blur of activity. There was the promised dinner at the palace with white-gloved servants bowing almost continually making us feel most uncomfortable. The shiny face of the bishop seemed blacker than it should due to the white clerical garments with which it was framed. The eyes were not soft, but glistened with excitement as he told me how famous Cachonga had become and how its priest was now seen as a legend to his faith. I wasn't at all comfortable with that idea.

The next day there was a celebration service held in the National Cathedral where thanks were given for my safe return. All the local dignitaries had been invited, and I was required to stand next to the bishop as they left the church and be introduced to each one. It was almost more than I could bear to hear over and over again how wonderful it was that God had saved me.

"What about everybody else?" I wanted to shout at them all. "What about the deaths and the tortures and the kidnappings? What about the continued evil indoctrination being inflicted upon the captives?" Instead all I could do was to smile and nod with a blank expression concealing the anger.

The next day was even worse. It began well enough when the starched finery I had been required to wear for the thanksgiving service was replaced by a simple cassock of burlap. The bishop had been told by his public-relation people to abandon the sumptuous clerical garments he had selected. This special vicar of Christ was known for his humility, they insisted and such a simple garment as the one now presented to me was the style of dress with which I was identified, and with which my fame had spread.

"We must give the people what they expect, Jack," the bishop had said, his large, ringed fingers resting on my bony shoulder. "You cannot help it that you are a hero, and I must confess, a very useful one. Your reappearance, helped as it has been by the government of the day, has gained us much goodwill. I'm sure you understand."

I didn't understand and grew increasingly uneasy as I was taken to the new Christian Celebration Centre built at vast expense with donations from overseas. This lavish building surrounded by manicured formal gardens and gushing fountains could seat over three thousand people and was absurdly out of place in a country of extreme poverty.

I found the structure insensitive and rather disgusting and my irritation was growing about having no choice of action but to fill the role that had been created for me. I was not consulted, nor was I briefed as to what to expect. I was just presented with shows of histrionics and garish theatricals with myself as the unwilling centre-piece.

Finally, when the bishop told me that I was to lead the service at the 'Celebration Centre' and to read the speech that was handed to me to a congregation of thousands, I looked him squarely in the eye and refused.

The bishop looked at his protégé with surprise. The sparkle in his eyes turned to a hard glint as he stared at me for several seconds. Then he shrugged his shoulders and read the speech himself explaining to the crowd that his humble chaplain was too shy to read it himself.

The text that was read on my behalf expressed gratitude to 'God the Father' briefly and then with more pathos, thanks were given the 'Father of their beloved country' - the magnanimous President who had played such a supportive role to the creation of Cachonga; and finally to the bishop himself for the many wonderful things he had done, not only for Cachonga, but for all the towns and villages throughout the land.

The bishop then launched into yet more prayers of thanksgiving for my survival and for the government who had made it possible, and then asked for donations so that the work this brave priest had started could be continued.

The packed audience sang and ululated throughout the prayers, the choruses of 'Amen' echoing around the auditorium and audible from the throngs who had gathered outside to watch the proceedings on giant screens.

People cheered and cried out as I was paraded around the auditorium. They rose to their feet as I passed; reaching out, as if a touch or a glance would bring them salvation.

The hypocrisy of the whole show made me sick. I had been turned into a clown, performing for others who pulled the strings to make me dance for their own advancement. This had nothing to do with religion, but it was dressed up with all the trappings. Once again, here was the horrible nonsense of crowd manipulation that inspired the kind of mass hysteria I disliked so much. It made my blood run cold.

That evening, to my relief I was left alone to dine with Percival and Amrita in the guest wing of the bishop's palace which had been made over to us for the duration of our stay. My friends had been busy at the American embassy, trying to sort out a visa for Percival and secure travel arrangements to The States. Both of them were in high spirits and full of enthusiasm to tell me about their day, but their eagerness disappeared instantly when they saw the look on my face.

Percival asked the servants to leave us until dinner time. He went to the amply stocked bar and poured amber liquid into a large crystal tumbler.

"Twenty-one year old malt," he said, handing me the sparkling goblet. "I don't know what happened to you today, but there is nothing this stuff won't make a bit better, and there seems no shortage of such luxuries here.

"Amrita and I have news, but it can wait." Percival continued as he maneuvered Amrita and her wheel-chair towards the large French windows which led to a wide veranda. He pulled up two of the heavy guilt armchairs and unwittingly reproduced our habitual day-room at St. Mary's. "Tell us what has happened to you," he said as he pushed the glass into my reluctant hand.

I sank gratefully into the offered chair and looked from one of my friends to the other. I could feel my eyes watering as I struggled to put my emotions into words.

"I am so grateful to you two wonderful people for being with me," I started. "You can have no idea how much solace your presence brings to a life suddenly thrown into a new and unanticipated turmoil.

"These people are trying to make me into something I am not. I am being used as a puppet. Today they wanted me to say a mass communion for over three thousand people. They expected me to stand upon a dais in the middle of an auditorium of obscene extravagance and speak into a microphone that would carry my voice to crowds of people gathered outside as well as those inside. They gave me a prepared speech to read in which I was to thank God and the government for having saved me. To explain to the people how wonderful is their damn President and how powerful and caring are his ministers. It was a nightmare, and I refused to do it."

"Good for you," said Percival with enthusiasm as he re-filled both our glasses.

"But it made no difference," I continued in a small voice. "The bishop read the speech out himself, explaining that I was too shy to speak. That I was too humble – and the crowd roared with appreciation. It was appalling, quite dreadful. I felt such a traitor."

I took a gulp of the whiskey and looked beseechingly at my friends who obviously had no idea what they could say to help. Amrita nodded with sympathy, her eyes wide with distress.

"I was paraded around like some sort of pathetic super-hero," I continued, my voice getting louder now. "They are making a mockery of everything I've done here and ignoring the calamity that, in a single afternoon, swept any improvements I had managed to achieve away without trace. I am like a pawn in a revolting game where the chess players press-gang their pieces into compliance."

I paused, and without thinking, took another gulp from my glass. "And then they sent runners around the stadium with sacks to collect donations to support the work their government was doing in the name of Jesus.

"It was horrendous – people were throwing money, mobile 'phones, even car keys into these sacs and then sinking to their knees in gratitude for the spiritual wonders which they had been promised would befall them. The bishop was blessing their generosity but always suggesting that whatever they had given wasn't quite enough. You cannot believe how dreadful it was."

There was silence for a few moments, before Percival spoke. "Whether you want it or not, Jack, you're a celebrity now, and obviously a valuable one at that. It seems that the success you made of Cachonga, before its destruction, has taken on mythical proportions. The common man sees you as someone to whom he can relate, and the government wants to capitalize on your popularity – in spite of your color. If you can be seen as one of their tools, your glory will be transferred to them."

"What should I do?" I looked beseechingly at my friends. "Even the leader of the opposition party wants to speak with me – look, this message was thrust into my hand from someone in the crowd while we were leaving." I passed a crumpled piece of paper to Percival who straightened it carefully with his one hand. After a few moments, he looked up and smiled.

"This could be your way out, Jack," Percival said slowly. "If you were to meet this Tchonga person, the powers that be would soon know about it, and you would no longer be welcome here. They would not dare to harm you, you are too popular, but they would know that you might not be as malleable as they had hoped. You would be encouraged to leave. As long as they think you will help them, you will never be allowed to go home. This is your ticket out."

"Do you really think so?" I was incredulous. I took another sip of whisky. The liquid was warming my guts and sending a flush to my face that was not unpleasant. I felt some confidence returning slowly.

"Yes, I do," Percival was quick to answer. "But this must be handled carefully, and first, Amrita and I have a favor to ask you."

"Of course, Percival. You both know I will do anything for you. You two are my family – well I mean I think of the three of us as family. No-one else could understand what we have experienced and how our friendship has knitted us together in the knot of endurance.

"I hope I am not speaking out of turn," I added in a sudden lurch of insecurity.

"No, of course not." It was Amrita who was quick to respond. "That was eloquently put, Jack, and I'm sure I speak for Percival as well as for myself when I say that we agree wholeheartedly.

"However, our request might put you in a difficult position as far as your new life and beliefs are concerned."

"What is it you want me to do?" I asked in confusion.

"Marry us," butted in Percival, before Amrita could continue. "We want you to marry us – in church, if you wouldn't find that too difficult."

I looked at Percival in amazement, and then turned to Amrita, who gave me a slight nod and a wide smile. Her eyes were fixed upon mine, full of excitement.

"I know Percival is an atheist, and that I am on a limb of my own when it comes to religion, Jack. We also both know how you now feel about the church. This is not a religious request, but a secular one which needs the disguise of dogma and ritual."

"I want to be with Amrita for the rest of my life," Percival broke into the conversation with an energy I had not encountered before in my soft-spoken friend.

"Marriage is not as strong as the bond that exists between us, and therefore should be unnecessary," Percival continued. "But it isn't unnecessary in the eyes of the law.

"If we are married then I will be allowed into the United States where Amrita has a family and some contacts in the medical world who might be able to help us. If we are not, then I cannot accompany her on her next journey, and separation is something that neither of us wants.

"A civil service will take time to arrange, but a church service could be carried out quite quickly if we could use your sudden fame to expedite matters."

Amrita interrupted quickly: "Jack, you are our dearest friend, and as you have rightly said, we are family, the three of us. We all know exactly where each of us stands on these issues of organized religion, but now we are being faced with obnoxious legalities that can make or break what we are trying to accomplish.

"Can we not, the three of us, perform a piece of theatre which will keep the officials off our backs and allow us to live our lives as we wish? Would it upset anyone? Would it do anyone anything but good?

"And apart from anything else," Amrita continued, her eyes brimming with emotion, "Percival and I would not want anyone else to do this great thing for us. If we are to get married, it has to be with you – in whichever official capacity you care to choose."

"But I shall lose you." It was a pathetic remark, and I knew it as soon as I said it. The words had come unbidden.

"You will never lose us." I was unsure which one of them spoke first, but they both made the claim, and adamantly too.

"You'll go to America. I won't see you again." I gave a gasp. I was aware that I was being very stupid and very selfish, like a petulant child losing a favorite toy. "Oh I know I've seen this coming for a long time, but I'm still not ready for it."

There was silence for a few moments before I could continue. "Forgive me, my friends. I am being ridiculous," I said, "of course I will do whatever you want."

Then, in a voice as buoyant as I could make it, I continued rapidly: "there is nothing I desire more than to see the two of you together, for always, wherever that might lead you. So maybe we can give some pathos to this charade and make it meaningful to the three of us in our own special way.

"Let me make an application to the bishop before he realizes that I am a lost cause as far as political gain is concerned. I will speak to him tomorrow."

"Nothing fancy mind," it was Percival who spoke. "Just us three and whoever else needs to be there to make it legal."

"I'll see what I can do," I said. "Now, what about another draught of this amazing liquid with which to seal our pact?"

60. THREE PEOPLE AND A WEDDING

The three of us went to see the bishop the next morning and I explained our request.

"You shall have the cathedral," the nation's leading cleric shouted with excitement. "We will make a huge celebration. Perhaps the President himself could be persuaded to give the bride away. Oh this will be spectacular."

It was Amrita who managed to get things under control. Percival found it difficult to speak rationally he was so irate. He fully understood the unwelcome notoriety I had explained to them, and now found himself and his beloved Amrita being threatened with the same treatment.

"I'm so sorry to disappoint you, your grace," the bride-to-be spoke softly but firmly. "Please don't think us ungrateful for such a generous offer, but Percival and I are still coming to terms with our disabilities and would not be able to cope with the sort of attention such a service would bring. I'm afraid it's out of the question. Could we not have a simple service, here in your own palace chapel?"

The bishop looked taken aback, but Amrita had played a strong card and he couldn't think of a way to counter such a powerfully emotive argument.

"I know it's cheeky of me to ask, your grace," Amrita had not finished her tactical approach, "but Percival, Jack and I were all rather hoping that you might agree to give me away yourself. It would be such an honor for me, and you have done so much for us, while we don't really know the President at all."

It had taken all Amrita's persuasive powers to convince Percival and me to go along with this idea. Reluctantly we had agreed that playing on the disabilities angle, while distasteful and not altogether truthful, was definitely our best line of defense against the anticipated move the bishop would make to capitalize on the union. But the idea of asking the bishop to act in a parental role and give Amrita away had caused consternation.

"What does it matter to us?" Amrita had argued softly, "and playing to the bishop's pride in this way might make all the difference to having his acceptance or not. And without his approval and acceptance, none of us can do anything in this country. However uncomfortable it makes us feel, we all know that we need this man's help. We are his guests, but are we not also his prisoners?"

"I think Amrita has a point," I said reluctantly, "and when you think about it, it's a small price to pay for achieving the required result. Once he's handed Amrita over to you, Percival, he is out of the proceedings anyway, and if we are to use his chapel, we can't do so without him. If we try for any other church there's bound to be complications and delays, and we would have to go out of the building and - as you know - we are all constantly watched. We would have the press hounds on to us immediately."

Eventually Percival had succumbed and promised to remain silent during any conversation with their host so as not to risk voicing his real opinions.

The plan had worked, the bishop, while irritated at losing the grand show, settled upon the suggested plan and immediately began to question his media people about the correct robes he should wear for such an occasion. They set a date for the Tuesday of the following week, and the bishop returned to being an amiable host who couldn't do enough for his guests. He even offered, no ordered, that he be allowed to buy Amrita's wedding gown as his present to the couple on this very special occasion. Amrita had wanted to wear a simple sari, but realized this might throw suspicion on the Christian affiliation so necessary for everything to run according to plan.

They would need two witnesses, the Bishop reminded them, and he had two perfect people in mind. Amrita had interrupted him quickly:

"Oh thank you so much," she said in her calm voice that brooked no argument, "but we have sent word to Sister Mary and the nurse Nolisa who looked after us for so long. We have asked them if they would do us that honor.

"Oh, yes," Amrita continued quickly, "we also have another couple of guests we would like to ask, please, your grace, if that's alright with you: the lady who gave us her set of Dickens and the works of Shakespeare, and Father Merciful who was the bearer of so many gifts during our time in hospital."

"Boniface the boatman, and your curate Jamu would also be most welcome," I took up the theme. "Boniface could bring Sister Mary and Nolisa down river and perhaps Jamu could meet them and accompany them here." I looked nervously at Percival and Amrita, for this hadn't been previously discussed, but they were both smiling and nodding in agreement.

"But we really don't want anyone else, please," added Amrita with a note of finality. "This really is to be just a family service with only people with whom we feel comfortable enough to relax and to enjoy the occasion."

The bishop had been surprisingly willing to agree to everything, and plans went ahead for the following Tuesday at eleven-thirty in the morning. followed by a small celebratory luncheon at the bishop's expense, with his guarantee that no-one else would intrude upon the occasion. The three of us congratulated each other on the successful outcome to our plan.

"What do you think he will bring me to wear?" Amrita asked, with laughter in her voice. "It's bound to be white and flouncy and quite over the top, but I don't mind – and neither should you," she added quickly glancing at Percival with a wide smile. "After all, it's me who has to wear it, and what does it matter? It will make no difference to the vows we give to each other."

It was Sunday evening, and the three of us were watching the daylight fade over the roof-tops of the capital from the bishop's hill-top palace.

"It all looks so much kinder in the dusk," Percival indicated the jumble of buildings that spread out in all directions. "You can't see the chipped and graffiti-covered walls, sagging roofs, and the squalor of the gutters from up here, in the twilight."

Sporadic lights were appearing here and there. Not many of the streetlights worked; most were bent or lying horizontally along the sides of the roads. Many had been robbed of wiring, with gashes in their poles from where the flex had been extracted, looking like unhealed wounds. The only ones that stood straight and were illumined were those on the streets leading to the President's and the bishop's palaces around each of which was a squadron of heavily armed soldiers, complete with tanks parked on every corner. The surrounding streets, although lit, were cordoned off every evening until the sun was high in the sky the following morning.

"What are you going to wear, Percival?" I pulled my friend's gaze from the smoky picture before us.

"Goodness!" Percival exclaimed, "I hadn't even thought about it. What on Earth should I wear? Amrita, my love, what would you like to see this wretched body draped in on Tuesday? Should I wind a garland of flowers around my stump?"

Amrita ignored the last remark. "I don't mind what you put on, my darling Percival," she answered; "just as long as you're comfortable in what you're wearing and with what you're doing."

Eventually it was decided that I would take time out from the various functions the bishop had arranged for me the next day and the two of us would brave the bazaars to see what we could find. Jamu would undoubtedly accompany us - we never went anywhere without him - and know where best to look and the sort of money we should expect to spend.

Much to everyone's surprise, the wedding passed without a hitch. I asked Sister Mary to help me with the service, allowing her to lead the Creed and the most devout prayers. It was a joy to see the little nun looking so elated, and Nolisa also, who claimed to be the bridesmaid and had brought her formal tribal dress of bright greens with dramatic black slashes.

Boniface was so proud to be included that he looked as if he might burst at any moment, splitting the seams of the crisp western suit that had to be returned to the dress-hire shop first thing the next morning.

The bishop was decked out in full finery, with a row of incongruous military medals pinned to his pastoral robes. He strutted through his part as if it was he who was on centre stage, and not Amrita.

The bride was wrapped in a cocoon of white silk shot through with silver thread; the Bishop – or more probably Jamu – had done an unexpectedly wonderful job. Her dark hair was plaited with jasmine. Nolisa had brought the flowers and a hair-dressing kit and had done a wonderful job threading the tiny white flowers into Amrita's long black tresses. The wheel-chair had been polished, and there were bows of silver ribbon tied everywhere that was possible without impeding the motion of the machine whose rider's skin glowed with happiness.

Percival was resplendent in a pale blue caftan with gold embroidery around the neck, hem and sleeves. Sister Mary was glistening in starched white, Nolisa vibrated with color and I, by popular demand, in contrast with everyone else, wore my dour brown cassock.

Father Merciful and Jamu, dressed in heavily embroidered robes, assisted Sister Mary with the service, allowing me to slink into the background as much as I could. I hovered around the periphery of the altar, trying not to collide with a huge bouquet of exotic flowers, imported under the bishop's personal supervision from South Africa.

However, when it came to the marriage itself, I stepped out of the background and found an almost magical pleasure in binding my two dearest friends to one another by repeating the words I knew so well, but had never enjoyed so much.

After the ceremony, the small party moved to the bishop's private dining room where an embarrassingly sumptuous meal had been laid out, and another huge floral arrangement dominated the room. French champagne shimmered in sweating ice buckets and waiters hovered around more numerous than the guests.

Percival, in an uncharacteristic mood of generosity, gave a short speech thanking the bishop for allowing them to use his private chapel, for presenting him with his wonderful bride, and for his lavish hospitality. He concluded with:

"For all the honors you have given us, your grace, we are most grateful. However, I have to put things into perspective, for no matter how elaborate our surroundings or how bountiful these gifts, everything pales into insignificance compared with the honor Amrita has accorded me in becoming my wife.

"Ladies and gentlemen, please raise your glasses to drink to my great fortune, to my beautiful wife, Amrita."

"I cannot stand on my feet to honor my husband," Amrita's small voice was clear in the silence that followed the mumbling echoes to Percival's toast. "But I stand proud in my heart to call myself the wife of this most wonderful of men. I must also thank the bishop for his generosity – this wedding gown is a joy, and his kindness in allowing our celebrations to take place here in the privacy of his home is appreciated more than he can know.

"And to our dear friend, Jack, we both give our love and gratitude. You are part of our family, Jack," she said, turning to look me. "You belong to us, as we belong to you. No matter where we are in the world, we will always be together, somehow, in the magical ether of existence. I believe that is how it is, and always will be."

There was a confused silence following this speech. Perhaps, I realized afterwards, I had been expected to say something, as best man, so to speak. However, I had nothing to offer but a lump in my throat and the foreboding ache of parting.

Jamu rescued us all by rushing around with a newly opened bottle of champagne, spreading easy joviality amidst the emotions.

Percival sought out Father Merciful. "What happened to the old biddy who gave us her Dickens collection?" he enquired after looking through the assembled guests and finding no unfamiliar faces apart from the myriad of servants.

"Oh, you'll have to ask Jamu," Father Merciful answered evasively. "It was Jamu who rounded up the works on Sister Mary's list – but the bishop gave him the authority so to do, hence they are really the gifts of the bishop.

Percival looked particularly unimpressed. He went to find Jamu and confronted him with the same question.

Jamu blushed, "well it was someone from the British Embassy who found them for me, well for you, actually," he stuttered. "They told me about an old woman who had given her collection of books to their library, I may have given Father Merciful the wrong impression, I'm afraid."

Percival formed the impression that Jamu wouldn't have told him even that much if he hadn't been sampling the excellent champagne to which he was obviously not accustomed. He gave the priest a jocular slap on the shoulder and told him what a splendid chap he was, deciding to resume the conversation after Jamu had consumed a few more glasses of the sparkling liquid.

About half an hour later, Percival approached Jamu once again. It didn't take long to ascertain that all the books that had come to St. Mary's had been sourced and given by the staff of The British Embassy. The bishop's involvement was only to insist that it should be Father Merciful who would take the gifts up river, and that they be presented in the bishop's name.

Percival determined that the three of us would visit the British Embassy before leaving the country to convey our gratitude and explain why it had taken us so long so to do. He felt an uneasy feeling that nobody at the embassy would be surprised with the deception, but only, perhaps, at our naiveté.

After the luncheon, there were tearful farewells to Sister Mary, Nolisa and Boniface, the remaining guests dispersed and I went to my room, as Percival and Amrita retired to their newly adorned joint suite.

It had been an emotional morning, and I should have been grateful for a moment to myself. However, I felt an unusual restlessness and paced my room for a while before finally stopping on the balcony to watch the busy workings of this messy capital city.

Below, in the beautifully manicured gardens and sweeping gravel driveways, there was an unusual degree of activity. Two large grey vans, with all sorts of antennae, appeared to be the centre of attention, and I watched with detached interest as the bishop himself came out to question some of the people around the vehicles. There was much nodding and smiling and shaking of hands, and then he withdrew to his palace while the vans absorbed the crowd and slowly made their way out through the many security barriers.

Turning away from the glaring white sun, I waited for my eyes to adjust, then changed quickly into some jeans and a shirt. I would go for a stroll, I decided, and explore this city on my own, to assuage this restlessness.

To my amazement, I was stopped at the first barrier.

"Bishop's own orders, Sir," the guard said unnecessarily loudly, the last word spat rather than spoken. "Nobody is to leave the palace."

I was startled when I heard myself say "do you know who I am?"

"Yes, Sir," came the response. "The order is especially directed at yourself and your two friends."

I stared at the man in disbelief. I felt suddenly very weak, as if someone had attacked me from behind and leveled a strong stick against the back of my knees. At the same time, the muscles in my stomach contracted making me want to retch. I could taste fear returning with speed, the impact making me reel. However, I did not let it show, but nodded slightly and turned back to the palace whose lavishness did little to conceal its fortress-style architecture.

That evening, Amrita and Percival and I, had dinner together in the newly-weds suite. I told my friends about our apparent imprisonment, which Amrita had already guessed, and we all decided that it was time to leave Africa.

"But first," Percival proclaimed, "we must visit the British Embassy to thank them for finding us our books. If we had known the truth, we would have done so already. In any event they probably have a better understanding about what has been happening to you, Jack, than you do yourself.

"And I don't see how anyone, even the bishop, can stop us from visiting our embassy."

"It's time to activate our escape plan," I said, "but, after this afternoon, I think I would feel safer doing so with the embassy's approval and assistance. The bishop's plans for me during the next three weeks are horrendous. Jamu, bless him, told me all about them towards the end of lunch today. He should drink more champagne, it makes him much easier to understand."

"Do you think they've found out about your suggested meeting with the opposition?" Amrita asked.

"How could they?" I said. Then suddenly, all three of us stopped breathing for a moment. We looked around the room with a trace of panic in our eyes. Percival put a finger to his lips, and Amrita and I nodded in agreement.

The rest of the evening past quickly with banal conversations where the three of us made a point of poking fun at the various dignitaries we had met since arriving at the capital and discussed the weather and the lavish flowers with which the palace was filled on a daily basis.

The next day, I expressed our desire to visit the British Embassy to Jamu who was in charge of all day-to-day activities. I explained that there were certain technicalities about my return to England that had to be sorted out. I no longer had a passport or any papers of identity, and although the bishop had promised to arrange this, it was obviously necessary for me to visit the embassy in person.

"Of course, we quite understand," Jamu answered with an eager nodding head. "In fact we are ahead of you, Father Jack. The bishop, always mindful of your needs, has sent word to your embassy and, in order to save you inconvenience, their emissary is on his way to meet with you here at the palace, as we speak. I was about to tell you of this first appointment of your day. He should be here in about half an hour."

This did not sound to me like a happy coincidence. With a sinking sensation in my stomach I had to confront the idea that our suspicions of being listened to were correct.

Edward Collins, from the British Consulate, was a neat man in his early forties. His manner balanced diffidence with confidence; he was obviously a professional and efficient diplomat. He introduced himself to us with the soft voice of a BBC broadcaster.

"The bishop's gardens are famous throughout the capital," Mr. Collins stated unexpectedly. "Being a keen gardener myself, I wonder if I might use this opportunity to observe them. Would you object to our strolling as we talk?" he asked.

Jamu looked nervous as our small party made its way out of the French windows onto the terrace. Massive terracotta pots overflowed with exotic plants, their colors spilling onto slabs of sandstone. Percival and Amrita were asking Jamu about the flowers' names and origins, their progress stopped by Amrita's wheelchair, as Mr. Collins, briefcase in hand and I, walked briskly down a set of broad steps and turned towards the rose garden.

Jamu watched our disappearance with alarm. He did not want to offend these gracious people who he had come to respect and like, but his orders had been clear. He was to stay with the man from the British Embassy and report whatever he heard to the bishop. They were not to be left alone.

"I expect you will have discovered by now," Mr. Collins spoke quickly and quietly so that I had to bend slightly to catch the words over the crunching gravel, "that the bishop spies upon his guests. Every room is bugged, and some have cameras as well as microphones. Those extravagant arrangements of Proteas hide a wealth of subterfuge. We must speak quickly.

"Your position here Jack, - you don't mind if I call you Jack"

"No of course not, please continue." Anxiety was creeping up my spine with cold fingers.

"Your position here is secure for as long as you continue to play the government's game. You have no documents of identity with which to travel, but I am organizing those. Presumably you would like to return to England?"

"Yes, of course, as soon as possible. My friends are going to America. I do not wish to stay here." My words tumbled out, panic edging my voice no matter how hard I tried to sound calm. "The leader of the opposition wants to have a meeting," I continued. "I thought if that happened, the bishop would no longer require my presence and I would be let go. What do you think?"

We walked in silence for a moment; "Yes, that could work," Mr. Collins said carefully. "It will not be without risks. You have become a national treasure, a valuable commodity, and yesterday's wedding won the hearts of the people."

"What do you mean?" I asked incredulously.

"Ah, I wondered if you knew." Mr. Collins smiled without mirth. "You didn't think the bishop would let a coup like that slip between his fingers did you? The whole thing was filmed and taped – and carefully edited,

I suspect. It was shown on television last night and the newspapers are full of it today. Here take a look."

Mr. Collins balanced his briefcase on a raised knee long enough to unlock it and extract a newspaper. A photograph of Amrita in her garlanded wheelchair, with Percival and myself behind, and the Bishop beaming at her side, filled the front page. "The speeches were obviously doctored, you could tell from the jerky film footage, but most of the population won't have noticed. Your friends are quoted here – he turned the page where there were photographs of the lavish lunch, with the bishop's beaming face ever-present.

"'For all the honors you have given us, your grace, we are most grateful,' says Percival, and then his wife responds:

"I cannot stand with my feet, but I stand proud in my heart to thank the bishop for his generosity – this wedding gown is a joy, and his kindness in allowing our celebrations to take place here in his home is appreciated more than he can know. You are part of our family, we belong to you. I believe that is how it is, and always will be."

"That last bit was said to me, not to the bishop," I was exploding with indignation and anger.

"Whoops, we have company," said Mr. Collins, returning the newspaper to his briefcase as Jamu could be seen approaching as quickly as his dignity would allow. "Leave the arrangements to me. I will talk to people at the embassy and we will make the necessary plans. Be ready, we may have to move quickly."

Bugged Bouquets

Percival and Amrita were also aghast when I told them how we had been betrayed and portrayed for political gain.

Percival and I had managed to maneuver Amrita's chair down the banked lawns onto the gravel path, and now the three of us were crunching along together.

"We kept Jamu busy for as long as we could," Amrita said, somewhat unnecessarily. "But the poor chap was desperate to do his master's bidding, and eventually we had no choice but to let him go."

"At least I had a few minutes," I said, "and what informative minutes they proved to be. How can we have been so stupid?"

Nobody spoke for several minutes, each busy with our own thoughts as we tried to adjust to the situation and deal with surges of anger and resentment. It was Amrita who broke the silence.

"My dear friends, we are looking at this situation with only negative thoughts. We must resist this temptation and recognize that this is a two-way street. We were using the bishop for our own personal gains – he has used us for his. The consequences are that we have both achieved what we set out to do.

"Percival and I are married. We will have the necessary documentation that will result in a green card for Percival. After all, if the wedding was seen on television, its validity cannot be questioned by the American Embassy. All we need to do now is work out how quickly we can get out of this country and the mess in which we find ourselves."

"Mr. Collins said that he would sort something out for us," I told them. "I think he liked the idea that I meet with the leader of the opposition. He said that he would make a plan. We should be ready to leave at short notice.

"I have told Jamu that I do not feel up to any more functions, that I want to go home. He didn't seem surprised or even annoyed, he just bowed and went off to see the bishop."

"We should make an appointment to go to the U.S. Embassy," Percival jumped into the conversation with sudden enthusiasm. "They can't stop us, can they?"

"There's only one way to find out," said Amrita, and turning around we headed back to the palace.

61. A MEANINGFUL MEETING

"Forgive me, Father Jack, for asking to meet with you," Tchonga began. "I know you have a busy schedule," he added with a rye look that was difficult for me to interpret. The leader of the popular opposition party, was a tall, thin man in his early forties. His grave face loomed over me, his mouth unsmiling, his eyes deep and penetrating. We were in a small room of what Mr. Collins had described as a 'safe house' somewhere in a not particularly affluent suburb.

Mr. Collins had collected me from the bishop's palace just after nine that morning and taken me to the British Embassy. One of the bishop's security guards escorted us "in case you need protection" Jamu had said, smiling. He accompanied us into the embassy and to the door of the passport and visa section where he was told to wait.

"Our own security will take over from here," Mr. Collins had insisted, and closed the door to the interview room firmly in his face. I had then been led swiftly through the embassy, donning a proffered red base-ball cap and green jerkin en route. I was taken through the immaculate embassy garden at the back of the building and directed to a small pedestrian gate set in a high wall at the far corner.

Mr. Collins – having replaced his suit jacket with a red and white T shirt with 'Man U' emblazoned across the back - took a small key from his pocket and unlocked an insignificant-looking padlock. He pushed the door open carefully and looked outside.

Being satisfied with what he saw – or rather with what he didn't see - he gestured to me to accompany him across the litter-strewn pavement to a clapped-out car of rusting beige. Behind the wheel lounged a young man whose dreadlocks spilled out from beneath a multi-colored cap and in the passenger seat, a young black woman was busily chewing gum.

As soon as the passengers were aboard, the car jolted into life and coughed its way to an intersection where it joined the moving traffic and became absorbed in the vehicular chaos of taxis, buses, cars and tricycles. It banged and clumped its way in many circles before arriving at a driveway beside a nondescript house with toddlers' toys strewn across the rough grass between the house and the pavement.

Mr. Collins and I got out and thanked our driver who gave a broad grin. We entered the house by the kitchen door and I was led, through a strong smell of cabbage, to a room at the back of the house where I found myself face to face with Tchonga.

When the introductory pleasantries had been exchanged, Tchonga went on speaking. "Please believe me that it is not a political motivation that directed this request for a meeting, but a spiritual one," his voice was low and strangely emotional. "My soul is in turmoil, Father, and I do not know anyone who is better qualified to help me with my dilemma than yourself, after what you have been through."

My heart sank. I had not been looking forward to further embroilment in the political machinations of the country, but a request for spiritual guidance was even more worrying. It was not at all what I had expected, and the last thing I felt capable of providing. "Please," I began, in a small voice, "please don't expect me to have any answers."

"If not to you, then to whom can I turn?" Tchonga's political carapace of confidence was abandoned. His eyes moistened as they grew wide. He grasped my hands in both of his, leaning into my breathing space. There was a hint of desperation as he continued.

"You have to help me, Father. I have been a good Christian all my life. I never missed Sunday school while I was small, or a Sunday service after I was confirmed. I have tried to follow the teachings; to be a good man; to honor my elders and protect and direct my children with proper Christian values.

"I was called for this political role against my wishes and persuaded that it was God's will that I represent the down-trodden people of this country. It was my church leaders who thrust this position upon me, and I believed that I was fulfilling God's purpose when I agreed to stand as leader of one of several opposition parties.

"As soon as I accepted the nomination, the rest of the opposition parties joined us, and suddenly I found myself at the head of a powerful political machine which I did not know how to steer.

"Of course there were others who knew exactly what needed to be done, and I was their tool, just as you have been used by the present government as their vote-gathering instrument. I tried to keep control; to put everything on the straight and narrow and not to compromise. It was difficult, but with the support of my family and close friends, I believe I did not sell my soul, I kept my values, and that was the way we went into the election, with our party being ahead in the polls sixty-nine to thirty-one percent.

"Then came the voting day," Tchonga paused; he dropped my hands and took a handkerchief from his pocket. He blew his nose and dabbed at his eyes before folding it carefully and putting it back. "Our supporters were confronted as they approached the ballot booths.

Some were fortunate and were only beaten about the shoulders before they ran. Others had their fingers cut off at the knuckles so that they couldn't hold the pen with which to vote, others lost their hands. Many staunch supporters disappeared completely and have never been found."

The tall man paused again. His shoulders had sunk, making him look suddenly smaller; his hands fell towards the floor, the fingers reaching as if they were involuntarily dropping something precious.

"Hundreds died," he continued in a low voice. "Thousands were maimed and wounded in horrible ways. We lost the election and our party was humiliated in the eyes of the world. I was – am – consumed by guilt and grief that my actions could have caused so much hurt and harm.

"I pray to the Lord for forgiveness a hundred times a day, and more importantly, I pray for understanding and guidance. How could something that I meant to be so good, turn into something so evil? Have I let my God down or" he stopped speaking, swallowed hard, and, raising his eyes to meet my reluctant gaze, he continued in a whisper: "has God let me down?"

I could not turn away from the man's tortured stare. I could feel my own eyes filling with tears, and no amount of swallowing could hold them back. I had no idea what I should say.

"You must have suffered a similar situation, when your village was destroyed," Tchonga continued softly, lifting his hands to grasp mine once again. "I have been thinking about your situation ever since I heard about you and what you had achieved at Cachonga, and then suffered with its destruction.

"I have sought your help as a man of the cloth who has experienced the same sort of disaster of intentions as I have; but you have more credibility with the Divine, you are one of God's own special advocates.

"Please share with me the secret of your continuing faith. Tell me how I can still cling to an idea that has become increasingly slippery as my grip tightens. I am in terror that I shall lose hold; that I shall fall forever."

In Tchonga's desperation, I recognized my own. The difference between us was that I had already let go. I had accepted the void in my soul and slowly come to terms with the vast emptiness. In the months with Amrita and Percival I had seen glimmers of other kinds of philosophies, but how could I offer such a fragile uncertainty to this man who was looking to me to reinstate the faith of his childhood, to justify the dreadful actions experienced under the watch of what had been perceived by both of us as a benevolent God?

I moved my eyes away from the supplicant. I was staring into the distance somewhere over Tchonga's left shoulder. There was no focus in my gaze as I pondered the available options.

The work of a vicar of Christ was to reassure this damaged man. To heal the hurts with promises of God's purpose; pointing out the fallible nature of mankind and our inability to understand the workings of the deity. I should emphasize that it was an act of hubris for a mere mortal to try to comprehend God's actions in this world.

I knew that I should explain how mankind should accept everything with the certainty that we are all fulfilling God's role for us, and our duty is to meet that role with humility; to carry it forward to the best of our ability. Only in that way could one really serve the Lord – with unquestioned devotion and trust.

This was the meaning of Faith and these dreadful happenings were a test for a man's soul, like Abraham being asked to sacrifice Isaac.

Tchonga's grip tightened slightly and brought me back from my thoughts. I felt my mouth opening and closing a couple of times, but no words came out.

Suddenly Tchonga fell to his knees, pulling me down with him, so that the two of us were only inches apart, the impartial cold of the stone floor seeping into our knees.

"Please, Father, please." Tchonga began to sob. Big tears were running down his sunken cheeks, leaving trails like a snail's. They fell unheeded onto his carefully ironed blue shirt making spots of a darker blue at random across his chest.

I focused upon the man's eyes and made ready to tell him the doctrine I had been taught, but when I opened my mouth still no words came forward. The ache of empathy in my chest was growing, spreading through my abdomen and up into my throat. I became aware of a strange moaning sound. It was circling the room, and then suddenly I knew, it was my own keen I was hearing.

I shook myself involuntarily and pulled my thoughts back with what felt like a physical effort. I tried again to utter words of reassurance, but instead found I was blurting out unprepared statements of honesty.

"I can't help you, Tchonga," I heard myself say, "because I, myself, have let go. I have abandoned the God of my childhood; abandoned those ideas of sweetness and light when faced with the true ferocity of existence. I have deliberately turned my back on all the promises. Promises that haven't been kept, that cannot be kept, that serve only to keep us subjugated to those who already know them to be false. People who use our gentleness and open-hearted ways to inflict dreadful atrocities; who control men of kindness with the oppression of the cruel.

"I have let go," I finished, in a quiet flat voice. "I shouldn't be telling you this. It is not what you want to hear, but I can't tell you anything different. You asked the questions, I'm sorry not to give you positive answers, but I haven't any."

We both remained motionless for a few moments, each staring at the small patch of floor between us.

Suddenly Tchonga let go of my hands and lunged forward encompassing me with his long arms. He hugged me to him so that I could feel the heaving of the man's chest and the dampness of the shirt against my cheek.

My arms moved from beneath the embrace and circled around Tchonga's waist. The two of us rocked from side to side, shifting weight slightly from one knee to the other. Eventually, our arms dropped and we each rose stiffly, unconsciously rubbing our knees.

"Thank you, Father," Tchonga spoke quietly but with a steady voice. "You are right, that what you have said is neither what I was expecting to hear, nor what I wanted to hear – at least I didn't think it was." He paused, and in the silence that followed our shallow breathing sounded unnaturally loud.

"However," Tchonga continued in a more confident tone, "I suddenly feel as if a great weight has gone from my shoulders.

"I have been struggling for so long to keep my faith, to look for good within dreadful men of dreadful actions. You have released me from that struggle.

"I agree with you. Suddenly I understand that it is necessary to let go. I have been using God as an excuse for my own failings. It is time to stand alone and to be stronger for doing so, rather than weaker.

"It is such a relief. You have no idea how liberated I feel. I will still grieve for my friends who have been killed and maimed, but I can grieve honestly now. I can see the crimes in the rawness of reality, without trying to understand awful deeds with whimsical ideas of a Divine plan. I no longer need to make sense of the senseless, to justify the unjustifiable, of searching for good amongst deeds of evil. I am free."

I was nodding agreement without wishing to do so. I was stunned by what I had said and done, but there was no pulling it back. I had to go forward and find something to offer this man who had so emotionally asked for my help.

"Tchonga," I said slowly. "I have undoubtedly spoken out of turn. We have both felt abandoned by God. That doesn't mean that there isn't something else for us to find. However, in the meantime we have to stand alone, as you say, and accept the solitude of mortality and the responsibility that comes with it."

Tchonga looked at me quizzically.

I thought for a moment and continued: "I believe the moral values we have inherited from the religion of our youth are just as valid with a God or without one. We cannot expect everyone else to have such a view, of course, and we are both aware of a large number of people who appear to have an agenda for life that is devoid of morals. However," I remembered Percival quoting from Shakespeare, "'This above all, to thine own self be true,' an English poet once wrote, and I can see a deep validity in that idea. That's what I mean by the responsibility of independent thought. We have to be content within our thoughts, to be confident of the correctness of the motives behind our actions, to be at peace with ourselves."

"Why?" Tchonga spoke the single word with vehemence.

I had been thinking out loud. I had been voicing thoughts as they came to me, without premeditation or any idea as to where they were leading. Tchonga's question blew a draught of cold air into my head, like a knife cutting a channel through the miasma of philosophy.

"I don't know," I answered slowly. "I don't know in any way that can be explained. But for me, personal honesty is paramount. I have never vocalized this principle before, but as I say it, I realize that I believe it. This is no kind of spiritual belief – at least I don't think it is – just a straightforward grasp at maintaining a moral compass. How else can we keep any sort of even keel as we travel through life?"

"In spite of being someone who values personal honesty so highly," Tchonga said slowly, "you appear to have been happy to present an entirely false impression to the public of this country - if what Mr. Collins told me earlier, about your belief in democracy and so on, is true. How have you allowed yourself to be so used by the government?"

"I have been abused, by the government, Tchonga," I answered quickly, stressing the first syllable strongly, "and most unwillingly, I assure you. None of us had any intention of being such pawns, but I'm afraid we were innocents in a vicious game.

"Now we have learnt how our words have been edited and reproduced, how our privacy has been invaded and our conversations misrepresented, we all three of us feel dirty and deeply angry.

"The bishop and his cohorts have trespassed into our personal space. They have stolen intimate concepts and rearranged them for their own purposes. We will not let that happen again. My meeting with you today is an expression of my no longer being a tool in his hands."

Tchonga looked at me with a hard, unwavering gaze. "I believe you," he said softly. Then suddenly the grave face split with an unexpected smile, the whiteness of his teeth putting the darkness of his skin into sharp focus. "Well, my friend," he continued, "you have given me much to think about, and much to be grateful for, I assure you.

"I cannot pretend to understand all your ideas, but I will try, as time passes to absorb them. I am still reeling with the sense of liberation you have condoned –

willingly or accidentally, I'm not sure which, and I don't mind either.

"Suddenly there is a whole new world waiting for me. A world in which I must take responsibility for my own thoughts and actions. I no longer have a God from whom I must seek guidance or towards whom I can direct excuses for failures. It is frightening, this freedom, but at the same time, somewhat exhilarating."

There was a knock on the door, and Mr. Collins entered without waiting for an invitation.

"It's time we were going, Jack," he said, a note of urgency in his voice. "Mr. Tchonga, I'm afraid we have to cut the meeting short. If you wouldn't mind staying here for a little while, it would be safer for all concerned. We can give you some lunch, and some newspapers if you like. A car will be here for you shortly."

"I would be grateful for the lunch, Edward," Tchonga had resumed his dignified composure and addressed his host with the familiarity usurped by leading politicians, "but I will not need the newspapers, controlled as they are by the present government, there is little truth in them – and anyway," he added, "I have plenty to think about thanks to my friend Jack here."

I wondered if Mr. Collins noticed how the title of 'Father' had been dropped, but if he did, he didn't show it.

Tchonga turned back to me and offered his hand. "Thank you for your guidance, Jack," he said. "If things ever change here, in this great country of ours, I hope you will come back to visit us. You will always be welcome, and I would appreciate your counsel. You have a permanent invitation - from me, personally. Please take advantage of it, I would appreciate it more than you can imagine."

We looked at each other in silence for several seconds before releasing the handshake.

"Goodbye, and good luck," I said, and then added "with everything." It sounded rather lame, I thought, but hoped Tchonga knew what I meant. I followed Mr. Collins out of the room, closing the door softly behind me.

62. AN UNEXPECTED FLIGHT

Amrita, Percival and I left the country that had so altered our lives in a swirl of cloak-and-dagger excitement.

Upon leaving the 'safe house' – this time through a back door into an unkempt garden, and over a style in a broken wooden fence – I found the same jalopy waiting at the end of a narrow path smelling of urine. Mr. Collins climbed into the back beside me, and immediately the car eased out of the siding and lost itself in the slow bustle of the suburbs.

Buses loaded with more passengers than could have been thought possible, their roofs piled high with everything from furniture to caged goats, ploughed through the mass of bicycles, ox-drawn carts, bouncing taxis and the occasional black four-by-four with sinister darkened windows and gleaming chrome bumpers.

There were swarms of mopeds, rusted vans and bicycles, plus a constant stream of pedestrians wandering around with the nonchalance Africans seem to display towards self-preservation.

Horns sounded incessantly, dust was everywhere, I had no idea where we were going, and didn't care. I closed my eyes to better reflect upon what had just transpired between myself and Tchonga and wondered which of us had been the most affected by the conversation.

We travelled for over an hour. Once we had left the urban sprawl the journey became less of a lottery. Now there were only the pot-holes to avoid and the steady, but diminishing stream of pedestrians. I wondered, as I had so often in the past, why it was always the women who carried great burdens of improbable things upon their heads, as if to counter-balance the children slung around their waists. The men walked unencumbered, usually in small groups, chatting and smoking.

Soon the number of hawkers, selling carefully stacked arrays of vegetables and fruits, or immaculately stacked towers of identical pieces of firewood, became less frequent, and their potential customers also. Now there was only the occasional band of children offering live worms for recreational fishermen heading towards the great lake to the East of the country, and small boys armed with long sticks trying to keep herds of scraggy cattle and goats off the road without much success.

Without warning, the car turned left into a dirt track and drove for two or three jolting miles before stopping without having arrived anywhere. The track continued in front, the dust settled behind, the tall grass waved quietly in the breeze, cutting off the view on either side.

Mr. Collins looked at his watch, then at me and put a finger to his lips. We sat in silence for nearly a quarter of an hour, the buzz of flies, the chirrup of crickets and the occasional sound of something slithering through the dried grass being the only sounds. I began to doze, relieved to have handed over the control of my existence to someone else for the moment. I was awakened by the sound of a vehicle approaching from behind.

The driver in front of me adjusted the rear-view mirror and stared steadily, after several seconds he started the motor. I turned and saw a cloud of red dust approaching out of which emerged a small transit van bumping along towards us.

Our driver threw the gear lever into position, and the car lurched forward. We drove on, the transit van following, for another twenty minutes until finally the track left the tall grass and entered a wide area of sparse bush-land.

The two vehicles continued travelling without a trace of either road or track. We wove between bushes and trees of different shapes, colors and sizes. The flame trees hurled their vivid flowers towards the sky, the sharp reds arguing with the clear blue, heavy with heat. An occasional baobab tree, with stunted limbs protruding from stately trunks seemed like silent giants of great wisdom. The acacia trees spread their flat branches to offer roofs of deep shade. It was under one of these that the car finally stopped, and the van drew up alongside.

We disembarked, shirts sticking to our backs with dark stains. I looked towards the van as the side door slid backwards and Percival jumped out. He waved at me, as a kid might do to a sibling on a beach holiday, then turned back to the van's gaping side. Slowly and carefully he reached for his burden and re-emerged with Anita held gently in his arms.

I bounded across the space between the vehicles to envelope my friends in an expansive hug.

"What's going on?" asked Percival. "We were expecting a morning at the U.S. Embassy, not a bumpy ride to the middle of nowhere.

I shrugged my shoulders and was about to reply when the sound of a small aircraft close above us seemed to arrive from nowhere.

We watched in silence as the airplane dropped into a space between the vegetation – a space which only now could be recognized as a possible runway.

The Cessna 182 – for that is what was written between the door and the tail – circled neatly after landing and taxied towards our little group. It came to a halt amongst a cloud of dust, the door slid to one side and a cheery hand beckoned to us from the opening. The engine was still running, the single propeller swirling at the nose.

"This is where we say goodbye," Edward Collins had come up behind me and was extending his hand. He gave me two bulky manila envelopes. "Here are all the documents you need," he shouted above the noise of the engine.

"You will travel with Gus, here, across the border. Someone will drive you to the airport where you will take a scheduled flight to London – the tickets are in here" he said, handing one of the envelopes to me. "Everything you need to know is in there, keep it safe, and enjoy your trip.

"This one needs to be given to your pilot," Collins added handing over the second package that was surprisingly heavy.

The diplomat shook my hand, and in an uncharacteristic gesture that caught all of us by surprise, he bowed to kiss Amrita lightly on the cheek. Her soft eyes brimmed with tears in reply. He nodded to Percival and indicated the door of the 'plane from which had descended some slender steps. The pilot was bent in the doorway, his arms extended to take the precious bundle.

Percival was reluctant to let go of Amrita and tried to climb the ladder without giving her up. I was quick to add support from behind.

"Don't be so bloody stupid," the pilot shouted down at us. "What do you think you're trying to do? Pass her to me, and quickly, we don't want to be here a moment longer than necessary."

Reluctantly Percival lifted Amrita away from his chest. She uncoiled her arm from around his neck and gave him a quick nuzzle with her forehead before stretching her hands towards the small, swarthy man in the doorway. It wasn't the most dignified of transitions, but somehow Amrita was hoisted aloft and strapped into one of the two tiny back seats. Percival leapt up and crammed his tall frame into the other one, as I, with a backward glance at Edward Collins, climbed into the seat beside the pilot.

Edward and the drivers pushed the steps up into the body of the tiny 'plane and swung the door closed. They stood back to wave goodbye.

I mouthed 'thank you' to the group, and Edward mouthed 'good luck' back. Then the 'plane was moving in a tight circle, before the engine revved as the pilot pushed the throttle forward and we advanced through the bush at an ever increasing speed.

Once airborne, the pilot indicated a pair of earphones that were hanging on a hook above the windscreen. I took them down carefully, and, following enthusiastic nods from my companion, put them on.

"Welcome aboard," came the voice of my neighbor. "I'm Gus Bridger, your captain for this adventure. This little beauty has a variable pitch propeller; that's how we can land and take off in such a small area. Effective, don't you think?"

I nodded as if I understood.

"I hope you're all good travelers," Gus continued in a jovial tone. "This bus is affectionately known as 'the vomit comet' due to the fact that I have to fly low enough to baffle any radar; this means dodging the trees and the termite hills. Nap-of-the-earth flying, they call it."

I was not sure how to respond to this, and looked anxiously back at my friends. Gus fiddled beneath his seat for a moment and placed a package of sick bags on my lap, with a wink.

"Just near the border are some power lines," Gus continued. "I have to fly underneath them on the way into this wretched country, and that's a bit hairy. However, coming home, we can risk going over the top, as by the time we come down we will be safely over the border – if all goes well.

A Brand of Faith ~ D.G.A.Pritchard

"Of course there's a chance someone spotted me on my way here, and if so they'll be on the lookout for my return. I'll cross further North from where I came in, but they may still have a pop at us."

I was unsure what to make of this information. I decided I should watch where we were going and not think of anything other than controlling my stomach as the little aircraft zigzagged its way through the undulating landscape just fifty feet above the ground. I passed two of the bags to Percival, realizing that they only had the side windows for reference.

It was a wonderful journey from a game-viewing point of view. There were herds of elephant, buffalo, Impala and two or three stately giraffes. We were close enough to the ground to watch the warthogs run, their tails straight up with the rigidity of radio aerials. Everything started running madly as the 'plane came towards them and Gus had fun chasing the various animals which crashed through the bush in panic. There were hawks and eagles above us and stately storks and herons below, cocking their heads inquisitively as we buzzed past.

After nearly an hour, Gus looked at me and pointed ahead. "There are the power lines. Hang on, this could be exciting," he said as he gave the aircraft a sudden burst of power and pulled the butterfly-shaped joystick towards him.

The 'plane leapt into the air, climbing so steeply that all view of land disappeared and I could see nothing ahead except for the blur of the spinning propeller. My back was forced into the seat and I found I was clutching the armrests with white knuckles. I didn't dare turn to see how the others were managing.

Suddenly there was a flash of light just ahead of us, slightly to the left. It turned to black smoke as a great bang shook the aircraft. "Come on baby," Gus was crooning to his machine, "just a few more feet and we'll

612

be above trouble." He was watching the altimeter, and, with a sigh of satisfaction, began pushing the stick carefully forward. The 'plane leveled off just as another bang was heard directly beneath us. The 'plane shuddered slightly but kept on flying.

"Those RPG's can't go more than nine hundred meters without exploding – less if they are fired straight up," Gus turned to me with a broad grin. "And the launcher is a way off on the port side so I reckon that now we're up here at eight hundred and fifty feet they can shoot away as much as they like and never get near us, given the RPG is travelling along the hypotenuse. But you see why I had to go under the lines on the way in!"

I didn't understand anything. Cold sweat was trickling down my spine and I could feel it bubbling on my forehead and at my temples. I wanted to wipe it away but daren't move my hands from where they gripped the armrests.

"What's an RPG?" I finally managed to ask.

"A Rocket Propelled Grenade" answered Gus as if he was discussing a type of chocolate éclair. "These will be RPG7s, kindly donated to your friends below by either the Russians or the Chinese. Fortunately the militia here don't use them with the greatest accuracy, but given that their orders are to shoot down anything that crosses the border, in either direction between the two official crossing areas, one does have to be careful.

"The danger's over now," Gus continued, "so you can all relax. "We'll have you down in just fifteen minutes and then it's a three hour car journey to the airport, and a long flight home.

63. BACK HOME

E ven though it was the middle of winter, England looked soft and green as the aircraft circled over Heathrow, waiting to land. I could not help a lurch of affection climbing to my throat and making my eyes sting as I viewed my native land. After all the browns of Africa, burnt dry by the sun or by man, England was a sponge of fecundity.

A slim young man from the Foreign Office was waiting for us at Heathrow, a wheelchair at the ready along with warm winter coats. He introduced himself as McManus in a voice as Scottish as his name, and whisked all three of us through immigration and customs and on into London in a shiny black car with the minimum of fuss – after all, we had no luggage.

We were to be de-briefed by a panel whose members specialized in Central Africa, McManus explained, but hastened to add that he knew nothing more about the arrangements that might, or might not, have been made for us.

Another wheelchair waited for Amrita as we arrived at the Foreign Office and Percival and I busied ourselves making her comfortable. We were all three suddenly feeling rather nervous.

McManus led the way along a tall corridor lit by fluorescent lights, from which highly polished wooden doors led to unknown destinations on either side. Finally, he stopped, and opened the last door on the right hand side. He stepped back to allow his charges to pass in front of him. It felt like entering a head-master's study, I thought, or that of Father David.

Percival pushed Amrita's chair into a high-ceilinged room with great Georgian windows overlooking St. James' park. I followed and McManus, without entering himself, closed the door softly behind me. I could hear the sound of our guide's footsteps diminishing along the corridor we had just left.

There were two empty chairs set in front of a long table at which sat a panel of six immaculately groomed men varying in age from thirty to sixty, I guessed. They were chatting to each other casually, but stopped talking as their visitors entered. An exceptionally tall man with dark hair graying at the temples stood up and introduced himself simply as "Matthew, the chairman of the committee." He indicated that Percival and I should take the empty chairs, with Amrita's chair pulled up alongside.

In spite of all the formality, we were greeted cordially and welcomed by Matthew on behalf of all the members of the Central African committee and two gentlemen from the U.S. Embassy who had been invited to join them. He said that they understood that the new arrivals had all had a rough time and expressed sympathy for what we had endured.

Percival, Amrita and I were all exhausted from our long journey. However, we answered the questions that were put to us by the soft-spoken, irritatingly polite interviewers, without difficulty. There was nothing much to tell, really, it all seemed so common-place, and we were surprised at the amount of detail that was sought over what seemed like simple and ordinary actions.

We were asked about the layout of the bishop's palace, of how many floral arrangements we had observed and their locations. There were questions about St. Mary's and the attention we had received there, about the river transport opportunities, about the presence or absence of utilities in the capital.

I was asked for my opinion of Tchonga as a possible future leader of the country. If he were to be elected, how long did I think the new president would take to embrace corruption – there was no 'if' implied, just a 'when.'

The interview lasted for just over an hour, and then I asked if we too could have some answers.

"Yes, of course, Jack," Matthew replied in a most accommodating tone. "What would you like to know?"

I said that we were all very grateful to be back in England, and thanked whoever was responsible for organizing the documents and our escape route, but we wondered why it had been necessary for us to leave in such a manner. Could we not have simply taken a scheduled flight home?

"I'll answer that, if I may," said a white-haired gentleman in a pin-striped suit, sitting to the right of the panel's spokesman. Having received a nod from Matthew, he continued: "the President of Aruba and his cronies, headed by your friend the bishop, had a lengthy propaganda tour organized for you, Jack. They planned to keep your two friends as hostages in the palace to make sure you went along with their demands.

"Accidents can happen to even the most revered public figures, and you were all far from safe as long as you stayed in that turbulent country."

"Our people over there didn't want to see our citizens used in such a way." It was one of the Americans who spoke next, a thickset man with a square face and carefully cropped ash colored hair. "And besides, none of us are enthusiastic about encouraging the present regime to stay in power."

"This is all top secret, I'm afraid," said a balding man, sitting on Matthew's left, who also spoke with an American accent. "But I for one feel that you should know the truth about what has happened," he looked at his neighbor, who gave a slight inclination of his head.

The American took a deep breath, and continued: "our intelligence was that the three of you were considered to be expendable. As soon as your usefulness had been exploited to the full, your murders had already been planned. They were to be carried out in such a way that the fingers of guilt would point at Tchonga's people – erroneously, of course. A full scale massacre of vengeance was the next anticipated step giving the government an excuse to completely wipe out the opposition.

"It was therefore necessary for us to remove you all quickly, secretly and safely."

There was silence for some time after this speech. Percival, Amrita and I were all three staring at the speaker. We didn't move, we seemed to stop breathing as the information sank into our minds.

"Well, it's all over now," Matthew said calmly. "Everyone here believes that we have done the right thing in bringing you out. We must ask for your assurance that what you have just heard will stay within this room.

"Do we have such assurances?" Matthew continued, following several seconds when nobody spoke.

"Yes of course," it was Percival who first found his voice. "And I feel that a 'thank you' is also in order. It appears that we owe you our lives as well as our freedom."

Amrita and I both nodded gravely, neither of us trusted ourselves to speak.

"Well, now that we have that sorted," Matthew spoke briskly as he rose to his feet, "our panel thanks you for your co-operation and for the information you have given us. It has been more helpful than you can guess.

"We have arranged for somewhere for you all to stay tonight. McManus will sort everything out. Then tomorrow, Percival and Amrita are booked on the ten-thirty flight to Washington, D.C. I assume you will be making your own arrangements Jack?" he queried.

I nodded, not knowing what to say. I hadn't any plans except for a vague idea of asking Thomas if I could come and stay for a few days. I needed time to adjust and the prospect of visiting the Allworthy family was both pleasant and safe for my bruised spirit.

"Please let McManus know what you decide to do," Matthew continued. "Your superiors in the church, who have given you more support than you can know, are eager to catch up with you once you are rested. We have promised to keep them informed as to your whereabouts."

I didn't appreciate that idea, but forced myself to smile and nod agreement. I followed my two friends out of the room to find McManus waiting for us in the corridor.

A special mini-bus was drawn up outside the entrance of the Foreign Office. Its back doors were open, with ramps descending to the road. Inside was an area designed especially for wheel-chairs. There were conventional seats also, towards the front, and when all three passengers were loaded, McManus himself climbed into the driver's seat. We set off towards the West End.

For our last night together, we had been billeted in a small hotel situated between the Cromwell road and South Kensington. We were shown into a suite with two bedrooms leading off a central sitting room and a balcony looking into a small park in the centre of a square of Edwardian houses.

I telephoned Thomas with some trepidation. My friend was ecstatic to receive the call and eager for me to make Thornton a home for as long as possible. He wanted to come up to London immediately, but I persuaded him to wait until the next morning when, I said, I would be grateful to be collected. I gave Thomas the address and hung up with a smile. It had been good to hear my old friend's voice and wonderful that my request had met with such an enthusiastic response.

First, I had to face saying goodbye to Amrita and Percival. We had a quiet evening together, nobody speaking very much. There was so much to say, but nothing that hadn't been understood already. We ate a light supper almost in silence and, exhausted, said our goodnights and went to bed early.

In the end, it was all over in a rush. We had all slept deeply and were late waking. There was a panic to get Amrita ready for the journey and to collect our few things together before joining McManus in the hotel lobby where a black car could be seen through the revolving doors. We exchanged hasty hugs and promises of reunions and keeping in touch, and then suddenly, they were gone. I was on my own.

64. THORNTON AND THE ALLWORTHYS

Throughout the long flight home, I had thought about what I should say to my parents, Father Justin, Rufus and to Thomas and his family when I should meet them. I realized they would all require an explanation for my unannounced return and of the change of character they would undoubtedly discover sooner or later. I did not relish the idea of the telling of my experiences over and over again.

I also knew there was no use in pretending to Thomas that my beliefs had not changed. I had left the religion of my youth behind in a morass of anguish and disappointment. If Thomas chose to live by the old ideas of his childhood, that was his prerogative, I was not going to try to persuade him to change his life, and I was certain that Thomas would not be able to persuade me to return to my former faith, although I knew my friend was bound to try.

What reason did a vicar in an English village, with a loving wife and healthy, adoring children, have to question the blessings of his deity? And what right did I have to throw the pain and disenchantment of my own experiences into Thomas's safe and untroubled world? None, I decided.

The last thing I wanted was to abuse Thomas's hospitality by making my host question the beliefs of his profession. Somehow I had to find a way to skirt around religious issues and leave Thomas's faith secure.

Thomas looked much the same, I thought, as he bounded into the hotel lobby, although rounder in both face and waistband. My friend's youthful demeanor made me realize how much my own face had changed. I had been so busy with the mental alterations in my life that I had not paid attention to the physical ones.

During the drive from London, Thomas was careful with his questions. He had only sketchy ideas of what I had been doing in Africa, and, in spite of his anticipations, was obviously shocked to see my gaunt frame and a face that looked so much older than it should, the trim beard doing little to disguise the hollow cheeks.

I decided that it was best to give Thomas the basic facts of what had happened to me, sparing the grisly details, as soon as we were out of traffic and on the M1 heading north in the winter sunshine.

Thomas listened carefully, keeping his eyes on the road. The only sign of emotion came from the occasional movement of his eyebrows, and I thought his eyes glistened with moisture briefly. I kept my tone as matter-of-fact as possible and played down the dramas as best I could. I did not give a graphic account of my own injuries or of those of anyone else. But I knew Thomas was filling in the gaps I was leaving, and, although my friend's imagination was bound to fall short of the truth, it would be enough to cause distress.

There was a jubilant welcome for me at the Thornton Vicarage. Sandra was standing on the doorstep smiling and waving, as she had done many years before. She had spread towards middle age and Alicia and my namesake, Jack, were nearly in their teens now. There was not much difference in heights as they stood together on the doorstep smiling by direction. Neither of the kids would remember me, nor would the two dogs – a black Labrador and a shaggy lurcher – who sped to greet the master's car.

Jack seemed genuinely pleased to see his God-father, and I realized with a shock that he had nine years worth of presents owing. The boy had grown into a thoughtful young man who looked very much like his father, apart from his eyes, which had the same shape and sparkle as his mother's and his hair that had turned to russet brown.

"Where's your luggage?" Sandra asked after the initial hugs had been exchanged as the dogs pushed for attention.

"Gosh, I never thought," said Thomas in alarm. "I was so pleased to see you Jack - I forgot about the luggage, did we leave it behind?"

I smiled at my friend's consternation. "No, no, Thomas, don't worry. I haven't got any luggage, Sandra. I think you'll need to take me shopping. I have only the toothbrush I brought with me from the hotel." I pulled a bright blue toothbrush from my breast pocket and brandished it with mock pride.

There was some confusion following this remark, so many questions hung in the air.

"What did you think about the new car?" my god-son asked, unaware that he was smoothing over an awkward moment.

"Oh," I said, turning to look at the vehicle that had brought me from London. "I'm so sorry, I wasn't paying attention. It's very smart, isn't it?"

"You're in your usual room, Jack." Sandra had recovered herself and was leading the way into the hall and up the stairs. "Make yourself at home, and we'll have lunch as soon as you are ready. After that, I can feel a shopping spree coming on," she said over her shoulder as she opened the guest-room door.

I spent the next few days strolling in the garden or accompanying Thomas on his pastoral tours. I had been startled to find that I had nine years worth of salary in my bank account – I hadn't given money a thought for such a long time, and now I found I was quite well off. Sandra had enjoyed spending some of it and had picked out an entire new wardrobe for me. The few clothes I had left with them upon my departure for Africa were all too big for me now.

In the evenings, Sandra would tactfully leave Thomas and I together, and we would chat amiably about what had happened that day, or what the future might hold. I realized that Thomas was letting me choose the time to talk about Aruba, only if and when I was comfortable to do so, and I was grateful. He did, however, talk of his own continuing faith, in the hope, I suspected, that his words might echo somewhere in the soul of his friend.

"I have never had cause to doubt the fundamental Truth of Christianity -although sometimes I question the ways in which it is expressed in our services," Thomas said one evening. "However I realize that I have not met the challenges you have, Jack, or suffered similar pains, both emotionally and physically – so maybe you could say that my faith has never been significantly tested. I don't know."

I was staring into the fire, the port in my glass making me think of Father Justin.

"What I do know," Thomas persevered, "is that sometimes, when I am preaching or counseling, ideas that I express seem to come 'through' me rather than 'of' me.

"There are times when I don't fully understand the essence of what I am saying. I find myself beginning a sentence not knowing how it is going to end. It's as if I am sensing things that need saying, even if I don't completely grasp the validity of what is being said. I am feeling my way forward and being pushed from behind at the same time. It usually does the trick for my audience, so I don't question its ingenuity or source. I am just trying to be an honest and true conductor for ideas that seem to come from elsewhere.

"Does that make sense to you, Jack?"

"That is just what I never had," I responded with a sense of injustice in my voice. "I have never had the feeling that my words have been guided by God, even though I used to pray fervently and frequently for such guidance.

"There I was, in Islington, straight from the seminary, being asked to advise on teenage pregnancies, drugs, alcohol, marriages and even masturbation – I so needed to feel a wisdom coming 'through' me – but I didn't, I just wallowed along as best I could feeling permanently unqualified and out of my depth.

"That's one of the reasons I left. All my best intentions went wrong. People I tried to help, just kept coming back again and again. They all wanted more from me than I had to give. I was trying to get them to stand on their own, but all I did was to encourage them to lean the harder."

We sat in silence for a while, each busy with our thoughts.

"Do you remember that awful man Simon Mountford?" Thomas said, all of a sudden.

I grimaced and nodded.

"Well, he was pretty much responsible for my being sent to this rural backwater, instead to a more demanding parish in a city. Of course I was upset about it at the time, but when I met Sandra, I realized that the whole Simon episode had been for a reason.

"With Sandra and the children I have understood the love of God in an entirely new way, entering another dimension, if you like.

"Thornton is definitely where I belong, and I feel strongly that it is God who placed me here – although it was a strange way to go about it," he added with a mirthless chuckle. "My life with Sandra, our wonderful children, the peace and love that surrounds us, are gifts that I never take for granted. I thank God over and over again, every day. I have no ambitions to leave this wonderful community, they keep adding more parishes, it's true, and that is enough of a challenge to keep me on my toes. I know I am doing God's work, in the place where God wants me to be.

"My great good fortune," Thomas added with a smile, "is that where God wants me to be is also where I want to be. My life has not the challenges of someone as adventurous as you, my friend, but I am happy and well satisfied with those I have. If I can meet them with success - and with God's help and my family's support, I will - then why should I wish for more?

"Our friend Simon, however, has raced up the ecclesiastical ladder, stepping over much more likely candidates. He had a high-society wedding a few years ago, with all the trappings, in York Minster, no less, where his uncle is still the bishop. He married an heiress with some sort of connection to the Archbishop of

Canterbury. He will be a bishop himself before too long – and a most inappropriate one. But God must have his reasons, I suppose."

I looked at my friend with a mixture of affection and envy. How wonderful to have such an unquestioning acceptance of what I now thought of as an archaic theology. I felt as if my selection of previous beliefs had been like picking beautiful flowers only to have them slip through my fingers and turn into briars.

"What makes you think there is a Divine Plan?" I asked softly.

"Because I can't afford not to," replied Thomas without hesitation. "I just don't have an alternative, nor do I want one. It's as simple as that."

The logs had turned to ashes in the grate, the port decanter was empty and so were our glasses, it was time for bed.

When Sunday came, Thomas asked me to accompany him in the presentation of the service. I had thought about this problem knowing that it was bound to arrive, and was ready with my answer.

"Forgive me, Thomas," I said softly, "but I won't be coming to church with you today. I would prefer to go for a long walk through the countryside."

"But it's raining, and cold," Thomas said in surprise, and then realizing the unimportance of the weather, he continued "I've written a special 'welcome home' sermon for you Jack. A thanksgiving to God for bringing you home safely." Poor Thomas could not have said anything less likely to make me change my mind.

"I have my smart new Wellingtons, and the ridiculously expensive waxed coat and hat Sandra chose for me, I will not mind the rain, and I shall enjoy the exercise." I said more brusquely than intended. "There are some woods I have been eyeing up just outside the village, with a footpath sign which looks most inviting.

"I'm sorry to let you down, my dear friend," I continued in a softer tone, putting a hand on Thomas's shoulder. "I have enjoyed visiting your church with you when we had it to ourselves, but I'm afraid I don't feel like participating in any kind of service now, or in the future," I added with a note of finality.

"Oh, Jack, I'm so sorry, so very, very sorry." Thomas was almost in tears. "I don't know what has happened to you, but I realize that it has done more damage than I could possibly imagine. I will change my sermon for today, but I will not tear it up. I hope to use it at some time, when you are ready."

I wanted to shout that he should rip it to shreds, that there would never be a time when I was ready for such a treatise, that I wanted nothing to do with this God of Thomas's, I was finished with all that. Now and forever.

But I didn't. I just nodded quietly and went into the hall to fetch my wet-weather gear.

The sky was heavy with grey, but the rain had stopped by the time Thomas and his family left for church and I was ready for my ramble. I looked at the cumbersome waxed clothes and the pair of shiny Wellington boots and decided to leave them behind. I set off at a good pace, eager to leave the anguish I had caused my friend. The dogs had sensed my intentions and were waiting at the door, tails wagging and eyes filled with expectation.

I took a short-cut to the end of the village through the copse that bordered Thomas's garden. The dogs bounded ahead of me, looking back every now and then as if to say, 'this way, this way, hurry up.' Their exuberance was infectious and soon I felt the hurt and irritation slipping away. I stepped out with firm strides emulating the joy of the dogs and sharing their freedom.

The path met the road, and I crossed with care, a finger lodged in each of the dogs' collars. I let them go as I approached the style with the footpath sign, and watched them scrabble through and over the rails and disappear up the muddy track into the wood.

The walk did me good. The wet earth seeped into my inadequate shoes, and it was not long before the rain began again, this time in earnest. I trudged on, enjoying the icy water running down my neck and spine. I was walking quickly enough to keep warm and reveled in the solitude of the dripping woods and the undemanding company of the two dogs who swooped into my vision every now and again, tongues lolling, as if with laughter, as they rushed back into the vegetation.

We were all three drenched to the skin by the time we returned to the vicarage. Thomas and his family were not due back until tea time, there being some celebratory luncheon happening in the village hall after the church service, and I enjoyed having the house to myself. I shut the wet dogs in the kitchen where they spread themselves out by the Aga, and went upstairs for a hot shower.

I was trimming my newly shampooed beard, steam rising from my naked body as I leant over the washbasin, when the door behind me opened.

Sandra came bustling in, and stopped in dismay. I caught sight of her expression in the mirror as her eyes rested on the cruciform scar which rose across my buttocks; the unmistakable sign of the cross still clearly visible in spite of the skin grafts.

The scream was quite involuntary, and Sandra clapped a hand over her mouth as she backed away into the corridor, pulling the door shut behind her.

The muffled words: "I'm so sorry, Jack," hung in the air as her footsteps could be heard running down the stairs. Somewhere a door slammed, and then all was quiet once again.

I put down the scissors carefully and picked up the hand towel, rubbing my hair and beard before wiping my face. Everything seemed to be happening in slow motion. I wrapped a towel around my lower body and returned to my room, leaving my wet clothes in a heap by the shower door.

I dressed slowly and then went downstairs to the kitchen. I found Thomas and his children seated around the table while Sandra was busy putting plates of food in front of them.

"We were wrong about the luncheon," Thomas said with a false brightness in his voice. "It's next week, not today. So come and join us, Jack," he continued as he pulled out a chair next to him, "Sandra's raided the larder with great success."

65. THE WORLD IN A ROBIN'S EYE

After lunch Sandra, Alice and my godson Jack went off to visit some friends and Thomas and I were alone in front of the fire in the sitting room, cradling cups of coffee.

Thomas turned and spoke in a soft voice. "Please, Jack, you have to help me deal with this. Sandra told me what she saw when she burst into the bathroom. You have to tell me what has happened to you, to your body, your beliefs, your faith, your calling. I don't mean to intrude, but I need to understand, and I don't think I can wait any longer."

I stood up and walked over to my friend, putting a hand upon his shoulder for the second time that day. "I'm sorry, Thomas," I started. "I am being a lousy guest and a lousy friend. I realize that my reluctance to talk about what has happened is selfish when it comes to communicating with you. Your caring means more to me than you can know, and I am insulting that care with my silence."

I moved to stand in front of the fire, picked up the poker and prodded the logs, adding a new one to the blaze. I noticed how the log was perfectly cut, just the right size for the Victorian grate. Thomas' life was so carefully shaped, even down to the size of the firewood. I turned again and told him the pieces of my story that I had omitted before. I spoke slowly and carefully and found it easier than I had imagined, as if in the telling, the tale was being diluted.

When I finished, the silence hung heavily in the room, only the crackling of the fire and the ticking of the clock on the mantle-piece disturbed the stillness. Thomas was staring at his feet, he said nothing.

"As to my faith," I knew the real area of Thomas's interest, "that went with Loveness's screams and the life blood of the elders.

"I have faced a void, Thomas, and slowly I have got used to it. However," I added, thinking of Amrita's gentle ideas, "there are possible alternatives to the Christian God with whom I grew up."

I recounted Amrita's analogy of the underground lake and spoke of her determination to 'filter the positive elements from the darkness.' As I spoke, Amrita's pretty face came to my mind with a force that was almost tactile. I remembered her insistence of the existence of good, of the positive force of creation which only man could corrupt; of the love between people being a manifestation of that goodness, and of the elements of positivity that infuse the energy field from which we were created and in which we exist. I did my best to communicate Amrita's thoughts and found it quite exhausting, but, at the same time, exhilarating.

Thomas was silent for several minutes, I left the fire and took my coffee back to the armchair.

Thomas broke the silence at last. "An all-invasive force-field that unites seemingly disparate energies and courses through all aspects of Life, is that what you're suggesting?" he asked, framing his sentence with care.

"Yes, I think so," I answered, equally cautious. "It's a pulling together of the positivity of existence, and at the same time there's an energy that pulsates outwards from the Earth's core, in such a way that particles are pushed apart and held together at the same time. Not an easy concept, I know. A cohesive expansion from the centre to the circumference, moving with enormous speed and yet perfectly still, so that the centre and the circumference are one, no matter the distance. A collection of paradoxes, I'm afraid."

There was an excited sparkle in Thomas' eye. "Say that again" he said with a sudden eagerness.

"Don't be silly, Thomas," I was getting tired now, and my friend's enthusiasm was horribly misplaced.

"You talked about the positivity of existence, didn't you?" Thomas insisted.

I frowned, thinking back over my almost subconscious ramblings. "Yes, I was describing all that is left for me now – a jumble of opposites without divinity."

"What did you mean by positivity?"

"Well, this fundamental field of energies has positive elements, it drives forwards, enthusing existence from minute particles."

"So it's a positive force?"

"Of course," I answered, trying to keep the irritation I was feeling from showing. Thomas was pressing on like a horse running through the bit.

"Positive is good, isn't it?"

"Positive as in the opposite of negative."

"But is this force evil?"

"No, definitely not, it pulsates with a clean light, only man defiles it."

"So the light is good, as in the opposite of evil?"

"Well, I suppose so." I was wavering, feeling as if I were being trapped.

"An immaculate light until contaminated by man?" Thomas continued, relentlessly.

"Yes, that sounds about right, somewhat over-simplified, but yes."

"It is an energy of goodness?" Thomas' excitement made me smile in spite of myself. Why was I being so obdurately negative, so reluctant to embrace Thomas's enthusiasm? There were so many reasons, but they were in the past now, and Thomas was a dear friend who meant me nothing but good.

"Go on," I told myself, "give him a break. At least pretend to be human." Then out loud I said: "Oh all right, I suppose so".

Thomas leapt from his chair and grabbed me by both hands, pulling me upright so that we were standing only inches apart.

"Faith, Jack, you still have it, you just don't recognize it any more."

I blinked, feeling my eyes widen. He had caught me by surprise. I felt as if I had been snuck up on from behind and ambushed. I did not understand the excitement in Thomas's voice, in fact I found it irritating – an irrational reaction, I know, but that's how it was. Somehow I felt he was pressing into my personal space without an invitation, he was invading my pain and devaluing it somehow with this talk of positivity.

"Your identification of the positive nature of your force-field is Faith," Thomas continued. "The fact that you believe the energy to be one of essential goodness, is Faith – don't you see? Faith, with a capital F."

Something seemed to shift inside me. In my mind it felt as if a miniature bucket was being pulled up from a long disused well. It was only the size of a thimble, but there was water in it, that special water of Amrita's analogy. As it reached the top of the pulley the bucket swayed and a tiny drop spilled out, splashing on the edge of the well where it caught the sunlight in a bright flash before falling into the dust.

Was it really still there? Was there really a germ of hope? I looked into the black pit where my God had once filled my soul with light. It was still the same black pit with a fathomless emptiness that threatened to drag me down to hell once again. But when I strained into the blackness there was a sense of something new. Something had changed. Somewhere amongst the density I glimpsed a tiny particle of non-blackness. It was not light exactly, more a reflection from a distant source. As the marble of the Taj Mahal draws in the moonlight and sends it out transfused, muted, different, with a magic all of its own, so Thomas' insistence had placed a small seed of luminance in the part of my soul where the carapace had been softened by Amrita's thoughts and ideas.

I was staring into Thomas' fervent gaze. My eyes were unfocused and unblinking. Then, gradually clarity returned, I found I was sweating and feeling dizzy. Thomas' steady grip of hands and eyes were all that kept me upright.

"Faith?" I queried, my voice seemed small and came from far away.

Thomas sat me back into the armchair with great gentleness, his eyes never breaking contact. He was kneeling at the side of my chair, a lock of hair falling over his forehead as he bent.

"You of all people, Jack, should know that nomenclature is irrelevant. Your belief in the fundamental goodness of your energy field is Faith – what else can you call it? The positivity of existence is apparent in every flower that buds, every far star shining, every wave that brings its force onto the shore; when the sun rises or sets; the warmth of its rays through the magic of an autumn mist; the way your heart surges with the breath of a new day and lifts with the birds' songs and the light trapped in a dew drop; dancing cobwebs through the bracken in a Yorkshire dawn; the way the clouds chase and dance; the feeling of rain upon an upturned face; the kiss of the wind amongst the apple blossoms – is all GOOD for which the word God is just an abbreviation. I still remember your sermon back in the College – the one about the magic of a chitted seed – nothing has changed."

"But everything has changed," I insisted, "I have abandoned the God to whom I dedicated my life. I have rejected the whole idea. I have deliberately turned my back upon the whole concept of deity. I despise it." I felt a choking sensation in my throat as despair threatened to unleash itself again.

"Everything has not changed, Jack." Thomas was talking softly, his eyes still holding my reluctant gaze.

"It is you who have changed. You see things differently now, and it is not surprising after what you have been through. But what we have discovered here, just now, is that although you have lost your religion, you have not lost your Faith. Religions are just the vestments of Faith. Ways to dress up an idea and make it graspable, ways of supplying hope.

"And if you have Faith, Jack - by admitting that your basic concept of existence is a positive one, one of goodness – then you must also have hope. The Immaculate Conception is an analogy for your immaculate light. Your metaphor of the centre and the circumference being one and the same is an ancient Hindu concept – or is it Buddhist? This was your specialty, Jack, not mine."

Thomas was smiling now, the depth of delight and excitement in his eyes was infectious. Again, I felt something stirring in the blackness, the grain of soft light was growing. Hope. I thought of Tolstoy's character

Ivan Illych in the book Percival had insisted I read. The dying man had seen death as a black tunnel, black like the void I had been carrying where my soul used to be. There had been a light at the end of Ivan's tunnel that grew through the pain into something beautiful. Using the parody of the birth canal, Tolstoy had pushed his protagonist through the transformation. Ivan Illych had conquered fear and death, he had fallen out of his tunnel and into the blissful light of …?

"Remember the light at the end of the tunnel could be that of an on-coming train," my intellect reminded me. I had experienced that, I had been railroaded, crushed, and broken.

'Instead of death there was light.' Tolstoy had written. Could it be that my soul was being reborn with this small glow that Thomas had recognized? Was this the chitted seed of my first sermon?

I remained skeptical, but didn't want to disappoint Thomas who was clearly deeply moved and delighted by his findings. "I shall keep my thoughts to myself," I decided, and, determined not to upset my friend further, I rearranged my features into a cautious smile.

"Well that's given me something to think about. Thank you Thomas for your faith in me and for your love and friendship that has given me back a modicum of hope."

"Ah, so you think to humor me by disguising your doubts" Thomas laughed. "You forget, I know you too well. Don't rush it, Jack. Give the seed time to grow, but nurture it every now and then with a glance as to its welfare.

"That's enough for now, I feel as if my world has shifted, even if yours has not, and I will need time to realign my own beliefs. What we need is a cup of tea, and maybe a slice of something from the larder. I think there is still some Christmas cake left – how very appropriate!"

Thomas stood up and moved to the fireplace where only ashes were left aglow. He pulled a log from the basket and dropped it onto the coals. "I'll bring tea in here, I won't be long" he said as he reached the door. He turned as he opened it and gave me a broad grin of delight. "Don't look so solemn, Jack. Try to let the blackness go." He shut the door softly but firmly behind him.

I listened to Thomas's footsteps echo down the tiled corridor towards the back of the house where the high-ceilinged kitchen was flanked by a larder, pantry, flower-room and acres of deep-shelved cupboards. I got up, turned my back to the fire that showed no sign of being coaxed back into life, and walked to the window.

Outside the garden was crisping with frost. The heavy clouds were dispersing but there was no hint of warmth to soften the blades of grass that stood stiffly to attention. The tall trees at the bottom of the garden were shadowy in the fading light with black blots in their top branches where the rooks had built their untidy town.

A robin was perched on the edge of one of Sandra's cherished garden pots in which an old rosemary bush seemed to shiver in the cold. The bird's bright eye moved in staccato style. It seemed to be looking me up and down in an interested fashion.

Everything looked the same, and yet everything was different. There seemed to be a new clarity of vision, as if my eyes had been re-focused to account for a new dimension. I thought of Amrita's idea of trees and mountains. Was there really a spark of hope coming back to my seared soul? The thought made me giddy, and I found myself gripping the windowsill for support.

The robin was startled by the movement behind the glass. It cocked its head on one side and hopped off the plant pot onto the stone slabs of the terrace. Instead of moving away, I watched as the little bird picked its way amongst the patches of moss, moving purposely towards the window. With a slight flutter of wings, the robin alighted upon the window ledge.

The bird was so close to the glass that I could see the red breast rising and falling beneath the feathers. A tiny bright black eye struck me with awe; so much life, the instincts of ages, the precision of gaze. Someone had once seen the world in a grain of sand, now I saw it in a Robin's eye. A tiny black globe of intelligence taking in information like a sponge.

Suddenly the bird flew away. Thomas had come in with the tea tray and the draught from the door caused the fire to leap into life. The room was light and cozy as the winter afternoon darkened into early dusk.

There was no sign of the robin but its imprint remained in my mind as I drew the curtains and turned

back into the nest of sofa and chairs around the fire. It is still with me today.

The Robin's Eye

66. THE JIG-SAWS OF LIFE

Thomas must have seen the confusion in my face when he returned with the tea. He set the tray down on the table behind the sofa and looked at me intently over the teapot. It was apparent that he had been thinking hard while waiting for the kettle to boil.

"Over the years," he began, in what I recognized as his sermon voice, "I have developed an analogy to help me deal with the changes that occur in beliefs as life confronts us with various challenges. Let's see what you make of it."

Thomas busied himself with cups and saucers, sugar bowl and milk jug, as he began his theory. "Imagine that one's Faith is like a jigsaw puzzle. Each one of us is given a box of hundreds of pieces to put together to form a picture. During childhood, the children are encouraged to look at the picture on the box lid to help them put the puzzle together. Parents and teachers, both religious and secular, are responsible for providing this guidance and watching with pride as the child joins up the pieces to achieve the desired finished picture, a picture that will provide foundations of that individual's physic strength as he grows and matures, a picture manipulated by the ideas of his elders.

"I believe both of us had our puzzles pretty nearly completed when we arrived at St. Augustine's. During our years there, the still-evolving pictures we were building were refined and our own impetus encouraged to tweak the final image into something profound; always within the original parameters however. There were some disruptions en route – a few pieces dislodged and needing to be brought back into position – but on the whole, by the time we were ordained, our individual puzzle-pieces were all in place, and glued together with our convictions, giving us a strong and stable base upon which to build our new lives."

Thomas finally handed me the cup of tea he had been cradling as he spoke, and started preparing his own cup. "As our lives unfolded, we have had to confront major upheavals of our puzzle pieces. These disruptions may be caused by illnesses, deaths, the troubles of our parishioners we find hard to cope with – your young Jamaican girl, for example – accidents, decisions that go wrong, and so on. You get the idea. These problems assault our carefully glued together jigsaw and fragments are blown away, jumbled up, scattered. Through careful prayer, meditation, or just stubborn mental perseverance, those pieces can be found, dusted off and re-positioned. Of course, the complete picture will be changed in the process, but the over-all image remains the same."

Having finally filled his own teacup, Thomas walked around the edge of the sofa and sat down, stirring carefully. He looked up briefly, a worried smile was evident only for a moment, and I realized that he was sharing something immensely private with me. I tried to push my skepticism away and honor the privilege with which I was being presented.

"I have used this analogy to help me re-build parts of my faith which have been ravaged by doubts, horrors, sadness and complacency. I have carefully reviewed the missing pieces of my personal picture, and found them using prayer to over-come pain and belief to conquer doubts. It is a constant struggle to keep the pieces where they belong, where they have to be if the picture is to look whole and glorious once again. Every night, when I say my prayers, I am looking at the frayed edges, or gaps even, in my picture, and trying to mend and restore the image.

"Now I understand that what happened to you in Africa didn't simply dislodge a few puzzle pieces. No, it completely destroyed your whole picture, scattering the pieces in a whirlwind of excruciating disaster. I accept that your original picture is gone forever – but, Jack, and it is a big BUT, those pieces are still extant, even though they are apart and probably spiraling outwards, blown further and further by the strength of your disillusionment.

"What I am so excited about today, is that I believe that you have tripped over a piece of your puzzle. Oh, I know it's just one piece of thousands, and it may not be a corner, but it is still a beginning, and I believe that other pieces will follow, if only you will allow them to return. You will still be responsible for engaging them –

whenever you get enough to warrant such an exercise – and then an entirely different picture will slowly be pieced together. This time, there is no picture on the box lid to guide you. You are on your own on an exciting journey.

"Let it happen, Jack. Please let it happen."

Thomas was staring at his cup with the intensity of a gypsy tealeaf reader. I got up and poked the smoldering logs, then took a turn around the room. There had been a shift within me with which I was not completely comfortable. Thomas's analogy was useful, I felt, and as I began to take it on board I thought of how much Amrita would have enjoyed it. I found myself suddenly caught up with the image.

"You know, Thomas," I began, "my friend Amrita would enjoy your analogy, and she would be the first to suggest that the picture does not start out as a jig-saw puzzle, but as a perfect individual image brought into this world by each child. She would claim that the fragmentation of the jigsaw comes into play during early education and the pieces re-arranged by enculturation to fit a particular template, with only tiny individual differences. She would say that it is our mission to recreate the original picture we were given at birth."

I sipped my tea and allowed my thoughts to run. "I really like your idea, Thomas," I continued. "I am interested with your vision of our pictures – yours and mine - being glued together while at St. Augustine's. Indeed I would go so far as to say that institutionalized religion not only instructs upon how to complete the picture, but, once finished, it traps the pieces – or tries to – so that they can no longer be moved about."

"Well, I assure you, Jack," Thomas responded, "my pieces still shift around a good deal, but I am grateful for the adhesive supplied by the church. It provides me with comfort and direction when I try to fit the pieces back together again. Institutionalized religion may not suit you, but for me, and thousands like me, it provides a safety net of security. Our church services provide people like myself and Sandra – and I hope our children – with a steady reassurance of the positivity of existence of which we were speaking earlier. If the words of our prayers are looked upon as a mantra to appease the soul and nothing more, it doesn't matter. What is important is that there is magic in the rituals and in the repeated prayers. There is familiarity, security, and inner calm. There is communication with the Divine, the Infinite, call it what you will. The Church – by which I mean both the buildings and the moral ideas that provide each denomination with its identity – gives us a communication channel with things beyond our immediate ken. There is magic in our churches, Jack – even you must have felt that, although I know, now, you prefer to visit them when they are not holding services."

I thought of Estelle's dowsing for lines of power through the church in Islington, and nodded in agreement – how I wished she had been with me now. Estelle would have known what to do with my seared soul; but she was far away, I knew not where.

67. A RETURN TO SERVICE

The church authorities left me in peace for two weeks before writing to tell me of a meeting I was to attend with the head of the Missionary Service at their headquarters in Whitehall.

I showed the letter to Thomas and Sandra.

"What will you wear?" was Sandra's first concern, and although it sounded flippant, she had raised a good question.

Thomas felt strongly that I should not abandon the clerical collar and offered to lend me one. "You must dress like a vicar, Jack," he insisted, you still have a job, after all." But I was adamant that the collar was a garment from my past, as was the title, and that neither one had a place in my future. If the ministry insisted on such accouterments, then I would have to resign, I told him.

Without the dog-collar to anchor the rest of my attire, we discussed the available clothes options. I didn't own a suit, but Sandra was enthusiastic about buying one for me. Again, I declined; so in the end we settled for some heavy beige corduroys, an open shirt, pullover and a thick tweed jacket to keep out the cold.

The proprietary role Sandra had given herself concerning my wardrobe amused me greatly. I did not object to it, in fact it gave me a sense of being looked after in a very pleasant way. I knew the whole family was genuinely fond of me. The knowledge, even with the resulting fussiness, gave me a warm feeling inside, akin to my friendship with Percival and Amrita. It was as close as I could come, I decided, to a sense of belonging.

The following morning Thomas dropped me at the station in Newport Pagnell in time for the nine-thirty train to Euston Station from where I would take the tube. After nine years in Africa the London Underground took on a ferocious appearance of rushing modernity. Here, it seemed that a travelers' slightest hesitation on direction was viewed as social anathema by the mass of people moving with hurried certainty. I steeled myself for the ordeal and managed the journey to Whitehall having to ask for help only once.

The Reverend John Illingsworth, head of the Missionary Service of The United Kingdom, rose from behind an enormous leather-topped desk and offered a hand across the paper-strewn surface. A heavy-set man in his mid-sixties, he wore an immaculately tailored suit and a conventional shirt and tie. Half-rimmed spectacles balanced at the end of a large and somewhat ruddy nose, his thin grey hair was brushed side-ways across a shiny scalp. He indicated a carver chair, upholstered with the same leather as the desk and with the same worn veracity of age, and I sat down obediently, although he remained standing.

"I have been looking at your dossier with interest, Jack," the Reverend tapped a green file in front of him with a gnarled index finger. "It makes fascinating reading. It seems you have become quite a hero in Aruba."

I winced involuntarily, Illingsworth noticed the reaction with the flick of an eyebrow, but continued as if nothing were amiss.

"You obviously accomplished great things in your village," he paused, his eyes dropping to the papers in front of him for a moment. "Cachonga," he added, pronouncing the word with care. "Something you should be proud of," he continued. "It is hardly your fault, or the fault of your achievements, that the community was destroyed. That thug would have come through there anyway. You can't hold yourself in any way responsible for the disaster." Illingsworth peered at his visitor over the top of his glasses with penetrating eyes. "You can't and you mustn't," he finished, and sat down.

"But, if I hadn't made Cachonga such a prize, would that revolting man have bothered with it?" I spluttered in an unexpected, slightly argumentative outburst.

"Oh yes, Jack," Illingsworth continued calmly, "all my intelligence tells me that Mungutu was on a rampage and anything he came across was plundered and then reduced to ashes. All you did was to give him more things to destroy, and you must fight hard not to let him have destroyed you at the same time."

There was silence between us for some time. I stared resolutely at the carpet, it was Oriental and obviously of considerable age. I noticed how the colors had faded where the light came in through the tall windows, and decided that it had probably been in its present position for as long as the desk and the chair upon which I was seated. I wondered how many generations of missionaries had sat at either side of the desk as Illingsworth and I were doing at that moment.

"Anyway, Jack," my superior interrupted the reverie, "if you don't mind I'd like to ask you some questions about what you did at Cachonga. I am asking you to put aside what happened when you left the village, for the moment. I am interested in how you achieved such progress in an incredibly backward area when so many others, in similar situations, have failed.

"For example, how did you get the village witch doctor to go along with your ideas of building a new church? I am told that not only did he not object, but he actively supported the project."

I found it hard to talk about my relationship with Umboto to start with, but with careful, probing questions from Illingsworth, I eventually found myself speaking with enthusiasm as the positive times at Cachonga were relived during the interview.

Illingsworth had a list of all the machinery, seeds, tools and materials that I had ordered over the years, and the questions which were directed to me followed the same chronological order as the requests for items and the subsequent deliveries.

Everything that had been requested, no matter how unimportant I had thought it at the time, had been recorded and reports sent back to headquarters with each delivery.

I learnt that it was the Missionary Service of the United Kingdom – my employers - who had supplied me with all the things that Boniface had brought up river and for which the Government of Aruba had taken both the credit and the bribes for allowing the items to be forwarded to Cachonga. And it was the same organization that had arranged for Mr. Umvari to travel to St. Mary's to do my operation and funded my time there with all the different treatments I needed.

In return, Illingsworth learnt how I had succeeded in teaching the indigenous population about sanitation, agriculture, dairy farming, specialist crops and their marketing. How the church had been built with the support of the whole community, how I had baptized the entire population of the village prior to the first communion service witnessed by Father Merciful and Jamu.

"By the way," Illingsworth had interjected at this point, "in your memories you mustn't be too hard on those two worthy clerics. They are both devoted to you, and always will be, I believe. They just have to work within the parameters of the pedagogues who provide them with their livelihoods and – to be blunt – with the permission to live.

"The moment the bishop is unsure of their loyalties, Jamu and Merciful will disappear without trace, and there are plenty waiting to take their places. These are both brave and good men, Jack, never forget that, please."

At some point during the discussions, someone came in with a jug of water, two glasses and two plates of sandwiches. Illingsworth and I were so deep in conversation that we hardly noticed the interruption, we did however avail ourselves of the nourishment in between sentences.

Later, the same unidentified person arrived with a tea tray. He cleared the lunch plates and left a plate of scones with delicate dishes of cream and jam along with the pot of tea, slices of lemon, and two cups and saucers. He also turned on the lights - the English winter was closing in around us.

It was after six by the time I rose to leave. The last hour had been occupied with discussions about my future. I was still an employee of The Missionary Service, Illingsworth reminded me, which had invested a great deal in my welfare.

I had much to offer in return, the employer pointed out, with my experiences 'in the field' and my achievements in transforming a small, backward village into a productive Christian community. If I would be willing to teach these skills to hopeful missionaries from around the world, then there was still a place for me in the Service, and, at an increased salary.

"Please understand, Jack," Illingsworth was looking at me directly, "that, although this is a Christian organization, with the spreading of that religion as its main objective, I am not asking you to undertake any kind of proselytizing. I fully understand that would be inappropriate for you at this time. However, there is a vital role you can fill by talking to the zealous first-timers about the pitfalls of working in the developing world - particularly out in the bush.

"Your understanding of indigenous cultures, and your ability to assimilate different ideas under a Christian umbrella, are assets that are very rare. If you can get across the message of how to motivate people to farm productively, to educate their children – and themselves – and to build a homogenous community out of disparate, bickering tribes, you will earn every penny we are offering, and we will be very grateful to you for your efforts.

"We would like to give you an assignment to tour both the United States and Europe, visiting missionary academies and lecturing upon the development of agriculture in the third world," Illingsworth declared. He went on to stress that I should concentrate upon the motivation of both extant and potential workforces; and the ways in which Western ideas of progress can be integrated within existing tribal rites.

"That is the area where, in my opinion, your expertise lies," Illingsworth told me. "In addition, of course, you will be expected to lecture on proper stock management, irrigation system possibilities, the ideal choice of crops, and suitable ways and times for their growth including the generation and use of compost and the building of contours.

"But there are several lecturers covering those agricultural topics – none with as much hands-on experience as you have, Jack, so possibly you will have the edge on other speakers there – however, I must stress that, as far as the Missionary Service is concerned, your greatest achievements have been in people management without which all agricultural improvements do not get off the starting block.

"That is where so many agencies go wrong." Illingsworth came round to the front of the desk and I stood to meet him. "They throw money and equipment into outlying areas; they give tractors, ploughs and seed, but they don't get the people's motivation worked out.

"I can show you pictures of tractors being used as taxis in Afghanistan – have you any idea how many people can travel in, on and around a tractor? – and refrigerators used as chicken coops. Big, American refrigerators sent to villages without electricity, ploughs sent to desert communities with no possible tilth to work. I could go on for hours, it is one of my big objections to the way in which the West distributes its largesse.

"You interest me especially, Jack, because you, with God's help, of course, succeeded where so many others have failed, and that is why the Missionary Service is prepared to offer you a generous salary to teach others what you have taught yourself.

"I have never been so impressed with the achievements of one man, as I am with yours from the reports I have received of your successes. Not one piece of equipment you requested was unsuitable or was not put to good use without delay.

"I know it will be difficult, but you must put the horrors of Cachonga's destruction behind you and concentrate upon the positive work that you achieved there. Do you think you can do that?"

I found myself nodding slowly. Illingsworth's speech was sinking slowly into my brain. "Yes," I said, raising my eyes, and added with a certainty in which I didn't truly believe, "yes, I can do that."

Then, after a moment's pause, I asked in a faltering voice: "does it matter that, in order to win the cooperation and support of the villagers of Cachonga, I needed first to have the backing of the N'anga Umboto. To get that, I'm afraid I somewhat marginalized Christianity and allowed his beliefs to merge with my own."

"Try not to stress that angle too much, Jack," Illingsworth responded quickly.

"But it is absolutely necessary, right at the start, if you are to win respect," I said, a note of urgency in my voice. "These villages are all Christian to a degree, but many of the old ways of magic and animism remain. To fight them head on makes the old ideas stronger by taking them out of your sphere of influence, and at the same time makes the witch doctor more powerful and sets him up in active opposition.

"If you can assimilate their ideas and pander to the status quo, then improvements to their standard of living can be achieved. It takes patience, a great deal of patience, and understanding."

"However, if you are successful," Illingsworth interjected, "and you are able to work with these people as part of a team, as you did, you can achieve ever greater things, and slowly the Christian values can overtake the local mumbo-jumbo. Isn't that true?"

"First," I was quick to reply, "you have to stop thinking of other people's values as 'mumbo-jumbo' and give them the benefit of the doubt. Nobody has the right to decree one belief over another just like that. If you can't respect their ideas, however foolish they may seem to a Western mind, how should we expect them to respect ours – let alone adopt them?"

Illingsworth smiled, and with a gesture totally out of character for his role as head of the Service, he put both his hands on my shoulders and looked me straight in the eye.

"Everything I have been told about you is true, Jack. You are definitely worth every penny of the salary that has been suggested, indeed, I intend to increase it. I don't want someone of your straight talking and genuine knowledge - that can only come from working in the field - falling for some inflated offer from one of the many charity organizations that know how to collect money better than they know how it should be dispersed.

"No, no matter what you think, Jack, you are one of us, and I feel sure we can count on your loyalty to stay with us, and to share your hard-earned knowledge with Christian missionaries around the world. "Am I right?" Illingsworth's question hung in the air like a raindrop caught on a spider's web.

"Yes, at least I think so," I answered eventually. "You have given me a lot to think about. I will go home and prepare for the lectures you wish me to deliver, and then I will submit some suggestions for you to look at. If you are happy with the contents, then the Service can offer me a contract, and we can consider it together. If, however, you don't approve of what I would want to say to missionary candidates, then we will have to rethink the whole idea. Is that fair?" I was looking at Illingsworth directly. I knew that if the contents of my lectures were to be censored in any way, I would be no good for the job I was being offered. I had had enough of being used as a puppet.

"I agree," said Illingsworth, thrusting his right hand towards me. "Let's shake on that. I'll see you back here in three week's time – no make that three and a half weeks. Give me a synopsis of your lectures within three weeks and let me have a couple of days to absorb them and to take advice from my colleagues."

When the handshake was completed, Illingsworth returned to his side of the desk and opened a heavily embossed leather book that looked more like a bible than a diary. He flicked through the heavy pages, and paused.

"Eleven-thirty on the fifteenth be alright with you?" he asked. I gave a shrug of acceptance in response. "That means I will need the synopsis of your lectures by say, the tenth. Is that enough time?"

"I have no other plans, Sir," I replied. "I will get you my ideas, in outline at the very least, by then and look forward to seeing you again on fifteenth."

We shook hands once again, this time in parting, and, feeling a sudden flush of affluence, I took a taxi to the station to find a train back to Hertfordshire.

68. A Welcome Visit to Friends

The American lecture tour that the Missionary Service organized began and finished, at my request, in Washington D.C. allowing me time to visit Amrita and Percival. I arrived two weeks before my first lecture was due and Amrita had planned all sorts of excursions for the three of us.

Percival and Amrita were renting a small bungalow in a pretty tree-lined suburban street not far from the hospital in Bethesda where Amrita was both working and being worked upon.

"There are all sorts of experiments being done with stem-cell treatments," she told me, "and I've volunteered to be a guinea-pig – after all, what have I got to lose?

"It's wonderful being able to work again, and I am not as limited in what I can do as you might think. Doctors use their hands much more than their feet, and beds can be lowered so I can examine patients from my chair."

Percival had also found employment. He was now a lecturer in literature at a nearby junior college, and was enjoying every minute of it. The two of them had grown even closer as their relationship matured and the stresses and traumas of Africa sank slowly into the background. Their love for each other filled their house and I shared their happiness with delight.

My two weeks holiday in Washington passed in a blur of activity. While my friends were working, I was sent 'down town' on various assignments. My first, by Amrita's dictate, was to the National Cathedral on Wisconsin Avenue.

To my surprise, although this is a modern building, the architecture was medieval. The grand edifice followed all the structural rules of the great cathedrals of Europe – except that this one had enjoyed the advantage of the use of cranes and hydraulics in its construction.

There had been no modern intervention with the stone masonry, however, and I was intrigued, and delighted, to find Indians chasing buffalo around the tops of some of the stone columns, sculpted in the traditional way. The American civil war was also depicted, as were herds of wild mustangs.

I enjoyed this visit to the cathedral more than I had anticipated. I found the merging of the old with the new very powerful, and wondered what my friend Estelle would have made of the building's situation, at the top of a long steady rise from the Potomac. Indeed, I was hit with a sudden longing for that lovely lady's company – a feeling I hadn't experienced as intensely since dowsing for the site of the church in Cachonga.   Although I thought of all my former parishioners from time to time, Estelle's conversations came back to me with greater clarity and fondness. I suppose she must have married that high-society chap with all the fast cars by now and be living an exotic life somewhere. I hope she's happy, I thought and came as close to saying a prayer as I had in a very long time.   Maybe the Cathedral was having its effect – or maybe it was still Estelle's influence that was swaying me? I shook my head and resumed my attention to the building.

The Cathedral's towers could be seen from many miles around.   Had the topography been solely responsible for the choice of location or had ley-line powers come into play? While missing my Islington mentor's opinion I eventually decided that it didn't matter much either way. It was an impressive building for whatever reason.

Another day took me to The Smithsonian Institute and sculpture garden where I was amazed to find Rodin's 'Burgers of Calais' looking somewhat out of place, I thought, but powerful nevertheless.

From the Smithsonian, it was a short stroll to the Air and Space Museum with its suspended sputniks and a view of the Capitol framed in every Eastern facing window.

After that, my mind spinning with aeronautical wonders, I enjoyed strolling along the mall and letting my mind absorb all the sights which were so familiar from photographs, but so new in three-dimensional reality.

Around the Jefferson Memorial the cherry trees were in bud, the blossoms promising an explosion of perfection. The water of the tidal pool reflected the cloudy sky suggesting sinister movements beneath the still surface.

Lincoln's statue left me unexpectedly breathless. The giant, still figure, with a powerful, unshrinking gaze, made me feel suitably insignificant as I read the great man's words of wisdom literally carved in stone in panels on both sides.

The monuments that moved me most, however, were the slabs of remembrance to the fallen in Vietnam. All those names representing people who had lived and loved, and been loved, who no longer existed on Earth. I suddenly felt unworthy of the life I could feel pulsing through me. The strength of these feelings took me by surprise and I tried to take an objective view of my reactions. I decided that my humility came from my good fortune at being alive, while so many of my contemporaries were dead. I remembered Umvari's words about how I would be able to leave a normal life when so many others . . .

I sat down on a stone bench - I wanted to savor this feeling of good fortune and to analyze it, to bring it to some sort of conclusion. "Life is a positive experience," I thought, "that is the only explanation for the feelings of grief I feel for these fellow beings who are no longer in a position to enjoy it."

"But what about all the dreadful things that happen?" my mind was hosting a dialogue. "How can they be seen as positive?"

"I don't know," my psyche wanted to shout back at the intruder. "But, surely, positivity is always an option. If we are strong enough, we can triumph over negative elements – that doesn't mean that we are not hurt by them, it means that we have alternatives that are stronger, with which we can win a battle."

The exchange that had been going on in my mind left me tired but exuberant. I felt as if I had won an important victory. A niggling voice in my sub-conscious warned me that I may have won a battle, but the war was still raging. All at once, I didn't mind. For some unknown, unidentifiable reason, I felt I had gained something. Perhaps Thomas's small seed of light was growing.

That evening, over supper, I discussed my feelings of the afternoon with the only two people I could trust to understand.

"I was delighted to realize how happy I am to be alive," I said, "but it took seeing all those lost names to shake me into the discovery. Along with the realization, however, came a new rush of bitterness for those who have gone. Snuffed out with violence from their fellow beings. I still struggle with haunting scenes of pain and horror from which so many of my friends – my congregation, in fact – will never return."

"I've got something interesting for you to read," Percival answered slowly, but with deliberation. "I have been investigating Spiritualism and have come across some interesting ideas which have helped me, a little, in dealing with the problems we all share in this regard.

"Did you know that the creator of Sherlock Holmes - Arthur Conan Doyle himself - was an ardent follower of Spiritualism?" I shook my head.

"Nobody can claim that such an erudite man could have the wool pulled over his eyes easily," Percival continued. "As Conan Doyle's own journey on this Earth drew towards a close, he promised his favorite medium that he would return to talk to his fellow enthusiasts after his death, through the channels she provided.

"According to the great author's wife, and his fellow Spiritualists, such visits did occur after he left this dimension of life and were documented in a book called 'The Return of Arthur Conan-Doyle' in which the levels of existence available to us as we move through various patterns of psychic existence are described.

"First come the astral planes. There are seven of these followed by three mental planes and finally three celestial planes." Percival had risen from the table and was talking over his shoulder as he looked at an over-loaded bookcase, his finger running along the spines of the books. He reached the book he was looking for, removed it and returned to the table, turning the pages as he did so. He handed me the open book. A chart covered the whole of one page entitled 'Spheres of Evolving Life and Consciousness According to A.C.D.'

"These ideas would have us believe that advanced souls are able to travel from one of the lower planes to another while still having two feet in the temporal zone, so to speak. Have you come across the idea of 'astral bodies' Jack?" Percival asked.

"I studied that concept in some detail while I was at college," I replied with enthusiasm.

"Well, I think it is those astral bodies, akin to what many refer to as 'souls' that do the travelling. In this book, whoever is writing it – obviously it is meant to be Conan Doyle dictating to the medium from another plane - refers to man's 'etheric body' as the part of mankind that does the travelling but 'astral memories' are mentioned as well."

I had put down my knife and fork, leaving my supper half eaten and unnoticed. I was studying the strange chart and listening intently to Percival as he continued: "Some auras can visit from the 'middle mental' to the 'lower astral planes' after they have died; i.e. left their physical bodies behind; hence ghosts are often described as being surrounded by hazy light, or a swirling brightness. These are moments when even the uninitiated can glimpse the astral body of their visitor.

"Even more advanced souls can return to the astral planes from the celestial levels. These we know of as Avatars – Gods-made-man. Jesus Christ came back from such a high level to help mankind to 'see more clearly and love more dearly.' He is often portrayed, in scenes after the resurrection not only with a halo, but with light shimmering all around him. His ascension was his final return to the third celestial plane – "the cosmic or universal sphere of atonement - at-one-ment.

"My idea from all this is to think that as souls visit higher levels while still based in the temporal zone, so too can they travel to the lower planes. This is where the ideas of evil and the devil come from. Souls who are attracted to evil will sink ever lower in their evolutionary journey, while their victims – whose temporal bodies are often abandoned early because of the deeds of others – have a quicker route upwards. This concept helps me deal with the pain of the premature departures of so many.

"What do you think, Jack," Percival sat down and resumed his supper.

"That's an intriguing idea, Percival," I responded, still looking at the chart. "I will try to assimilate it, as I can see the balm it can give to grief.

"Only the good die young," Amrita joined in the conversation. "Isn't that what they say? This idea of yours, Percival, would fit in with that. Early release from this plane, by whatever means, would provide a short-cut, so to speak, to a higher level of consciousness."

"Exactly," Percival said with conviction. "It is indeed a chink of light in the darkness."

The rest of the evening was spent discussing Man's journey – or those of his aura, spirit, soul or astral and etheric bodies.

On the first Saturday after my arrival, neither Amrita nor Percival had to report to work. Amrita had planned our day, and when I arrived in the kitchen for breakfast I found her busy packing a picnic basket.

"The dogwoods are nearly finished here in D.C." she said brightly as she wrapped mysterious parcels in tin foil, "but they are in their prime in the Blue Ridge Mountains, and that is where we are going today. A taste of the countryside for you, my dear Jack. Not the dusty-dry countryside of rural Africa, but the lush farmlands of Virginia, West Virginia and Maryland, awakening from the harsh winter and quite literally 'full of the joys of spring.' We are taking a picnic and are out for the day, so help yourself to some breakfast and get ready!"

The three of us piled into the car that had special controls on the steering column so that Anita could drive. The wheelchair and picnic basket were packed in the back and we headed North through the country around Boyds, Maryland, where almost every field hosted two or three horses. We turned South to take White's Ferry - a splendid chain driven vessel - across the Potomac and into Virginia. There was something about the small craft and its old-fashioned stately passage that was delightfully out of place in this hurrying modern country.

It was nearly mid-day by the time we reached the Blue Ridge Mountains, and climbed to the road that creeps along their spine. To the right spread the farmlands of the state of West Virginia, and to the left, between the trees, could be seen the undulating pastures of rural Virginia.

"There is something wondrous about the dogwood blossoms," Amrita said as she steered the car along the winding road, the dogwoods, beeches, and oaks jostling on either side. "I have tried hard to analyze why they should be so special," she continued. "I finally decided that it is because their horizontal petals give the impression that they are falling, like giant snowflakes, and the eye makes an effort to grasp their beauty before it falls. The flowers have an ephemeral quality to them that demands maximum attention. They have always bewitched me, ever since I was a child, and I'm so happy to be able to share this sensation with you both."

"I like the uncurling leaves of the oaks, also," said Percival. "The way they coyly reveal their delicate colors, like a new born baby uncurling its fingers. 'The sticky green leaves of spring,' I think it was Dostoevsky who described them like that. A most apposite phrase, I must find it and quote it to my students."

It was, indeed, a splendid journey even though the road was clogged with other people making the same pilgrimage. We stopped at one of the ridge-top picnic areas offering magnificent views across West Virginia to the Appalachians, and ate a meal of samosas and bhajis supplemented by some moist slices of Virginia ham.

The route home took us through the gentle countryside surrounding Warrenton and Middleburg and from there we turned east, past Dulles airport with Irané Saranson's wonderful building swamped by new additions. The original design, which on its own had suggested 'lift-off' so dramatically, is now tethered to the ground by appendages necessary for the complexities of modern travel.

On past Manassas and the battle-fields of the civil war to the ever-humming Beltway, back across the river and finally home again.

On Sunday, Amrita's family had invited us round to their home, just a few blocks away. It was a large sprawling house with an expanse of carefully maintained lawn between the gleaming windows and the street. It was full of people, and I was introduced to everyone in turn and became totally bewildered.

Watching Amrita surrounded by her family and friends, I understood how right she had been to come home, and began to realize how much she had given up by staying as long as she had in Aruba. But then, she had Percival, and it had all proved to be worthwhile, and I thought selfishly of how much I had benefited from her prolonged stay at St. Mary's. How the calm acceptance of her calamity had helped heal my own physical and mental anguish. How her quiet positivity had slowly countered the bitterness and despair that had threatened to destroy me.

I looked at my two friends, chatting comfortably amid the throng, and remembered Mr. Umvari's words again: "There's no reason why you should not lead a perfectly normal life again. In that respect you are a great deal more fortunate than the other patients in this hospital." The surgeon had gone on to admonish me - with instructions to pull myself together and to stop self-pity ravaging my mind - all mixed up with the grief of losing everything and everybody in Cachonga.

As I flexed the fingers of my right hand and walked confidently about the house as neither of my friends could do, I felt suddenly angry with myself for the self-indulgence of the past. The admiration I had for Amrita and Percival took another leap forward and I wondered why the two of them, in spite of their physical handicaps, seemed to be doing so much better than I was on the mental front. I decided, with new resolution, to commit myself to the lecture tour ahead with the same vigor that had fueled my successes in Cachonga. To concentrate on what was still possible and available in my life instead of dwelling upon what I had lost.

'If I can inspire a new generation to spread their beliefs without trampling upon the traditions of others,' I thought, 'I will do so in the names of my lost friends. Maybe I can still make a difference.' All at once I felt stronger in all sorts of ways and began to look forward to the challenge that was about to begin.

69. THE IMMENSITY OF AMERICA

The University of Maryland has a department of Environmental Resource Management & Development, which was where I was to give my first lecture. I tried not to show the trepidation I felt as I approached the rostrum. Once I had made a start my anxiety soon left as I warmed to my subject, and the lecture was well received. Afterwards I was the guest of the faculty for an informal lunch where I found myself answering the barrage of well-meaning questions easily and enthusiastically. I explained why some of their ideas wouldn't work in the bush, while others would, and gave alternatives to the former and amplified the latter suggestions with some of my own innovations. My second lecture that afternoon was well attended and well received.

The day passed quickly, and the excitement my visit engendered gave me confidence for the next stages of the tour.

My visits to Atlanta, Memphis and New Orleans passed in a blur. Almost all the students in these three cities were black Americans eager to search for long lost roots and bring help and enlightenment to their brethren.

I found their ignorance of the realities of life in rural Africa quite painful. This generation of relatively affluent students had no idea how to survive without a steady supply of electricity, food, running water, sanitation, and so on. How could I possibly prepare them, in two or three lectures, for the flies, mosquitoes, dirt, smells, litter, hunger and general discomfort of life in an African village; a place without either ATMs or credit card terminals, and locations without landlines or coverage for mobile 'phones?

I realized with some surprise that, when I had arrived in Cachonga, I had taken the lack of everyday conveniences with an almost masochistic pleasure. It was as if my being dirty, unkempt and uncomfortable would make up for the unsolicited protestations of affection declared to their neat and tidy vicar by so many of my Islington parishioners from whom I had fled. Somehow, by not indulging in any sort of physical pleasure or luxury I was purging myself of the guilt I felt following those unexpected barrages of emotions. Any sexual urges had similarly been bleached from my person as unsuitable and undesirable, and that was the way in which I continued to live.

By the time I had forgotten about my previous parishioners and become the vicar of Cachonga I was used to the surroundings and primitive way of life. I saw the austere nature of my existence as both unremarkable and enjoyable.

Before being hospitalized at St. Mary's I had not owned a pair of shoes or any undergarments for over seven years. I had not eaten with a knife and fork or brushed my hair or teeth with anything other than twigs and sticks. A flushing lavatory was something quite forgotten. None of those things had seemed important to me.

I looked at the scrubbed faces of the eager students attending my lectures, their cheekbones obscured by enough subcutaneous fat to lose the angular qualities I had seen in so many faces in Africa. I noticed the carefully coiffed hair - on the men as well as the women - and the manicured fingernails and soft hands. I couldn't help feeling that no amount of lectures could prepare these people for the life they thought they wanted to lead.

Dallas, Phoenix and Denver offered a different but similar array of eager faces. In these cities the white faces outnumbered the black, but the same naive stares followed my presentations and the same questions concerning facilities were asked repeatedly.

"Please understand, that it is people like you and me who are responsible for providing the facilities we take for granted here in the West. Don't go out there expecting to find any; go out there with the idea of helping the people to create them," I found myself saying over and over again.

The students would nod excitedly, but I knew, with a sinking heart, that the possibility of these people staying more than a month in the bush was as remote as the locations that so desperately needed their help.

Travelling by air from one city to another I didn't get a chance to experience much of the great North American continent until I arrived in Colorado. There was a couple of days break in my itinerary between lectures in Denver and those planned for Salt Lake City and I was delighted when one of the International Missionary Service organizing gophers suggested that we should drive, rather than fly to Utah.

"I'm assigned as your guide anyway," Jason Bertrand said, as we left the last lecture in Denver, "but the organization – while happy to pay for your airfare – insist that I should drive. It is an order that I embrace with delight for the topography is startling, and you get a real feel about what the founding fathers of the Mormon faith encountered on their search for a home – for themselves and for their beliefs. If you don't object to travelling by road instead of by air I would be delighted to have your company."

Jason was a likeable young man in his early twenties. His whole demeanor suggested a generosity of spirit that preferred to give than to receive, and I was eager to accept the invitation. We set off early the next morning, driving out of Denver with its immaculate streets and orderly suburbs.

I thought of the chaos of African cities; of bent lampposts, pot-holed streets, non-functional traffic lights, broken-down cars, rusted buses, and of the litter that flowed along the roadsides and collected in heaps at the intersections.

In Denver there were no men busy selling telephone cards, fruits, sun-glasses, or newspapers with smudged writing and out of focus photographs. Unlike in Africa no sinister-looking bottles of refreshment were pushed at us when we stopped at intersections, nor the bizarre large inflatable toys and blow-up paddling pools which used to be randomly displayed amongst the myriad of wooden carvings and stone sculptures. In Aruba, wherever a set of traffic lights was working and cars were stationary for a moment, vendors - festooned with their wares - touted for business and beggars pressed emaciated faces against the vehicles' windows, waving crutches or stumps of limbs.

The smells, the dust and the flies that hovered everywhere in every town of Central Africa came back to me when I closed my eyes. I felt I could almost touch the children, dragging babies with one hand and reaching out for money with the other, and the misshapen men and women who thrust their misery towards any vehicle that slowed. Memories came back in a rush until I opened my eyes and surveyed the stark cleanliness and order of the streets of Denver, lined with well-stocked stores selling a plethora of sophisticated items.

Once out of the city, freeway 170 climbed into the Rocky Mountains. The flat arable lands were left behind and prairie country rolled gently upwards to merge with the foothills. I opened the car window and inhaled the cold, clear air. With every outward breath I pushed the thoughts of heat, dust and poverty away.

There were cattle ranches, fields of horses and much to my delight a buffalo farm, the top-heavy beasts looking very black against the sandy grass-lands; more like a painting of long ago than a twenty-first century landscape.

Buffalo alongside the Highway

One of the cameos that I remember from this trip was of some slow-moving vehicles with flashing lights directing traffic out of the fast lane of the freeway that they were occupying. As we passed, I saw a collection of men in florescent suits collecting litter from the central reservation, following them in stately procession was a canteen and a mobile lavatory in its space-styled pod on wheels.

'The Americans really have got everything sorted,' I thought with amusement. 'No wonder everywhere looks so tidy.' It made me appreciate how much I needed to teach the 'would-be-missionaries' to prepare them for the dishevelment of Africa.

As we continued to climb, I began to understand why Colorado was so called. Where the freeway had been carved through the mountains, the red cliffs rose dramatically on either side. The road itself was a monument to engineering; when Jason told me that one of the world's most famous ski resorts had been named after the chief engineer of its construction, I felt it was a fitting tribute. We passed Vail with a nod of recognition and admiration. The end of the ski season was approaching and winter sports advertisements were being replaced with those for hiking tours, mountain biking, tennis and paragliding, although the mountaintops were still snow-covered and ski-laden cars filled the roads leading to the parking lots.

Our descent to the West took us through Glenwood Canyon where the different shades of rock strata shone dramatically in the sunshine, then down to the great flat-lands of Utah. It was indeed a stunning drive. Salt Lake City shimmered in the distance, circled on two sides by mountains; the massive Salt Lake itself disappearing into the lowering sun.

From the City's ring-road that runs along the mountains' roots, I looked down at Utah's famous capital and the headquarters of the Mormon Church.

"We're lucky to get such a good view," Jason told me. "Usually the whole city basin is filled with smog and just looks like a grey spongy mass from up here. Today it is windy, and hence the air is reasonably clear."

Jason found our accommodation in the foothills above the city and we grabbed a quick meal at the local deli before retiring to our rooms. My head was full of the magnificent vistas the day had given, I was tired but exhilarated by the journey and excited about exploring the Mecca of the Mormons the following day. There was a strange lightness to my body and mind that I didn't recognize at first, but, just before I fell asleep, I realized - I was happy.

It is a requirement of followers of The Church of Jesus Christ of Latter Day Saints that all young members spend at least a year and a half of their lives doing good deeds throughout the world, proselytizing their beliefs at the same time. Their missionary involvement is accordingly enormous, and I had been assigned to the Mormons for a series of lectures in their Utah capital.

The streets leading to Temple Square were busy with morning traffic as Jason drove me to the vital heart of the City. The wide road, lined with billboards, was an avenue of gigantic automobile emporiums, fast-food restaurants, and pawnshops. The feeling was one of American suburbia at its most tacky rather than an approach to a stately city centre.

The Tabernacle, John Smith's Memorial Hall and the Temple itself are encircled by a high wall with entrances that can be easily and carefully monitored. I asked Jason to treat me like any other tourist and not to mention my missionary connections. If I was going to lecture to these people, I needed to learn about them as the lay person I felt myself to be, and not as the experienced missionary priest I was introduced as, prior to my lectures.

As soon as Jason and I set foot inside Temple Square we were accosted by eager young faces offering assistance and a tour - wandering on our own apparently was not an option. Every one of the scrubbed young people was neatly dressed with a badge of identity pinned to their blazer pocket. In the end it was a 'sister' from Honduras who landed the prey and led us forward; she was buzzing with excitement and enthusiasm from her catch.

Sister Catalina's English was very hard to understand and Jason and I stood mesmerized by the tumult of language with which she accompanied her gestures, pointing hither and yon with dedication. Fortunately our plight was recognized by another 'sister' - Esmeralda - from The Philippines, so her badge informed us - who joined us. She was both intelligible and eloquent. Both the guides were eager to tell us how proud they were to have been assigned to Salt Lake City for their months of missionary work.

Jason and I had been caught and soon realized that escape was impossible. We were herded from one building to the next until the cloying scripts that were recited to us got too much for me. Once again I was being confronted with a suspension of rational and independent thought. I felt claustrophobic – as if smothered by all the "peace, love and serenity" which gushed from these two girls as they recited their homilies.

"Thank you sisters, very much," I said suddenly, as we exited one building and were being propelled towards the next. "We have enjoyed our tour, but I think we have seen enough for today. I presume we are not allowed in the temple itself?" I asked after a slight pause, looking at the Gothic-style building built of local grey granite in the mid to late 1800s.

The two sisters shook their heads with great solemnity. "Only true followers of the Mormon faith are allowed inside," they said in unison. "It is a wonderful place," Esmeralda added in a hushed voice. "People come from all over the world to be married here and to be baptized for themselves, or for the members of their families who have passed away without the promise of eternal life in heaven. This is how families are reunited upon the other side. Isn't it wonderful?" she finished, gazing at the building with wide eyes and a quick inhalation of breath. I was unsure whether the little Philippine girl was referring to the baptism of dead souls as wonderful or to the building itself.

"Of course, it is early in the year, yet, and very quiet," Esmeralda went on, "but in the summer we have over ninety weddings performed each day and easily as many baptisms."

I wondered how so many functions could take place within such a relatively small building. I thought briefly about telling the two sisters that I had once baptized more than one hundred and twenty people in one day, but decided against it. The thought made me smile secretly to myself.

Jason and I thanked our guides who did little to hide their disappointment that the tour had been cut short, and the conference centre, that was next on our tour, had not yet been visited.

"We'll come back and see it tomorrow," I promised sincerely. I knew I would indeed be doing so, as the first of my lectures was scheduled for the next day in that very building. However, the girls would still not let us leave without obtaining our home addresses. I wondered with amusement what Thomas would make of the visit from a Mormon missionary that would undoubtedly follow my writing of the Allworthys' address in the great visitor's book.

Having finally disentangled ourselves from Sisters Catalina and Esmeralda, we crossed the road looking for somewhere to have something to eat. The grey granite of the holy buildings was reflected in the cloudy sky. The roads were tarmac grey, the pavements: concrete grey, the surrounding office blocks: cinder block grey. Even the cars, muted by the winter road-crud, had grey carapaces over hidden glints of muted color. Everything seemed to echo the same slightly grubby and sad aspect of the low sky, as if all was in a state of hibernation.

When Jason realized that he couldn't get a beer or a glass of wine at any eating establishment within walking distance of Temple Square, he persuaded me to return to our hotel where he had supplies imported from Colorado.

I was glad to be back in my room and alone with my thoughts. The rest of the day was spent preparing my lectures for the ardent students I knew I could expect to meet the next day and contemplating the weird experiences of the morning.

As darkness fell, I felt like a visitor from outer-space as I stood on the balcony of my hotel room, looking down on the lights of the city and up into the lights of the sky. The clouds had gone, and the scattered stars sparkled in the night. The hum of traffic seeped through the air like the workings of a single machine; exhaust fumes mingled with smells of spilt petrol and cooking oils. The railing beneath my hands had a patina of urban grease.

I thought back to the sounds of the African bush at night under an almost solid canopy of stars; how the staccato grunts of the hippos and trumpeting of elephants during the daytime were replaced with the occasional lion's roar or squeal of hyenas. I remembered how, when the rains came, the constant chirrup of cicadas was augmented by the glottal songs of the frogs and toads.

The noises of a Cachonga morning flooded back, unbidden, as I rocked against the balcony rail: the crow of the cockerels that heralded the approach of every dawn and the flood of bird-song that followed as a greeting to each new day. I always suspected that the birds competed with each other to make their presence felt, a competition which became more intense as the sun made its climb above the horizon. Hoopoes, finches, rollers, pipits, shrikes and plovers whooped, chirped, fluted and chuckled. Once the sun was clear of the horizon, they returned to their daytime regime of just the occasional trippet.

Once the sun was up I would never emerge from beneath a shade tree without scanning the skies for the many different kinds of eagles, buzzards and hawks that might be hovering overhead – or the ever-sinister vultures. My head raised itself in an involuntary motion.

I remembered my baths in the crocodile-free zone of the river I had created. How I would stop my ablutions to watch the kingfishers as they hovered and dived while stately storks looked on with disdain from the far bank. How sudden snorts from the hippos made me jump as they raised their nostrils above the river's surface and blinked their piggy eyes at me with disbelief, their ears flapping to shed water and hear more acutely before the huge head disappeared into the muddy waters.

Sometimes, when I went to the river, herds of impala and dik-dik would be drinking and cavorting on the opposite bank, their springing leaps defying gravity with unimaginable grace and agility. At other times a herd of elephants might have come to the river. I would watch from my 'bath' as the big cows pounded the water with their trunks to frighten the crocodiles away before they allowed the young ones to approach for a drink. The bulls kept watch for any danger that might come from inland, stamping dust around themselves to give the impression of a much larger herd. Only when the young and the females had finished drinking, and the cows had returned to relieve them on patrol, would the male elephants slake their thirsts.

I shut my eyes and visualized the sun rising behind the Msasas and how its rays shimmered through the Fever Trees as it set. I was amazed to find that I was homesick for Africa, in spite of everything. I turned back to my room and opened my lecture notes once again – it was time to fill them with more positive tones, I decided, to balance all the negatives that tended to dominate my talks on life in the bush.

Should we have a new chapter start here? Maybe it could be called The Wonders of the West Coast – or something like that?

From Utah I flew to Los Angeles, reluctantly leaving Jason to do the journey by car. Several talks at UCLA had been scheduled and I was not allowed the time to continue by road.

My confidence had grown a great deal during my trans-America peregrinations, and I found myself looking forward to each lecture with energy and excitement. Now I managed questions with the surety of someone who knows his subject intimately; the only time I had a moment's hesitation was when I was asked how to deal with the political upheavals so common in Africa. I had paused for only an instant before replying that my specialty was with local communities, their people and their agriculture – for political advice, the student must ask elsewhere. Then I quickly took the next question and was able to talk about the successful use of vetiver plants to uphold contours while I recovered my equilibrium.

The lectures were well attended, as had been the case wherever I had travelled. This time there were many Hispanic students attending the classes; they all asked intelligent questions and seemed well motivated. However, there was still the problem as to how these people would cope with a missionary's life, without the luxuries they took for granted in the U.S.A. There seemed even more life-enhancing gadgets in Southern California than anywhere else. I decided to leave that for someone else to sort out. 'I can only do my best to warn them,' I thought; 'after that, they're on their own, and it's important that I keep things positive.' This was a new angle of thought, I realized, that had crept into my psyche unbidden, but – I reflected – it was welcome. I had seen such a variety of places on this tour and met so many interesting people and encountered so many natural marvels that my ability to wonder was steadily returning. A healing process was taking place: I couldn't deny it, nor did I want to – and there was more to come.

Jason had arrived in L.A. shortly before I was due to leave, to drive me to my next stop, San José, where I had one lecture before three days in San Francisco. I was as delighted to see him as I was with the idea of being back on the road again.

I couldn't help enjoying the glamour and glitz of Los Angeles, although I didn't like the idea that there was nowhere suitable for walking within the hundred square miles of concrete and tarmac. After nearly a week in this urban sprawl, I was pleased when Jason came to pick me up and we headed off along the magnificent Pacific Coast Highway.

Jason knew this part of the country well, he told me, having himself been a student of UC Santa Barbara with a girl friend in San Francisco. "We used to do this drive, in one direction or the other, every couple of weeks. Of course if we were in a hurry, we had to take the mid-state freeway, but whenever we could, we came along Route 1. It's never the same twice."

We started at Venice Beach with its display of muscle men and voluptuous women, then drove alongside surfing beaches on our left while to our right steep-sided canyons wound their way into the hills.

The road took us past San Simeon, newspaper magnate William Randolph Hearst's magical folly, which reminded me of one of my father's favourite films, Citizen Kane. I had been dragged, along with Alice and Robert, to the Classic Cinema especially to see it, and being overwhelmed by how Orson Wells' face seemed to fill the screen to overflowing.

We stopped for lunch at a place Jason claimed to be his favorite restaurant in all of California – "if not the world," he added enthusiastically. 'Nepenthe,' a restaurant built on a rocky piece of coastline, offering outstanding views in all directions. Inland, to the east, rise the soft hills of Great Sur National Park clad in Ceonothus and Rosemary, growing wild amongst the rocks, their scents infusing the ocean winds with mystery. California oaks, twisted and stunted from the winds, seem to hang against the steep slopes with strange dignity.

To the west is the Pacific Ocean, stretching forever, waiting for sunsets to give it a defining line. To the North and South are vistas of the surf crashing against the first piece of land to be encountered for thousands of miles.

Looking down at this impressive and turbulent view, I could see seals sunning themselves on the rocks below us and the heads of others bobbing in the crashing waves. Sea birds swooped, hovered and dived in and out of undulating fields of kelp that glistened with every backwash.

"Well, I can see why they call it Nepenthe," I said as we took a table perched over the edge of a continent.

"You mean you know what it means?" Jason answered in a surprised tone.

"It's a drug named in the Odyssey, isn't it?" I said, mentally thanking Percival for the knowledge, "the one that banishes grief and invites forgetfulness."

Jason looked disappointed. "I had been hoping to tell you that," he said, "I suppose I should have known better than to try to teach you anything."

I looked at my friend in astonishment. "But, Jason, you can - and do - teach me a great deal every day. Look at the journey you took me on from Denver to Salt Lake, look how much I am learning from our journey today."

"Oh, and I have something even more spectacular for you tomorrow," Jason's natural buoyancy had returned and he was smiling again.

Just north of Monterey, Jason headed east and picked up the highway to San Jose, I was sorry to leave the coast. I had enjoyed visiting the town where Clint Eastwood had been mayor, and wanted to stay beside the surf. Jason explained that Route 1 had to make a slight detour here as the world famous Monterey golf course took over the next section of coastline.

"But don't worry," Jason had consoled me, "we'll pick this road up tomorrow on our circuitous route up to San Francisco."

My lecture at San Jose State University the following morning was once again over-subscribed and well received. I had lunch in the faculty dining room and felt quite the celebrity as professors from the departments of anthropology and sociology crowded around questioning me on what life as a missionary in Africa was 'really like.' I was careful with my answers.

Jason collected me just after lunch and we set off into the San Andreas Mountains towards Santa Cruz and our return to the Pacific coast. I wondered what Estelle would think if she knew I was crossing one of the most famous fault lines in the world. Suddenly her dark eyes came back to me with a jolt of recognition, the swirl of her chaotic blond hair, her smile and her encouraging voice as she shared her knowledge and understanding of a different dimension. I felt a twinge of guilt that I wasn't busy dowsing for energies – but then my rods were long gone and so was Estelle – or so I thought at the time.

As the road rose away to the West from where the San Francisco Bay ends at San José, I became aware of thick woodland on either side of us. The trees were majestically tall with ram-rod straight trunks. Immaculate drives snaked into the deep shade and disappeared around stately curves; Jason told me they lead to splendid houses of the rich and famous participants in the silicon revolution.

All of a sudden, Jason left the freeway and turned right into a winding road. The trees rose on either side of us making the car seem pathetically small. We passed more driveways curling away on either side, with solitary mailboxes standing sentinel by each one. After a ten minute gradual climb, Jason turned right again and entered some gates displaying a modest sign saying 'Henry Cowell State Park.'

"We owe the State a great debt of gratitude for creating this park and saving a magnificent forest from the developers. It is one of God's great cathedrals, undiluted by man's vanities, just a straight forward – or upward – declaration of the inestimable soaring force of life."

I looked at Jason in surprise. I had underestimated this young man, I decided. "There you go teaching me something amazing, again, Jason," I said and patted my chauffer's shoulder affectionately. "Was this what you were promising me yesterday, at Nepenthe?"

Jason nodded as he pulled the car into a painted slot of the almost empty car-park. We paid the ranger at the entrance to the park and began walking on the earthen path that led into the dusk created by the canopy high overhead.

"California Coastal Redwoods are part of the Sequoia family," Jason explained. "They grow faster and taller than the giant Sequoias of the Sierra Nevada Mountains, but never attain quite the same girth or have the same extraordinary longevity." These momentous trees were indeed spectacular, and I found myself gasping in admiration and awe as I walked deeper into the forest as they rose ever taller and their trunks ever wider on either side of the path. Jason's analogy had been an accurate one, it was indeed like walking down the nave of a Cathedral such as the one in Salisbury, where the columns rise high enough to emphasize the insignificance of man before branching out to interlock their stone fingers and support the unseen roof above.

"This is my favorite spot," Jason said, touching me lightly on the arm and indicating to the right. He stepped over the path's guardrail, and, pushing through some low reaching branches, suddenly disappeared. I followed with a sense of adventure and excitement. I also brushed through the branches and found myself entering a perfect circle of these grand giant trees, the diameter of which must have been at least fifteen yards. Jason was standing in the middle, the floor beneath his feet empty of any kind of undergrowth. His head was bent backwards towards a glitter of blue sky and the slanting rays of the California sun, some fifty or sixty feet over his head.

I advanced carefully to join him in the middle of this astonishing circle. The trees had to be well over two hundred years old. How did they manage to be so perfectly positioned, I wondered. I looked at Jason, my eyebrows raised enquiringly.

A Coastal Redwood

"The bark of the sequoia is impervious to fire," Jason started talking softly. "Only if the flames can penetrate the interior of a tree, through some sort of scar, does the tree burn. That's the reason for these trees living so long, in spite of the forest fires that rush through the mountains every twenty or thirty years.

"Sequoia's don't only propagate by seeds," Jason, was obviously enjoying our reversal of roles. "They also spring up from burls or the knobs of roots where they break through the soil. Obviously, a long time ago, the huge tree that once grew where we are standing, must have burnt down, leaving only the bark-covered roots. It seems that new trees sprouted out of these roots, and hence the seemingly magical circle in which we find ourselves today."

I nodded with understanding. "It still looks miraculous to me," I said, "and it feels miraculous also. There is a genuine sense of the mysterious here, don't you think, Jason?"

"I knew you'd appreciate this Jack," Jason's smile showed genuine pleasure. "I only bring very special people here; it means so much to me. I would hate to have people with me who were unreceptive to the powerful vibrations I feel within these trees."

"Thank you for that vote of confidence, Jason," I replied. "It means more to me than you can imagine." I was moved by Jason's belief in my ability to respond to the awesome nature of this forest, and with that encouragement, I did indeed open myself to the calm but strong earth energy that seemed to pour into me with each intake of breath and spread through my anatomy with every exhalation.

The trees seemed to be holding hands, imparting a collective knowledge of the infinite, which was made all the more powerful by the absence of interfering dogma. This force was one to be felt viscerally, not intellectually. It seemed to feed the dim glow that I had discovered at Thornton in the dark emptiness of my soul. The Light was cautiously growing brighter.

I could not get the impact of those giant trees out of my mind. As Jason drove back to join Route 1 at Santa Cruz and turned north again, I kept dwelling on the stately sentinels I had just met. It had been hard for both of us to turn our backs on such silent beauty, and drive away. 'I wonder if I'll ever see them again' I thought to myself.

Jason's thoughts were also with the giant Redwoods it seemed, because he suddenly asked: "Do you know where the word Sequoia comes from?"

I shook my head.

"It was the name of a famous Cherokee who invented a syllabary for his language," Jason looked pleased. "Well, that makes up for your knowing about Nepenthe," he said with a grin.

"More than makes up," I answered, "I'm afraid you've overtaken me – what's a syllabary?"

"It's a collection of characters which represent whole syllables rather than individual sounds. One symbol for a collection of several letters, if you see what I mean."

I nodded. The connection between giant trees and a form of writing wasn't apparent to me, but I was pleased with the Cherokee connection.

We were driving along the top of tall cliffs, the Pacific throwing its huge waves beneath us. "There's a seismograph on the other side of the mountains," Jason was now on a different tack, enjoying being the teacher once more. "It straddles the San Andreas Fault to measure the Earth's movements at one of the globe's most volatile points. Even though it is a goodly distance from the coast, with these mountains in between, you can tell how big the waves are at any time of the day or night, without leaving the building. You just watch the needle measure the shudders in the Earth's crust every time a roller hits the shore."

Jason paused, and then added quietly: "there's so much that is awesome going on around us all the time, isn't there Jack, and so few people take heed of the many wonders that permeate their everyday lives."

"I know what you mean, Jason," I replied in an equally soft tone. "Those of us who are receptive enough to pick up on these things are a privileged few."

"But that's just what missionary work is all about," Jason now spoke enthusiastically. "Sharing the privileges with others, helping other folk understand and appreciate the many wonders of God's magnificent creations. And you don't have to travel the world to do so. There are many that need the guidance right here, at home."

I turned my head to the left, across Jason for a moment, and looked at the massive ocean that stretched until it hazed into a soft horizon, glinting greys, blacks and slate blues as it heaved towards the coast. 'The world is not only full of good,' I thought sadly to myself, but I said nothing.

I was delighted with San Francisco and the excitement in the air across the Bay Bridge at the U.C. Berkley campus where most of my lectures were to take place. The students were a wonderful mixture of races and somehow seemed more robust than their contemporaries in the southern part of the State. I didn't feel as if many of these people would be overly fazed by being in a land without credit cards or mobile 'phones and found my enthusiasm in the lectures mounting. The questions I was asked were also more realistic and earth-bound. I enjoyed the exchanges, and found the talks over-running the time schedules on a regular basis.

From San Francisco, I was to go North again to Portland, Oregon, and time dictated that I travel by air. I was sorry to lose Jason after sharing so many adventures. The two of us had so little in common on paper, but we had opened slices of our souls to each other, and I found it hard to say goodbye. With bags checked in, and boarding pass in hand, I arrived at the departure gate with Jason at my side.

"How I wish you were coming with me," I said, taking Jason's proffered hand. "I will be lost without your guidance in so many ways. I have so enjoyed being your friend and sharing the delights of life with you. We must be sure to stay in touch." We hugged each other in silence, knowing that it was unlikely that we would.

My disappointment at being back in the air dwindled when my window seat allowed amazing views into Crater Lake, a jewel of blue within the craggy drama of the Sierra Nevada Mountains.

Similarly, the flight from Portland to Seattle showed me the magnitude of Mount Shasta and its newly re-arranged foothills and parasite volcanic cones. I kept thinking of Jason's idea of the privilege of being open to the wonders of the Earth.

The positive views I had developed of the students in San Francisco were equaled in my visits to Oregon and Washington State. In both places I found my lectures invigorating and felt sure that the fervent notes the students were taking would be put to good use in some far-flung outpost of the world.

70. THE BEAUTIES OF BOSTON

It was time to turn East. While I was glad to be heading back towards Amrita and Percival, I was sorry to leave the wonders of the West coast. The next stop was Chicago.

Four lectures in two days meant I saw little of the Windy City before being bundled onto another airplane en route to Boston. Here I was met by a tall woman in her early twenties whose unruly light blond hair reminded me of Estelle once again – how I missed the easy companionship we had developed during our dowsing adventures and chats over tea in the Priory Café. Still I had a new life now and one I was beginning to enjoy more and more – but it would have been even better with a kindred spirit like Estelle with whom to share it. I shook myself from my reverie remembering that in a couple of days I would be back with Amrita and Percival, the closest friends I could ever have.

"Hello, Father Jack, I'm Alice," my new guide greeted me.

"I have a sister called Alice," I answered unexpectedly. "She must be a little older than you now. I haven't seen her for a long time," I added in reply to my companion's raised eyebrow.

"Welcome to Boston, Father," Alice resumed her speech. "We have several hours before your reception at MIT this evening, so I have been sent to escort you on a tour of the City of Boston before taking you to your hotel. I hope that is all right with you, and that you are not too tired for a bit of tourism?"

I was delighted with Boston. Of course it was so much older than the West Coast cities I had been visiting and there was a flavor of Europe about the narrow streets and formal squares and gardens. But the area that impressed me most was the block that incorporated "The Mother Church" of Christian Science.

Alice had insisted that we park the car and wander amongst the elaborate fountains and reflecting pools as we admired the great white building that stretched towards the New England sky. I remembered studying Christian Science at one point in my journey of spiritual exploration, but found that I had forgotten whatever I had learned. I asked Alice to remind me. "Isn't this the religion that doesn't allow doctors?" I asked.

"Oh dear," Alice replied, shaking her head, making her hair shimmer in the sunshine and her looped earrings dance. "That's such a popular misconception, and not at all true. The followers of Christian Science have nothing against the use of doctors whenever and wherever they are needed. It's just that – unless in very unusual circumstances – Christian Scientists themselves don't have need of the medical profession."

"They are very fortunate, aren't they?" I responded. "I mean, what happens if they get ill?"

"Well that's the whole point, you see," said Alice enthusiastically. "Mary Baker Eddy, the founder of Christian Science, unlocked Christ's messages from the prisons imposed by other followers of Our Lord's teachings. You never heard of Jesus having a cold, or cough did you?"

I shook my head, indicating with an open palm that she should continue.

"Not only was Christ never ill himself, he also healed those who were suffering from what he could see were the delusions of matter. Jesus could heal people by channeling the truth of a pure mind and spirit into the body of someone else and expelling the illusion of illness encouraged in them by matter."

"You've lost me there," I was struggling to keep up. "Surely Jesus Christ was the Son of God, and as such had super-natural powers, hence he could heal the sick and so on."

"But aren't we all sons and daughters of God?" Alice turned to me with a smile and twinkling eyes that indeed made her appear to be a child of the Divine.

"But, surely you aren't suggesting that each of us can perform the same miracles as Christ? Wouldn't that be blasphemous?" I was rather enjoying this exchange. I liked Alice, I decided, and was eager to keep her in conversation, especially this one that was apparently important to her, and was intriguing to me.

"Jesus Christ, Mary Eddy tells us," Alice continued unabashed, "was the first man we know about who perfected the art of what she called Christian Science – after its founder, so to speak. He was a man of ultimate goodness, who understood the powers that are available to all of us but achieved by only a few. His understanding of the spiritual nature of mankind lifted him above the material world in which the vast majority of us flounder. He always told us what he could do, we could do also; it's just that there aren't many people who have the faith or the understanding to believe those words enough to act upon them."

"I still don't understand this completely." I couldn't think of anything else to say in the silence that followed. We were sitting on a bench, the great church behind us, it's image bouncing from the pools in front where fountains sent frissons across the reflections and added an extra dimension to the pictures.

"Perhaps it would be best to quote you Mary Baker Eddy's 'Scientific Statement of Being.'" Alice answered slowly. "I may not get it word perfect, but if you can follow the ideas, you should understand the crux of this philosophy."

I sat still and silent, watching Alice out of the corner of my eye as she arranged her thoughts with a slight frown of concentration.

"'There is no life, truth, intelligence nor substance in matter,'" Alice recited with a seriousness that made me think of Amrita and her mantras. "'All is infinite truth and its infinite manifestations. For God is all in all. Spirit is immortal truth, matter is mortal error. Spirit is the real and eternal, matter is the unreal and temporal. Spirit is God, and man is His image and likeness. Therefore man is not material, he is spiritual.'"

Alice paused before turning to me with another of those wonderful smiles. "Q.E.D." she said. "Sort that out and you have the whole concept of Christian Science in a nut-shell.

"It's a shame you're not going to be here for a Wednesday evening, that's when the most interesting services take place – as far as I'm concerned that is. During those sessions, when selective readings from the Bible and from Mary Baker Eddy's textbook: 'Christian Science with Key to the Scriptures,' are delivered. There is a section during the service where members of the congregation stand up and tell everyone of the 'demonstrations of Christian Science' they have experienced, personally. Other people might call these quietly spoken experiences 'miracles,' but for a follower of C.S. they are just demonstrations of their faith."

"You seem to know a lot about this, Alice," I ventured.

"My mother is a Christian Scientist," Alice responded quickly. "And I went to their Sunday school as a child – well until I was twenty-one, actually. But, somehow, I just didn't feel I could be good enough to follow that route completely. It's very demanding. Just as they don't need doctors, nor do Christian Scientists need stimulation of any kind – such as alcohol and cigarettes to start with, and then as you advance, tea, coffee and even sex," Alice blushed an attractive rose color. "I admire them enormously, and if you knew the troubles from which my mother has lifted me during my life, you would respect the faith as much as I do. One day, maybe I'll be good enough to follow it completely."

Silence hung in the air between us for several moments, both of us lost in thought.

"Goodness, look at the time," Alice started from her reverie and jumped to her feet. "I will be in trouble if you're not at MIT in time for your welcome dinner, and we haven't even been to the hotel yet.

"I'm sorry, Father, but I'll have to rush you," she finished, gesturing me to follow her back to where we had left the car.

"My name is Jack," I said firmly, catching her arm. "Please don't use the 'Father' title, I am Jack Bolden, a lecturer on missionary agricultural and sociological activities, that is all."

"All right, Jack," Alice answered in confusion, "I don't mind what you're called, we need to hurry!" And off she bounded with me in pursuit.

71. BACK TO FRIENDS

Over the next two days, I saw a lot of Alice and enjoyed her company as I had that of Jason. When my visit was over, we shared a buoyant farewell dinner with a mixed faculty from MIT and Harvard. I was catching the last 'plane to shuttle South, eager to return to Percival and Amrita. I had opted for the late flight rather than spend another night in a hotel. I was sorry to say goodbye to my charming guide as I went through the security gates for my flight to Baltimore's Friendship airport, and again found myself making promises of continuing communication that we both knew were unlikely to materialize.

As it happened, my flight was delayed, and I had time to reflect upon what I had learned from my visit to Boston and all the other cities I had visited since I had last been with my friends in the Washington suburb of Silver Spring. I was so looking forward to sharing all these experiences with them, especially the irony of the teacher being taught that had followed me on my travels, from Jason to Alice.

The delay was extensive and by the time I arrived in Baltimore it was four in the morning and I had long missed my train to Washington D.C. The airline offered to put me up in a hotel, but I had other plans, and in an excited act of independence, I rented a car and set off down the Parkway with a map at my side and a new feeling of freedom.

Navigating onto the Beltway took a lot of concentration, even at this early hour. This huge road was far from crowded compared to other times of the day, but the signs confused me as the lanes changed beneath my car so that I would find myself almost exiting on one side of the road or the other without any intention of so doing. I was constantly looking at the signs strung above the road, trying to stay in the centre lane, when the road curved gradually to the left and suddenly I saw a golden figure hovering in the darkness, just to the right of the ten-lane highway. The sun was yet to be seen on the horizon to my left, but this single statue, being at such a height, was catching the first rays as if under a spot-light.

Seeing the dawn light illuminate this solitary golden figure, while all around was bathed in shadow, took my breath away to such an extent that I pulled over onto the hard-shoulder and stopped. I turned off the car's lights to concentrate on the rising dawn and the magic of this floating golden figure and to absorb the experience.

I sat still, amongst the dizziness, as the traffic passed unnoticed, allowing the sight to fill my consciousness. I found that I was holding my breath as I watched the sunlight slowly slide down the shaft which held the statue aloft and then to the building that supported it. All the lines of this gleaming white edifice suggested upward motion of which the statue was the pinnacle.

I envied the passion of the architect who had designed such an inspiring presentation, I yearned to be filled with such certainty, to know of a Divine plan such as the one suggested by this creation.

As I leant forward upon the steering wheel, gazing at the building that seemed now to be floating above trees still swathed in the diminishing night, I became aware of more lights, different colored lights, that seemed to be playing across the dashboard of the rental car. They sparkled in my eyes, as if Tinkerbell's wand had swept over the scene dispensing magic.

My idea that I was experiencing something miraculous was cut short by the reflection in my wing-mirror being blocked by the silhouette of a policeman's body approaching from a patrol car parked behind mine, its lights flashing with urgency and power. This sinister figure was in the process of removing the top strap from his gun holster, and shifting his pistol for easy access.

"Stay where you are and keep both hands on the steering wheel where I can see them" came the unexpected command in a voice that gave no room for argument.

I froze. My hands tightened upon the steering wheel but did not move. An icy chill seeped into my spine and spread steadily up to my neck and down to the coccyx.

The policeman opened the driver's door with a sudden jerky motion of his left hand. The right hand held the pistol.

"Explain your purpose and position," came the instruction.

I was totally bewildered by the arcane vocabulary and by the aggression evident in the tone. "I stopped to admire the beauty of the sun-rise on the statue on that building," I said in a small voice. "I didn't think I was doing anything illegal," I added, feeling exceptionally pathetic.

"Repeat," came the command, "and loud enough so that I can hear."

I did as I was told. There followed a few seconds of silence while the policeman's left hand removed a torch from his belt. A sharp light was directed into my face.

"Are you for real?" the policeman asked, in a slightly less belligerent tone.

My confusion with this question must have been evident in my illumined features, for the policeman didn't wait too long for an answer.

"Driving license" came the next instruction. "And for God's sake turn your lights on."

"Can I move my hands?" I asked carefully.

"Yep, but I've got you covered remember. One false move and you won't know anything anymore."

Somewhere in my subconscious there was disappointment that my interrogator had not insisted that he had "a Magnum 45, the most powerful hand-gun in the world . . ." I reached cautiously for my wallet and removed my British driving license which still had me identified as 'The Reverend Jack Bolden.'

The policeman looked at the license, removing the torch light from my face as he did so. "Just a minute," he said, "don't move." And with that he turned and went back to his car. I could hear him talking into his radio.

Eventually, I heard the crunch of returning footsteps, and to my surprise, the passenger door opened and the policeman climbed in.

"Well, Reverend," the title was rolled around in the American accent, "it seems you are legit. I just checked out the rental car. It also seems you are unaware of our laws concerning stopping to sight-see while driving on The Beltway, in the dark, and without lights. Tell me again exactly what you were doing."

"I'm so sorry officer," I used my most conciliatory voice. "I just saw that golden statue up there, illumined by the rising sun – just the statue, nothing else. It was so overwhelming I had to stop and watch as the sun came up and the rest of that extraordinary building appeared beneath it. Would you mind telling me what it is I am looking at?"

"That's the Mormon Temple," the policeman explained in a thoroughly friendly voice. "And that is the Angel Moroni that you have been looking at. It's quite something isn't it? People who are not here at dawn miss an amazing sight. I'm not going to fine you as I should, because I appreciate why a reverend, such as yourself, should find the sight so moving, and now that you've got your hazard lights flashing, you're not such a danger to yourself or to others. But please don't do anything like this again."

"Oh I won't, officer," I was quick to respond. "I realize how stupid I've been, and thank you very much for your understanding. As a matter of fact this is the first time I've driven in the States, and it's all a bit frightening. Especially a road as big as The Beltway with its exits on both right and left sides of the road. It's quite unlike anything we have in England."

"Well, you're lucky not to be here during rush-hour." The policeman responded. "Where are you going?"

I told him about my friends in Silver Spring, and how the delayed flight from Boston had made me miss my train. To my amazement the policeman offered to escort me. Having given the address, I watched the officer return to his car, and then pull out carefully, beckoning me to follow him.

It was seven-thirty by the time the police car drew up in front of Amrita and Percival's house, and Percival was in the kitchen making their morning tea. He came rushing out in his dressing-gown with a look of astonishment and concern upon his face.

"Just delivering your friend here," said the policeman with a broad grin. "These limeys take a bit of looking after, and I wanted to make sure he got to where he was going safely. Do you accept delivery of the Reverend Bolden?"

"Jack," said Percival with worried delight. "are you all right?"

"Oh sure, he's fine," replied the policeman as I parked the rental car carefully in the driveway and climbed out. "You look after him now, and make sure he doesn't decide to stop on the Beltway again, especially in the dark, without lights.

"I'll be off now. You-all take care now, d'ya hear?" and with that he jumped back in his car and disappeared with a friendly wave and a big smile.

Percival escorted me into the house and ordered me not to move until he returned with a sleepy Amrita in his arms. The three of us hugged and shed tears of excitement at being reunited. Percival fetched the tea and then demanded to know how I had obtained such an impressive escort.

I began to describe what I had seen that had caused me to stop the car. "What an amazing building," I said as I finished the account. "Compared with the slightly grubby church in Temple Square, Salt Lake City, this one must be even more impressive inside."

"Sadly, it's not," Amrita said with a wry smile. "I agree that it is truly splendid from the outside, but, as with all Mormon temples, in spite of their lofty exteriors, they are not cavernous inside like European cathedrals but have many stories. There are management floors, huge areas housing ancestral records and dozens and dozens of holy rooms for the performance of different rituals – the marriages and baptisms of relatives long dead as well as those of the living. When that building was first built, before it was consecrated, they allowed non-Mormons to come and have a look at some parts of it. My parents and I went along, it was quite fascinating. Very grand, but not in the way we had imagined. The reception area was just like that in one of the world's most famous hotels, only larger and with an atmosphere full of beneficence."

"That's how they manage so many in one day," I realized out loud, "I just couldn't get my head around all the marriages and baptisms they told me happened every day in Utah. Now I can see how it works. But what a shame to clutter such an immense space like that."

I wondered what Joseph Smith would have made of this building's extraordinary testimony to the faith he had started. I told my friends of my visit to Temple Square, and then to The Mother Church in Boston.

"How extraordinary it is," I said more to myself than to my friends, "that seemingly random people can take an idea, dress it up with a bit of this and a bit of that, and start a whole new religion – or in both these cases, new aspects of an existing religion – surrounded by controversies which seem to attract followers rather than to put them off."

Percival took up the theme. "Remember Amrita's analogy of the wells? I think here are two such well diggers. Each busy constructing their own route to enlightenment and salvation, and then finding others pressing them to share the 'water'."

"There must be a combination of courage and arrogance in someone who deliberately decides to start a religion," it was Amrita's turn to join the discussion. "However, I'm not sure that the arrogant side of the situation comes from the founder. I think it refers more to the followers who push the founder to the fore. It must be hard to hang on to humility having received divine inspiration. These are very different faiths we are talking about, started by two very different people."

"Well," said Percival with a broad smile, "it doesn't take us long to get back to our philosophical debates, does it? You've only just got here, Jack. How about some breakfast? But first, I've got something to show you."

Percival disappeared upstairs leaving me looking quizzically at Amrita.

"Just wait and see," Amrita said with a smile. "I think you'll be impressed."

Percival came downstairs and back into the sitting room, he was now dressed in jeans and a long-sleeved shirt. His right arm was behind his back.

"Ta-da," he pronounced most uncharacteristically, and brought his right arm forward. From the shirt cuff protruded a prosthetic hand. "Watch this," he continued, and with much concentration, the fingers began to twitch with small jerky movements. "It's still very new, and I'm not very good with it, yet. However, you should see what some of the guys I train with can do. It's amazing."

It was an emotional moment, I found my chest heaving and stood up to give my friend an all-encompassing hug. "Oh, Percival, that's just wonderful. I had no idea they could make such realistic things."

"It's absolutely fascinating." Percival said, his face red with the effort of sending messages through his truncated nerves to the artificial hand. The index finger began a beckoning motion. "The real-skin-look comes from mixing resins with synthetic materials. They make improvements almost every day it seems.

"And not just with the skin replications. Until recently, tiny pumps were used to create movement. They were minute hydraulic devices, but still relatively bulky and difficult to conceal. Now computer technology has made it possible for tiny sensors to establish a biological connection with the remaining limb as well as creating contours which clothe the structure with life-like 'muscle tone'. It's extraordinarily exciting - even in these rudimentary stages.

"Prosthetics like this one have to be custom made, of course, because of the different limitations of different patients, so while they build the individual electrical sensors, they try to match the individual skin color and also ensure that it makes a suitable pair with the remaining human hand.

"One of my fellow amputees has a prosthetic foot, ankle, lower leg and knee – all fitted with biosensors that connect to the nerve endings extant in his thigh. He can change the settings, somehow, to adjust the movements to cope with uneven surfaces, swimming – and even rock-climbing, would you believe.

"This hand of mine cannot cope with rock-climbing, by the way. I was asked if I was willing to sacrifice verisimilitude for greater agility, and I decided not to bother. "

"However," Percival continued, holding his two hands out and trying to stretch the fingers of the prosthesis to match his real one, "some of the trainees I work with have several hands. They choose which one they need depending upon what they are doing. For example, one chap is a carpenter who lost his hand in an accident with a circular saw – he has a prosthetic hand specifically designed for working with various sizes of hammers, screw-drivers and so on. Then he changes hands when he is going out for dinner. Pretty amazing, isn't it?"

I nodded in agreement. "Amazing indeed, Percival, I don't think I've ever known anything about prosthetic devices before, let alone rock-climbing hands and so forth."

"Never heard of dentures?" Percival asked, with a mocking smile. "Any one with false teeth is a prosthesis user. Then there are glass eyes . . ."

"O.K. Percival," I interrupted with a big smile. "I get the message. I'm very ignorant on the subject – at least I was. I am learning now. How do all these researches help in your trials, Amrita?" I asked, turning to the seated figure who was watching her husband with affection and pride.

"Well, believe it or not, they might help, one day." Amrita turned her gaze to me; there was a sparkle in her eyes. "It seems that researchers at MIT have developed a new algorithm to create 'neural prosthetic devices' which are designed to convert brain signals into action in patients who have been paralyzed as well as those who have had limbs amputated. They use biosensors – electronic devices that monitor the neural signals that reflect an individual's intentions.

"Of course there's a long way to go yet. But it's exciting, just to know that this sort of research is going on. And to be a part of it, they have agreed to use me as one of the early guinea-pigs. The engineers' approach to paralysis and amputation is different to the medical. It's intriguing, isn't it?"

I nodded enthusiastically, trying hard to understand the things my two friends were saying and to put things into perspective.

"Of course," Amrita continued, a note of realism replacing excitement in her voice, "There is a huge distance between the prototypes they have functioning in the laboratory and someone like me. Algorithms have a long way to travel before they reach their goal. But this merging of science, engineering and medicine is inspiring and has given thousands of people in my situation – and those considerably worse off – reason to hope. And with hope comes vitality."

I bent down and gave this dear, dear friend a gentle hug. "Oh, Amrita," I whispered in her ear, "you will always be perfect both to me and to Percival, you must know that. But if anything could happen to bring you joy, then we will share your hope, join you in your optimism and wait, full of excitement and anticipation."

"Thank you, dear Jack," Amrita responded, smiling, as I stood tall once again. "I know I have your support, as I have my husband's – and I never get over the thrill I feel when I address him by that title. No amount of paralysis can stop that sort of delight tingling all through my body. Love is an amazing emotion – I'm sure I can feel my love for Percival all the way to my toes. I have so much to value in life. I will not let ideas of physical miracles that are possibly whimsical block the value of the here-and-now. After all, there is no disappointment without anticipation."

"Amrita," I said carefully, "you have no idea how much I miss your wisdom when we are apart."

"Aren't I the lucky one?" said Percival with a broad smile, as he moved behind Amrita's chair and put his hands lovingly but lightly on her shoulders.

Amrita was looking at me fondly, her eyes full of caring. She took a deep breath and said: "And you, Jack, how are you dealing with your demons? You may have recovered physically, but there was deep bitterness in your heart when we parted in London. Have you managed to deal with it?"

I was surprised by her question and had no ready answer. "What exactly do you mean?" I asked, buying time to gather some thoughts, feeling suddenly on the defensive.

"Have you come any closer to dealing with the concept of evil?" Amrita was still looking at me steadily. "I ask, because it is something I have been working on for some time now, and I have some ideas to share with you if you think they might help."

I was instantly relieved that I was not expected to describe the battle I faced on a daily basis whenever Loveness's face hovered in my head. As time passed, Rosie and Loveness had merged together somewhat in my mind, evil was a tangible part of both their lives; an aspect of their existences I had to confront whenever I thought about them. My own confrontation with evil was also still with me, of course, but I had shut it away somewhere in a cold, black area of my psyche.

"I would be very interested to hear your ideas, Amrita," I said with sincerity. "I confess that I have not confronted the darkness as I probably should have done, and am still angry and bitter about what happened to so many good people. Only a couple of days ago I snapped at a delightful young lady who insisted on calling me 'father' – so I would be very grateful for some help out of this quagmire."

Amrita was smiling at me; love and friendship filled her eyes. I felt humble to have this lady as a friend. "Well," she began in a tone which made me reach for a chair – this was going to be a conversation where I needed to be at the same level as my teacher; "I'm going to start with some ancient wisdoms.

"Forces of energy have been recognized by mankind - and probably by all living things - from before our knowledge can relate. Indeed maybe it was this recognition, the "naming of the whirlwind" as it has been called, that was the beginning of what we call 'knowledge'.

"This mixture of energies is called by many names: Numen, Tao, Anima Mundi, Divine Source, for example. It can be visualized as a twisting helix of opposites whose blending together creates infinite harmony. The Masons refer to this as "The Great Architect of the Universe," so now we are putting a personal identity to the flux – but in nomenclature only, I think.

"Many religions divide the opposites and come up with two identities to represent the different faces of the 'force' – hence we get God and the Devil, Shiva and Kali, Allah and Shaitan, and so on.

"But I digress: to return to the original idea, the Ancient Egyptians believed that every spirit of human existence contains a spark of this divine energy. That the force we are trying to identify flows through everyone, leaving an individual light static within – creating a soul, so to speak - while the creative force itself continues to flow in perpetuity. Their belief was that for this spark to be coaxed into a flame, souls must descend to the lower planes of existence to do battle and grow, one way or another, as a result of confrontation. Thus the positive elements of existence had to merge with the negative in order to shine more brightly - or to tarnish, dim, and sink deeper into darkness.

"It is not only the Egyptians of several centuries before Christ who believed that every human being travels into this world carrying a spark of the Divine within the newly created body. This is a concept familiar to members of almost every religion extant on the planet. The Roman Catholic idea that the spirit/soul is evil until 'saved' by baptism into Christ's church gives a negative slant to that original spirit, but it doesn't deny the idea. 'God – by whatever name - is within us' is a universal idea and one expounded by Christ himself, as you will know, of course.

"Again, many faiths are confident that this life we are in at the moment is just one of many, and the direction in which a soul travels from one life to the next depends upon its experiences, challenges and successes in each incarnation. You are familiar with the Hindu circle of re-births, I know, but there are many other faiths that have multiple lives as part of their philosophies.

"For the moment, let us assume that souls are indeed on a journey of many lives. In order to develop individual dimensions of reality, evil must be confronted and dealt with, one way or another – it must be embraced or defeated.

"Recently I read a book about 'pods of inter-active souls' who travel through their multiple life-journeys connected to each other in some way. Maybe in one life a soul will take the role of a daughter and then a wife, and in the next a son, husband, lover and so on. The important thing is that, throughout their interactions, they are bound together by love.

"Have you ever met a complete stranger and felt the Earth shift with an unintelligible recognition?" I hadn't, but that is precisely what happened to me in Rome a few months after this conversation – and I was to revisit this scene with a new dimension of understanding.

Amrita didn't wait for a response. "This is what happens when inter-connected souls bump into each other on a new plane of existence - an expression of 'destiny'. Each soul has a chosen role to play in the interaction, all with the aim of rising towards perfection and a final liberation.

"Now here is the nub of this idea." Amrita paused, and looked first at me, and then turned to look at her husband. "I am still 'playing' with this suggestion, it is very powerful and needs digesting slowly and with care.

"It is: that in order to progress, challenges must be overcome with a positive outcome for the soul concerned. It could be a member of your 'pod'- maybe the one whose love is the strongest - who 'volunteers' to put you through such a trial during your next Earthly existence. A soul who deliberately chooses a negative role in order to give your spirit the chance to rise. A soul who sacrifices its own chance of advancement to allow yours to progress – or maybe, if the motives are genuine, – it can also develop in a positive way? I'm not sure, I am still working on this complicated concept."

There was silence for several minutes, each of us busy with our own thoughts. It was Percival who spoke next.

"You are giving a new slant to the idea of 'loving your enemies,' aren't you, Amrita?" he began. "You are suggesting that maybe some soul has put you through the mill for your own advancement, someone who loves you enough to play the necessary 'bad' part in your new journey, at their own expense. A soul who deliberately flirts with evil in order to allow another soul to conquer a necessary hiccup in its own advancement."

"Yes, I think so," Amrita replied softly. "The thing is there are some deeply evil souls lurking through history, I'm sure you can suggest a few?"

She paused and looked at Percival who volunteered: "Attila, perhaps, and more than a couple of Roman Emperors."

"Phillip of France and the Inquisitors - for what they did to The Templars, among others," I volunteered.

"Stalin, Hitler, Amin, Mugabe," Amrita had come back in control, "your own nemesis, Mungotu?" People who are responsible for atrocities on huge scales.

"Then there are those strange lunatics who take a gun and storm into a school and shoot lots of children and teachers for no apparent reason. How do we deal with that sort of seemingly random evil?"

"And natural disasters," I said, disturbance in my voice echoing that in Amrita's, "millions killed by earthquakes and their tsunamis, hurricanes, tornadoes, floods and the like?"

"Yes," Amrita said sadly, "maybe there were thousands of souls ready to rush forward in the spiritual evolution, and this was a way to fast-forward them to the next level while, at the same time, challenging those left behind with the agony of their loss.

"Perhaps the idea of an intimate collection of spirits fits best when we look at relationships that have gone bad. Marriages that begin with such positivity and love and then turn sour and ugly – maybe the one who is inflicting pain upon the other is doing so for a loving reason unrecognized in the present sphere of existence?

"It's a vast idea, but it has ropes of hope dangling from it, and there is an idea of purpose and progress inherent within the concept that provides comfort and strength to deal with the trials we have to confront on a day to day basis. It also helps turn bitterness into acceptance and even, perhaps, to gratitude. An extraordinary reversal of feelings from the negative to the positive."

I looked at this beautiful young woman, trapped in her chair through no fault of her own, who had put herself in danger in order to help others, who had to deal with the indignities and frustrations paralysis forces upon its victims twenty-four hours a day, who was smiling at me with calm acceptance. How pathetic my own problems seemed in comparison.

"Thank you, Amrita," I found myself speaking softly and reaching out for her hands with both of mine. "You have given me a lot to think about. I will do my best to absorb your ideas and let you know how I get on."

"Please do," she answered, smiling as she disentangled her hands. "Now how about doing something special to celebrate your return, Jack. Percival and I are full of questions about your lectures."

During the two remaining days we had to share together the three of us never stopped talking. I told Percival and Amrita about my travels they, in turn, filled me in with news of their professional lives and ambitions. Our attempts to come to terms with the problem of evil were left for another day. Amrita had given both of us enough to think about and it would take many months of contemplation to absorb her ideas and then decide how to react to them.

When it was time for me to leave, I extracted promises that they would come and visit me wherever and whenever I settled. "It's your turn next," I said, knowing that it asked so much more for the two of them to travel than it did for one able-bodied person like myself. "And if you don't come and see me, then I will have no choice but to make a nuisance of myself here once again. You had better alert the police if I do!"

Amongst the jocularity, there was much pain in our parting. Percival and Amrita had each other and –I reminded myself forcefully, as the 'plane took off from Dulles – I had the Allworthy family to whom I was returning. I watched the lights of the North American continent disappear into the blackness of the Atlantic, as my latest adventure slipped into the past.

72. EUROPE

John Illingsworth said he was delighted to see me across the desk from him once again. The same green file had been placed upon his desk as for the first visit, but it was looking even fatter now and was held together by a piece of string.

"Well, Jack," the head of the U.K's Missionary Service couldn't conceal his pleasure, "what a success your American tour has been. I have had nothing but positive reports from each place you've visited. Everyone wants you to make it an annual trip, and we would like to organize a similar tour to Europe. What do you think?"

"I think that would be very possible, sir," I answered. "I can't deny that I learnt a lot from the experience myself, and it was good to have my lectures so well received. Of course there was the advantage that a form of English is spoken on the other side of the Atlantic, so that, with only the occasional misinterpretation, what I talked about was easily understood. I'm not so confident when it comes to the different countries and languages of Europe."

"We'll give you interpreters, where necessary, Jack. But you know most of our European neighbors are kind enough to speak English, indeed it is an obligation for all missionary students apart from those traveling to the former African colonies of Portugal, France and Holland where the languages of their former colonizers is still spoken."

I didn't take much comfort from this information. It was true I had found the American tour not as challenging as I had anticipated but felt that this was partly due to the easy acceptance that English people were lucky enough to have from an audience in the USA. Such a concession was not going to be forthcoming in Europe - in fact I suspected the reverse would be the case.

"Your tour takes you through France, Germany, Austria, Switzerland and Italy," Illingsworth continued. "We have bought you a Europass which is valid for sixty days; however your lectures will only take up twenty-four of those. They are somewhat spread out, but I thought you might like to take advantage of the rail pass and fill the spaces between your commitments with visits to places of interest - Eastern Europe, perhaps? You are a free agent, Jack, and The Missionary Service hopes that you will use your time wisely, in ways that might rejuvenate your religious feelings of the past.

"The official tour ends in Pisa, but The Service has accommodation in Rome and I have booked a room for you there for the final three weeks before your rail pass expires. I thought you might appreciate visiting a special library which isn't open to the public, but to which The Service has access."

"That's very kind of you, Sir, that all sounds quite wonderful." I was surprised by these plans, made on my behalf, with such generosity.

"Well, Jack," Illingsworth answered carefully, "you see I have a personal mission to attract you back to the fold. I hold you in great respect and would like to think that, as the years pass, you will be able to include Christ in your lectures and to understand the strange path that has led you here. I still believe that we are governed by a Divine plan, and that you did not arrive here, in this office, by accident."

"I hope it isn't a condition, sir," I answered quickly, "that I revert to my former beliefs, in order to accept the program you have for me. If there is a Divine plan, and the destruction of Cachonga and the rape and murder of my congregation was part of it, I am not interested in paying homage to the perpetrator of such a revolting scheme.

"No, I'm sorry, sir," I continued in a quiet but strong voice, "if that is what you want from me, then I had better refuse the appointment altogether."

"Calm down, Jack." Illingsworth rose to his feet and lent forward across the desk. "It isn't a condition, it's just an explanation of how and why I decided to organize various options for you. You don't have to follow my suggestions, but they are there, along with your salary and free accommodation in every city in which you are to lecture, and also in Rome, for whatever dates suit you."

I was embarrassed by my outburst. "I'm sorry, sir," I spoke quietly once again, but this time with a softer tone. "I just don't want to disappoint you. I am gaining confidence in my new life, and finding it stimulating and satisfying. What you are offering is very generous and I look forward to seeing where my footsteps take me."

"Use your time wisely," Illingsworth reiterated with a smile. "I'm sure you will, and I look forward to hearing all about your adventures when you come home." He extended his hand across the desk, as I rose from the chair. "Good luck, Jack, and God bless you," he said as we shook hands solemnly.

While I was in London, I went to visit my old mentor, Father Justin. It was strange to be back at St. George's and I was sad to find the priest looking much older than when I had last seen him. In turn, he also expressed a dismay in how much I had aged since my departure. I told him briefly of my years in Africa, of my recent travels in the United States, and the missionary's plans for my next trip.

I did not hesitate to tell Father Justin of my reversal of faith – somehow, I knew he would understand, especially as I was keen to discuss with him the various alternative ideas I had been cultivating. We had an interesting discussion and I left feeling lighter of soul, in some way.

My journeys across Europe were exciting and depressing at the same time. I loved walking around the great cities and took time to visit Prague and Budapest that were not on my itinerary.

As the trains took me this way and that across Europe I noticed that every place I visited had its scars alongside its splendors. Amongst the spectacular architecture and artwork of places of worship, learning and government were an equal number of memorials to victims of atrocities and wars of one sort or another, from the very recent to those whose origins were lost in time. 'Man's inhumanity to man' was mourned in every town.

Slowly I was putting the catastrophe of Cachonga in perspective when viewed in a global and historical context. I stared at the war memorials that adorned every city and dominated every village the train passed through, thinking of the horrors they represented.

On a journey from Germany to Austria, when the conductor announced Dachau as the next town, I decided upon another unscheduled stop. I put my luggage in a storage facility on the platform and walked out into the sunshine and a bustling parochial town.

A bus was waiting at the train station announcing a schedule for journeys to the concentration camp as if it were taking people to Disney World. I climbed aboard and joined a party of German school children in their early teens.

I expected a place of such horror to be far removed from civilization, hidden in some remote forest, and mentally prepared myself for a journey of some distance. However, after only fifteen minutes of slow urban travel, the bus turned left through some sinister metal gates into a large parking lot.

I didn't know how to deal with the fact that this place occupied a block of land alongside a busy road, with factories on either side of it and some sort of office block opposite. It was unashamedly part of the urban sprawl with people passing it every day on their way to work, or to school, or maybe out for a stroll in fine weather. A sign advertising a McDonalds restaurant flashed on the other side of the tall wire fence behind which so many thousands of innocent people had suffered and died.

I left the tour before it got as far as the gas chambers. My energy had been drained by the vibrations of the place, my head and heart bursting with horror, hurt and anger. The simple memorial to all the dead, with "Never Again" written in every language I could imagine, and a single flame of remembrance, was very moving, but not enough. Nothing, I decided, could ever be enough.

Percival's tales of his experiences during the genocides in Eastern Europe, and subsequently in Africa, came back to me. This memorial flame had been flickering away throughout those years, I thought, the stark statement written in so many tongues, ignored. Was it in fact a statement, or was it a command or perhaps a plea? "Never Again" - maybe it was all three.

All the angst I had felt after Cachonga returned in a sudden rush. It infused every portion of my body. I was angry, deeply angry. I climbed back into the bus and waited to be taken back to the station. The bus driver was sitting in the front of the vehicle reading a newspaper and eating a sandwich. This was just another stop on his daily route.

How could people go on with their lives with such acceptance? My thoughts were scrambling. How could the gaggle of school children returning from the tour be busy teasing one another and making jokes of what they had seen, some mimicking death beneath the grotesque 'shower' heads? How had life continued for all these years, in close quarters, to such a heinous construction?

I abandoned trying to make sense of this ghastly experience. There was no way I would ever begin to understand the why's of the world. I attempted to close my ears and my mind, along with my eyes. I tried to imagine I was somewhere else, I had to. This was a time to abandon Amrita's concept of the 'Now' it was too painful, too destructive.

I felt the energies about me to be in a state of pain and panic. I wanted to leave, to be transported away from this dreadful place. I sought solace from memories of elsewhere; of our trip along the Blue Ridge Mountains to see the dogwoods, of my drive with Jason through the red mountains of Colorado, the peace and wonder of the circle of redwoods. I hung on to those views as the bus finally drove away and deposited me back at the station.

I collected my bags and waited for the next train in a daze. The horror of Dachau threatened to invade my defenses as my journey continued towards the Alps. Only when the train was deep within the mountains did I become aware of my surroundings once again, and allow my mind to return to occupy the same place as my body.

The experience of Dachau stays with me, alongside the devastation of Cachonga, to this day, and I expect it will never leave. That day, as the distance between me and that place of pain increased, and the inner hurt began to abate, I had to wonder why physical or temporal distance should make any difference to the horrors I had seen and learnt about.

Evil, I decided, should not just be noticed at a particular time or in a particular place. Certainly, time should allow healing – but should we ever forget? Would not forgetting or worse, denying, make repetitions of past horrors easier? Had this not already happened over and over again? If the horrors of Cachonga were so insignificant amongst the atrocities of which mankind was capable . . . what was the point of mankind's existence? How could all the good in this world justify evils of this magnitude? Evils that kept repeating themselves in one corner of the globe or another.

Lying awake in some obscure hotel room in some obscure European town, I tossed these thoughts backwards and forwards. Anger boiled and bubbled throughout my body as I tried to sleep. Resentment was growing within leading inevitably to self-pity, until I was rescued by the vision of Amrita's sweet face shining through the quagmire of my mind.

Along with Amrita's calm expression, came her ideas of how emotions of despair provide the devil with an open door. "Despair and self-pity, write 'Welcome' on the entrance mat of your soul," Amrita had said, sometime, somewhere. I struggled to visualize her tiny form, encased in a wheelchair. Her hands would be lifted towards me in a gesture of greeting or assistance. I thought of her words of encouragement as to how we should defy negativity and turn to the positive. I remembered the words of Mary Baker Eddy that Alice had taught me: 'Stand porter at the door of thought." I must not let these dark stains forever damage my psyche – or was it my soul?

Had she been there, I decided, Amrita would have admonished me for allowing pointless anger to take over my heart and to allow negativity to flood my being in such an invasive fashion.

"But how can I justify or understand the dreadful destructive powers of my fellow beings?" I would have defended myself.

"Why do you have to?" Amrita would have answered. "Your purpose in this life is to maintain the positive aspects within your own energy field. You cannot be responsible for the actions of others. It is hard enough to take full responsibility for one's own thoughts and deeds. Keep yourself straight, Jack," she would have insisted, "and cope with the pain and anguish of others as empathetically as possible without allowing yourself to be destroyed or diminished in the process. Sympathy must replace empathy if your own aura is threatened by the darkness. Love is a powerful tool with which to help the victims of disasters; along with the compassion of sorrow, it is all you can offer."

I remembered Amrita's advice, given one afternoon as she tried to ease my anguish over the lost souls of Cachonga. I was not sure I really understood her meaning, but had found comfort in her words, and found it again now, as I recalled the conversation. Finally, I fell asleep.

The students to whom I lectured as I travelled around Europe were as enthusiastic as their American counterparts, but more realistic with their expectations and more mature with their questions. I found the exchanges I had with each group exhilarating, and even with the language problems, I managed a good rapport with all the different audiences.

However, the schedule was tiring and all the travelling was taking its toll. I was ready to be in the same place for a while, to take stock of all the different things I had seen, of the sights, scenes and experiences I was trying to absorb. It was with relief that I unpacked my things, and put my suitcase away, in the small room that had been assigned to me in the Missionary house in Rome. Three and a half weeks in the same place seemed an immense luxury.

73. SURPRISING ROME

No more lectures, no more travelling. I slept well and awoke feeling strong and excited about my coming explorations. My host was a kindly man in his seventies called Signor Valdi who gave me a front-door key so I could come and go as I pleased. He also gave me a card of introduction that would admit me to the library of which John Illingsworth had spoken. He marked its location on a map of the city and indicated that it was for my use. There were no other guests.

A continental breakfast was provided every morning and Signor Valdi was eager to help with directions and information as much as he could. However as he spoke little English, and I had even less Italian, our communication was necessarily limited. Breakfast was the only time we met.

I wandered through the streets of Rome with delight. There was a charming restaurant not far from my lodgings that spilled out onto the pavement of a tree-lined street. I stopped there for a coffee on my way to and from the library, and returned for dinner when I had finished writing my notes. It took just two days to establish a routine with which I felt comfortable and excited at the same time.

The library itself was within the Vatican and offered thrilling opportunities to examine religious texts in their original format. However, I found my knowledge of Latin and Greek too poor to allow me to take full advantage of these wonders, and having enjoyed the experience of handling antique texts and breathing the atmosphere of ancient learning, I opted for a more conventional ecclesiastical library outside the Vatican walls.

I hadn't spent time in a library since I was at St. Augustine's, but it was as if the years in between had faded away as I found myself once more drawn to the writings of the mystics of the East. I took up my studies of Taoism and Zen Buddhism where I had left off a good fifteen years earlier. Inspired by Amrita, I poured over The Upanishads, the I Ching, the writings of Kahil Gibran and the hymns of Zarathustra. Percival and his wife were always in my mind, and I missed being able to discuss my findings with them. I wrote long letters instead which I found helped me both organize and analyze my thoughts and discoveries.

At the beginning of my second week in Rome a most extraordinary thing happened. I was seated in my usual place on the pavement in front of 'my' restaurant, stirring a large cup of filter coffee and contemplating the day ahead. Yesterday, as I was leaving the library, I had noted a new edition of The Egyptian Book of The Dead. That would be my project for today. I was looking forward to it.

"Excuse me, but are you Father Jack?"

I looked up in amazement, the coffee spoon halted in mid-air. I felt a jolt between my shoulder blades, as if someone had pushed me in the back, but there was nobody behind me. In front, however, stood a beautifully dressed, attractive woman in her early thirties, perhaps; she was looking at me quizzically. The fair hair that swirled around her face formed a naturally chaotic halo, unlike the rest of her physique that seemed carefully manicured. The deep brown eyes that gazed at me were familiar in a most unsettling way.

"Yes," I found myself replying involuntarily, "and 'no'" I added, equally unrehearsed. "I mean I am Jack Bolden, do we know each other?"

"Have I changed so much from our dowsing days?" the lady answered with a smile – that smile rolled back the years, I recognized Estelle, from a different time and place – a different life, it seemed – standing before me, asking if she could join me at this small table in front of a small café, in the middle of Rome.

"Well, it's not quite the same as The Priory tea-room," I responded, leaping from my chair, so that it fell over and clattered on the stone slabs of the piazza. "But you would be most welcome, Estelle. How amazing that you should be here, and that you should recognize me amongst all this strangeness."

"Indeed," said Estelle, beaming with delight as she pulled out the chair opposite and sat down with a delicacy that belied her frame. "So it is you!

Italian version of the Priory Café

"Do you know I have been circling this table for nearly five minutes trying to decide whether or not you really were Father Jack."

"Just call me Jack, please," came the hurried response, and before any awkward silence had time to form Estelle rejoined: "And please call me Stella. I have left the Estelle you knew behind on my travels, as it seems you have abandoned your former title. But I'm sure we are still the same people inside, somewhere. We may have new trappings, of course, but something of the old Estelle and the former Father Jack must exist for me to have recognized you – and I'm so pleased I did.

"How are you, dear Jack?" Stella continued in a lighter tone. "I have thought about you so often during the last decade, and missed your counsel."

"And I have missed yours," I found myself responding without thought. "I have wanted to talk to you so many times in the space that has happened between our meetings. You have no idea how often."

I paused, but the words were coming unbidden and I had no choice but to let them flow.

"Oh how you would have laughed to see me dowsing for sacred lines in the middle of the African bush, miles and miles from any kind of what we call 'civilization.' I dowsed for ley lines, as you taught me, and with the rods you gave me. I searched for water too, and for fertility – agricultural, that is, - and most important of all, for the perfect place to build a church."

"And did you find it?" Stella bent to place a polished handbag carefully on the floor between her feet. "Did you build your church?"

"Yes," I answered, but the excitement went from my voice, and the atmosphere went suddenly flat.

A waiter was hovering alongside the table, fixing us with a raptor's eye. His presence diluted the situation, and I brought my thoughts back to the present.

"Will you join me," I asked somewhat unnecessarily, seeing that my companion was already seated in front of me. "What would you like?" I added rather lamely.

"I'll have an espresso, please," Stella answered, more to the waiter than to me. Then she turned back to our conversation and said, "I always knew you had the talent, Jack, you just weren't quite ready to use it all those years ago. I'm thrilled that you didn't forget it, and that you kept the rods I gave you. Have you still got them?"

"No," I said sharply, "but never mind about all that," I had found a few seconds in which to pull myself together and back to the present. "Let's talk about you," I insisted with relief and genuine interest. "What are you doing here, and how has life treated you since I last saw you?"

It was sometime around eleven in the morning when Stella had stopped by my table. We were still in deep conversation at just after one-thirty when the ever-hovering waiter produced the lunch menus. He had already provided Stella with a bottle of Verdiccio, at her request, and was quick to refill her glass whenever it approached being empty, the bottle hovering over my full glass before being poured into Stella's.

I learnt that following Stella's marriage to Chicago things had gone well for a couple of years while her skills in designing cosmetics had been absorbed into her husband's pharmaceutical business and become very successful. She had resigned from the company to concentrate on having a family, because Chicago thought that her failure to conceive was the result of her being too absorbed in work.

At this point, unsolicited, and to my embarrassment, Stella had interjected that she could not have talked to anyone else about these things; how she was amazed that elapsed time had done nothing to interfere with the confidence she had to speak to me in such a manner. She felt, she said, as if the two of us were still in Islington.

"You must understand, dear Jack," she said, "that I have kept all this bottled inside me for so many years. It is quite unfair to unburden myself like this upon you, all of a sudden, but after all, I may not see you again for another ten years, and I must take advantage of what the forces of existence have provided for me. Will you forgive me?"

I had only to nod agreement for the monologue to continue. Stella, having ordered some tagliatelle alle vongole for both of us – she assured me it was the best choice on the menu – went on to explain that, after many tests and a great deal of heart-ache, she had been pronounced barren for no apparent reason.

"The difficulty is, you see Jack, that if doctors can't find a reason for your inability to conceive, they also can't find a cure. There must be an identifiable problem before it can attract an identifiable solution.

"So, that was that."

I was unsure what to say. I loved listening to Stella's sparkling voice and was only taking account of about half the words. I nodded or shook my head slightly when I thought it appropriate, but otherwise just enjoyed watching her gestures and her dancing eyes. Those deep brown eyes that I remembered so well, now with tiny lines forming at the corners.

Stella stopped talking and concentrated on her tagliatelle for a few moments. Her thoughts seemed to have moved into the distance somewhere, and a frown deepened between the finely shaped eyebrows.

I had abandoned the idea of visiting the library, and suddenly, watching Stella eat thoughtfully, realized that I was hungry. The delicate aroma of clams and garlic that rose from the plate that had been put in front of me some time before finally penetrated my nostrils and I began to eat with an altogether new sense of appreciation.

"What happened next?" I asked when I realized that the silence was becoming heavy enough for Stella to start asking me questions, and I didn't want to be the one talking.

Stella finished her glass of wine and looked accusingly at the bottle now resting upside down in the ice bucket. "Shall we have another?" she asked. "Do you like this, or would you like to try something else?"

"No, this one's fine," I answered, raising my glass to prove the point. Indeed, now I was paying attention, I found the wine quite delicious.

"Well, what happened next is not the nicest part of the story," Stella continued after gesturing to the waiter to replenish the wine supply. "When I tried to return to work I found I had been excluded from the Company. During my time away from the office many changes had been made, and my share of the business now belonged entirely to Chicago.

"I expect I probably signed some papers at some time or other. Papers that I didn't read, or care about, amongst the physical tests that were taking up my time and my mind. After all, I trusted my husband and had no idea what was going on behind my back.

"I don't think you ever met my friends Ashok and Peter?" I shook my head, and Stella continued: "no, I didn't think so. We were at University together and the three of us formed a little company after graduation. I was the one with the ideas, and they were the ones who made the ideas into products. We were a good team and always got on well together. When Chicago took over the business, he took over Ashok and Peter as well."

Stella had finished eating. She leant back in her chair, twirling her glass slowly between her fingers. "I should explain," she continued, lowering her voice slightly, "that my two friends, of Indian descent, send most of their money back to India where they each support very extended families. The homosexual relationship they have enjoyed for nearly fifteen years now, is illegal in India, and if the authorities were to find out about it, everything that has been purchased with their money would be confiscated and an entire community left destitute.

"Chicago threatened my friends with exposure unless they agreed to continue working for him, even though I was now being excluded. To sweeten the deal, he increased their salaries so that money that should have come to me, was now split between them in addition to their previous wages.

"Our marriage had become a farce. Chicago would refer to me as 'the barren bitch' and did not hesitate to bring a collection of girlfriends around to our flat – all of them very young, pretty and impressionable. His flash cars and lavish lifestyle drew nubile wenches like moths to a candle; he put our flat up for sale and told me that he was beginning divorce proceedings.

"Shut out from a business that I had created from scratch and built up with diligence, I did not know what to do. I had an allowance from Chicago, but it wasn't large enough to keep me in London, nor did it reflect the amount of money my ideas and products were bringing into his company."

"What ideas?" I questioned, trying to understand this strange story.

"Well, the most successful of my products at that stage was a face cream I had developed after many months of experimentation. Ashok and Peter helped, of course, but it was my recipe that finally achieved the result I was after.

"What I wanted, Jack," Stella lent towards me in a conspiratorial fashion, "was to produce a face-cream that would not only soften the skin but be attractive to the opposite sex at the same time.

"You see, even when we were getting along well, Chicago always complained if I came to bed smelling of grease. He said he found all women's lotions to be unattractive at close quarters. The smells, he claimed, no matter how disguised with perfume, were no good for the libido."

Stella laughed. "What a strange conversation to be having, Jack, but you did ask. I have to tell you, as it was this situation that put the idea into my head of developing a cream with a scent which would arouse passion rather than diminish it.

"Ashok and Peter were my testing guinea-pigs. They had the advantage of experiencing – at least in some way - both male and female urges and they were enthusiastic about the project. Each morning they would let me know what they thought about yesterday's recipe, and eventually we found one that was declared a complete success. 'Turn-On Cosmetics' was born and the cream and the lotions that followed became the best selling products in the whole of Chicago's business.

"Chicago took all the credit, but I didn't mind because of the rather embarrassing nature of the product – embarrassing for a woman, that is. And anyway, we hadn't long been married and I still trusted him completely.

"Don't worry Jack." Stella refilled both glasses. "You can smile now, for the story has a happy ending. Ashok and Peter proved their friendship by putting aside the extra money Chicago was paying them. They opened a bank account in my name, without telling anyone. The three of us bought a small cottage about an hour out of London, with a shed in the garden that we turned into a laboratory. I would work there during the week, and they joined me at the weekends, bringing whatever we needed for the experiments from the factory in London, plus ample provisions for my kitchen and larder.

Together we started a new company: Lio. The dot of the 'i' shows the arrow of the male symbol, and the bottom of the 'o' sports the cross of the female." Stella retrieved her handbag from between her feet, and found a pen. She picked up a menu, and wrote the i and the o, decorated them with the symbols and framed them on two sides with a voluptuously flowing capital L. "Like that," she said, pushing the menu across and leaning back with a sense of satisfaction.

"Lio" she said, pronouncing the individual letters carefully and pointing to her diagram, "stands for 'Libido Inducing Oils' and our concoctions started being sold in sex shops across Europe and filtered into the more conventional beauty shops with amazing speed.

"Chicago was living high on the hog with the income from 'Turn-On Cosmetics' and his cars were more and more extravagant. One day, about eighteen months ago now, he hit a patch of black ice travelling on the M40 at 120 mph and overnight, I became a widow."

The Lio Symbol

Stella sipped slowly at her glass of wine. Her cheeks had taken on a rosy glow that was not unattractive.

She shook her head slightly and brushed a lock of hair from her forehead.

"It turned out that my husband had never proceeded with the divorce, I think he liked having me as an excuse not to take any of his other relationships further – he was in what he called his 'catch-and-release' phase. He also hadn't changed his will since we were first married. So I inherited the business I had put so much into and everything that went with it.

"Ashok, Peter and I are now free from threats and intimidation and we are enjoying ourselves. We sold off the bits and pieces of the business with which we weren't identified, and which we didn't want, and merged the cosmetics into the Lio business. I moved back to London and bought a house in Chelsea. Suddenly everything was positive.

"And here I am," Stella emptied her glass once more, "enjoying a holiday. We closed the factory for three weeks, giving everyone a break. Ashok and Peter have gone to visit their village in India, and I decided to visit Rome, and," she said abruptly, standing up with a scraping of her chair on the flag-stones, "if you'll excuse me, Jack, I need to find the loo. Please don't go away."

I watched Stella weave her way uncertainly through the tables on the pavement and disappear into the restaurant. I looked around me as if I couldn't remember where I was. I looked at my watch, it was half-past four, and the shadows were beginning to lengthen.

During the next few days I spent increasingly less time in the library. I found I was waking later, having slept with luxurious dreams. I breakfasted quickly and hurried to my studies trying to focus my mind upon the research ahead instead of dwelling on the plans Stella - as I was now accustomed to calling her - and I had made the night before about where we should meet for lunch.

The afternoon's studies were then abandoned as my companion suggested one historic venue after another as a more potent addition to my learning than "anything you can find in a library. . .

"You can pick up a book almost anywhere, or better still, go on line to see the 'original' while sitting at home," Stella insisted. "It's far better to experience the physical locations while you have the chance. To amble and absorb the atmospheres of churches and temples while we are here, living in the 'Now.'" Amrita's philosophy of the immediacy of existence was part of Stella's also.

When daylight faded and the amphitheaters and museums closed, we explored the narrow streets and broad avenues of whichever district we were in that day, looking for a suitable place for dinner. Sometimes we walked for hours, comfortably silent together, at other times we would share this or that point of interest with excitement. Mostly we talked; especially when settled at a corner table of a bistro or restaurant whose starched linen-clothed tables spread onto the pavement. During the day we chatted over coffees or ice-creams; throughout lunches - that could be standing at a kiosk or a five course meal in an establishment overlooking the Vatican - we never seemed to run out of things to say to each other.

During our conversations, much of what Stella said, or implied, referred to the numinous and ideas of esoteric communication which reminded me of Amrita and her deep wisdom. A wisdom that ran beneath Earthly worries and setbacks - such as being paralyzed from the waist down.

As the days passed, I found myself talking of my two friends more and more frequently Inevitably, this led to questions from Stella as to how the three of us had met and come to share such intimate discussions.

Over a variety of meals, walks through churches and museums, sips of tea and coffee at pavement cafés, strolls amongst the tourists and the vendors and the population of Rome going about their everyday lives, I told Stella all that I had to tell. She pulled the story out of me delicately, asking quiet questions whenever I came to a stumbling block, questions that gently encouraged me to continue from where I had left off, or, more frequently, took me back to an unfinished part of the tale where I had previously broken the narrative.

The details of Cachonga's destruction I kept to myself. For the first time, I realized, my reluctance to talk of the horrors came not because I didn't want to share them, but because I didn't want to upset her with the gruesome details that seemed so out of place in our life together in Rome. I did not want to cause this lovely creature any pain. I would never want to cause her anything but happiness.

The two of us walked arm in arm as we toured the city – I was not sure how or when that had come about, but it felt so natural and warm that I was happy not to question it. Each evening, when we said goodnight in the lobby of Stella's hotel - which was conveniently close to my digs - before returning to our solitary beds, there was always a kiss to both cheeks and an indication of a hug that, as the days passed, grew into a complete embrace. On the night Stella asked me to accompany her upstairs, it seemed the most natural thing in the world.

There were two weeks left before I was required to return to England and re-evaluate my life when Stella tripped over me on that amazing morning - that's how I always thought of it, and still do – in spite of subsequent revelations. The time passed in a blur of new discoveries, firstly in giving myself over to Stella's introductions of the magical places of Rome and subsequently to the even more magical demonstrations of the physical wonders my body had hidden from me during all the years. Most astounding of all was my introduction to the extraordinary wonders of the female anatomy. It was a journey that I had never anticipated, and now that I had started, I never wanted it to finish.

I found myself gazing at the female population of the city as they went about their day to day activities, trying to understand that each one of them possessed those delicate petals between her legs; that they too had nipples that could be teased erect and hard; that all of them must also be capable of the ecstasies that I had watched erupting through Stella's beautiful body as we merged and blended into each other.

I was awash with the new sensual dimension that had invaded my life, affecting every atom of my being. Food tasted sharper and more intense than I had imagined possible; drinks sparkled across my tongue and tickled the back of my throat; my nostrils vibrated with the intensity of the aromas which assaulted them; my feet seemed to float over the pavements, up flights of steps, across restaurant floors; my fingers had a new sensitivity so that everything I felt reminded me of the exquisite sensation of touching Stella where she had first placed my fingers with an encouraging smile. Life was amazing, life was beautiful, life was full.

Whenever I closed my eyes now, my mind – which had become one with the rest of my anatomy in a most unexpected way – would take me back to that initial moment when Stella had taken me in her arms as we lay naked together for the first time, on her massive hotel bed. How her hands slid along my body making every fiber shudder under the caress. How when she found my excited manhood, hot and full, she had murmured with delight instead of disgust, and had led it into that beautiful softness. How I could do nothing to stop the spiraling surge forging through channels so long unused until I exploded all over her with an agony of embarrassment that threatened to quench any positive feeling, until I heard sounds of her delight purring in my ear.

I would re-live the moment I had been transported from fear into wonder as I looked into those deep brown eyes and saw her joy. Stella had been talking, but I didn't hear the words, just the soothing and positive sound of her voice. She was happy, and hugged me with an exuberance that rushed into my body from hers and spread through every part of my being, and beyond. Where was that beyond? I couldn't identify it, but I knew it existed and that somehow it still belonged to me even though it was outside my physical anatomy. I knew this with a certainty that was beyond argument. It was an exquisite and liberating experience. And that was just the beginning.

How could anything so immensely wonderful be considered dirty and sinful?

Now, wherever we went, we walked either hand in hand, or with my arm around her shoulders and her arm around my waist. We would stop for no reason, turn towards each other and kiss, or just look at each other and squeeze. Our eyes danced, our mouths smiled, there was laughter and love in every movement either of us made towards the other.

"I love you, Jack," Stella had whispered in my ear, early on in our sexual encounters.

"And I love you," I had replied without thought or question. It was a most delicious and exciting truth.

As the days slipped past, and I missed more and more breakfasts with Signor Valdi, and spent less and less time in the library, we confronted the fact that we had to look to the future and what would happen after we left Rome.

"You realize what you have taken on?" Stella was perched atop me one morning, looking down at my disheveled hair with loving eyes. "Having someone love you, as much as I do, gives you new responsibilities, whether you want them or not. Responsibilities to keep yourself safe and well. To look after yourself for me, not for yourself – I need to say this because I don't suppose you've ever bothered to look after yourself for you or anyone else. When you tell me about your living conditions in Aruba, I have come to understand how little personal comfort has to do with your requirements. Now, however, you have me to consider, and I, my lovely man, have you.

"Why not come and live with me when we return to London. My house is big enough to cope with us both, and I can work out a way for you to have your own space. Surely, we cannot waste any more time being apart. What we have is to be cherished, nurtured, enjoyed – but not squandered. It will never be squandered. I know that deep within my soul."

"And so do I," I answered, looking with amazement at the beautiful woman sitting astride me.

So it was decided that we would return to London together, and I would take Stella with me to Thornton and explain my move to London. At first the idea took my breath away, but I got used to it slowly, and by the time my rail-pass ended back in Victoria Station where it had started, Stella was by my side and full of enthusiasm for our new life together; an enthusiasm that swept me along in an invigorating way.

74. A NEW LIFE

A weekend visit was planned during which I would introduce Stella to my Thornton 'family' and collect my few possessions, making my move to London official. Thomas and Sandra were delighted with the change in my circumstances and full of excitement and curiosity as they waited for Stella's car to arrive at the vicarage. They looked at each other with raised eyebrows as a sleek Aston Martin purred across the gravel towards them.

"It's the only car of Chicago's I kept," Stella told me when the tour of her house in Chelsea ended with a visit to the garage – itself a great luxury in this part of London. "I only use it on special occasions, it's a treat and, I admit, I like it."

The visit to Thornton was obviously a special occasion and it was my first trip in the luxurious machine. It was a silvery blue, with cream leather seats and a walnut dashboard. Stella had changed the number plate from Chicago's initials to L 10. She drove with confidence and obvious enjoyment. I felt as if I were taking part in a film as I watched people's heads turn towards us as the car purred past.

Stella was an instant success with the Allworthy family. The weekend passed quickly in a rush of getting acquainted and sharing thoughts and ideas. My initial shyness soon faded and, looking at the faces round the table at dinner on Saturday night, I thought I had never felt such deep contentment, nor imagined that such a feeling was possible.

After dinner Stella insisted on helping Sally with the washing-up, leaving Thomas and myself to enjoy a quiet glass of port together in the drawing-room. I was expecting questions about my relationship with Stella, so was relieved when Thomas started the conversation, eagerly, on a completely different subject.

"Do you remember the last time you were here, Jack, in this room?" Thomas asked, "how I bullied you into admitting there might be a glimmer of faith left within you?"

"Of course," I replied, "and you weren't really a bully, just an enthusiast – and a good friend," I added after a pause.

"How has that little seed progressed since then?" Thomas asked cautiously. "If, of course, it has progressed at all."

"Actually, Thomas, it has come along quite well," I replied. "At first I thought of it as a seed of hope, rather than of faith, but then I asked myself 'what exactly is the difference between the two?' I decided it was really just a matter of degree, and that it was silly to split hairs. That, in itself, was a big step forward, don't you think?"

Thomas looked at me quizzically. "I see faith as understanding that we can't understand," he said, "and being content with that situation and the existence of the imponderable. Hope, on the other hand," Thomas started to smile with a trace of mischief in his expression, "is defined by Oscar Wilde as 'the triumph of optimism over experience.' I think he was referring to those who marry more than once, so it really shouldn't apply to this conversation – I couldn't resist it, that's all. No, the hope you're talking about can certainly be seen as a precursor to faith, so I think you are correct in looking from one to the other without trying to define where one stops and the other begins."

I nodded and continued, carefully: "I have been nurturing that seed you discovered most diligently and, you should be pleased to know, there is definitely something more substantial growing now. My jigsaw puzzle – your metaphor from that same day, I think – is beginning to take on a new design, and I'm finding the challenge much more exciting than I could have envisaged in the past. It is not at all the same picture as the one I had at St. Augustine's, but a picture is beginning to form, and maybe some of the original pieces are still involved – they just make up a different image."

Thomas nodded with a smile. "That's exactly what I meant by that analogy, how well you have grasped the concept. I have never shared it with anyone else, but I knew you would understand the different aspects of the idea, and the possibilities – the same pieces being re-arranged to create a new picture."

"Maybe some new pieces have been introduced also," I said with a smile. "After all there is now Stella in my life, and for her, I think I need totally new pieces."

Embarrassed by my admission I continued quickly to tell Thomas of Amrita's ideas about confronting evil and how she had helped me to shed some of the bitterness that had been weighing me down for so long. He was quick to seize on the idea of the force of existence running through each of us.

"God within us is a central concept of many Christian sects, especially the Quakers, I believe," said Thomas enthusiastically. "One of their essential truths is 'there is that of God in every man.' We are back to nomenclature again, aren't we?"

"Yes, I suppose so," I agreed, "but the more I think about these ideas, the more titles become obstacles rather than signposts. I am beginning to get a feel for the necessity of evil in order to put goodness in perspective. Virtue cannot shine without a backdrop of something sinister. If there is no possibility of failure, why should we try so hard to succeed?

"I cannot justify evil, but I must come to terms with its existence and fight to minimize its influence on my life. Perhaps 'conscience' should be seen as the Divine aspect of 'consciousness' as it is the side of our thinking that steers us towards the light, and our consciousness is just a part of the continual flux of existence. It is how we develop our conscience that determines the direction our souls will take within that flux. Belief in the final triumph of good over evil constitutes faith – that is what you told me in that last discussion we had here, by the fire – and now I will not argue with you, I believe you are right."

Thomas was obviously delighted with my ramblings. "We'll get you back, yet, Jack – just wait and see!" he chortled, putting an arm across my shoulders.

"Well, I wouldn't say that, exactly," I responded quickly, but I gave him a smile and added "but I am enormously grateful to you, Thomas, for your faith in me, apart from anything else, and your insistence that there was still something positive and good in the blackness of my misery. I just needed you to point it out and force me to recognize it for what it is. You are a very wonderful friend, and I am sincerely in your debt," I added softly, suddenly realizing how true that was.

Thomas refilled our port glasses and, with shining eyes, turned the conversation to lighter topics.

Three boxes of books, my diaries and numerous sketch books were brought down from the attic, a small suitcase of clothes and a few photographs made up the total baggage of my past. They were loaded into the boot of the Aston Martin, after lunch on Sunday, the lid clicking shut with a sense of finality. Stella and I said goodbye to Thornton with promises that Sally and Thomas would come and see us in London and let us return some hospitality. This talk of 'us' still sounded strange in my head, but in a wonderful and exciting way. I shut the door of the Aston and waved a cheerful goodbye as the car purred its way south.

My new home was a Georgian house in a small square in the centre of which was a charming garden surrounded by a tall wrought iron fence. All four sides of the square were made up of similar buildings all painted white, with columned porches over tall front doors with highly polished brass fittings. There was a discreet air of affluence combined with a friendly community spirit more like that of a village than a city.

Stella had re-arranged things in a flurry of activity when we first arrived from Rome. She moved piles of clothes into one of the guest rooms and created a study for me, at the top of the house, where her dressing room had been. There were plenty of shelves for my books and the oak desk she had used as a dressing-table was returned to its original purpose. It was situated beneath a large window at the back of the house that overlooked a patio and some buoyant flowerbeds. The little garden backed on to that of a house in the next street and, between the two properties, two large plane trees blocked the view of other people's windows. It was a pleasant view and could have been deep in the countryside if it wasn't for the ever-present burr of traffic.

A redundant computer was brought from Stella's factory and set up in the new study. I was introduced to the internet and was entranced to find access to books and all spheres of education at my finger-tips. While Stella disappeared to her office during the day, I sat in my eyrie and explored an unanticipated world of knowledge.

The sabbatical I had started with my three weeks in Rome had been extended by the Missionary Service. I now had three months in which to re-arrange and expand my lectures to form a complete university-style course, entitled "People and Land Management in the Third World," to be taught at the UK's leading missionary school, in London. It was Illingsworth's idea, and it was at his instigation that my tin trunk and suitcase were recovered and sent back via St. Mary's. I looked forward to the challenge of collecting slides and making diagrams to be shown during my lectures, and of having the time to develop and deliver all my ideas. The internet allowed me to work at home, and I grew to love my little study at the top of the house. The shelves were filling up with reference books on one side, and a quite different set of texts on the other, for my studies were no longer restricted to agricultural practices in Africa.

My discovery of romance and the resulting sexual experiences had opened an extra dimension to my life and given a new direction to my pursuit of the numinous. I was in no doubt that there was something mystical about the physical love I shared with Stella and I knew when I looked into her eyes, at certain moments of intensity, that she felt the same. There was indeed magic happening between us, with us, through us. A power so awesome that it left us both breathless, and not only because of the physical exercise involved. I suspected that this power came from the joining of our astral as well as our physical bodies. I remembered my discussion with Percival and Amrita on this subject and decided to research the idea in order to better understand what was happening to us during our lovemaking.

75. Entwining Astral Bodies

I had first come across the idea of astral bodies at St. Augustine's in the anthropology section of the college's library where I read books by Juan Carlos Castaneda. In 'The Teachings of Don Juan' he described bundles of luminous fibers that swirl around our physical bodies emitting different colors depending upon a person's emotional and spiritual state of awareness.

Sometime later, in a theosophy journal, I found 'astral' defined as 'a supersensible substance,' and an 'astral body' as an "astral counterpart of the physical body." From these two diverse sources I deduced that there are energy fields that interact with human beings, or rather are a part of them; swirling with, through and amongst the visible cells of the anatomy. Perhaps, it would be better to say that the physical body is part of the astral body, rather than the other way around?

Fascinated with this idea, I worked my way through the Seminary's library looking for references to these auras and found many in both Eastern and Western philosophies. Now, many years after those initial studies, I burrow through my books to find my scribbled notes on the subject, and so armed, I order yet more books for my new study's shelves.

When I read those books at St. Augustine's I formed my own views about how and where the extensions of human forms worked. I learnt, and still believe, that brujos, wizards, magicians, holy men and psychics can see these auras. That, amongst the swirling lights, an individual's Chakras glow. I want to be able to see them for myself but know I've a lot more to learn – or unlearn, perhaps- before my mind can be ready for such visions. However, even though the luminous fibers are not visually apparent to me, I am beginning to feel their presence and to look at people in a new way.

When I was in London I realized that in everyday interactions astral bodies must be forced to overlap but I was sure they maintained their individuality. Rush-hour in a tube train, for example, would see such a jumble of auras. People 'shrink inside themselves' as their energy fields compact but interaction of some sort is inevitable. Expressions such as 'I need my space' describe this feeling of entrapment due to the restricted movements of a person's astral fibres. As long as emotions remain neutral there is no danger or need for discomfort from such overlapping.

I notice couples in crowded places, how they share their space with gentleness and comfort because their auras are joined in harmony, becoming stronger in the process – the whole being greater than the sum of the two. The result is that other people tend not to crush them. I have experienced the same sensation when travelling with Stella. We feel secure in our shared space no matter how many people are jostling around us.

'In their own little world' people said of couples in love. How apt for a pair of astral bodies which have expanded and joined in magical togetherness; a merger of shared energies with a double protection of mutual love.

However not everybody has positive auras.

With reluctance, I turn my thoughts to the darkness of evil. Emotional and sexual energies can be as negative as they can be positive, and violent and aggressive forces can be present between people as readily as the peaceful and harmonious. I can see how one person's aura might overwhelm another's in a take-over bid and absorb someone else's energy field to augment their own. How controls could be established, pain inflicted, and ultimately rape and murder committed. A theft of someone else's energy. Such stealth may succeed during this lifetime but, with the act of murder, the victim's energy has the ultimate escape.

Horrors such as my experience in Cachonga must be brought about by a clash of journeying souls: those who milk energies from their captives meeting those of open and giving dispositions. I think and hope that such destruction is only temporary in the swirling forces that dictate the many lives available to each individual's inner self. Now, it seems, I have adopted the Hindu concept of Samsara.

As Percival had intimated, I recognized these energy fields as another name for souls - they were of the body without being dependent upon the body. When the physical body is discarded, the astral dimension of a person continues to the next plane. The victory of the negative on the temporal plane would only serve to sink the perpetrator lower into the mire of sorrow while those who suffered the victimization would find their souls elevated as their auras rise.

Had these ideas anything to do with faith - with the new light I was nurturing in my own soul? My ideas could not be proved, so faith - or Faith - was necessary for such beliefs to be maintained. True, I had the proof of the interchange of energies between Stella and myself, but it was only apparent to the two of us alone.

There is evidence however of learned and attuned monks, magicians, gurus, brujas, and so on, being capable of 'astral travel' where their souls move without their bodies. Only highly evolved psyches can do this safely and find their way back to their physical forms. Suitable protection needs to be in place to safeguard the travelers from the highwaymen of evil who wait in the ether for the unprepared. Perhaps the kind of decorporealisation Father Henry had experienced through drugs and I - through nearness to death - are small examples of astral travel. Fortunately we were both 'true' men in heart and mind and were not assaulted by alternative energies while in our vulnerable state. Also, of course, neither of us traveled very far.

Further research led me to believe that it is through astral bodies that healers work. They pull in cosmic forces through the top chakra as they inhale - once again, only when suitable protection is in place - and use the overlapping astral bodies to transfer purifying energies from themselves to their patients as they exhale. Some highly evolved healers can heal over great distances as their powers do not recognize physical space and can communicate with a willing and open recipient whether they are in the next room or on the next continent. This is just another form of astral travel.

I began to see the importance of maintaining an honest soul, not just for the sake of morality but for mental survival and physic advancement. Being true to oneself, as Percival had admonished me, quoting

Shakespeare at St. Mary's, became crucial if one was going to investigate the astral plane. I became nervous about the vulnerability of Stella's and my souls as our sexual activities merged our energies into one and opened us to interact with mighty forces – there was no doubt that our activities were of cosmic proportions. But then I decided that our love for each other was so strong, and so immensely positive, that it should create enough protection. However, when I found the Yogini Tantra with its recipe for protection, I taught it to Stella and it became one of our rituals of foreplay. I felt happier and stronger as a result.

As my research expanded, I could not help wondering why it was that so many of the philosophies of the Western world worked diligently to obstruct the liberating experiences I was learning? By clothing sex with the negative shroud of shame and by demanding the denial of natural instincts, institutionalized religions had created yet another way to control their followers. A ready source of guilt - and guilt was obviously a powerful by-product of the restrictions imposed in this area - meant more clout for those who claimed to have forgiveness in their power.

"Love enjoyed by the ignorant, becomes bondage. The same love, tasted by one who understands, brings liberation," I read in the Cittavisuddhiprakarana. Individual liberation, I knew, was not something that was encouraged by the religious hierarchy.

"I have as much authority as the Pope," Percival had said one day at St. Mary's. "I just don't have as many people who believe it." I remembered the conversation with a smile.

While much of Western thinking denigrates man's physicality, Tantric law dictates that the body should be revered. That if a person cannot truly love him or herself then they are incapable of loving someone else.

Loving yourself should start with an appreciation of your body; your body as a temple, a shrine of the Divine, of your own divinity.

The unnatural restrictions certain dogmas place upon bodily sensations create tension in both mind and body. Tension closes doors, restricts the flow of vital energy, limits possibilities. It is vital to unblock preconditioned restrictions, to learn to love your body, if you are to let the energies flow through open channels of appreciation for all that is good about what you have been given. Yoga, is one science which concentrates on unlocking such tensions; meditations of Taoists and followers of Zen are designed for the same purpose.

If the body is a temple that can provide access to the numinous to all who seek diligently enough and in the correct way, then it is right to pay homage to our physical being. This kind of 'worship' moves sexual activity from the profane to the sacred and went a little way towards explaining the mystical experiences Stella and I were so enjoying. "Love thy neighbor as thyself" is one of the basic commandments of Christianity, what we forget so often is that means one must love oneself first if the similar affection for one's neighbor is to be of any value. However, I did have trouble loving my own scarred body.

Stella was my teacher. Her love for my body, which had so embarrassed me at the start of our relationship, was slowly giving me confidence in many different ways. Her sensuous love of her own body slid over my own in an extraordinary exchange of admiration and passion.

I had been so worried about her reaction to my ugly marked buttocks – I remembered Sandra's scream only too well. I had seen pity in Stella's face, but never horror. I had seen and felt her love as she ran her tongue carefully over the cruciform mark and later, when she rubbed a variety of her oils carefully over the affected area, there was actually pleasure shining in her eyes, just as when she ministered to any other part of my anatomy.

Another of my studies led me to Lingam Meditation and what the Taoist teachers referred to as 'solo cultivation.' The idea was simple enough – if your body is a temple, then self-pleasure should be seen as a form of worship and an opportunity for intimate self-knowledge and self-appreciation. In this light, masturbation should be viewed as a sacred act if performed with suitable reverence.

I thought of my teenage years – and into my twenties – when I had explored my juvenile physicality with a silk cloth designed for use during communion. I had been mortified by these recollections in the past. Now, I began to realize, that I hadn't been committing a terrible sin. My thoughts had always been upon what I then thought of as the Divine, I had been offering the essence of my being to God and had indeed seen it as a form of worship; I just failed to articulate it as such.

I didn't ignore Western religions in this new direction of research. Christian mysticism I found was full of tales of 'ecstasies, raptures, visions, trances,' and even 'convulsive seizures' - all, I now realized, must be references to religiously induced orgasms.

I remembered some of my readings while at St. Augustine's and the painting of "The Ecstasy of Saint Teresa" I had seen reproduced in one of the books. I obtained a copy of St. Teresa's autobiography and found her sensuous mystical experiences recorded in detail.

"Like imperfect sleep which, instead of giving more strength to the head, doth but leave it the more exhausted, the result of mere operations of the imagination is but to weaken the soul. Instead of nourishment and energy she – the soul - reaps only lassitude and disgust; whereas a genuine heavenly vision yields to her a harvest of ineffable spiritual riches, and an admirable renewal of bodily strength." Here St. Teresa succinctly describes the difference between self-pleasuring with profane thoughts versus channeling sexual energy towards an idea of the Divine.

I had also written notes on Anslem, Benedictine Archbishop of Canterbury in the eleventh century. Although he viewed monastic life as the only way to attain salvation, it did not stop Anslem's devotions taking on physical expression. He prayed: "Oh God, let me know you and love you so that I may find joy in you," which is conventional enough until juxtaposed with his writings to fellow monks concerning the 'amitié particulière': "Most beloved . . since I do not doubt that we both love the other equally, I am sure that each of us equally desires the other, for those whose minds are fused together in the fire of love, suffer equally if their bodies are separated by the place of their daily occupations . . . If I were to describe the passion of our mutual love, I fear I should seem to those who do not know the truth to exaggerate. So I must subtract some part of the truth. But you know how great is the affection that we have experienced – eye to eye, kiss for kiss, embrace for embrace."

Suddenly, with this new understanding, a mantle of shame and guilt that I had thought of as part of my persona, disintegrated as mist when the sun rises. I found myself grinning involuntarily, my whole being seeming lighter, more flexible, buoyant even.

76. NEW DIMENSIONS

My studies into the development of spiritual experiences initiated through sensual activity were becoming more and more interesting. I began to study Tantric writings some of which dated from as long ago as 600 B.C. Buddhism had embraced Tantric thinking – as it had many other philosophies – and in this assimilation recommended looking for the 'Ultimate Meaning' through actions rather than words.

In Taoist thinking I found the idea of the attraction of opposite forces and the harmony that results when they join. I could see that the synchrony illustrated in the Yin-Yang symbol referred to the coupling of males and females – and other entities - in a very powerful way. Apparently Taoist doctors used to prescribe physical intercourse to their patients both to heal and to keep them healthy. Different positions would be suggested for different ailments of both body and mind. I was surprised to note that, when talking of erogenous zones – of which there were more than I had dreamt – the most powerful of them all, they claimed, was the brain.

Taoists call carnal energy 'Ching-Chi' and recognize it as a revitalizing force that helps men and women to keep in balance with themselves, with each other, and with the world. I was keen to pursue the Tao of Loving that proclaimed that when two people unleashed their sensual energies and allowed them to mesh into one, that 'one' could also be merged with the spiritual energies of existence.

A whole science had been developed to unlock the vital forces of mankind and to allow souls to plug into more than just one another – to connect with the source of all - whether it be called the Tao, or Prana, or Chi, or anything else, and augment their otherwise limited supply of energy. To re-charge their batteries, so to speak and stretch both philosophical and physical boundaries.

"He who realizes the truth of the body realizes the Truth of the Universe." I read in the Rat Nas Tantra.

"Your body will understand before your mind puts words to it," the Shiva Sutra proclaims.

When Stella came home from work, I would pounce upon her with enthusiasm, filled with excitement from my readings, and lead her to the bedroom.

Stella would laugh as I undressed her, fumbling in my eagerness, and telling her about my research of that particular afternoon. The two of us would then embark upon one experiment after another to expand the feelings of our bodies and souls into another dimension of being alive. It was a spectacular journey.

After studying Pranayama and Chi - Taoist breathing sciences - for example, we would concentrate on matching our breathing patterns, with foreheads and toes touching to circulate the sexual energy between us, breathing deeply, taking oxygen deeper into the body than we had ever done before. Another time, we would regulate our breaths so that one was breathing in as the other exhaled, passing passion to each other in a crescendo of exchanges. When we embraced and felt our hearts beating against each other it was impossible to tell which pulse of energy belonged to which body - as if there was just one heart fueling us both.

One of the Tantric texts taught that the sounds of breathing and of the heart beating - which I found I could hear if I concentrated hard enough - can be used as a most personal mantra. "When the breath is unsteady, everything is unsteady; but when the breath is still, all else is still" the Goraksha Shataka recounts. So Stella and I would sit cross-legged, facing each other, holding hands lightly, and meditate by listening to these powerful sounds and feeling the energy they represented pulsing through our bodies.

"My mother uses breathing techniques in her healing work," Stella confided to me as I was telling her the results of that particular day's research. "She says she draws in the Cosmic Power through the crack in the top of the skull, and directs the vital forces throughout her body's interlinked energy paths – or that of her patient's – to cleanse and carry away pain and negativity. Inhaling brings in the positive forces, exhaling expunges the negative ones, pushing them out of the body with determination."

"I'm looking forward to meeting your mother," I said, encouraged by the way Stella's words gave credence to my own thoughts. "You told me she is a Druid but it seems she has much Eastern-style philosophy within her beliefs. It is fascinating how fundamental ideas cross over, under, or through religious barriers, unaffected by restrictions that affect the superficial elements of 'religious thought' that are really nothing more than cultural controls."

Stella gave me one of those looks that I had come to know meant I was talking too much, and there were other urgencies to be dealt with to which speech was a hindrance.

As my readings continued, I began to appreciate that Stella was a most consummate lover. I was only too aware of my ignorance and inexperience in this sphere and was eager to learn how I could bring her pleasures in return for the extraordinary things she did to me. I asked her to teach me, but she was uncharacteristically shy about her own physicality. "I get pleasure from giving you pleasure, my love," she would murmur softly, her tongue darting in my ear, "and, anyway, you know what we do together is magical. What makes you think I am not enjoying it as much as you?"

"It's just that you do things to me while I just lie there and groan with ecstasy. I am the passive recipient of your extraordinary attentions. I would like to be able to do that for you. As well as sharing the pleasures we give each other when we are both active, I want to know how to initiate your pleasures on my own, with you being the passive one. But I need you to teach me what to do."

These discussions always ended by Stella's kisses stopping my speech and spreading warmth and excitement in such a way that any passivity from either of us was out of the question.

Then one day I was reading about The Yellow Emperor – the founder of the Chinese civilization, many centuries ago. Three women were put in charge of the young Emperor's sexual education, each one being physically different and with different areas of expertise. The smallest, Su-Nü, was responsible for teaching her royal pupil how to 'pleasure a woman.' Finally, I had found myself an instruction manual, and Stella, in spite of her experience, found herself on journeys that led in previously unimagined directions.

I would go down on my knees at the side of the bed and, with a new sort of worship in mind, I would pull Stella's prone form towards me until her legs were over my shoulders.

"I thought the idea of women 'bursting' was a myth," she said after one such session, looking in bewilderment at the puddle on the bed.

"The Taoists call that 'moon flower water,'" I said, thrilled with what I had achieved. "And the Tantrics refer to it as 'divine love nectar.'"

"I had heard about it, but never believed it could really happen," Stella was filled with amazement. "Look what you have done to me! I am now the student, and you the master, my love. These mysteries just keep growing, don't they?"

I was delighted. Following instructions given originally to the Yellow Emperor I had awakened Stella's

'Goddess Spot,' as Tantric texts called this source of Shakti power, centuries before Dr. Grafenberg claimed to discover the 'G-spot.' In addition, gentle but steady stimulation of her other delicate petals and the mysterious pistils in between seemed to assist this glorious out-pouring. Our experiments were teaching us exciting physical secrets, secrets previously hidden from ourselves as well as from others.

Shakti is the Tantric Goddess of Creation. The Universe and whatever lies beyond are created by her dance with the great God Shiva. It is a sexual dance of bliss, and mortals are invited to copy the coupling of the divinities and to become one with the source of all life and creation.

I had watched Stella dance at the parties to which I accompanied her. I was both thrilled and aroused by the freedom with which she moved when the music seemed to take control of her body. I had asked her what happened to make her move with such fluidity, abandonment, and obvious enjoyment.

Stella told me that when she 'let herself go' as the expression so succinctly puts it, she could feel the earth's energies running up her spine, as if the music was a conduit. "Dancing allows you to feel the excitement of unity with disparate forces," she explained during a break between dances. "Your energy mass expands to mix with and embrace that of others in the immediate present and beyond. Can you think of a culture that doesn't dance?" I admitted that I couldn't and thought of the tales of magic whipped up by the whirling Dervish tribes.

It was true that our intimate encounters had now become like many dances merged into one stream of thrilling activity. It was impossible to tell where one of our bodies ended and the other began. Our nerve-endings seemed to tingle in unison and bind us into one being, without physical boundaries.

Now we were discovering things together and Stella was entering new realms of experience along with me as an equal guide at last. Our journeys had become adventures of discovery for both of us.

The summer passed in a rush of new experiences – not just in the bedroom. Stella had a busy social life, and I was introduced to so many people I got them all muddled up. I enjoyed having the house to myself during the weekdays. Occasionally I would emerge to potter about the neighborhood on domestic errands. I loved shopping for Stella and myself. Looking in the greengrocer's for something special to accompany whatever I had selected from the butcher's for us to have for supper. However, so often, there were guests who appeared without notice, and the housekeeper took over the cooking to cater for the extra mouths.

Stella's friends were obviously used to her having 'open house' and didn't see why that should change because she now had a live-in partner who they tolerated with politeness. It was a life Stella had become used to, and I saw no reason why I should initiate any changes. However, I found myself retreating to the sanctity of my study more and more frequently.

At weekends there were always people coming to visit us, or we were off to join a group at some important function in the social calendar - often for which special attire was necessary. There was the tennis at Wimbledon, the regatta at Henley, races at Ascot, Cheltenham and Goodwood, Polo at Windsor and The Grand Prix at Silverstone. Stella had special passes and tickets for all, and a group of enthusiasts attached themselves to her for every event and made it apparent to me that the precedent had been set well before I arrived on the scene.

Stella had taken charge of my hair and beard both of which were now neatly trimmed on a regular basis. She encouraged me to try contact lenses, but I was uncomfortable without my glasses and hated poking things at my eyes. My mentor consoled herself by choosing several pairs of stylish glasses, suggesting which ones were appropriate for each outfit she bought me. I had never had such a wardrobe, but remained happiest in jeans, although I had to let the belt out a couple of holes as my new life encouraged an unaccustomed enjoyment of food and drink. Even the angular lines of my cheeks began to soften.

On a weekend in late June, when the Allworthys came to stay, Rufus joined us for dinner on the Saturday night, complete with his exotic wife of Jamaican descent. Her name was Pearl, and she was the most striking woman I thought I had ever seen. She arrived on Rufus's arm, draped in a brightly colored garment of reds and blues which showed off her tall sinewy figure and seemed to make her dark skin glow. When she smiled, her teeth shone like her name, and her eyes danced with merriment.

It was one of those magical summer evenings, so special in England for being so rare, when there was not a breath of wind, and the sun showed no intention of going down. Stella had champagne on ice set out on the patio, and Thomas, Rufus and I celebrated our reunion in style and chatted with animation while our partners got to know one another, seated around a small wrought iron table heavy with white paint.

It looked as if they should have little in common, these three women. Estelle, the gracious hostess, in her sophisticated designer dress of pale mauve and matching silk shoes with perilously high-heels. Her fine blond hair was swept around her face in entropic confusion; she wore Boliviana ear-rings which caught the light and sparkled with expense, with a necklace, bracelet and ring to match. Then Pearl with her dramatic Afro of teased black curls, her ears decorated with hoops of brightly colored plastic, matching the swirls of her ethnic costume. A plethora of bangles danced on both wrists, and dramatic sandals with wedged heels and red ribbons climbed above her ankles, showing off her long toes with brightly painted nails. Finally, there was Sandra with her delightful lack of make-up, naturally wavy short hair tucked behind her ears, and a straight dress of pale green without ornament apart from a small gold cross that hung around her neck.

Despite their differences, whatever it was that had caused these three women to choose their male partners seemed to bind them together in instant friendship. Before they had finished their first glass of champagne they were chattering away like finches, their talk interrupted regularly by laughter.

Meanwhile, I was catching up with Rufus and was especially keen to know what had happened regarding Father Henry and his somewhat unorthodox ideas.

"Well, we did well for several years," Rufus answered my query in a quiet voice. "But there were rumors, and chit-chat, even though our coffee mornings were now completely legitimate. Eventually pressure came from the hierarchy of the Church, and Father Henry took early retirement. He lives in an establishment known as The Castle and seems very content – I visit him at least once a month to give him a report upon the parish he built up. He loves his life in The Castle where he has the company of many erudite men."

"What do you think really happened that night he 'flew' and saw the crack in the masonry?" I asked. I had my own ideas about this, of course, but I was eager to know what my friend thought.

"Well, as I understand it," Rufus answered carefully, "it is possible, if you take more of a drug than you should, to decorporealate – that is for your spirit to leave your body. It happens to people who are very close to death also, so I have been told. If you overdose, or if the person close to death actually dies, then the spirit never returns to the body, but in this case, I think father Henry was simply 'flying high' as the expression goes. I truly believe that his spirit soared to the beams of his beloved church and that he saw the dangerous cracks that needed attention. His body, meanwhile, must have stayed in a heap behind the altar, where they found him the next morning. He was lucky that his spirit was not ready to leave and found its way back."

"Yes," I said, "I have had a similar experience," and then wished I had said nothing. Raising my eyes, I was relieved to find that Rufus and Thomas were deep in discussion about the value and dangers of drugs and had not heard my revelation.

"Oh, by the way, Jack," Rufus turned to me with enthusiasm. "I forgot to tell you, Pearl is Raymond's sister, so I now have Raymond as a brother-in-law and Winston as something closer still – it's as if he's attached to us somehow. The congregation of St. Luke's continues to swell and we are blessed with a peaceful and friendly parish where once there had been such hostility and aggression."

The evening was a great success, and I was deeply grateful to Stella – and proud of her also – for having arranged everything and provided such a wonderfully warm atmosphere for my friends, as well as all the food and drink.

"You made them feel so welcome," I said as I thanked my generous lover. We were lying facing each other in the mystical midnight twilight of June in England. The bedroom lights were not on, but the curtains were open and the aura of mid-summer spread shadows across the room.

"They're your family, Jack," Stella responded, her fingers running lightly across my chest. "And now they're my family too. I'm so pleased it went so well.

"When am I going to meet your other family, Jack? Your parents, brother and sister? I hope you're not ashamed of me," she added with a twinkle of humor that betrayed her confidence in my answer.

"But I've not met your parents either," I was quick to point out. "Your family of friends is enormous, I'm still trying to work my way through all that lot, but if I am to impose my biological family on you, then you must allow me to meet yours."

"Of course, my darling," Stella's hands were moving downward, the circling motion causing havoc with nerve-endings deep inside my abdomen. "And my parents are looking forward to meeting you. Which should we do first?"

"Let's talk about it tomorrow," I answered, I now had other things to think about. I pulled Stella into my embrace and began my own caresses.

77. A DIFFERENT WILLENBURY

My parents had moved out of the Hall when Robert got married some four years ago. A gardener's cottage in a corner of the grounds had been extended and smartened up to accommodate them. My father, Charles, had retired from the business when the outset of Alzheimer's had been diagnosed and thrown the family into confusion.

I had visited them very briefly during my stay at Thornton, before going on my travels - I had wanted to thank mother for providing the missionary service with the prescription for my glasses. Thomas had accompanied me for moral support, for I felt suddenly nervous about the visit. The idea of my father with

Alzheimer's was very uncomfortable, and the thought of Robert lording it in the house of my childhood was also unattractive. I had not visited since.

Now, approaching Willenhall in the purring Aston, with Stella behind the wheel, I found my nervousness reappearing. I felt like a small boy again, with the awkward clumsiness and lack of confidence that had pursued me during my years there. Was it possible that such a pathetic person as Jack Bolden could be returning with a glamorous and intelligent girl-friend? I put a hand on Stella's thigh; she turned to me with her beaming smile and I smiled back, my worries only slightly reduced.

My mother opened the cottage door to our knock and looked Stella up and down with undisguised curiosity. Stella had chosen a conventional tweed suit for the occasion that seemed to meet with approval, as her hostess gave a slight nod as they shook hands.

I bent to kiss mother's cheek and thought how much older she looked than when I had last seen her. She seemed bowed somehow, and the sparkle of energy that always fueled her movements had faded. As we followed her into the house, down the passage to the sitting room, I noticed how much her stride had shortened and felt a sudden sadness.

Father was sitting in an armchair, but he rose as we came into the room, smoothing the front of his V-necked sweater with fluttering hands. His eyes had a watery, vacant look.

"Hello, father," I extended my right hand, and with my left, pulled Stella gently closer to me. "This is Stella," I continued, trying to sound relaxed and chatty. "We are living together in London. She is a pharmacist," I didn't know what else to say.

The once powerful business magnate shook hands with both of us solemnly; there was no recognition evident in his face.

A tea tray had been put ready on the table in the window, and mother busied herself handing things round. The little party sat perched on chairs, stirring tea and balancing a plate of sandwiches on our knees. Father had a small table for his convenience. The conversation was stilted and interrupted every now and then by a question from father as to the identity of his visitors. Mother either ignored him or answered in a cross tone that he had already been told several times.

All of a sudden, mother rose and approached Stella, turning her back on her husband.

"Stella, dear," she started in an uncharacteristically soft tone. "Would you mind looking after Charles for me for a few minutes? I am anxious to speak to Jack privately for a moment, it's very awkward, but I would be most grateful."

I had never seen mother nervous before. I rose quickly and went to her side. "What is it mother?" I said anxiously, but she was still looking at Stella.

"I would be delighted," said Stella, managing to get up without spilling her tea or dropping her plate. "Please, don't worry at all, I quite understand, you haven't seen Jack for quite a while."

"We'll just be in the garden," mother gestured to the door. "If you have any problems, please call me."

"Everything will be fine," said Stella soothingly. "Take your time." She reached out and gave my hand a squeeze.

Seated on a wooden bench with a view through the trees towards The Hall, mother told me that she had been diagnosed with cervical cancer and was about to undergo an operation. She spoke in a matter-of-fact voice, but I could feel the emotion quivering in the background.

"I know I haven't been the best of mothers to you, Jack," she said softly. "I'm deeply sorry for that. None of us really understood you, did we? You seemed so different. I know I have a difficult road ahead of me, and I need your forgiveness and your help to see me through. I need some of your faith – of course I have always been to church, you know that, but I haven't the depth of conviction that you've always had. Please show me how to find it and give me your blessing."

Fear had been the first emotion to hit me as I listened to this speech. Fear for what lay ahead for her, fear that I would not be able to help her. The beliefs she wanted from me I had abandoned completely – how could I tell her that? Such information would remove the only thing she had to hold on to?

For a brief moment, I contemplated confiding in my mother, telling her of my trials and the resulting rejection of my original faith. "I would if I could, Mother, but," I started.

"Oh, don't deny me your help, Jack, please," she interrupted me quickly misunderstanding my comment. "I know you must resent how I favored the other children over you, I can understand that, and I'm sorry, so very sorry. But please, forgive me and give me your blessing." She was looking at me fervently, with the affection I had so longed to see in my childhood. Now she needed me, as I had needed her for so many years.

I knew she was in a state of panic and that my own experiences were of no more interest to her now than they had ever been. The immediate personal problem dominated her thinking, suddenly I had become of use to her – or at least she thought I could be.

She took hold of my hand with both of hers. "Please don't be angry with me, dear Jack," she said in a pleading tone. "I can make things up to you, really I can. Charles has left you nothing in his will – he was always frightened that you'd give anything you had to charity, and he wanted to know exactly where his money went. But now I have power of attorney and will change it. It's quite unfair for Robert and Alice to have everything, especially as we've been pushed into this tiny cottage and abandoned. We hardly see anything of either of them," she added, a note of bitterness entering her speech.

"Well, I've hardly been an attentive son," I said softly, "but I always seemed to get in the way, here. I decided I'd be less of a nuisance to everybody if I stayed away."

"I know, I know," mother began to sob quietly. "I'm so sorry. I don't blame you for not being here. It's not as if you live just along the garden path, is it?" she said pointedly, glancing towards her former home. "But please don't abandon us in your thoughts and prayers. We need your help, both your father and I."

"Of course you have my support, dear mother," I was also feeling tearful as I watched mother dab at her eyes. "What exactly do you want me to do?"

"Pray for me, Jack. Please pray for me. I am due to go into hospital next Wednesday – I was going to telephone you, but you beat me to it when you rang to ask if you could come and visit. I thought maybe God has not forgotten about me after all, and that He sent you to see me. Your visit's a great comfort and has given me hope. Maybe the hysterectomy will solve the problem, maybe I won't have to die just yet."

"Of course I'll pray for you," I hated seeing my mother crumbling before me. I knew she needed the comfort of her traditional religious ideas, and not to hear of how I had rejected them and was now pursuing knowledge of ultimate life forces in an entirely different way.

"And you'll forgive me?" She raised her eyes and looked hard at her younger son.

"There's nothing to forgive, mother," I responded.

"Then, give me your blessing," mother was quick to return to her request. "Here and now, please, Father." And with that unusual form of address hanging strangely in the air, she sank from the bench onto her knees, bowed her head and put her hands together in front of her.

I hesitated, but then compassion filled me and I rose slowly and turned to face her. I gave her the conventional blessing she required, making the sign of the cross as I did so. The words and actions coming automatically even after years of disuse.

78. AMANDA & GORDON

The visit to Stella's parents was a much more positive experience. We had been asked for the weekend, their home in Avebury being a considerable distance from London. We planned to arrive in time for tea on the Saturday allowing for a leisurely drive and to stay until after lunch the following day.

Avebury is a startling village encircled by a famous array of standing stones – one of the largest henges in Britain, dating back to 2,300 B.C. The Marchants' cottage, situated behind an array of deep red hollyhocks had a wonderful view of several of the gnarled, lichen-covered relics from the end of a garden busy with flowers. The impressive mound of Silbury Hill could be glimpsed in the distance.

"Come in, come in, and welcome," Amanda Marchant stood in the open doorway of her home, smiling. Two long-legged slightly shaggy dogs rushed towards the gate, tails wagging and lips curling in excitement. I took our small suitcase from the boot of the Aston and followed Stella up the little path, trying not to trip over the bounding animals.

Stella enveloped her mother in a hug and received an equally enthusiastic one in response. Then to my surprise Amanda turned and, ignoring my outstretched hand, she hugged me also, giving me a kiss on the cheek as she squeezed.

"I'm so thrilled to meet you, Jack. It seems you have transformed our daughter's life, and both Gordon and I are eager to welcome you with warmth and gratitude for bringing Stella such happiness."

"Here, here," came a deep voice from just inside the house, and a tall man with white hair appeared behind his wife. He shook my proffered hand with enthusiasm. "I'm Gordon," he said, "and I echo my wife's sentiments. You are indeed welcome."

I felt instantly at home in the cottage that was much larger than it looked from the outside. "We call it our Tardis – from Dr. Who, in case you missed the series" Stella had informed me during the drive down. "We will be sleeping in the guest room in the attic. It's a charming room, but you must be careful not to stand up straight, those beams are very hard."

Amanda led the way through the house to a conservatory at the back, the doors and windows open to the garden sunshine and the view of the stones. Stella had reminded me that her mother was quite advanced in the Druid hierarchy as well as being a professional dowser. Her father, she told me, was high in the ranks of the Masons, "so, you see, they're both deeply involved with energies of all kinds," she said. "I think you'll find the visit interesting."

"I'm sure I will," I had answered enthusiastically. "I'm especially fascinated by the dowsing; do you think your mother would mind talking to me about her skills?"

"No, I don't think so" Stella had said after a moment's pause. "As a matter of fact, I have already warned her. I told her of your initiation in Islington, when we dowsed for ley lines, and of how you took your rods to Africa and used them there. She doesn't usually talk about her skills in any detail, but I'm sure, with you, she'll make an exception."

I was as excited as I was intrigued and it was with great interest that I looked around me as I followed my hostess through the cottage, glimpsing rooms full of jumbled furnishings with strange symbols decorating any space of wall that wasn't covered by either bookcases or paintings.

The dogs bounded ahead of the party straight through into the garden where they stood waiting expectantly. The conservatory stretched the whole width of the back of the house, the central corridor led straight into it and there were doors to the right and left leading from the sitting room and the kitchen. Through the windows I could see into the two rooms, the latter dominated by a dark green cast iron Aga cooker upon which was a steaming kettle.

"Shall I make the tea, mum?" Stella asked.

"Yes please darling," Amanda replied. "It's all ready, you'll find everything on the kitchen table." She gestured to me to sit down on one of the wicker chairs festooned with cushions. A sleek black cat was curled up on one, another pale grey cat lay stretched in the sunshine.

The conversation flowed easily. Unlike my mother who had asked nothing about either of us, Amanda and Gordon Marchant seemed genuinely interested in everything we were doing. They were eager to know how I liked my new home and how my lecture preparations were proceeding. It seemed that Stella had been keeping them well informed.

I was eager to turn the conversation to dowsing and waited for an opportunity to ask my hostess for a demonstration and, more importantly, for an explanation. It was Gordon who initiated the subject, however.

"Stella told us that you are keen to learn about dowsing, Jack." Gordon had risen to his feet, his teacup and saucer in hand. "I also understand that your interest is genuine and that your mind is open and uncritical. That being the case, I have encouraged Amanda to speak to you about this – something she rarely does – and if you are to have a go yourself at this ancient mystery, I suggest you both get on with it or, knowing my wife as well as I do, we might be very late getting our supper.

"If you'll excuse me," my host continued, "I have explorations of my own to pursue, so I shall leave you if you don't mind. I wish you well, you are in for a fascinating experience, I'm sure you will find it as worthwhile as it is interesting."

I sprang to my feet also but was waved back to the chair as Gordon turned to leave the conservatory. Amanda looked at me, one eyebrow raised questioningly.

"Will you educate me in the mysteries of your profession, Amanda?" I stammered. I glanced at Stella but she was not looking in my direction. I was on my own. "I know I'm asking a lot, and am humble in my request, and enormously excited at the prospect of your sharing knowledge with me, and very grateful also."

"I don't proselytize, you understand." Amanda started. "I do not intend to open myself to ridicule, so I rarely acquiesce to interviews. The world is full of skeptics, and, as far as I'm concerned, they're entitled to their views just as I am entitled to mine."

"I hope I don't qualify as a skeptic," I said in an urgent tone. "Stella and I have done some dowsing together before, many years ago, as I think she told you." Again I looked across at Stella – this time we exchanged smiles. "I have faith in the use of rods - so much so that

I took them with me to Africa and used them to the best of my ability to site a church. However, I know I am only an amateur and am frightened to be using forces that I do not fully comprehend. I want to know more, to try and understand why and how they work."

"Well, you are right to be wary Jack," Amanda answered, smiling at me. "I am only sharing my private beliefs with you, because you have asked me to in a frank and open way, and because Stella confirms that you have a genuine interest in understanding what I do. It is for my daughter that I will risk sharing these ideas with you. It shows how much I trust her judgment."

I felt humble and awkward at the same time.

"It's all about energies, Jack," Amanda was stirring her tea, being careful not to spill it. "Energy is indestructible. Oh, it can change, of course, and does so frequently, but it is continuous nevertheless and is everlasting.

"To understand dowsing, it is important that you are comfortable with the idea of the Universe being filled with inter-connecting forces, all swirling together without bumping into each other, like a flock of starlings on a mission. But, unlike the birds, these forces often converge, combine, split and reconnect in different guises. We hope for serendipity with these connections, but it is not always so.

"This force goes by many names, the most accepted of which is the Tao -pronounced Dow. Not so long ago, well probably about the time you were born, Jack, a Hollywood producer made a film called Star Wars, with "The Force" described quite eloquently. I remember going to see it with a group of friends from college.

"I couldn't decide whether I was pleased that the idea of universal energy was being so well illustrated or upset that such a mighty and awesome concept had been displayed in a modern-day fairy tale! I was impressed with the way the neutrality of the energy was indicated in the film, by showing the attractions of both its positive and negative aspects. Anyway, that's an aside, a discussion for another day, perhaps. Today you want to know about dowsing.

"So, we return to the concept of universal energy. Let's concentrate on how it flows through this planet and its atmosphere. Energy is not restricted by solid mass. It flows unhindered through air or granite, through water or metals. Our bodies live by it and our thoughts and ideas contribute to it.

"We are all made up of universal energy, but we also produce it. If all living things could be more circumspect in the type of energy they produce, the Earth would be a better planet; but there I go again, off on another old tangent. Sorry Jack."

"Please don't apologize, Amanda," I said earnestly. "I'm fascinated by your views on this subject and hope we may be able to discuss them together at a future date. It is a topic I have been studying for some time."

Stella had risen during this interchange and was handing round a plate of shortbread. Her mother considered the plate for a moment, and then waved it away.

"No thank you darling," Amanda fixed her daughter with a loving gaze. "I need my concentration if I am to explain these complexities efficiently."

She turned back towards me. I was busy munching one of the biscuits and balancing a cup and saucer on my knee, in a strange parallel to our visit to Willenbury.

"Now, suppose you are driving a car," Amanda resumed. "The radio is on, and Stella is chattering away to you about something or other. There is also the sound of the car engine as an ever-present background drone. You are not consciously listening to it, and yet, if the noise of the engine changes, however subtly, your hearing will select any dissonance out of all the other sounds and give it special attention. You then stop listening to your passenger and to the radio, now it is their turn to become the background noises, while you listen intently to the engine, trying to identify what it is that is going clunk. Your hearing has given the engine noise priority. This is not the most romantic analogy, but I hope you find it useful.

"If you think of the huge bombardment of information that the brain is taking in through all the body's senses, at any one time, it becomes apparent that priorities have to be selected to avoid over-load. These priorities can be changed.

"As we grow up, cultural indoctrination and education seep into our minds and set priorities for us. We become comfortable within our own society with people who share the same values. Non-selected information, which still lurks within the brain, sinks steadily deeper into the sub-conscious.

"I believe that we are all born with the ability to feel and sense energies that come to us, through us, and even from us. As we grow, these energies are filtered by the conscious brain, and those that are not prioritized are pushed into the subliminal areas of the mind. For some people, certain energies refuse to be relegated to the subconscious and demand attention. These people are heralded by the rest of humanity as either geniuses or lunatics. I think this is how the likes of Mozart, Blake and Michelangelo came into being.

"Coleridge and Byron used laudanum, the opium tincture popular at the time, to facilitate their access to subconscious energies. Pop groups nowadays use all sorts of hallucinogenic drugs for the same purpose."

"Like Huxley's Doors of Perception?" I enquired, remembering Rufus's story of Father David's experience, "and the group who named themselves after that book?"

"Indeed," answered Amanda. "Perhaps it's not just a coincidence, but 'The Doors' was one of my favorite bands when I was a teenager.

"Anyway, my belief is that communicating with the Earth energies is one of those abilities that lies dormant in the vast majority of people, but that can be called up from the sub-conscious relatively easily by those who bother to try.

"Before I go any further, I must tell you that this package comes with a health and safety warning." Amanda smiled at my raised eyebrows. "Those who delve through the realms of the subconscious to the energy flow itself, need to do so with great care. If you are going to open doors – to use your friend Huxley's analogy – that lead to the 'rushing flux' of the essence of existence, you need strength to filter the forces you encounter. You have to be able to select the positive and to withstand and exclude the negative."

I thought of the Tantric guide to liberating the soul and connecting with the forces of existence through physical intimacy that I had been studying and with which Stella and I had been experimenting. Here again, a warning was given about selecting the positive energies and being careful to close the portals to negative influences through establishing an aura of psychic protection around the merging astral and physical bodies.

The Yogini Tantra had provided me with a recipe to ensure this sort of protection. It allowed us to abandon ourselves without fear of negative intrusion through the aspects of existence that were opened by our powerful love-making.

Ever since I found that Tantra, Stella and I always commenced making love by following its instructions: "with the first two fingers touch the partner's head, forehead, eyes, throat, earlobes, breasts, upper arms, heart, naval, thighs, feet, and sexual organ. Charge these places with the vital energy of transformation." Even though I wasn't sure how to follow that last instruction, the ritual seemed to imbue us both with an inner calm, at odds with the outer excitement that always resulted from the exercise. These sexual portals needed guarding as much as any other but I chose not to share such ideas with Amanda who was sitting, head tilted on one side indicating curiosity, looking at me steadily.

I pulled my thoughts out of the bedroom and back to the Avebury conservatory. "'Stand porter at the door of thought,'" I quoted. "It was Mary Baker Eddy who said that." I was remembering my time in Boston and the phrase that stayed with me most insistently from that visit. I thought also of Amrita and her underground lake, and told Amanda of the analogy and how essential it was that the magic water was filtered of impurities by the careful maintenance of a correct heart. I realized once again how greatly I missed my friends. They would so have enjoyed this experience, and Amanda and Stella would have enjoyed meeting them also. Perhaps one day . . .

"Exactly so, Jack," Amanda interrupted my thoughts. "Although here we have to be extra careful as we are standing porter, as you say, to the door of sub-conscious thought. The Hindu Brahman and the Buddhist Bodhisattva have this down to a fine art through their strength of meditation. The Adolf Hitlers and Robert Mugabes of this world allowed the evil forces to invade, and kept going back for more.

"We mere lay people are not diving so deeply, but we must still be careful. Always, before I dowse, I ask for positive powers to protect me against the negative, and only when I am confident that the protection is in place do I proceed. A friend of mine, a really experienced dowser, was in a hurry once, having arrived late for a job, and omitted his protection plea. He never finished that job, he became too ill to stand within half an hour. We got him back to health eventually, don't worry, but it wasn't easy – but anyway that's another story."

Stella was doing a round with the tea-pot, but I shook my head to her. I was leaning forward, trying to catch Amanda's words and the meaning that lay behind them. I decided I would never avoid the Yogini Tantra before making love, even if physical desires suggested urgency. I didn't relish a fate such as the one that had beset Amanda's dowsing friend.

"It's easy to envisage the brain as a computer," Amanda continued, unaware of the directions of my thinking her words had provoked. "But you must also try and see it as a radio transmitter and receiver. One part of the brain supplies the computer element with information for analysis. It also sends the brain's waves of messages and energies outwards. Obviously discipline and understanding are necessary if we are to open up our radio receiver to unknown forces – things go awry when people take drugs that blast open doors before the necessary defense filters are in place.

"Did you ever play Planchette or mess about with a Ouija board in your youth, Jack?" Amanda asked, holding her teacup out to Stella who filled it from what seemed an inexhaustible pot. "Did you know that the word Ouija was made up from the words for 'yes' in French and German? But I digress again," she added with a smile.

I confessed to knowing nothing of either pastime.

"Never mind," my hostess replied, stirring her tea thoughtfully. "It's just a demonstration of one of the many diverse forces that flow around, about and through us. People are different as are the energies they select and the results they wish to achieve. The dowser won't select the same energies as the spiritualist, for example, or from the faith-healer or the clairvoyant. When you have done your preparations and are ready to dowse, the first thing you do is to select the particular energy with which you wish to connect. The one you wish to give priority, if you will.

"In other words, we are seeking to tie into the energies of the Earth upon which we live and which provides us with succor: our Mother Earth. But we cannot cope with all Her energy forces at once, we must be circumspect and as precise as possible."

I thought of my cherished parish of Cachonga and the spiritual forces my parishioners could feel coming from the ground they tilled. I wondered what Amanda would have made of their revered deities of the soil, river, forest, bush, clouds and sky, and of the way I had incorporated those beliefs into my own church. I remembered the niches I had built into the walls of St. Thomas' to provide homes for the natural spirits, dressed anew in Christian forms, and how Loveness had decorated each one, every morning, with fresh palm fronds and any scraps of color she could find amongst the inhospitable plants of the bush. Once again I could feel the ever-present dust in my nostrils and felt my eyes involuntarily squint against the hard sunlight.

As always, when I thought of Cachonga my mind constricted with pain and I found myself swallowing to stop the rising bile that blocked my throat.

"Are you alright Jack?" It was Stella's voice that brought me back to the soft light of England and the cool breeze that stirred the grass, the oh-so-green grass of the fields surrounding the colorful garden.

"Yes, of course" I said giving myself a quick mental shake. "Sorry about that." I looked at the concerned faces of mother and daughter and felt I owed them an explanation. "I was just thinking of the Earth spirits my parishioners in Africa used to placate in various ways as they turned the soil. It was rude of me, I'm sorry."

"Not at all, Jack," Amanda answered with a gentleness that was almost super-human. "You're with family here, and I am sharing my innermost thoughts with you, you should have the comfort and security, here, to do the same."

"Maybe another time, Amanda," I answered cautiously. "I would very much like to talk to you about those beliefs. There must be lots of parallels with what you are talking about. But as you say, 'that's for another time' and I really do want to learn about dowsing." For all the love I had for Stella and the respect I had for her mother, I knew I wasn't yet ready to talk about the disintegration of Cachonga in any detail.

Amanda set down her cup and saucer on the patio step and stood up. She picked up her rods from the glass-topped wrought iron table and looked at them with affection. "Now, Jack, as I just intimated, I am about to share something very personal with you. Please suspend any indoctrinated bourgeois preconceptions and judgments and try to take in what you observe without engaging your critical faculties."

I tried hard not to look either indoctrinated or bourgeois, although was unsure how to achieve the best result, but I must have done a reasonable job because Amanda continued with the lesson.

79. A RETURN TO THE RODS

"I am going to indulge in some verbalized thinking for your benefit," my hostess started, handling the rods carefully and with respect. "When I go out on a job, I do not say these things out loud, it is not necessary, and would only bring derision on my profession. But I think them succinctly, and direct them to the energies with which I wish to communicate. I use the rods as both conductors through which these communications take place and interpreters of the answers to my questions. By amplifying energy waves that my body is feeling at a level below which my conscious mind can travel, the rods enable me to converse with these forces.

"What would you like me to dowse for, Jack?"

The question took me by surprise. "What do you mean?" I stammered.

"Just what I said," Amanda replied with a smile. "Are we looking for water, seismic powers, oil, or how about gold? Although I have to warn you that if you choose either of the last two, we are in for a very dull afternoon!"

"Oh, I see," I said, still looking confused. "But don't you need different rods for different elements?"

Amanda gave an unexpected hoot of laughter.

"Oh dear, you haven't been listening very well, have you. But never mind, it's a common illusion, and some dowsers actually promote the myth by having several sets of rods marked with a variety of colors for different requirements. All rods are exactly the same of course, the colors are purely decorative, but it adds to the mystique."

"Let's make it water, then," I said in a rush to divert her attention from my evident stupidity.

"Water it is then," she responded with a smile.

"I'm going to leave you to it," Stella said as she stood up and started collecting the tea things onto a polished wooden tray. "I'm off to dowse the refrigerator for some supper. I'll see you later. Look after him, mother, he's very special." And so saying, she picked up the loaded tray and left the conservatory.

Amanda looked at me with a wide smile, as my face colored. I shrugged my shoulders, not knowing what to say.

"Right then," Amanda took a deep breath. "First we have to establish a code – I always ask the rods to turn towards each other for a positive answer and to stay still, pointing down, while in neutral mode. There is no hard and fast rule about this, other dowsers have different codes. The important thing is that specific instructions are in place."

Amanda stood very still, closed her eyes, and took a deep breath. Then she spoke in an ordinary, every-day voice to no-one in particular.

"Please indicate, by rotating inwards, that we have protection to dowse for water today, and that no evil forces will be allowed to usurp the channels we may open."

The rods twitched inwards in her hands in one swift motion and then resumed their position pointing down. I had seen no movement in Amanda's fingers, thumbs or wrists.

"Thank you," said Amanda, opening her eyes.

"I've been doing this for a long time, Jack," she continued, "so don't be surprised that I can get a response so quickly. It all comes with practice. It takes time to allow your feelings to run freely in this unknown jungle of energies. Time to learn what questions to ask and how the answers manifest themselves.

"Now, we are looking for water which flows underground. I must ask my sub-conscious to concentrate on sending a signal on the 'water frequency' into the ground then, when it encounters a subterranean stream, the water will respond because it is resonating at the same frequency. That's how communication is established, augmented by the rods. I pull all my thoughts together and turn them into an image of water flowing through a tunnel. The rods will conduct this thought-energy into the Earth.

"If I have been commissioned by a farmer to find the correct point to dig for a well, for example, I will have done my homework before arriving on site. That means I will have studied the geological maps of the area in detail, and these will give me ideas of where to look. That, of course, is a science in itself, and we won't go into that just now.

"So, having selected a particular area of the farm, where the maps indicate that water is most likely to be found, I begin to walk in an organized manner until something happens. I'm cheating here, in my garden, because of course I've done this many times, and always get the same information. But let's pretend it's a new site and see what happens."

I was walking carefully alongside Amanda, watching the rods and her hands as if bewitched.

"When the water energy is transmitted from its underground course to the surface," Amanda continued, "the frequency alters as it meets the new medium of air. This causes a reflected wave of energy that spreads out along the Earth's surface like ripples in a still pond when a stone is thrown in – only in this instance it is the energy resonating outwards, in response to my own energy where I am standing – that causes the ripple effect. You start off by finding the echoes of the true source that are weaker than the real one and then pursuing the energy to its source. Just watch."

As we proceeded slowly across the lawn, the rods in Amanda's hands twitched inwards and quivered slightly.

"There, you see," Amanda stopped our progress. "That's our first suggestion that there is water running underground somewhere relatively close by. Now I have to decide in which direction to walk. If I was out on a job, I would stake this point, so that I can find it easily again if the direction I choose yields nothing.

"Using this stake as a centre point, I walk several meters away, and if nothing happens, I return to the stake and walk out in another direction, going away from the stake in lines like the spokes of a wheel. If you are a well-practiced dowser you can take a short cut by asking the rods to show you which way to go to find the true course instead of the echo. Let's try. Once again I will verbalize my thoughts for your benefit."

A small frown of concentration joined the other wrinkles across Amanda's forehead.

"Is this the true course of underground water?" she asked nobody in particular.

The rods swung back to facing downwards and twitched slightly away from each other.

"Thank you. Please show me the direction I should take to find the true course." Her tone was polite and matter-of-fact. She might have been asking the way from a friendly policeman.

The rods twitched again both moving towards Amanda's right. They settled pointing diagonally in a two o'clock direction.

"Thank you," Amanda repeated.

"All right Jack. You see the way we should proceed? Come with me and see for yourself."

Turning our steps in the direction indicated by the rods, the two of us walked slowly forward until the rods gave another inward twitch, considerably stronger than the first one.

"Well, we're getting closer, or maybe that's the valid spot," said Amanda. "Let's go a bit further and find what comes next. Again, if I was doing a job, I would mark that spot also, and the first peg would become irrelevant, as the response here was stronger."

We walked on again until the rods moved together with terrific speed.

"Well, that's the strongest yet," I suggested.

"Yes indeed," Amanda answered. "But we'd better make sure. Remember this spot – well if you don't the rods will – and we'll keep going."

The stately walk continued, and once again the rods twitched together, but not as insistently as before.

"Now you see, the signal is getting weaker again, so that last one must be the real thing, and these others merely echoes. Let's go back."

We retraced our steps until once again the rods moved violently towards each other.

Amanda shifted them in her hands, until they were once again facing down.

"Is this the true water course we are seeking?" she asked the space in front of her. Immediately one of the rods jerked inwards, and then came back to its original position without a quiver.

"Thank you," said Amanda. "Now please could you show me the direction of the flow?" The rods spun to the right. Amanda turned to the right and the rods came back to their central position.

"Thank you," she said again. "Now please tell me how deep below the surface is this water course. Is it ten feet down?" the rods stayed motionless. "twenty feet, thirty feet," she intoned slowly, and continued with no response until she got to "seventy feet" at which point the rods leapt into action, turning so that they almost poked her in the stomach.

"Too much," she explained, and she started counting down: "sixty-nine, sixty-eight, sixty-seven," and here the rods stopped their quivering and stayed quite still, pointing inwards.

"So, we have a water course running in this direction," she nodded her head towards a bank of azaleas, "which is sixty-seven feet below the surface. Let's see what else we can find out."

Amanda's conversation with the rods continued for several minutes and by the time she had finished she claimed they had told her how many liters per minute it could produce should a borehole be drilled at that point, the salinity of the water and even its pH measurement.

"Well, that really is quite remarkable, Amanda," I was trying hard to follow the initial instructions of suspending my critical faculties. "I'm absolutely stunned. I had no idea you could extract details like that."

"Now it's your turn, Jack," said Amanda turning to her pupil with a smile.

The rest of the afternoon saw the two of us solemnly marching backwards and forwards across the lawn and then standing together, heads bowed, as the rods jerked about in my hands.

After supper that evening, when Stella and I had mounted the steps to our attic room, I told Stella the details of my induction into the art of dowsing for water and what an amazing experience it had been.

Stella did not look surprised and was obviously delighted by how her mother and I had established such a good rapport. We curled into each other in the big oak bed and chatted idly about the wonders of the Universe until we fell asleep.

80. THE MYSTERIOUS AND THE URBANE

Sunday morning was spent exploring the Avebury stones and climbing to the top of Silbury Hill.

My first stop was at a particular megalith I had seen from our attic window. It had fascinated me from a distance, and up close it was even more impressive.

"It's called 'The Devil's Chair,' Stella told me, noting with delight my enthusiasm and interest. "They say if you run around it a hundred times in an anti-clockwise direction, you get to hear the devil's voice."

"I think I'll give that a miss," I answered with a smile. "It sounds far too energetic, and I'm not sure that I want to know what the devil has to say. It is an awesome stone, though, isn't it?"

"It's one of the largest anywhere in Britain," Stella said. "It marks the entrance to these sacred circles."

"What sort of 'sacred' are we talking about here, Stella," I asked.

"No-one knows for sure," she answered. "It pre-dates all the formal religions we know about. The experts say that this was an important site of great rituals for over a thousand years, but by as long ago as 900 B.C. it had fallen out of favor. Since then various fanatics of more modern religious beliefs have tried to destroy the magic of these circles. They dug away part of the great bank and used the stones to build houses and barns inside the circle. Mother and father's cottage is one of those houses; it dates back to the seventeenth century but of course the stones with which it is built date back centuries before that – you can see why they were both so excited when it came on the market."

Stella cut short our tour of Avebury's stone circles and the avenues of menhirs that led to them. "We can do the rest another time, my love," she said gently, as my face obviously showed disappointment. "We still have Silbury Hill to explore before lunch. This is an experience I am looking forward to sharing with you."

I smiled and let Stella lead me by the hand to the Aston. It was only a short drive to the small car park at the base of this extraordinary mound.

"So tell me about this," I asked as we started on our steep climb.

"This," Stella began with a definite note of pride in her voice, "is the largest prehistoric man-made mound in all of Europe. One of the guidebooks says it is made up from thirty-five million baskets of earth, which would have taken eighteen million hours of work, and must have taken at least a hundred and fifty years.

"There are various ideas as to why this Neolithic hill was created. The one I prefer is that it marks a convergence of ley lines – and you know what I feel about ley lines," she added with a smile. "Let's see if you can open your sub-conscious and let the powers of this multi-lined cross-roads run through your body and mind, as well as running through each other."

The view at the top was spectacular and we sat in silence, short-breathed from the climb, and let our eyes wander over the rich English countryside.

At Stella's suggestion we sat cross-legged and back to back, with spines aligned against each other, our shoulders and heads lightly touching. The backs of our hands rested on our knees, the fingers curled open, thumbs and middle fingers pressed lightly together to allow the forces to circulate.

"Open yourself to the energies of the Earth, Jack," Stella spoke in a soft voice. "Close your eyes and feel the forces flow through you with each breath, pull them up through your spine and let them spread throughout your body."

I was familiar with 'The Royal Road' of Hindu philosophy. The path that linked the seven Chakras started with Kundalini at the base of the spine. I remembered how, early in our intimate physical explorations, Stella had used some of her special oils to massage the scar tissue on my buttocks, her fingers sliding into personal places, how my feelings had slowly moved from distaste and embarrassment to the deeply erotic.

Stella had been working to unlock 'The Root Chakra' and allow the powerful creative energy of Kundalini to flow. She attributed my sexless past to the locking of this vital power source by the trauma and scarring of the dreadful assault. "Your sexual muscles have atrophied, my love," she had said as her fingers worked their magic. "They have been put into an enforced slumber, and I will awaken them, like sleeping beauty, with a kiss." And indeed she had.

Now, as I inhaled slowly, I could feel a surge of energy spiraling upwards from my coccyx and the first

Chakra to the second – the Sacral Chakra in the pelvis from where it tingled down my thighs. As I exhaled, the energy continued to rise and to spread outwards; now it had reached the Solar Chakra at my naval. It was progressing to the heart, home of Chakra number four, from where it seeped across my chest and down my arms. With the next breath, the Throat Chakra sparkled with activity as the energy moved to Chakra number six: The Third-Eye, and my mind seemed to expand with intangible knowledge. Finally, it reached the Crown Chakra, that opening in the top of the skull from where it spun into the atmosphere, linking my awareness with the essence of life. My whole being was filled with an intense feeling, as if every nerve-ending had been awakened and made to dance in unison. And in the midst of the intensity, there was a mighty calm.

With each breath, the flow of energy purred through my body from the Earth beneath me into the blue sky above, and still further. I had become a link in a chain of vitality, a small part of an amazing whole. I was floating, my eyes were closed and my body seemed to scatter into thousands of tiny pieces merging and cavorting with particles of other energies, of existence itself. I was at peace amongst the activity and filled with a joy that made me feel like shouting – maybe I was shouting?

Silbury Hill

Neither of us knew how long we sat there, atop the mighty and extraordinary mound of Silbury Hill. The spell – for that is indeed what it felt like – was broken by the sound of two children calling to each other as they raced ahead of their parents, up the winding path. They rounded the corner and almost bumped into us as we sat, still facing in opposite directions. The children, two girls of about eight and ten with cheeks flushed from their climb and fair hair blowing in the breeze, stopped short, looked at each other and began to giggle.

I felt myself smiling, and then felt laughter following the energy path through my body, indeed, it was part of that same energy; it came bubbling up through my being, exiting through my mouth. It was a splendid laugh, and Stella joined in. We turned towards each other, uncoiling our legs and standing slowly as our mirth mingled. We stood and hugged, chuckling with delight, as the girls stared at us open-mouthed.

"Let the wise person forcibly and firmly draw up the Goddess Kundalini, for She is the giver of miraculous powers," I quoted from the writings of Shiva Samhito. "What an amazing experience. How did things go with you, Stella?"

"They say that Silbury Hill is the womb of the Earth mother," Stella answered slowly. "I could feel her powers flowing through me and out into the Universe. I had this wonderful feeling of connectedness, of being at one with all creation. It was quite awesome."

"And the same for me," I said with glee. I felt like a child discovering a new and special toy. "It was a mystical experience, and I am so excited with the knowledge that I can feel in such a way; that I am no longer closed to the numinous, that I have found my way home."

The two of us walked down the hill slowly, our arms around each other's waists.

With the end of the summer came the end of my sabbatical. I had worked hard on my lecture series and felt ready for the new task. I had acquiesced to Illingsworth's request that I wear a dog-collar while at the missionary college. "I know I can't persuade you to include Christian dogma in your teachings Jack, but at least do me the favor of looking the part." It seemed a small concession to make, and I had grown fond of Illingsworth. I viewed the collar simply as part of a uniform that allowed me to fit in with the other members of staff at the college. It also had the advantage of saving me from wearing a tie. I became quite used to it once again.

The college was full of worthy souls – teachers and students alike - all intent upon bringing enlightenment to the dark corners of the globe. I had little in common with the other members of the college's faculty all of whom started and finished each day with prayers in the staff-room. My habit of leaving the room as soon as these services started was quickly noticed, and any close friendships which might have matured, were snubbed by suspicions of my lack of religious commitment.

However, I enjoyed my rôle as a professor. I knew my subject well; my experience 'in the field' gave me confidence and credibility; and I liked the students. They were all dedicated and eager to learn just what would and wouldn't work in whichever part of the world to which they were sent. I felt that I was achieving and contributing something valuable, much more than I had been able to do on the one day lectures I had given across America and Europe.

My mother's operation had been a success, and Robert had engaged a splendid woman to look after her and father while she convalesced. The 'carer' came from South Africa and had a voice that was used to being obeyed, but she was warm and kind underneath the bossiness. Stella and I visited them at Christmas time, taking presents for everyone. Mother was delighted to see me back in the clerical collar and thanked me over and over again for my prayers, which made me feel fraudulent in the extreme. However, I didn't contradict her, for her mistake obviously had beneficial results.

At home, in London, Stella had organized a large Christmas tree to be erected in the drawing room next to one of the tall windows looking onto the square. Its twinkling lights could be seen from the street and gave me a warm feeling as I made my way home from college in the December darkness. As always, the house was full of people coming and going, enjoying the endless jostle of Stella's hospitality.

Amanda and Gordon came to stay for Christmas and I was pleased for the opportunity to get to know them better. We had long discussions about the mysteries of the Universe finding so many similarities within the different structures of our beliefs.

Ashok and Peter, Stella's business partners, joined the family for Christmas lunch along with various other friends who had no family of their own - 'Stella's waifs and strays' Amanda called them. There was a huge pile of presents under the tree to be distributed, plenty of champagne and much laughter.

Amanda gave me a framed card – "to help you with your research and to stop you from getting too serious" she said with a wink. It was entitled 'Religious Truths' and read as follows:

> *Taoism: Shit happens.*
> *Buddhism: If shit happens, it isn't really shit.*
> *Hinduism: This shit has happened before.*
> *Islam: If shit happens, it is the will of Allah.*
> *Catholicism: Shit happens because you deserve it.*
> *Protestantism: Let shit happen to somebody else.*
> *Judaism: Why does shit always happen to us?*

It made me laugh and I hung it in the study to remind me of the power of humor and the vagaries of philosophies.

The part of Christmas I enjoyed the most was when everyone had gone to bed and I had Stella to myself in our bedroom at the top of the house. It seemed I was seeing less and less of her these days and our evening and morning romps were curtailed by fatigue or the need to 'get to work' in a hurry.

Stella, Ashok and Peter were busy working on ideas for a new company. Erostique Ltd. was to be launched in the Spring with products such as Sensual Soaps and Bathing Bliss, an oil for men called Homus Erectus, and a jell for the ladies entitled Semper Paratus. Much time was spent designing the packaging and making sure the recipes were kept secret from any opposition.

I visited the little factory in Wembley one day to see how everything worked. I was fascinated by the bottles of different oils and the jars of gruesome-looking powders. There were oils of distilled ylang-ylang, peppermint, evening primrose, juniper, rosemary, geranium, lavender and sandalwood plus preparations from rose otto and tagette. The powders were of various types of chilli, ginger, peppercorns - white, red and black - and something suspicious with the name of 'Spanish Fly.'

A clutter of pestles and mortars, glass tubes, mixing bowls, saucepans, filters, Bunsen-burners and different sized spoons of wood and porcelain littered the shelves and worktables. A variety of aromas hung in the air in strata, or lurked in corners and cupboards. It was an astonishing place and I felt completely lost. Stella, Ashok and Peter moved about the place with confidence pointing out this and that, but my bemusement only increased.

The products of Erostique Ltd. were distributed to suitable shops in early May amidst a flurry of publicity.

Stella was busier than ever, and I was also occupied with marking papers as the academic year drew to a close. There seemed to be even more people in the house these days, and I spent an increasing amount of time in my study. Stella had given me a wonderful music machine that produced startling sounds from its tiny speakers and I worked my way through symphonies and concertos, cocooned in my personal space as I worked, read or just stared out of the window trying to recreate the mystical experience of Silbury Hill.

81. THE CASTLE

In June, when the exam papers had all been marked and the students dispatched on the next section of their adventure in life, I was once again summoned to Illingsworth's office. I assumed I would be given the schedule for the next American tour, and was looking forward to visiting Amrita and Percival once again. Stella was off to Royal Ascot in yet another extravagant outfit, I was glad of the excuse to abscond.

John Illingsworth looked worried, I thought, as we shook hands over the venerable desk. We sat down and a strained silence persisted while I waited for my boss to start the conversation.

"I'm in trouble, Jack," Illingsworth began at last. "I have come under a lot of pressure, and I'm sorry to say that it is all about you. I thank you for wearing your clerical collar to college, it has made my job a little easier, but unfortunately not easy enough.

"It seems that some of your peers at the college," Illingsworth looked at me over the top of his glasses, "have been voicing their opinions as to your lack of commitment to the Christian faith. Several have signed a letter, written to Bishop Paul, to whom I have to answer, suggesting most strongly that you are not imbuing your lectures or your students with Christian beliefs. They point out that this is a college for missionaries and that the faith the students are indentured to spread is not reflected in any of your classes.

"Now I know, Jack," Illingsworth continued with a big sigh. "I know that what you are teaching those students is worth more than they will learn in any other course or any other lecture at that college. Yours is a course on survival. It provides more relevant information than all the other courses put together. You are offering them a recipe for success. However, I can no longer defend you regarding the total absence of Christianity in your talks. I am outnumbered and outranked. I have done my best with Bishop Paul, and have argued enough that he now wants to meet you, to form his own opinion. You have a meeting with him scheduled for next week, on Wednesday, in the Cathedral, no less, just before Evensong."

We sat in silence for a few moments. I was digesting what I had been told.

"What are my options, Father?" I asked quietly.

"Well, as I see it," Illingsworth replied after a moment's hesitation, "you can either change your approach in order to bring Christ into your lectures, or you can say goodbye to your post at the college, any international lecture tours, and, indeed to your salary. I'm really sorry Jack, you know how much I admire you and how much I feel you are bringing to the education of young idealists. I had hoped that your faith in God would return, but it seems that we are not being given enough time for that to happen. You're going to have to make up your mind as to where your future lies."

"Are there no other options?" I asked.

"Well, there is one other, but you are very young for this particular option. 'The Castle' houses men many years your senior; however it remains an option."

I raised my eyebrows questioningly. I had heard of The Castle several times since being ordained, but I couldn't remember what exactly I had been told.

"The Castle, Jack, is an institution run by the church very much out of the public eye." Illingsworth coughed nervously and dabbed his mouth with a large white handkerchief. "It is a wonderful house, so I am told, to where members of the clergy, who have become disenchanted with their calling, have retired. If you like I will arrange for you to have a visit there, it would be best to see it before you meet with the bishop."

The Castle

"Yes, I'd appreciate that," I answered quickly. "I can hardly be expected to make important decisions if I am not acquainted with the alternatives. When do you think I would be able to go?"

"I will have to make a few telephone calls. I'll give you a ring as soon as I have something organized, but I will make sure it happens before next Wednesday evening."

As it happened, Illingsworth couldn't arrange my visit to the Castle until Wednesday morning. I left the house early, leaving Stella still curled up among the pillows. I took the tube from South Kensington to Euston, and found a train to Leicester. It was a journey of an hour and a half and I enjoyed a leisurely breakfast while watching the countryside slide past.

"Hello, sir, I'm Broadhurst," a tall, middle-aged man in a smart uniform greeted me at Leicester station. "I do the running around for the gentlemen in The Castle. You know, gardening, waiting at table, grocery shopping, fixing things, and so on. Including meeting guests at the railway station," he added with a smile. He led me to the car park as he spoke, stopping next to an old, but highly polished, dark blue Rover.

Broadhurst drove the machine with care and obvious pride. As we left the city and drove into rolling countryside he chatted away about how much he enjoyed his job. "It's a real privilege to work for a collection of gentlemen as kind and appreciative as those in The Castle," he said. He told me of life in the nearby village, where he lived with his wife, who was the housekeeper. "The only female to enter The Castle is my Edna," he said proudly. "She's in charge of all the laundry and the pantries. She knows when we need to order different things and she supervises the provisioning of the larders and the cellars. There are some very grand dinners at The Castle, Sir. Very grand indeed."

We had turned onto a single-track lane that dived into a valley only to climb steeply up the other side. We were travelling between fields of lush grassland with cattle and sheep dotted hither and yon. Once, we met a car coming in the opposite direction, and Broadhurst had to reverse until he found a gateway into which to tuck the Rover as the approaching car passed by with two wheels on the grass verge and a cheery wave from the driver.

At the top of another steep hill a clump of woodland opened up for a moment and a gravel drive disappeared into the trees. Broadhurst turned the car through a pair of large gates set back from the road.

"Here we are sir," Broadhurst announced as we followed the curving drive and emerged from the trees onto a broad forecourt in front of an enormous house of amber colored stone. It was four stories high - counting the basement windows whose upper halves could be seen behind the flowerbeds on either side of the stone stairway that led to the entrance – and had a turret at each corner linked by castellated stonework. A pillared porch held sway over the pair of grand front doors. The car drove up to the steps and crunched to a halt.

I got out and looked up at the building with a sense of awe. There was a special aura about the house. I felt it at once, even though I couldn't identify it exactly, it was deep and peaceful, warm and welcoming.

Broadhurst led the way up the steps, but the doors opened before we arrived and a good-looking man in his early fifties came out with his right arm stretched out in greeting.

"You must be Jack Bolden," he said as we shook hands. "I've heard a lot about you, not only from John Illingsworth, but from your friend Rufus McKinney. I'm father Henry. I was Rufus's mentor in Brixton."

I was delighted. "Oh, how splendid," I said quickly. "This is a real treat. I've also heard a lot about you, Father, and am delighted to be able to put a face to the stories I've heard."

"I know Rufus let you into our little secret," Father Henry led the way into a large two-story hall with a black and white slab floor and a gallery running around the landing of the first floor. Broadhurst had returned to the Rover with a polite salute. "And I believe you gave him some very good advice," Father Henry continued. "I also know that Rufus's trust in your discretion was well placed. It's good to meet you, Jack.

"My job, today, is to show you around The Castle." Father Henry made a sweeping gesture with his arm. "I am not to discuss the reasons for us being here, that is for someone else to do, this evening, I believe. I am merely a tour guide. So, if you're ready, we might as well get started straight away, because I know you have an important date back in London this evening, and lunch is served in just over an hour. We will begin with the most important room of all - the library." So saying, Father Henry turned to one of the six grand doors that led off the hall. He turned the shining handle, and the heavy door opened without a sound.

"When you enter here," my guide spoke softly as he led the way into a tall room lined with soaring bookshelves of polished wood, "you leave all pain and guilt outside, along with any pretensions of faith.

"Belief is to be rebuilt – or not . . . it is unimportant. Is God in here – maybe, or maybe not, but mankind is in here without savagery – and there is something Divine about that. We live with the great thoughts of great humans who have discovered their own truths – or transferred the truths of others into their own."

I looked at rows and rows of heavy leather tomes with amazement. The room seemed to be divided into five sections, denoted by the three tall windows that looked out across the forecourt to the parkland beyond. In each section, on both sides of the room, were beautiful spiral staircases on wheels, six of them in all. They allowed access to books on the upper shelves that rose some eighteen feet from the floor. Elegant trestle tables of dark brown, highly-buffed wood, stretched along the centre of the room with chairs waiting randomly for occupants. There was an intoxicating aroma of leather, parchment and furniture polish.

Father Henry let me wander along the room's length. He knew better than to disturb the magic of the initiate to this hallowed space – at least that is how he thought of this room. "I remember so clearly my first view of this collection of man's knowledge," he said, ushering me inside, "and my excitement at being so close to so much wisdom."

I walked slowly, trying to take in all the possibilities this room had to offer. I looked at the immaculately constructed library stairs and, unbidden Amrita's borehole analogy sprang into my mind. Here it was, in reverse, I decided. Inside this room the thirst for knowledge went up instead of down. The stairs offered anyone who was allowed to climb them access to the collective wisdom of mankind. And for once, man 'kind' seemed to be an appropriate noun.

Here, nobody could get between the reader and the distillation of man's cultural and philosophical development. The wisdom of the world was presented without dogma or ritual. As I paused alongside a shelf I glanced at a heavy tome with gold letters embossed into the leather: 'Corpus Hermeticum' it read. Where else could a man find such an edition? My hands itched to pull it out, lay it upon one of the central tables with the reverence it deserved, and to have time to absorb the contents without pressure.

I also noticed a volume of the Upanishads that looked as old as the wisdom it contained. The Rig Veda and several editions of the Koran I spotted along with the I Ching and editions of the Bible in Greek, Latin and a variety of English versions. The shelves were clogged with volumes of the philosophical discoveries of the ages. I never wanted to leave.

I continued ambling amongst the shelves. Once or twice I reached for a volume, looked at Father Henry, and having received a nod of approval, removed it carefully from its place and opened the sacred pages. It was if I wanted to check that the books were real. And they were. I felt as if I had entered the inner sanctum of existence. I was at home, if the 'home' accepted me.

From the library, we went to the dining room, because luncheon was about to be served. This room, as tall as the library, had stained glass windows whose colors fell across the refectory tables in a dapple of blues, gold and reds. The first impression was of ecclesiastical motifs, but when I looked carefully, I noticed that there were no images of the crucifix, martyred saints or pietas; in fact all aspects of pain were absent. Instead there were rising suns and moons, growing crops, birds flying, trees bearing fruit. Everything was positive and productive.

Men were drifting in from various doors leading into this impressive space. They chatted to each other, as they took their seats, with a relaxation I didn't think I had ever experienced before. I took the place indicated by Father Henry and looked around in astonishment.

There were forty or so men eating lunch at The Castle that day, all of them residents apart with myself as the one exception. Most of them, I thought, were in their seventies, a few were significantly older and a few were vibrant men in their sixties. Father Henry was one of the youngest, and still some twenty years older than me.

Lunch was served from large platters handed round by several waiters over whom Broadhurst seemed to have charge. It was an uncomplicated meal of a rich beef stew, potatoes mashed with parsnips, and some green beans. There were various cheeses and fruit to follow. Talk was of the value of home-grown horseradish and mustard mixed with someone's latest interpretation of astral travel and the questionable benefit of mixing mysticism with clairvoyance.

The absence of traditional faith within my soul seemed to be echoed by everything I saw, heard and felt within this building. Outside this house, everywhere I looked – especially within the college where I had been teaching and the church services I now spurned – I saw the connection between religion and control, religion and power, religion and manipulation. Where was the numinous amongst all that ritual and mumbo-jumbo as Illingsworth would call it? Here, in this dining room, things were reversed and as much a home for me as there could ever be.

After lunch, the tour resumed with Father Henry leading me through various sitting rooms and studies, all with highly polished oak floors, the occasional Persian rug of awesome proportions, sumptuous arm chairs, desks, card tables and side-boards groaning with decanters and glasses. Large paintings and tapestries covered the walls wherever bookcases were absent.

The top floor contained the bedrooms and bathrooms - nothing like as many of the latter as there were the former. The bedrooms were stark and reminded me of St. Augustine's. The narrow wooden-framed beds were far removed from Stella's super-kingsize acreage of mattress. The bare floors and tiny wardrobes and chests seemed a relief from the thick carpets and closets of clothes and shoes that had been foisted on me in Chelsea. The bathrooms were delightfully simple and free of any sort of cosmetic or lotion.

All of a sudden it was time for me to leave and catch my train back to London. Father Henry said goodbye with warmth, adding "I'm sure we'll be seeing you again," as he waved from the top of the steps, outside the heavy pair of front doors.

Broadhurst was waiting at the car, one eye on his watch. "I think we'll make it, sir," he said as they drove down the drive, "but we've cut it a little close."

I caught the train back to London, and had time to reflect upon all I had seen and felt in that extraordinary building.

82. CHOICES

The meeting between Bishop Paul and myself - the errant priest - was scheduled to take place in the sacristy of the Cathedral where the Bishop was shortly to officiate at an evening Eucharist. Nowhere, in the realm of the Church of England, could have been more impressive, or more intimidating, to a reluctant missionary who had so blatantly kicked at the traces.

Fresh from my visit to The Castle, I wondered what I would have to say to so eminent a cleric as Bishop Paul. On the train journey back to London I formulated answers to the questions I expected to be asked. Never-the-less, when I approached St. Mary's, in Parliament Square, I did so with suitable trepidation. I entered the great doors of the cathedral and was excused the admission fee when I explained my purpose. One of the tourist guides led me to the sacristy and deposited me at the door.

"So this is the Jack Bolden who has been putting my flock in such disarray," the bishop said, as I was ushered in by the guide who was hovering to make sure my claim of meeting the bishop had not been an excuse not to pay. Bishop Paul's smiling face took the sting out of the statement and made me feel unexpectedly at ease. "You have made a good friend in John Illingsworth, Jack. He cannot speak highly enough of what you have to offer our missionary service, and he is not a man to be easily impressed. He is also a man whose opinion I value, and he's a friend. Therefore, I am glad to meet you," he concluded as we shook hands.

The bishop was already in his full regalia, ready for the Evensong Communion service he was about to perform. He looked over his half-moon glasses and stared steadily at me. "Now why is it that you refuse to pray with your fellows at the college and omit all references to religion from your lectures?"

I had prepared myself for this interview and had my answer ready. "As I understand it, your grace, I was hired to teach missionary students about farming and trading in the developing world. Two skills that are vital to any rural community that wants to be self-sufficient. The spiritual guidance of any such community is for someone other than me. It is not an area for my particular expertise."

"That's exactly where you have gone wrong, Jack," the bishop spoke firmly, but with kindness. "It is your calling, the one you took when you were ordained. I have done my research and spoken to father Justin. He tells me your work in Islington was a success and that the parish grew while you were ministering there. Spiritual guidance was the purpose of your ordination. Primitive agriculture and social anthropology have merely been sidelines – impressive ones, I admit, but sidelines nonetheless. Everyone knows what a marvelous success you made of Cachonga, and we all assume that it was not just for the agriculture that you went there."

I winced visibly, but the bishop continued fervently. "I know you have experienced great wickedness. We are all sent trials of one sort or another. It is not for us to question Almighty God. Our job is to do His work to the best of our ability and to learn from the evils with which we have to deal, and by that learning to turn awful deeds into something positive."

The bishop paused. He looked down at his hands and the great ring that obviously meant much to him. "That's what true faith is all about, Jack," he said slowly. He raised his eyes and looked straight at me once again. "The unquestioning belief and trust that God has everything in hand and that, in spite of how dreadful things may look to us mortals, Divine wisdom is always at work."

There was silence in the sacristy for several moments. I could not hold his gaze and dropped my eyes to the floor, trying to keep my emotions under control. I noticed how the bishop's polished black shoes peeped out incongruously from under his white and golden robes.

Bishop Paul then invited me to join him in the service that was about to commence. I declined the invitation as gently as I could. "No, thank you Father; it's a kind and wonderful suggestion, but it is inappropriate for me to participate in the sacrament anymore." Then, sensing the prelate's disappointment I continued: "But I can come back after Evensong, if you like."

I was eager not to cause offence. "I would like to know more about the options Father John set out for me. I visited The Castle this morning. It was an amazing experience."

We talked a little while longer and agreed that I should dine with the bishop that evening as had been the original plan. "I have a special guest joining us, Jack. One whose company I know you will enjoy. Come and find me after the service and we'll walk together to dinner."

I left the cathedral as members of the congregation were filing in quietly, choosing their seats amongst the pews and sinking to their knees. Out into the evening sunshine I felt the self-imposed restrictions slipping away from me. I found a telephone box and rang home to tell Stella what was going on. There was no reply, just the answering machine with Stella's sparkling voice, so I left a message explaining why I wouldn't be back for supper; I felt an unanticipated feeling of guilt as I did so.

In London there is always a pub 'just around the corner' and I was pleased to find that Parliament Square was no exception. Across the road from the 'phone booth was a narrow pub of black timbers and diamond-paned windows; its ancient walls squeezed between office blocks of steel and glass. The pint of draught bitter I ordered was quite wonderful, bringing relief to the tension of the last half hour. The second one tasted even better.

I thought back through my day with the many sensations I had experienced. I tried to imagine who the bishop's other guest might be and wondered again about how Rufus's Father Henry had been selected to show me around The Castle. I had liked Father Henry instantly - in fact I had liked everybody I'd met at that strange and wonderful house.

As arranged, I met the bishop as he left the vestry, his robes carefully stored and replaced by an immaculately tailored dark suit. We walked together along the embankment, across the river, to Lambeth Palace, with its astonishing fig tree.

"No-one knows how old it is," the bishop told me when he saw me staring at the girth of the trunk and the expanse of twisted branches. "It's part of the fabric of these wonderful buildings and produces remarkably good fruit if the English summer is ever hot enough."

A door man, looking as stooped and ancient as the fig tree, appeared out of the shadows and unlocked a heavy oak door for the bishop, muttering "Good evening, your grace," with a strong cockney accent. "Your other guest is already admitted," he added as he looked me up and down with undisguised suspicion.

"Thank you, Stevens," the bishop responded with a nod of the head. "Father David is staying the night here but Father Jack will be going home, so please wait to lock up after him. I don't think we should be too late."

"Doesn't matter to me, your grace," Stevens grunted in reply. "I'm here until well past sun-up, as you know."

"Good night, Stevens," the bishop called over his shoulder as he led me along a dark corridor to a sitting room of oak panels and heavily framed portraits.

I recognized the former head of St. Augustine's as soon as he rose from the armchair by the window. I rushed across the room with delight and an outstretched hand.

"Father David, how amazing that you're here. The bishop said he had been doing his research, but I didn't realize it went back so far. It is wonderful to see you.

"Thank you Father Paul," I turned to the bishop who was chuckling with pleasure.

"We nearly persuaded my old classmate Father Justin to join us," said Father David, shaking my hand warmly. "But at the last minute, his courage failed him, and he left me with a message admonishing you to visit him in your old quarters beneath the vicarage at St. George's."

I felt greatly humbled that the bishop had gone to such trouble over an insignificant missionary worker. I didn't know what to say and felt suddenly out of my depth.

"You see, Jack," the bishop began as he reached for the whisky decanter, "I had anticipated your reluctance to be drawn back into what I can only call the 'true' faith. John Illingsworth had warned me, but I had to try. That's my job," he added with a smile.

"Father David, here, left St. Augustine's some four or five years ago?" The bishop looked questioningly at his other guest, who nodded in response. "He is now a resident of The Castle, but was not there to meet you today because I had asked him to come and see me early this afternoon to tell me about how you were as a student.

"Please understand, Jack, I don't usually take this much interest in 'a lamb who has gone astray.' But your history intrigued me and, I have to confess, I like everything I've heard about you. Your resilience, your courage, your honesty and your inventiveness"

My embarrassment was eased when a liveried servant announced that dinner was served and the three of us moved into the dining room next door where one end of a long table was immaculately set.

Distracted by the presentation of a marvelous dinner and the chatter of finding out what had been happening at St. Augustine's since I left, the serious nature of the dinner was momentarily put aside. However, as the cheese arrived, with a decanter of port following close behind, Father David began to talk about his new life.

"You see, Jack," he began, "the members of the Castle have an eclectic view of the Universe and are no longer restricted by an exclusively Christian doctrine."

I raised my eyebrows, my hands lifting from the table in an involuntary gesture.

"Yes, I know Jack," Father David continued quickly. "You were a bit ahead of me with your philosophies at St. Augustine's. It took me a long time to catch up! But now I have overtaken you.

"However," he continued briskly," you've had the hands-on experience through your ministry in London, Africa and elsewhere, which I lack. But maybe now it is time for you to catch me, in turn; to try the esoteric experience of the Divine, an experience supremely powerful as it has no limitations – spatial or intellectual. It is therefore not a journey for the weak or the timid.

"Such a commitment requires an ascetic life, of course, uncluttered with physical requirements, so that the self can fuse with the life force of the Universe. This is what is possible in The Castle.

"Are you familiar with the rain-drop analogy, Jack?" Father David asked.

I shook my head.

"Well, imagine yourself to be a drop of water, falling. Do you identify most with the water itself or with the defining line which gives the drop its shape as it falls?"

I put down my glass of port carefully, studying the elaborate pattern of the cut glass. Then I looked up at Father David and said: "If you had asked me that question when I arrived at St. Augustine's, I would have said I identified with the water. However, during my years in Yorkshire, the teachings of the College aimed at changing my ideas, so that when I graduated, and during my time in Islington, I would certainly have identified with the defining line. St. Augustine's gave my faith shape, and shaped me with it.

"During my time in Africa, before the disaster, I would have continued to identify with the defining line. I was so different from everyone around me and felt that it was my beliefs and knowledge that gave me credibility both as a priest and as a person. It is what made me of value to that community."

There was a pause as I took another sip of port. Buying time, I raised my napkin to my lips before continuing. "Now, all is changed again," I said softly, "and I will go back to identifying with the content of the drop, with the water itself, although, of course, the water will now have more dimensions than I would have noticed previously. It's a bit like the trees and mountains of the Buddhist metaphor.

"Does that answer your question, Father David?"

"Well, indeed it does, and with greater clarity than I anticipated," Father David said. "It's a good answer too, because, you see, to finish the analogy we have to follow the falling drop until it splashes into the ocean, river or lake. Once that happens, the water merges and continues to swirl and sway with the one great body. The defining line, however, is lost forever."

We sat in silence for a few minutes, each with our own thoughts. Surprisingly, I was the one to speak next.

"I missed out a piece of my story, Father David," I was smiling slightly. "There was also a time when I would have denied the existence of the water altogether, falling drop included. However, now that I am back in the flow, so to speak, if the Castle is an echo of the Universe, I should fit in as the water drop does when arriving in the sea."

The Bishop stood up suddenly, gesturing to his guests to stay seated. He folded his napkin and set it down carefully beside his plate.

"Gentlemen, please excuse me for a moment. There are things you two should talk of without my presence. I am not a candidate for The Castle, and therefore have no business in hearing of its secrets – not yet anyway.

"Please join me for coffee in the 'drawing-room when you are ready." He bowed his head and muttered 'benedictus, benedicat' before turning away, leaving the room through a massive paneled door.

Father David looked across the table at me. 'I remember you, Jack, as an ungainly youth who turned up at my door full of ideas, not so very long ago, or that's how it seems," he said, giving an involuntary sigh. He refilled our wine glasses from the heavy glass decanter and started to talk of The Castle.

"It doesn't matter whether there is a God or not – what there is here, in the ever-present, is life to be lived and learning to be milked to enrich personal knowledge and Knowledge - with a capital K - as a whole.

"If you exchange knowledge, you become a link in the chain of information which is passed from one generation to another. It is an honor to be part of that chain and the possibility should not be offered to just anybody. We invite only those to join us who share the same quest, those whose questions have shown them to be worthy and who will not arrest the smooth running of the links in the mighty mechanism by bringing unnecessary impedimenta to the chain.

"When you became a missionary, you undertook to spread the teachings of the bible. You, as it happens, chose to do more than that, you involved yourself in agriculture also and all aspects of village life. When your parishioners had enough time to think about existence, when they had full bellies and full larders, then you were there to answer their questions. The bringing of knowledge to such a place is the bringing of the Apple of Eden - thus casting such a missionary as the snake.

"Knowledge sets man free from stupidity, but it makes him less malleable. If knowledge is used badly, then it can take on the mantle of power and limit other people's capacities instead of enlarging them.

"The snake is a very positive emblem in many different cultures, as I'm sure you know. It is the belief of those in the Castle that the allegory of the snake in the Garden of Eden is positive; that the apple gave Adam and Eve freedom. They became free to make mistakes, yes, but also free to expand their souls. Have you noticed the icon for Apple Computers – there is a bite out of the apple. It is the bringer of knowledge.

"By the time we are old enough to appreciate the wisdom we have accumulated – fed through the prism of personal experiences – we have lost the inspiration of careless youth. Inspiration that is often doused by those a little ahead of us on the chronological ladder, those who resent the equal status that the years will bring, they tend to slap down those on their heels.

"The people who refuse to be slapped down or inhibited, who hang on to their wild notions and persevere with their ideas, are the bold visionaries of the Castle. They can inspire and encourage – their wisdom and excitement are shared with others so that it can grow, unfettered by governmental or ecclesiastical institutions. Their potential damage to the outside system is controlled by being hidden, but it is not lost, and can be handed on.

"We are not talking about an innocent, accepting faith here. No, that sort of belief is the narcotic of the hopeless. But it was our best-selling product while we were preachers!

"We are talking about the machinations of the human mind – why did Blake call his God 'Urizen'? 'Your Reason' is what he meant – he was a grand master of the Druids, Blake, did you know? Anyway, it doesn't really matter what name you give to where our studies lead us. It is the journey that is exciting.

"I know you've been through some dreadful experiences, Jack. But so have many others. The world is not a nice place, and these happenings serve to put Truth into perspective.

"So you see, the great secret of The Castle, and every other religious inner sanctum, I suspect, is that there is no secret. Once you have discovered that, you have to be either admitted or expelled.

"Your time of trial is over. The Church has failed to win you back into its conventional fold. Instead, you have passed into the realm of true knowledge, a realm not to be shared with the uninitiated who are happy with the Valium of organized religion and who should be maintained in their non-abusive state.

"Our duty, on this plane of existence, is to use the balm of belief to reassure those whose minds are not ready to travel to further levels. That done, we can concentrate on increasing the dimensions of knowledge available to those whose minds are ready to proceed; ready for the journey into knowledge, to embark upon the search for ultimate wisdom, freedom, nirvana, sartori. . ."

Father David paused, took a long sip from his glass and watched the light dance across the cut crystal.

"The Church has been good to you, Jack," he continued. "However, as I said before, it has failed to get you back, and their offer of a life in The Castle is all there is left for you if you are to remain a priest. You have become a loose canon, full of ideas that would be welcomed in The Castle, but most unwelcome anywhere else within the Church. If you do not wish to join us, you must leave the priesthood and the Missionary Service altogether."

It was late when I left the Bishop's palace, but I felt invigorated rather than tired. I had made my choice and could already feel the peace of The Castle's promise seeping into my soul.

The wet roads were deserted at so late an hour, only the occasional taxi or delivery van splashed through the glistening streets as I crossed the Thames. I paused to look up and down the great river and admire the buildings that rose upon its flanks. I could feel the heart of the city, coming from under the water, beating with the regularity of Big Ben.

Turning my collar up against the damp night air I walked on towards Piccadilly. Here the late hour had called forth the excitement-seekers of the night, and people were all over the place. In the doorways, crossing between the moving traffic, bumping into each other on the crowded pavements, all busy with individual dark time pursuits. The rain had stopped and left pictures of multi-colored lights along the curbs.

I heaved a big sigh of relief and contentment, looking up at the sky as I walked. There was too much city light to see the stars as they should be seen, but there was still a feeling of awe, and a strange sense of having arrived. Life was pulsing through me with new vigor. I was as alive in every pore as I had been on Silbury Hill. I felt like dancing with Shiva, swimming with Poseidon, flying with Mercury.

I turned a corner and there was the famous central statue of Piccadilly Circus. Eros, perched so delicately on one toe, his bow and arrow stretched and poised for flight. How was I going tell Stella of my choice?

Stella, who had given me so much, who had enlarged my understanding of the world, its people and, most of all, of myself.

"She has been a wonderful experience," I said to myself with slow deliberation; "but like all experiences, it is time to learn from it and move on. She has had lovers before, many of them, and will have lovers again." Why did this part of my reasoning irritate me? "She will survive, and I've probably grossly over-emphasized my importance in her life. Just because she was so earth-shatteringly important to me, doesn't mean that the same is true in reverse. Perhaps I was just another adventure."

Head bowed now, strides lengthening, I left Piccadilly behind, crossed under Hyde Park Corner, and walked through the lights of Knightsbridge as my thoughts rambled along with my feet. It was a good long walk to Chelsea.

By the time I rounded the corner into Stella's street I had convinced myself that I had been a mere blip on her radar screen and that my absence from her life would be only a temporary loss of pride. I climbed the steps to Stella's house, feeling for the house key.

As my hand grasped the key, deep in my right pocket, I felt a surge of guilt for having taken it and all that it symbolized. I turned the key over and over in my hand before straightening my back and placing it in the lock. "I've been just another blip," I repeated to myself.

83. SWIRLING EMOTIONS

The house was quiet and dim except for a light that had been left shining on the upper landing. I looked at my watch, it was after 3 a.m. My walk had taken me a good while, but I felt relieved that I would not have to face Stella until the morning.

I went carefully up the stairs and turned towards the bedroom. A light shone from the door that had been left ajar. It was my bed-side light, and through the partial opening I could see my side of the bed neatly turned down, the quilt and sheet placed in a welcoming V.

I moved carefully towards the half-opened door, pushed it fully open and stopped. On the far side of the room, Stella's part of the bed was empty but ruffled, in sharp contrast to my nearer side with its unwrinkled invitation.

Stella's head was the first thing I focused on in my confusion. It was bowed onto the bed over folded arms, her hair glinting subtle reds amongst the blond in the slanted light. She was kneeling on the floor, on the far side of the bed, so that from the doorway, only the head and arms were visible. I had only seen Stella on her knees in a very different way before and hesitated in the doorway not knowing how to proceed.

Stella raised her face revealing tear-streaked cheeks and swollen eyes that strained to focus on the figure in the doorway. Suddenly she leapt to her feet and clambered straight over the bed to throw herself around my neck so that I felt the hot wetness of her face through my shirt.

"Oh God, oh wonderful God, thank you God, thank you." She exclaimed, clasping my chest against hers so that I could feel the swell of her breasts against my taught frame. "You have come back to me, my darling. I was so frightened that you had left. Look how, without even trying, you've converted me into a creature who will go down on her knees and pray, and try to believe with my whole self in my supplications – and it has worked. You have a true convert on your hands, my darling Jack, now that you are home again, where you belong. I promised the Almighty, and I will keep that promise. I haven't been on my knees in prayer since St. George's days. This is the gift I was begging for – your return to my arms. Oh thank you God, my darling has come home.

"Oh Jack, I have been scared, so scared," she continued, still with her head buried in my chest, her arms clinging around my back now with a strength that surprised me. "My love for you has made me so vulnerable in a place I didn't know I still had. A place from the time of innocence, from when I thought the world was fair. I thought that place had been closed up for ever, and now I find it open, soft, horribly available to pain."

I was stroking her hair – an automatic gesture - while the other arm supported the shuddering waist. Without cogent thought I burrowed my head in her hair, my mouth against her ear, whispering: "it's alright, it's alright, I am here now, there's nothing to worry about." The drama of the moment had taken over and I was playing a part which somewhere deep inside me was being denied. I found myself holding her away from me with exquisite gentleness and wiping the tears from her cheeks with my thumbs.

Stella pulled herself upright and gazed into my heart. "We'll move," she started, her words rushing out of her. "We'll leave London to give you space and quiet. Whatever you want, wherever you want. I have been thinking about our life together, you are more important to me than anything else. I can be happy anywhere, as long as I have you – and a garden," she added after a slight hesitation and with a hint of a smile amongst the tears. "I've out-grown the parties and the noise and the business. You have shown me an inner tranquility of my own which I want to share with yours.

"What do you say, my love, my dearest man. We'll move and find somewhere in the country, as remote as you like. You are my rock now, my anchor, the keeper of my soul. My peace after all these years of turmoil. Thank you, Almighty God, for bringing my Jack back to me."

"Sh, sh," I was cradling, leading her gently around the bed. I moved my hands until they rested upon her shoulders and applied gentle pressure to sit her down on the bed amongst the ruffled sheets she had previously thrown aside. Very gently, I lifted Stella's legs and twisted her body to settle her back against the pillows. I kissed her on the forehead, smoothing the puffy cheeks. I could not bear to look into the beseeching eyes. Something in her distress had aroused me in a way too difficult to handle. I pushed the confusion away and hoped that the ache in my groin would go with it.

"You do love me, Jack, don't you?" Stella was aware of me avoiding her gaze, and the panic started to creep back into her voice.

"You know I do." I said softly as I stood up and began to fuss about the bedclothes. "Hush now, I'll come and join you in two ticks." I turned towards the bathroom, but she caught my hand and tugged urgently.

"No," Stella's tone was frightened and insistent. "Look at me, Jack. Look at me and tell me that you love me and will stay with me forever."

I sighed, turned slowly and sat down on the bedside. I put my hands on Stella's shoulders and looked straight into her eyes; deep brown chasms of love and yearning, a layer of tears shimmering along the lower lashes. I was trapped. She held my gaze without blinking. "I have to know, Jack, you don't know how important it is that I have to know. Please tell me the truth."

"I love you, Stella." I said quietly but firmly, "and I'll never leave you. Somehow we will always be together."

Stella's arms rose slowly, her hands reaching for my neck to pull me down for a soft kiss with no trace of the wild passion that usually accompanied her embraces. It was a kiss of trust that I could not fail to return. Slowly I pulled myself away and stood up, looking down at the face I loved, now with a shy smile curling the moist lips, making her look like a child.

"Now, let me get ready for bed, and no more nonsense," I said, following the sense of youth that her trusting face had adopted. I was making a desperate effort to sound calm in spite of the turmoil of emotions in my chest, belly and below.

Stella made no further attempt to stop me, but I could feel her eyes following me into the bathroom. Stripping off my clothes that I left where they fell, I tried to avoid looking at myself in the mirror over the wash-basin. I stood in the shower, feeling the water pound my skin as I turned, but there was a mirror in the shower also. I watched my reflection, as if from a distance. I saw the water running down my taught frame, making rivulets around the small scar in my side which was all that remained of the angry gash necessitated by the colostomy bag.

Continuing my slow turn I looked over my shoulder and forced my eyes down to the reflection of my buttocks. The dark red cruciform still showed beneath the grafts, the creases of the stretched skin radiating outwards from the wound. But it didn't look angry anymore and I was amazed to find that it didn't make me feel angry either, it was just a mark, empty of any power.

I turned off the shower and looked back towards the water-spattered mirror, holding the gaze of my reflection, aware of my nakedness as the water glistened in my beard and pubic hair, slowly forming into droplets and falling to join the pool at my feet as it swirled towards the darkness of the plug hole. I felt aware of all those drops of water, aware of myself in their midst, loosing my defining line. Perhaps I could slide down the drain and disappear in a merger of unidentifiable atoms all, most suitably, going down the drain.

I tried to think, to dig into my psyche for answers. My eyes continued to stare back at me, slightly out of focus without my glasses. There was only emptiness and the sound of the water gurgling softly into the aluminum vortex.

Totally without thought, I stepped out of the shower and absentmindedly pulled a soft white towel from the rail, winding it around my shoulders and letting it slip slowly to my waist. I was suddenly dreadfully tired and, dropping the towel in a heap with my clothes, I left the bathroom, walking softly onto the deep carpet of the bedroom.

To my relief, Stella was asleep. She was lying on her side, curled towards the edge of the bed. Her face had softened and there were no signs of all the tears that had gone before, apart from tiny traces of salt in the creases around the closed eyes. Her deep auburn hair was spread behind her over the pillow, the light from my table once again catching highlights of red and gold amongst the waves of yellow and brown and the flecks of grey at the temples.

I slipped quietly into bed and turned off the light, sliding my still moist body between the cool, crisp sheets. Stella turned with the movement of the bed. I could feel her weight shifting on the mattress, and then she was nuzzling my shoulder, first with her nose and then with her mouth as she nibbled her way up to my ear lobe.

"Good night, my darling," she whispered, as she squeezed her left arm under my back and wrapped it around my waist while her right arm crept across my chest and up to my neck. "We'll talk about it all tomorrow. Our new life is about to begin – more than you know. My wonderful Jack, maker of miracles, man of my dreams."

Stella's tongue flicked inside my ear, and then her head squeezed against my shoulder as her arms hugged my body. In just a few seconds, the pressures loosened and her breathing became deep and regular. Stella's body relaxed around me. I didn't move a muscle for fear of waking her. I was trying to understand her words, looking for the hidden meanings that the depth of her voice had intimated. I was confused, and, without knowing why, more than a little scared.

84. REVELATIONS

Stella had left the bedroom by the time I awoke and there was a smell of bacon coming from down-stairs indicating her whereabouts.

I lay still, trying to piece together all that had happened the day before. Memories of last night's scene in the bedroom came back with painful confusion. What had happened to cause such an out-pouring? I resolved to explain everything to Stella now, in the light of day, how I do love her, but also, how I am committed to another life, and so on. She will come to understand, in time, I persuaded myself, and we could always be friends.

With a sigh of relief and determination I threw off the bedclothes and went to the bathroom. When I emerged I found Stella standing in front of me holding out my dressing gown. She was swathed in her robe of Indian silk - a present from the 'boys' at the factory - her head tilted slightly to the left, a large smile on her face and her eyes sparkling with joy. I thought I had never seen her look so beautiful, and my heart gave a lurch in my chest as the now familiar tingles began to spread up my inner thighs.

"Good morning, my darling man," Stella's voice purred, and those deep eyes washed over me with such strength that I thought I could feel them physically caressing my body.

"Put this on, and come with me." Stella wrapped me in the dressing-gown, snatching a quick hug as she did so, and then took me by the hand and led me out of the room and down the stairs.

When we got to the kitchen I looked in amazement at the breakfast table in the gable end of the room. It was bathed in sunlight spilling in from the garden and was laid for two with a fresh, starched cloth of white linen, a single deep red rose in a thin vase stood in the centre. There was fresh orange juice in a crystal jug and – most surprising of all - a bottle of champagne reclining in a sweating silver ice bucket.

"I've cooked your favorite, my love," said Stella as she pulled out my chair for me with a lavish gesture and spread a clean white napkin across my lap. "Eggs Benedict with some crispy American-style bacon. But first, we are starting our day in style – we have something to celebrate" and she handed me the dripping bottle of champagne to open.

"'Gracious me Stella, it's only just nine in the morning – can't this wait a bit?" I asked nervously, but I found myself obediently untwisting the wire.

Stella watched me lovingly, her eyes sparkling. "No, it can't wait, my darling. Open her up, I'm all ready" she added as she picked up two champagne glasses from the table and held them towards me with excitement.

I stood up, the napkin falling to the floor. I was turning the bottle carefully. "What is all this about?" I said, easing the cork out with a satisfying hiss. I poured the sparkling liquid into the tilted glasses, watching the foam crawling up the sides, replaced the bottle in the cooler, and took the proffered glass in bemusement.

Stella took a step towards me so that we were almost touching. "I have a confession to make, my darling Jack," she began.

"My world has been turbulent – not as turbulent as yours, of course, but still, in its own way, not an easy ride. I was depressed and lost, and my attempts to find distraction with different men only made me feel worse."

Stella sipped her champagne thoughtfully. A blush rose to her cheeks as she continued: "as you know, I was reading a lot about the possible path to enlightenment through physical experiences. I never got anywhere with my experiments however, apart from using them as research for Lio. My somewhat random sexual dalliances always left me feeling let down, tarnished somehow. It became obvious to me that I could not travel this sensual path to spiritual enlightenment with any of the men I was dating. With my regained wealth, I had plenty of candidates from which to choose, but none of them pressed the right buttons, if you'll excuse the expression," Stella's blush deepened, "and I was never sure if they genuinely liked me as a person, or just for the trappings." She stopped talking for a moment and contemplated her champagne.

"You underestimate yourself, dearest Stella," I said softly. I was touched by what I was hearing and saddened for this lovely, intelligent woman who had so little self-confidence. Chicago had done much damage to the sparkling young woman I had met in Islington.

"You're not offended by my talking like this?" Stella raised her eyes, and smiled as I shook my head and smiled back at her – my planned conversation would obviously have to wait. "That's just one of the many wonderful things about you, Jack. I can – and do – talk to you about anything and everything. There is nothing that needs to be hidden. At least I hope not – this next piece of the story will see if that's true."

I raised a quizzical eyebrow, and decided that a sip of Champagne might be a good idea after all.

"At home, at night," Stellla continued, "I would wash away the dirt of those petty relationships in a deep bath full of bubbles of my own creation, and every time, I would find myself thinking about you.

"I know we didn't have much of a relationship during our time in Islington, but I always felt at home with you. There was never any need to act, I could just be myself and feel as if I belonged where I was, at your side. I couldn't get thoughts of you out of my system; instead of growing weaker with time, they grew stronger. Eventually I gave up trying to push those thoughts away and went to find Father Justin to ask what had happened to you."

Stella pushed me gently back into my chair. I was gazing at her, my mouth slightly open, my breath short. My champagne glass shook slightly as I placed it carefully on the table. She went to her chair, pulled it away from the table and sat down so she was facing me, the single rose between us, shedding its delicate perfume. I was reminded of the first time we sat together like this in Rome, and before that, in the Priory Café.

"Dear Father Justin was not hard to find, you know where he is now, living in what used to be your basement flat. He was touchingly pleased to see me and we had a cup of tea together with a splash of whisky from the bottle I brought him. I asked after you and explained why I needed to find you. He seemed to understand immediately and was wonderfully supportive, I couldn't believe it. He told me of your brief visit after returning from America, and how much you had changed. He told me of your trip to Europe and assured me that you would be pleased to see me. He promised to investigate on my behalf and to find you.

"I was impatient, and kept ringing him up. He repeated that he was working on finding you and that he would have an answer soon.

"One day he called me and said I should come and take a cup of tea with him again, and he would tell me what I wanted to know. And so I did."

Stella took another sip of her champagne. "Father Justin had found out that your European tour was due to end soon, in Rome. He told me, with a smile, that the church was busy sending you on assignments 'to keep him out of trouble'. He had found out when and where you would be staying.

"And so, you see my darling, our meeting in Rome was far from a coincidence. I went to Rome for you. Well not for you, actually, it was for me. I knew where to find you, and I waited. I followed you from your house to the library. I noticed your visits to the coffee bar, and after a couple of days of nervousness, I set my trap."

Stella was looking worried now. A small frown dipped between her eyebrows. She drank the rest of the champagne in a gulp, and refilled it herself.

"Please don't be angry with me, dear Jack," Stella continued, afraid to raise her eyes. "Everything seemed so right. I knew if I found you I would find peace and happiness, and I have. And we have found excitement together with our lovemaking opening doors to the magical mysteries of spiritual love.

"And now it seems," her voice fell to a whisper, "I have found something even greater."

Stella picked up her brimming glass slowly, and raised it up, above the rose, towards me. "A toast to my miracle worker," she said carefully, looking straight at me. "After all these years, God has answered my prayers, he has allowed me to find you and we have loved with a new depth. You're going to be a father, Jack, you have made me pregnant."

My world froze. There was a strange stillness all about. I couldn't move. My eyes were locked with Stella's but everything had lost its focus. It seemed a long time before Stella spoke again.

"Say something, Jack," she urged. "Speak to me for heaven's sake. This is wonderful news, and you are looking as if you've been hit by a train."

I shook myself back into reality, into Stella's kitchen, to my position at the little table. I looked at Stella with her raised glass and pleading eyes. Slowly, I raised my glass and focused my gaze:

"My wonderful woman," I began, with a voice that seemed to come from a long way away. "What astonishing news, what amazing news, what a miracle indeed. Forgive me, I was just too stunned to say anything" I ended rather lamely and took a gulp of champagne.

Stella's joyous laughter sprang around the kitchen. "Isn't it awesome, Jack?" She rushed into speech. "Just wait 'til I tell mother, she will be over the moon.

"Oh, and darling, what an exciting voyage we are embarking on, what wonders lie ahead for you and me together, bound anew by this miracle. I have never felt so happy. You see now why I got myself in such a state last night when you were so late coming home?

"I'm really sorry about that whole scene, but I was so frightened, so very frightened. I thought that - just when I felt the closest to you that I have ever felt to anyone, just as I discovered this wonderful physical bond between us, just at the most important moment in my life - that I had lost you.

"I should have known better, of course, my love," the words were tumbling out as she leapt from the table and rushed towards me, dropping on her knees by my chair and seizing my left hand she pressed it to her cheek.

"I should have had more trust. I promise I won't be such an idiot again. I know we will be together for always, and now it isn't just the two of us." She dropped her eyes coyly towards her stomach, patting it gently. "The fruit of our love" she added softly and turned to kiss the palm of my hand.

The parameters of my existence had moved. I stood up slowly; a strange warmth was spreading from behind my navel, deep inside me. It moved through my skeleton, through muscles, into veins, to the extremities of my body. My scalp tingled, toes clenched and my fingers spread out as if the force coming from within was too much for them to hold.

I found myself raising Stella from her kneeling position and clasping her gently in my arms. Our energies merged, joining us in an exquisite rush of emotion. I let my mind widen, abolishing thought, and felt with my essence the powers of existence that bound our two bodies together. As I concentrated upon the sensation, I became aware that in the midst of all that power and light, there was the fluttering of a new energy, a different essence, with us, of us and yet separate.

"Can you feel it?" I whispered softly in Stella's ear. The head that nuzzled in my shoulder nodded a little, as she tightened her grasp around my waist.

85. TODAY

So here I am, in my quiet study overlooking a garden reaching into the rolling farmland, towards Leicestershire. My notes are all in order, the tin trunk and boxes finally emptied. It has been a cathartic experience, this arrangement of my past, and I believe I have put my life in perspective to some considerable degree – but for what purpose, I wonder?

The months between the revelation of Stella's pregnancy and the move have been a blur of activity, as exciting as it has been disruptive. Stella kept her promise that we would move out of London and that I should choose the location of our new home. My thoughts turned immediately to The Castle and the surrounding undulating farmland. I might not be able to be an inmate of that wonderful establishment now, but I was hopeful they might admit me as an 'outpatient,' especially if I came off the Church's payroll.

I had a meeting with John Illingsworth, who, as he is no longer my employer, I feel flattered to call a friend. He was amazed at the story I had to tell him about Stella and how she had 'found' me, and of course, of my approaching parenthood. He was the only one I told of how close I had come to telling Stella of my decision to leave, and how grateful I was that circumstances had intervened and I had learnt about the depth and determination of her feelings for me, and of the pregnancy, before I told her of my plans. It seems I wasn't just a little blip on her radar after all. I needed to re-consider in a hurry, and re-consider I did. I had new responsibilities ahead of me, I realized, which pushed my own desires out of the lime-light. Responsibilities towards which I was looking with excitement, delight and, of course, some anxiety. I shared all this with Illingsworth as I felt I had to justify having used up his and the Bishop's time in my contemplation of life at The Castle, and to demonstrate that I had been serious at the time.

Illingsworth accepted my resignation - with relief, I suspect - and promised to speak to the Bishop on my behalf and to do what he could to allow me to visit The Castle if the existing residents were happy for me to do so.

Stella and I had set off to Leicestershire to visit estate agents and look for an appropriate dwelling. The house in Chelsea went on the market, much to the chagrin of so many of Stella's followers. "But I will keep a flat in town," she promised them, "I will have to, for business reasons, so you will all be welcome to visit me there." Somehow the throng remained unconvinced, they were probably wondering where they would be spending their weekends, I suspect, and who would gain them access to all the social events after Stella became a mother.

The Welland valley is a verdant stretch of England laced with hedgerows. Towards the eastern end, it is crossed by an astonishing viaduct of eighty-two arches, each of which is forty feet wide and it joins the two counties of Northamptonshire and Rutland. Built in the late1870s to carry the steam trains traveling north and east from the capital, this extraordinary feat of Victorian engineering rises sixty feet above the valley floor and, although it is still in sporadic use, the arches are homes to an assortment of birds, plants, insects and wildlife of various kinds. The village of Harringworth nestles alongside the Northamptonshire end of the structure on the outskirts of which a three-bedroom stone cottage was for sale. This has been our home now for several weeks.

A five minute stroll takes us past the church to the village centre where there is small grocery shop and a pub. Our neighbor sells eggs from the chickens that run around her cottage during the day and are shut up safely at night, for there is a large population of foxes in the area. A short ride in the car takes us to a dairy farm where fresh milk and butter is sold to local people from a small shop at the back of the buildings, the bulk of their produce going to the urban sprawls of Corby and Peterborough. The Castle is a twenty minute drive through rich farmland, and Leicester a forty-five minute commute.

I mention Leicester as, having obtained a wonderful reference from John Illingsworth, I now have a job at the University there, lecturing two days a week on 'farming in the developing world' as part of their agricultural program. As there is a predominance of students whose parents came originally from India and Pakistan, there is no call for any Christian influences in my lectures, and I am free to lecture as I see fit and appropriate. I start in the autumn by which time I should have been a father for around six weeks.

I lunch at The Castle every Wednesday and the inmates are kind enough to allow me to use the library from whenever I arrive – usually around ten in the morning - until I leave at tea-time. I am not allowed to take any of the books home, but I take copious notes and greatly enjoy the privilege of being in such a special place. I am making new friends during the lunch hours and have fascinating conversations as I exchange ideas of the numinous with some immensely knowledgeable people. I am keeping notes of those interchanges also.

Stella is coping with the pregnancy well, only a couple of weeks to go now. She has stopped going to London, happy to deal with business matters via Skype or email. So far, we are loving our peaceful time together and the excitement of preparing for the new member of our family and trying to cope with the feeling of vulnerability in an unknown area of our psyches.

All of a sudden I have a purpose for my life and new questions. This cathartic exercise of re-arranging my experiences might well lead to a philosophy I can pass on to the next generation, to my child – an unknown quantity who will need guidance, but at the same time, the freedom to explore. How am I going to help this visiting soul? I must use these last months of exploration into my past to build a future for someone else – someone who's part of us and yet separate.

There's so much to learn ahead of us. How will the experience of parenthood affect our philosophical wanderings, I wonder, what – or who - will be our guides? It will be an exciting journey, and a demanding one, but not one I will be taking on my own.

I am slowly getting used to the fact that I am no longer a free-standing individual but a swirling half of a composite whole made up of Stella and myself. Soon there will be a third dimension to these energies, one, as yet unknown, who will slowly disentangle itself from us as the years go by and step away to lead an independent life. That will leave Stella and me back where we are now – a single unit made of two enmeshed halves.

I know now that I will never be on my own again. I have my side of our entropic aura as Stella has hers, and we are both free to expand those as much as we like but neither of us is an individual anymore.

So it is together that we embark on this new voyage of discovery and growth. A journey full of mystery and no small amount of anxiety but one to which I am looking forward enormously.

A Bridge Across Uncertainty ~ The Welland Valley Viaduct

ACKNOWLEDGEMENTS

To all those who have been helpful and inspirational with the writing of this book and to those few whose acts of unkindness have unwittingly provided grist to the mill.

Thank you.

ABOUT THE AUTHOR

D.G.A. Pritchard has travelled the world widely and lived within several different cultures. Spending significant periods of life in Europe, Africa and USA, DG is well versed in the challenges that have faced these cultures during difficult times of social upheaval.

Educated in the UK and Switzerland, with dual degrees in English Literature and Comparative Theology from Georgetown University, in addition to studying at The Department of History & Philosophy at Kings College, London, DG has grappled with searches of the soul on a personal basis. A Brand of Faith is one step on that journey.

Visit the author online at

www.dgapritchard.com

Printed in Great Britain
by Amazon